Praise for

Finding Fraser

"Jamie Fraser would be Deeply Gratified at having inspired such a charmingly funny, poignant story—and so am I."

—Diana Gabaldon,
#1 *New York Times* bestselling author of the Outlander series

"A must-read for *Outlander* fans eagerly awaiting their next Jamie fix."
—Bustle

"A humorous yet relatable self-discovery tale."　　　—*Us Weekly*

"I loved this book. It transported me to a Scotland I wished I'd grown up in. Everything about it is a delight, and it's all authentic—the environment, the characters, the dialogue, and the sheer enjoyment of it all."

—Jack Whyte, bestselling author of the Guardians of Scotland series

"For everyone who ever fell in love with a fictional character. Dyer blends humor, a love of Scotland, and romance into a page-turner that will keep readers cheering on the main character and turning pages."　　　—Eileen Cook, author of *You Owe Me a Murder*

"An absolute must-read for any Outlander fan. The story is both hilarious and romantic, as well as guaranteed to have readers turning the pages until the wee hours to discover if the heroine finds her very own Jamie Fraser."

—Laura Bradbury, bestselling author of the My Grape Escape series

Eighty Days to Elsewhere

kc dyer

JOVE
NEW YORK

A JOVE BOOK
Published by Berkley
An imprint of Penguin Random House LLC
penguinrandomhouse.com

Library of Congress Cataloging-in-Publication Data

Names: Dyer, K. C., author.
Title: Eighty days to elsewhere / kc dyer.
Description: First edition. | New York: Jove, 2020.
Identifiers: LCCN 2020010649 (print) | LCCN 2020010650 (ebook) |
ISBN 9780593102046 (trade paperback) | ISBN 9780593102053 (ebook)
Subjects: GSAFD: Love stories.
Classification: LCC PR9199.4.D93 E38 2020 (print) | LCC PR9199.4.D93 (ebook) |
DDC 813/.6—dc23
LC record available at https://lccn.loc.gov/2020010649
LC ebook record available at https://lccn.loc.gov/2020010650

First Edition: August 2020

Printed in the United States of America
1   3   5   7   9   10   8   6   4   2

Cover art and design by Vi-An Nguyen
Book design by Kristin del Rosario

For M&J
Because of whom I crawled backwards
into a hole beneath the ground.
No regrets.

chapter one

IMAGE: Bookshop Reflections
IG: Romy_K [NYC, March 14]
#TwoOldQueens #ShopWindow
#AnUnexpectedProblem
13 ♥

Almost there.

I type the last few letters of the caption, hit the "upload" button, and flick the app closed. Glancing at the time, I see I'm late, but only a little. Still, it's at least a week since I've uploaded anything to Instagram, so it had to be done.

It's been a long morning already. Up since before six, I've been toiling over the bookshop's social media accounts. Two Old Queens Books & Tea has been operating in this same unfashionable East Village location since long before I was born. Since before my uncles were born, in truth, though in those days the name over the door was different. Bagshaw's Books, maybe? I think there might be an old photo somewhere in Merv's back room. I should try and find it. Might be a nice visual counterpoint to the piece I added this morning. But not today. I'm late enough already.

Luckily, I don't have far to travel to work. My studio apartment is three flights of stairs above the shop. I've lived here almost two years, since the—literal—professional clown who used to rent the space disappeared overnight, leaving behind a disturbing number of popped balloons and sprays of confetti.

At least, I *hope* they were balloons. That's what I told myself as I cleaned them up off the floor, and out of the tiny closet. And from inside the shower drain.

Anyway, this morning I got caught up posting a few new acquisitions to the shop's #Bookstagram account, and lost track of the time. Generally, I agonize how to best present the latest book, shoot a few dozen possibilities, then narrow it down to my favorite. I post the shot first to Instagram, which auto-feeds it to Facebook, and then I post it separately to Twitter and Snapchat, so the full image appears, and not only a link. All of this takes time, but it drives more traffic to the bookshop's site, and ultimately to the bookstore. At least that's what I tell myself. And Merv.

Right about the time I graduated from college and started working full time at the bookshop, I promised my uncle that a few decent social media accounts would help us build our community. He grumbled that pictures in the ether didn't sell books on the ground, but I know it's made a difference.

But this morning? It's only made me late.

Trying to keep the sound of my heels to a minimum, I hurry down the back stairs. These lead to the lane behind the building, but also to the rear door of the shop, which is always kept locked. Going this way means I can't avoid the smell of the dumpster parked outside the back door, but it also means I might be able to sneak past the unblinking eye of Uncle Merv's partner, Tommy, who is never averse to pointing out my shortcomings.

As I slip into the back room, the warm aroma from Tommy's old coffee urn supersedes the dumpster stench, and—bonus!—there's no one around. Immediately, I hurry over to finish a job from last night: sorting through a pile of books bequeathed to us by an old patron.

This happens a lot at Two Old Queens—somebody dies, and their kids or grandchildren aren't readers, so they dump all the family books on our doorstep. Most of what comes our way in this fashion we can't really use. I mean, we already have a full shelf of Jacqueline Susann paperbacks with lurid seventies covers, right? So, as low girl on the employee totem pole, it falls to me to sort out the dregs, and then take any titles that appear even moderately appealing to my Uncle Merv for the final decision.

By the time I finish culling the pile, I'm feeling pretty pleased with myself. I've got social media locked in for the bookstore, finished my assigned task, and mapped out my plans for the week in my bullet journal, all without being called out by Tommy for showing up a little late. There's a long workday still ahead of me, it's true, but tonight I've got a plan for a night in. It involves a giant bowl of pho and a *Black Panther* DVD I found in our discard pile, loaded with outtakes of Killmonger with his shirt off.

Don't tell me I don't know how to live.

Flipping open my bullet journal again, I cross off all the tasks I've accomplished for the morning. Then, making a careful largest-to-smallest pile of books to take out front for my uncle, I ass-backed my way through the swinging door and onto the sales floor.

I need to pause here to give a sense of what it is to work in Two Old Queens. I mean, if you peer in through the glass of the front window, I guess it looks normal enough. There's a lovely wooden sign depicting Queen Victoria gazing disapprovingly at Queen Elizabeth—who stares serenely back—in the transom above the door. The store's located on a corner within sight of Tompkins Square, which is pretty much the center of the East Village in New York City. This means we're far enough off the tourist trail to be generally pretty quiet, and not close enough to Soho or Greenwich Village to be hip. Our window display, courtesy of my uncle's partner,

Tommy, changes seasonally, and sometimes even monthly, when he's feeling creative. You might also spy the wee tea bar, tucked into one corner; leaf tea only, darling. And there's the standard cash desk, mostly filled by an old register with buttons so stiff, it hurts my fingers to press them.

The register does, however, make a satisfying *cha-ching* when I complete a sale.

Supervision is provided by Tommy's cat, an elegant, aloof, green-eyed tabby called Rhianna. Literally all the boxes ticked for a self-respecting indie bookstore, right? But where Two Old Queens sets itself apart is in our merchandise. You know how in the library, they refer to the bookshelves as stacks? *Hey, don't mind me, I'm only heading over to the stacks to look up a book on paleontology.*

Well, when *we* talk about the stacks in our shop, it's literal.

Every surface is stacked high with teetering piles. Until they stop teetering, and tumble—usually Rhianna's doing. When this happens, everything comes to a halt, and all hands converge until a new pile appears once more. Faster when a customer is underneath, of course.

It's a chaos with which I've battled as long as I can remember. I have spent my time—So. Much. Time.—trying to organize Uncle Merv and his systems. Whenever a tiny bit of progress is made—I find a new computer program for arranging book intakes, or an inventory system relying on something more comprehensive than the alphabet—inevitably, the wheels fall off again.

Still.

The shop is always warm. Every reader is welcome. It smells of old books and sweet tea and the heady scent of ten thousand stories, trapped between the covers.

And a little bit of cat.

Currently, the front of the shop boasts a dozen "book pillars"; floor-to-ceiling spirals of new acquisitions. I've been laboring over them for weeks, and have managed to work my magic and stack three of them from largest to smallest. Still, with having to sort Merv's most recent acquisitions, it's been slow going.

By the time I take a final pivot around the waist-high stack of family bibles—there's been a run on funerals in the neighborhood recently—I stop in surprise to find two men standing beside the cash register with my Uncle Merv.

As noted, our little shop is definitely off the beaten path. We have what I like to think is a pretty typical amount of foot traffic—mostly regulars, and once in a while the odd tourist gets lost and stumbles in. Business *has* been a bit brisker since the Starbucks down the street relocated elsewhere, but we're never remotely crowded. It's rare to have two customers in the shop at one time, unless it's Christmas or one of the local book clubs decides to do a Jane Austen reread.

However, as I stagger up to the desk, the two-man element of this scenario is less surprising than the expression on Merv's face. Merv came of age as a gay man in 1970s New York. He's survived bashing, the AIDS crisis, and Tommy's histrionics when I set the table and forget to put the forks on the left. Merv's live-and-let-live ethos rules his life, and explains a lot about the condition of the bookshop. There's not much that can knock him off his stride.

So, when he looks worried—there's usually a good reason.

I pause, chin resting lightly on my stack of books, and take a closer look at the two men standing by the desk. The first is a short, overweight man with bleached hair and a spray tan. His camel overcoat is crumpled, and he's left a trail of dirty snow all the way from the front door. I can't help glancing around for Tommy, who will have an absolute bird when he sees this, but thankfully he's nowhere in sight. The orange man is clenching the soggy nub of a well-chewed, but blessedly unlit cigar between his thick lips.

Uncle Merv is at least a head taller than this guy, but as he catches my eye, his expression doesn't relax.

"Ramona," Merv says quietly, "this is Mr. Frank Venal. Apparently, he is the new owner of our building."

"Ya got that right," Frank Venal says, his New Jersey accent thick as buttah. "Won the whole buildin' last night on two pair and a cement poker face."

He squints in my direction, and with his thick tongue, moves the cigar to the corner of his mouth.

"Ramona?" he asks, glancing at one of the papers in his hand. "As in, Ramona Keene, suite 2B?"

I take advantage of his moment's distraction to slide my pile of books onto the sales desk. As I do, Venal's companion shuffles his feet uncomfortably. He's closer to my age, and taller; with tawny skin and wavy dark hair that just brushes his shoulders. I know instantly I've seen this guy somewhere before. He's attractive enough that under normal circumstances, I'd be wracking my brain to remember where.

But at the moment, the circumstances feel pretty far from normal.

All the same, I slide sideways a little to try to catch the young guy's eye. When I do finally manage it, he glances away, maintaining a carefully blank expression.

"That's right," I answer, at last. "I'm Romy Keene." I look past the younger man and exchange a worried glance with my uncle.

"Well, as of midnight last night, doll, this building is mine," Venal says smugly. "And seein' as nobody in their right mind reads books anymore, I'm guessin' this place don't pull its own weight. Consider this your official notice. You pay what I'm askin', or you got forty-five days before the wreckers come in."

He turns and bares his teeth at the younger man. "I'm thinkin' micro-condos, Dom. Them things are the way of the future."

He waves a piece of paper that reads "Property Deed" in Merv's face.

Merv takes a step back, and Venal clutches the younger man by the arm.

"This is my—ah—*nephew*, Dominic," he says. "He'll be by to collect the rent every month."

"We always pay by direct deposit," Merv says, but Venal waves this away with a menacing chuckle.

He slaps a new lease agreement on the counter.

"I prefer the personal touch," he says. Except he pronounces it *poisenal*. Then he marches out the front door.

The taller man shoots a startled look at Venal's retreating back, pausing as the bell jingles on the front door. "He's *not* my uncle," he whispers, then hurries out onto the street.

Merv slumps on a stool behind the counter, looking stunned. This act in itself shows how upset he is, since he has always equated sitting behind the cash desk with the most contemptible laziness. At this moment, Tommy, swathed in several scarves and with a large Soviet-era fur hat on his bald head, comes bustling in the front door, laden with patisserie bags.

By the time he's got his coat off and the pastries under the glass display domes on the tea counter, Merv's told him the whole story. Tommy bursts into tears at the news.

This is no help at all.

In the end, I tuck Tommy into the comfy sofa in their tiny apartment behind the bookstore. I leave a cup of tea, a plate piled in chocolate éclairs, and his favorite telenovela on to distract him. Hurrying back into the shop, I find Merv has summoned our neighbor, Mrs. Justice Rosa Ruiz, in the interim.

Mrs. Justice Rosa—seriously, that's what we call her—is eighty-six, and a retired circuit court judge. She's among our regulars, stopping by weekly to pick up her copies of the *Times* and *Hola Latinos*, a cup of tea, and whatever sweet treat Tommy can entice her into. Today, she's wearing a tracksuit in vivid magenta and a pair of Birkenstocks that show off her turquoise pedicure.

It's hard to decipher some of the document's legalese, but once I find her a magnifying glass, Mrs. Justice Rosa lends us her thoughts and we determine the extent of the bad news.

The new lease spells out that since Venal's acquisition has negated historic rent controls, he will now be charging triple the rent, something the bookshop can never sustain. Two Old Queens needs to pay up by May 1st—less than seven weeks away—or face eviction.

I spend the rest of the very long day running back and forth between the cash desk and the little apartment behind the shop, bearing fresh cups of tea. Mostly this is in aid of keeping Tommy calm, as his inclination to burst into tears is upsetting to Merv.

Tommy and Merv have run this Lower Manhattan bookstore together for more than thirty years, and the thought of losing it is horrifying to all of us. After Mrs. Justice Rosa leaves for her daily nap, the two of them huddle in the back, knees together on one of the overstuffed sofas, reading and rereading the new lease document in hopes of finding something the old lady judge has missed.

When the midafternoon lull hits, I tiptoe into the back to see if the uncles have made any progress. I peek around the corner to see Tommy has fallen asleep, head tilted against the back of the couch, mouth open. Rhianna is curled on his lap. Merv is still holding the document, but he's not looking at it. Just staring blankly into space.

As he catches sight of me, Uncle Merv tries to manufacture a smile.

"Any breakthroughs?" I whisper, not wanting to wake Tommy. His tear-stained face is propped against one wing of the sofa, and at the moment, he's snoring gently.

Merv shakes his head. "I think we're screwed, honey," he says, and even through his whisper I can hear the catch in his voice. "You know our Rosa is the sharpest in the business, and if even *she* can't see a way out . . ." His voice trails away.

I tuck myself in between the couch and the old coffee table and drop to my knees beside Merv.

"Listen," I say quietly. "I've got twenty-seven hundred dollars in my film school account we can put toward the rent. It should help for a month or two, at least."

The look of horror on Merv's face dries up everything else I was going to say.

"Absolutely not," he hisses, and then freezes as Tommy stirs. Rhianna shoots me a dirty look and leaps lightly to the back of the sofa.

"You've looked after me since I was thirteen years old," I manage, barely holding it together. "Let *me* help *you* for a change."

Merv reaches across and pats my knee. "We're *not* touching your money," he whispers fiercely. "But we'll find a way, I promise."

The front doorbell jingles, and as I leave, Merv is tucking Tommy under one of his tulip-pattern crocheted throws.

The customer out front wants to hunt through our Nora Roberts collection to find one she hasn't read before, so I leave her to it, and risk the cardinal sin of pulling out my phone on the sales floor. With one eye on the back door to make sure Merv isn't about to catch me, I speed-text the only person I can think to talk to in this situation.

Jerz—you busy?

About to give a talk. Call u 2nite?

Can you come over? Things are bad

Shit. Emergency?

NO. Not really. It can wait til tonight

I can call after 8

Okay! Talk then

I manage to tuck my phone back into the drawer under the cash desk when Merv emerges. A close call, but worth it. Talking things through with a friend always helps. Jersey will know what to do.

All the same, for the rest of the workday, as I hunt down books for customers and sell several pots of tea, I worry. I know, even though Merv did not point it out, my gesture is futile. With the increase in rent, my savings can buy us little more than a month's extension to Venal's threat.

A sense of doom settles on the place like a shroud. It's so bad that when Jonah Dross walks through the door before closing, I actually agree to leave with him.

chapter two

IMAGE: China Teacup
IG: Romy_K [NYC, March 14]
#TimeforTea #AnUnwelcomeOffer
5 ♥

So. Jonah Dross. Every woman knows a Jonah Dross. I mean, he's a nice enough guy, I guess. Tall in a gangly way—all large feet and pointy elbows. Manages a call center in one of the buildings across the street. He works nights, so he stops by almost every day before closing to buy a cup of tea.

No books, because Jonah Dross doesn't have time to read. He's a working man, isn't he?

Which, quite frankly, says it all.

I happen to know he lives with his mother, in an apartment overlooking one of the runways outside of Newark, but I'm completely unwilling to ever bring this up in his presence.

A typical visit from Call Center Jonah starts something like this:

Bell rings at front door and then Jonah slopes in, hands in pockets. Around him floats a miasma of Axe, or maybe its dollar store cousin.

"Morning!" he shouts, cheerily, to whomever might be in the shop that day.

It's never morning.

Of course, if a customer dares point this out, he beams, pats them on the shoulder, and says, "Maybe not for you, but it's morning for me!"

If there is no unfortunate customer around, Jonah will nod at Merv, who returns the nod, says "Jonah" in an undertone, and goes back to whatever it is he's doing.

In the meantime, at the first ring of the bell, I've bolted to hide behind the tea counter. Jonah, after pausing at the graphic novel display, will spot me—particularly if I've been slow off the mark—and then veer straight over. He'll smack his hand on the counter and smirk.

"The usual, wench!" he'll say.

Every day.

For the first year, I inevitably replied, "Please don't call me *wench*, Jonah."

To no effect. Jonah has a litany of excuses, including "I'm only ribbing you," "It's just banter," and the ever-popular, "Jeez, Romy, can't you take a joke?"

Worse—Jonah is a toucher. Nothing serious, of course. He's never copped a feel or even brushed against me in a questionable way. He merely wants to touch my arm when he talks to me. Pat my hand when he pays for his tea. Squeeze my shoulder when something good has happened at his work. I cannot count the number of hugs I've dodged on statutory holidays when the shop is open, and he's so delighted, he must "thank me properly."

I've tried ignoring him, heading for the back room as soon as I spot him, and even patiently explaining my problems with his behavior. Nothing works. After a while, I caved. For the past six months, I've made his tea and collected his money in silence, trying, at the very least, to minimize our interaction time.

The only result is that Jonah has added "Cat got your tongue?" to his store of stock phrases.

However, two months ago, someone called immigration on Jonah's company. I watched the ICE sweep from across the street, my stomach in knots. When the dust—or in this case the snow, since it was just after Christmas—settled, half of Jonah's team was gone. To his credit, Jonah was horrified by this. Three of the staffers who ended up deported had worked at the call center longer than he had. He stepped up and vouched for a half-dozen workers who were legal but had misplaced papers or other legitimate excuses. But mostly, he hugged people goodbye and scrambled to fill the positions with documented workers.

Since the raid, he's been after me to come work for him. It has become part of his regular repertoire:

"Morning!"

"The usual, wench!"

"Whatsa matter? Cat got your tongue?"

"C'mon, Romy—I can give you a better job than this. Work for me and we'll have a riot every day. What do you say?"

And up until now, I've said nothing. Usually, after he's loaded his pockets with sugar packets, he winks at me a couple of times before finally heading in to his work.

But today? I crumble like a New York cheesecake.

On the dot of 4:45 p.m., the bells attached to the front door jingle. I sigh and put down the books I'm shelving. As I trudge over behind the tea counter, the expected voice rings out.

"Morning!"

Merv is not behind the cash desk, and so by the time I pull out the tin of Earl Grey, Jonah has made it to the counter. He slaps his hand down.

"The usual, wench!" he says, smirking.

"Earl Grey?" I reply, interrupting before he has a chance to bring up the damn cat.

A look of stunned surprise crosses his face. "Yes!" he says joyfully. "That's right—Earl Grey. *Thank you,* Romy!"

He's so thrown off, he actually accepts his tea before reengaging his autopilot. "C'mon, Romy," he begins, but before he can get the rest out, I cut him off.

"Okay," I say.

He stares at me, mouth open, and then twitches with shock. This sends a small wave of boiling tea across both his hand and the counter, which he apparently does not even register.

"Wha—what?" he mutters.

I pass him a wad of napkins for his hand, and use a rag to wipe up the spilled tea.

"Okay. I'll come with you and have a look at the place," I say. "No promises, though."

Jonah leaps behind the corner and grabs my hand, shaking it in both of his. "Wonderful news," he says, looking dazed. "I can't believe it!"

"Neither can I," I mutter, and toss the cloth into the sink.

By the time I grab my coat, Uncle Merv is back in his spot behind the cash desk. His stunned expression echoes the one on Jonah's face.

"I'm going out," I say. "I'll be back in time to help balance the till." And I march through the door.

Call Center Jonah is back on form even before we make it across the street.

"This is so fantastic," he cries, squeezing my shoulder. "We're going to have a riot every day, I promise you!"

I pinch my lips together and manage to dodge the spontaneous hug he tries to extend while we wait for the light. I do, however, allow him to hold open the door for me when we get to his building. Between his tea and the door, it means both his hands are busy.

I need to take these tiny wins where I can find them, okay?

The call center is even more depressing than Jonah himself. Five floors below ground, the place has McJob written all over it. The elevator doors open into a giant space, entirely divided up into hundreds of small cubicles. The air smells of dust and something chemical—maybe old Freon? Most of the cubicles are populated with folks whose glazed expressions don't even flicker as we walk by. The ceiling is grey, the walls are grey, and the fabric of the cubicles is—you guessed it—grey.

Someone has strung up grimy, pennant-style flags that sag limply from the acoustic ceiling tiles. Each flag boasts a different motto: "Be the change!" "The promise of tomorrow is today's joy!" "Get in the zone!" My favorite is "Think Different!" which I'm almost sure has been lifted from Apple. Maybe *all* the flags were lifted from somewhere, but if they were, it wasn't recently. It looks like they've been hanging around for a long time.

This dank atmosphere is filled with a low drone made up of one-sided conversations, humming air conditioners, and buzzing fluorescent lights. The place holds none of the musty joy of our old bookshop, and seconds after I step into this low-ceilinged office, claustrophobia begins to squeeze its stealthy hands around my heart.

As Jonah enthusiastically tours me through the call center, he so thoroughly mansplains the details of the position, I can't even work in a single question. When at last we end up in the small glass box that is Jonah's office, he presses me to take a seat, so he can fill out my application on the spot. I only make my escape by taking a paper copy, promising a decision by the next day, and enduring one last, overlong, congratulatory hug. He's offering what seems to be an impossibly high salary, but at what cost?

After the meeting, I stumble out of the building and back across the street to the bookshop. Merv brightens when he sees me, and waves away my proffered help with the cashing out. Instead, he cheerfully inquires about what he refers to as the "call center opportunity."

I don't dare tell him the salary Jonah's quoted. Instead, I mumble something and flee up the stairs to my tiny apartment above the bookshop. Worse than the situation itself, is seeing how thrilled my uncle seems at the possibility of my impending employment elsewhere. One less worry for him.

It's a sickening thought.

chapter three

IMAGE: Cookbook Aisle
IG: Romy_K [NYC, March 14]
#BookshopLove #HOTReader
2 ♥

It's ten past eight by the time my phone rings. My friend Jersey is two months and two days older than I am. She has russet skin, round brown eyes, and a smile that's wide and white and warm. She's also an inch taller, and shares my general disregard for any kind of team sports. Two tall girls who don't play basketball. It is a friendship for the ages, I promise you.

"Look, I'm sorry I can't come over and drink wine with you. My advisor needs to see me at eight thirty. What's going on? Tell me everything."

Since my own bottle of wine is already open, I take a big sip and do exactly as directed.

The most important thing to know about Jersey is she's smart. Like rocket-scientist smart. We met and bonded in secondary school; two nerdy girls who loved to read. She, in defiance of her name, actually hails from Long Island, but moved to the East Village when she turned thirteen. Our friendship endured, in spite of the fact she shot past me in school. By the time I was into the first year of my B.A., Jersey? Was starting her master's in art history.

These days, she's getting ready to submit her dissertation in museum studies. The actual title is "Suppressed Identities: The Role of Race in Contemporary Collection Curation." This is her second dissertation, to be perfectly clear. She's going to be a double doctor at age twenty-seven. A double doctor, and a friend who gives good advice.

After I finish my tale of woe, she's so quiet, I'm worried I've lost her.

"No, I'm still here," she says. "Is—is Call Center Jonah really so bad, Romy? I mean—can you choke down working there for a few months, maybe?"

I pull the phone away from my ear and stare at it for a minute. "I guess there's really no other choice," I whisper, at last. If Jersey can't see a way out, all hope is lost.

An uncomfortable silence falls, and I hear a knock on her end of the line.

"Shit," she hisses. "It's my advisor. I've got to go."

"Thanks for talking it out with me," I say, but she's gone.

I sit on the couch and last ten full minutes before I start to hyperventilate. Since it's too late to go to the library, I pull out my bullet journal and make a list.

Jobs I'd take over the call center:

1. *Library reshelver*
2. *Barista*
3. *Library cafe barista*
4. *Janitor*
5. *MTA station employee*
6. *Library bag checker*

Available jobs that pay better than the call center:

. . .

When I can't think of a single item to add to my second list, I flip open the lid of my computer and look through the job listings on Monster, and even—universe forgive me—LinkedIn. But the city's in a downturn. Even after scrolling all the jobs I can find, there's still not one that pays better than the call center.

Maybe Jersey's right. Maybe Jonah's not so bad.

In the end, I fall asleep on my couch and dream of working for an octopus.

The slimy thing has eight arms, and the face of Call Center Jonah.

Sometime after two, I wake with a start. Staring up into the dark, I remember where I've seen Venal's nephew before. It was in the shop, of course, since I'm rarely anywhere else. At the time, I thought he was an ordinary customer—but was he? Could he have, in fact, been checking us out on behalf of his Evil Landlord uncle?

I lie back in bed and replay the whole interaction in my mind.

It was last Tuesday, I think—or maybe Wednesday. I remember I had been sorting through a newly donated collection of fantasy paperbacks. The books were in pretty good shape, which was a bonus. They'd been bequeathed by a regular customer I knew only as Old Harold, to his daughter Janice. Janice is a customer, too, but while she's a reader like her dad, her tastes run more to Judith Krantz and Danielle Steel. In fact, I only learned that very morning that Old Harold had passed, when Janice lugged in a big carton of her dad's Wheel of Time and Game of Thrones books. After giving Janice a hug and seeing her off to the funeral home, I'd spent the rest of the morning sorting through her late father's collection.

The Evil Nephew made it almost to the back of the store that morning, before I noticed him. Morning shoppers are inevitably retired folks who have the freedom for a leisurely daytime browse, so when the front doorbell jingled, I hadn't even glanced up. But as I dropped the last of the unwanted Robert Jordan paperbacks into the discard pile, a movement caught my eye. My first glimpse was of the back of his head, above the shelf in the cooking section. He was tall, with dusky skin and dark hair tied into a low ponytail. As I stared at the back of his head, he made a triumphant little noise and disappeared from view. Seconds later, as he was striding toward me carrying a large book in his hands, I got my first clear look at his face.

I have to admit, it made for compelling viewing. Of course, I had no idea at that time of his role as the Evil Nephew. As far as I was concerned, he was merely a customer of unusual youth and beauty. Dark hair, flashing eyes, and the lanky, easy gait of an athlete. As a result, as is the case with all such customers, my mind clicked straight into the HOT Reader rating system. The HOT Reader—Handsome, with Outstanding Taste—rating system was invented back when Jersey and I were working part-time for the uncles during the summer we turned fifteen. Good-looking guys walking into the bookstore were a comparative rarity even then, and Jersey was determined to make the best of any potential dating material that crossed our paths. She considered anyone who rated over a 7.5 as flirt-worthy.

In our defense, what sets this system apart from the usual, sexist one-to-ten scale is that it doesn't matter how good looking the guy is—the rating system is based purely on the quality of his reading material. The book's format is inconsequential—we don't downgrade guys reading graphic novels or even comic books, as long as the source material is interesting. Jersey's a fan of thrillers, but if the guy slapped a Dan Brown on the counter that summer?

3.5, tops.

As for me, I invariably awarded bonus points for any kind of romantic content, regardless of genre. Back when we were fifteen, Jersey and I agreed that a ten on the HOT Reader scale meant definite marriage material. I guess it says something about the pathetic state of my love life that I still haven't ever met even one customer who has ever rated that elusive ten.

All this is to say that when a good-looking guy wearing chef's whites under his parka placed a copy of *The French Chef in America* down on the cash desk, I couldn't help feeling intrigued.

"Julia Child," he said, and grinned at me. He smelled of cinnamon and cloves and warm bread, which was a little on the nose, considering his book selection.

"That's—uh—not her cookbook, you know," I mumbled. His grin was distracting, and I was doing some rapid calculations in my head at the time. I hurriedly jotted a 7.5 on the pad of paper on the desk, so I could remember to tell Jersey.

His left eyebrow rose, forming a sharp triangle. "Yep—I know. I already have her cookbook. I want to read about her life."

I scratched out the 7.5 and replaced it with an 8.5. I'm not great at small talk at the best of times, and I hadn't actually read this book beyond glancing at the summary when I shelved it. So, in that moment, I just stared at him like a tongue-tied idiot.

"Are you a chef?" I blurted, at last.

His smile faltered a little. "I used to be."

I found myself suddenly in that weird netherworld where I was desperate to know his whole story, and completely unable to find the words to ask without sounding nosy.

In the end, all I could manage was: "That'll be four fifty."

He slid a five across the cash desk, and when I handed him back two quarters, he dropped them into the "Save the Children" collection tin on the counter. Mustering up a smile again, he said: "Have a great afternoon, Ramona," and marched away before I could even offer him a bag for his purchase.

In the moment, I'm ashamed to admit I thought he'd read my name tag because he liked the look of me.

"Thanks!" I called out, to his back. "Same to you! See you . . ."

But the jingle of the door cut me off, and he was gone.

". . . next time," I finished. So much for liking the look of me.

I was so sure I'd never see him again, I hadn't even called Jersey to discuss his rating. And that's where things stayed until this morning.

So. Was his visit last week a setup? Not a chance encounter, but a case of him scoping the place out, prior to his Evil Uncle making a play for our bookshop? A wave of shame washes over me at the memory of giving the guy a HOT Reader rating, when his goal is clearly only to destroy my family's little business.

As I stare with burning eyes into the dark, it seems forever before the guilt and worry ebb away long enough for me to fall into an exhausted sleep.

chapter four

IMAGE: Assorted Delectables
IG: Romy_K [NYC, March 15]
#LifeChangingPastry #AFlyerintheWind
13 ♥

By the next morning, the snow has stopped, but many of the back streets are still sporting a sheen of black ice. Tommy's picked up a cold somewhere, and so I wrap my head in a scarf to protect myself from the wind whipping between the buildings, and head out to Claire's Patisserie for croissants. After taking a single step into the street, I dash back inside to grab my camera. The grey overcast hemming us in for weeks has blown away overnight, and the sun is rising through low fog like a ripe red dragon's egg, way down the end of our street.

I've been taking pictures as long as I can remember. My dad was a photographer before I was born, and there were always cameras around the house when I was small. He shot for AP overseas—Falkland Islands during the conflict, and Ireland too—but after I came along, he mostly freelanced. And when I made it into NYU, I majored in photography. I've always planned to take it further, but—well, you know. Life gets in the way. With this news about the bookshop, the chance of returning to film school is looking increasingly unlikely.

These days I mostly scratch the photo itch by posting to Insta-

gram, almost exclusively in black and white. I live in the best place in
the world for fascinating subject matter, so why not? I've always got
my phone at hand, so it's my go-to, but I still like to pull out my dad's
old Canon, for the special ones.

Freezing my fingers, I take shots of the sun, being careful not to
look straight at my subject. Only when it vanishes behind the towers
of Stuytown do I sling my camera back around my neck and head
off to the patisserie.

Claire is as French as I am, but her baking skills are top-notch. I
go through a mental checklist of favorites I need for the tea shop—
the croissants, of course, both almond and chocolate; a dozen Danish
pastries; and maybe some petit fours, if they aren't sold out already.

About halfway down the block, the wind swirls, blowing my
scarf off my head. I pause beside a light standard to readjust. As I'm
tucking in the ends, a page flapping on the pole catches my eye. The
flyer reads:

JOB OPPORTUNITY

ExLIBRIS EXPEDITIONS—

OPENING THE BOOK ON ADVENTURE

Help Wanted: Special Projects Planner

Apply in Person

The text of the flyer has been done on a computer, but the phone
number is repeatedly handwritten on little pull-off tabs at the bottom.

I finish tucking in my scarf and dash into the patisserie, but while
I'm selecting the day's choices, my mind keeps going back to the flapping flyer. Aside from photography, the one thing I'm really good at
is organizing. This is inevitable, after all my years toiling at an independent bookshop. It takes a lot of work to keep Uncle Merv together.

I've never heard of ExLibris Expeditions, but if it involves planning, I'm their girl. I've been planning things my whole life.

Planning to go to film school.

Planning to get out more.

Planning to meet the perfect boyfriend.

I'm so distracted by this last thought, Claire has to ask me twice to pay for my purchases. I hand over the money, and step back into the wind, clutching my brown paper bag of deliciousness.

I aim straight for the light standard.

Someone has seen the flyer before me, because one of the little tabs is missing. As I yank another one off, the whole page comes loose and sails away down the street.

I tear the seam under the arm of my coat chasing after it.

When I finally corral it, the flyer has blown up against the brick wall of Jonah's call center building. It's completely crumpled, and I dismiss the idea of reattaching it to the pole. For one thing, I don't have tape or staples or anything of the sort. And for another . . .

The little tab has the phone number, but the address for ExLibris Expeditions—which, what even *is* that?—is printed in a tiny font on the bottom of the flyer. Clutching the page, I glance upward at the hideous orange, blinking logo for Jonah's company, Digi-Dial. Inside, deep underground, a grey office decorated with dusty, sagging flags awaits me. Making up my mind, I jam the page into my coat pocket, and fight the wind all the way back to the bookshop. Nothing—I mean *nothing*—can be worse than accepting a job with Call Center Jonah.

The rest of the day is taken up with helping customers and alphabetizing the new inventory. After closing, as I'm giving the cash desk a last tidy before heading up to my place, Uncle Merv calls me from the back.

Merv and Tommy's apartment behind the bookstore is bigger than mine, and rightly so, seeing as it houses two men and a cat. The living room is filled with overstuffed chairs that are threadbare with age, and awash in the smell of Tommy's homemade potpourri. I've spent many happy hours here over the years, but I settle into one of the chairs feeling worried at the expression on Merv's face. I can hear Tommy in the kitchen, alternately coughing and singing along to his favorite aria from *La Traviata*. Smells of basil and garlic come wafting out, strong enough to almost defeat the potpourri.

Almost.

Merv clears his throat, his expression serious. "I've had several calls today," he says. "From Jonah Dross."

Shit. "Listen, I'm really sorry. He's been bugging me for months to come work for him, and I only went over there to get him to quit bothering me about . . ."

Merv holds up a hand. "It's not a bad idea," he says quietly, which silences me completely. "I can certainly arrange to cut back your hours at the shop so you can go to work for Jonah, if it's what you want."

"Uncle Merv," I stammer. "I'm not—not even really considering it. You've got to know my whole heart is here at the bookshop, with you and Tommy."

Merv reaches forward and squeezes my hand. "I can't afford to pay you anymore, love," he says, and the tone of his voice causes something in my heart to break.

Neither one of us can speak for a moment, and we both sit and listen to a paroxysm of coughing coming from the kitchen.

Somehow, I recover my voice again. "I'll find a job," I promise my uncle. "Do *not* worry about me." A feeling of panic, pure and raw, is firing adrenaline from my gut right through me. I jump to my feet.

He sighs. "Will you stay for dinner?" he asks. "I don't think Tommy's contagious."

Jamming my hands into my pockets so he can't see them shake, I plaster on a fake smile and shake my head. "There's something I've got to do," I say.

"Sure thing, honey," he answers mildly. "Wrap up warm."

chapter five

IMAGE: Library Lion
IG: Romy_K [NYC, March 15]
#NYPL #PatienceorFortitude #OrderfromChaos
6 ♥

There's only one way to soothe a panic this deep. After wrapping up warmly as admonished, I stand on the street and check my phone. Luck is with me. It's a late-opening day.

Of course it is. The library always knows.

Generally when I'm home, getting to the New York Public Library means hopping the 7 train to get to the Main Branch. The Mulberry Street branch is way closer, of course, but for a feeling this bad, only the Main Branch will do. Besides, history has taught me the best thing for a panic attack is action. I decide to hoof it.

It's always tourist season in New York—even on a windswept March evening—and soon I'm close enough to the fashionable part of Manhattan to adopt the native New Yorker walk. Head angled down, stride long, speed high. Of course, the real key is to make eye contact with no one. This serves to keep all the hawkers at bay, and tonight? It also means no one can read the fear in my eyes.

I'm full-out running by the time I spot Patience and Fortitude, the two stone lions guarding the front door of the library. Glancing at my phone, I see it's after seven. Less than an hour until they shut the place down, but that's okay. What I need won't take long. I stand in the line to show the guard the inside of my handbag, and then I'm through.

Stepping to one side for a moment, I stop and just breathe the place in. Considering our respective inventories, it smells remarkably different than Two Old Queens. Of course there are the scents of books and ink and paper, but here at the library, it's more—careful. The temperature is better regulated, and the shelving radiates the comforting smell of lemon polish.

Most visitors end up in the General Research area with its windows and high ceilings, or maybe take a wander over to Manuscripts and Archives. Not me. I veer away from the crowd, make a hard left, and head straight for my favorite room.

I'm not sure who Miriam and Ira D. Wallach were, but—folks? You don't know how many times you've saved my sanity. The Wallach Room is the photography archive for the library, of course, but it's also my happy place. You want to find a specific daguerreotype from 1850? Or maybe you're looking for something from the Annie Leibovitz collection? Or what if you need the entire history of everything appearing on film? The Wallach Room is your go-to.

But truthfully? I almost never look at any photos in here.

I mean, I have. Lots of times. When I was still in school at NYU, I was here weekly for that very purpose. When you're chasing an arts degree with a focus on photography, this place holds a lot of answers.

These days, though? Well, mostly I come here—to remember how to breathe.

To sit in a very proper, upright wooden chair at a desk in which my position is actually numbered. To rest my fingertips lightly on a polished surface unobscured by piles of papers, unsorted magazines, or books of every genre and condition. To watch—in a totally non-creepy way, I promise—the resident librarian as he glides from his seat behind the front desk across the room, retrieving stray elements of the collection. Sorting them. Filing them. Returning them.

This is the organizational center of the universe.

This library is the second largest in the country, third in the world. It's got a collection topping fifty-three million items, and a staff of more than three thousand people. And it is the tidiest place I know. I can take a chair at my numbered seat in my favorite room, and within minutes—within seconds—the peace of the place wraps itself around me like a cloak. Like one of those heavy blankets that people—people who don't suffer from claustrophobia, I hasten to add—use to calm themselves into sleep.

Of course, you might think it's crazy for a person who works in a bookstore to find comfort in a library. What can I say?

Maybe it *is* crazy. But you know what? It works.

Tonight, the polished desks in the Wallach Room are almost completely unoccupied. A lady wearing a carefully pinned silk scarf around her neck sits at the table nearest the door. She's got three folios spread out in front of her and is so engrossed in her work, she doesn't lift her head as I come skidding into the room.

The librarian looks up immediately, a frown darkening his features. Horace is a guy who's had a grey buzz cut and black horn-rimmed glasses since I've been coming here. Which is to say, long before buzz cuts and horn rims made it back into vogue. As soon as he recognizes me, his brow clears. He does make a little patting gesture with his hand, indicating I should cool my jets, but I've already slowed to a walk. I give him something in the vicinity of a smile, and practically meander down to the end of the third table, my favorite.

I haven't even taken my seat yet and I already feel better. Horace has one of the old card catalogue drawers out on his desk. The sight of him returning the little rectangular squares carefully back to their correct alphanumeric locations makes me smile for the first time since before the new Evil Landlord made his presence known in our lives.

Pulling out a book to use as my cover, I slide my bag under the table and take my seat. I always have a book in my bag, in case I find myself on a train, or stopped at a light. Today's title is the latest Denise Mina mystery, set in Glasgow. At the moment, I'm still too roiled to read, but I open it anyway, turning my bookmark sideways to hold the pages open.

This is officially a Quiet Room, which means as soon as the disruptive noise I make getting to my seat ceases, absolute peace descends. Two aisles away, Elegant Scarf Lady reorders the contents of one of her portfolios. The soft shushing noise of the documents sliding against the table only adds to the comfort of the place.

Everything is going to be all right. It has to be. Our new Evil Landlord and his minion, the Evil Nephew, can't prevail. They can't because it would mean chaos would have a foothold, and my whole goal in life—my whole reason for existing—is to eliminate chaos. To make things run smoothly. To emulate what I see—what I feel in my very bones—around me right now. When I'm here, I know everything has a place. I have to believe this works in the wider world too. On some kind of larger, cosmic scale, even Frank Venal has a place somewhere, there is no doubt. But not in my life. Not in the lives of the people I love most.

I hear a rustle behind me, and instinctively turn the page of my novel. When I look up, I find it's only Horace. He shares the supervision duties of this department with a woman named Judith, but as she generally works mornings, I run into her less frequently. Horace and Judith have been here since long before I first came to discover this room, and together they are a well-oiled machine—toiling methodically and serenely to ensure no one who ever enters this room leaves unfulfilled.

Over the years, Horace and I have never discussed my need to come here, to find order when the rest of my life is a mess. We don't have to. We are simpatico. Possibly the fact I live and work with two sixty-something gay men doesn't hurt in this regard.

Nevertheless, it is unusual enough for Horace to float out from behind the front desk, that I turn enquiring eyes in his direction. His face, winter pale, breaks into a soft smile. Already, my own problems are fading.

"Everything okay?" Horace breathes near my ear, managing to effectively communicate his concern without violating my personal space.

"It is now," I whisper back, knowing that's enough. Horace never needs details.

There's a gentle whooshing noise, and suddenly a photograph lies on the polished surface in front of me.

"This crossed my desk last week," Horace says, his words a gentle zephyr in my left ear. "And I knew, somehow, it was meant for you. That is, for me to share with you."

After staring at the photo for a moment, I shoot him a sideways glance. His face reflects his usual serene state, his beatific smile broadening a little.

"Where—where did this come from?" I manage.

My newly found calm, while not shattered, is more perturbed than I can ever remember in this usually safe place.

"The provenance is not completely clear," he murmurs. "I believe it is one of a collection, taken in the Westfjords of Iceland, and photographed by a renowned traveler who goes only by the handle of Alex. Her—or his—collection, however, has been gaining notoriety over the past few years, and we have begun to amass a folio of their work."

He smiles, and angles the photograph more precisely on the desk in front of me. I stare down at it, mesmerized. The picture is of a grey wall, scarred and pitted and altogether unlovely. There's a tracing of ice along the ground and in one corner, a small pile of dirty snow. The wall is peppered with graffiti tags, but the photographer has focused the lens on a motto, scrawled in vivid magenta paint. It reads:

DO MORE OF WHAT MAKES YOU HAPPY

The word *happy*, unlike the rest, is rendered in a rainbow of colors.

"At first, I was ready to dismiss the work as trite," breathes Horace, after a moment. "But the more I look at it, the more I find it speaks to me."

For the first time in our acquaintance, Horace touches a hand to my shoulder.

"Perhaps you, too, may grasp the truth encapsulated within this work?" he asks.

Without another word, he rises, and returns to his desk, leaving the photo with its haunting message behind.

What makes you happy, Ramona? it whispers to me.

"This library," I whisper back. "My work. Making order out of chaos."

The woman two tables over looks up at me sharply. Her scarf has somehow come unpinned.

And suddenly? I know what to do.

Carefully scooping up Horace's photo by the edges, I return it to his desk. When he lifts a fist to me, I bump it with my own, and hurry out the door.

chapter six

IMAGE: Flatiron Building
IG: Romy_K [March 16]
#*ExLibris* #OpportunityorDisaster #DesperateTimes
6 ♥

The following morning, the address on the crumpled flyer leads me into a building that could not be more different than the call center. After riding one of the posh chrome elevators up forty floors, I step out to find a 360-degree view of New York City. It's been a long time since I've seen such a panoramic view of my home, and I pause for a moment to drink it all in. Then from behind me, I hear a quiet cough.

I turn to see a young woman with classic pre-Raphaelite features—dark hair and eyes, and skin the color of fresh milk. She identifies herself as Powell—just Powell—assistant to the CEO.

I give her my name and force myself to keep the crumpled page in my pocket. "I'm here to apply for the planning position. Is it still open?"

She rises from her seat and smiles kindly. "I don't believe a final decision has been made as yet. Let me take you in to see the boss."

"This is some view." It's impossible not to feel impressed.

There isn't a limp flag in sight.

Powell smiles. "You should see it from the penthouse. Breathtaking."

She walks me down a glass hallway to a set of heavy double doors. Embossed in gold leaf is a name plate which reads "Teresa Cipher, CEO ExLibris."

This throws me a little, as I expect to meet someone from human resources, not the CEO. But Powell taps lightly on the door, then swings it open. The CEO gets to start every day by looking out over the Flatiron Building, with the East River glittering behind it in the morning sun. The room itself is a study in understated elegance; all mahogany and glass and rosewood, with a floor-to-ceiling bookshelf along the inside wall.

"Ms. Cipher, this is Ramona Keene. She's here to inquire about the—er—new opening."

Behind the desk, Teresa Cipher gets to her feet. She is a statuesque blonde, with platinum hair, large carefully manicured hands, and a tight sheath dress. Around her wafts a cloud of equal parts Chanel No. 5 and cigarettes. Her flawless, powdered skin puts her somewhere between forty and sixty, though she may have been there awhile. Balancing an amber cigarette holder in one hand, she has a Hermès silk scarf fashioned into a sling on her other arm.

I don't know if I should offer to shake hands or not, and so I just stand there awkwardly as the assistant closes the door behind me. After a long moment while she takes me in from top to toe, Ms. Cipher speaks. "Please sit down," she says, in a cultivated baritone.

As I pull up an elegantly minimalist chair, I think of the many "No Smoking" signs I passed on my way through the building, and manage to suppress a sneeze.

Ms. Cipher opens our conversation with a brief précis of the company. ExLibris, it turns out, is a firm that specializes in replicating literary journeys. "If the book has been written," she says, "we find a way to re-create any experience depicted."

I don't even know how to respond to this. I can hear Tommy's voice in my head saying, *Some people have more money than sense,* but I crush that thought as it rises up.

"That's—incredible," I manage, at last. "So, you organize all the details behind the scenes?"

Her shoulders lift a fraction. "Well, travel can always be unpredictable. It helps that I am, at heart, a bit of a gambler. But I promise you, we've never disappointed a client. Our record is my proudest achievement."

She swivels her chair and gestures broadly at the book-covered wall. "ExLibris offers our clientele the journey of a lifetime. We produced the first Outlander tours in Scotland," she notes with a smile, pointing to a row of books on the shelf behind her. "Now the series has found a whole new life on television, our influence has become a trifle less exclusive over there, I have to admit."

I lean back in my chair, my eyes running across the huge collection of books on her shelves. The selection would please my Uncle Merv if he could see it. Ms. Cipher goes on to explain how the literary journeys she organizes run the gamut from re-creating the feast scene in Henry Fielding's *Tom Jones,* to a street tour of Gabriel García Márquez's Colombia.

"If a scene exists, we will take our client there in person, no matter how distant the setting," Teresa Cipher says. "It is our goal to create an adventure they will never forget."

I can't help smiling. "Just like *The Amazing Race?*" I ask. "Adventures all over the world?"

Ms. Cipher's face takes on a frozen expression. "Certainly not," she says derisively. "This is no tawdry reality show. We are offering as close to the genuine experience as possible, drawn from the pages of the client's favorite book. This is a *literary* endeavor, I assure you."

I shrink a little in my chair. Some of my favorite memories are of cuddling between my uncles as a child, watching *The Amazing Race* on the television that sits inside Tommy's antique armoire. With the exception of a school field trip in fifth grade, that show is the closest I've ever come to real travel. But clearly, Teresa Cipher doesn't share this view.

A large clock on the wall ticks loudly through this moment of awkward silence. When I can't stand it any longer, I clear my throat and ask about the job opening.

Teresa Cipher crushes out her cigarette and straightens her spine.

"ExLibris has been booming recently, and the company is short-staffed. One of my high-end clients, a Jules Verne fan, has decided that he'd like to retrace the journey of Phileas Fogg, on his round-the-world adventure. Due to the complexity and expense of such a journey, the organization would, under normal circumstances, be entirely under my purview."

She pauses, cautiously lifting the arm encased in the sling. "Unfortunately, I broke my arm last week after slipping on black ice. There's no way I can even carry a bag, let alone record the details of such an elaborate project."

She raises an eyebrow at me. "You are familiar with the story, I take it?"

I have been sitting pretty much in stunned silence all this time, but I nod at this. "Absolutely," I say, clutching at a vague memory of reading the book as a teen.

All the same, as the CEO opens a case on her desk to extract another cigarette, I can feel my eyes narrowing. For one thing, I'm quite sure the woman sitting in front of me has never carried anything heavier than a clutch purse in her life, let alone luggage.

I decide to take the plunge. "Can you tell me what the position entails?"

Ms. Cipher flicks a gold lighter and inhales deeply before answering. "The job," she says, the smoke trickling out slowly with her words, "is to follow in the footsteps of the famous protagonist Phileas Fogg. Specifics of the journey—including recommended modes of travel, suitable accommodations, and associated activities—are then reported back to our offices here at ExLibris. From here, our staff compile this information and generate a safe, contemporary adventure for the client."

I can feel my jaw drop. "So, not only organizing, then? I would— I mean, the person who gets this job—would need to actually take a trip around the world?"

Teresa Cipher nods. "The chosen candidate will be provided with a camera-equipped smartphone, and a prepaid credit card, allowing for a reasonable per diem to cover sustenance, accommodation, and travel. All methods of transportation are acceptable, with the single exception of airlines."

I hold up a hand. "Excuse me? How can it even be possible to get around the world without airplanes?"

She shrugs. "The goal is to make real the travels of the fictional Phileas Fogg. There can be no commercial aircraft involved, naturally, as the book was written before the advent of tourist-based airlines. Of course, our timeline is very short, so we can't expect there will be *no* air travel, but nothing of a commercial nature is acceptable. Our client wants to re-create Fogg's actual experience, warts and all."

The very idea of this stuns me into silence.

After a moment, Teresa Cipher leans forward. "Do you hold a valid passport?"

"I have a passport," I reply carefully. This statement is only *technically* true, but I'll worry about the details later.

"Excellent," continues Teresa, crushing her cigarette into a crystal bowl. "The idea is that our selected candidate will keep in close communication, connecting with our office at each checkpoint. We expect regular e-mails, reporting each leg of the journey and the suitability for the client. This may include photo documentation, and brief interviews with a few of the more unique and amusing individuals encountered along the way. Should the chosen mode of travel prove too arduous, of course, alternatives must be determined and presented in these reports."

I squeeze my hands together under the desk so the trembling doesn't show. "Very *interesting*," I croak.

Perhaps sensing my anxiety, Teresa Cipher locks her eyes on me. "You *are* fond of travel?" she asks.

I hope the heat I can feel rising on my neck stays below my collar. "Absolutely," I insist, with as much bravado as I can muster.

Desperate times call for desperate measures, I think, pasting on a confident smile. After all, the situation with my uncles and the bookshop could *not* be more desperate.

"Excellent," says the CEO, and I allow myself to breathe again.

Abruptly, Teresa Cipher uses her good hand to push back her chair. "This client is an American," she says, reaching for one of the leather-bound editions on the shelf behind her desk. "And so, the decision has been taken to start and end the quest right here in the most quintessential of American cities—New York."

As she slides the book carefully off the shelf, I see "Jules Verne" written in gold leaf on a half-dozen other titles nearby. "Obviously," she adds, "circumstances are different today, a hundred and fifty years on from when Verne wrote this story."

With a single fingertip, she slides the volume across the desktop. It spins slowly, so by the time it reaches me, the title is face up.

"The goal is for our contemporary traveler to hit the same touchpoints as Fogg did, to experience how the world has changed since the time the novel was penned, but also to see how it remains the same."

As it seems expected, I flip open the cover of the book, and can see right away that this volume is a recent reissue. It has an elegant leather binding with the requisite gold leaf for the title, but the inside holds none of the charm of most of the old books in my uncles' shop.

In fact, it looks like this edition has never been read.

In the quiet of the elegant office, my mind is racing. There's no question about it. This opening is a chance to see the world, all expenses paid.

And I've never heard anything more frightening in my life.

The CEO's voice breaks in on my thoughts. "I should add that additionally, this trip is to serve as a testing ground. Should all expectations be met, on successful completion, the candidate will be offered a full-time position with ExLibris."

"Is that so?" I reply, working hard to keep the fear out of my voice.

"Indeed. The starting salary is only fifty thousand dollars a year, I'm afraid, but we will offer a project completion bonus of ten thousand dollars to the successful candidate."

My heart is pounding so hard, I'm quite sure she can hear it from her spot across the giant mahogany desktop. Not knowing what else to do, I slide my résumé across the desk. It's only a single page long, and I regret not having taken time to pad it up a bit. One look, and she'll know how desperately unqualified I am for this position.

But Teresa Cipher gives the page only the briefest of glances before turning her attention back to me.

"Photographer, hmm? What is your experience on foreign soil?"

I don't even have to think hard about this one, since I've only been on foreign soil once in my life.

"I—ah—recently had a wonderful time photographing the Bonhomme at Carnaval in Quebec City," I reply, wondering in what universe fifteen years ago counts as recent. And then, remembering the school report I must have on a hard drive somewhere, I add: "I can forward you the review I wrote at the time, if you'd like."

Teresa Cipher delicately extinguishes her cigarette. "Not necessary," she says. "This company is unlike any other, of course, so most of the required insight is acquired on the job." She slides my résumé back across the desk. "Thank you for coming in. Please drop this off with my assistant. I'll consider your application along with the others."

"The others?"

"Oh, I have interviewed several other potential candidates," she assures me, smiling.

I know I'm expected to leave at this moment, but I feel somehow frozen to my seat. During the whole of this interview, I've been mostly in a state of shock. The desk job I thought I was applying for is in fact so much more. But the sorry truth is that I have never—not even once—traveled anywhere alone in my entire life.

Suddenly, in spite of my tiny résumé, I'm determined to admit no such thing to this chic person patiently waiting to usher me out of her elegant office. And in spite of the fear clenching my stomach, the idea that someone else could snatch this opportunity away is unbearable.

This job is the ideal solution to every one of my problems. It's an opportunity to add some international flavor to my photography portfolio. An opportunity to avoid taking a job in Call Center Jonah's seventh level of hell. And an opportunity, as terrifying as it seems, to see the world for myself, instead of waiting for adventure to walk through the door of my uncle's bookshop. Even better, expenses are covered, so all the money earned can go straight to saving the shop from our evil new landlord. And, if everything works out, I will even have a real job to return to.

Still, I can't help feeling the whole thing seems too good to be true. Instead of getting up to leave, I lean forward.

"What's the catch?" I blurt, before I can stop myself.

Teresa Cipher, who had half risen out of her chair, resumes her seat and crosses her legs. From where I'm sitting, I can see how one of her shoes, which is likely worth more money than I've made in the last year, casually dangles from the toes of that foot.

"No catch," she replies. "But of course, there are certain— parameters. Our chosen candidate must be ready to embark almost immediately, and to follow the literary itinerary as provided. We expect frequent, detailed updates, this last being nonnegotiable, as we require sufficient, timely information to generate the program of travel for our client. ExLibris will, of course, provide the communication equipment, and the candidate simply has to find an appropriate location to upload a digital file of text and photos at each checkpoint."

She stands, and I slowly make my way to my own feet. "Of course, should the candidate not fulfill any of these requirements, or, indeed, neglect to cover the entire distance in the maximum allotted time, their eligibility for the position, obviously, will be forfeit."

Ah, I think. *So, there* is *a catch.*

"The maximum time?" I ask softly. "You mean eighty days?"

For the first time, Teresa Cipher laughs. "Oh my goodness, no," she says. "Our client expects to depart in June. The reconnaissance trip must necessarily be very brief—and completed before the first of May, to allow sufficient time to get everything set for our client's journey."

Shooting a glance down at my phone, I'm stunned into silence at the sight of the date. Of course, this *is* the twenty-first century. It can't take more than four or five days to fly around the entire planet by air. I'm sure I read somewhere that the space station circles the planet every ninety-two minutes. How hard can it be to make it on the ground in seven weeks?

Another thought occurs to me.

"And if I return early? Before the beginning of May, I mean."

Teresa Cipher's face lights up. "As long as you've attained all the designated stops on the itinerary, and kept your reports up to date, we will consider the contract fulfilled."

Swinging open the door, she steps aside to allow room for me to pass. "My assistant, Powell, will give you an application form to complete before you leave. We'll be in touch."

To my surprise, she reaches out with her unencumbered hand as I walk past. It's her left hand, so the shake is awkward. Her grip is much firmer than I expect, but I do my best to reply in kind. This contest of wills is so brief, it's over almost before it begins, but her eyes twinkle at me as she releases my hand at last.

Deeply confounded by the whole encounter, I shake out my slightly crushed hand and flee down the corridor.

chapter seven

IMAGE: Around the World, First Edition
IG: Romy_K [March 16]
#JulesVerne #TheBookThatStartedItAll #LifeImitatesArt
13 ♥

You have to be the least qualified person on the planet for a job like this, Romy," says Tommy. His nose is red and raw from his head cold, but I can tell he feels he has to say something. Uncle Merv is so shocked, he can't even articulate a word. "You've never even been out of the city!"

"Have too," I counter quickly. "Fifth-grade field trip, Quebec City. It was *Carnaval, n'est-ce pas?*"

It's after nine thirty at night and I'm sitting with the uncles at their tiny kitchen table. Tommy has cleared the plates, and Merv is standing with the afterdinner teapot still in his hand. He finally sets the pot down, and shakes the heat out of his fingers, looking stunned.

I'm speaking with forced jocularity, pushing down the inner anxiety that is threatening to swamp me, but my terrible French is fooling no one. "If I get the job, the salary is fifty thousand dollars, Tommy. *And* there's a bonus of ten thousand dollars at the end. That's enough to buy us time to figure out how to save the bookshop."

Uncle Merv looks shaken and sighs heavily. "Darling girl, I'm moved that you'd even consider something like this, but you know it's a crazy idea, right?"

Before I can reply, he disappears through the door to the store. Tommy huffs impatiently and, without asking, pours me a cup of tea. I mutter my thanks and manage to avoid his gaze by fiddling with the sugar tongs. Two minutes later, Merv bursts back into the kitchen with a dusty old book in his hand.

"All the same, Phileas Fogg didn't fly commercial either, and he made it round in eighty days," he says as he hands me the book. "I guess you could do worse than follow his lead."

The cover of the book in my hand is green, and fairly battered around the corners. The title on both the spine and the front cover is outlined in gold leaf, and the pages still bear a trace of gilt on the edges. When I lift the cover, it smells something like a garden after a spring rain—raw and earthy and old. "Is this a first edition, Merv?" I whisper.

He nods. "It's dated 1873 on the title page, and this copy is even signed by the author," he says. "If you don't get the job, we can get ten grand for it—maybe twelve on eBay. But you hold on to it for now, for luck. Maybe it'll help you get the gig."

Tommy gives an impressive sniff, which manages to convey disdain and be slightly disgusting at the same time. "Don't encourage the child," he says, clattering the dishes in the sink with unnecessary vigor.

Merv pats my hand, and though my stomach is still in knots, I smile. I know how valuable this book is, and his faith touches me.

Later that night, as I turn out the lights in my wee apartment, my phone tings. It's an e-mail, but I don't recognize the sender at first— K. Powell. Then I see the e-mail domain is @exlibrisexpeditions.com, and I remember Ms. Cipher's assistant.

Writing on behalf of the CEO, Powell thanks me for my consideration, but politely indicates the position has been filled. She notes the successful applicant is a young photographer with extensive travel experience, *and* ten thousand followers on Instagram. Worse, this individual is apparently fully prepared to depart as soon as tomorrow—March 18th. On behalf of Teresa Cipher, Powell wishes me nothing but the best in my future endeavors.

Dropping my phone onto the pillow beside me, I close my eyes and desperately think back to the application form. Where did I go wrong? I *had* noted that I'm between boyfriends in the "Anything Else You'd Like to Share?" section. At the time, I reasoned that it might put me ahead of any applicants who have to worry about leaving behind relationships or families. But maybe it was too much information?

Grabbing the phone again, I scroll through the message app. It doesn't take long to find what I'm looking for, seeing as it's the final note from my last boyfriend.

The ignominy of being dumped by text rises up to swallow me again. I mean, it wasn't the great tragedy of my life or anything. Luis and I had only been going together for five months at the time of the dumping. All the same, I'd really liked him. I thought we had something special. When he'd invited me to visit his cousins over the New Year in Guadalajara, I'd embraced the idea at first. But as the date crawled closer, I found myself coming up with every possible excuse not to go. My uncles needed me over the holiday season. I was considering applying for an online course, and they were going to let me know in January. Mrs. Justice Rosa was going off to visit her grandchildren, and she'd asked me to look after her parrot.

In the end, I think it was the parrot that did it. I pull up his text and read it again.

What are you so scared of? he wrote. **You chose a freakin bird over a visit in the sun with my family?**

It's a long-standing obligation, I replied. I'm sorry. Can we meet for coffee and talk about it?

His final text came two nail-biting hours later. Nah. The parrot sez it all.

And that was it. He didn't answer any of my further texts.

I flip back over to my e-mail and read Powell's message again. At least *she* didn't throw a parrot in my face.

I drop the phone and pull my pillow over my head, forcing myself to face the truth. I hadn't gone with Luis, because it meant leaving the city. What kind of weirdo is willing to give up on a relationship with a lovely guy because she doesn't want to leave home?

"Something's got to change," I mutter aloud. "And if you're going to help save the bookshop, that something is you. *You* have to change, Romy. This might be your only chance."

I jump out of bed, too wired up to sleep. *I'll show him,* I think, scooping up the phone, and deleting all of Luis's messages for good measure. Justice Rosa's damn parrot will haunt me no more.

Since space is at a premium, I always store my out-of-season clothes in an ancient suitcase under my bed, and I pull it out now, and stare at it for a long moment. It's brown leather, more scuffed than a hobo's shoe, but all the hardware works fine. There's a single label affixed to the lid, a sticker made to look like an Alaskan license plate. The top of the sticker has worn away, but along the bottom, "The Last Frontier" is still readable. I run my finger over the words, just once, and then flip the lid open.

I spend the rest of the night alternatively gathering my very few belongings from around the tiny studio apartment, and writing lists. Once I've got everything packed, I sit down and jot a note to my uncles, filled with false optimism and inauthentic statements intended to make me sound bravely adventurous.

Fake it till you make it, Romy.

Next, I open Instagram, trying to scope out the competition. This is a big city, and it's filled with photographers. In the end, I narrow it down to three possibilities, each an increasingly photogenic young New York woman who has traveled the globe. I lose almost an hour clicking through their Insta stories, many of which feature artfully skimpy outfits. Two of the women have more than twelve thousand followers, and one has a hundred thousand.

I have thirteen.

I spend another twenty minutes trying to mimic their perfect over-the-shoulder smolders in my full-length mirror, but I have to quit when my neck starts to cramp.

Reading the names of the places they've been makes my throat close up. The jungles of Vietnam? Ice fields in Norway? One even worked as a janitor in Antarctica, purely for the opportunity to visit the seventh—and final—continent on her "bucket list." It makes this little race around the world seem like a walk in the park.

Not for me, though. Not for me.

I rub my sore eyes and try to swallow down my self-doubt. Even with the thought of beating out these smug faces, it takes concentration and quite a bit of deep breathing to convince myself I'm doing the right thing. My eyes fall onto the copy of Jules Verne's book, and I think about how, even in the face of Tommy's doubt, Merv still believes in me.

I glance over at the alarm clock on my bedside table and see it's 5:00 a.m. My Uncle Merv always rises at six, so—it's now or never. I clutch the handle of the old suitcase, tiptoe down the stairs, and leave the note for my uncles under the iron knocker on the door to their flat. Then I sneak out onto the street.

It's time to talk Teresa Cipher into giving me the job.

chapter eight

Packing List for Absurd Attempt at Traveling Around the World

Laptop, plus accessories
Phone, plus cord
Hair straightener
10 pr underwear
Bras—2 regular, 2 sports bras
Jeans—3 pr . . .

A bunch of streets are blocked off, and I worry there's been some kind of police incident, when I remember the date. Nothing stops traffic in New York City more effectively than the Saint Patrick's Day parade. Avoiding the preparations that are already in full swing, I slip down the stairs into the nearest station. This early, I have to wait fifteen minutes before a train pulls up. I use the time to list out all the things I've jammed into my college daypack and the old suitcase I pulled from under my bed.

It's a long list. I'm already regretting the fact the suitcase doesn't have wheels.

It's nearing six as I stagger up to the front of the towering home of ExLibris Expeditions. I expect to find the building locked up tight, but in fact, the front doors are already open. Inside, there's no guard behind the entrance desk, but the elevators are running. My plan to waylay the CEO before she arrives is thwarted when I find her office door open, and Teresa Cipher already at work.

Weirdly, she doesn't look at all surprised when I tap on her door. Or tired either.

"Lovely to see you again," she says, tucking a file folder away into her desk. "Ramona, isn't it?" When I nod, she adds: "I've been up all night, sorting out the details for our new candidate."

"About that," I say, and take a deep breath of the cigarette-scented air. Before she can get in a word, I throw back my shoulders and immediately launch into all the reasons I'm the best person for the job. Skirting my whole lack of travel experience, I whip out my bullet journal and read a list of every organizational-related skill I can make even the vaguest claim to. I wrap up with a catalogue of possibilities for increasing the company's social media follower count, which basically boils down to finding an audience by making a better use of hashtags.

As I finish, I look up to find Ms. Cipher listening intently. "Ramona," she says. "I need someone who is a quick decision maker and excels at planning on the fly. Can you do that?"

I straighten my spine, the better to squash the imposter syndrome that is swelling inside me. "I am the most organized person I know," I say, knowing this part, at least, is true. "I can do this."

"That's quite an impassioned defense of your abilities," she says. "But I need to make something clear. ExLibris is not some kind of high-end travel agency. Our mandate is to reproduce journeys from books as closely as possible. This very rarely ends up being a luxury experience, you understand?"

I nod silently.

"Good. Well then, if you had to pick one of your strengths, what would you say sets you apart? Why should I choose you?"

I bite down the urge to plead with her on behalf of Two Old Queens; to tell her the whole tale of the Evil Landlord and throw myself on her mercy. Instead, I reach into my pack and dig out the book my uncle gave me.

"I'm following in literary footsteps," I say as firmly as I can manage. "And I've grown up inside a working bookshop. You may find someone else with more travel experience or more social media followers, but no one can compete with this."

I carefully place the copy of Uncle Merv's book on the polished surface between us.

Teresa Cipher reaches across the desk, and without a word, flips open the cover. She gently touches the onionskin protecting the frontispiece, then runs her finger across the signature scrawled below the title.

Silently closing the book again, she stares wordlessly across the desk at me. The clock on the wall behind her ticks away the seconds, each one seeming longer than the last. When I think I can't stand the silence any longer, she leans back in her chair and shoots me an evil little grin. With a single smooth motion, she opens a drawer, extracts something, and slides it across the desktop.

It is a temporary credit card.

"This will do for you to get on with, Ramona Keene," she says. Retrieving a single sheet of paper from a folder on the desk, she lays it beside the card. The title reads "Projected Itinerary."

"I'll get the rest of your materials together today. If you *truly* are ready to take on this challenge, make your preparations and I'll see you back here in this office sometime before midnight."

"Are—are you serious?" I stutter. My bowels have suddenly turned to water.

Her grin broadens. "Absolutely. But the clock starts right now, and I need you back here in the city by the first of May. If you are going to have any chance at all, you'd best leave by tomorrow."

I jump to my feet, grab the card and the itinerary, and bolt from the room before either of us can change our minds.

chapter nine

IMAGE: Passport and Tequila
IG: Romy_K [NYC, March 17]
#PassportToAdventure #TakingMyBestShot
15 ♥

Not daring to go near the bookshop, I hop back on the subway and make my way to the passport office, down on Hudson Street. Since this only takes twenty minutes, I stop to grab a cup of tea at a nearby coffee shop, before heading toward the doorway under the American flag. Clutching my warm cup of tea, I wait outside for the place to open at nine.

Even at almost an hour early, I'm still five people from the front when the doors open. Nevertheless, I *am* early enough to qualify for an emergency renewal to my passport, provided I can show proof that I will, in fact, be leaving immediately.

This is starting to feel like it's meant to be. I fill out the forms, pay the fee with my new ExLibris-issued credit card, and then, fired up on caffeine and adrenaline, I lug my suitcase out the door. The next item on my list is to book a ticket for a speedy exit. Once I do, I can return and collect my new passport.

Outside, I pause for breath. This is really my first moment of still-ness since the caffeinated tea kicked my brain back into gear, and the magnitude of the undertaking hits me like a brick. A tsunami of exhaustion, fear, and—I can't quite believe it myself—excitement sweeps through me.

I decide the only thing to do is embrace the excitement and ignore the rest until it's too late to look back. Teresa Cipher's paperwork notes the name of a recommended travel agency, which is only a ten-minute walk away, according to my phone. It's a testament to my level of caffeination that I stride up to Go Global a mere seven minutes later.

Dropping my suitcase by the door, I pause outside to smooth out the itinerary, which has become crumpled and sweaty from being clutched in my hand on the way over. Suddenly the door flies open beside me, and as someone comes rushing out, I stagger back, trip over my suitcase, and go flying.

My daypack takes the brunt of the fall, so while I'm winded, nothing really hurts. But the instinct to leap back to my feet is stymied by the heavy suitcase, which is pinning one of my legs. I flounder around on my back, stuck like a turtle overturned on its shell.

"I'm *so* sorry," comes a deep voice from behind me, and a pair of large male hands quickly set me back on my feet. It's not until I'm vertical again that I realize who the hands belong to.

Before me stands the Evil Nephew himself.

"I'm sorry," he says again. "Are you okay?" He's red in the face, clearly embarrassed to have knocked me over, and it takes him a second or two longer to recognize me. I recoil in horror and snatch my arms away.

"What the *hell* are you doing?" I splutter.

"I—I didn't see you behind the door," he says defensively. "Are you okay?"

"I'm fine," I mutter, quickly scooping up my scattered papers from the floor. "It doesn't matter. The only thing that matters at the moment is the fact that your uncle is trying to take away the livelihood of my family."

"He's *not* my uncle," he says.

"So—you're just his lackey, then?"

His expression darkens. "What exactly do you mean by *that*?"

Grabbing my suitcase, I push past him and stomp to the closest desk. By the time I think of a suitably cutting reply, he's gone.

Just as well, since I have no time to waste exchanging barbs with the guy who may or may not be Frank Venal's Evil Nephew. What I need is to find a way out of this city, and soon.

Booking the first leg of this insane adventure takes longer than I expect, mostly because the travel agent is so skeptical of my choices. I need to leave the country by tomorrow—but not on a plane? Things get a little smoother once I explain the parameters of what I'm trying to do.

The travel agent, whose nameplate reads "Lakeesha Jones," smirks at me.

"Girl—you heading off on a round-the-world trip by yourself? Planning on a little *Eat Pray Love* action while you're on the road?"

I can feel myself blushing, which irritates me. "Of course not. It's for my job. A—uh—potential job, anyway."

"Uh-huh," Lakeesha says. "Well, let's see what I can do for you." Her fingers clack away on the keyboard, and after a minute she swings her screen around to show me what she's come up with.

"A—boat? Like a cargo boat?"

"It's a container ship. But they occasionally take passengers. You got lucky, Ramona. Openings like this usually need to be booked months in advance."

Rubbing my suddenly damp palms against my jeans, I try again. "I was thinking of something more like—a cruise ship, maybe?"

She laughs out loud at this. "Leaving New York mid-March? I don't think so."

In the end, since I don't have any better ideas, I slide my new credit card across the counter to her, and she hands me a ticket.

As I race back down the street to the passport office, my mind returns to the interaction with the Evil Nephew. I suppose it *is* possible he has no say in Venal's business, and might, in fact, not be evil at all. On the other hand, he might be lying through his teeth. Who knows? All the same, I feel guilty for snapping. The whole lackey thing was a step too far. *I've had this job less than a day and I'm already on the moral low ground,* I think gloomily.

A more worrisome thought strikes me. Evil Nephew or not— what the hell was he doing at the travel agency?

The worst part of sitting in the passport office is the anxiety. By four thirty, my guts are churning. Apart from a short tea and bathroom break around two, I've been sitting here in the waiting room all afternoon. What have I gotten myself into?

The truth is, I'm not sure what makes me feel worse—the worry that they won't be able to sort out my passport in time, or that they will. It's not until ten minutes before the end of the business day that my name is finally called.

The woman behind the booth is dressed in a green satin blouse tucked into a navy skirt and her name tag reads 'Juanita.' She pulls a file folder across the desk and looks through the glass at me, her dark eyes crinkling at the corners.

"You're the last of the day," she says, stamping the date on my paperwork with a practiced hand. "It's good luck, yeah? Luck of the Irish!"

"I—hadn't even thought about that," I mutter, and her smile broadens at my expression.

"Don't look so worried. This is *good* luck, not bad." She glances at her screen. "You have to be traveling in the next forty-eight hours to qualify for this quick renewal, right? Let's see your ticket."

I slide the ticket from the travel agent under the glass partition. Juanita's eyes widen as she glances at it, then she looks back at me and winks.

"An adventurer, huh? I can't say you look the part."

Somehow, this rankles. "What does that mean?"

She leans closer to the glass and gives me a slow once-over.

"You're too tall," she says, at last. "And with that red hair and pale skin, you look like you should be playing basketball for Bryn Mawr, and then changing into flats and taking tea in the library."

I narrow my eyes at her, and shuffle my Chucks under the overhang of the desk so they won't show. "Isn't that a little personal, coming from a government employee?"

She chuckles. "You're my last client of the day. I could always . . ." She mimes tucking the paperwork into a drawer.

"I went to NYU, not Bryn Mawr," I say hurriedly, skirting the whole library thing, which is a little too close to home. "And there's a first time for everything, right?"

I'm trying for hearty enthusiasm, but even to my own ears I sound more like I've lost a puppy.

She taps the ticket. "This your final destination, then?"

I shake my head and slide the itinerary through to her. She glances at it, then tucks it with the receipt into my new passport, and slides the whole thing back under the glass partition.

"You goin' all these places? You're gonna need shots," she says, reaching to flip a 'Closed' sign behind the glass. "You got all your shots?"

This time, she laughs out loud at the look on my face. "Wait a sec," she instructs, and ducks out of sight. Dropping to one knee, she digs around inside the bottom drawer of a file cabinet, and then yanks out a piece of paper.

"The clinic on Madison Avenue is open till seven," she says, glancing at her watch. "Better to do it here than in some grotty place on the road, right?" She slides the page under the glass, lifts a hand in farewell, and disappears into the back.

The security guard holding the door gives me a big grin. "Bon voyage," he says. "Right in time for some green beer too!"

And I decide on the spot he is absolutely correct.

Sometime after nine o'clock, passport in hand, I make my way up the elevator to the ExLibris offices. While not technically pissed out of my gourd, I'm two glasses of green beer and a tequila shooter less anxious than I was before I hit the travel clinic.

Which is another way of saying I got all my shots, okay?

When the elevator doors open, the entire floor seems to be in darkness, apart from the city light pouring through every window. I concentrate on keeping a straight trajectory down the corridor toward Teresa Cipher's office. As I near, I see the yellow light of a desk lamp spilling out through the door.

Dropping my suitcase in the hall and clutching on to the doorframe, I swing myself into the office with a little more enthusiasm than I intended.

Teresa Cipher looks up at me over a pair of red reading glasses.

"Good evening, Ms. Keene," she says, her voice holding the sooty rasp particular to smokers of a certain age. "Did you have a successful day?"

"Believe it," I crow, slapping my newly acquired paperwork onto her desk. "And check this out." Yanking my NYU hoodie over my head, I show her my arms, each bearing several Band-Aids. Glancing down, I see my left bicep has already taken on a gentle blue tinge.

Teresa Cipher raises an eyebrow, perhaps because my arms look like they have survived an attack by a deranged porcupine, or maybe at the smell of my breath. Not sure which, actually.

"Are you still feeling up to the task at hand?" she asks, after a moment.

I slump into the chair in front of her. "Abso-freakin-lutely," I say as convincingly as my thick tongue will allow.

She raises her eyebrows skeptically, but after examining my ticket and passport, the CEO slides my papers into a large manila envelope and hands me a waiver to sign.

She collects the pen from my hand and then leans forward to lock eyes with me. "Ramona," she says quietly. "I'm taking quite a risk here. ExLibris is relying on you. There's still time to walk away if you don't think you are up to the challenge."

Any residual tipsiness falls away from me instantly. "I can do this," I say aloud to her—and to myself. "I'm *going* to do this."

Teresa Cipher looks down at the Rolex on her wrist. "Good. I'll forward the further necessities—including visas, and a credit card issued in your own name—to one of the checkpoints in Europe. You'll receive more information from my assistant shortly."

Europe. The very word makes my hands shake, so I clutch them together, and manage to squeeze out a thank-you. Then, snatching up the papers and my luggage, I stumble down the corridor toward the elevator. Once inside, I drop my hands to my knees and force myself to take deep breaths all the way down.

chapter ten

IMAGE: Loading Crane
IG: Romy_K [NYC, March 17]
#LoadingDock #BonVoyage #GoodbyeCruelWorld
13 ♥

Almost two hours later, I find myself sitting inside a dingy waiting room beside something called a "Lading Office" on the docks in Brooklyn. This is the Red Hook neighborhood, which I know only because there's an IKEA here, serviced by a water taxi, which is free-with-purchase to Manhattanites.

Like anyone could walk into an IKEA without buying something.

Until today, wandering the halls of a Swedish home store is the most exploration I have done in the Red Hook area, I'm ashamed to admit. I have a slightly better understanding of the neighborhood now, since I've endured a fairly thorough walk-around. On my way here, I caught the F train with no trouble, and alighted at Carroll Street, but I misread the map on my phone, and ended up at the Brooklyn cruise ship terminal, by mistake. After finding myself at the so-empty-it-echoed terminal, I walked out as far as I could toward the water, and caught sight of the cranes on the other side of the little enclosed bay. They were all lit up so I kept them in sight as I trudged around, and found this Lading Office at last.

Based on the general ambiance of this place, I'd much prefer to be at the Brooklyn cruise terminal. Of course, Old Romy wouldn't have considered a cruise in a million years. She would never have committed to traveling around the world, let alone having her arms shot so full of vaccines that they feel ready to fall off. To tell you the truth, sitting here in this dark, silent waiting room, me and my sore arms are missing Old Romy.

Still. I'm here. The decision is made. The green beer and tequila-fuelled bravery has long since drained away, and everything has taken on a dreamlike quality. The sort of dream where you're lost in a place you've never been, and have no hope of finding your way home. So, more of a nightmare, in point of fact. A nightmare, smelling of tar and old rope, with an undertone of secret decay.

Taped to the glass of the office window is a handwritten note. The note reads: *Keen Passenger, wait here for Lading Officer. Back at midnight.*

Hoping this means me, and knowing there may never have been a *less* keen Keene passenger, here I wait. There can be only one outcome if I leave New York. But it's too late now.

To take my mind off what's coming, I pull the papers from the envelope Teresa Cipher handed me. A quick glance shows me the first page is a blank report—what looks like a pretty standard outline of the information she expects me to provide at each stop on this insane journey. The second is the copy of Phileas Fogg's imaginary itinerary. I still haven't even cracked the cover of Merv's book, and I have only the faintest recollection of the story at all. This reminds me, with an added pang of guilt, that I ran out of time for a final return to the bookshop. I'd planned to head over there after collecting my passport, but the trip to the travel clinic put an end to that idea. Time is no longer on my side.

Maybe this is a good thing. I wouldn't even begin to know how to say goodbye.

Affixed above the office window with the note is an old clock, hanging a little askew, and loudly ticking away the seconds as they pass. The face of the clock is rusted, and it reads three minutes off the time registering on my phone. Either way, I know there's barely thirty minutes before I leave New York for the first time since I was a kid. Without even finding time to say goodbye to the people I love the most.

In order to avoid thinking of this, I focus on the list of mandatory checkpoints noted on the itinerary in front of me. The list seems pretty straightforward: ExLibris Offices, New York → the Reform Club, London → la Tour Eiffel, Paris → Brindisi, Italy → Suez Canal, Egypt → Aden, Yemen → Mumbai, India → Kolkata, India → Victoria Harbour, Hong Kong → San Francisco Train Station → ExLibris, NYC.

Ten stops by the end of April. The ticket Lakeesha Jones issued gives me a room on the only seagoing vessel heading east on March 18th. It's a cargo ship called *Guernsey Isle*, destined for Liverpool. Until today, I didn't even know cargo ships let people ride along.

The only mental image I have of a sea journey is from a movie. In my mind's eye I see Kate Winslet as Rose, wearing her enormous purple hat, boarding the *Titanic*. Maybe an iceberg will get me too.

In any case, the *Guernsey Isle* is no ocean liner. While Lakeesha booked a private room for me to sleep, all other facilities are apparently shared. I've never had to share a bathroom with anyone, apart from Jersey at college, and she's a neat freak.

A ship's horn sounds with a deep, resonant boom, startling me to my feet. For the first time, I turn to look out the window facing the water. My whole view is taken up with the side of a giant container ship, painted green and sitting tight against the broad dock. There's no evidence this behemoth even rests on the water. No bobbing. No motion at all, apart from the men driving forklifts purposefully to and fro along the dock. I can't see a departure gate, or any kind of a sign indicating the *Guernsey Isle* is leaving at all. In fact, I can't even see the name of the ship anywhere. The letters "MSC" are emblazoned on the side, so the little handwritten note on the window is the only evidence I'm even in the right place.

There's a sharp knock behind me, and I turn to find a man with a red, heavily creased face squinting at me through the office glass.

"You Keene?" he yells.

When I nod, he points at the door, and walks away without another word. Clutching my pack and my battered old suitcase, I hurry through the glass doorway and follow him up the gangplank to meet my fate.

chapter eleven

IMAGE: Deck Guernsey Isle

IG: Romy_K [Atlantic Ocean, March 18]

#AllAboard #TheFirstofSevenSeas

11 ♥

The red-faced man turns out to be the port agent. He introduces himself, but I'm so tired I immediately forget his name. He then walks me into an office where a female immigration officer awaits us. She's dressed, at nearly 1:00 a.m., in full uniform—complete with a grey, flat-topped, peaked cap and sidearm—but smiles at me kindly, all the same. She stamps my passport and then instead of returning it to me, hands it to the man beside her. He is stern-faced, and when he speaks to her, it's with a thick German accent. He's wearing a heavy, burgundy cable-knit sweater stretched across his broad stomach, and a navy wool beanie pulled down to his enormous eyebrows. Though he looks nothing like the dapper captain on the *Titanic*—or even Captain Kirk, for that matter—he turns out to be one Captain Gerhardt Anhelm.

The captain's face holds a slightly startled expression as he glances up from my passport to my face. It turns out my cabin had been reserved until yesterday by an old Swedish couple who are apparently semi regulars on this route.

I follow Captain Anhelm into a small elevator. "You were very lucky to get this spot," he says in a thick German accent. "Einar must be doing poorly. His health has been a little bad lately."

The elevator door opens onto a dizzyingly high gantry that allows us to cross from the Red Hook shipping offices over to the vessel itself. I'm so unnerved by the height that I keep my eyes locked on a strand of wool that has unraveled on the back of the captain's sweater. It's left a small hole and all I can think is that Tommy, had he been here, would have it mended in a hot second. In fact, he likely would have embroidered over the repair with something manly and nautical, leaving it better than it had been before.

But Tommy isn't here. I'm alone, following this man—who, with his muttonchop whiskers, looks more like a Teutonic Smee than any kind of ship's captain—to my doom.

As we step over the threshold of the ship's entryway, we are met by a crew member, who salutes smartly. The captain clasps the man's arm, speaking a few urgent words in German. The crewman's eyes suddenly glisten. I can't understand a word of German, but I recognize enough to realize the news of Einar Svensson—the passenger I've displaced—has been passed along. Both men wipe their eyes, and then the captain hands me over to a woman he identifies as his second officer. She hangs an ID badge on a lanyard around my neck and escorts me to my tiny quarters.

We pass several other rooms on the way to my own—many of them with bathrooms and showers—but apparently, these are all assigned to crew members on this journey. I am the sole passenger. And so, I find myself taking the space of a sorely missed Swedish couple, who from the size of the room must have a very close marriage indeed.

My room very sadly does not have a shower, but does contain a tiny cubicle with a sink and toilet. I have just enough time to get settled in and read the information pamphlet provided by the second mate before the ship's horn sounds again. With rain spattering against my window—my porthole!—the *Guernsey Isle* is underway.

In spite of the rain, the movement of the ship feels smooth and stately under my feet. A deep thrumming from the engines vibrates through my entire cabin. I jump up to peer out the porthole, but rain and dark cloak everything. The feel of the engine through the soles of my feet as we pull away from the dock gives me a shiver of fear so visceral, it sends me running for my little bathroom.

I'm leaving New York. Leaving America for the first time since I was a child. Leaving North America for the first time in my life. Outside my porthole, the darkness is suddenly replaced by a figure awash in white light. It is Lady Liberty, looking out across the ocean toward France, the country of her origin.

One of the countries I'm about to visit.

In person.

I lean over the toilet, convinced the feeling inside me is nausea. Is this what facing death feels like? But I'm not sick. Not yet, anyway. I am, it turns out, wildly, deliriously, flamboyantly excited. Excited in a way I cannot remember feeling ever before.

This delicious, anticipatory feeling lasts just about nine hours.

Most of which? I sleep through.

Rollercoasters have never been my thing. Whenever our class visited Coney Island, I was always the kid who stayed on the ground. I held everyone's bags while they roared overhead, shrieking; upside down and enjoying every minute.

I enjoyed every minute too, because I was never the kid who threw up. I was never the kid who had to go sit with the teachers until the dizziness passed. I stayed on the ground, organizing the daypacks alphabetically for when the unnecessary risk-takers returned. I liked it that way.

Of course, these days the MTA gives me excitement enough. Subways are a way of life in Manhattan. I've got a monthly MetroCard, and hop on and off all the time. I've never had any reason to believe I would be subject to motion sickness.

It doesn't take much time for me to learn the sorry truth.

I awaken, still fully dressed, lying atop the tiny bed. The strange euphoria of the night before is so far gone, it might never have happened at all. Instead, my dreams have been filled with the deep certainty of exactly what happens when people go out into the world. The world is dangerous, and I know from experience that sometimes? They never come back.

I almost choke on the sob that emerges from my throat, and when I reach to rub the sleep from my eyes, I find my face is wet. Yanking up a corner of the tightly tucked sheet, I wipe the tears away. I haven't dreamt of my parents in years.

Before I have a chance to think this through, I realize I'm looking up at my feet. I stare at my socks, brain addled with sleep, as my feet, unmoved by any effort on my part, drop out of my line of vision once more. On the floor, my suitcase slides across the room and hits the door with a thump.

Sitting bolt upright, I clue in to the long slow roll the ship is making. Through the porthole, the window is awash in spray, but outside I can see a grey line, limned in white. The horizon. It slides briefly by, before the prow of the ship points upward again.

I don't see much else, apart from the inside of my toilet bowl, for the next forty-eight hours. The second officer, a dusky-eyed, no-nonsense Italian woman called Sylvia, pops by several times, worried when I don't show at meals. Once she establishes that I have not thrown myself off the side, she returns periodically—the first time with something called barley sugar, and later with ginger ale.

While it feels closer to a full year, it's really just three days that pass before I'm able to show my face outside my cabin. Time crawls painfully when one is hanging over a small metal toilet bowl.

I wake the morning of the third day to find the ship has once again resumed the stately forward motion she exhibited on leaving harbor. Perhaps not so coincidentally, I'm ravenous. After a meal of spaghetti Bolognese that might be the best thing I've ever tasted, I hunt down Sylvia, who reluctantly gives me the password to the ship's internet.

"It's a satellite," she whispers, in an accent thick as the sauce on my pasta.

She hands me a scrap of paper with the password scrawled on it. "Don't leave this anywhere, eh? We have problem with some of the guys watching pornos, and eating up all the bandwidth, you know?"

"I only need to check my e-mail," I assure her. "And send my boss a report."

She pats my hand. "Good girl," she says. "I trust. You no watch that filth."

Which, of course, makes me wonder what I've been missing.

She perhaps senses this, and doesn't release the scrap of paper until I swear that I won't download so much as a YouTube video.

Clutching the precious password, I power up my laptop, only to have it die after less than a minute. My brief moment of panic vanishes when I remember that I carefully packed charger cords for both the laptop and the new phone. They are at the bottom of my suitcase, neatly coiled under my hair straightener, which I haven't had a moment to put into use. Vowing to do a better job of personal grooming after my next shower, I smugly fit the cord in place, only to find—my cabin has no outlets.

This seems wildly improbable, considering there's a small lamp screwed firmly into the wall beside my bed. But when I pull out the plug, all I find is a weird round sort of two-slotted thingy which will not take my charger, no matter how hard I push. In the end, I'm forced to return to Sylvia, who explains the ship is wired to European standards, and the weird round thing *is*, in fact, an outlet. Luckily, she has an adapter she can loan me, but I trail back to my room feeling ignorant.

I mean, I would have Googled it, but how do you Google something you don't even know exists?

I'm a well-read person. I've got a degree. You'd think I'd know the rest of the world doesn't necessarily channel electricity the way Americans do. But until today?

Nope.

Once I'm safely plugged in, I start to get a sense of just how much work I have to do. It's enough of a job documenting the ship in pictures and firming up my itinerary for when I reach land, but as soon as I get online, a new problem arises. I open my e-mail to find a veritable flood of messages from Tommy, ranging from worried to guilt inducing. I decide to find a way to placate Tommy later, and settle myself into writing my first ExLibris report.

chapter twelve

IMAGE: Sea Birds
IG: Romy_K [Atlantic Ocean, March 21]
#StormWarning #Seasick #50Shades
25 ♥

ExLibris Transit Report, submitted by Ramona Keene

TRAVEL SUMMARY: The *Guernsey Isle*, an Algol-class ship, is
among the fastest in the world. Currently traveling in excess of 33
knots, aided by a substantial tail wind, and heavy seas. Suitability
for elite traveler: low. Will investigate other options that may be
available on the client's timeline.

TOP PICKS TO SEE AND DO: Not much aboard ship. I can't really go
up on deck, because it turns out sea spray is pretty much freezing in March . . .

Even though I modify the format a bit, the report is four full pages
long by the time I finish it. Tucking my feet under the thin blanket, I press send and flop back onto the metal cot that serves as my
bed. This is the first update I've managed in three days, what with 1)
the whole unexpected vomiting thing, and 2) the raw fear of leaving
home by myself, for the first time ever.

It's possible the awareness of 2) has led pretty much directly to 1),
now that I've stopped barfing long enough to think about it. To take

my mind off this, I open my e-mail again. Merv has never taken to e-mail, so I read through all the irate notes from Tommy.

"Is this your shot at *Eat Pray Love*?" he writes, adding that Merv has been unable to sleep, plagued with worry since I've been gone.

"Just tell him it's a sort of one-woman *Amazing Race*," I reply guiltily, trying to ignore the mental image of Teresa Cipher's disapproving expression as I type the words. "It's all fun, no risk, I promise."

The last thing I want is to worry my uncles, but it's too late now. My relationship with Tommy has always been a bit rocky, but his disapproval has never felt quite so overt. My e-mail must have caught him while he was on the computer, because fast on the heels of my reply comes another note, informing me that Call Center Jonah has been around the shop for tea.

"He's deeply disappointed you didn't take the job," writes Tommy. "He thought he sensed something special between you. And I must admit, I did too."

All of which I'm deeply grateful to leave behind, as I steam across the Atlantic Ocean.

The next day, Captain Anhelm grants me an interview. This is the perfect kind of detail to add to my ExLibris report, and I'm determined to get all the extras Teresa Cipher's special client could ever ask for.

We sit in the captain's office, which holds several tables piled in rolled charts, but he dismisses my questions about them immediately. "We don't use these anymore," he says, and points instead to a sleek monitor. "All nav is online these days."

For a moment, I'm at a loss what to ask him, as all my Captain Ahab questions dry up in the face of this modern technology. But behind his desk, I see that his shelves are lined in copies of books of every description. I toss my prepared questions aside and pull my uncle's copy of the Jules Verne book out of my bag. The rest of the interview is taken up by the captain's theory on how *my* trip will compare with the story, which turns out to be one of his favorites.

I also learn he expects to make Liverpool in nine days total, which means we still have five more days at sea. This seems a horrifyingly long time, compared with what it takes to fly. Still, there's nothing I can do about it, so I upload another report with a review of how easy the journey has been. I carefully avoid any mention of my metal berth. And that night, I settle in to read Uncle Merv's book, gingerly turning the old pages and smoothing out all the dog-ears. I fall asleep as the members of Fogg's Reform Club, one by one, turn against him, and lay wagers on his failure.

The next morning, I'm wakened by being pitched from my cot onto the floor. We are south of Iceland, and anything easy about the journey vanishes. Sylvia tells me that we've hit what's called a Force 10 storm. The ship's internet is satellite, so the conditions prohibit me from looking up what that even means. In any case, I'm not looking at much besides my toilet bowl again. Sylvia appears once more, but only to pass on the news that I'm to be confined to my quarters for my own safety. Her eyes are wild—she tells me there's a very real danger of cargo going overboard.

After another endless day of being trapped in my tiny rocking room, and still desperately seasick, I creep up onto the deck in search of relief from the vomiting. The sea is every color of grey—fifty shades and more. She's also deeply into domination, which I learn as the first wave lashes me with an icy hand. The spray is freezing the ropes the crew are using to further tie down the huge cargo bins, but the icy air feels good in my lungs, and smells so clean. I snag someone's hat as it blows past me and jam my hair under it, then make my way into the central section, where most of the crew are working.

Sylvia points wordlessly toward the stairs when she catches sight of me.

"Please let me stay," I bellow into her face. "I'm so sick down below."

She rolls her eyes, but minutes later, she returns to stuff a weatherproof life suit into my arms, complete with heavy work gloves. With a glance over her shoulder, she helps me into it.

"If you stay, you work," she hisses in my ear. "And keep that hat on. You so tall, captain no spot you, long as your hair cover."

As soon as I'm suited up, she drags me off to work under the supervision of a crew member whose name might be Carl. I spend the rest of that long night tying knots in the comparatively safe—but still freezing—central section of the outside deck, and I don't vomit even once.

chapter thirteen

IMAGE: Ferry Cross the Mersey
IG: Romy_K [Liverpool, UK, March 26]
#ManOverboard #AnotherPlace
27 ♥

I awaken to the sound—of no sound. The wind has gone, the labored clang of the engines is muted to a low hum, and we are mercifully, mercifully, no longer rocking. Everything I own is strewn across the floor of the tiny cabin except for my laptop and camera, which, in the end, I took into bed with me. I figured if I got dumped onto the floor in the storm, I could at least protect my electronics with my own body.

Priorities, man.

As I glance out the tiny porthole, the horizon is pink and gold where the water meets the sky. Either we've survived the massive storm or this is the entrance to a watery afterlife, bathed in an appropriately celestial glow. Throwing on my heaviest hoodie, I grab my camera and head upstairs to see if I can somehow capture the astonishing colors for my Insta page.

The sight that meets my eyes as I hit the deck renders me fully speechless. Dashing toward the stern, which has the only really open space near a railing, I'm shocked to see we are no longer in open ocean, and in fact, appear to be gliding toward the mouth of a river. The golden glow is still there, but the sun is streaming not across the vast expanse of water but over a low rise of land, speckled with a few small oblongs that mark distant buildings.

We have made it across the ocean.

Yanking out my phone, I check the date. March 26th. Which can't be possible. The captain had said nine days, absolute fastest.

Seconds later, footsteps clang up the metal staircase, and I whirl to see the first mate pop out of the stairwell, carrying a clipboard and a tablet, one in each hand. This is Sylvia's boss, Martin Sixsmith, whose name I know only because she's pointed him out to me, using hushed tones. He's always running somewhere or doing something, and I haven't exchanged more than a hello with him for the entire trip.

But now, Sixsmith pauses a moment, and points at me. "Oy—Ramona, is it?"

His cockney accent is so thick, I have to strain to recognize my own name.

"Thanks for the assist last night, luv. Your extra pair of hands helped save them containers. Captain's right chuffed—a storm like that can cost us dearly in cargo when luck ain't on our side."

I was only trying not to vomit, I most certainly do not say. Instead I smile, as if wearing a survival suit and hauling rope and chains is all in a day's work for me. "No probs." Jabbing my thumb at the coastline, I add: "Is that—Ireland? How . . . ?"

He laughs delightedly. "Oh, y'er behind the times, luv. We blew past Ireland two hours ago—that's why it's so calm in here. What you're looking at is the Welsh coast. We'll be pulling into the Mersey within the hour."

"The Mersey?" I say slowly. "Isn't that . . . ?"

"Liverpool. That wanker blew us in more than eighteen hours early. Eighteen hours! How brilliant is that, then?"

He tucks the clipboard under his arm and trots off to where a group of the crew is gathering near the bow. I lean against the railing. Eighteen hours early? Suddenly, it's like all the fear and nausea of the past few days never happened.

I grasp the handrail and take a deep breath of the chill morning air, suddenly feeling on top of the world. I've survived my first ocean crossing—and early too. I'm determined to take the extra eighteen hours and use them to their greatest advantage. Martin Sixsmith said we'd be entering Liverpool within the hour, which gives me just enough time to pack up and write a killer report for Teresa Cipher.

Turning back to face the rising sun, I start taking shots of the coastline to illustrate my report, when I notice something strange. A man—I think it's a man—is standing waist-deep in the water along the shore.

I crank my telephoto to the highest setting, and sure enough, there he is. It's too far to make out his face, or even what he's wearing. But waist-deep in the icy waters of the Irish Sea in March?

All my good feelings drain away, and fear rises in my throat. There's no reason—no good, *non-suicidal* reason—for anyone to be where he is standing. I tuck my camera strap around my neck and wave at him with both hands.

"Hey—HEY! What are you doing?"

My voice is whipped away by the wind, so I try a series of wild jumping jacks, waving my arms and leaping in the air to get his attention.

"Hey—buddy! BUDDY!"

Nothing.

The deck of the *Guernsey Isle* is horizontal, and the ocean—or more properly the Irish Sea, I guess—is very calm, but waves are still splashing the man. We're moving so fast now, he's almost out of sight.

I turn, ready to dash up to the bridge to alert the captain, when I hear Martin Sixsmith's voice in my head. *Eighteen hours early. How brilliant is that?*

Eighteen hours.

Even if the captain takes time to report a suicidal man on the beach—what if no one on shore can help? What if the captain has to stop the ship and drop one of the rescue boats over the side?

What if reports have to be made to the local police?

How much of the eighteen hours is that going to cost?

I swallow hard, and put my camera to my eye again. I can barely make out the man's outline, but I swear, he looks like he's walked in deeper. Only his shoulders and head are visible.

Dropping the camera, I grip the ship's railing with both hands. No alarms have rung out. Clearly no one else has spotted him. If I don't report what I've seen in the next minute or two, the man's life choices will be in his hands alone.

Is this stranger's life worth slowing the ship for?

Before I realize it, I'm running down the deck toward Martin Sixsmith.

"Help! Martin—help! Man overboard!"

My voice is blown away once again by the wind, which might not be a bad thing. After all, the guy has not exactly gone over the rail. I try again, waving my arms at him this time.

"Martin! Emergency! Look!"

Either he hears me or catches sight of my waving arms, but he looks up at last, as I thunder down the deck toward him. He turns to the crew and says a few final words, and the group disperses. Having given all my wind to the sprint up the deck, I point wildly off the side of the ship toward the beach behind us.

"A guy," I gasp. "In the water! Back . . ."

The ship has slowed noticeably in the last minute or two, and suddenly up ahead, I see someone else standing in the water. This man is closer to shore, but as we approach, his face disappears behind a wave. I grab my camera to focus on him, and as I do, another man appears. This one looks like he might be kneeling. And beyond him, a head, bobbing in the waves.

"What the hell . . . ?" I mutter, and turn to Sixsmith.

"It's—it's gotta be some kind of mass suicide!" he says urgently. "Look at the fuckers!"

As the boat cruises forward, the water is suddenly full of men, all marching into the ocean, spread out along this stretch of otherwise deserted beach.

"What's going on?" I gasp. "Can you radio the captain?"

Martin's eyes are cartoonishly round. "It's too late for that," he says, setting his clipboard and tablet on a nearby bulkhead. He begins to strip off his jacket. "I'll have to go in myself!"

"You can't do that," I cry, reaching out to grab his arm. I come away with only the sleeve of his jacket as he pulls out of it and reaches for his boots. "It's too dangerous!"

He pauses, kneeling with his hands on the laces of his boots, and looks up at me. "There's no other choice," he says. "Look at them— all out there in the water, like bleedin' lemmings."

I grab my camera again. "Maybe it's a cult," I say, desperately trying to focus in on the faces. "What if we call the . . ."

My words fail me as the camera finally locks onto one of the desperate men's faces. A wave washes right over his head, and he disappears from view for a moment. Twisting the lens, I catch sight of him again, and for the first time, something doesn't seem—quite right.

A wheezing sound from beside me penetrates through my fog of panic, and I drop the camera again to see the first mate draped across the rail. His jacket is puddled on the ground beside him, but his boots are still on.

I place a hand on his arm, but he's doubled over, the wheezing sound louder than before.

"Martin," I say urgently. "It's okay. Don't worry. I can run up and tell . . ."

He stands upright at last, and for the first time I get a good look at his face.

"Martin?" I say slowly. "Are you *laughing?*"

This sets him off again. He drops his hands to his knees. "Maybe it's a cult," he manages. "Oh my God—it's got to be a bleedin' cult!"

Bewildered, I turn back to look at the shoreline. I no longer need my camera to see the dozens of men—perhaps as many as a hundred—in the water. And for the first time, I notice that none of them are moving.

Turning, I find Martin has his jacket back on, an arm wrapped around the shoulders of a newly arrived crew member. Carl from last night, maybe?

They're guffawing helplessly. "A cult?" Carl repeats, incredulously. "Wait'll Sylvia hears this!"

"Why are there hundreds of statues in the water?" I demand, but this only makes Martin lose it again.

"Not statues," he gasps. "It's a *cult!*"

As Carl heads off, I straighten my spine. So much for "thanks for the assist, luv."

Carl waves at one of the night crew whose name I can't remember, and within seconds, the two of them are glancing over at me and roaring.

Martin, wiping his eyes, retrieves his tablet and clipboard. "God love you," he says, slapping my shoulder altogether too heartily. "I'll drink free tonight, sister, thanks to you and your cult!"

Refusing to dignify this with a response, I turn on my heel and stalk back to the privacy of my cabin, my report—and Google.

B y the time off-loading begins in earnest, I've completed my report, gathered my possessions, and am standing on the bridge, shaking hands with the captain.

He squeezes my hand. "Are you sure you are ready to leave? You seem to have found your sea legs, and I heard—ah—a rumor that the extra hand on deck last night was a true asset during the storm."

I grip the handle of my suitcase, not sure if I'm more relieved that he's okay with me being on deck in the storm or that he hasn't mentioned the statues along the beach.

"Quite sure," I say hurriedly. "The storm bought me some time, and I plan to make good use of it. If I manage to catch the express train to London today, I can hop the overnight to Paris and get ahead by two full days!"

The captain looks quizzical. "Do you not want to see anything of the country before you move on?"

"Oh yes. I need to find the Reform Club in London before I head to . . ." I check my notebook. "Pancreas Station."

"That's Pancras, *Liebchen*. As in the saint, not the organ." He pauses as I jot an embarrassed note. "No time for a tour of Liverpool, then?"

I shrug. "Tight schedule. But I live in a port city. Liverpool can't be much different than New York, can it?"

He chuckles gently. "Don't let any of the natives hear you say that," he says, and reaches into an inside pocket. "I'd like to offer you this memento, Ramona Keene. To put you in mind of our chat and your first Atlantic crossing, yes?"

He hands me a slim paperback copy of Verne's *Five Weeks in a Balloon* that must come from his own library. I'm so delighted to have something new to read on the train, I throw my arms around him in a big hug. This may have been a mistake, as he kisses me soundly on each cheek at least twice before I am able to make my escape.

chapter fourteen

IMAGE: Fab Four
IG: Romy_K [Liverpool, England, March 26]
#WrongWay #Liverpudlians #AMusicalEducation
30 ♥

After the captain's effusive send-off, I hurry down the ramp toward the customs office. While I'm very proud of finding my sea legs, it feels fantastic to be on land again.

As my feet hit the dock, I stop a minute and let the rest of the crew stream past. Setting my feet on foreign soil actually feels a little surreal.

"You made it," says Second Officer Sylvia as she strides by.

"I did," I reply, beaming at her. "I almost can't believe it."

She doesn't stop walking, but winks back at me over her shoulder. *"Ciao ciao, bella,"* she calls, before vanishing through a doorway. "One foot in front of the other!"

Following her advice, after taking a deep breath of British air, I carry on along the dock and through the door. I'm sure I can still feel the sway of the ship, and the thrum of the engines beneath my feet, even inside the building. I have to ask the customs officer to repeat himself twice, as his accent is so thick, but as soon as I realize it's not much different than talking to someone from the Bronx, I feel better. He looks bored as he stamps my passport, but I feel a real surge of triumph as I hurry off in the direction of the exit. I'm on my way—and well ahead of the careful schedule I've worked out.

Vowing to update it as soon as I get onto the train to London, I step out into the street to wave down a passing taxi, and am suddenly yanked backwards. I trip over the curb and sit down hard. Where I was standing, a truck whistles past, the wind blowing my hood right off my head. I've only just missed being flattened.

"Christ sakes, ducks!" cries a voice. "That lorry would've done for yeh, I swear!"

A round, pink-faced lady, her bleached curls tucked tightly inside a black hairnet, looks down at me, shock written across her face. "All right, luv?" she squawks. She's still clutching one of the straps of my daypack.

"I think so." I take a shaky lungful of air, and scramble back to my feet. "Thank you for that. I did *not* see him coming."

"Oh, y'er an American? Well, that explains it, don't it?" she says as I dust myself off. Apart from a sore butt, I can't feel any damage. "Yeh need to look to the *right* first, luv. Maybe look both ways before yeh cross, to be safe, aye? Y'er not in Kansas anymore."

She chuckles at her own witticism.

"I'm from New York," I say, scooping up my dropped suitcase. "I've never actually been to Kansas."

"New York, eh?" She nods at me approvingly. "I got a cousin there—more of a second cousin, really. Been there since we both were kids. We talk all the time on the Facebook. I do love the Facebook." She glances down at the watch on one plump wrist. "Ooo, must be gettin' on. There's a taxi stand at the bus station, just up the way. You can't miss it."

A tiny green man lights up on the walk signal across the street. As all the traffic screeches to a halt, pedestrians pour out onto the road, walking across, and even diagonally through the intersection. Feeling like I'm somehow breaking the rules, I scurry off in the direction of the taxi stand.

The smell of the sea fades as I get deeper into the city, and over-head the golden skies of early morning swiftly vanish under a grey fog. In seconds, it's pouring. Spotting a cab, I wave, and glory of glories, he actually pulls over.

Flinging my suitcase straight into the back, I jump in after it. Again, as soon as I open my mouth, the cabbie has me pegged.

"You from America, then?"

"I am," I say, trying to find a dry spot on my cuff to wipe the rain off my face. "New York, actually."

The cabbie beams delightedly at me in the rearview mirror. "Was there last year with the missus. Pilgrimage to see the Dakota, y'know."

"John Lennon?" I guess.

In the mirror, I watch all the cheeriness drain from his face.

"My uncle loves the Beatles," I say. "Were they from near here?"

The vehicle swerves sharply as my cabbie's eyes bulge out of his head.

"You are sorely in need of an education, young woman," he says. "You wanting the coach or the train today?"

"Train. I need to get to London. Then Paris. Hopefully today."

"Ah. Then it's Lime Street Station for the express. And that way I can drive yeh past a little local history, eh?"

"Okay."

His shoulders relax a little, and I spend the next fifteen minutes with my nose to the window, absorbing Beatles trivia, and copying most of it down into my notebook. Merv is going to be impressed, but more importantly, it'll add local flavor to my ExLibris report.

"And that's the pub Paul dropped into last summer," the cabbie says, as we screech up to the curb at the train station. "Played the piano, and everythin'. Imagine singin' 'Lady Madonna' while sharing a pint with the man?"

He wipes his eyes, and then gestures roughly through the window.

"Here you are. Sure I can't convince you to at least take a magical mystery tour while y'er here?"

"It's on my bucket list," I promise, collecting my credit card. "Thanks for the ride—I'll e-mail my uncle tonight. He'll be so jealous!"

The cabbie gives me a cheery wave as I head into the station. And all his Beatles stories bring me luck after all, as I manage to snag a ticket on the last express train of the day to London.

chapter fifteen

 IMAGE: Reform Club, The Pall Mall
IG: Romy_K [London, England, March 26]
#WhereItAllBegan #DressCode
37 ♥

ExLibris Destination Report, submitted by Ramona Keene

CITY/REGIONAL SUMMARY: Liverpool, fourth largest city in the United Kingdom. A must-see on the way to London.

TOP PICKS TO SEE AND DO: The home of the Beatles, so don't miss the original Strawberry Fields. Can you find the secret symbol on each of the Fab Four at their statue on Pier Head? For readers, the Central Library has been recently remodeled, and is on William Brown Street.

WHERE TO STAY: Best hotels can be found near the city docks at One Water Street.

WHERE TO EAT: For fine dining, you can't beat the Art School on Sugnall Street, but don't forget to try the plaice & chips, served in newspaper, from a chippie by the sea.

WHAT ELSE: Fear not, if you witness what looks like mass exodus into the waters of the River Mersey. This installation, known as *Another Place*, is a collection of iron figures, each sculpted in the image of his creator. *Glub glub!*

My train pulls into Euston Station as I complete the finishing touches on my report, and I'm feeling dangerously accomplished. I'm ahead of schedule, my stomach is full, and I've even bought myself a bag of something called Worcester sauce flavored crisps—which I'm almost certain are potato chips—for the train to Paris. Not only that, but my follower count on Instagram has taken a real leap while I've been at sea, with my posts regularly scoring over thirty likes—more than double what they were before I left New York. I feel a flush of pride heating my cheeks as I jump onto the platform.

Near the ticket booths, a small orchestra, populated mostly with a selection of balding elderly gentlemen, plays an uplifting march to speed me on my way. They are the Great Western Players, and I hurry past them to collect my ticket from one of the machines along the wall. The Paris train doesn't leave from here, but from another station called St. Pancras—*not* Pancreas, thank you, Captain Anhelm. Embarrassing public mispronunciation is the curse of us introverts, who learn more words from books than from other humans. I'm just saying.

En route to St. Pancras, I need to find my London checkpoint: Phileas Fogg's Reform Club. The glow of self-satisfaction fades a little when I realize how far across the city I have to travel in the hour before my train departs, but not for nothing am I a New York girl. Clutching my fresh feelings of confidence as tightly as the handle of my suitcase, I head down into the London Underground.

One train—two, if you count the District line car I jumped on by mistake, and got off only by jamming my suitcase into the doors as they closed—plus a ten-minute walk later, and I've made it.

The place where it all began, at least for Phileas Fogg.

The Reform Club exists in real life, looking more like a stately townhome on an elegant street than a private gentleman's club. Not that I've ever seen a private gentleman's club, in any case.

The sun is setting, but as the rain has stopped, I use my Canon to take a couple of shots of the club flag flapping out front. Then, careful to look both ways in case of random vehicles, I drop my suitcase on the curb and pull out my phone. It's time to take a quick selfie by the front door.

I've just centered myself beside the number when the door swings open behind me.

A sharply dressed young man wearing a suit jacket and striped tie stands inside the doorway. "Deliveries are taken around the side," he says, making a shooing motion with one hand.

"I'd love to get a picture inside . . ." I begin, but he raises his palm to cut me off.

"This is a private club, madam," he says, giving me a sweeping glance from head to toe. "We have—a dress code."

I admit to being a little travel creased, but I'm wearing jeans that were freshly laundered yesterday on the *Guernsey Isle*, and even my Converse are mud free at the moment. "You have a dress code for selfies?" I ask.

"Denim is never permitted," he replies with a sniff. "As for selfies?" He pronounces the word like it tastes bad in his mouth. "Selfies inside this premises will not be tolerated."

As the door swings shut in my face with a muffled sort of boom, I grin up at the closed-circuit camera above the transom. For the first time on this insane journey, a feeling of well-being washes over me. The members of the Reform Club had scoffed at Fogg too. In any case, regardless of this fellow's disapproval, I've got my picture. The first checkpoint on my itinerary is officially crossed off, and ahead of schedule too.

It's time to catch my train to Paris.

My confidence lasts all the way to St. Pancras Station, and right into my *très* comfortable coach seat on the Eurostar train. The service provides complimentary—and even functional—Wi-Fi. When I log on, there's a single e-mail sitting unread in my inbox, sent by one Frank Venal.

Subject line? "Eviction Notice."

chapter sixteen

IMAGE: Eurostar
IG: Romy_K [London, England, March 26]
#ChunnelBound #StPancrasPlease
37 ♥

<FRANKVENAL@HEATTMAIL.COM>

MARCH 26

TO: Ramona Keene, Suite 2B

RE: commercial and supplemental space currently occupied by

Two Old Queens Books & Tea Shoppe,

Second Avenue, East Village, New York

Consider this written formal notice from landlord of above noted property. Should current lessor Mervin Keene-Knocker not disburse to the undersigned the agreed-upon increase in rent on or before the first day of May, as a sub-lessor of supplemental space attached to above-noted commercial space, you are ordered to depart the premises known as Suite 2B, conjugate to the above-listed property.

Your compliance with this directive on or before the first day of May will prevent any legal measure, including action of eviction, being taken against you. You are hereby notified of your right to avoid eviction by completion of assigned payments on said date.

Respectfully,

Angelina Sweetmeat, LLB

Cohen, Avenatti, and Sweetmeat

Legal Counsel to Mr. Francis Venal, Property Owner

Action being the best answer to fear, after reading this horrifying missive, I log off the internet and concentrate on writing my latest ExLibris report. This takes me a full hour. But even after padding it with a list of activities I hadn't even begun to research in person, giving it a cheery, adventuresome tone, and sending it off, I still feel haunted by the lawyer's threat. It speaks to the level of my anxiety that as the Eurostar hurtles through the tunnel deep under the English Channel, I don't give a single thought to the massive body of water that is literally right over my head.

Over my head, and just waiting for a single pressure crack in the structure to come flooding in, trapping me inside and drowning every passenger before rescue can even be attempted.

Okay, so maybe one thought. Or two.

Still, my uneasiness in the Chunnel can't compete with the anxiety over everything happening at home. Why would Frank Venal have his lawyer e-mail me? Is his plan to frighten me into paralysis, the way Rhianna stares down a mouse before snapping it up?

"Ramona Keene is no mouse," I mutter, slamming the lid of my laptop closed. I don't actually mean to say this out loud, but the woman sitting across the aisle gives me a startled side-eye. After a minute, she folds up her magazine and relocates further down the car.

This shunning convinces me to focus the rest of my nervous energy on Paris, which must be a good idea, because after I sort out my plans, I even manage to fall asleep.

As the train pulls into the Gare du Nord—the North Station, according to the translator on my phone—I'm ready. I've written a plan to conquer Paris in my notebook, and before my phone dies, I manage to file the lawyer's hideous e-mail in a folder labeled "Asswipe"—the spot I generally stash Jonah's missives.

Whatever it takes, I'm not going to let Frank Venal ruin my life.

In spite of not enough sleep and this underlying worry, my first goal is accomplished with almost ridiculous ease. A bank of ticket machines line the train platform, with the delightful bonus of having instructions available in English. I manage to book an express train that will get me all the way to Brindisi, Italy, in a mere twenty-six hours. This is amazing. Brindisi is one of the Fogg checkpoints, located near the spike heel of the Italian boot, and I had scheduled two full days to make the trip from Paris.

Even better, the train doesn't leave for three hours, which gives me the rest of the morning to glimpse the City of Light.

Slinging my daypack around my neck, I hoist my suitcase and aim myself toward the nearest subway sign. But just as I'm about to trundle down the first set of stairs, I spot a luggage storage company. My mind flashes back to the trouble I had hauling all my stuff through the London Underground.

The store owner scoffs at the very sight of my suitcase, and tries to sell me one with wheels. That's never going to happen, so I redirect him to the all-in-one travel adapters, since I had to return Sylvia's. Five minutes later, suitcase safely stored with my new travel adapter inside, I head out the door with only my camera around my neck, ten euro tucked into my daypack, and a free tourist map of the city in one hand. I get to see Paris without having to ferry all my stuff, *and* I'll be able to charge up my equipment on the train to Italy. Win-win!

Turns out that Paris has not only a subway—called the Metro—but also commuter trains, trams, and a complicated bus system. In light of the traffic clogging the streets outside the station, I don't even glance at anything above ground. It's been shocking to learn that London—and now Paris—both have subway systems even more complex than the one I ride every day in New York. Of course, the other thing they have in common is that each is far too much city for a traveler to cram into a single day.

But a girl's gotta do what a girl's gotta do.

Thundering down the steps into the nearest Metro station, I have to acknowledge that this whole crazy undertaking is *not* travel. Not really. It's an assignment, no different from the ones I faced down and conquered in school. And like in school, success is only going to happen if I stay focused. The beauty and romance of Paris I know from all the books I've read need to stay right there—inside the covers. As much as I want to, there's no time to visit the charred towers of Notre-Dame Cathedral, where Quasimodo roamed and pined for Esmeralda. I have to give a pass to the Arc de Triomphe on the Champs-Élysées, where my other favorite Hugo characters fought and died in their *Les Miz*-ery. Even the Père Lachaise Cemetery, resting place of Jim Morrison, one of Merv's musical heroes, is off the table. I have three hours to do one job: take a perfect shot of the Eiffel Tower.

A shade under thirty minutes later, I step onto the Tour Eiffel Metro platform. For the first time since I filed away the Evil Landlord's message, I'm feeling confident. Even if I dawdle over the picture taking, I've got plenty of time to get back to the Gare du Nord. Once I hop on board, the train is going to have me all the way through Italy and on the cusp of leaving Europe *three full days* ahead of the timeline I planned on the *Guernsey Isle*. A tiny glow of accomplishment ignites deep inside me. I'm going to ace this test. By end of day tomorrow, I'll be saying goodbye to my second continent. And in less than a month, I'm going to count that money into Frank Venal's hand myself. Maybe in dollar bills, just to show him.

Clutching my camera, I grin triumphantly at the staff member manning the Metro gate. *"Vive le France!"* I say, cheerily feeding my tiny ticket into the slot.

"Merci," he mutters back. *"Tu parles comme une vache espagnol."*

Which I assume is a compliment, since I'm pretty sure he's detected my excellent Hispanic accent.

On the street, I only need to turn around once before I spot the tower, a little further along the riverbank. The sight of it stops me in my tracks. So much of this trip has been on ocean waves and under the ground in trains, it feels surreal to see the solid iron structure, almost close enough to touch. It stretches up, lacy and grand, high above the Paris skyline. I'm not sure how it would rank if transplanted onto the streets of Manhattan, but here, there are no skyscrapers to detract from its majesty.

I take special care crossing the street until I see the vehicles have all miraculously migrated back to the right side of the road. Another win! I do have to dodge an electric scooter careening by, but since it turns out I'm standing on a section of pavement marked for bikes, it's my own fault.

Just like the streets outside the Gare du Nord, this area teems with traffic. A nearby patisserie scents the air with traces of cinnamon and sweet almond paste. Cars and motorcycles clog the streets, while bicycles and scooters—most of them motorized—buzz past like giant mosquitos, jockeying for position with pedestrians along the sidewalks. Rising above it all, the silhouette of the Eiffel Tower feels as familiar to me as if I had grown up beneath its sturdy iron legs.

A light drizzle begins to fall, but in spite of the grey day, my heart soars. This monument is so different from my beloved Empire State Building. But halfway around the world here in France, it's doing the same job: giving we insignificant humans a chance to touch the sky.

"Bonjour, mademoiselle! Comment ça va?"

A young man materializes at my elbow, holding up a tattered card offering guided tour services.

"No thanks," I say firmly, but he glues himself to my side, still chattering away. He's short, with sallow skin, but it's his dirty fingernails that seal the deal. There's no way this guy is legit.

"I don't speak French—and anyway, I'm not interested," I say.

At this, he reverts to broken English, babbling something about showing me a secret apartment hidden in the tower. I know when I'm being had.

"Non, merci," I repeat, and then march over beside one of the armed guards standing near the Metro entrance.

Immediately, my so-called guide melts back into the crowd. I can't suppress a grin. *Game goes to Romy,* I think as I aim my viewfinder up at the tower. *My New York grifter-avoidance instincts come through every time.*

For all the Eiffel Tower's familiarity, as I get closer, a few unexpected details begin to appear. The mechanisms that shoot up the legs look less like elevators and more like funicular railroad cars. They glide up and down so smoothly, I could happily stare at them all day. But time is moving on. Even with my good zoom lens, I can't quite manage to get the whole tower into a single shot, so I hustle over onto a nearby bridge crossing the Seine.

The river is wide and brown, and fairly fast-flowing beneath me. As I prop one elbow on the stone railing, a sturdy riverboat motors below the bridge. Beneath the glass roof, only a handful of tourists take up seats. I try not to think about how much I'd like to be one of them, leaning back and taking in the sights of this compelling city at my leisure. Instead, I resolutely turn away, and framing the tower in the most dramatic fashion I can manage, I take a few dozen shots, just to be sure.

Under the awning of a nearby tourist booth, I scroll through the photos. A few minutes with the black-and-white filters on my computer, and I'm sure the result will rank in popularity with the best shots of the Empire State on my Insta feed.

Feeling completely satisfied with the day's work, I swing my camera over my shoulder, turn, and step straight into the path of an electric scooter.

The collision is gentle enough that I'm not even knocked over, but the girl driving the scooter somehow tumbles to the ground.

"I'm so sorry," I say, bending to help her to her feet. "Are you alright?"

The girl, who appears to be about my age or slightly younger, brushes herself off shakily. "*Oui, oui.* I believe so." In spite of the rain, she's wearing only a flippy little black skirt and a cropped t-shirt, but at least none of her exposed skin appears injured. No blood. Not even a scraped knee. I reach for the handlebars and stand the scooter upright.

"I think your scooter's okay," I say, but her expression is doubtful.

"*J'ai un petit peu mal à la tête,*" she says, touching one side of her head.

"I'm *so* sorry," I repeat. "Do you need a doctor? Is there anything I can do?"

"I sink—I *sink* I am A-OK," she says in a charming accent. "But now, I am late to meet my boyfriend."

Maybe you shouldn't have been driving so carelessly, I most definitely do not say.

As she steps onto her scooter, the handle wobbles wildly.

"Are sure you're good to drive?" I ask instead.

She turns her round, damp eyes to me. Her eyeliner is smudged a little in one corner, which somehow makes me feel worse. "I think maybe I should walk. Is not far."

She stumbles a little as she starts away, and the scooter nearly topples.

Choking down a little sob, she reaches for my arm. "Could you— do you mind to walk with me? My flat is only around the corner. Near the Metro."

Guilt surges through me. This girl is injured because I thoughtlessly stepped in front of her scooter. That she was driving too fast shouldn't matter. The least I can do is walk with her for a few moments.

"No problem," I say. "I'm heading for the Metro, anyway."

"Oh, *merci*," she replies breathily, and links one arm through mine. "There is a—a how you say?—a quick way?"

"A shortcut?"

"*Oui!* A shortcut. Through La Petite Ceinture, down this way."

In my own defense, when they rob you in New York, it's not complicated. At home, theft generally involves knocking you down, grabbing your handbag and whatever else you've dropped, and bolting.

I've only been mugged once, and since it was for my lunch money in fourth grade, I'm not even sure it really counts. Maybe that's why it isn't until we walk down a crumbling old ramp, past a gate that's had the wire center cut out, and around a sharp corner, my spidey senses go off. And by then, of course, it's too late.

The ramp stops abruptly above a quiet, surprisingly green stretch of clearly abandoned rail line. The stale, petrol-laden air of the street is replaced with the faint scent of moss, earthy and moist. Every surface is covered in tags and graffiti and the tracks below stretch out toward the mouth of a tunnel that is almost completely overhung with ivy.

Waiting around the corner is a handsome young Frenchman, perhaps two inches shorter than I am, with a charming smile and one hand ominously in his pocket.

"Elle est américaine," the suddenly not-at-all-injured girl says. Her grip on my arm swiftly turns to iron, and she clutches me so close that I can smell the minty essence of her shampoo.

"Rad," he says mockingly, before leaning over and kissing his villainous girlfriend passionately on the lips. This is PDA of the worst sort, since she retains her grip on me, making me an unwilling party to the whole thing. When they break apart, his hand is on my camera.

"I'll take *this, mademoiselle,*" he says. "And your handbag too, *s'il vous plaît.*"

Ignoring this directive, I try shaking my arm free. The girl doesn't release me, but nevertheless, I'm sure I can feel a fractional loosening of her grip.

"You don't scare me," I say, bending my knees a little and glaring at him. "I'm from New York, bitch." Clenching every muscle, I wrench my arm back, but as I do, the girl suddenly releases me, and I stagger sideways and tumble off the ramp to the tracks below.

chapter seventeen

IMAGE: Eiffel Tower
IG: Romy_K [Paris, France, March 27]
#SpringtimeInParis #PetiteCeinture #Connards
47 ♥

The only good thing about the next few moments is that I somehow land not on metal rail lines or crossbeams, but on chipped wood. Also? Perhaps because I wasn't expecting to fall, I land like a limp rag. My camera strap catches painfully around my elbow as I fall, wrenching it from the young Frenchman's grasp. The camera bounces once with a sickening crunch against the cement ledge, before landing beside me on the ground.

"*Merde,*" spits the girl. Her pale face, framed in long dark hair, appears over the edge.

A fierce, hot anger shoots through me. "You *ass*holes," I gasp, scrambling to my feet. The back of my shirt is crawling with splinters from landing on the woodchips. "You've broken my camera!"

The girl's face is replaced by her boyfriend's. "What's this?" he snarls, waving my daypack at me. "Ten stinking euro?"

"My camera's worth a lot more than that," I shout.

"Not anymore," he smirks, and vanishes.

Something comes fluttering off the ledge, and I dodge out of the way until I see it's only my daypack. Before I even scoop it up, I know it's empty. They've taken the money, but have generously left me the free map of Paris.

And my broken Canon.

A sudden angry exchange erupts on the ledge above me. I can't understand a word, but feel a certain bitter satisfaction to hear them yelling at each other. As the sound of their argument fades away, I scoop up my camera, and glass tinkles out of the lens. The weird, grey-green light down here is too poor to tell if it's repairable or not. With a sigh, I drop it into the daypack, and only then spot the luggage tag tucked inside. At least most of my valuables are still safely under lock and key. So it is with this single tiny feeling of relief that I turn and trudge across the woodchips to find a way back up.

There isn't one.

No ramp. No steps. Nothing but a solid, if slightly pockmarked, brick wall.

Peering upward, my best guess is the stone ramp I'd been standing on once led down to another structure—perhaps wood?—which has long since rotted away.

"Hey!" I yell, but the voices above me, and the people they belong to, are long gone.

"Hey," I yell again, louder this time. "You can't leave me down here!"

As it turns out, they can. And they have.

After a moment or two—or maybe even five—of self-pity, I take myself in hand. I'm stuck along what is clearly some kind of abandoned rail line, without any visible exit. This section is open to the air, but at least twenty feet below street level. Against the far wall, the corpse of an electric scooter, like the one Thieving French Girl crashed into me, lies stripped and abandoned.

My only remaining assets are a daypack empty of everything except a freebie map, and a broken camera. No money. No phone. No way of getting back to the Gare du Nord. To the train that will leave without me in ninety minutes.

I run my hands over the wall, but even if I knew how to scale the thing, there's nothing to give me any kind of purchase. Climbing out is not an option.

"Hey!" I yell again, trying to keep the panic out of my voice. "Can anyone hear me? Hey!"

No response. Even the traffic noise sounds distant.

I spin around. There has to be a way out. Underfoot, the wood-chips I tumbled onto earlier quickly give way to packed, grey gravel. Stepping right into the middle of the tracks, I try to take stock. I'm more or less equidistant from a pair of train tunnels which, like the walls, are faced in brick. Two dark semicircles, leading to who-knows-where. Below the ivy, every surface is awash in graffiti as far as the light carries, and in all likelihood, far beyond.

Above me, the rain begins to fall again, this time in earnest. Re-luctantly, I hustle across the gravel to take shelter inside the mouth of one of the tunnels. The sky suddenly opens up, and the wind swirls icy March rain into the tunnel. I take a couple more hesitant steps into the darkness. With the first step, the gravel crunches under my sneakers. With the second?

A voice shouts *"Arrêtez!"*

Jumping backwards, I'm suddenly blinded by a brilliant halogen light.

Shining from a hole in the ground, right beneath my feet.

It's lucky I don't have a heart condition. If I did, and the robbery or the fall hadn't killed me, having my ankle grabbed by whatever is climbing out of the ground would surely have done it.

Even so? The next few moments are—complicated.

Once all the scrambling, kicking, and shouting dies down, and we settle on a language most of us understand, things become a little easier. I stop flailing my broken camera around like a weapon as soon as I recognize that the two filthy creatures emerging from the ground under my feet are not spawning orcs or carnivorous monsters. Instead, I'm faced with my second Parisian couple of the day. This pair are young, and while they are clearly male and female, that's where all similarities end.

"We're *cataphiles*," the girl says proudly. She pushes up her headlamp so it points at the ceiling rather than my face. "We explore the tunnels and caves beneath Paris."

She pronounces it *"Paree,"* but I've been taken in by a charming accent once already today. I narrow my eyes, and tighten my grip on the strap of my shattered camera.

"For work?"

The girl shakes her head. *"Pour s'amuser,"* she says. "For fun. We post pictures to our Instagram too."

She's tiny—perhaps a shade over five feet tall—and dressed in full-length orange coveralls, over which she's strapped thigh-high hip waders. The pale skin of her face is mud spattered, and her hair may be brown. Or that might be the mud too. I put her age at somewhere south of twenty.

"C'est illégal," adds her companion, swaggering a little. *"Trés illégal!"*

He's maybe an inch taller than I am, and looks about the same age as the girl. His skin is so dark, the mud shows up as lighter smudges on his face. He's wearing dirty rubber boots and what look like a pair of yellow dishwashing gloves. In spite of the mud and the getup, he's ridiculously good looking. A younger, muddier Michael B. Jordan.

All the same, I cross to the other side of the train tunnel, in order to keep a little space between myself and these mole people.

"Apologies for grabbing your ankle," the girl says. "But you nearly stepped on my head."

She points a mud-caked glove at her companion. "This is Rol. And I'm Emilie, but you can call me Rox."

"Cos we ROX AND ROL," the boy says, shooting finger darts at us both.

Emilie-known-as-Rox rolls her eyes. "He has almost no English," she explains. Her own English is not bad, though heavily accented. "His name is Roland, so he goes by Rol, *n'est-ce pas?*"

"*Tu lui dit que je la trouve belle, non?*" Rol says, and waggles his eyebrows suggestively at me.

I don't understand a word, but the eyebrows alone send me another two steps back along the tunnel.

"I'll tell her no such thing," she says sternly to him, before turning to me. "It is illegal, what we do," Rox says. "So we all use nicknames, in case the *flics* show up and catch us in the caves. Big fines, maybe jail time, eh?"

"*Cataflics,*" says Rol, nodding sagely. "Cops."

"Okay," I reply cautiously. It's becoming clear that these two are only adventuring teenagers, and they look harmless. Still, I've had my fill of run-ins with Parisian criminals for the day.

"Back to the caves you mentioned," I say, flashing on a sudden memory from my Paris research. "Are you talking about the Catacombs? Where they store all the old bones?"

He nods but Rox shrugs.

"The Paris Catacombs are only a small part of a very large network," she says. "And they are really for tourists, eh? Anyone can get in. What *we* do? Is special."

She points at my camera. "This? Is no place for tourists. You are unprepared for the dangers below."

"Look," I say, trying not to sound impatient. "I'm not a tourist—not really. This is the *last* place I want to be. I was robbed, and I've no idea how to get out of here. I need to get back to the Gare du Nord to catch a train in, like, an hour. And my money's been stolen, so I have to walk."

Rox's face falls.

"Ach—*je suis désolée*," she says to me, before pausing to explain to Rol.

"It's too bad about *les voleurs*," she adds. "You should know all Parisians are not this way."

"*Connards,*" spits Rol, shaking his fist at the universe.

"Thanks," I say. "Can you point the way out of here? I need to get going."

Rox scratches her nose with a gloved hand, which leaves a fresh smear of muck across it, and points deeper into the train tunnel.

"*D'accord.* If you follow the tracks here, maybe two kilometers? Just stay to the left, to the end. When the tunnel opens up, you'll find a spot where there is a hole cut in the fence. Climb through, then up the bank, and *voila!* You will be one street only from the RER yellow line."

She turns to Rol, who has neglected to flip his headlamp off, so his light bounces painfully off the dark walls. "*RER jaune, oui?*"

"*Mais, oui,*" he replies. His smile is a white slash in the darkness beneath the bobbing headlamp. It's the sort of smile that's destined to break hearts in a few years.

"Two kilometers? Is that more or less than miles?" I mutter, hoping it's less.

"Less," she says, lifting my spirits for a millisecond. "But not much less. And is all the way in the old tunnel, so you must take care where you step. Running is not a good idea."

I can't suppress a sigh. If I miss this train, it will throw off my schedule by a minimum of two days, and all the lovely gains I've made will be gone. "I have to at least try. I'll walk along the rail ties."

"In an hour?" says Rox doubtfully. "You'll never make it. Is twenty minutes to catch the RER, then almost the same for the ride to la Gare du Nord. And didn't you say the thieves take your money?"

"Shit," I mutter under my breath. I step carefully onto the next rail tie. "I still have to give it a shot."

"Wait!" shouts Rol, proving he has at least one other English word. He starts to undo a zip on his jumpsuit. *"J'ai une autre idée!"*

He pulls something from an inside pocket and they share a brief, incomprehensible exchange. When Rox turns back to me, she has a small plastic folder in her hand. Her expression reflects a mix of hopeful skepticism.

"How *confortable* are you in—ah—tight places?"

I'm starting to get a very bad feeling about this. Outside the tunnel, rain is pelting down onto the tracks. She points past my feet into the black hole in the floor.

"It looks bad, I know," she says. Removing her headlamp, she shines it into the muddy gap in the rock. "But once you go through, it opens right up. Inside, we stand upright, I promise you. The passage lasts maybe one hundred, one hundred fifty meters. Then we climb a little ladder and *voila!*"

I swallow hard, and drag my eyes away from the cave entrance. "Voila what?"

"La Metro. Tour Eiffel station. Maybe five minutes' walk from there, no more."

I look from her serious expression to his cheerful one. "Is there no way to make it above ground?"

Both heads shake in unison. "Not from here, unless you have

ropes," she says, and holds up the plastic folder. "Rol's Metro pass. I have no cash, but he can tap you through."

I look over at him. He's finally remembered to flip off his headlamp, but my eyes have adjusted and I can see the glint of his broadening smile. "Why would you do that?"

He shrugs, and points at the cave entrance. "Down 'ere? We 'elp each ozzer," he says.

My eyes are drawn back to what is essentially a crumbling crack in the tunnel floor. It looks big enough for maybe a Pekinese. "I'll never fit through there," I mutter.

"You will," says Rox firmly. "Rol's bigger, and he has no problem. We go in arse first, eh?"

"Dis-donc ça, c'est un joli cul," Rol adds appreciatively, and hands me his yellow gloves.

I swallow hard, try not to think about all the bones I read about in the Catacombs, and climb backwards into the hole.

chapter eighteen

IMAGE: Cave Entrance Under Paris
IG: Romy_K [Paris, France, March 27]
#CrevicetoHell #CrazyCataphiles
97 ♥

Things I learn under the ground in Paris:

1. Ancient miners, toiling under what would one day become the city of Paris, and using only hand tools, dug up something called Lutetian limestone, leaving behind more than two hundred miles of winding quarries, hundreds of feet below the ground.

2. Below the sewers. Below the electricity tunnels. Below the subways.

3. The first official quarries were documented in thirteenth-century Paris, but may have been going for centuries before that in what has to have been among the worst work environments ever. This place makes Jonah's call center look like a day at the spa.

4. When the overcrowded cemeteries of Paris began to collapse into people's basements, hundreds of thousands of bones were dug up and dumped into the tunnels. The Catacombs were established later as a tourist attraction, and represent only a fraction of all the bones that were originally

dumped. They've somehow lost track of exactly where the rest of the bones are.

5. The sewers are high above, but the tunnels are conduits for not-quite-icy, often knee-deep ground water.

6. Regardless of the weather outside, the temperature underground stays at a steady 57 degrees Fahrenheit all year round. Related fact: 57 degrees is damn chilly when wading through not-quite-icy knee-deep ground water.

7. 150 meters translates to 160 yards, or approximately the length of a hundred thousand football fields. Underground football fields. Dark as pitch.

8. Stalactites are the ones that hang from the top and smack you on the head when you don't duck quickly enough. Stalagmites are the ones you trip over.

9. Graffiti artists have no fear.

10. Never listen to a short person when she says you can stand upright underground.

Rox cheerfully shares facts, oblivious to my horror at these new surroundings. Since I dressed this morning for a day of sightseeing in Paris—and not in head-to-toe protective gear—I'm immediately soaked to the skin, my leggings mud-caked. And just when I think squeezing backwards down through a hole in the ground is the hardest thing I've ever faced, a maze of low, rocky tunnels opens up in the bobbing light of her headlamp. Rox leads us onward, illuminating the way while we shuffle, splash, and stoop our way through any rational person's worst nightmare.

Suddenly, the stone walls of the tunnel around us begin to shake.

I clutch the back of Rox's muddy coveralls in a vise grip, convinced I'm going to die.

"Just the RER," she whispers. "It is a deeper rumble than when the Metro passes above."

A tiny cascade of dust showers down onto my face as she resumes walking.

All the blood in my body has been replaced with pure adrenaline. I push my free hand against my chest, sure that any moment my heart will collapse under the strain. And yet somehow, over the sound of my thundering heartbeat, I hear Rol humming quietly to himself as he splashes along behind me. He's bent over at the waist, the light from his headlamp bouncing off the walls and the water around our feet.

It's strangely reassuring.

Rox starts to speed up, though the muddy water we're running through is knee deep and filled with invisible tripping hazards. I follow behind, in a hunched half crouch, with my free hand held out front in case I fall.

"This water's from the ground, not the sewers," she says as I wade through a puddle that reaches well above my knees. "So it won't make you sick."

"That's reassuring," I gasp. It feels like we've been down here an eternity. When she stops suddenly, I nearly crash into her. And behind me, I feel a hand on my butt.

"Ah, pardon, pardon," says Rol. *"Tu as arrêté trop vite!"*

Even in French, I'm pretty sure it's a lame excuse, but I have larger worries at the moment. I remove my posterior from his vicinity and peer into the darkness.

Rox points her headlamp down an opening in the wall. The ceiling inside drops down to half the height below where we're standing.

"We went that way once," she says. "But the roof is coming down, you see? And Rol found a femur. So, we don't go back."

"He found a what . . . ?" I say, but suddenly, the space in front of me is completely dark.

"Just here," calls Rox, and I realize she's not vanished into thin air, but has instead taken a sharp right turn. I hurry around the corner, with Rol literally on my tail.

The air inside the tunnels has a strange, muffled quality to it. I always thought caves were echoey places, but that is really not the case here. So when I spot a tiny flickering light in the distance, I don't hear the accompanying shout for at least a full second or two. And suddenly, more lights join the first—many more lights, all bobbing in our direction.

"*Merde,*" spits Rol, and grabs my arm. "*Cataflics!*"

He pushes me right into Rox, who is standing in a sort of hollowed-out area, surrounded by what looks like concrete, rather than rock. I clutch her sleeve, and she pulls me close, pointing her headlamp up.

"Good news," she whispers. "Our way out."

Water is raining down freely here, but when I follow the light from her lamp, I see a series of iron rungs implanted into the side of a round, concrete tube. The rusted rungs are green with algae and the air smells so metallic, I can taste copper on my tongue. About twelve or fifteen feet up, a corrugated metal panel blocks the passage. In it, a small square hole is cut through to allow progress up the rungs.

"*Allez, allez,*" hisses Rol, pushing past me.

"You see that panel?" Rox whispers. "That's one story up. We get past that, they can't see us from down here."

I've already grabbed the bottom rung.

"Not so fast," she says.

I'm sure I can hear splashing footsteps in the distance, and I convulsively clutch her sleeve, as her whisper continues. "Rol goes first. There's a manhole cover at the top, eh? Too heavy for you."

It is a measure of my raw fear in this situation that I neither object to this sexist assumption, nor go anywhere near a manhole joke. Instead, I obediently follow Rol's muddy butt up the slippery, endless series of rungs. I have no feeling in my feet as we start the climb, but by the time we squeeze past the metal panel, the effort of hauling myself upwards warms me right up.

The bad news comes out as I pull myself through the tiny square hole.

"We can stand here, for a rest," pants Rox, as she pulls herself through behind me.

In the light of Rol's torch, the tunnel carries on above us, complete with a second corrugated panel, twelve or fifteen feet up.

"You mean there's another one?" I whisper, once my breath returns.

Rox nods and the light from her headlamp bounces around inside the little shaft. "Only three or four more," she says. "Oh, and keep one foot on the rungs, eh? Sometimes these panels, they pop out."

"L'effondrement!" says Rol, mimicking a swift collapse with one hand.

Below us, I hear a sudden babble of voices. I catch a glimpse of the whites of Rol's eyes, widened in fear, and then we are immersed in darkness as they extinguish their headlamps simultaneously.

I can't suppress a squeak of sheer terror.

The darkness? Is absolute.

There's no need to wave a hand in front of my face, and seeing as both of mine are currently clutching rusty ladder rungs, I couldn't do it if I wanted to. For the first time in my life, I literally cannot tell if my eyelids are open or closed.

Just as I think I'm about to go mad from sensory deprivation, a sudden beam of light shoots up through the square hole cut in the corrugated metal we've just climbed through. Above my head, Rol's feet turn sideways on the rung, and a shower of rusty particles rain down onto my face. Beneath me, Rox thrusts herself flat against the concrete wall, and instinctively, I do the same.

"Bonjour?" calls a deep voice, so startlingly loud I'm sure its owner is right beneath my feet. Which he likely is.

In the ray of light, I can see Rox push an imploring finger to her lips. After a long moment, in which the only sound is dripping water, the light flicks out. I feel Rox reach up and put a cautious hand on my foot. After a moment, a low scrape and another gentle shower of rust tells me that Rol is on the move. I clutch the nearest iron rung convulsively, and we start up again, this time in total darkness.

For the first few steps, this darkness consumes me, but I'm soon overcome by an even greater fear. Considering I'm only hauling up my own body weight, the act of climbing makes the burning in my legs and arms almost unbearable. Only my fear of falling back down into the black abyss keeps me going. It is a step-by-step, agonizingly slow climb; my arms and legs trembling with the effort. We squeeze past four more metal panels before we are through, and in the end, it's only pure desperation that gets me up the last set of rungs.

At long last, I'm forced to stop for an endless, horrifying moment before Rol, emitting a string of French expletives, grunts, and a wash of cold fresh air sweeps over me. There is a ringing clang as the metal cover crashes onto the pavement.

Seconds later, I'm collapsed beside Rol and Rox, gasping on cobblestones that are wonderfully, mercifully above the ground. I feel like I could lie here in the grey daylight, with the gentle rain on my face, and drink in the sweet, sweet smell of city air forever. But according to my phone, there's a shade over half an hour until my train departs from a station across town. I make it to my knees before Rol reaches over to give me a hand. After he helps me to my feet, he pauses before planting a gentle kiss first on one cheek, and then the other.

"Merci, ma cata-amie," he says tenderly.

Rox rolls her eyes as she carefully replaces the manhole cover. "Those *cataflics* are no joke," she says. "It was good you kept your head."

Since the last thing I want is to be arrested on my lone day in Paris, I can only nod in agreement, and then stagger along behind her on my still-wobbly legs. As promised, she leads us out of the dingy alleyway and across a busy intersection to the Metro station.

Minutes later, Rox engages the station guard with a question long enough for Rol to tap me through the turnstile. Before I can do more than shout a word of thanks, my two mud-covered rescuers melt away into the commuter crowds. And I?

Drenched and exhausted and stinking of mud, but astonishingly, deliciously alive, I step aboard the Metro. And somehow? This miracle of modern civic transportation rockets me back to the Gare du Nord in time to grab my suitcase and make my train.

chapter nineteen

IMAGE: Left Bank, Seine
IG: Romy_K [Paris, France, March 27]
#AuRevoirParis #CleanatLast #StrangerontheTrain
85 ♥

A guard on the station platform gives a piercing blast on his whistle as I hurl my suitcase up the steps of the train. The man swings up behind me, and tucking his whistle aside, kindly offers to help stow my suitcase as the train pulls out. I decline, since I need to find a change of clothes first, so he bustles off, without even giving my mud-caked appearance a second look.

The train rocks back and forth, gathering momentum, as I flip open the lid of my case and pull out a pair of clean yoga pants, underwear, and an oversized sweatshirt. Even with these items removed, the case is so jammed, I have to sit on it to snap it closed again. I slink my mud-caked self into the train washroom, vowing to reassess my inventory. In any case, there's no way I'll be able to return the clothes I'm removing, filthy from the caverns beneath Paris, back into my luggage again. Instead, I roll them into a stinking, muddy ball to deal with later. As I use a scratchy paper towel to wipe the grime off my face, I think about how Fogg, as a gentleman of his time, preferred to see all the sights through the eyes of his servants. I feel a wave of tremendous gratitude wash over me for everything I have been lucky enough to see with my own eyes. And after that run through the Paris caves, I'm convinced that nothing can ever scare me again.

It turns out my assigned seat is actually three cars up, so ten minutes later, freshly clad in clean clothes, with as much of the visible muck as possible washed away in the lavatory basin, I fall into my seat at last. My hair is no longer sticking up, and my heart finally settles into something resembling a normal pace. Closing my eyes, I take a deep, shaky breath. *It's all right,* I tell myself. *You've made it. You've made it.*

When an older gentleman from across the aisle tries to engage me in conversation, I close my eyes and pretend to be asleep.

What feels like seconds later, the conductor is standing over me.

"Des billets," he says. "Tickets."

By the time I've dug through my daypack for my wallet, found my ticket, and handed it over, the passenger across the aisle is chatting with a woman dressed in a little black suit that fits her like a glove. She is the human embodiment of chic, and the man never looks my way again.

There's no one in the window seat beside me for the moment, so I slide over, out of the view of the chatting couple, plug in my phone, and attempt to log on to the train Wi-Fi. Pronounced, according to Monsieur La Conductor, *"Wee fee."* When the Wi-Fi signal proves to be surprisingly robust, I try FaceTiming Merv.

Through some internet miracle, the line clicks right through.

He is still in his pajamas, and is delighted to see me. The pj's are a surprise. Unlike Tommy, who, given the chance, would swan around in his silk dressing gown all day, Merv is always up and dressed early.

"Where are you?" he says in a stage whisper. Tommy must still be asleep. This proves to be correct, as Merv hurries into the kitchen, the image bouncing up and down across his pajamas, which are patterned in a selection of blue and green cats. For all his delight to see me, he still sounds worried.

"I'm on the train, in France," I say, hurriedly plugging my earphones in. As I recount the details of the journey so far—the good parts, anyway—a strange feeling of pride sweeps through me.

"I can't believe you're really doing this thing," he says as I finish. His beaming smile warms me right through the ether.

I grin back at the screen of my phone. "You're talking to a whole new Romy," I tell him. "I'll be crossing into Italy tonight. The third new country in my passport!"

"I don't think they actually stamp your passport when you cross borders in Europe these days," Merv says doubtfully. "But I still can't believe it. It feels so strange, speaking to you when you are on the other side of the world. This new Romy is freaking me out a little."

"I'll be back home before you know it," I mutter, using the same tone with him that I've had to take with myself so often, recently. "And when I get there, all our money troubles will be history."

He sighs at this. "I keep thinking about that *Eat Pray Love* book," he mutters.

"Have you been talking to Tommy?" I ask suspiciously. "This trip is nothing like that book. I'm not taking a journey to find myself. I'm doing this to prove I can plan an event for ExLibris. This is a chance to show my organizational skills, okay?"

Merv shrugs. "Seems like a bit of an adventure for you too," he says in a sensible tone.

"It's not the same thing at all," I huff back at him.

"Well, you never know. You might end up like she did and fall for some guy in Asia."

"That's *not* going to happen," I insist. "For one thing, I won't be stopping long enough to meet anyone."

"Well, I think you should keep an open mind," he says, chuckling. "Even I would have trouble turning down Javier Bardem, is all I'm saying."

"Merv—that was the *movie*!" I say, horrified, but he winks and toasts me with his coffee cup.

"Maybe when you come home you can patch things up with Luis?"

"That's not going to happen."

"Why? He was a nice boy. I want you to be happy, Romy."

I try changing the subject, but things go from bad to worse when he asks about the visas I'll need to cross into Egypt and India. Between avoiding everything that happened in Paris, old boyfriends I don't want to talk about, and visas I haven't yet received, the conversational ground has become altogether too rocky. I make an excuse about the train Wi-Fi, blow him a kiss, and sign off.

But as I tuck away my phone, my worries return. The robbery and the run through the tunnels beneath Paris pushed all of my ExLibris concerns aside, but now they come charging back. Not only do I not know what's happening with the visas, I still don't even have a credit card in my own name. I haven't heard a word from Teresa Cipher. I flick open my phone and double-check all my folders in case I've missed something. Then I fire off an e-mail, copying both Teresa and her assistant, Powell, at ExLibris:

I'm leaving France on a train to Italy, and have still not received the rest of my travel materials. Can you please clarify?

After staring at my empty inbox for a further twenty minutes, my stomach squeezes painfully, and I decide that a trip to find the nearest washroom might be a good idea. Sliding my arms through the straps of my daypack, I head back to where I changed my clothes earlier. As I walk up, the *"occupé"* light flicks on.

Stepping aside while I wait, I lean back against the carriage wall and think about my conversation with Merv. I'd never told anyone the real reason Luis broke up with me. Even Luis didn't know the whole story, because I'd never come clean with him either.

But things are different now. New Romy has made it at least a third of the way around the globe; run past Big Ben in London and through ancient crumbling tunnels under Paris. Maybe Merv is right. Maybe now I've broken through my whole fear-of-travel barrier, Luis and I can talk again. I decide to at least reach out to him when I get home.

The pride I was feeling earlier during my conversation with Merv returns. I've conquered the Paris underworld, after all. There's nothing I can't handle.

Behind me, the door between the cars slides open. Someone is trying to come through, but since I've been half leaning on it, I lurch backwards. The door hisses shut, catching my daypack. As I yank it free and spin around to apologize for blocking the way, a man in a black leather jacket steps through the open door from the neighboring car.

My words die on my lips. It's the Evil Nephew.

The Evil Nephew is on my train.

He opens his mouth to speak to me, but I'm so freaked at the very sight of him that I panic and bolt the way I came. When I reach my seat and gather the courage to turn around and look back, he's gone.

chapter twenty

IMAGE: Train Tunnel
IG: Romy_K [The Wilds of France, March 27]
#TensiononttheTrain #AlpineAdversity
81 ♥

t's past dinner time, but instead of heading to the dining car, I'm curled up in my seat, freaking out. It was fantastic to talk with Merv, but now my homesickness has been replaced by something so much worse. What the hell is the Evil Nephew doing on my train? My brain starts doing that thing where it spins in sick circles, each problem magnifying the one before.

And there's no organized, quiet, public library to restore my calm.

I try writing a Paris report for ExLibris, but it's going to need more research. If I take out the robbery and the completely illegal race below the Catacombs, there's not much left. In any case, the memory of the Evil Nephew's face keeps floating across my keyboard. Just what in the name of all that's rational is going on here? Coincidences this big don't happen.

Sometime later, when I have bitten one thumbnail right down to the quick and have just started on the other, the conductor returns to adjust my seat into what he calls a *couchette*. This is well named. He pronounces it *coo-shette*, but really, since it's about half the size of a normal couch, *couch-ette* feels more accurate. And there are three others in this section of the car, so privacy? Not really a thing. The French couple never reappear after dinner, and are instead replaced by a pair of giggling teenage girls who ignore me and stream anime on their phones. I'm exhausted with worry, but sure I won't be able to sleep at all, between the jerking stops of the train and the strains of *Totoro* wafting through the cabin. This proves to be wrong. Sometime later, pretzeled into this rocking, toddler-sized bunk, I'm jolted out of lonely and worried dreams by a sudden thought.

What if the Evil Nephew has been following me the entire way?

By the time a pale pink light gleams through the windows, I'm up and dressed, determined to hunt the Evil Nephew down and demand some answers. Being dressed turns out to be a good thing, as the conductor shows up almost immediately after I return from my morning washroom visit, to convert the beds back into seats. I leave him dealing with the groaning teenagers, and head out to search the train.

My initial fear has been replaced by a new resolve. The old, easily intimidated Romy is gone. This new Romy isn't afraid to leave home. She's a world traveler. She's conquered a stormy Atlantic and the bone-chilling caves beneath Paris. Dealing with an Evil Nephew should be a piece of *gâteau* for new Romy.

Armed with fresh resolve, I march through the train from my seat all the way to the front, and then all the way back again. While the warm smell of dark espresso permeates the train, less than half of the sleeping cabins have been restored to regular seating. I head back to search the dining car, but the Evil Nephew is still nowhere to be found. There, the bouquets of toast and bacon join the coffee, and I decide to fuel up before continuing my search. I'm just brushing away the last delicate crumbs of a *pain au chocolat* when the train begins to slow.

Peering out through the window, I see, to my surprise, that we are surrounded by a towering mountain range. The Alps! Until this moment, the tallest mountains I've ever seen are the Adirondacks in northern New York State, which I have to admit look like a handful of gently rolling hills by comparison.

There's a long announcement over the intercom in French, followed by the briefest of English explanations, of which I can still pick up only a few words. "We regret to inform . . . unscheduled stop . . . *cinq minutes . . . desolé.*"

Once we stop, I can see the station sign through the window: Chamonix-Mont-Blanc. Outside, a picturesque village encircles the station. Grabbing my wallet and my phone, I jump outside for a breath of air. The platform is suddenly filled with smokers, some of them lighting up before they've even stepped off the train. So much for the breath of air, I think moodily, and stomp off further along the platform.

Still, the view smacks me in the face with its raw beauty, and every trace of crankiness is immediately blown out of my head. In fact, the air is crisp and cold enough to leave me feeling a little breathless. I'm relieved to be wearing my heavy hoodie. The platform has no roof, and while the station is clear, I can see piles of snow crusted farther along the tracks.

Near the front of the train, a little signpost indicates the names of some of the peaks surrounding us. The track follows a narrow valley, and apparently the white-cloaked monster towering above is Mont Blanc. The series of sharp-toothed peaks jostling for space across the valley include both the Dent du Caïman and Dent du Crocodile. Further along from these reptilian monsters is a mountain called the Aiguille du Midi, which, from this angle, looks higher than all of them. Behind the glacial white of the mountaintops, the sky is a crystalline blue.

122 · kc dyer

In the distance, near the top of one of the toothier peaks, there's a sudden flurry of what look like miniature, brilliantly colored butterflies against the snow. It takes me a minute to realize these are actually paragliders. As I watch, a dozen more take to the skies, hurling themselves off the cliff face, and then swooping away on the mountain currents. I take a few shots with my phone, though the specks of color are far too tiny to be of any use for posting. They've lifted my heart a little, and after all the worry of the night before, that has to be enough.

The crowd around the train is beginning to thin when I spot the back of a black leather jacket near a coffee kiosk. Fury surges back into my gut, and before I can even formulate a plan, my feet are racing down the platform.

He turns as I arrive, out of breath and furious, and as he catches sight of me, an expression I can't read crosses his face. Before I can say a word, the conductor who reconfigured my seat this morning steps off the train.

"Mademoiselle Keene," he says. "Apologies for the delay. *Pour vous.*" He hands me an envelope, and then turns to the Evil Nephew, and gives him one too.

My planned tirade is derailed for a moment while the two of them have a brief conversation in French. Instead, I glance inside my envelope, and see—to my relief—it contains papers from ExLibris. The missing visas and credit card from Teresa Cipher. Now I can e-mail home to reassure the uncles.

"Merci, monsieur," concludes my enemy politely, as the conductor clicks his heels at us before vanishing back onto the train.

Stuffing the envelope into the pocket of my hoodie with my phone, I clutch the sleeve of his leather jacket. "Just what the hell is going on?"

"I think it's pretty obvious, isn't it?" He thrusts his hands into his pockets, his startlingly clear eyes boring into mine. I notice he's tied his hair back neatly, but hasn't shaved anytime recently.

"No—no, *nothing* is obvious. What are you doing here? Are you following me?"

He gives an incredulous little laugh. "You're kidding, right? I've had a ticket on this train since I left New York. *You're* the one who jumped on at the last minute."

"How—how do you know that?" I say slowly.

"I saw you. At the Gare du Nord." He closes his mouth abruptly and takes a step backwards. He's wearing faded jeans under his leather jacket, and is managing to look way more at home here than I feel.

Behind him, the engine coughs, and then revs again.

"Okay, so we've established you were at the Gare du Nord. The question is—why? Has your hideous uncle sent you to follow me?"

His face creases in an expression of annoyed confusion. "What? No. I'm trying to qualify for a new job with a company called Ex-Libris. Which I have to assume you know about, seeing as you're here too."

I stare at him, stunned into silence.

"ExLibris?" I manage at last. "How—how did you even find out about the job?"

He shrugs and pulls a tiny scrap of paper out of his wallet. When he holds it out to me, I see it's got a handwritten phone number on it.

"I spotted it on a street corner near the bookstore," he says quietly.

As I stare at the crumpled scrap, I remember the posted page that blew off the pole on my way to the bakery that day. I'd torn my coat chasing that poster down, after it blew away in the wind. It had been missing a single tab.

Releasing his sleeve and snatching up the tab, I'm still not quite able to believe my eyes.

I turn on him. "It's not bad enough that your uncle is trying to ruin us, but you're stealing my job too?"

I'm shouting now, to make my voice heard over the engine; all the fear and fury and homesickness bursting out of me in a torrent.

"It's not your job yet," he says, but he takes another step back.

"The least you can do," I continue, "is to tell your uncle to quit hounding me."

The Evil Nephew's face blanches. "What? He's been hounding . . . ?"

"By e-mail," I say, reaching for my phone. I have a moment's struggle pulling it out of my pocket, and then bring up the lawyer's threat on the screen. He glances at it, and then stares at me, wordlessly.

I fold my arms across my chest. "So, I'm supposed to not only accept this level of harassment from your uncle . . ."

"He's not my uncle," he mutters.

"Well, whoever he is to you. I don't really care. He's obviously set his sights on destroying my family, including throwing me out of my apartment."

The Evil Nephew looks uncomfortable. "I—I don't know what to say. He's a total shit. But I have no control over what he writes to you or to anybody."

Somewhere up near the front of the train, a whistle sounds. Dom punches the button by the train doors, and they hiss open. He steps back onto the train.

As I reach for the handrail, something flutters out of my pocket. It's not until I'm standing inside the train that I see I've dropped the ExLibris envelope onto the station platform.

With the whistle shrilling out again, I leap onto the platform and scoop up the envelope. But as I whirl back to the train, the door hisses shut in my face. The train begins to pull away.

"Wait!" I yell, racing the car along the edge of the platform. Ignoring the piercing sound of a whistle behind me, I smack the side of the train as it hastens past. "Hey—wait!"

I reach the end of the platform as the final car of the train accelerates by. My momentum is so great that I have to grab hold of the wire fence by one edge so as not to fly out on the tracks. I still have a death grip on my phone, but the whoosh of wind from the train's departure rips the envelope from my hand. The torn envelope and its contents swirl onto the tracks behind the departing train.

chapter twenty-one

IMAGE: The Alps
IG: Romy_K [Chamonix, France, March 28]
#ReptilianTeeth #GoingUp
91 ♥

In shock, I watch the red lights on the back of the train as they race off into the perfection of the snowy mountain morning.

This is a disaster. Leaving aside the fact that a competitor I didn't even know existed has now got a lead on me, the train is gone, and all my things with it.

Suddenly, someone grabs me from behind. *"Arrête je dis!"* comes a breathless voice. *"Qu'est-ce que tu penses faire, petite folle?"*

Turning, I find an old man with an enormous white moustache and a pristine uniform clutching my arm. His face is a mask of horror. *"La vie est belle, mademoiselle,"* he says. *"N'essaie pas de la terminer—surtout pendant je bosse!"*

I hold up both hands. "I'm sorry," I gabble at him. "I can't speak French, *por favor.*"

His look changes to one of complete bafflement.

"Shit. Sorry, that was Spanish." I take a deep breath and try again. *"Je no—uh—habla français, monsieur."*

His eyes clear. "Ah," he says, not unkindly. "American?"

I nod. "I have a seat on that train, and it left without me—can you call them to stop?"

And of course, in no way surprisingly, he cannot.

What he can do, now that he understands I had no intention of throwing myself under said train, is to climb down and retrieve my envelope and its scattered papers.

"Here you are, *mam'zelle*," he says, puffing, as he climbs back up a recessed ladder from the tracks. "All is well once more, yes?"

"No sir, it's not." I slump onto a nearby bench with my wallet, phone, and the contents of the envelope from ExLibris. "Apart from this, everything I own is on that train."

He gives me a kindly smile. "I promise you, *mam'zelle*, we can arrange to have your bags collected at the next stop, and book you a seat on another train. Where are you headed?"

"Brindisi."

His face falls. "Ah. Well, tomorrow is a public holiday, so the next train destined for the south of Italy doesn't come through here for two days. It *can* be arranged, but . . ."

While the kindly station guard chatters on, my mind is racing. Even if I'm able to collect my bags at the next station, waiting for another train will put me two full days behind schedule by the time I get to Brindisi.

And also? Behind the Evil Nephew.

Worse, Kindly Station Guard tells me the highway tunnel connecting France and Italy is closed over the holiday.

"Annual repairs and maintenance," he tells me. "Only commercial vehicles allowed, and even they can't get through until after midnight."

By losing my train, I've effectively trapped myself in Chamonix, unless I hike over Mount Blanc into Italy and catch a train there.

I stare up into the sky, watching a new batch of paragliders flit like spring butterflies across the face of the mountain when the idea hits.

A New Romy sort of idea.

The station guard is winding down, and has already lifted his hat to me twice when I grab his arm and point at the paragliders.

"How do those people get up there?"

"They—I believe they take the gondola, *mam'zelle*."

"Which is . . . ?"

He points mutely at a signpost near the station entrance. It has a pictogram of a skier striding toward a chairlift.

I stuff my wallet and phone into the torn envelope with my Ex-Libris paperwork, and run, before Old Romy can find a way to stop me.

After following the signs, I end up at the entrance to what is clearly a major tourist attraction here in Chamonix. A church bell tolls eight times as I hurry up the steps. This mountain is called the Aiguille du Midi, and according to the poster on the wall, it is home to the longest and steepest cable car in the world.

I stare up at the thin black line tracing across the snowy, jagged cliffs above me. A tiny silver and red car hangs precipitously from the line about halfway up, bobbing like a single, dangling Lego block, until it vanishes out of sight. On a parallel wire, another Lego block breaks the clouds to head down toward me. Somewhere in the back of my brain, Old Romy's voice starts to yell.

A pale young guy with a blond man bun and an overbite lounges against the entrance, smoking.

"*Nous ouvrons à dix heures,*" he says through a cloud of sweetly skunk-scented smoke.

"Do you speak English?" I ask, racing up the steps. "I need to get up to those paragliders."

"Hell yeah, I speak English," he says, holding out his joint. "Always willing to share a smoke with a fellow American."

"No thanks," I say quickly. "Listen—it's a long story, but I need to get to the next train station, like—right away. It's in . . ."

"Courmayeur, Italy," the guy says, narrowing his eyes to take another drag. "I ski there all the time. Bummer about the tunnel being closed. You can normally bus there in about twenty minutes."

"Listen, if you can get me up to the top, I'll hire one of those paragliders to fly me down."

The guy stares at me for a long moment before he starts to laugh. It is a quintessential stoner laugh too, one that goes on for about twice as long as it should. By the end, he's doubled over, the teeny burning remainder of the spliff clenched between his fingertips, hands on his knees, gasping.

"I'm not joking," I say, trying not to sound huffy. "And I'm really, really in a hurry. Will you take me for a hundred bucks—er—euro?"

Still chuckling, Stoner Guy stands upright at last, drops the end of his joint, and steps on it before reaching out a hand.

"Eric Neville," he says. "Born Terrytown, New Orleans. At your service."

"Romy Keene," I say, shaking back. "New York City born and bred; currently desperate to catch a train."

He grins. "Well, it just so happens I'm about to send up the first supply car of the morning. And, much as I admire your moxie, I think I can save you the whole kite trip. Follow me."

I trail after him through the entranceway, but my mouth dries up as the next cable car jostles to a stop. Close up, the car seems bigger, and has a kind of futuristic sleekness. All the same, it's still dangling from what looks like a few pulleys and a bit of overstretched wire.

"It—it doesn't seem very safe," I mutter.

"You never been on a chair lift?" Eric asks incredulously. "This thing's safer than one of those, for sure."

"How—how often . . . ?" I start, and then I have to stop and swallow hard to quell the voice of Old Romy in my head. "Have there ever been any accidents? I mean—do those things ever fall off?"

He holds out a hand. "Not this one," he says, flicking his fingers at me impatiently. "But I'd save Googling it until after you're back down, hear?"

I manage a nod, and he leans a shoulder against the wall.

"So, here's the deal. Much as the idea of your dramatic flight down into Italy appeals to me, it's not going to happen. Instead, you're gonna take this cable car to the top of Midi. Then, there's a bit of a walk over to a gondola that crosses the glacier at the top to Pointe Helbronner. After that, it's a quick trip down on the other cable car into Italy. Piece of cake, right?"

The relief at the lack of paragliding alone is enough to have me opening my wallet.

"Atta girl," Eric says approvingly.

I take the ticket he hands me and follow him into his Lego block of doom.

The view? Is breathtaking.

Literally. As the car surges upwards, the town of Chamonix shrinks to the size of a toy village almost immediately. In an effort to keep Old Romy from screaming, I turn away from the incredible shrinking village and gaze at the face of the mountain itself as we race by. This doesn't help. The shiny black cliff face is suddenly much closer, and we whiz past icicles that drip into the sheer, plummeting drop below.

Only yesterday, I left Old Romy's fears behind as I crawled through the claustrophobic darkness of that tunnel entrance. Clutching the rail that encircles the interior of the gondola, I tell myself that New Romy can survive this too.

The interior of the cable car is empty, apart from Eric, pushing buttons inside a tiny control booth, and two tiny Asian ladies who whipped aboard before he closed the doors. So, the only positive thing about the panic attack I have inside this dangling pod of death is that I'm not alone with my fear. Both women are dressed in identical red trousers and puffy jackets. Both are wearing daypacks similar to the one I've left on the train, emblazoned with a tour group logo, and each has a name tag neatly pinned to her collar. Neither says a word.

As the car rockets over the first support pillar, it swings wildly back and forth. My hands squeeze convulsively on the railing, and the lady closest to me—name tag: "Yang Jin"—squeaks like a frightened mouse and skitters across the car. The second lady—"Li Yun"—wears a pink surgical face mask, so I can't really read her expression, beyond the flash of pure terror in her eyes. Instead of following her friend, she sidles over beside me and clings tightly to the handrail.

"No worries!" hollers Eric, stepping out for a moment from his opaque plastic booth. "It's completely safe, I promise you. The car's meant to hold at least fifty people, so since we're almost empty she'll sway a bit." He shakes an admonishing finger at the two ladies, and adds, "This is what comes from getting the jump on your tour group, right?" Then he vanishes unhelpfully back into his little booth again.

Across the car, Mrs. Yang giggles nervously and pulls a camera out of her daypack, which she is wearing back to front. Either she's taken heart from Eric's words, or is determined not to show her fear. The lady beside me—Mrs. Li—hiccups loudly, and then looks up at me, her eyes imploring above her mask.

"It's okay." New Romy speaks up somehow, using my voice. "Just maybe don't look at the view."

Mrs. Li hiccups again, and then, on the exhale, emits a rolling, thunderous burp. With her travel partner all the way across the car, she redirects her grip onto my wrist, and above the mask, her eyes squeeze shut. For the rest of the trip up, she clings to me, hiccupping on every inhale, and loudly, fragrantly, burping on each exhale.

I've always thought nothing could be worse than my own racing heart and inability to breathe during a panic attack.

I was wrong.

Convinced my new best friend is about to be sick all over me, I try sliding my hand gently out from beneath her own. As if in response, the car rocks again, this time with a little side-to-side shimmy for good measure. We're crossing a second support tower, and Mrs. Li's grip tightens on my wrist. In seconds, I've lost all feeling in the fingers of that hand, and I'm consumed with a desperate need to disentangle myself from this visibly terrified woman. I open my mouth to suggest she stand with her friend, when I realize there are silent tears leaking from her tightly closed eyes and down into her mask.

Outside the window, the icicles have coalesced into frozen mounds, clinging precipitously to the cliff. Mrs. Li's burping does not change in volume, or regularity, but has at least not resulted in anything worse. Mrs. Yang maintains a careful distance from both of us. She has regained her initial composure, and, having ventured to the outward-facing side of the cable car, is taking in the view through her camera lens. Her diligence is rewarded when the dense grey fog enveloping the car is abruptly replaced with a brilliant glow, as if a thousand klieg lights had suddenly slammed on above us.

Squinting my eyes against the glare, I find we have emerged from the low layer of cloud, and the entire earth has unfolded beneath our feet. I've only been in an airplane once, but it's hard to not feel like we are soaring through this incredible landscape. The crystal blue of the sky above delineates sharply against the black rocks and the brilliant white of the snow and ice beneath us. The sight is incredible enough to make New Romy want to join Mrs. Yang in her photography, but Old Romy is not completely unhappy about being pinned to the rail near the rear of the car. Over Mrs. Li's still-convulsing head, I watch the endless, serrated-topped spectacle of the Alps stretching away to the horizon.

We bump over another support tower, and as the car swings wildly, something catches my eye through the window on the mountain side. I turn my head in time to see an enormous chunk of ice dislodge from the tower beside us. I can't hear the ice fall, but within a second or two, a wave of sound envelops us—a low rumble, deeper than thunder.

Eric leaps out of his booth at the noise, and the four of us stare down the side of the mountain in shocked silence, punctuated only by the mournful burping of Mrs. Li.

Before he can say a word, Mrs. Yang strides across the car.
"What the fuck was that?" she blurts, in what I'm embarrassed to hear is an Amercian accent.

Mrs. Li's hiccups are sounding increasingly urgent, but Eric ignores all of us, craning to look down the mountain.

The cable car itself doesn't falter, but continues to sweep upward, before dipping suddenly. Without answering, Eric leaps back into his compartment. The car makes a final stomach-dropping swoop, and then slows. On the mountain side, a structure looms closer—a twin to the one at the base. We've reached the top at last. The snowy ground is now only a few feet below the base of the car, and in the lee of the building, the swinging settles almost immediately. On the platform, a young woman with pink hair, skin the color of nutmeg, and a puffy coat, steps over to meet us. We rumble into the enclosure, and before the car has completely stilled, the doors hiss open.

My traveling companions both beat me outside.

This turns out to be a good thing. Mrs. Li pushes past the young woman and out onto the large viewing platform. She clutches the rail with both hands, and standing on her tiptoes, vomits copiously over the side. Ignoring her friend's plight, Mrs. Yang throws herself into the girl's arms.

Eric, who has emerged from his little enclosure, steps out of the car to stand beside me. "Sorry," he says, and reaches up to pull what looks like a walkie-talkie off a clip on the wall. "Minor glitch."

"Minor glitch, my ass," says Mrs. Yang, releasing the girl with the pink hair at last.

The girl, looking not at all perturbed by Mrs. Yang's hug, holds up a cell phone.

"Ice fall," she says. "Not so bad for us, but it block the tracks below, eh?"

I look from her to Eric. "Blocked the tracks? You mean the train tracks?"

"Yes," she says, in an accent that sounds more German than French to me. "But my colleague tells me this ice fall was not so big. Not like a real avalanche, you understand? They clear the tracks in an hour, two, maybe. No harm done."

Eric hops out behind me. "Good luck to you," he says to me, then looks at Puffy Coat Girl. "So, we are okayed for the trip down?"

She nods, but before either of them can move, the two Asian women march past them back into the car.

"Mesdames," Eric says, making a polite shooing gesture. "Time to continue your journey."

Both women shake their heads firmly in unison. Mrs. Li, no longer hiccupping, points down the mountain. *"Il faut que nous descendons tous de suite,"* she says firmly, and even with my pitiful French, her meaning shines clear.

"Vraiment?" he asks, looking surprised. *"La vue est trop belle!"*

"Vraiment," she repeats firmly.

"Too right," mutters Mrs. Yang, and raises her camera. "Already got what I came for."

Eric shrugs, lifts a hand to me, and steps back into his car. Beside me, Puffy Coat Girl flips a switch, and the car lurches out the door.

"Ready?" she says, and I turn to see a second cable car descending to meet us from above.

"What?" I yelp. "This isn't the top?"

She smiles. "You're only halfway. I take you up the rest. It's very quick, I promise."

And this, at least, turns out to be the truth.

chapter twenty-two

 IMAGE: *Aiguille du Midi*
IG: Romy_K [The French Alps, March 28]
#TheNeedleAtNoon #DocumentDisaster
93 ♥

Things I learn above the Alps in France:

1. Puffy Coat Girl's name is Nathalie, and her trip up the mountain with me is the 807th time she's piloted the cable car without ever once falling off the mountain.

2. The Aiguille du Midi translates to "the stroke of noon," and is one of eleven peaks in the Mont Blanc range. Mont Blanc itself is the highest point in Western Europe, but this particular peak tops out at more than 12,600 feet, which is several million feet higher than I've ever been before.

3. The last few years have seen a total onslaught of climbers up Mont Blanc, resulting in overcrowded peaks, trash-strewn trails, and the deaths of several inexperienced climbers.

4. The Grand Couloir, a broad swath of open mountainside, is also known as Death Alley, for the rocks that come tumbling down without warning. Half of all the mountain fatalities in France occur on the sides of the mountains below us.

5. Climate change has come at double the rate in Chamonix that it has elsewhere around the world, resulting in an explo-

sion in the number of snow and ice avalanches. Which I can now attest to, personally.

6. As the result of a collection of rogue paragliders, a recent law has been enacted to disallow them from landing anywhere near the peak of Mont Blanc.

And with this last piece of fortuitous information, Nathalie has to stop feeding me facts long enough to steer our car into the berth at the top. I scramble out, breathless and a little headachy, but with a rush of sheer delight at the sensation of solid earth under my feet again.

Because I'm her lone passenger, Nathalie takes a moment to step out with me onto the platform. The view is magnificent. It feels less like being on top of the world than being perched high on the blue-white canine tooth of some ancient beast who, for the moment at least, is too busy gaping at the view to eat me.

Nathalie zips up her puffy vest and lifts a practiced arm to sweep across the panorama.

"Welcome to the peak of Aiguille du Midi," she recites, only a little robotically. "The paths are still mostly packed snow, and are safe as long as you stay within marked boundaries. Explore all you like, but you must take the car down by fifteen hundred hours, yes?"

"I'm not going back down," I say, and show her my ticket. "That is, I need to get down the other way. The Italian side."

"Ah, *schade!*" she says, and rolls her eyes. "That Eric. He should have radioed me to say." She gestures for me to follow, walks through the exit and points along a snowy path. "You need to take the gondola over to Pointe Helbronner. It's five kilometers, *wunderschön*, across the Glacier de Géant. From there, you can get the Skyway back down."

I take a deep breath. "A gondola and *another* cable car?" I ask quietly, desperately wishing I'd listened more closely to Eric's explanation at the bottom.

"Yes," Nathalie says joyfully. "It is your lucky day, hey?"

And, in fact, while I never do manage to catch my breath the whole time, she turns out to be completely correct. The gondola ride is as wonderful as described, and holds a handful of German tourists, having made an early start from the Italian side. As we sweep across the glacier, my eyes are glued to a jagged blue-black crack on the surface—a crevasse with a faint trail leading to it, but nothing on the other side. Beside me, the two youngest of the tourists—eight or nine years old, by the looks of them—whoop joyfully as the gondola bumps over the first tower and sweeps out across the unblemished blanket of white filling the enormous valley beneath us. It's impossible not to smile at the children's enthusiasm, and dragging my eyes away from the thoughts of death in the deep, I realize I have been shamed into enjoying myself.

We are so high that, above my head, the sky is showing me a side I've never seen before. It begins as a crystalline blue that darkens through navy to almost indigo by the time I crane my neck all the way back. Around us, the rippling coverlet of white is broken only by the jagged peaks, poking through the snowline as far as the eye can see. The sun beams down like a searchlight overhead—a warm deity, benevolently overseeing us miniature, meaningless specks beneath.

Nothing like a mountain range to deliver a sense of perspective, is what I'm saying.

By the time we reach Pointe Helbronner and prepare to descend the Skyway down what has now become Monte Bianco, I'm feeling quite embarrassed about my earlier panic attack. As the two children leap eagerly aboard the enormous Skyway car, their mother leans over to me.

"Apologies," she whispers in a thick German accent. "Their papa is ice-climbing today, and this was all I could think of to keep them entertained."

I smile at her and follow her on board. "Anything to keep them off the computer games, right?"

She looks puzzled. "No—no—they wanted to go with him, but I couldn't face recoiling all the rope again today."

So, there is that.

Though this is also a two-part journey down, the Italian cars are even larger than the ones on the French side, and the ride is comparatively smooth. This car rotates as it travels downward, and this time, I remember to take a few shots for my Insta page. Unlike the route up, I can see tracks in the snow beneath us, visual proof that Nathalie's stories were not just intended to frighten a nervous American.

Near the end of the ride, a mammoth, rainbow-striped balloon floats by, close enough that I can see two people, heavily bundled up, inside. We all stand near the window as the children leap up and down at the sight, cheering with delight when the operator fires their burner, and the balloon shoots suddenly upward, before floating away.

At the bottom, the car slows to a crawl so that we can all step out. As soon as my feet are on solid, less alpine ground, I aim straight for the receptionist to ask about the avalanche on the other side of the mountain. She confirms that all trains are delayed, and then points me toward a tourist booth for more information. But before I can get there, a serious-looking man in uniform steps up to meet me.

"Papers, please."

Flustered, I hand him the envelope of papers from ExLibris. He pulls the pages from the now-crumpled envelope, glances through the paperwork, and then hands the whole thing back to me in a messy pile.

"Your *passport, per favore,*" he says, holding out his hand.

I'm guiltily aware that it was likely the motion of our particular cable car that set off the avalanche, but—the police?

"I'm so sorry," I begin, but he sighs and waggles his fingers at me, so I pull my passport out of my wallet and hand it over.

"I was only riding on the gondola. I don't really know what happened. Perhaps the motion of the car . . ."

Ignoring my babbling, he marches toward a counter marked 'Polizia.' I follow on his heels, but he steps behind the counter and slams the low door closed between us. He punches numbers from my passport into his computer, and I'm trying to remember what I know about Interpol, when he leans across the counter.

"*Grazie, senorina,*" he says, and hands my passport back. "Welcome to Italia. Next!"

Behind me, the German lady passes across a handful of documents. I sidle out of the way, and pretend—not for the first time—that I knew what was going on all along.

I start to slide the papers back into the envelope, when I stop, frozen. Both pages are mostly covered not only in languages I don't understand, but also alphabets. The Egyptian visa is identifiable by the pyramid stamp on one corner, and Arabic script. The Indian visa, too, is written in what must be Hindi, but luckily also in English. Outside, a shuttle bus gives a last-call honk on his horn, but I can't take my eyes off the three English words typed near the top of each of the papers in my hand.

Dominic Makana Madison.

chapter twenty-three

IMAGE DETAIL: Italian Slate Roof
IG: Romy_K [Courmayeur, Italy, March 28]
#ARailJourneyResumed #FirstClassFabulosity
47 ♥

It takes a late bus trip and a long cab ride to get me from the base of the Skyway cable car to the train station. It's so cold; there is frost on the slate roofs of the houses we pass. By the time I get there, the doors to the station are locked and the place is entirely empty. Even the platform is deserted—not even a security guard to gaze at me suspiciously. In the end, I drop my envelope onto a bench under the overhang, pull my hoodie over my head, and fall asleep with the envelope as my only pillow.

It's light when I awaken, but barely. I'm not sure if it's the sound of raised voices or the cold that jerks me awake. My fingers are warm enough, stuffed inside the pocket of my hoodie, but my toes are solidly numb. I sit up in time to see a security guard rousting some old guy from under a pile of cardboard further down the outside platform. Above his head, red LED lights traveling along a display board click over to read 6:03. My neck has developed such a solid kink from sleeping on the bench, I can't turn my head to the left at all.

I'm desperate for a toilet, but even more so for information. Stamping my feet to bring the feeling back, I scoop up my envelope, wipe the sleep out of my eyes, and try to look like someone who has just arrived at the station. As I walk over toward the security guard, the conversation has gotten louder, but I can't pick out a single word. The old guy who had been sleeping rough under the cardboard catches sight of me, and extends his splayed hands out in my direction before replacing them pleadingly on his own chest.

The implication is unmistakable.

The security guard turns to look at me, his eyes narrowing suspiciously. He's a trim, tiny man, perhaps five and a half feet tall.

"Avete dormito bene?" he says in a sarcastic tone.

I adopt my most innocent expression. "I'm sorry, I don't speak Italian. Has the Brindisi train been through yet? I have an assigned seat."

The guard rolls his eyes at me.

Cardboard Guy's triumphant smile is half a dozen teeth short of a full complement. *"Americana!"* His breath makes me stagger back a few paces.

"Ticket?" the guard demands in English, holding out a hand to me.

I shake my head. "You don't understand. Everything I own is still on the train."

He rolls his eyes theatrically. "The train that has not yet arrived?"

Taking a firm grasp of my upper arm, and a similar grip on Cardboard Guy, he marches the two of us across the concourse.

"Wait!" I try to pull my arm out of his grasp, but my shoulder doesn't really work due to the stiff neck. "This is a mistake. I've got a seat on the Brindisi train, I promise you!"

Meanwhile, Cardboard Guy clings to his tattered box as the guard hustles us along toward a door marked *"Stazione Capo."*

"Uno momento," the guard snaps at me impatiently. Since he

hasn't got a free hand, he kicks the door with the toe of his boot, none too lightly, twice.

There's no answer from inside the door, but a voice from behind us calls, *"Scuzi!"*

We all turn to see a tall, handsome man striding across the concourse. He has the bearing of a soldier and is immaculately turned out. His shoes are so highly polished, they reflect the overhead lights, and I could shave my legs on the creases in his uniform trousers.

By this time, more of the public are wandering through, including one woman who curls her lip at me before marching over to open a tiny coffee kiosk.

"Problema?" says Debonair Officer. He's wearing a flat-topped cap similar to that of the Kindly Station Guard back in Chamonix, and is exuding a definite Oscar Isaac vibe.

Except taller. And more Italian.

He sweeps his hat off as he nears, tucking it under one arm.

"My name is Ramona Keene," I say hurriedly. "The stationmaster in Chamonix said he would contact you?" I add, *"Por favor?"* and hope it's close enough.

Debonair Officer offers us all a gleaming smile, and reaches into an inside pocket to retrieve his cell phone. Without a word, he rapidly scrolls through the messages, and then, oddly enough, holds the screen up beside my face.

"You are indeed," he says, in perfect, swooningly accented English. "Ramona Keene."

I peer at the screen, which he obligingly tilts toward me. On his phone is a screen grab of the most repellant-looking creature I've ever seen. Windblown hair in a rusty tangled knot, face red and swollen from crying. Not a speck of makeup, apart from the streak of day-old mascara trailing down one cheek.

144 · kc dyer

"Oh my god," I mutter. The fact this picture exists leaves me feeling worse than being arrested with Cardboard Guy.

Who am I kidding? The person in this picture *deserves* to be arrested with Cardboard Guy.

I try smoothing my hair behind my ears before dragging my attention back to Debonair Officer.

"My esteemed French colleague forwarded me all your details," he says soothingly. "The tracks have been cleared, and your train is due shortly. Your personal items have been collected for safekeeping by the conductor on board. Your seat is still waiting for you."

For a moment, I forget all about the screen grab and the clump of hair that won't stay tucked behind my ear. Tears of relief spring to my eyes, and without thinking, I clutch the sleeve of his uniform. "Thank you so much," I say, at least a dozen times in my terrible bodega-Spanish. *"Gracias, muchas gracias."*

Before he can reply, the air around us begins to rumble gently with the sound of an oncoming train. Debonair Officer escorts me to the correct platform, trailed by the cranky security guard and Cardboard Guy.

As the train pulls up, the stationmaster delicately extricates his uniform sleeve from my clutches. "Your seat awaits, *signorina*."

"My seat?" says Cardboard Guy, in terrible—but hopeful—English. "I with she."

And my heart breaks a little when Debonair Officer looks at me inquiringly.

"Have I missed something . . . ?" he says, but Cranky Security Guard comes to my rescue. Without a word, he snatches up the folded cardboard, tucks it under his own arm, and marches my would-be travel companion away.

Seconds later, the familiar, if a little sleep-deprived face of the train conductor appears, ready to hustle me back on board. The voluble flow of apologies pouring from his lips leads me to understand that he feels at fault.

I begin to tell him it was me who dropped the envelope, but the words die on my lips as he leads me to a first-class cabin. My suitcase and daypack are there, with the phone in the front zipper pocket where I left it.

"To make up for your troubles, *mademoiselle*," he says, sweeping out an arm.

The cabin has a *Futurama* vibe, with beige walls and ceilings and a zesty zigzag pattern extending across the seat cushions and throw pillows.

Because yes, there are throw pillows. Lavender-scented.

"This—must be a mistake," I stammer, as my better self takes hold of my speech centers. "Isn't this first class?"

The conductor beams at me. "It is indeed, *mademoiselle*. Premiere class, private. The rest of the journey takes place in daylight, it is true, but a word from you and I will make up the bed, so you may catch up on your—beauty sleep."

This is first class at its finest. The temptation to lie down on one of these softly padded couchette cushions hits me like a punch to the head, but I make one last, half-hearted attempt at clarification.

"*Monsieur*, I didn't pay for this," I mutter, gingerly feeling the luxurious fabric of the tablecloth with one finger. "Are you sure . . . ?"

"*Absolument*," he says before I can even finish my sentence. "*Bonne journée, mademoiselle.*"

And he is gone.

I bounce across and lock the door behind him before he can change his mind. Then I do a final scan through my things to ensure all my possessions are indeed present, before succumbing to the temptation to check if the crisply encased pillows are as soft as they look.

146 · kc dyer

I awaken to the sound of a quiet knock on my door. Scrambling to my feet and wiping away the crust of drool from one side of my mouth, I throw the lock and peer out to see a young woman dressed in a crisp blue uniform. She is standing beside an elaborately laden cart.

"Tea or coffee, mademoiselle?" she asks, and when I point to her elegant silver teapot, she leaps into action.

Before I know it, my table has been extended and reset, and a full tea service is laid out, complete with china pot, cup and saucer, and a three-tiered tray loaded with tiny rolled sandwiches and a variety of pastries. By which I mean dark chocolate and whipped cream in every possible configuration.

"Bon appetit!" she says, and steps out of my room. Before she can close the door, I reach over to catch it.

"Wait—can you tell me where we are?"

"We are not long past Rimini, *mademoiselle,*" she says politely. "Because of the delay in the Alps, our anticipated arrival in Brindisi is now nineteen thirty this evening."

She bobs her head and closes the door.

I'm suddenly ravenous, and I tear through the entire repast in an embarrassingly speedy time. But the tea has helped, and as I brush away the last chocolate crumbs from my face, I begin to think clearly again.

Checking my phone, I see that Italy shares the same time zone with France, which means I must have slept for at least six hours.

Sliding gingerly past the table, which looks like a hurricane has swept across it, I reach for the recessed handle of a door in the wall. My hopes for a toilet are rewarded. But as I stand at the open door, the train swaying gently beneath my feet, I can't help staring open-mouthed. This is no public train car lavatory. The room is absolutely tiny, containing a sink, cleverly situated above a compact toilet, and to one side? A private shower stall.

Half an hour later, I emerge from my cabin in a cloud of rosemary-scented steam—hair washed and fashioned in a chic high ponytail, and with a clear goal in mind.

I need to find the Evil Nephew, otherwise known to the world as Dominic Madison.

Over the rest of the journey, I search the train from end to end, and back again. No luck. There's no evidence the Evil Nephew has ever been aboard.

When I return to my cabin, all signs of my nap, my meal, and even my steamy shower have been completely eradicated. The gently swaying room is perfection once more.

I plop down on a seat by the window. Now my stomach and brain are once again working in concert, I try to make sense of everything that has happened.

It *can't* be a coincidence that Frank Venal's nephew—or gopher or whatever Dominic is to him—is trying to steal this opportunity out from underneath me. And regardless, even if he is legitimately going for the ExLibris position, it will still ruin my chances to help my uncles hold on to their bookshop.

My brain ticks along with the wheels of the train. I think back to the snarling, slightly orange face of Frank Venal that day inside Two Old Queens. And further? The threatening e-mail from his lawyer. There can be no question. The Evil Nephew can pull his innocent act all he wants. Frank Venal is behind this, somehow. He has to be.

Outside the window, the sun glints off water bluer than I think I have ever seen. We pass a cluster of windmills, all spinning in the balmy salt breezes off the Adriatic coast. Farmers are out in their fields, turning over the soil and sowing crops. The train flashes by a grove containing low, twisted trees that I don't realize must be olives until we are long past. The lush rich soil of Italy provides a far more varied landscape than I ever imagined. I don't know if it's the hypnotic rocking of the train, or the beauty of the view, but my thoughts feel more focused than they have in days. As the train slows down, one thing is obvious.

I run my fingers across the packet of papers that I've carried since they blew out onto the tracks behind the train. A certain Mr. Dominic Makana Madison is going to need these visas. And I will happily exchange them for my own. But not before a few questions get answered.

Suddenly, this trip around the world takes on a whole new dimension. No matter what happens, I decide to keep a smile on my face and to update Teresa with the sunniest and most comprehensive tour information ever. There's exactly zero chance I'm going to let Frank Venal and his nefarious nephew Dominic have things their way. The prize money is going to keep the bookshop safe for Uncle Merv and Tommy. After all I've been through so far, I *have* to succeed. And whatever happens next, I know that I'm 100 percent up to the challenge.

After, perhaps, I find a decent plate of pasta. This is Italy, after all.

chapter twenty-four

IMAGE: Ancient Pillar
IG: Romy_K [Brindisi, Italy, March 29]
#Mediterranean #AppianWay
99 ♥

ExLibris Transit Report, submitted by Ramona Keene

TRAVEL SUMMARY: True luxury is not a thing of the past. Case in point: Pendolino high-speed trains, with their superior-class cabins, which have a tilting technology that allow them to travel the rails of Italy at speeds up to 200 mph. This speed is, of course, limited by weather conditions and such things as landslides or avalanches.

TOP PICKS TO SEE AND DO: First-class travel on this vehicle is unbeatable, from the downy pillows of the couchette to the ensuite shower for lovers of luxury. Let's take a look at high tea as an example of onboard cuisine . . .

The temperature when I step off the train offers the most pleasant of shocks. For the first time since I left New York, the air is warm. It's got to be at least 65 degrees Fahrenheit this evening, and I'm definitely not unhappy about this at all. A gentle breeze blows my hair off my forehead as I walk through the town of Brindisi, and I feel like a new woman. Being clean and somewhat rested helps, and the plate of pasta that appears before me in short order does not hurt either.

I honestly do feel different. The Romy who left New York what seems like an eternity ago bears little resemblance to the one lingering over fettuccini in this ancient seaside town. It's more than my weird level of comfort, sitting here alone, eating pasta in a rich sauce of mushrooms and possibly almonds, in this most foreign of foreign countries. I feel *confident* for the first time on this trip.

For the first time I can remember, if I'm being truly honest.

My life since I left college has been—well, I wouldn't want to say I've been drifting, but . . .

The plan to go on to graduate school has always been there—it has—but now that I really stop to look at it, it hasn't been anywhere near the front burner. For good reason; there's no question Merv needs me. I know that Two Old Queens would fall apart if I wasn't there, overseeing and improving systems every day. But while it will always be home to me, the shop is Merv's baby, not mine. Of course, I love it. I've grown up within its walls. But halfway around the world, sitting here beside my now thoroughly cleaned plate, the significance of all this dawns on me at last.

Immediately after departing the train station this evening, I secured my passage across the Mediterranean Sea. Just past the parking lot, I spotted a travel office, with an ex-pat Brit in the agent's chair. Luckily, she only asked if I had been issued a visa to enter Egypt, and I wasn't forced to admit the one in my possession doesn't exactly have my name on it. Old Romy would have melted down right then, and gone to pieces over the missing visa and the nefarious actions of one Dominic Madison.

New Romy is sitting here, dipping a biscotti so buttery, it actually melts away if I hold it for more than a second in sweet rich Italian tea. Not a care in the world.

I have a place to sleep for the night. I have a berth on the only ship leaving port in the next three days. She is called the *Isa Minali*, and is a refrigeration ship, carrying some sixty tons of frozen fish across the sea to the Suez Canal. In three days, the *Diamond Empress* will also dock here in Brindisi, and it was on that ship that I had set my sights originally. But the loss of three days in this place, regardless of its beauty, is something my schedule will not allow. I'm proud to say I easily won the battle of wills with the local travel agent, who was appalled at the thought that I would take a room on such low-class transport. After collecting all the agent's cruise ship information for Teresa's ExLibris client, I booked the faster, cheaper, and definitely lower-class transport without a second thought. And sometime soon? I will submit a report extolling the virtues of the *Diamond Empress*, without ever quite admitting that I didn't actually float across the Med in one of her fancy cabins.

I've just spent almost sixteen hours in a luxury first-class train cabin, *with en suite shower*. Nothing can ever top that, anyway.

My wee room in Brindisi has the comfiest bed I've come across since I left home, luxury train accommodation included. The inn faces out onto the street, and my balcony is made from iron wrought more than a century ago. Corso Giuseppe Garibaldi is the main street leading down to the town's inner harbor, where one remaining marble pillar marks the end to the Appian Way. As established by the Roman Empire, no less. Brindisi is one of Italy's oldest and most important trade seaports, and the harbor is gorgeous.

Aside from a cursory look at the waterfront while searching out my little inn, I don't have time to check out the town any further, as there's ExLibris work to be done. The Wi-Fi in my room is sketchy, so I spend the early part of the evening scouring tourist pamphlets culled from the innkeeper.

Brindisi may be small in size, but it is mighty in history. The city was once the government seat for the Kingdom of Italy, but these days is better known as a bustling port on the Adriatic Sea. It's about halfway down the heel of the Italian boot, and the closest natural harbor to the place where the Adriatic meets the Mediterranean. One of the innkeeper's pamphlets insists (in poorly translated English) the city was founded by Diomedes, the Greek hero from the Trojan War, but since the Wi-Fi in my room has given up completely, I can't really confirm. Regardless, it's been a city since before we started keeping dates going forward, so it's altogether too much history for one small ExLibris report, anyway. I settle on noting the balmy temperatures and the palm-lined streets, paved in ancient cobbles. And I reserve most of my space for the Italian cuisine, since I've got six local menus to refer to.

I'm writing while sitting on the balcony, the better to keep an eye on the road below for a particular suspicious character. Dominic Madison's dark hair will blend right in with the Italian norm, yes, but he can't do anything about his height. Standing head and shoulders above most of the resident population of this seaside town is not something he can easily hide. So far, there's been no sign of him, and now that it's full dark, I'm beginning to worry that he's somehow managed to surge ahead of me. Still, Brindisi is one of the checkpoints from the novel, and even if he managed to stay hidden on the train, he's going to need to come out at some point, if only to take a photo to prove he was here.

Around nine, I tuck my laptop into my daypack and head out to see if I can find a local cafe with better Wi-Fi. The door to my little inn hasn't even closed behind me before I am swept up in a spontaneous parade leading down to the waterfront. I never do discover which saint is the focus, but without any warning, the entire main street is teeming with celebratory Brindisians. Led by a brass band, all the local clergy are represented. White-frocked choir members in full voice are trailed by a collection of priests in varying levels of clerical garb, followed by an abundance of nuns, most of whom appear to be in their eighties. Just as the parade of clergy slows, the rest of the town leaps into the street in solidarity. By the time the last of the children in strollers are wheeled by, almost all the shops are closed. So much for any shot at better Wi-Fi.

I manage to squeeze into a gelato place just before they shut the doors. The girl behind the counter twists my arm into sampling three varieties, served in a large, pressed paper bowl: *stracciatella*, which tastes like vanilla studded with tiny dark chocolate chips; *nocciola*, which I'm pretty sure is filled with hazelnuts; and something called *zuppa inglese*, a rich, custardy concoction which the card on the wall translates to "English Trifle Soup."

It might be the best Italian food I've ever eaten.

I have an early morning departure on the *Isa Minali*, so even though I still haven't heard from Teresa Cipher about the mix-up with the paperwork, I head back to my little inn with a full stomach and the goal of a fresh start in the morning. I've gone from frosted rooftops to palm trees in a single day, and I have to believe that things can only get better from here.

Leaving Brindisi turns out to be both easier and more complicated than I expect. The complicated part comes first, when the balance of my temporary credit card runs dry as I go to pay my bill at the inn. There's a long moment while the innkeeper and I stare at each other, and then, out of pure panic, I pull the card with Dominic Madison's name on it out of the tattered manila envelope. I stumble through an offer to read the numbers out so he won't see the name, but the innkeeper holds out an imperious hand, and like a schmuck I fork it over.

I fully expect him to ask for my PIN or at least check the signature on the back, but to my everlasting relief, the innkeeper doesn't look at the card at all. Instead, he taps it against his machine, the machine beeps, the transaction goes through, and my complication disappears. I have a moment of vindictive satisfaction at the thought that Dominic Madison is now paying my bills, but it passes when I remember all the charges go through to ExLibris.

While a round Italian girl with no English makes me a cup of tea in the cafe across the street, I have enough time to log in and upload my e-mail. Reasoning that I'll have plenty of time to read and reply on board the *Isa Minali*, I grab my tea, drop the last of my change into the tip jar, and head for the water.

Dockside, the Brindisi harbor smells of salt and seaweed and tar, and is packed full with bobbing boats. As I hurry along the oldest end of the docks, heavily armed guards patrol the entrance gate leading to an Italian naval vessel moored behind razor wire. Outside the fence, a couple of tiny, decrepit rowboats have been discarded on the shore, next to a collection of multicolored fishing vessels. Above them all, the morning sun reflects off the Sailor's Monument, memorializing Italian sailors since sometime between the two world wars. At the far end of the cobbled street, I find the commercial port, which, like the naval section, is behind a guarded gate.

No submachine guns here, though. Commercial fishing vessels are moored next to high-end yachts, two of which sport visible swimming pools on board, and one with its own helipad.

The *Isa Minali* is moored in the outer harbor, and I have to pass through a customs facility before I can even get close. Like the moment with Dominic Madison's credit card, I stand with my heart in

EIGHTY DAYS TO ELSEWHERE · 155

my throat, waiting for the customs officer to ask to see my visa. Instead, he stamps my passport, wishes me a *buon viaggio*, and waves the person behind me forward.

I'm through, and on my way to Egypt.

The captain of the *Isa Minali* introduces himself as Giuseppe, though I never learn if this is his first or last name. He tells me that given good seas, the ship is expected to approach the Suez Canal in as little as two days. He also tells me there's no Wi-Fi available on board. The idea of going incommunicado for the length of the journey is unnerving, but I don't really have any other viable choice, so I follow a crew member down to the tiny quarters assigned to me. One of the walls of my room is frost covered, which is something I don't recall ever seeing before.

"We're a refrigeration vessel," the crew member, whose name is Joachim, explains. "All the rooms on this side are up against the freezer."

He leaves me to my unpacking with a wink, and an offer to "warm me up anytime" that I have no intention of taking him up on. After dumping my bag on the cot, which proves to hold a single sheet of worryingly thin foam over a metal frame, I lock my door and head up on deck. I'm in time to get a last view of beautiful Brindisi, the first checkpoint on this trip where nothing has gone wrong.

I can only hope it won't be the last.

I spend most of the day on the deck, trying to stay out of the way of the crew, and taking pictures of the glittering Mediterranean for my Insta page. I don't think I've ever seen this many shades of blue.

When the light begins to fade, I find a spot out of the wind to read through my e-mail. Tommy writes me, reporting on Frank

Venal's first rent-collecting visit. He says that when Merv expressed surprise at seeing Venal instead of his nephew, Frank Venal complained bitterly that he'd gone off on some wild goose chase. When Uncle Merv remarked on the coincidence of my departure, the two men got to comparing notes. Tommy said Venal became incandescent with rage, convinced that Dominic has applied for the ExLibris internship to shirk his family duties. Apparently, he loudly blamed my bad influence before stomping off.

Without thinking, I write Tommy as reassuring a note as I can muster, insisting that *of course* I have zero influence with Venal's nephew. After pressing 'send' twice, I remember the lack of Wi-Fi. It'll be almost two days before my reply can go through.

Swallowing my frustration, I turn to the second e-mail. This one is from Teresa's assistant, Powell, in response to my frantic questions about the switched paperwork. Irritatingly, this note informs me that I will still need to connect with Mr. Madison—*Mr. Madison!*—before entering customs in Port Said, Egypt, as replacement visas cannot be forwarded in time.

Considering I spent almost the entire time I was in Brindisi on the lookout for Mr. Madison without any success, this is not good news. I can't reply to either e-mail, so I close the lid of my laptop and lean back into one of the last rays of the setting sun. The air smells fresh and slightly salty, with a fishy sort of undertone that's not strong enough to be unpleasant. I should be basking in the moment, sitting in the sun for the first time in weeks—months, really, since we've had such a hard winter in New York. Instead, I have a growing suspicion that Dominic Madison has ditched me and dumped my visa into the Mediterranean.

With a sigh, I decide to go down to my cabin and collect up the cruise ship pamphlets in order to work on my next transit report. As

I descend the iron steps into the bowels of the ship, the fishy odor grows stronger. Downstairs, several crew members whiz past as I approach my cabin. Joachim, racing by with a wrench in each hand, stops to tell me the freezer unit in one of the holds has failed.

"At least there'll be no frost on your walls," he says before dashing off.

And just like that, my shipboard priorities change. I spend the rest of the voyage in a near-fruitless effort to keep away from the smell of the hold. My room is uninhabitable, so with Joachim's help, I lug my bedding upstairs and create a little nest in my writing spot under the eaves on one corner of the deck. It's not ideal, but it's out of the wind and has the freshest air to be found on this suddenly stinking ship.

The next required checkpoint is at the docks of the Suez Canal. Trying to put Dominic—and the reek of rotting fish—to the back of my mind, I fill the day writing a glowing report of the *Diamond Empress* as transport across the Mediterranean. That I haven't even seen the cruise ship at a distance, let alone stepped on board, leaves me feeling no guilt. Whatever it takes to defeat Dominic is fair game.

That night, lying under a pile of blankets tucked into my wee corner of the deck, I dig my copy of *Around the World in Eighty Days* out of my suitcase. The cover is in remarkably good condition, all things considered. Inside, I pull out the decals I've been collecting from each country, and on a whim, apply them to the top of my old suitcase. When I'm finished, the orange and green on the tricolor Italian flag add a bit of variety to the red, white, and blue of the Union Jack and the French flag.

The old decal of an Alaskan license plate is on the bottom, but I'm careful not to look at it at all.

Instead, I trace the shape of the flags on the top with my fingers.

Three countries down, but so many more still to come. The thought, like the sight of the old decal on the bottom of my case, makes my stomach clench. Why is it always harder to find New Romy in the dark?

In the end, to comfort myself, I sit up late as the *Isa Minali* glides along the coast of Turkey in the gradually warming dark. In the glow of my computer screen and the stars above, I write my uncles an e-mail, to send off when I reach Egypt.

chapter twenty-five

 IMAGE: Ship's Chimney, the Isa Minali
IG: Romy_K [Port Said, Egypt, April 1]
#ASecondSeaSailed #AnAprilFool
85 ♥

Spring is kind to the Mediterranean this year, and my odor-challenged ship makes it across the calm seas in record time. Also? As I get ready to leave, I can't help noticing my hair looks maybe the best it ever has—soft curls where it's usually frizzy, and even a few sun-kissed highlights. Maybe the time I spent on deck in the Mediterranean air and sunshine is paying off, after all. Still, the relief at being able to leave the stinking hold of the *Isa Minali* behind carries me all the way down the gangplank.

As did the fictional Fogg, I find myself in Port Said, an Egyptian city on the Mediterranean side of the Suez Canal. As I trot along the dock, I breathe in the scents of tar and gasoline, and when the breeze stirs, I have to blink a salty grittiness out of my eyes.

Egypt is the first country that expects a visa, and I have one—just not in my own name. Clinging to the knowledge that I *do* have my own passport, I decide the only thing to do is brazen it out. It's not like I haven't grown up with a great role model, after all. I mean, when Tommy gets on his high horse about some perceived slight, nothing can get in his way. His eyebrows do this imperious thing that I'll never be able to manage, true, but I can only try. Throwing back my shoulders, and tucking my definitely cuter hair behind my ears, I aim for the customs sign.

These new, Brazen Romy thoughts push me forward for the entire ten minutes it takes to get to the front of the queue. When, at last, the customs official holds out one white-gloved hand, I give him the passport.

After riffling through the pages, he asks, "Your visa?"

In the moment before I reply, I swear his eyebrows go into full Tommy mode. It's uncanny. And as he reads Dominic's name on the visa out loud, Brazen Romy folds like an old paper doll.

"There's been a little problem," I whisper, but that gloved hand lifts again.

"These names don't match," he says, and points to a dingy-looking door across the room from the exit sign. "Further clarification is required."

I glance over my shoulder, trying to judge the chances of bolting back in the direction of the ship, but before I can so much as take a single step, two guards materialize out of nowhere, and escort me through the dingy wooden door. Both are dressed in identical blue uniforms, with peaked caps pulled low, I barely see their eyes. They swiftly relieve me of all my possessions—camera, suitcase, everything.

Behind the door is a hallway, and at the end of the hallway is another door, but instead of wood, this one is made of rusty iron bars—and fear.

"Wait a minute," I say, turning to look at the woman on my left. Her eyes don't even stray in my direction. Instead, she takes a grip of my arm above the elbow, and pulls out an enormous, rusty key from the jingling bunch at her belt.

"Look, this is only a misunderstanding," I babble, trying the male guard on my right. Brazen Romy is only a distant memory at this point.

His eyes don't turn either. As the female guard unlocks the rusty iron door, he reaches with his free hand to hold it open. In unison, the two of them thrust me inside, and slam the door behind me.

Together, they turn and march back down the corridor.

I briefly think about pressing my face between the bars, but up close, they look so grimy, I reconsider.

"Wait!" I yell at the retreating backs. "Don't I get a phone call? Is this even legal? I need to call the American . . ."

The dingy wooden door at the end of the hall slams shut behind the guards.

". . . embassy," I finish.

A wave of fear and discouragement washes over me that is so strong, I forget about my distaste and cling to the iron bars, trying my hardest not to cry.

A mistake, as it turns out, since the bars are sticky, as well as rusty.

It is April first, and I am in jail.

I don't even have time to berate myself for being a literal April fool before I feel a hand on my arm.

A heavily accented voice whispers, "Pretty lady," in my ear.

I leap almost straight sideways, and whirl, so my back is against the bars of the cell wall. The gap-toothed smile of a tiny old man in a pristine white turban shines up at me. He's wearing sand-colored baggy pants and what looks like a soccer jersey with "FIFA" printed across the chest in blue letters.

"Pretty *American* lady," the man repeats, and reaches toward me again.

"Don't touch me," I snap, my fear tamped down for the moment by sheer annoyance. I have been pawed by pervy old guys on the subway enough times that this one holds no terrors for me. Most of them have more teeth than he does too.

Since my suitcase and all my papers have been taken away from me, I don't have anything that I can use to defend myself, so I ball my hands into fists.

The fact I've never been in a fistfight in my life doesn't stop me.

In response, the old guy folds his hands together in prayer position over his heart and gives a little bow. "Pretty American?" he says, and this time it sounds more like a question. "American dollar?"

"In your dreams, bud," I say, but as the words come out of my mouth, I realize there are at least three other people sitting against the wall behind the old man in the dim recesses of the cell. I press my back into the bars as one of them unfolds himself to loom over the old man.

"No American dollars here, sir," Dominic Madison says, resting a hand lightly on the man's shoulder.

At the sight of him, the most peculiar combination of relief and loathing flows through me. But before I can gather my thoughts into an actual English sentence, someone physically shoulders him aside and reaches an arm out to the old man.

"Leave the nice lady alone, Jaddi," says a young woman. Olive-skinned, she's wearing jeans, a long-sleeved cotton t-shirt in pink and white stripes, and a matching pink headscarf.

She turns to me, her lips curling up in apology. "He doesn't mean any harm."

She steers the old man away, over to a low wooden bench that is the only furnishing in the cell.

Dominic leans against the bars. "Fancy meeting you here," he says.

I glare up at him. "It's *your* fault we're in here," I hiss.

"Wasn't me who mixed up the documents," he says with a shrug. "Though I must say I'm happy you've made it at last."

"At last? When did *you* get here?"

He glances at his wrist, and then rubs it absently. I realize they must have taken his watch.

"Not sure. Three hours ago? Maybe four? When you weren't on the dock, I thought I'd wait outside the customs office, but the officials were not really open to it."

"Did they take your passport?" I ask, glancing around the cell. Apart from the girl and the old man on the bench, the room is thankfully empty. It gives off a smell that is remarkably similar to some of the older subway tunnels back home. Damp, with a faint metallic undertone of urine.

"Yeah. All the paperwork, and my pack too," he replies.

My mind races. "Okay, that has to be good. I'm sure once they match the paperwork with our correct passports, we can be on our way."

He shrugs. "You'd think so."

Peering through the bars, I scan the dim corridor for any sign of movement. "Hey!" I yell. "Can you let us out, please?"

There's a tiny giggle behind me, and I turn to see the young woman has covered her mouth with one hand. "I'm sorry to laugh," she says, looking contrite. "But it's always funny to see how Americans think."

Before I know whether to work myself up into taking offense over this, Dominic slips over to sit down on the bench beside the two others.

"Ramona, this is Huda and her grandfather, Tariq. They traveled aboard the same ship as I did from Cyprus."

"Cyprus?" I hiss at him. "What were you doing in Cyprus?"

He shrugs. "Making my way here."

The girl, Huda, nods her head at me. "Nice to meet you," she says with a shy smile. "I live in Cyprus, but now I am take Tariq back to my mother's home in Cairo. He is too much work."

In spite of the bleak surroundings, I can't help smiling back at her. "Was he visiting for long?"

"Long enough," she says, rolling her eyes. "A week with my husband and me. I have to take extra day off work to bring him home, and my boss at the office, he is not happy. Then last night, Jaddi take all our papers and throw them over side of ship. So, who knows when I get home?"

Suddenly, my own situation doesn't seem quite so grim.

I look at the old man in a new light. I've watched several of the bookshop's oldest customers retreat into senility over the years, and it has always been so sad to see.

"Pretty hair," Tariq says brightly to his granddaughter. "American dollar?"

Huda shakes her head at him and then turns back to me. "Sorry. He doesn't have much English." She squeezes her grandfather's hand and speaks to him softly in Arabic.

The dingy door down at the end of the hall opens suddenly, and a small man appears, striding toward us.

"Huda Al-Amin?" he asks.

When she rises, he follows this with a stream of Arabic of which I cannot understand a single word.

In the time it takes Huda to help her grandfather to his feet, the man is unlocking the cell door. He ushers the two of them through the door, and then swings it closed.

"Wait a minute," I say, reaching through the bars. "What about us?"

The small man gives me a scornful look and neatly sidesteps out of my reach.

"You wait," he barks, and walks up the corridor.

Huda glances back at me with a sympathetic look. "My mother has come to collect us," she says. "Peace be with you."

"American dollar?" says Tariq hopefully, and they are gone.

As the door closes behind them, I can feel tight fingers of panic squeezing my stomach, and in the silence of the room, the pounding of my heartbeat in my ears sounds like a bass drum.

Looking over at Dominic, I see that he doesn't appear much more confident than I feel, but he must be able to read the fear in my eyes.

"It's going to be okay," he says, trying to sound reassuring. "I'm sure they'll sort it out soon."

"And you know this how?" I snap at him. The worry makes me sound angrier than I mean to, but I don't owe this guy any encouragement. It's his fault we're here, after all.

As if he can read my thoughts, he gets to his feet. I'm nearly five foot ten, but standing beside me, Dominic is at least four inches taller than I am, maybe more. He's wearing long cutoff jeans that look like they've been hastily chopped, which make his legs look even ganglier.

I take a step back, wanting to keep at least an arm's length between us.

"Look, what happened on the train was an accident," he begins. "Once we get out of here, we can talk things through, okay? And I'm . . ."

The door at the end of the corridor opens again, and we turn in unison to see the female guard from earlier. She's taken her cap off, and is holding an American passport in each hand.

"Dominic Makana Madison?" she asks.

"That's right," he responds, sounding relieved.

"I'm Romy—uh—Ramona Keene," I say as she walks toward us. "Is that my passport? Ramona Paige Keene?"

The woman unlocks the door and points at Dominic, who shoots me an apologetic look.

I make a dive for the opening, but she slams the iron bars closed in my face.

"I'll do what I can for you," he promises, and follows her down the hall. "Try not to worry."

"Hey!" I yell at the guard's back, as panic settles over me like a thick black cloak. "Hey—don't leave me here! Dominic—don't let them leave me in here!"

But before I can finish my plea, they are gone.

The next twenty minutes, I have to say, make me look back to the vaults below Paris with a kind of fondness. By the time the guard returns, I've mentally replayed every scary prison movie ever made. Even once she unlocks the door, it's a full half hour before I stop shaking.

She hands me a tissue and seats me at a desk in another, slightly less dingy room. Behind the desk, a man in a pristine customs uniform—no cap—smiles brightly at me. He theatrically stamps my passport, and bids me good day as if nothing is out of the ordinary.

Which perhaps nothing is, for him. No explanation offered.

My relief leaves me weak in the knees, and I stumble out onto the streets of Port Said. And I can't say it's a surprise when there's no trace of Dominic Madison. Spotting a familiar green and white logo, however, I hurry away from the customs building toward the one place I know I can find comfort in this strange land—a Starbucks, near the entrance to what looks like an American-style hotel.

After downing a close-to-scalding cup of English breakfast tea, sweetened with three packets of sugar and heavily slaked with cream, I begin to feel a little better. On the plus side, all my possessions have been returned to me—my broken camera, my phone, and my correct paperwork from ExLibris. The visa now stamped into my passport is good for thirty days.

On the negative?

The mess at the border means I've missed my assigned place on a ship that left two hours ago. Way back in Brindisi, the travel agent suggested that picking up transportation out of Egypt might not be as easy as booking a train ticket in Italy. On her advice, I booked a berth on a Red Sea steamer called the *Wahash Mahat*. At the time, the steamer's planned route seemed perfect. Down through the Red Sea, across the Arabian Sea, docking in Mumbai. It's as long a voyage as the one I took across the Atlantic, and the *Wahash Mahat* was the only ship she could find that was still accepting passengers.

But now—that ship has sailed. Steamed. I don't know—whatever it is that ships do.

I still feel completely furious with Dominic for being at the root of the problem. Determined to distance myself from him once and for all, I decide to spend the rest of the day looking for an overland route across the Horn of Africa.

Port Said is a unique place in a number of ways. It perches on the Egyptian shoreline, at the mouth of the Suez Canal, which was built by the Brits in the nineteenth century to better facilitate their exploitation of all the nations they subjugated overseas. The skyline from the water is stunning, filled with sumptuous architecture. While the palm trees look much the same as those in Brindisi, there is no question that I am now in Egypt. Across the water on the eastern bank is Port Said's twin city, Port Fuad. This is one of the rare places in the world where two cities essentially cohabit across continents, as Said is on the African side of the canal, and Fuad is in Asia.

According to a handsome young man I meet who claims to be the harbor master, the canal sees an average of more than forty ships pass along its 120-mile length every day. Of course, this same handsome young man insists he is in search of an American wife, so I'm inclined to take anything he says with a pinch of salty canal water.

You'd think that with that kind of traffic, hitching a ride would be a piece of cake. Yet, over the course of the day, I'm refused passage on an oil tanker and two smaller passenger vessels. The single travel agency I find that has an employee who speaks English is baffled by my request and keeps trying to book me onto cruise ships. When I suggest traveling across the Arabian Peninsula, the woman laughs, and apparently Yemen is even worse.

Sometime in the afternoon, exhausted by the heat and the discouragement, I buy a lamb shawarma from a street vendor. It is greasy and delicious in the moment, but leaves me with a kind of sinking sensation in my gut afterwards. So about on par with the rest of my day. By nine that night, I've managed to find exactly zero ways to move forward.

The only success I experience the entire day, apart from being sprung from custody, is finding a tiny villa to spend the night. I can't even take credit for finding it, as the English-speaking clerk at the travel agency slid a card for the place across her desk to me, when it became obvious that I was going to be stuck here for life.

The card, luckily, has a tiny fragment of map on the back. It doesn't look too far from the main street, so I follow the directions, and circle into the marketplace, which is where I find the Resta Ramal. It's an old sand-colored building laden with intricate cast-iron balconies, and is tucked around the corner from what looks—and smells—like a hookah bar. As I walk in the front door, I'm greeted by the proprietress, who introduces herself as Madame Nephthys.

She is dressed in a red, high-necked tunic and brown trousers, and her hair is covered with a scarf in matching colors of red and brown. Both wrists are loaded with jingling bangles, and she is wearing several gold necklaces of varying lengths, each bearing heavy medallions. Even with what are clearly at least three-inch wedges, she still tops out under five feet tall.

I show her the card from the travel agent. "She called," Madame says kindly. "I expect you. Tell me what you need, yes?"

I manage to give her the short version of my story without crying. An accomplishment I'm proud of, I have to say.

Within minutes, Madame has me seated at a tiny table outside a beaded curtain that leads, I think, to a kitchen. At the sight of my ExLibris credit card, she winks both eyes at me, and reappears with a steaming bowl of couscous, and an uncorked and unlabeled bottle of what is clearly red wine.

"You eat this," Madame Nephthys says, tucking a long-tined fork into the bowl. "Is good. You feel better. Tomorrow another day, yes?"

"Is this *wine?*" I hiss at her. "Isn't that illegal?"

"No wine here," she says loudly, in the direction of the door. She turns to me, making a slashing motion across her throat with one hand. "Keep voice down. You want get me arrested?"

She reaches for the bottle, but I manage to grab it before she can snatch it away.

"I'm sorry," I whisper. "Thank you."

She sighs loudly and then, glancing at the door, reaches across what is clearly a bar, and snags a long-stemmed glass. She slides it across the table at me. "You drink quiet," she commands, and I meekly proceed to do just that.

chapter twenty-six

 IMAGE DETAIL: Guesthouse
IG: Romy_K [Port Said, Egypt, April 1]
#NoRoadsOutofEgypt #TravelersTummy
105 ♥

Madame Nephthys is right—her couscous is the best thing I've ever tasted. It's loaded with roasted onions and pine nuts and sun-dried tomatoes. I've never been a huge fan of olives, but the ones in this dish are finely sliced and briny and perfect. Before I know it, the bowl she's set before me is almost empty. As for the wine, there's about a half a glass left in the bottle, and I've drunk enough to feel a little reckless. Not reckless enough to show my face on the streets, but enough to consider drunk-Googling. I'm not actually sure if drunk-Googling is even a thing, but if it isn't? It should be.

My daypack is leaning against the legs of my stool, and I reach down and pull out my laptop. There's got to be some way for me to get out of this mess. So far, even Madame Nephthys, who gives off the aura of being able to solve any problem life throws at her, has been no help when it comes to getting me out of Egypt.

Let alone the rest of the way around the world.

In desperation, I type *Help Romy* into the search bar, and scan the results. For the most part, what comes up are crowdfunding pages for other women named Romy who are struggling in one way or another. There's also a site for a transgender woman looking to legally change her name.

Of course, that Romy needs support too, when it comes right down to it.

This gives me a thought, and I wonder what Teresa Cipher's name was before she changed it. Before she legally became Teresa, that is. I have no doubt that she's always been Teresa, no matter what her birth name was. It's an interesting thought, but of course it does nothing to help me with my current problem, and Google doesn't help me there either. I cross my arms on the bar, and drop my head down onto them.

A worried voice immediately barks out from behind the bead curtain.

"Missy not feeling well?"

Madame Nephthys bustles out, hands dripping and holding a dish towel. "Missy need to go to room?"

"It's okay," I say, lifting my head to stare at her blearily. "I'm not sick. Only . . ."

Worried? Depressed? Completely stymied? And maybe . . . okay, maybe a little sick too. My stomach gives an ominous gurgle.

As my thoughts turn inward, the door to the street swings open, and Dominic Madison walks in.

Of course he's here. He's here because only bad things are happening to me here. And really? He's the ultimate bad thing.

"Hey," he says, as if he hadn't disappeared on me earlier.

As if we were in some bar in New York, and not in a little guesthouse on the other side of the world.

"How did you know where I was?" I ask, eyeing him narrowly. "And what are you doing here, anyway?"

"I'm staying here, of course," he says, and slaps a fresh bottle onto the table beside the remains of my couscous. "I think we need an exchange of information."

I stare at him, feeling defeated on every level.

"Okay," I say, at last.

But Madame Nephthys has thoughts. "Afraid not. No alcohol in this house. We could lose our good rating."

I look from the bottle of wine she provided with my dinner to her face, and back.

She flicks her towel along the bar and sniffs. "I don't know where his bottle come from. You could be agents, try to shut me down. Try to make me lose hospitality license."

Dominic slips the bottle into his pack. "Nothing to see here," he says to her, and slides a handful of Egyptian pounds across the table. "For the couscous," he adds, though what he's offered is about triple the actual price on the menu.

The bills vanish into Madame's apron before I can blink. "Thank you, Mr. Dominic. But no funny business, eh?"

He assures her that he has exactly zero funny business in mind, and then scoops up my suitcase from the floor. "Let's go talk in my room," he mutters, but Madame's eyes widen.

"Talking only, Madame," he promises. "No funny business. You have my word."

She smiles at him, but turns slowly to me. "Your word too?" she says, reaching her hand toward me, palm upward.

I jam my hand in my pocket, grab all the rest of my remaining coins, and carefully pile them into her cupped palm. "My word too," I say.

She sniffs dismissively at my meager offering, but drops the jingling handful into the pocket of her apron all the same, and vanishes back through the beaded curtain.

Dominic's room turns out to be far more spacious than my own, with a window onto a tiny, enclosed garden nestled at the center of the inn. In addition to his bed, he has a small table with two chairs, decorated with a bowl of colored fruit made from, on closer inspection, papier-mâché. From a shelf over the sink, he produces two shot glasses, which he slaps down on the table beside the bottle. He yanks out a chair for me, points at it, and then folds his lanky frame around the other one.

"Who goes first?" he asks.

"You do," I say flatly. "This was your idea, after all."

And so, over the course of the next hour, Dominic Madison's story comes out.

He is, as he's repeatedly stated, *not* Frank Venal's nephew. In his regular life, he trained first as a cook, and then as a pastry chef, at the International Culinary Center over on Broadway—less than a mile from Two Old Queens. At some point, he pulls out his phone, taps the screen, and then slides it across the table at me. His Instagram feed is loaded with a dizzying assortment of cakes and pastries. I have to bite back my admiration as I swipe through the pictures. It's an impressive variety, and his number of followers is even higher than Teresa quoted, but I'm not going to tell him that. Mostly I'm embarrassed that I never thought to look him up on Instagram.

Instead, I lean back in my chair and remember Teresa Cipher's description of my competition for the ExLibris position. So, *this* is her New York photographer? Not quite one of the glamorous, smug-faced girls I'd been worried about.

I give him the side-eye as he pours clear liquid from his bottle into the two shot glasses. His smooth, amber skin is tinged with sunburn, and his eyes are tired, but—I have to admit, he's better looking than any of the girls I'd been worried about. I remember back to the 8.5 I'd given him on the HOT Reader Scale. A rating like that would firmly place him into Jersey's "gorgeous, and therefore flirt-worthy" category.

All the same. Gorgeous is as gorgeous does, right? His HOT Reader score came before I knew who he really was. His association with Frank Venal negates it all. Besides, there's something more important to take from this than what this dude—my sworn enemy—looks like. I'm missing something important. I just need to wrap my foggy brain around it.

Closing my eyes, I force my thoughts back to the last night at ExLibris. So much has happened since that night, it feels like it could be two years ago, rather than two weeks. One thing about this adventure—it has slowed time right down.

I'm a gambler, Teresa had said. At the time, I thought she meant she was taking a gamble by hiring me. Maybe she was. And maybe? There was more to it.

"So," I say, enunciating carefully. "The night before I left, Teresa told me she'd planned to give the job to some Instagram influencer. Obviously that was you, right?"

He grins. "She called me an *influencer*? I must be more persuasive than I thought."

"Okay, whatever. That's not the point. The point is, at the time, I thought she'd given the job to me. But obviously, she's clearly promised the job to both of us."

He leans back in his chair. "She never told me about you either. But I began to suspect it, when you crashed into me in the travel agency."

"*You* crashed into me," I say with as much dignity as I can manage. My lips have begun to feel numb. "So, it *is* a race, then, and not just against the clock."

His smile broadens. "I guess it is."

For courage, I shoot the clear liquid in my glass down in a single burning gulp. As my eyes begin to water, I point at the photo page still up on his phone.

"You're an *influencer*," I say, putting as much venom into the word as I can muster. "You don't need this job. Why are you even here?"

He drains his own glass and, for the first time, looks me square in the face.

"My mom's Samoan, born in Hawaii," he says quietly. "She met my dad in Honolulu, when he was there on vacation one summer. When they learned I was going to show up on the scene, she married him and moved back to his family in Connecticut. They tried, I guess, but they couldn't make it work, and my dad's never really been in the picture. My mom wanted to go back to Hawaii, but she ended up in New York, and she took a job as a housekeeper for Venal. She's worked for him ever since. I grew up in a little coach house on his property."

"So, do you work for him—for Venal—too?"

Dom shakes his head. "No. Not really. But it's—complicated. And I need this job to help untangle things a little for my mom. Last year, Venal found out she's been helping some of the local immigrant families with childcare during the day. Since then, he's literally been blackmailing her, threatening her with exposure, and the families she helps with deportation."

He looks moodily at the bottle, and refills both our glasses.

I slide mine away. "I'm already having trouble concentrating," I mutter. My stomach gives another ominous gurgle.

The truth is, between my upset stomach and the unaccustomed alcohol, forget concentrating—I'm having trouble staying upright.

But I'm not about to say that.

Instead, I crack the bottle of water that Madame Nephthys has left on the table by the door, and take a big swig.

It helps, a little.

"Look, complicated or not—you *know* what my situation is. Your guardian or whatever he is, is about to ruin my uncles' lives. Merv and Tommy have run Two Old Queens since before I was born. That bookstore is their whole life—they live there, they work there. And your—and Frank Venal is going to take all that away, pretty much on a whim."

Dom sighs. "I know. He's a total asshole, there's no denying it. And, honestly, if he wasn't holding my mom's life to ransom, I would not be here. But she's got no one else, and I need to find a way to get her away from him. I didn't know it was you, I swear. Not for sure, anyway, until I saw you on the train in France. And now—well, it's too late."

I slam my fist on the tabletop. "It's not too late," I say, filled with a sudden fury. "You said it yourself. You have a little problem to un-tangle. But for me, it's my family's whole livelihood that's at stake."

"Take a breath," he says, glancing over his shoulder. He grabs my glass and drains it too. "The situation's bad for both of us, obviously. That's why I came in here to talk to you."

He leans back in his chair, his face flushed. "That day we all met at the bookstore? He left an article about how to report people to ICE on her kitchen counter. It made her cry, Romy. I knew right then that I had to find some way to get enough money to pay for a decent law-yer, and fast. After we left your bookstore, I spotted the ExLibris flyer on a telephone pole up the street. That night I applied for the job."

His eyes suddenly look more tired than ever, and he leans back in his chair, and rubs them. Outside the window, it's full dark, and some kind of sweet, exotic scent begins to waft in from the garden. Suddenly, it's all I can smell—pervasive and foreign and strange.

"*I'm* the foreigner here," I mutter.

"What?" Dominic asks. He tucks a strand of hair behind his ears and leans forward.

"Nothing. I should probably go," I say, but he holds up a hand.

"Just a minute, here. I've basically bared my soul to you and you haven't told me anything. What about your parents? Why do you live with your gay uncles? What's the story there?"

"What does being gay have to do with anything?" I snap, my earlier animosity returning.

"It doesn't, it doesn't," he says soothingly. "Only—your parents . . . ?"

My eyes fill with sudden hot tears, which makes me even angrier. "I don't want to talk about it, okay?"

"Okay."

He's quiet a minute. "But if you ever do . . ." he begins.

I shoot him a glare, and he subsides into silence again. Grabbing the bottle, I pour two more shots. When he picks up his glass, I clink it with my own. "To not talking about the shitty stuff," I say, and he drinks.

I manage to swallow the whole thing without gasping this time.

"Did you have any luck finding a way out of here?" I ask as he sets down his glass.

He shakes his head. "I found a dive ship, but it's local. I thought about getting a bus or something across the desert to Dubai, but there's a travel advisory for pretty much all of Saudi Arabia right now. Not great for Americans."

"Yeah, I tried that too," I say. "One guy I spoke to just laughed. He still tried to take my money, though."

I lapse into silence and concentrate on drinking as much water as I can choke down. Strangely enough, it doesn't taste nearly as good as whatever is in Dom's bottle.

"Listen," he says after the silence stretches on endlessly. "I don't know what Teresa's up to, but—what do you say we make an agreement?"

"What kind of agreement?"

He shrugs. "We could try—for now—to work together. Put our heads together to get out of here, at least."

I stare at that handsome face. It's a face I want to believe. A face that I would—under almost any other circumstances—want to learn more about. Would follow anywhere, truth be told.

But now? I'm not sure I can trust Dominic Madison as far as I can throw him, which would not be at all far, considering the amount of alcohol I've put away in this teetotal country.

Still. I decide I'm drunk enough to agree to at least give it a shot.

"An agreement," I say, reaching across the table.

"A gentleman's agreement—and lady's," he adds hastily as he shakes my hand. "Teamwork."

I think it's the handshake that does it. I'd been sitting almost motionlessly for the past hour, trying to quell the growing unease deep inside. But as I lean across the table to shake his hand, I realize there's more than unease lurking inside me. And whatever it is?

Wants out.

I get as far as the door before the retching doubles me over. Suddenly nothing, not even the humiliation of vomiting in my greatest enemy's room, can stop the tidal wave. Before I can move, Dominic is there, and rather than tossing the contents of my stomach all over his floor, I find myself barfing into the large decorative bowl from his table.

Those papier-mâché fruits are never going to be the same.

I'm kneeling on the floor, retching into the bowl by the time I realize that Dominic is still there beside me, holding my hair back out of the mess.

"Oh—this is so gross," I groan, when I can finally speak. "I'm so sorry."

"It's probably the grappa," he says apologetically. "I bought it in Cyprus, and it's really strong."

I shake my head. My stomach's feeling better already—as long as I don't look at the contents of Dominic's bowl.

"It's not the alcohol. I think it might be the shawarma I ate for lunch." I chug half the bottle of water at one go.

"You ate street meat—in *Egypt*?" he asks incredulously. "Not a great idea. But don't worry—it doesn't really count as sick until it starts shooting out the other end."

My stomach rumbles again, and I dart a panicked glare at him before dashing for the toilet down the hall.

I just make it. As I sit there, listening to my body produce noises I've never even heard before, I pray he's still back in his room. He might be my enemy, but no one deserves to hear that.

Twenty minutes later, when I'm feeling completely hollowed out, I risk heading back to my own room. The hallway is blessedly empty, but as I put my key in the door, Dominic emerges from his room. He's carrying a new water bottle and a small white box.

My head feels wobbly on my neck, but I shake it anyway. "I don't need medicine," I mutter as I stumble inside. "I've had all my shots."

He rattles the box. "They can't give you a shot for traveler's—uh—tummy," he says.

"It's okay. You can say diarrhea."

He smiles and rattles the box at me. "I was trying to avoid the power of suggestion," he says. "Take one of these. They're antibiotics."

But before I can even grab the box, I need to run back to the toilet.

I guess I might be suggestible after all.

chapter twenty-seven

IMAGE: Onward Routes
IG: Romy_K [Port Said, Egypt, April 2]
#RottenResearch #AReluctantAgreement
101 ♥

Waking the next morning is—no fun at all. Yes, I'm tucked safely into my own bed in the little guesthouse. I have a vague recollection that Dominic and I had spent at least part of last night talking in this very spot, but for the life of me I can't remember how I got here.

Or what was said. Or if anything else happened.

I fling the covers back to find that I'm fully dressed in my usual night attire of t-shirt and boy shorts. My copy of the Verne book is sitting neatly on the night table.

I heave a sigh of relief. The evening appears to have been completely innocent, after all. Thank goodness. There will be no sleeping with the enemy on *this* trip.

I lie back in bed and pick up my phone, which has magically been plugged into my universal charger. The enemy. I need to know more about the enemy.

Having only the vaguest of recollections of our conversation last night—mostly due to the barf-o-rama that was happening at the same time—I do for the first time what I should have done long ago.

I Google Frank Venal. And what comes up? Is not good.

Frank Venal: Bon Vivant, Man About Town, and Real Estate Cutthroat

New York Post Exclusive

He might be known for his support of the Philharmonic, or his nights at the opera, but one of the richest self-made men on New York's real estate scene has a secret ace up his sleeve—he loves poker. For Frank Venal, the path to success traces from a childhood steeped in poverty, but he joins the top-ten self-made men list this year with an estimated worth of $250 million. Much of this stems from the real estate brokerage empire he began building before the turn of the century, first with Bronx Builders, and later with his eponymous brokerage firm, Venal Ventures.

"I love my work," he says between sips of coffee—black—in his palatial home. "I knew from the time I was a teen that real estate would be my calling. I've never been afraid to fail—and so I never have."

Venal, sixty-one, has made his fortune acquiring, renovating, and reselling property in Manhattan, Brooklyn, the Bronx, and beyond. Last year, his brokerage firm was responsible for the sale of almost $25 billion in real estate, netting more than half a billion in sales. When asked about expansion, Venal laughs.

"I could have a stable of a thousand agents by now, believe me," he says. "I got an offer on the table from a firm in London as we speak. But I have to tell you, I like having my own fingerprints on my work. It makes it personal, you know?"

When asked about his humble beginnings, Venal, a notorious raconteur, uncharacteristically demurs. "Where you come from is less important than where you're headed, huh? And I'm always going somewhere big."

I flick my phone off and drop it on the bed. What chance have I got against this guy? He's rotten to the core. And as I sit up, things go from bad to worse.

A pain that I'm sure has Frank Venal's name on it sets my head spinning. And after the gut spinning of the night before, this isn't good. Dominic's antibiotics seem to have worked their magic with my digestive system, but my head is *sore*.

I swing my legs off to the side of the bed, and keeping my eyes down, rest my bare feet on the cool tile of the floor. This room smells of dust and maybe some ancient air freshener—nowhere near as good as Dominic's room smelled last night, or at least until I filled up his fruit bowl.

I stumble down to the communal bathroom to brush my teeth, which helps a bit. Once I finish, I find I can actually stand completely upright for the first time. All the same, I'm going to need serious drugs for this headache.

Back in my room, as I reach for my Tylenol bottle, I notice something for the first time. Fear clutches at my still-sour gut, and I have to clench my teeth to stop from retching again. My computer is safely tucked in the back of my daypack, but all my papers—passport, visas, everything—are missing. Also? My wallet.

The clenching of teeth no longer does the trick, and I have to race back for the bathroom. It's close—but I make it. For the next half hour or so, I alternate between throwing up and resting my face against the cool tile of the bathroom floor, grateful for Madame's impeccable housekeeping standards.

I'm so sure Dominic has betrayed me, I'd cry—if I could only stop throwing up.

When the worst appears to have passed—literally—and I'm able to sit up long enough to wipe any stray splashes off the toilet seat, I hear a tiny noise behind me.

Clutching a fresh wad of toilet tissue to wipe my streaming eyes, I turn to see a young girl, maybe twelve or thirteen, standing with both hands clutching a bucket.

"Madame see you?" the girl asks.

I stare at her blankly, clearly having vomited any intellect out along with whatever Dominic poisoned me with the night before.

"I clean," she says, tugging at my arm. "Madame fix you, yes?"

"I'll wipe it all up," I say hurriedly. "As soon as I feel a bit better."

The girl makes shooing motions. "I clean," she says again. "I clean sparkle."

There's no arguing with her, so I stumble back to the violated space that is my room. With no bottled water in evidence, and mindful of all the warnings I've been bombarded with since leaving Italy, I decide to head downstairs.

Zipping all the open pockets of my pack closed, I remember at the last moment to jam my legs into yoga pants and to don my shoes. I don't even make it to the bottom of the stairs before Madame is there, bearing a steaming mug and a kind smile.

This morning she is wearing an eye-searing combination of hot pink tunic and flowy black trousers. Her hijab is a silk scarf patterned in jagged slashes of black and matching hot pink. She winks one perfectly kohled cat eye at me.

"You got headache?" she says. "I make tea."

She sets the steaming cup on the table I was sitting at last night, and I flop bonelessly into a chair and pour half of it down my throat in a single gulp.

It is searingly hot, not just in temperature, and it tastes of something foul.

"That's terrible," I splutter, and the words are out of my mouth before I realize how insulting they sound.

Madame doesn't look the least put out by my insult. "Is hideous taste, yes. But drink it all up. You need hydrated, yes? And painkiller?"

"I have more Tylenol," I say, reaching for my pack, but Madame waves it away.

"You no need. Hold nose. Finish tea. I bring breakfast."

"Oh, there's no way I can eat anything . . ." I say, but she vanishes behind the bead curtain before I can finish my sentence.

I think about calling out for a bottle of water, but feeling too defeated, I slump back in my seat and stare gloomily at my phone. My Instagram numbers have been steadily growing, and with the crossing into Egypt, I've finally broken the hundred followers barrier. But, when I flip over to Dominic's account, I see he is cruising in on eleven thousand followers. Eleven *thousand*. How can I ever compete with that?

Madame Nephthys bustles back carrying a basket piled high with steaming pita bread, and a bowl of what looks like a greenish sort of paste. It is a tribute to whatever is in Madame's foul tea that I'm not sick at the very sight of the contents of the bowl.

"Oh, no . . ." I begin, but that's all I have time for. Dropping the plates on the table, Madame lifts the cup to my lips.

"You drink," she demands. "You better."

I don't know if she means I'd better drink or else, or I'll be better if I drink, but either way, I have no fight left in me. The liquid has had a little time to cool, at least, though when I swallow it, it still retains its peppery fire. It might even taste deadlier than whatever Dominic was pouring last night. But as I set the cup down, I realize I can turn my head without pain. I gently move it forward and back and then side to side for good measure, but the worst of the pain appears to be gone.

Unfortunately, what Madame's Miracle Cure brings with it is also a dose of reality. As the pain subsides, one thing is perfectly clear.

I'm in *big* trouble. Mr. 'Let Me Help You' Madison is following in some scary, evil footsteps.

Madame reappears, this time with a bowl of sliced citrus fruit. She takes up a quarter lemon in each hand and squeezes the juice over the contents of the bowl.

"You eat," she says. "You feel better with food."

"I already feel better," I admit to her. "But, listen—this is important. You know Dominic—the guy from last night? He's stolen all my stuff."

Madame gives a little chuckle, and ignoring my words completely, takes a pita bread from the still-steaming pile.

"Like this," she says, ripping the bread, and then expertly dipping it into the paste. "Fava bean. Delicious."

And then, as if she were feeding a baby, she holds the loaded bread in front of my mouth. When I try to protest, she pops it in.

She's right, of course. It *is* delicious.

My stomach groans so loudly, she nods her head. "You see? You need food. Your stomach call for food." She reaches out to pat my hand.

"That boy no steal from you. He's a good boy." She points at my pack, sitting on the floor beside my chair. "He no take your stuff."

"No!" I have to shake my head at her, because my mouth is still full. I swallow and try again. "He *did*. My wallet, my passport. I need to go to the police . . . or maybe . . . Where's the nearest embassy? The American embassy? They must be able to . . ."

Before I can finish this sentence, the front door swings open and Dominic walks in, looking fresh as a daisy.

"Ah—Meester Dominic!" says Madame cheerfully. "You find what you need?"

"I have indeed, Madame," he says, and lifts a piece of pita from my basket.

"You all packed up?" he says to me, eyeing my bag.

"Just a minute," I splutter, spraying fava paste indelicately across the table. "Where's my stuff?"

Dominic affects a hurt expression. "I've found us a way out of here," he says, wolfing down another piece of bread from my basket. "This pita," he says, turning to Madame and putting his fingers to his lips. "It is"—he blows her a kiss—"perfection!"

Madame turns bright red and giggles like a schoolgirl, but I'm not buying any of this.

"Where's my stuff?" I repeat, more effectively this time, as I've stopped spraying food. "My wallet? My passport?"

Dominic swings one leg over the other chair at my table, and reaches into his pack.

"Look—I'm sorry you were worried. I thought for sure I'd get back before you even got up this morning, which is why I didn't leave a note."

He slides my wallet across the table. I open it to find that the small amount of Egyptian currency I'd changed with the otherwise unhelpful travel agent is still inside.

"You're not going to believe this. I've got us both spots on an NGO helicopter—crewed by Swiss nationals—which is heading out to deliver supplies."

He reaches into an inside pocket of his jacket and pulls out both passports, visas safely tucked inside. "I needed to show them all our paperwork, to prove we are legit," he says, handing mine back. "You weren't worried, were you?"

I think back to the article on Frank Venal. Can I afford to trust this man? Can I afford not to?

In the end, I shake my slightly tender head, submit to a warm hug from Madame, and follow Dominic out the door.

chapter twenty-eight

IMAGE: Last Sunset Over the Sea
IG: Romy_K [Suez, Egypt, April 2]
#GoodbyeMediterranean #NGO #Choppertime
103 ♥

M adame Nephthys has a niece who has a friend called Abdul who has a car, which means that—for a price—we have a ride to our departure point. This turns out to be a helicopter pad in the middle of a dusty field. I spend the whole way there firing questions at my old enemy / new travel companion. Dominic admits that, last night he, too, was at his wits' end about the next leg of the journey. But this morning, while I was trying to recover from his grappa—whatever that is—he was scoping out the neighborhood, thinking to hire a driver.

"Wait a minute," I say, holding up a hand. "Why no hangover?"

He shrugs. "I drank some of Madame's special tea before bed," he says, "plus about a gallon of water. And after a second cup for breakfast—no problem."

"So—you were out trying to find a driver?" I ask, dragging him back to the topic at hand.

"I drive for you!" pipes up Abdul, from behind the wheel.

"Yes, thank you, Abdul," Dom says, grinning. Then he mouths *a long-distance driver* for my benefit.

Abdul fires a baleful glance into the rearview mirror. "I drive long distances," he says. "Why you not ask me? I drive all the way to Sharm El-Sheikh. To Wadi Halfa. You safe. I guarantee."

"It's all looked after, Abdul," I say, rotating one finger to indicate Dominic should finish his story.

"We're going to the helipad," Dominic says to the driver, then turns back to face me. "I was on my way back to the Resta Ramal when I spotted a couple of men loading a truck with food and medical supplies. I chased it down the road to the airbase."

"Airbase?" I say doubtfully as Abdul takes a final, sharp corner and screeches to a stop inside a wire fence.

"Airbase," Abdul repeats, beaming. He sticks his hand, palm up, right into Dominic's face.

As I step out of the car, the wind, which has been blowing out of the north all morning, suddenly drops, and the curtain of fine particles in the air slowly settles to the ground. The contrast to the brilliant blue of the Mediterranean could not be more pronounced—or dusty. Across the field, I spot a vast machine, with two figures running back and forth shoving boxes inside from the back of a flatbed truck parked beside it.

"Holy cow—that thing is huge," I breathe.

The helicopter has twin rotors on the roof and a dusty, sand-colored body that blends in perfectly with the surroundings.

"It's ex–U.S. Air Force," Dominic says as he climbs out of the car. "Armored, so it's heavy, but really fast, and can carry a ton of cargo."

His eyes are gleaming in a way I do not like at all.

"Is it safe?" I ask, but my question falls on deaf ears.

Abdul, having collected his money from Dominic, whips around the back, pulls our luggage from the trunk, drops it in the dirt, and leaps back behind the wheel. He squeals away before either of us can react.

"Nice," says Dom, and stoops to hand me my dust-covered suitcase.

One of the figures beside the helicopter catches sight of us, and waves.

"I don't know, Dominic . . ." I say, but he's already hurrying on ahead.

"It's not an airplane," he yells back at me. "Teresa never said anything about helicopters."

"But—don't we have to make it to Yemen?" I say, trying to Google the distance on my phone as I jog along behind him.

Of course, there's no Wi-Fi signal, but it seems impossibly far, even for such a giant bird.

Meanwhile, Dominic has been wrapped in an enthusiastic embrace from Waving Man.

"Romy, this is Captain Andrew Tracks," he says. "He's from Switzerland, and he flies cargo for an NGO called Doctors Without Borders."

"Médecins Sans Frontières," says the captain with a broad smile, "And everyone calls me Anthrax." He's almost as tall as Dominic, but fair haired, and sporting a wicked sunburn. Nevertheless, he shakes my hand with enthusiasm.

I shake back, and ask about the distance.

"It *is* too far, really, for this craft," he explains, with an accent that sounds German to me. "Normally we fly in with a cargo plane full of medical materials and personnel. But this is the only one available to us at the moment, so we use what we have."

Then he inexplicably throws his arms around me, and points to one of the pallets. "This is because of you," he says, tearing up, before releasing me at last. *"Merci vielmall!"*

Before I can ask what exactly he's getting at, he produces a couple of pairs of giant ear protectors, and hands one to each of us. Fortunately, these protect us from the unrelenting sound of the giant machine, as it lifts us skyward. Unfortunately, they also prevent me from getting any kind of answer from Dominic as to *how* he secured this particular passage, after all.

A t the risk of stating the obvious, I have never been one of those people who aspires to living life on a perilous edge. Remember the grade school rollercoasters? I mean, part of the draw for this particular quest—aside from the desperation element—was that air travel was *not* involved. Put me on a machine, hurtling along narrow tracks at high speed below the ground, and I'm perfectly comfortable.

I am a New York girl, after all. I have third-rail current in my blood.

It's not as if I haven't been on an airplane before—see aforementioned trip to Quebec City with my fifth-grade class. Mind you, on that trip, I spent the whole flight with my face buried in my teacher's shoulder. She was a patient woman, Mrs. Johns.

The difference between a short-haul trip across the snowy wastes of Canada, buckled safely into a padded airplane seat, and being cinched onto a metal fold-down in the back of a cargo copter is no small thing, is all I'm saying. Not so long ago, I thought nothing could be more frightening than being locked alone in a dark, urine-scented cell in Egypt.

I was wrong.

By the time Abdul dropped us at the airfield, any hint of the city's greenery had been left behind. Now, in midair, I can see a couple of scrubby bushes against low, distant hills, but everything else is sandy brown. Or plain sand. The wind, having died down long enough to give us a glimpse of the machine that would ferry us south, rises up again with a vengeance after we lift off. Over the course of the rest of the day, the giant metal bird is buffeted in all directions by the desert winds. When we do get a glimpse of anything below us, it is either a gorse-flecked, but otherwise empty, desert landscape or the white-capped surface of the Red Sea.

By the time we begin our descent into a tiny airport outside the desert city of Port Sudan, I feel exhausted and completely battered. As we set down, Anthrax turns in his seat and grins at us. "What a ride, eh?" he yells, and, in the pure elation of it being over, I can't actually disagree.

While Captain Anthrax consults with the ground crew over re-fueling, Dominic and I walk across to the terminal to seek out sustenance—and something to drink. My mouth feels like I've spent the entire trip dragging my tongue through the desert. Even my throat feels full of sand.

Dominic can't stop talking about the helicopter ride. "That was the best thing I've ever done," he says, his eyes aglow.

"It scared me to death," I answer, but clearly, every bump that made me close my eyes in terror only added to his fun.

"When we lurched sideways over the water? Man—I thought . . ."

"We were going to die? Because that's what I thought."

He laughs.

"I'm not joking," I say, but he lopes on ahead of me toward a nearby Quonset hut, still grinning like an idiot.

Now that we're safely on the ground, it's hard not to smile at such joyful enthusiasm. And yet, somehow, I manage it. Who is he to feel so joyful, anyway?

My heart does lift a bit at the familiar red and white sight of a Coca-Cola machine, but on closer inspection it proves to be empty. The lock on the front is rusted and snapped, and the door is hanging ajar. Next to it is a large white plastic water carrier about half full, a kettle, and some teabags. Grabbing a cup with a broken handle, I

192 · **kc dyer**

turn the spigot and run water straight into it, but Dominic snatches it away from me before I can drink.

"Unless you want to be peeing out your butt by nightfall, we need to boil that first," he says, and dumps the contents of my cup into the top of the kettle.

"Elegantly put," I say drily. Literally drily—my lips are sticking to my teeth. "I'm just so thirsty."

He sets the kettle on a little gas burner. "I've basically given up urination altogether," he says, grinning. "Saves a lot of time, actually."

Five minutes later, he hands me bitter, black tea, steaming a little in the handle-less cup. No sugar, no milk.

Nothing—*nothing*—has ever tasted so good.

It's over our second cup of tea that I finally learn the truth, and it's not lost on me that I don't hear it from Dominic. When Captain Anthrax joins us inside, Dominic hands him a cup of tea. Anthrax pulls a packet of sugar out of one of the pockets in his cargo pants, adds it to his tea, and then swallows the whole cup appreciatively.

He clinks cups with us after drinking, which I'm not sure counts as a real toast, and I tell him so.

"I just want to celebrate you two," he says cheerfully. "When you see the camp, you'll know how important these supplies are. Half of the people—more than half, actually—are kids."

"This camp is *where* in Yemen, exactly?" I ask.

Anthrax looks puzzled. "Not Yemen," he says. "Eritrea. In the deep south, outside Asseb. I drop you in Aden, afterwards."

"I thought . . ." I begin, but he's not finished.

"Your *schtutz* means we can bring a full complement of emergency supplies," he says, and clinks my empty cup again. *"Prost!"*

As soon as he leaves to begin his preflight check, I turn on Dominic.

"What did he mean—*schtutz*?" I ask.

And for the first time, Dom's smile falters. "I think he means money," he says. And then, at last, it all comes out. To secure our place on the chopper, he has maxed out both our credit cards.

It is possible I have an opinion about this.

Which I'm quick—very quick—to share.

"There *was* no other way," he says, after I run out of words at last. "And it was for a good cause, right? Our fare covered the costs for the last pallet of dehydrated food going to feed hungry kids."

"A good cause? *A good cause?* What about *our* cause, Dominic?" I demand, feeling shocked to my core. "How are we going to get the rest of the way *around the world* with no more available credit?"

"I really tried, Romy." He narrows his eyes. "As I recall, you didn't have a better idea. This was all I could come up with."

"Really? *Really?* The only option was to spend all our money?" I jump to my feet. "I missed the ship in Suez because of you. *None* of this would have happened if you hadn't switched those envelopes in France."

"I didn't switch them," he explodes, throwing his arms up in disgust. "Jesus! I'm not out to undermine you at every turn, you know. Of *course* I want to win this thing. I told you—I *need* this job. But we agreed to work together, and this was my best shot at helping us both."

He stalks off toward the helicopter.

Anthrax, oblivious, sees him coming and gives a double thumbs-up.

Time to go. My anger washes away, and suddenly, I feel sick about getting back into this helicopter with things so bad between us.

"Dominic—wait." I hasten my pace to catch him, but he doesn't slow down.

"Look, I feel really torn about this, okay? I know it's a good cause, but—it's like on an airplane where they tell you to put your own mask on first. We need to help ourselves before we can help other people, right?"

Dom stops suddenly in his tracks, the dust swirling in a little cloud around his sneakers. "Okay, maybe you're right. And I feel bad about including you now, I do. I shouldn't have used your card without asking."

He turns, and lifts a hand to Anthrax to indicate that we are coming.

"I couldn't leave you behind," he blurts, turning back to face me. "I want to win this thing fair and square, but if it meant stranding you alone in Egypt, I couldn't live with that. Not after I'd promised to work together."

"I can look after myself," I reply huffily, but I can't really dredge up the same level of animosity anymore.

"I'm sure you can," he answers, his whole body radiating stiffness. "It won't happen again, believe me."

He points toward the horizon, where the silhouette of the city of Port Sudan rises up against the pale blue sky. "There's a train station in town. You're totally welcome to take another route. Do what you want."

And with that, he turns and strides off to the helicopter.

Maybe I will, I manage to not say out loud. The rotors on the helicopter begin to slowly revolve as Dom jumps in through the back hatch. I see the window to the cockpit slide open, and Anthrax's arm pops out, waving me over.

The sunlight reflects off his watch, blinding me, but also reminding me of the bitter truth. Dominic maxed out the limit on my Ex-Libris credit card. Angry or not, I have no money for train fare.

As the rotors pick up speed, I take a deep breath of sand-filled air, and crouch-run toward the chopper.

chapter twenty-nine

IMAGE: In Flight
IG: Romy_K [Port Sudan, Sudan, April 3]
#AstonishingAfrica #AirborneEritrea
151 ♥

In spite of what feels like an even bumpier ride, at some point I fall into an uneasy and uncomfortable sleep in the back of the helicopter. As we sail on through the dark African night, I'm tired enough that I actually miss the landing completely.

Later, I learn that Anthrax set the giant bird down sometime around three and fell asleep in the pilot's seat. As for me, I awaken before dawn. There's the faintest hint of a chill in the air, and only a whiff of breeze that, when it touches my face, feels like it has crossed water. The back of the chopper is empty of human life, and when I stick my head through the door to the cockpit, there's no sign of Anthrax. The huge loading bay door is open, and so I step out that way to take a look around.

I can't see any of the usual indicators one would expect from an airport—runway, terminal, airplanes. Instead, there's a metal Quonset hut, and beside it, a collection of large white tents. I scurry along in that direction, looking foremost for a washroom or latrine of any variety at all. I finally spot the familiar-looking green plastic siding of a porta-potty and make a beeline for it. This particular version comes equipped with an outside sink, but once I'm finished inside and I attempt to wash my hands, I find the water is not hooked up.

There is, in fact, no sign of water anywhere.

My memories of Egypt are verdant compared to this place. The wind is still mercifully low, but dust skitters along ground dry as a Mojave riverbed. As I emerge among the tents again, I see a line of dust billowing up along the horizon, which—after a moment's squinting—resolves into a convoy of heavy trucks headed this way.

Right at that moment, Anthrax emerges from a doorway at the end of the Quonset hut. He's carrying a paper cup in one hand, steaming gently from the top. Behind him Dominic appears, a steaming cup in each of his hands.

I take a deep breath and aim myself in that direction.

There's no tea to be had, and the coffee is terrible, but it's hot and clears the last of the sleep out of my skull. When I drain my cup, Anthrax points at something behind me. "That's where it's all going," he says.

For the first time, I turn and look across at the vast expanse of desert behind me. There's no border or fence in evidence, but as far as the eye can see is a collection of low, widely spaced buildings.

I use the word *building* loosely. Most of the small structures are made from scrap wood, corrugated iron, and tent canvas. Some of the buildings are framed, but not one has glass in the windows or doors of anything more substantial than cloth. The trees, when there are any, are low and scrubby, with dusty trunks and sparse, needley foliage. Among the buildings are people of all sizes and shapes—too far away to make out distinct facial features, ages, or even genders—but close enough to see they are going about their business as a new day dawns. Many of them appear to be hurrying toward the approaching trucks.

Between the so-called heliport and the edge of this enormous settlement stretches a long fence laced through with lethal-looking razor wire. Following the fence line with my eyes, I see the first of the trucks slow to a stop beside a tiny hut. Someone steps out of the hut beside what I realize is a low pole gate. After a moment, the figure leans onto the pole and the gate swings open. The truck lurches into gear and the convoy drives straight toward us. The first truck has a large open storage area in the back, framed by a flapping tarp.

The second has a machine gun on the roof.

Any saliva I've managed to generate from my morning coffee dries up in my mouth. I clutch on to Dominic's arm.

"Is that a gun?" I mutter. When his arm closes around me instinctively, I do not resist.

We both turn to look at Anthrax, who shrugs.

"The official war is technically over, but there are still problems with local warlords and smugglers stealing supplies," he says, as if he's describing a neighborhood football match. "Which means we really have to scramble to get these supplies to the people who need them."

I can't find the words to reply before the first truck pulls up.

Anthrax waves as the crew—all men—jump off the trucks, then offers us a tense smile. "The faster we get stuff unloaded, the sooner we're out of here," he says.

Without a word, Dom and I both turn and head for the ramp at the back of the helicopter.

As we work together, I learn that most of the volunteers on the trucks are local people in the employ of the various nongovernmental agencies in the region. This camp is found along what is known as one of the deadliest migrant routes in the world. People running from war and famine trek from East Africa through to Libya, with the faint hope of catching a boat across the Mediterranean and finding asylum in Europe.

"The resources are so few for these displaced people," says Anthrax as we lug the final boxes of supplies out of the back of the chopper. "And the need is so great—we have to do what we can."

By the time we finish loading the last of the trucks, I can see a long line of people forming near the heavily guarded airport gate.

"There are so many children," I say to Anthrax, who can only nod.

He lifts a hand to the last of the volunteers, and the truck engines roar as they circle around to head back to the gates.

Suddenly, I hear a pattering sound—like raindrops on a tin roof. Instinctively, I look to the sky, but it has hardened into a crystal clear blue. Not a raincloud to be seen.

Without a word, Dom clutches my hand, and I barely manage to keep my feet as he pulls me into a full run.

"Get on the chopper," yells Anthrax, a little unnecessarily, considering we are already racing up the loading ramp as he shouts the words.

Dominic pushes me inside and yanks the door shut behind us. Above us, I can hear the rotors begin to whine, which means—I hope it means—Anthrax has made it to the cockpit.

The noise from the rotors intensifies, and then suddenly the floor rises up to meet me, and I crumple to my knees as we become airborne.

Anthrax yells something from the cockpit, but I can't hear a word over the roar of the engines. I crawl on my hands and knees to the nearest window, and look down to see three heavy jeeps that have pulled in front of the first truck, outside the airport gate.

Turning, I find Dominic beside me. He's wearing the ear protectors and is holding out the other pair for me. I grab them, but instead of putting them on, I reach up and push the ones he's wearing away from one of his ears.

"They're stealing our supplies," I yell straight into his ear. He jumps back a little, wincing.

The helicopter banks suddenly to one side, and we're both thrown to the floor. Dominic grabs me by the arm, and half crawling, hauls me over to one of the flip-down seats.

"I need to talk to Anthrax," I yell at him, trying to push his hands away. "We have to go back!"

Dominic widens his eyes at me, and then yanks the seatbelt across my lap, strapping me in.

"No!" he yells, clamping the ear protectors on my head. Then he takes my hands in each of his so that I can't undo my seatbelt.

Since, between the noise and the ear protection, neither of us can hear a thing, what follows is the most awkward miming conversation I've ever had in a careening helicopter.

Which, as you might expect, is the only conversation I've ever had in a careening helicopter.

In any case, the gist of it boils down to—all decisions at this point rest with our pilot.

Relying on the judgment of someone whose nickname is an infectious disease seems—questionable. But he is the one experienced in this region, in the end. As there is not a single other option open to me, I sit back, stare out the nearest window, and wait to see what's going to happen next.

Below us, the camp vanishes almost immediately, and the land, dry and desolate, stretches out as far as I can see. There isn't a single

patch of arable land within eyeshot. I do spot a handful of goats crop-
ping at the ground—tiny little dots on a hillside—but that's it. How
can anything survive in this climate?

After half an hour, the helicopter resumes what passes for level
flight, and Anthrax flicks the red signal light above the cockpit door
at us. I look over at Dominic to make sure he's not going to dive over
and re-strap me in, but his face reflects the same expression of shock
that I'm feeling. We both unbuckle and stagger unsteadily toward
the front.

Anthrax glances over his shoulder as we open the door to the
cockpit, and he gestures under the seat beside him. I bend low and
pull out a pair of pilot earphones similar to the ones he is wearing.
While steering with one hand, he flicks the other at me to indicate I
should put the earphones on. There's an umbilical that attaches the
earphones to the dashboard, and suddenly Anthrax's voice is in my
ears.

"Sorry about that," he says quietly. "What a fuckin' disaster."

"Were they warlords?" I ask. "Will they steal everything?"

"Sit down," he says, and I slide into the empty copilot's seat.

Dominic, still wearing his own ear protectors, is deaf to our conversation but nods at me encouragingly. He takes a wide-legged
stance between the two seats, and I realize he's waiting for me to
hear what our pilot has to say before taking his own turn.

Looking out the windscreen, I feel my stomach surge as the world
stretches out beneath us, the jagged shoreline separating the dry tan
earth from the deep blue of the ocean.

I look away from the passage of the earth beneath us—which is
making me a little sick, anyway—and turn to Anthrax.

"We're unarmed," his voice says in my headset. "Nothing more
than a flare gun on board."

I know this, since I'm one of the people who helped empty out the helicopter, after all, but I don't say so. Instead I ask, "But—did they take it all? Everything you've worked for?"

I hear him sigh through the earphones. "I don't know," he says at last. "But it would be so much worse if they hijacked the chopper too. It's only on loan to us."

After a minute, I ask, "What's going to happen now?"

"I need to take this bird down to Aden," he says. "I can let you off there. You are sure to be able to get a ship onward."

"Okay," I say quietly. "Thanks."

"I'm so sorry, Romy. I wish this had ended differently."

I reach over and squeeze his hand, then stand up and hand off my earphones to Dominic. He slides into the copilot seat as I head back to strap myself into the empty hold.

Later, as the chopper swings wide over what must be the port city of Aden, I spot a large tanker moored at the docks below. After we land and bid Anthrax a subdued goodbye, we discover the ship in question is none other than the *Wahash Mahat*, the very vessel that I missed boarding in Suez.

The captain agrees to honor my ticket, and I board before he can change his mind. Dominic follows me up the gangplank, and I'm so stunned and exhausted, I don't even think to question why.

chapter thirty

IMAGE: Endless Ocean
IG: Romy_K [Gulf of Aden, April 4]
#AnUnexpectedDevelopment #AtSeaAgain
129 ♥

The speed of our visit doesn't lessen the shock of everything we saw in Eritrea, and I can't seem to think of anything else. Climbing onto the tanker, I can't even manage to generate a sarcastic comment for Dominic. I don't see any evidence that he has a ticket, but somehow there's magically a berth for him. His endless good luck is galling, but I feel too wrung out to react.

Instead, I follow one of the deckhands to my assigned cabin. This will be my home for the journey across the Gulf of Aden and the Arabian Sea, all the way to India. The cabin is by far my nicest shipboard accommodation of the journey, fully appointed with a double bed tucked between end tables, a desk, and chair, and even an easy chair for gazing out the porthole.

I spend the entire first day of the journey in my room, mostly sleeping or staring blindly out the porthole at the distant brown line formed where the deserts of Yemen and Oman meet the impossible blue of the gulf. My period's arrived, leaving me crampy and sapped of energy. I'm behind in my reports to ExLibris, having submitted nothing since the one I sent off before I got sick at Madame Nephthys's place. But the sight of the desperate people in the camps, of the hard-faced men on the jeeps with the guns—has somehow drained my interest in writing anything at all.

Sometime, long after darkness has fallen, I lift the lid of my laptop.

ExLibris Destination Report, submitted by Ramona Keene

CITY/REGIONAL SUMMARY: Port Said, Suez Canal, Egypt

TOP PICKS TO SEE AND DO: This city is a tiny oasis in a sea of sandy sadness. The canal itself is a model of modern engineering, built mostly by colonialist overlords using slave labor . . .

As I type, something splashes the back of my left hand, and I realize I'm crying. What is the use of anything—anything at all—when there is such terrible hate in the world?

At the sound of a quiet tap on the door, I jerk my head up and hurriedly wipe away my tears.

I open the door to find Dominic standing there. The warm air from the deck swirls his hair around, and he is backlit by a clear, starlit sky the likes of which I haven't seen since I was in the Alps.

Which was less than a week ago.

"Holy shit," I blurt at the thought.

"And a kind good evening to you too," says Dominic, rolling into my room without an invitation. "I haven't seen you since we boarded, so I thought I'd better check that all is well."

He places a small, tinfoil packet on the desktop and glances at the screen of my computer.

"Not exactly a rave beginning," he says.

I leap across from the door and slam the lid of the computer closed, which unfortunately leaves us both standing in utter darkness.

"That's private," I snap at him, desperately feeling around the wall beside me for a light switch. "How is it they let you stay on board, anyway, when you hadn't even booked a ticket?"

There's a click, and the lights go up. Dominic has flicked the switch by the door. His smart-ass grin has been replaced by a more guarded look.

"Well, I don't have a nice room like this, I can assure you. I've got a bunk with the crew, and I've spent the day down in the galley, baking bread." He gestures at the small packet he's dropped on the table. "I brought you some, since I'm pretty sure you haven't had anything to eat since we boarded."

"I'm not hungry," I reply coldly, even though—now that he's mentioned it—I'm feeling so hollow, it's making me a little wobbly.

Of course, my stomach chooses that moment to growl, and Dominic raises an eyebrow at me skeptically. "Okay, whatever you say. I'm only checking you're all right."

Flopping back down into the desk chair, I can't suppress a sigh. "I'm not all right," I say bitterly. "I feel wrecked after the last few days. All those suffering people—and the only ones who do have money spend it on guns to rob the others of what little they have. There's nothing good to say about any of it. It feels hopeless."

Dominic is silent for a moment. Beneath us, the hum of the ship's engine chugs on. The smell of salt water and engine oil drifts in through my open window.

"Look," he says at last. "I've never seen anything like that either. I had no idea things were so bad, but maybe that's part of the problem. I know we can't fix any of this, but . . ."

"I don't know what you're talking about," I say, cutting him off. "That kind of attitude is nothing but apathy. Those warlords have taken all our supplies—the supplies Anthrax and his team paid for—away from the people who desperately need them."

"You didn't let me finish," Dominic says. "The fact is, you

wouldn't have seen any of it if I hadn't essentially stolen your credit card to buy us a seat, and to cover the cost of those supplies. I had to make that decision without you, and when I told you about it, you were really upset with me."

I swallow hard. "That's not fair. That was before I saw what it was like. How bad things are."

"My very point," says Dominic, swinging open the door. "Those people have been hungry a long time," he says, "but maybe seeing that changes us. Maybe we need to learn more about the place before we impose our ideas of what will work on them."

He walks out and the heavy door swings closed behind him with a slam. I stare at the back of the door, feeling totally speechless at his callousness. How can seeing people go hungry make a difference?

I jump to my feet, determined to follow him and straighten him out, when I realize, suddenly, there's exactly zero I can do at the moment. I decide the best course of action is to accomplish what I set out to do. Which includes not spending another minute with Dominic. Instead, I'm going to put all my energy into beating him to the prize. I'll find a way to get some kind of support to those people in need.

Then we'll see who can make a difference or not.

The *Wahash Mahat* is classed as an LR2, or large-range tanker. It's considered a Suezmax, which means it's the biggest ship that can traverse the Suez Canal fully laden. Apparently there are much larger vessels than the *Wahash*, but I've never seen one. It's carrying a load of crude oil from Egypt to Mumbai, and is a fast and powerful ship. I spend the next full day rewriting my report, taking ibuprofen, and reading Wiki articles about East Africa.

That evening, since I'm feeling better—physically, at least—I head up to the galley and sit at a table with the first mate, a sailor called Ganesh. He's wearing a crisp, jewel-green short-sleeved shirt, open at the neck. When I ask if he's from Africa, he sets me straight right away.

"Born in Chennai, Tamil Nadu," he says, his accent carrying a distinct Indian lilt. "But I have family in Mumbai and London and many other places. Most of us are on the sea, somewhere around the world."

Ganesh is regrettably enthusiastic about Dominic's contribution to the menu. "Your friend—he's quite the pastry chef, eh? Did you try the sponge? I haven't tasted cake that fluffy since my mother's."

I roll my eyes and try to change the subject, but Ganesh will not be silenced. It turns out the crew are all massive fans of *The Great British Bake Off*, and Ganesh pulls out his phone to show me his favorite cakes, as featured on Instagram. Unfortunately, after this, he clicks through to Dominic's page. My heart sinking, I see his follower count has soared since I first found his account. He's posted a ton of pictures, dish after dish highlighting all the different foods he's come across in his travels, with a focus mostly on baked goods.

I use my own phone to show Ganesh my Instagram page, which he dutifully follows immediately. But while my following has definitely grown since I left home, I still don't have numbers anywhere near what Dominic is pulling.

"Woo-hoo," crows Ganesh, and waves across to Dominic, who has come out of the galley to deliver baskets of warm beignets to each table. "Look at the followers you have, bro!"

Dom drops a basket on the center of our table and shrugs. "I share the pictures, but I don't care about the numbers. I just like talking to people about food."

As he moves away, Ganesh sinks his teeth into a beignet, his eyes closing in pleasure. I pocket my phone, and bring the conversation around to what I saw in Eritrea. "I'd love to hear what you think about aid for the people stricken with famine and disease, Ganesh. Do you support donations of supplies, or is straight money the better way to go?"

Ganesh's face, which had been open and laughing while we went through the Instagram posts, suddenly shuts down. "So many people want to impose their own ideas to rescue Africans," he says with a sigh. "This? Is not what's needed."

He excuses himself and departs through the galley door. Inside, I get a glimpse of Dominic, wrapped in a giant apron and with flour dusted across his netted hair. As the galley door swings closed again, I can't help thinking that his growing connection with the crew— including Ganesh—isn't helping my cause at all.

If he's reaching them through their stomachs, then I'll go in through their hearts, I vow silently. Grabbing the last beignet from the basket, I take my phone outside. My head is full of possible new hashtags aimed at finding new followers. But the followers I find?

Are not exactly the ones I expect.

chapter thirty-one

IMAGE: Ship's Tender
IG: Romy_K [*Wahash Mahat*, Arabian Sea, April 7]
#OceanRescue #Refugee
129 ♥

I spend the next couple of days mostly in my cabin, which has the dual advantage of helping me avoid both the intense African heat *and* any contact with Dominic. On April 7th, the *Wahash Mahat* officially exits the Gulf of Aden and enters the balmy but more turbulent waters of the Arabian Sea. Since the heat of the day is mercifully cut by the gusty wind, I head up to the deck of the ship to try for a last photo of Africa. I've just pointed my viewfinder at the coast, when I hear a thin voice cry out. Way up at the prow of the ship, I see Ganesh wave frantically out to sea, and then, as he turns to look up at the bridge, I hear him cry out again. Other crew voices join his, and by the time I race closer, I hear the ship's engines change note.

We've come upon a small fishing boat, built of grey wood and riding incredibly low in the water. It's filled, stem to stern, with people. They are packed in so tightly, their knees are interlocking, with no room to move, let alone lie down. Waves slap across the gunnels of the boat, and most of the people on board are waving frantically up at us. The *Wahash Mahat* now has her engines in reverse, but it's no joke to slow down a ship of this size, and momentum carries us past the small craft. As it bobs in the waves below us, I can see the wood on the stern of the boat, where presumably there should be some means of propulsion, is cracked and broken. There's no sign of an engine, or even an outboard motor, but I can see the word *"Njeri"* hand-painted on the stern. The tiny vessel is completely dwarfed against the side of the tanker, and as I look down, it feels like a miracle that we didn't plow right over them.

Several crew members of the *Wahash Mahat* toss down ropes, and the *Njeri* is drawn alongside. The ship's captain, whom I've not caught even a glimpse of since the first day, comes marching out on deck, and engages in a loud discussion with two of his senior crew. Meanwhile, one of the *Wahash*'s tenders comes roaring around from the far side to moor itself beside the small boat. Again, there's more discussion among the crew on the tender, and what looks like two men, yelling from the back of the *Njeri*. Each time a wave slaps across the bow, my stomach clenches. We are close enough now that I can see the expressions of terror on the faces of the people. More than a handful of them are children.

In the end, the captain of the *Wahash Mahat* begrudgingly accepts the people on board, conditional to the ship dropping them all upon arrival in Mumbai. I watch from above as the group of refugees is settled onto a section of deck to the rear of the tanker, where the crew are rigging up a huge tarp. There's no other space to house this number of people, which to my rough count looks to be close to fifty, including the children. The group is strangely silent as they clamber on board, faces exhausted and drawn, clothing soaked and salt-stained from their journey.

That night, I corner Ganesh to try to get a bit more information. He tells me there's enough food on board to feed everyone, though he's not sure it's halal.

"He's not happy, I'll tell you that," Ganesh whispers. We're leaning against the outside wall on the starboard side, to get a break from
the unceasing wind. It's not so hot now, late at night, and it's definitely easier to hear him on this side of the ship.

"The captain?"

He gives a quick nod. "From what I can tell, they come from a
camp in Yemen, but most are Somali, displaced by the war," he says.
"The captain has a policy not to pick up refugees—there are so many
these days, and so many countries refusing them. But this ship was
sinking, so . . ."

"So, he couldn't watch them all drown," I whisper, barely able to
get the words out.

Ganesh shrugs. "They are lucky," he says. "I think the smugglers were taking them to Pakistan, but they lost their engine. We do
not stop until Mumbai, so what happens to them there is anyone's
guess."

He folds his arms, looking serious. "From my experience, there
are usually one or two of the human smugglers on board. You need
to stay away from these people, right? They are bad men."

"Okay, but one or two out of nearly fifty? Can't I try talking to
any of the actual refugees—at least get a few pictures and make a
connection?"

Ganesh blows air out his nose like a bulldog. "Listen, I know you
mean well. But most of these people have no English, and they are
all traumatized. Also, they have not been exposed to the same germs
and things you have—you could be a danger to them, you see?"

"Got it," I say.

But my wheels are turning. I didn't get to talk to the people in the
desert, and I have a chance to remedy that now. Operation Hashtag
Refugee is underway.

According to the itinerary I drew up way back in Suez, the *Wahash Mahat* is due to dock in Mumbai sometime in the early hours of April 12th, though the repairs back in Yemen will likely delay that date. Mindful of my late-night conversation with Ganesh, the following morning I head down to the ship's sick bay and ask for a face mask. He's right. I don't want to be the jerk who passes on a virus to these people, who have already suffered so much.

Still, for my sins, as soon as I walk through the door, the nurse practitioner sits me down and quizzes me about my entire health record. When I finally leave an hour later, I have a pocketful of condoms, two sample Ativan—which I can apparently stick under my tongue in case of anxiety—and a skin-tone face mask in no-one's skin tone ever.

The way things are going, I'm going to need refills on the Ativan long before I ever crack the package of even one of the condoms.

More-than-adequately equipped, I head back to my observation spot on an unused set of iron steps, above where the refugees have settled, to get a feel for the lay of the land. I'm tucked into a little nook, out of the wind, but with part of a large metal winch poking me in the back. Still, I don't think they can see me up here, so I can get on with my note-taking without fear of offending any of my subjects. It's worth a bruise between the shoulder blades, no question.

I'm relieved to see that most of the people have managed to make themselves a bit more comfortable than they must have been on the leaking *Njeri*. Clotheslines are strung about, adorned with brightly colored fabrics, drying in the wind. I do a quick count, and come up with forty-six people—twenty-eight men, twelve women, and six kids. Not counting babies, because I'm pretty sure at least two of the women have infants swaddled under their colorful robes.

About half the men wear turbans, and almost all the women are in headscarves, so it seems pretty clear the majority of the group are Muslim. My best friend all the way through public school was Maryam Khan, and she wore a hijab. Maryam was Punjabi, though, so I'm not sure if the same rules apply. I make a note to hit Google as soon as I can get a clear signal on the ship's Wi-Fi, and check.

I lost touch with Maryam after high school, mostly because she moved to Lahore for university. That girl taught me some bitchin'— *kutti'n*, according to Maryam—swear words in Urdu over the years, I have to say. Sadly, all I had to offer in return were the mean names that Tommy called the lesbian couple who dropped into the bookshop occasionally for tea and a book of erotica, so I definitely got the better end of the deal. I'm also reminded how much I miss her.

After watching the group for half an hour after breakfast, one girl stands out to me almost immediately. She looks to be maybe twelve or thirteen, and is tall but skinny as a beanpole. She wears a headscarf about half the time, over hair so immaculately braided I feel immediately ashamed of my own windblown locks. Curiously, twice, I watch her walk over to chat with different members of the crew.

Both of whom are Anglo white guys.

I pocket my notebook and scramble down the ladder. At the bottom, I remember my face mask and hastily don it before approaching the part of the deck cordoned off for the Somali passengers.

One of the crew members—I think his name is Terry—is standing nearby, taking a smoke break. His eyes widen at the sight of me, and he hastily steps behind a large yellow bollard.

I unhook the mask. "I'm not sick," I say hastily. "Just trying to be a—uh—good world citizen." I make an exaggerated gesture with my thumb, which immediately makes me feel like I'm a hitchhiking mime.

Behind me, a voice says, "You needn't worry about us. We were all inoculated at the camp in Yemen."

I turn to see the young girl I'd been watching has come to stand against the cordon. Her arms are crossed and her high, perfect forehead is creased in a frown.

"I know you," she says accusingly. "You're the woman who's been spying on us from the upper deck, yeah?"

"I—I'm—not spying," I say weakly. "Just—uh—observing."

"Huh. So, a western woman sits in her throne on high, looking down on us without speaking, and you say that's not spying?"

So, yeah, I'm rendered completely speechless by this kid in under a minute.

I take a deep breath and try to gather the tatters of my resources.

"Okay, yes, now that you describe it like that, I can see where it must have seemed offensive. But that is not at all my intention, I assure you."

I snap my mouth shut, to try to recover from sounding like I've stepped out of the nineteenth century, and then begin again.

"What I mean is—I'm sorry. Can we start over?"

I reach my hand across the cordon. "I'm Romy. I'm from New York City in America, and I'd love a chance to chat a bit with you, when you are free."

The girl takes my hand eagerly, all traces of her former hauteur banished by her giant white smile. "New York City?" she squeals. "That's so sick!"

And with that, I become immediate BFFs with one Sumaya Warsame, age fourteen and a half. In fairly short order, I learn that

Sumaya's excellent English has been learned largely through communicating with the members of her family who have emigrated abroad, and from watching YouTube. Her greatest regret is the loss of the smartphone, which had originally belonged to her father, into the water on the *Njeri*'s first day at sea.

When I ask, however, which of the people present are her mother and father, her face shuts down. "They're gone," is all she'll say. And from this?

I know, through bitter experience, not to push further.

chapter thirty-two

IMAGE: Limes and Beets
IG: Romy_K [Arabian Sea, April 11]
#NoScurvyHere #InterpretingStandUp
179 ♥

The air gets steadily warmer as the ship steams across the Arabian Sea. My path doesn't cross Dominic's at all over the next several days. The *Wahash Mahat* turns out to have excellent satellite Wi-Fi, which allows me to get caught up on my ExLibris reports, after I have rewritten them with a sunnier tone. It also allows me to keep an eye on Dominic's Insta page, where I can see he's still busy posting his culinary creations. Since the arrival of the Somalis, he's expanded his repertoire to include more main courses, but desserts are still his—well, I was going to say *bread and butter,* but you get my drift. Unfortunately, as a result, I hear about him at every meal, as the crew celebrates each new treat that comes their way. You'd think these people had never been fed properly before. Since I find this nothing but annoying, I deliberately take a shot of the cook's store of limes—and beets, oddly enough—rather than feature anything that Dom's had a hand in.

Aside from eating, I have taken to filling the long hours by interviewing any of the Somali passengers who are interested in talking with me. When I ask Sumaya for her help, she nods eagerly.

"I'm the interpreter," she says. "That's why they let me come along. No one else's English is as good as mine."

She points to a child aged about six, who is currently dashing across the deck, shrieking with delight. "Uuli's is close," she admits. "But she's too little for the job."

I start by interviewing Sumaya herself, careful to avoid any mention of her family. I ask open-ended questions, mostly so she can steer the discussion. As a tactic, it works pretty well. I learn, not unexpectedly, almost nothing about Sumaya's own story, apart from the fact that her ultimate goal is to reach her only remaining family, who have settled in Hong Kong. However, she's eager to share information about the other members of the group. When I ask about the human smugglers who put the group on the *Njeri*, she is dismissive.

"When we set off, we had a little inflatable Zodiac in tow," she explained. "One of the *tahriibintas*—uh, the closest English word I know is *pirate*—he said it was for emergencies. But the first night, soon as it got dark, they jumped in and zoom away."

I stare at her, uncomprehending. "They left you? In the middle of the ocean?"

"Mm-hmm. Our group has a midwife, and old Shamso, who's a healer, but no captain. Jula has been on a boat before, and Fatima was a fisherman's wife before her husband died, so she knew how to make the motor run, at least until the wood rotted, and it fell into the sea."

Her voice trails away for a moment, but then she brightens. "So, we were happy to see the *Wahash* come chugging by. Shamso was sure you would carry on, but you stopped!"

She can't seem to help throwing her arms around me in a hug.

I hug her back with all I've got, and it's a long few minutes before I can pull it together enough to talk again.

Not unexpectedly, the stories I hear from the Somalis who agree to speak are mostly horrific—tales of being torn from their homes by warfare or forced into camps by starvation. But peppered throughout these nightmares, I begin to hear little gems of hope, and even humor. This, I'm sure, is entirely due to Sumaya's involvement. She's quick to laugh and is good at remembering tiny incidents that bring my interviewees a little joy in the telling.

"Tell Romy about the pig," she says to Fatima, the fisherman's wife, and soon the three of us are nearly weeping with laughter over the story of a pig destined for slaughter who jumped out of the boat slated to take him to his doom, and instead swam back to the shore and bolted into the safety of the scrubby Lag Badana-Bushbush National Park lands.

Later, we speak with a woman called Hodan, one of the refugees with a tiny infant tucked into her *dirac*. Hodan's baby, a wee boy called Mohammed, was born on the beach, the night before the group set sail in the *Njeri*. Sumaya relates the story of the birth—how all the women present had gathered round and protected Hodan from male eyes. The birth had not been a secret, and Hodan's husband is present on the ship, but Sumaya has Hodan giggling over how the smugglers had not known of the baby's arrival until after the *Njeri* had departed.

"They asked many rials for each soul aboard," Sumaya relays. "But once we are at sea, they can't ask for more."

Sumaya grins and says something to Hodan, who smiles back. "I told her Mohammed is our little bargain," she explains to me, and we laugh together as the ship's engine hums along beneath us.

Sometime between interviews, I mention to Sumaya that while I don't have any aunties, I've lived with my uncles since I was thirteen. She doesn't meet my eye or ask me any questions, but something in the shift of her shoulders tells me that she's registered this information, and filed it away.

That evening, I sit on deck after dinner, near the Somalis but—mindful of Sumaya's spying remark—not close enough to impose on

218 · kc dyer

anyone's space. Listening to all the stories has given me more than enough material for my ExLibris reports. Since I'm now completely up to date, I turn to my e-mail and find a cheery note from Tommy, who has discovered my Instagram account. He uses the word *thrilling* to describe some of my shots, and even wishes me luck on the rest of the journey.

This touches me. Tommy has been in Merv's life since before I was born, and he has invariably been kind to me. But the relationship between us has always been more volatile than with my mellow Uncle Merv. It can't have been easy to find room in their lives for a devastated teenager. In the good-cop/bad-cop dynamic of middle-aged gay men saddled with a teen, Tommy has usually been the one to give the stern admonition.

Which is to say I consider his e-mail to be positively effusive.

Continuing the good news is a message from Teresa Cipher. She writes to say, without a word of complaint, that she has fully paid our balances, allowing us to use our credit cards once again.

This is such good news, I feel compelled to find Dominic and let him know, but when I seek him out in the kitchen, he's not there. Before I have to get up the nerve to ask where the crew quarters are, I spot him sitting on a deck chair watching Sumaya, who is telling jokes.

I walk up in time to hear Dominic cracking up and see Sumaya take a deep theatrical bow.

"That was fantastic!" he says, applauding enthusiastically. "I mean, apart from the dead dik-dik story. I—uh—think that could possibly be misconstrued if you're doing the bit in English."

Sumaya whips out a crumpled coil ring pad and jots down a few notes in pencil. "Okay—good. That's feedback I can use."

"What have I missed?" I say, and Dominic startles a little before turning around in his chair to look up at me.

"Well, hello stranger," he says, getting to his feet. "What you missed was an awesome set." He turns back to Sumaya, holding up his watch. "You were right—dead on three minutes of material."

She notes that down, too, before looking back up at me.

"More than anything, I want to be a stand-up comic when I grow up," she says.

In all our conversations, this is the first I've heard of it. I'm pretty sure my mouth gapes, so I fake a cough to cover it. "A—a what?"

Sumaya throws back her shoulders. "Yeah, you heard right."

"How do you even know what a stand-up comic *is*?" I ask, forgetting who I'm talking to.

She gives me a disgusted look. "The internet, how else? Duh!"

So. It turns out that this kid, like most of the kids I know, has grown up watching YouTube. Only—you know—in Somalia.

"I love Ali Wong and Maysoon Zayid," Sumaya tells me, after rolling her eyes at my ignorance. "And of course, Bilal Zafar, though I think most of his jokes would land better if he was a woman."

I don't tell her the only name she's mentioned that I've heard before is Ali Wong, and instead, make a mental note to look up the other two.

"Can you believe this?" I hiss at Dominic as Sumaya runs off to join a group of kids.

Dominic shakes his head. "Oh, trust me, speaking as a male with a Samoan-born mother, I understand exactly how something like this will be appreciated by Sumaya's family."

"As in, not at all?"

He shrugs. "Exactly. But she's young, and I feel like it's a way for her to work through things. Plus?" he says. "She's funny."

Since Sumaya has shut down her one-teenager entertainment committee for the evening, I start to walk away before I remember my original errand.

"Oh—I nearly forgot. I got an e-mail from Teresa, telling me she paid off our cards. She didn't even sound upset. So, I guess we're solvent again."

He grins. "Yeah, she wrote me too. But thanks for letting me know."

"No problem," I mutter, and turn away, feeling foolish. Of course she would write to him too.

"G'night," Dominic calls from somewhere behind me. I give him a wave without looking back. I realize my feelings are smarting from missing Sumaya's performance, when she'd taken the time to show it to Dominic. It bites me that she has any time at all for him, with his self-serving attitude.

Beneath my feet, a small shift in the engines causes the iron floors to rattle. The *Wahash Mahat* is due in to port sometime overnight, and when I pass Ganesh on my way to my cabin, he tells me I can expect to wake up in Mumbai. "Closest to home I've been in a year," he says cheerfully. This drives all thoughts of Dominic out of my head.

The very name of the city makes a shiver run up my spine. Mumbai. A place so exotic, it never even crossed my mind that one day I might get to see it for real. As I climb a set of outside stairs and work my way around to my cabin, I get a glimpse of the group of refugees on the deck below, settling down for their last night on the ship. Remembering Sumaya's complaint, I don't stop to gaze down upon them, though I really want to. I want to know what they're thinking—are they afraid? Excited? From what Sumaya has told me, I'm certain that none of them has any idea of what their future will hold.

Not that I have a clue about my own future either.

It's a long time before the deep thrum of the ship's engines manages to lull me into sleep.

chapter thirty-three

IMAGE: Gateway to India
IG: Romy_K [Arabian Sea, April 14]
#PassagetoIndia #Mumbai
150 ♥

Mumbai is the next checkpoint on Phileas Fogg's itinerary, except when he visited, of course, it was known as Bombay. The ship must have anchored sometime before dawn, because I awake to the absence of sound and movement. The engines have stopped and the cabin floor is completely still for the first time since we boarded in the Red Sea. I spent my last night on the ocean stowing my freshly washed laundry in my suitcase, so after leaping out of bed and brushing my teeth, I hurry to take in the view.

India first leapt into my imagination courtesy of *A Fine Balance*. Rohinton Mistry's book had been recommended by Oprah, and so therefore was immediately on Tommy's reading list. I found it on the coffee table and was instantly transported into the brilliant colors and tragic losses of twentieth-century India through the eyes of Dina and Maneck and the rest. I remember trying to wrap my mind around the caste system and peppering my uncles with questions about untouchables and Brahmins. My literary love affair with India led me on a high-speed dash through the works of Salman Rushdie, V. S. Naipaul, and Anita Rau Badami. Of all the places Fogg visited on his journey, it is India I am most eager to see.

In spite of the weight of my suitcase, I climb the iron steps up to the deck two at a time, excited to take in the sights and sounds of this ancient country. I can't wait to lay my eyes on the largest city in the second largest—by population, anyway—nation in the world. The romance of this historic place can't be denied, but even the logical side of my brain is excited. The systems they must have in place to ensure that everyone gets to school and work on time—the train schedules alone have to be enough to leave New York in the dust. I burst out onto the deck, and race over to the railing, desperate to take it all in.

Of course, I've forgotten the size of the *Wahash Mahat*, which is not docked, after all. The harbor here is too far away to see, and we are anchored at least half a mile from the closest pier. In the distance I can see a large, arched monument that looks strangely similar to the Arc de Triomphe, which I also have only seen from a distance. I'm distracted from the view by the hive of activity around the refugees on the deck below mine, as tarps are folded and belongings gathered. Further down, the ship's tenders are being lowered into the water, and a number of other small craft I don't recognize are buzzing nearby.

The reality of departing the ship washes over me. Glancing down at my phone, I'm shocked when I catch sight of the date. How can it be nearly the middle of April already? It feels like an impossible task to cross this country, and literally half of the rest of the way around the world, and make it back to New York in time. Which means, apart from this, the only glimpse of India I'm going to get will have to be from the inside of a speeding train.

Dominic hurries past and grins at the expression on my face. "What are you worried about now? I thought you'd be thrilled to be heading back onto solid ground."

I wave my phone at him glumly. "It's April fourteenth, and we have just over two weeks to travel half the planet."

"We can only do our best," he says, and then strides off before I can land even a single jab at his nauseating optimism.

Annoyed with myself for using the word *we*, I scoop up my suitcase and head down the stairs. I don't know what Dominic's plans are, and at this point I don't care. I have to put all my energy into moving forward.

Passing the door to the mess hall, I spot the group of Somali refugees gathered inside. I catch sight of Sumaya and pop in to say goodbye. My heavy suitcase snags on the doorframe and I drop it with a thud, right onto my foot.

As the pain radiates up from my crushed toes to my brain, the only thing I feel is shame. Every person in this room is leaving the ship with nothing but the clothes on their backs.

Except for me.

In a trice, I have my suitcase open on the nearest table. Into the lid, I drop all my underwear, my papers and phone, and two changes of clothes. I scoop up the Bowie t-shirt I sleep in and cross the room to say goodbye to Sumaya.

She seems extraordinarily cheerful and hugs me hard. I write out my e-mail address so we can keep in touch, and she folds it into the small cloth pouch she wears tucked beneath her robes. She seems preoccupied, likely with whatever unknown she's about to face, but when I hand her the Bowie t-shirt, her eyes light up with excitement.

"For me?" she says so sincerely, my heart breaks a little at her tone.

I point at the picture. "He was a pretty famous rock star . . ." I begin, but she holds up a hand.

"Uh—he was married to *Iman*," she says, clutching the shirt to her chest and rolling her eyes. "Only the most famous Somali woman in the world."

"Right—right. Well, I'm carrying too much stuff," I mutter,

equally delighted that she is happy and embarrassed that I've forgotten this detail. "Will you tell the ladies I want to share?"

She beams at me and hugs me hard, and we make a quick circle through the rest of the group, saying goodbye as I shake each hand.

"*Nabadgelyo,*" I say over and over, as Sumaya has taught me. By the time I reach the last woman, the main compartment of my suitcase is empty.

"*Wad mahatsantahay,*" they reply, clasping my hands joyfully. "*Ilaah ha idiin barakeeyo.*"

Not one of these women knows what lies in store in Mumbai, but they still take the time to wish me well. My heart goes with them as I watch the captain usher them out the door.

As I line up behind them to wait for my turn on the ship's tender, which will whisk us the last few hundred feet across the Arabian Sea, I watch every member of the crew step up to thank Dominic for teaching their cook his favorite recipe for *gâteau au beurre.*

My resentment about his popularity fades in the face of reality. By baking them something special, and then sharing his recipes, he's left part of himself behind with them. It doesn't hurt that his cake is delicious—moist with the flavors of rum and butter. But Merv has always said *food is love,* and I've never really understood it until now. Whenever the ship's cook makes that cake again, they'll think of Dominic.

All I have left behind me is a collection of travel-worn—though at least freshly clean—clothes. "American white girl overpacks" is not exactly a memorable legacy.

As Ganesh ushers Dominic onto the tender in front of me, he holds out a small white card.

"If you get stuck anywhere on the water on your journey," he says, "message me. I'm from a family of sailors. I've got connections."

I sling my now much-lighter suitcase ahead of me, but Ganesh holds up a hand to bar my way.

"This one's full," he says. "You're on the next one."

I step back as he swings the gate closed in front of me.

I try to wave at Sumaya, but her head is turned away.

"I thought she might want to ride in with me," I say to Ganesh. "But I guess she needs to go with her group."

He shrugs. "She asked specially to ride with Dominic."

"Who doesn't want to ride with Mr. Popularity?" I mutter, but Ganesh has turned to answer the captain, and doesn't hear.

As the boat speeds away toward the customs dock, I watch Dominic leaning against the railing beside Sumaya. She says something that makes him laugh. Then he catches my eye and lifts his hand to wave at me. Instead of the usual resentment, I'm struck by the most peculiar panicky feeling that I will never see him again.

The next tender pulls up almost immediately, and I spend the entire ride berating my subconscious for feeding me ridiculous emotions about a man who's not even my friend.

He's a rival. My only true rival. And if I don't see him again, it's a good thing.

It is.

chapter thirty-four

IMAGE: Crane, Sassoon Docks
IG: Romy_K [Mumbai, India, April 14]
#Colaba #TrainStationChaos
153 ♥

'm on the final tender, so I disembark with the last half-dozen crew members.

Ganesh grins at me. "I'm excited. We almost never get to go through the Sassoon Docks. Must be an overload at the main port authority."

I glance at him, feeling instantly worried. "Is this further from the center of town? I need to catch my train later today from Central Station."

He waves a hand dismissively. "Close enough. There's a metro rail station not far from here. You'll be fine."

Jamming his hands in his pockets, he rocks back on his heels. "I love this part of town. Anything in the world you want? You can buy here in Colaba." He waggles his eyebrows at me suggestively.

"What's that supposed to mean?" I say, but he's suddenly disappeared into the crowd.

I join what looks like a roughly forming line outside the customs office, and try to take in everything that's going on around me. The aroma of being back on land hits me first, but this is like nothing I have ever smelled before. Fish and hemp and the oily smoke of cooking nearby jostle for prominence, but I can also smell flowers and something that I think must be incense.

The pier itself looks very old, and it's lined with open wooden sheds along its whole length. The sheds shelter enormous piles of fishing nets, stacks of massive baskets, and huge wooden spools of the sort for rolling rope. To one side, dozens of tiny fishing boats are moored, painted in every color of the rainbow, but most in need of repair. With their flat bottoms and flat roofs, they look like jaunty little rowboats. I can't imagine they have the power to tow the enormous nets coiled on the dockside, but they must. Even at this early hour, as boats putter out of their mooring spots, new boats pull in to unload their catch, stored on the tiny decks in huge baskets like the ones piled on the dock.

Above the door to the customs office, a tall white crane with a lethal-looking black beak perches on the branch of a tree awash in red, fragrant blossoms. The crane gazes across the water toward a derelict lighthouse on the shoreline across from the pier, the rotting timbers of its structure visible through a dense forest of trees. Above the trees, the tower stretches to the sky, but where the light must have once flashed, a small tree has taken root, its branches sheltering the tower like a large, leafy umbrella.

"These docks were built by the Sassoon company in the nineteenth century," says Ganesh, who suddenly reappears beside the doors to the customs office. "They are Mumbai's oldest docks. You go in this way, yes?"

So, apparently what I thought was a line was not. As he shepherds me past the milling group of people outside, I feel sweat trickling down my spine beneath my shirt. It's just past eight in the morning local time, but the air already has a damp heat to it that doesn't bode well for the rest of the day. The breeze that buffeted the decks of the *Wahash Mahat* is most definitely not in evidence here.

Inside the door to the customs office, I expect to see Dominic ahead of me in line. Instead, Ganesh waves me over to stand beside him.

"Normally, you'd go to a line for foreigners," he says as we join the queue for processing. "At the airport or even the port authority, there's a special queue for foreigners with visas. But here, you muck in with us regulars."

I dig out my passport and clutch it nervously. The visa Teresa Cipher arranged is safely folded inside.

"Where are you heading next?" Ganesh asks as we take a few steps forward.

"Apparently I can take a train right across to Kolkata," I say. "I had a clear signal last night for about an hour, so I checked it online. It goes from the Central Station, I think?"

"You're braver than I am. I hate the crowds, so Indian train stations are not my favorite places. I always fly, if I can."

I swallow hard. "Not really an option for me," I mutter, moving forward with the line. "And it'll take too long to go by bus."

He bursts out laughing at this, and then stops suddenly when he sees my face. "Oh—you're not kidding? Okay, well, sounds like train it is, then. Make sure you look for the ladies' car."

Right then, the customs agent calls me forward, so I have no chance to ask if he's joking or not. As I step forward, Ganesh pats my shoulder, wishes me luck, and then heads off to a different agent. Waiting for the officer to examine my paperwork, I scan the room again, but the rest of the crew must have passed through already. When Ganesh gets waved on, I lose sight of my last familiar face.

The officer in front of me leafs through each page of my passport, before stamping it. He informs me that I am welcome to return any time for the next year to India without having to reapply for a visa. Then he kindly points me to another officer, who he promises can give me directions to the train station. But before I can even think of catching a train, I need to send in my report to ExLibris, and for that? I need Wi-Fi.

The information officer looks bored, and is clearly puzzled at my request for an internet cafe. Instead, he points me through a set of distant gates, and onto a busy street beyond. He answers me in English, but his accent is so pronounced, and he speaks so quickly, I have trouble catching all the details. In the end, I decide he's directing me to a hotel, which at least will be a good start. I thank him politely, determined to counteract everything I have read about the Ugly American abroad. Stepping out of the building, I am immediately swept up into the loud, terrifying, magnificent chaos that is twenty-first-century Mumbai.

As I exit the ornate gates that mark the end of the Sassoon Docks, the air tastes dusty and hangs heavy with the smell of exhaust from nearby traffic. The street is jammed with women wearing jewel-tone saris, and tunics with flowing trousers in brilliant color combinations, often topped with a contrasting scarf. People are busy chatting, walking, working. One elderly lady rolls an impossibly large bundle of laundry down the street. I stop to surreptitiously snap her picture, and then head out into the surging crowd.

The atmosphere is generally cheerful, but the sheer number of people is overwhelming. There's no way I can adopt the eyes-down, purposeful stride technique that I use daily in New York, because this tactic only works when you know where you are going.

My single advantage at this point is height. I'm not quite five ten in my sock feet, but here I literally can look over the heads of the crowd to orient myself a bit. After all, this number of people is little different than what I'd find in Times Square on New Year's at midnight.

The fact that I would never go anywhere near Times Square

almost any time of year, let alone New Year's at midnight, should not have any bearing. I can cope with these crowds.

I can.

Following the crowd as it surges out onto the high street, I spot a sign saying "Hotel Anand," and aim myself in that direction. This is no easy task, since everyone seems to have some important place to be, and no one is prepared to give way.

The thing about this journey is that, apart from my one quiet night in Chamonix, it's been cities all the way. I'm city-hopping my way around the globe. I'm a city-hopping city girl who has lived in and loved big cities all my life.

But Mumbai?

Mumbai is something else.

I know from a little onboard Googling that Colaba is a big shopping district in Mumbai. But I'll tell you something. Colaba is about as far from Fifth Avenue as this New York girl is ever going to get. I've always struggled with the presence of beggars on the streets of my own city. Every city has them, I know. Growing up, Tommy always took a tough stance . . . *Every penny you give them goes to drugs,* he would say disparagingly. *Don't give them a cent.*

As an adult myself now, I don't ascribe to this theory. My compromise is generally to carry an extra granola bar in my pocket to hand over when someone asks. Even if Tommy's right, I can say truthfully that never once has my offer been refused.

I'm under no illusions that this is helping, or doing anything apart from assuaging my liberal guilt. But that liberal guilt is being given a workout like never before as I walk the street leading to the hotel in Colaba.

Mumbai, I see before me, is a city of absolutely tremendous contrasts. The colors are brilliant: yellow, orange, pink, red flowers blooming, draped on tiny shrines inside the base of mighty baobab trees—even right here downtown!—and hanging from strings above merchant stalls. As I walk past, the heavy, rich scent of the flowers is soon replaced by the sweet tang of sugarcane, being chopped and ground up in a street stall. But the stalls themselves, and many of the buildings, are in an advanced state of decay and disintegration. Everywhere I look, things are dirty and falling down.

And while I stare in wonder at the city, Mumbai stares right back at me. More than any place I've ever been before, my presence marks me as a stranger. My height; my kinky, rusty hair; my pallid, awkwardly sunburned skin. I've never walked down a street and felt every eye upon me like this before. A Mumbai walk should be compulsory for every complacent white person in the world. *This* is what it feels like to be the Other. Twice in a single block, a teenage boy runs up to me, cell phone in hand, and takes a selfie beside me before I figure out what's happening. I feel like a freak.

Right now, I'm too caught up in my quest to think this through, but file it away for future consideration as I press on toward the hotel.

The street is teeming with traffic, an endless cacophony of horns and speeding motorcycles and dodging pedestrians. The sidewalks are crumbling, but are still overrun with local merchants, many with their goods spread out on tarps. Piles of watches, and bangles, and sneakers. A cart laden with small red fruits about the size of plums, but still on the branch. Later, I find out these are called lychees, commonly eaten to provide refreshment from the ever-present, humid heat of the city. Beside the cart, a man lays out jean shorts and plastic sand buckets and huge baskets of smoky, fragrantly roasted nuts.

Collections of tiny children—toddlers, really—run between the tarps, playing under the watchful eye of sari-draped grandmothers. There's no rhyme or reason to the retail—piles of bananas sit next to multicolored flip-flops; cobblers repair shoes sitting inside tiny work-shops on wheels next to sari-clad women deep-frying samosas and pakoras. The spicy-sweet smell of these last is almost intolerably deli-cious, but that rogue shawarma in Port Said is too close to my stom-ach to risk another leap into street food so quickly.

By contrast, the hotel is located in a freshly painted building. Three motorcycles are lined up neatly out front, and two turban-clad, elegantly uniformed doormen oversee taxi-hailing and keep the general public off the pavement outside.

By the time I reach the hotel doorway, I'm drenched in sweat. Even my daypack, tucked under one arm, is completely damp. Gross as this must look, the doormen immediately smile, bow, and hold the door open for me. I feel an equal mixture of embarrassment and relief.

This trip is really messing with my head.

As the doormen politely wave me inside the entrance to the hotel, it occurs to me that I'm in possession of exactly zero Indian currency. I'm going to need cash to buy some time online, some food—not street food—and a train ticket. I point my sweaty self in the direction of the front desk to find someone to explain the currency exchange. Just how much is a rupee worth, anyway?

An hour later, I have cash in my pocket, and directions to the near-est Mumbai Suburban Railway station, which the kind hotel clerk assures me is the quickest connection to the Central Station and my train out of town. Their Wi-Fi was down, but I'm sure I can find somewhere to log on when I get to the station.

Of course, as soon as these feelings of pride and accomplishment rise within me, I walk through the station entrance and everything goes to hell.

Inside, the crowds that fill the streets condense in a way that gives me pause. But by the time I've queued for my ticket, and then passed through the turnstiles, it's too late. The crush is immediate, and over-whelming.

I mean, I'm a New Yorker. I know how to endure a crowded subway. I know what walking down a busy street feels like. But step-ping inside Churchgate Station schools me.

You know nothing, Romy Keene.

The first hint I've made a big mistake comes to me as I emerge through the turnstile. There suddenly isn't a single woman to be seen.

Not. One. Woman.

The platform is a surging sea of humanity, and as the train pulls up, things swiftly worsen. I find myself being swept away from the tracks by a crowd as inexorable as a riptide. I'd slung my pack across my chest to go through the turnstile, so my front half is somewhat shielded. But trying to reach the train, I find myself swimming up-stream in an endless flow of grabbing, clutching, caressing strangers. I'm trapped in a school of slithering, hand-shaped fish, unable to escape. Unable to breathe.

Barely keeping my feet, I'm slowly, inexorably pushed away from the train. I don't know how long I spend caught in the crush—several lifetimes, maybe?—before I feel a whisper of cool tile against one arm. Galvanized by the feel of a wall at my back, I use my suitcase as a battering ram and slide along the tile until I'm close enough to the gate to draw the attention of a guard.

The disinterested expression on his face changes as he looks at me, and he flips the latch on the gate and steps out of the way. The crowd spits me out like old chewing gum, and I hit the ground hard with both knees, vomiting my fear—and my mercifully small breakfast—onto the station floor.

chapter thirty-five

IMAGE: Old Factory Sign
IG: Romy_K [Mumbai, India, April 14]
#Rescue #AlexanderHamilton #MumbaiCallCenter
429 ♥

The combination of revulsion and fear is too much, and I burst into tears. The guard has disappeared, my knees are battered, and beside me is a puddle of sick that I desperately scramble away from. I'm on my haunches, in the act of madly searching my pockets for a tissue, when a perfectly manicured hand swims into my vision.

It's holding a white cotton handkerchief.

Before me stands a small, smiling woman. She's an angel come to earth, albeit one dressed in a navy skirt suit, with a high neck and a colorful scarf. Her dark hair brushes her shoulders, and she's carrying a large leather messenger bag over one arm.

"For your eyes," she says, and then adds hurriedly, pointing at my puddle, "Stay away from that!"

Wiping away the tears on my face, I take a deep breath, roll onto one sore knee, and stand up.

"Thank you," I say, offering the handkerchief back, but she shakes her head firmly.

"Nose too," she says in a tone that reminds me so much of Tommy that I almost start to cry again.

Instead, I wipe my nose and repeat my thanks.

She smiles up at me, and a small bottle of Purell appears in her hand. "The floors in here are dreadful," she says, and waves the bottle.

"I think I made them worse," I mutter, and hold out my hands, palms up.

She squeezes a few drops into each of my palms, and then deftly sanitizes her own hands.

"My name is Priti Chopra," she says, and then shakes my newly sanitized hand with one of her own. "Let me . . ." she begins, then turns her back to me and gives a piercing blast on a small silver whistle that she's wearing on a chain.

The crowd, which has begun to fill in around us—though nowhere near the volume of bodies crammed onto the train platform—parts, and a station attendant approaches.

"Someone has been sick here, Gurdeep," Priti says to the man, her tone disapproving.

Making a sweeping gesture toward my mess on the floor, she says, "You must see to this right away before someone slips in it." She clicks her tongue. "Health and safety, you know."

"It's my fault . . ." I begin, but Priti gives me a warning squeeze on the arm.

"We'll be on our way, then," she says. Linking her arm through mine, she marches me away.

"A breath of air is all you need," she adds as we hurry along. "And a lick of good sense. You are American, yes?"

I nod, still hiccupping a little. We trot up the last set of stairs, and step out onto the street, where the heat hits me like a solid blow.

"Over here," says Priti, and keeping a firm hold on my arm, pulls me expertly through the traffic and safely across the street. We step into the shadow of an old stone building, and she pauses beside a heavy wood door, painted deep green. A worn and heavily tagged sign beside the door reads: "House of Exquisite Textiles." Expertly flipping a set of keys from one of her pockets, she has the door open and the two of us inside in seconds.

My first feeling is relief. There's no air-conditioning, but the thick walls of the building make it feel much cooler in here. My second is anxiety. As the door swings closed behind us, we are swallowed up in darkness.

"Tsk," she says impatiently as she releases my arm at last. "Let me get the lights. Don't move."

Seconds later, the lights rise up, and my anxiety falls away.

We are standing inside the entrance area of an office space filled with desks that looks so familiar, I nearly laugh out loud.

"Is this—a call center?" I ask, and Priti bobs her head. "From the sign outside, I thought it was a factory."

"It used to be, until we took it over," she says. "My brother is the manager." Glancing down at her watch, she adds, "He's late."

She leans across the counter to flick the switch on an electric kettle, and then pulls out a chair. "Sit down a minute," she says. "I'll make us some tea."

She drops her messenger bag onto one of the chairs in the reception area, and smiles as the kettle begins to whistle shrilly.

"Do you work here?" I ask as she unplugs the kettle.

Priti shakes her head. "It's a family business," she says. "I used to work for the transit authority."

"Which explains the whistle," I say, and she grins.

"Let me guess," she says, dropping tea bags into two sturdy white mugs. "First time in Mumbai?"

"Does it show that much?"

She heaps three spoons of sugar into one cup and one into the other before adding milk to both. Pushing the sweet tea into my hand, she takes a seat beside me.

"For the shock," she says firmly. "Drink it up."

I take a sip, and the warm tea flows through me like liquid energy. I feel immediately better.

She smiles at me approvingly as I take a second sip. "Good. Now, we have already established who I am. And you are . . . ?"

"Ramona Keene," I say hurriedly, and offer her my hand again. "From New York City."

Her eyes light up. "I *love* New York," she says. "I've been to see *Hamilton* three times!"

I can't help smiling back at her. "I haven't seen it yet," I admit. "Too pricey for me. I know all the songs, though."

"Me too," she says, and we both grin.

"When were you in New York?" I ask, and she laughs.

"Which time?"

It turns out Priti works for a company called Travel India, and while she spends most of her time touring visitors around her own country, she also takes tours overseas. This has meant a half-dozen visits to America, including two to my own city.

And then, because I have no self-control, I tell her about my own quest to get around the world, and why. Because the story is long enough already, I leave out all the bits that include Dominic.

Her eyes light up when I explain my efforts to get a job with ExLibris.

"Oh, I hope you get the job," she says. "We can be sisters in travel! And the next time I come to New York, we can go see *Hamilton* together."

I laugh. "It's a deal."

Her eyes still dancing, she puts down her teacup. "So, Ramona, tell me. Do you hop on the subway regularly during rush hour in New York?" she asks.

"It's Romy," I say, shaking my head. "And never—at least not if I can help it."

Priti jabs her thumb over her shoulder toward the front door. "Well, now you know. Same rules apply here. And it's maybe a little bit worse, even?"

I laugh. "A little. It was a stupid mistake."

She shrugs. "You didn't know. But now you do. Where are you trying to go today?"

"I need a ticket to Howrah on the fast train," I say. "I thought I could hop the local commuter train to get to Mumbai Central, and buy a ticket there. And I need to send a report in to ExLibris before I go."

Priti rolls her eyes at me. "Ever heard of the internet?" she asks. "You can use the office Wi-Fi to get your ticket organized. And send your e-mail too."

As she glances at her watch again, the door opens behind her.

"Hey, sis," says a cheerful male voice. "Thanks for opening up. Some asswipe was sick on the platform in the station, and they shut down all the turnstiles on that side. Took forever to get through . . ."

He stops speaking as he catches sight of me.

"Who's this?" he asks, his smile broadening. "Introduce me to your charming friend, Pritisita!"

Priti rolls her eyes.

"Prem, this is Romy, from New York. She's on her way to Kolkata, so no putting your famous moves on her, okay?"

She glances over at me before pulling something out of her bag. "Listen, Romy, I have to go to work now. But here's a map of this area. We are here, not far from Marine Drive, see?" She marks the spot on the map. "And here's Mumbai Central. It's a bit of a walk, but if you stay on Lamington Road, it will take you straight there. Or there's a stop right across the street where you can catch a bus that will take you there too."

"Thank you so much for this," I say, folding the map into my daypack. "And for rescuing me at the station. I was really scared."

She waves away my thanks. "It's my job," she says. "I've seen worse, believe me."

Prem smirks and gives me a familiar little pat on the shoulder. "Don't give her too much credit. She's *supposed* to make the tourists happy, right, Preet?"

Priti huffs impatiently and shoulders her bag. "Nice to meet you, Romy," she says, ignoring her brother's grin. She pushes open the door, and then she turns back and points dramatically at her empty teacup.

"I'm *not* throwing away my chai!" she sings, and then lets the door close behind her.

I laugh out loud, but Prem shakes his head. "I don't know what she's talking about half the time," he mutters, but as he glances at me, his face brightens.

Reaching over, he touches my arm, and I experience the strongest sensation of déjà vu I've ever felt in my life.

"So—you need to send an e-mail?" he says.

It takes maybe half an hour in total, between booking the ticket and sending in my report to ExLibris. All the while, a steady stream of workers enter through the front door. Prem greets them all—handshakes for the men, and effusive hugs for the women—and introduces me to every single person as "his friend, Romy, visiting from New York City."

At least two of the women roll their eyes at me over his shoulder before he releases them to hurry off to their desks.

And I'm struck by how, in spite of being literally on the other side of the world, Call Center Prem could be a brother to Jonah in New York. Shaking my head, I send in my update, with Prem's left hand casually resting on the back of my chair the entire time.

chapter thirty-six

IMAGE: Train Station Ceiling

IG: Romy_K [Mumbai, India, April 14]

#MumbaiMayhem #CityofDreams #Dharavi

165 ♥

After declining Prem's increasingly intense invitations to dinner—or perhaps a spot of tea? Or how about an escort up to the train station?—I hurry away from the call center. I've got a ticket on the Howrah Superfast Express, departing from Mumbai Central station in just under two hours. The heat immediately wraps itself around me like a warm wet cloak, but Priti's directions prove successful, and I spy the bus stop right away. Even better, there's a definite queue, and I hurry up to take my place in line.

Five minutes later, the bus pulls up. Inside, it's standing room only, and two of the window openings have men sitting right on the sill, legs dangling. I reevaluate and decide to make the walk. According to Priti's map, it's about three miles to the station and I'm a New Yorker used to walking. How hard can it be?

Things I learn walking the streets of Mumbai:

1. Street sitting—and lying—is a thing here. At noon, in the heat of the day, there are as many people sitting—and lying—on the sidewalks as there are pedestrians walking.

2. The roads are constant mayhem—a cacophony of honking cars, squealing brakes, revving engines, and roaring motorbikes. The air is so thick with exhaust fumes, I can taste nothing else. Lane usage is considered optional, as is signaling, parking lanes, and yellow lights. Horns, however, are mandatory.

3. Lunch delivery, in the city, is the most remarkable thing I've ever seen. Men called "dabbawalas" collect up commuters' lunches from their homes all around the district, and deliver them to Mumbai offices by the thousands—the hundreds of thousands—every day, without a mistake. Without a computer. I can only dream of being so organized.

4. Motorized rickshaws are the bomb. Essentially three-wheeled motorbikes, designed to hold three people. They never hold three people. I stopped counting after seeing one with nine passengers. Plus driver, of course.

5. Shrines are found in the most unexpected places, and are dedicated to the most wonderful deities. Gods with the faces of elephants and monkeys and beautiful women, tucked under trees and in tents and under little handmade sheds. Most are draped in flowers.

6. I spotted a single sacred cow on the streets, and discovered that you can buy hay to feed the cow for ten rupees. Afterwards, I learned that this particular cow is known to haunt a corner cafe, and has a fondness for iced lattes. Never have I felt such communion with an animal.

7. How to know when you're near a university: Outdoor study centers begin to appear, generally in tree-shaded areas, with built-in desks and benches. While mostly filled with young stu-

dents whose homes are too small to offer adequate study facilities, they are also hangouts for . . .

8. Stray dogs and cats. Mostly these guys lay around prostrate
in the heat. It's pretty clear spaying and neutering aren't
really a thing here.

9. India has a consistent time zone across the whole country,
but it's half an hour off the surrounding ones. I cannot get
anyone to give me a reason for this.

10. Bamboo scaffolding instead of iron. Flexible, cheap, and
eco-friendly. Who knew?

This list could easily be twice as long—ten times as long. Each
street holds a revelation in this astonishing city.

I stumble into the train station close to two hours later, exhausted
with the heat but exhilarated with the sights and smells and sounds
of Mumbai. As with any city, it presents a mixture of old and new,
but the extremes of poverty and tremendous wealth seem so much
more evident here than I have seen anywhere else. The walk took me
probably twice as long as it would have at home, mostly due to the
whole life-in-my-hands element of crossing the streets, but was worth
every minute. Every second.

I line up to collect my train ticket, and follow the ticket seller's
pointed finger in the direction of the platform. Unlike the local commuter station, this place is bustling, but not insanely crowded. Above
my head, the ceiling soars to elegant, ornate heights the likes of which
were nowhere to be found in the Churchgate Station.

My train to Howrah runs only twice a week, and I feel lucky to
have snagged a seat. The train company's online ticket service offers
six or seven different classes, but when I went to order a sleeping

berth, none were available. My seat ends up being near the middle of the train in a car without air-conditioning but with large windows that open. Also, only ticketed passengers are admitted, so there will be no clinging to—or dangling out of—windows, at least not in my car. Several seats remain open, in fact, and I have room to stretch my legs right out. The engine chugs to life, and I feel a sudden pang of regret. If Sumaya doesn't get in touch, I'll never know what happens with the Somalians rescued on the *Wahash Mahat*. The thought leaves me feeling strangely sick.

As the train pulls out, I slide over to the window seat, and spy what looks like a mammoth outdoor steam bath. It's only when I catch a glimpse of legions of white-clad men hand-scrubbing piles of sheets that I realize it must Dhobi Ghat—the city's most storied outdoor laundry. But as the train picks up speed, the laundry is replaced by rickety shacks and shanties draped in tarps, all jammed impossibly close together. I stare out at the slum, mesmerized by the crowded, filthy conditions.

My thoughts must show on my face, because I hear a voice nearby.

"Dharavi. The last census put the population at more than a million."

I turn to see a grandmotherly lady, stitching something she's holding on her lap with bright orange thread, and smiling at me from across the aisle.

"You mean the population of Mumbai?"

She shakes her head, and the loose skin under her neck wobbles gently. "No—no, only of Dharavi. Of course, these figures are never accurate. Some say that more than eight million make their home in the slums of this city."

The sheer volume of the poverty strikes me dumb. "Can—anything be done?" I manage, at last.

The lady shrugs. "Oh, there have been many initiatives. I'm not sure they've found one that will make much of a difference yet. Mumbai is known throughout India as the City of Dreams, you know. Many of the people who come—they are the ones you see living in Dharavi, or out on the streets. Not so many find their dreams here, after all. A hard lesson to learn, especially for those who come from far away."

She reaches into her bag, produces a packet of small crackers, and leans across the aisle to offer me one. When I decline, she says, "Suit yourself," pops one in, and returns to her stitching. I turn back to the window to watch mile after mile of shanties whiz past.

Two hours into the journey, when the train has left Mumbai far behind, I make my stumbling way through the carriages in search of food. Earlier, a train steward came by bearing bottled water, but I am ready for something more substantial. Three cars forward, I find a canteen where I can buy a thick vegetable broth that comes with breadsticks and butter.

Also? I find Dominic.

"Great to see you," he says as I step into line behind him. He's wearing an expression I can't read, and lapses into perhaps the most awkward small talk I've heard coming out of anyone other than Call Center Jonah. Or maybe Prem Chopra.

"Well, well, isn't this great?" Dominic repeats, with entirely false heartiness. "Where's your berth?"

When I explain the berths were all sold out and that I'm in a seat, he looks strangely relieved. "It *is* a fairly short trip, after all. And at least there's air-conditioning."

"Not in second class," I mutter.

He is saved from replying by the steward calling him forward.

"Oh, no—after you, after you!" he insists, stepping back to let me go first.

"Thank you," I say, using as much quiet dignity as I can muster with the man who has clearly taken the last berth on the train.

I collect my soup and hurry off, declining to reply to his overenthusiastic farewell.

By the time I get back to my seat, my anger has reached a full boil. I guess I shouldn't be surprised that he's on the same train, considering how infrequently they are scheduled along this route, but the fact that he didn't utter a word of commiseration about my second-class seat, let alone offer to switch me into the berth that should have been mine in the first place, really bites me.

The scenery outside my window is flying by so fast I can no longer make anything out apart from a generally green blur. Even Stitching Lady has fallen asleep across the aisle. No one can really hold a conversation over the swirl of tepid wind rushing in the wide-open windows. The only thing that makes it over the noise of the wind is a crying baby, sitting somewhere behind my seat. I slump down to eat my soup, then jamming my hoodie under one ear, I close my eyes and let the familiar rhythm of the train take me away.

chapter thirty-seven

 IMAGE: Ladies on the Platform
IG: Romy_K [Chhattisgarh State, India, April 15]
#ChapatiChallenge #SleeperShock
301 ♥

wake from the bleary doze I fell into before dawn as the train, once again, shudders to a stop. I've lost track of the number of stops in the night, each one rattling me into wakefulness. It seems excessive for what's supposed to be a high-speed train, is all I'm saying.

I glance down at my phone, to see that it is twenty past six. The heat is already stifling.

Outside the window, the sun beats down on a dusty landscape. There are trees, but where the train is stopped, all I can really see are fields, separated by low, scrubby brush. Apart from a sign on the tracks, written in a language I cannot even identify, there's no indication of where we are. The train's engine has stopped, and heat is rising in the carriage. The baby, who cried most of the night, has finally fallen asleep in her mother's arms. When I peek over the seat behind me, the mother herself is out cold, head leaning against the window, mouth open.

With the stopping of the train, all air circulation has ceased. I don't think I've ever been bathed in sweat before seven in the morning before, and as a sensation, I do not recommend it.

All I've had to eat in the last twelve hours or so is the soup I bought earlier—which was tasty, but hasn't lasted, so I'm hungry. Hungry, stiff-necked, and regretting not booking when I was on the boat, so that I could be enjoying the sleeping berth rather than having it wasted on Dominic. On the *Wahash Mahat*, he admitted to me that he has the ability to sleep under any conditions if he's tired.

I bet *his* neck isn't stiff.

There's a clatter of machinery from somewhere toward the front of the train, and the engine starts up again. I've never driven a car, but I've ridden in enough rickety cabs to know the sound of an engine on its last legs. A smell of burning oil floats back through the carriage, mingling with the scent of diapers and curry for what you might call a full gustatory banquet.

The train is doing little more than limping forward, and I check my phone again, worried. The trip across India was supposed to take a day, and because we lost a day on the *Wahash Mahat*, I was behind plan when I climbed into this machine from hell. At least we are moving forward. And I haven't had to put up with Dominic's relentless good cheer, so that's saying something. He's probably wallowing in air-conditioned luxury in his compartment.

I lean toward the window to try to catch whatever breeze is being generated by the slow motion of the train when I realize, with a pang of despair, the train is slowing down again. Half standing to look out the window, to my relief, I catch sight of what looks like a platform in the distance. I flop back into my seat and reach for my wallet. If it's a train station, at least there will be a chance of food. And perhaps there will even be a working engine waiting for us.

Across the aisle, the exhausted mother has awakened, though the baby is still mercifully asleep.

The woman gently slides herself over to the aisle seat. In the daylight, I can see the circles under her eyes. She looks like she could be my age, or maybe even younger. Nevertheless, had she not been up all night with her baby, I'm quite sure she would be startlingly beautiful. As things are, her face is tired and gorgeous.

"Auntie," she hisses, leaning out into the aisle between us. "Auntie— can you help me? I need . . ."

Her voice trails away as she nods vigorously toward the rear of the train carriage. I have a moment of raw panic thinking she's somehow been struck blind and mistaken me for one of her relatives, before the woman across the aisle lumbers to her feet, arms outstretched.

"I'll take her, *choti*. Give her to me."

The young woman jumps up to join her. When she smiles, all the exhaustion falls away, and I have to say, her beauty is breathtaking. White teeth gleam against her dusky skin, and the large gold ring in her nose catches a glint of reflected sunlight, dazzling me further.

"Thank you, Auntie. I need to use the toilet and call my husband. I will return immediately. A thousand thanks."

Stitching Lady makes a dismissive noise—*"Pfft"*—and waves the younger woman off. "It's no trouble," she says, having already nestled the still-sleeping baby in her arms. She settles into the seat beside me. "But bring me tea, will you?"

"Of course, Auntie," says the younger woman. "That was my plan all along. Forgive me for not mentioning it."

With a swirl of jeweled blue and gold, she's gone, hurrying toward the door marked "WC" at the back of the coach.

The baby makes an ominous little snuffle, but Stitching Lady exerts some kind of grandmotherly magic, and the baby cuddles in again.

It's only then I realize I'm effectively trapped in my seat by this sleeping child.

I, too, have a strong urge to visit the WC at the back of the train car, but don't want to risk waking the Child with Lungs of Celine Dion.

Stitching Lady, sensing my restlessness, gives me a calm smile. "She will not be gone long," she says, pitching her voice so low, I almost miss the comment under the screeching and clanking of the train.

I lean back in my seat and sigh. There's no way I'm going to be able to suggest this class of train service to Teresa Cipher's client. Rich people might claim to want the warts-and-all experience, but they also need an escape route back to luxury. I'll need to take a look into the first-class compartments to do a proper job of the report.

While the lady beside me croons under her breath to the sleeping child, I wriggle my laptop out from under the seat in front of me, balance it on the little half tray, and start typing.

"You're a journalist?" Stitching Lady says suddenly, startling me out of my focus.

She bobs her head at my screen.

"Ah—not really," I say, using my cuff to wipe away the sweat beading above my eyebrows. "I'm a . . ."

"Travel blogger?" she offers. "My nephew does that too. I'm meeting him in Calcutta because he wants a 'senior perspective' on the dining experience there."

This makes me laugh, and I clap my hand over my mouth, shooting a glance at the baby.

A pair of kohl-black eyes stare up at me from the folds of the blanket in the woman's lap.

"I'm so sorry—I didn't mean to wake her," I whisper, but the older lady shrugs.

"Her mother returns soon. So, what's so funny about me helping my nephew, hmm?"

Her expression doesn't change from one of pleasant interest, but I feel immediately that I have insulted her.

"Nothing—nothing. I'm more a photographer, actually. I put pictures on Instagram. Have you heard of it?"

"My nephew does that too. Blog and Insta and—Snapchat, yes?"

"Yes! You seem very well informed. My own uncle is a complete luddite. He's still got a flip phone."

The young mother walks up as my seatmate and I laugh together at my old-fashioned uncle.

She carries two cups of tea, which she sets down carefully on her own tray. At the first sight of her, the baby opens her mouth and howls.

Without a word of warning, my seatmate plops the baby into my arms. I'm not sure which of us is more shocked. The baby stops crying and stares at me with wide, frightened eyes. Her mouth falls open, but instead of resuming her cry, she hiccups gently and tries to stuff her whole fist in her mouth.

In the meantime, Stitching Lady, who is a woman of admirable dimensions, has undertaken the necessary actions required to pull herself upright. With the help of the young mother, she finally gets to her feet. Standing at last, she gives herself a little shake, and with a gentle tinkle, the bracelets on her arms and her sari and headscarf all settle neatly into place.

On my lap, the baby notes our seatmate's absence with alarm, and scrunches her wee face up as tight as a fist. There's no longer a sign of the round black eyes. All I can really see is a wide-open mouth: pink and toothless and strangely perfect. As she takes a deep breath, Stitching Lady reaches across the now empty aisle seat, and with another jangle of bracelets, scoops the baby from my arms and safely deposits her across the aisle. By the time I look up, the baby has vanished under her mother's sari, and the yelling has entirely stopped. One bare foot emerges from the folds of blue cloth, kicking contentedly.

"Thank you, Auntie," the young mother says, and then smiles over at me. "Thank you too."

I shake my head. "I didn't do anything. This lady handled it all," I say.

"Well, thank you for your patience. She's got a big voice already, my Rhupi. Would you like tea?"

She offers me the second cup, as the older woman has already started on the first.

I snap the lid closed on my computer. "Oh, no—I can't take your tea!" I say, horrified at the thought. "I need to go, uh . . ." I nod toward the rear of the train, not sure what the protocol is for the discussion of toilets with ladies in India.

If I was a travel blogger, I'd have all this in my mental knapsack. But, as I'm fairly certain the subject never came up in any of V. S. Naipaul's stories, I'm at a loss.

The older woman leans toward me. She's almost finished her cup of tea, and has not shown any sign of resuming her seat. "Go—go," she says, waving her cup recklessly. A few drops fly out and spatter the carpet as the train lurches into a long slow bend. "We are near the station, so you'd better hurry."

I don't need to be told twice. There's a lineup of two men before me, which is not a best-case scenario, but at least they both get the job done quickly. The teeth-grinding squeal of the train's brakes rings out as I finish flushing. By the time I've washed my hands, passengers are pouring out of the carriages onto the platform. I lean out the door to see a sign reading "Raipur." The station smells of spices and incense, and the air is so thick with moisture, it practically steams.

My heart sinks. Only Raipur? I have a strong recollection of the city being just halfway down the list of stops. The train conductor who checked my ticket earlier tries to squeeze past me onto the platform, but I reach in front of him to grab the handrail.

He shoots me an annoyed glance for blocking his way.

"Are we stopping here awhile?" I ask. "Can we transfer to a train that actually works?"

The annoyance on his face changes to puzzlement. "This train *works*, madam," he says, adding air quotes for emphasis. "It has got us to Raipur, has it not?"

I tighten my grip on the handrail, and the annoyance returns to his face. "Please remove your arm, madam. I need to check in with the stationmaster."

"Look," I say desperately. "We are already *so* late. I need to be in Kolkata, like, now. If there's no other train, will someone be fixing this engine so we can get there today?"

"Those matters are out of my control, madam," the conductor says stiffly. "I can tell you there are mechanics working on the engine as we speak, and we fully expect to be underway in the next quarter hour or so. Now, if you don't mind . . . ?"

Reluctantly, I release my grip on the handrail, and he vanishes into the teeming crowd on the station platform. Near the door to our train, a collection of ladies wearing jewel-colored saris sit in a loose, comfortable circle on the ground, chatting while they wait. After my experience in Chamonix, I'm loath to follow the conductor, having developed a deep distrust of the speed with which a train can exit a station. All the same, my short time in India leads me to believe I may have a little more notice before this train pulls out. And I'm most definitely hungry.

Further down the platform, I see my conductor muscling a new tea trolley onto one of the train cars, but with the number of people aboard, I know there's a good chance that nothing will remain by the time he makes it up to our car.

My stomach rumbles and makes the decision for me. I jump onto the modern-looking platform and aim myself toward a small girl with a large basket of plastic-wrapped items. She's handing them out and collecting money fast, her arms are a blur. By the time I push close enough to speak with her, only two items remain in her basket. I think they might be samosas, and my mouth spontaneously waters at the thought. The girl scoops up one of the remaining packets and hands it to a tall young man in a vivid yellow turban. He smiles at the girl as he turns away, and I can't help smiling back at him.

If I'd known the world held so many handsome guys, I might have gotten out of New York a little sooner, is all I'm saying.

I turn back to the girl to find a second handsome man has stepped in front of me. He has the last package in his hand.

"Hey," I say as he drops coins into the girl's hand. "That's mine! I was next—you can't take my samosa!"

Dominic turns and grins at me. "Too late," he says, tucking it into a pocket. "And it's a chapati, okay?" He places a hand on my shoulder, but I wrench out of his grip.

"That's really rude," I mutter. "That was supposed to be my breakfast."

His smile falters. "I was trying to point you toward that booth," he says. "They've got tea and sandwiches—and more chapatis, I'm sure."

I turn to see an elegant little kiosk set against the side of the station. From the silver samovars lined up on the counter, I surmise they have tea on tap.

I turn my back on Dominic and hurry over to join the queue. By the time I gain a spot in line, there's no longer any sign of him.

Good riddance. First he takes the last sleeping berth and then the last chapati? This has stepped beyond coincidence and into full-out warfare. I feel more determined than ever to win this thing.

By the time I reach the front of the line, the train is beginning to make suspicious rumbling noises. Fearful of missing it again, I snatch up an armful of plastic-wrapped food items of indeterminate provenance, along with the largest tea I can carry, and run for the train. By the time I work my way down to my seat, the train is clacketing its way down the tracks again, this time at a much more heartening rate of speed. Since I have arrived at my seat with more food than I can hope to eat myself, I offer some to the young mother, and to my seatmate, who both accept with large smiles.

As I reach across to deposit my teacup on the tiny half tray in front of my seat, I spot Dominic weaving his way down the car toward me. The older lady is showing signs of getting ready to haul herself to her feet, so I give her a quick smile and tell her to take her time and finish her chapati, as I need to go for a little walk. I quickly turn on my heel and work my way down toward the toilets at the back.

I can hide in there until he gets bored.

Unfortunately, there's once again a lineup at the unisex WC, and the toilet with the disabled symbol on the door boasts a large, hand-written "Out of Order" sign that appears to be Scotch-taped in place.

Dom squeezes past the people in the toilet queue and reaches out to me.

"Here—I wanted to make sure you didn't go hungry." He pushes a small packet into my hand.

I pull both hands back, letting the packet fall to the floor.

"I can look after myself, thank you."

As soon as the words are out of my mouth, I flash back to the train station in Mumbai, of course, and Priti's small hands, helping me up. I push the image of her kind face away and turn back toward my seat.

Behind me, I can hear Dominic's voice say something quietly, and then a much louder "Thank you, sah!" Ignoring all this, I walk back to my seat, hoping he will take the hint.

He does not.

"Look," I hiss, not wanting to disturb the baby, who is finally sleeping again. "It's perfectly clear you want to win this thing at any cost. I get that. But I do too. So you go on, putting yourself first. I'll make my own way. And we'll see who wins in the end."

His eyes widen, and for a minute he looks really hurt, before his face clouds over again.

"Me?" he splutters. "I'm not the one who's giving people handouts and labeling my photos "hashtag refugees." It might make *you* feel better, but that sort of white-savior thinking helps no one. I know this is a race. But this trip is also a chance to learn something—for both of us. We should be listening and watching. You need to check your privilege, not coast on it all the way back to New York."

"My privilege?" I can feel my face burning. "*What* privilege? I'm broke, my uncle's broke, and your evil boss is going to take what little we do have away. And if he doesn't, *you* will. How is *that* privileged?"

Too late, I realize I've forgotten to keep my voice down, and the baby begins to cry.

"You should leave," I say, pitching my voice lower. "We're done here."

Dominic bends toward the mother, and I hear him apologize. Without another word to me, he turns and walks off down the aisle.

I apologize to the young mother also, and to my own seatmate. As Dominic vanishes through the door at the end of the car, she rises to make room for me, and steps into the aisle.

Still fuming, I take my own seat.

I've never in my life been accused of benefitting from my race, which is what I think he's implying. Stuck in my seat as the train gathers speed, I can feel the fury bursting out of me.

"Privilege? How can he even say that? He doesn't know my life,"

I blurt to Stitching Lady, who has switched threads to a gentle shade of buttercup yellow.

She smiles at me. "You are on a journey together, you and your friend?"

I have to clench my teeth at this, in order not to frighten the baby. "He is *not* my friend," I hiss. "He's—he's . . ."

And I don't know if it's her grandmotherly vibe, or the fact that I've been alone too long, but before I know it, I've told her everything. The trip, my uncles, the bookshop, Frank Venal, and every single thing about Dominic. His betrayal of my family. His ongoing quest to beat me at every turn, including having a zillion more followers on social media. How unfair his accusations are. I tell her about my life in New York, the rainbow of friends and neighbors I have, the diverse choices I make when I read. All the times I have taken a stand against injustice, marched for change. How I only wanted to help Sumaya and her fellow travelers, and how hurt I was to not even get a chance to really say goodbye to her.

Everything.

In retrospect, I have to admit it's possible I went a teeny bit overboard. But I was provoked, okay?

By the time I finish, Stitching Lady has embroidered the entire bodice of a dress in tiny, delicate flowers. When I flop back into my seat, exhausted at this outpouring of emotion, she carefully folds her needle into a paper packet that she stows in her handbag.

"You say this man is not your friend. But it is our friends who tell us the difficult things. The things about ourselves that we may not want to hear. Our enemies do not try to help us in this way. This boy Dominic, he is African, yes?"

"Samoan," I blurt. "But only half. His dad was white."

Stitching Lady stifles a yawn. "All the same. He worries for his family too. He is a man, and he may see things differently, but he is speaking his truth to you. That's worth something, yes?"

And with this pronouncement, she rolls up her project and promptly falls asleep.

The train wheezes to a stop twice more before I'm all the way cooled down. When the conductor passes by after lunch, he confirms that while the train will arrive later than scheduled, three hours isn't that bad in the greater scheme of things. We had been due in around three, so our expected arrival should be half past six, or not much later, he insists.

When the old lady adjusts herself sideways in her seat, I slide by and go off to find Dominic. I'm not sure I agree with Stitching Lady's point, but I shouldn't have dropped the food he brought me on the floor. And he's right about the hashtag thing.

There are only six sleeper compartments on this train, which I know from trying, and failing, to book one. They are all in the first car, behind the engine, so I decide to head up there and apologize. No one answers my knock at the first three doors, but the fourth door is ajar, so I open it wider with one hand while tapping lightly with the other.

Inside, a table is set up with two glasses and a plate. The plate holds a crumple of foil wrap and a few crumbs, nothing more. A door to a tiny closet door is open, blocking my entrance. At the sound of my knock, a voice says: "Oh good, you're back. Did they have any more of the dal?"

The closet door closes, and I find myself staring in shock at the startled face of Sumaya.

chapter thirty-eight

IMAGE: Yellow Rik
IG: Romy_K [Howrah, India, April 15]
#KolkataBound #AChangeofPlan
350 ♥

The door swings closed behind me, and, on shock-induced auto-pilot, I shuffle to one side as Dominic brushes past. He's carrying a small tinfoil package in one hand and a spoon in the other.

"I thought I told you not to let anyone in," he whispers to her, but she shrugs.

"It's only Romy."

"*This* time. But if the conductor sees you, he could put you off the train. You *know* that, Sumaya. We've talked about it."

Feeling incapable of speech, I look from her face, which bears the slightly sullen expression teenagers from time immemorial wear whenever under scrutiny, to his, which looks mostly worried. Maybe a little defensive, actually, the longer I stare at him.

"What—are you doing here?" I whisper to her. "Are all the others here too?"

Sumaya shakes her head, and her lower lip protrudes a fraction.

"I'm going to find my auntie," she says. "Dominic is helping me."

I whirl to look at him. "What *the hell* are you thinking?"

"Look, you need to keep your voice down," he says quietly. "Why are you even here? I thought you were done with me."

"I—came to apologize," I mutter. "I mean, about the food thing, and anyway—*never mind* what I'm doing here! That's no longer the issue."

The berth is not exactly roomy, and by the time I'm finished speaking, I realize I've got one of my fingers pointed right in his face.

"I think maybe we need to sit down," says Dominic. "Let me double-check the lock." He hands the package and spoon over to Sumaya, whose face lights up, animosity forgotten. I sit down beside her as she peels the foil off the top and starts in on the contents.

Dominic slides into the bench seat across from us, and while Sumaya happily eats her snack, he starts to talk.

The story is not long. It boils down to Dominic helping Sumaya climb through a washroom window behind the customs office at the docks in Mumbai, while the captain was busy shepherding the rest of the refugees into the custody of immigration authorities. Sumaya's goal has always been to find her auntie, who escaped Somalia when she was tiny, and whom she believes is making her living as a hairdresser in Hong Kong.

While Dominic is clearly worried about getting caught, "I'm helping to get her to Hong Kong," he says defiantly.

"Don't be angry at Dom," interjects Sumaya, having expertly cleaned out her bowl with one finger. "It's on me. I talked him into it on the little boat ride over to the docks. Even the duffel bag was my idea."

"He is a grown man," I say sharply, and regret it instantly, when she cringes away from me.

"I only mean—none of this is your fault," I mutter. "You're just a kid."

"Which is why this is happening," says Dominic. "It's April fifteenth already. I've got almost no chance of making it back to New York on time. Since everything else on this fucking wild goose chase has been a fail, maybe one good thing can come out of it."

"Don't swear," blurts Sumaya, and then turns to me. "Are you going to tell the conductor?"

The moment of silence that follows her question feels like an eternity. An eternity where Old Romy and New Romy wrestle for supremacy—each with her own valid arguments and a strong will to live. Organization versus spontaneity. Status quo versus the great unknown. Fright versus right. There can be only one winner.

Old Romy takes a shuddering, final breath, and dies on the floor.

"Of course I'm not," I say, at last. "But let's go over the rest of your plan."

B y the time the train finally crawls into Howrah, we have the narrowest bones of a plan in place, and I'm back in my seat. Most of the travelers swing themselves off the creaking cars before they even grind to a halt at the station. Stitching Lady, whose name turns out to be Mrs. Gupta, wishes me well on my journey, as she collects up her travel bag.

"You have undertaken a great deal," she says. "I hope you find a way to enjoy it while it is happening."

This gives me pause. "How do I do that?" I blurt. "Every time I blink my eyes, something new is in front of me."

She chuckles, a low rumble deep in her chest. "This is true. But what you must do is settle on one thing. One thing you can see. One point of beauty, and focus on that."

"I'll do my best," I say, and thinking of Sumaya, manage a smile.

"I will make an offering to Ganapati for you, Ramona," she replies, patting my shoulder kindly. "I pray that he may remove all obstacles in your path."

And with that, she is gone.

I stuff my daypack into my much emptier suitcase and hurry out onto the station platform to look for a tall man carrying a large duffel bag.

Since this isn't a border crossing—at least not yet—things actually unfold pretty smoothly. Once we're out of the station, Sumaya climbs out of her hiding place and the three of us go in search of a good internet connection. Howrah turns out to be a fairly industrialized city, with the railway station just across the bridge from Kolkata.

In the time it takes me to reserve passage on a ship crossing the South China Sea from Haldia to Hong Kong, Dominic and Sumaya have found a taxi driver willing to take us across the river to Kolkata. We have a worrisome amount of distance to cover, but I can't see any alternative. Phileas Fogg took a steamer from Calcutta, so I book one for us too and hope for the best.

The taxi turns out to be a rik, the local name for the three-wheeled motorized rickshaws. This one makes the little yellow machines buzzing through the streets of Mumbai look like high technology. It's a three-wheeled, World War II–era motorcycle, with a torn canvas roof soldered onto what looks like a buggy in the back. It's designed to carry two passengers, but my time dodging over-loaded motorbikes in the streets of Mumbai was not for nothing. Dominic and I pile our luggage on the roof, squeeze Sumaya onto our laps in the back, and go.

A s we travel through the steaming heat, Sumaya dangles off the side, taking shots of the city on my camera phone. Dominic takes advantage of her distraction to confess in my ear that initially, back at the docks in Mumbai, he'd only planned to help her out the window.

"But once she was out—I couldn't leave her," he mutters.

I have a sudden memory of our awkward interactions on the train—when he took the last chapati, and later when I let his peace offering drop to the floor. At this moment, Sumaya swings back inside and lands in my lap, eager to show us the shot she's taken of the Howrah Bridge, currently lit up in vivid purple. She weighs so little, I have to swallow hard to keep from crying.

"You did the right thing," I whisper back to him. "Our plan is going to work."

Kolkata—known during the British Raj as Calcutta, and changed back officially in 2001—is home to India's oldest and largest river port. West Bengal state abuts Bangladesh, and Kolkata, its largest city, is connected to the region's biggest seaport, Haldia, by the Hooghly River. And our new little team? We make it all the way to the dockside before things begin to go wrong.

chapter thirty-nine

Plan to reconnect Sumaya with her auntie in Hong Kong:

1. R departs train by myself, while D & S get off the same way they got on, using Ganesh's old duffel bag.

2. Turns out Ganesh has been in on this with Sumaya all along, or at least since she confessed her plans to him on the Wahash Mahat. This kid might be the most persuasive individual I've ever met. And Ganesh? Has the world's best poker face.

3. Once train departure is effected, find local travel agent who speaks English. Failing that, go online, book fares on fastest container ship to Hong Kong available.

4. Once tickets secured, hire taxi or rik to transport us to correct dock. If ship sailing requires overnight stay, find a place on travel agent's recommendation, and take taxi there.

5. On boarding, check suitcases and packs, and carry duffel as hand luggage.

6. Long shot: If all the wheels fall off at any point, text Ganesh via WhatsApp. He has connections in Kolkata.

Kolkata is our last Verne-related checkpoint on the subcontinent. I've been plagued by a deep feeling of anxiety since we left the train in Howrah. The rik is so cramped, and it's not like we don't stand out at all.

Slightly sunburned white woman, crammed in with skinny Somalian girl and a mocha-colored, scruffily bearded young man, who is head and shoulders taller than anyone we've met so far. And it doesn't help that Sumaya is wearing the clothes she came off the boat in—a cotton dress printed in vivid red, yellow, and orange stripes. The colors have faded substantially from the sun and salt water, but they still pop against her smooth dark skin. I rarely saw her wear a headscarf on the *Wahash Mahat*, but Dominic must have picked one up for her at one of the train stops. She's had it on all day, but it, too, is in vivid yellow and orange—this time a floral pattern. Crammed into the rik, where Dom and I are basically sitting underneath our stowaway, it feels as though everyone we pass drops what they are doing to stare at us.

Thankfully, the drive is fairly quick. Shortly after crossing the bridge, the driver drops us outside a shipping company office near the Kidderpore Docks. I hustle Sumaya into the shadows while Dom lines up to collect our tickets. We fought over this in the rik already— who will stay with Sumaya and who will line up. Dominic was adamant that he was the least obtrusive choice to stand in line, but looking over at him, standing a full head and shoulders above anyone else in line, he's just wrong.

I create a little wall using my suitcase and Dominic's pack around her, but Sumaya keeps popping up to look at the sights. Just as she's about to scoop up a skinny stray kitten from the dockside, a man in a white uniform walks around the corner. He looks like he could be navy or police.

I hurriedly fasten my scarf over my hair, and turn my back, but it's too late. Worse, it's not a police uniform. I can clearly read the word "Customs" on the blue lanyard around his neck.

The man peers from my face to Sumaya's and back again, all the while slowly drawing a coil notebook—which, strangely enough, reminds me of Sumaya's stand-up notes—out of his front pocket.

"Kaagzaat," he barks, his eyes still beetling back and forth between the two of us.

I give Sumaya a little shove back, and step in front of her, holding out my American passport. "I'm afraid I only speak English, sir," I say, and hate myself for the quaver I hear in my voice. I clear my throat and try again. "We're picking up our tickets for Hong Kong."

I shove the passport into his hand. "Americans," I say more firmly.

"Thank you very much, madam," the policeman says, segueing easily into English. His head bobs gently side to side as he examines my passport. "This seems to be in order," he says, and unexpectedly smiles. His skin is dark, and the flash of his teeth is disarming. I can feel my shoulders relax.

"Everything okay here?" Dominic's voice sounds worried as he walks over.

Desperation grips me, and I slide my arm into his and pull him close. "Hi, honey," I say brightly. "Yes, we were telling this nice officer how we're off to Hong Kong in a couple of hours."

Dominic looks anxious, but he plasters on a smile too as he fans out the ship tickets to show the officer.

"All very good, very good," the officer says, tucking his notebook back in his pocket. "Now I need to see the girl's passport, and yours too, sir."

I feel him stiffen beside me, but Dominic digs out his own passport, and hands it over silently. The officer flips through it and hands it back without even really looking at it. "And the girl's?" he says, his voice taking on an oily quality I don't like at all.

"She's—she's our niece," blurts Dominic. "In America, minors can travel on their guardian's passport."

Behind the officer, I can see the whites of Sumaya's eyes widen in the shadows. Not even a fourteen-year-old buys this excuse. I see her take a cautious step sideways, to free herself of the danger of Dominic's backpack straps, and realize with a sudden jolt of fear that she's going to make a run for it.

Which is exactly what happens.

And which is how she ends up dangling by the elbows from the arms of two substantially burlier officers who step out of the alley behind us.

So it is that while Dominic follows the men, who turn out to be immigration officers, to plead Sumaya's case, I dash into the nearby customs building, clutching Ganesh's card. And while I have no Bengali, the clerk, after a long discussion with Ganesh—and apparently the ship's captain—over the telephone, agrees to issue Sumaya some kind of a refugee travel document.

"This is valid only on the condition of her departure from the country," he says to me. "We cannot, of course, guarantee the reception of the refugee in the receiving country, and she will be refused reentry to India."

After I show him our tickets on the ship, he stamps the form at last, before escorting me out the door. "Your ship departs in less than an hour," he says pointedly. "Make sure you are on it."

He flicks out the light switch and locks the door behind us.

Dashing back to the place Sumaya and Dominic disappeared into earlier, I find what essentially looks like a lock-up in every Western movie I've ever seen. With a Bengali in the role of sheriff.

The man sits at a desk in front of a jail cell with iron bars cemented in place from floor to ceiling. There are five plastic chairs—all empty—neatly lined up in a row, facing the desk. The sight of the cell reminds me of my experience in Port Said, and it takes all my strength of will to march through the door into the room.

Spotting Sumaya standing inside the cell does the trick, though I'm startled to see Dominic sitting inside with her, instead of in the waiting area. I can't ask him why, however, as when I enter the room, I discover the incarceration cell is behind a wall of presumably bulletproof Perspex.

Just as well I hadn't tried to blast them out.

When I approach the desk, the seated man gestures with his pen at the LED lights on the wall, which spell out the number 142. He then redirects his pen, pointing toward a ticket dispenser by the door. I hurry back to collect a ticket, only to find my number is 143. I race back to the desk and place Sumaya's document in front of him.

"I'm here to collect the girl, Sumaya Warsame?"

Without meeting my eye, the man reaches into his desk drawer and begins to fill out a double-sided long form.

Several times during this ponderous process, I reach across the desk to point out the departure time on our tickets, but my pleas for speed do not affect his form-filling rate in the slightest. When he finally comes to the end of the second side of the form, he stamps it with the date and signs his name, before sliding it back across the desk, along with Sumaya's travel document. I snatch them both up, and move over to stand by the door of the cell, only to see the man pull a second form out of his desk. From another drawer, he retrieves what is clearly Dominic's passport, and then begins anew the agonizing, laborious project of completing the second form.

Twenty endless minutes later, the three of us are running down the pier toward the assigned berth of our Hong Kong steamer. It's full dark outside, of course, but the pier is lit with sodium bulbs that cast a vivid orange glow along the entire length. A pair of seaplanes are moored to one side, bobbing in the river's current, while two or three wiry old geezers, all stripped to the waist, load goods into the back of one of the planes. It must have rained while we were inside, as the pier is peppered with large puddles, and the air smells like wet rope and seaweed, with a trace of cigarette smoke from the old guys.

As we run, Sumaya, who was apparently not at all bothered by her jail experience, tells me how she spent most of the time testing out new stand-up material on the burly guards.

"Do you speak Bengali?" I gasp, as we take the last corner.

"No. But Dom laughed, so the guards knew it was funny, and they laughed too."

Suddenly, a loud low tone fills the air. We hurtle up the dock to see the steamer is already more than a hundred yards into the shipping channel. Skidding to a stop, we reach the gangway as the ship's horn sounds again—a final, irreversible indicator that we have indeed, missed the boat.

chapter forty

IMAGE: Street Vendor
IG: Romy_K [Kolkata, India, April 15]
#MissedtheBoat #GoingAirborne
401 ♥

After a panicky discussion dockside, we can't come to an agreement. Dom argues for hiring a motorboat to overtake the ship, but I'm too worried it won't see us in the dark. And what if we go to the expense and it doesn't stop for us? In the end, we decide to head back to the place the rik driver dropped us, as Sumaya insists she spotted a hotel sign in English on the street. Around us, the street vendors are packing up their wares. Bananas, gold bangles, and knock-off sneakers are all being carefully packed into boxes. As we reach the corner of the pier, I agree to at least look into Dominic's idea, so we pause under the lights to examine the map on my phone.

It's a long way to Hong Kong.

The marina office is further along the pier, in the opposite direction of the street, so we agree to split up and meet in thirty minutes. Dominic trots off toward the marina office, and Sumaya and I head in the direction of the possible hotel.

We've only gone maybe three steps when a voice comes out of the darkness.

"Hong Kong, did yah say?"

The voice belongs to one of the men we'd run by earlier. He is quite possibly the tiniest, wiriest man I've ever met. His skin is brown as a nut, and his face gnarls up like a dried apple as he draws on a cigarette.

Sumaya and I listen silently as he speaks. And truthfully? While what he says scares the shit out of me, it just might be a solution to our problem.

Ten minutes later, the sound of footsteps running along the pier coalesces into the shape of Dominic. He slows as he sees us, still standing almost exactly where he left us, and his face is puzzled as he hurries up.

"No luck. The marina office is closed," he says, panting a little. "But it opens really early. We can head over there first thing in the morning. Did you find us a place to stay?"

"We didn't look," I admit. My heart is pounding, and I'm not sure if it's from the absurdity of our possible new plan, or the simple fear that saying it aloud will make it real.

"I have—another idea."

"A *better* idea," adds Sumaya, eyes gleaming in the darkness.

There's a clanking sound followed by a low rumble behind us, and the small man steps off the plane's float and back into the puddle of orange light on the pier.

"All preflight checks complete," he says, lighting a fresh cigarette from the stub of his old one. "Ready to take your gear on board."

"Our gear on board?" repeats Dominic faintly.

"Dominic, this is Klahan Wattana. He's a pilot from . . ."

"Thailand," offers Wattana. He reaches out a hand and Dominic shakes it. "Been a pilot since I was with the marines in the war."

"He's about to depart on his regular flight to Hong Kong," I add.

"In a *plane*," says Sumaya, directing a beaming smile up at him. "Like a *real plane*, Dom!"

"Can I—ah—talk to you for a minute, Romy?" Dominic says, and I follow him a few steps to the right. This takes us out of the puddle of light from the streetlamp. Behind us, I see Sumaya handing my suitcase over to Klahan Wattana, who hoists it into the back of the plane.

"A pilot since he was in the war?" hisses Dominic. "*What* war?"

"I—ah—didn't ask him that," I say. "But I saw his paperwork. It looks legit. *And* he's not worried about bringing Sumaya. In fact, he says it will be easier for us, since he's landing at a private airstrip."

Dominic waves his hand wildly in the direction of the plane, which is now fully lit up with lights on both wings.

"Even so—he's an *airplane* pilot. Isn't that against the rules?"

Strangely enough, having to defend my idea is making me more enthusiastic.

Or, at least a bit less scared.

"Look," I say firmly. "He makes a regular monthly flight to Hong Kong. The plane is not a commercial aircraft, okay? His specialty is flying seafood back and forth across Malaysia, but he says he's modified the plane to take passengers. And he'll take us right now, Dom. Instead of a week, we can be in Hong Kong in a matter of hours."

"Holy shit," he says quietly, and then glances over his shoulder. "All the way in that little plane?"

"Yes. It's a pontoon plane, modified from"—I pause to check the flyer Klahan handed me earlier—"an old Canadian Beaver. It was a bush plane, so not as many comforts as a commercial jet, but it'll get us there."

For the first time, Dominic snickers. "Really? A Canadian bush plane?" He holds out a hand and I give him the flyer, which describes the services offered by Klahan's company in English, Bengali, and what might be Cantonese. He glances over it and then nods his approval. "Seems legit."

"Not much different than your helicopter, really. And Teresa didn't say *no* planes at all, right?"

"You have a *helicopter*?" Sumaya says to Dominic as she walks up. "I've always wanted to ride in a helicopter!"

"It wasn't his," I say to her shortly. I can't help feeling disappointed that Dominic is not more impressed with my success. "We hitched a ride in one before we met you. Are you in, Dominic? He says he's ready to leave."

Dominic steps back into the lamplight, pausing to look from my face to Sumaya's and back.

"Are you sure about this?" he mutters. Behind him, I see Klahan step across from the edge of the dock onto the pontoon of his plane.

"Yes. No. I don't know." I stare up at him. "It's only—he's here. It'll get us there faster. And . . ."

"And I think it's a brilliant idea," adds Sumaya. "By this time tomorrow, I could be with Auntie Nkruna."

Dominic takes a big shaky breath, and then puts a hand on Sumaya's shoulder.

"Let's go," he says. "Before I change my mind."

I feel a little less sure of things myself as Klahan helps the three of us into the back of the plane.

"Is that—duct tape?" I say, pointing to a silver patch on the inside of the door.

Klahan shrugs. "It inside door. Don't matter so much on inside." He slaps the fuselage of the plane fondly as Sumaya clambers up the fold-out steps. "This old gal strong as ox."

"I hope so," I say, climbing over my suitcase to reach the seats. "I really hope so."

Sumaya practically levitates through to her own seat, her face alight with excitement. *"Ammaanta Allah!* We get to *fly!"*

She holds up the ends of the seatbelt.

"Peace be on his name," says Dominic, absently, as he shows her how to clip the seatbelt in place. He hands her his earphones, which she immediately places right over her hijab.

"And luck on ours," he whispers to me. "Are you sure this thing is actually airworthy?"

"You doubt me?" says Klahan, appearing out of nowhere. His voice is low—different than before. Growly. "You doubt my plane? My angel?"

"No, no . . ." begins Dom, lifting his hands placatingly. "It's only . . ."

"YOU DOUBT ME?" yells Klahan. A little saliva flies onto Dominic's face.

Dominic, thoroughly alarmed, leans back. "No, man, it's . . ."

"Good!" says Klahan, suddenly grinning. He reaches with one thumb and wipes the drop of spittle off Dom's forehead. "'Cos that would be cray-zee."

He pulls the door closed, then pushes past Dominic and swings himself into the pilot's seat.

Dom looks at me, the whites showing all the way around his irises. *You sure about this?* he mouths.

The engine revs, loud and long, drowning out any possibility of a reply. I give up trying to talk, shoot Dom a tremulous smile, and strap myself into a seat beside Sumaya. She is still beaming all over her face, having missed the little exchange, and bopping to whatever is coming through Dom's earphones instead.

Dom is still trying to find the buckle side of his seatbelt when the little plane starts to taxi. In seconds, we're hurtling along the water, bouncing so much as we hit each wave in the river that I'm convinced we'll never make it in one piece, when suddenly—the plane is airborne.

"WHOO-hoo!" shrieks Sumaya, throwing her arms in the air.

And we're on our way.

chapter forty-one

Klahan handles the plane as if he was born in a pilot's seat, which boosts my confidence long enough to get us in the air, at least. Maybe takeoffs are always this bumpy in a small plane? But even after we burst through the grey mass of cloud, the plane never seems to settle, trying its best to rattle my teeth right out of my head. It's far too noisy to talk, so I plug in my earbuds and scroll through the playlist on my phone. According to the screen, it's after midnight Kolkata time. Exhaustion hits me like a truck, but with the shaking of this tiny plane, there's no way I'll be able to sleep.

When I can't sleep at home, I generally find that something orchestral does the trick, but at the moment, all I can find for some reason is Wagner. Since it already feels like we are living through the "Ride of the Valkyries," I give up and switch it off.

The thing about flying, I am learning, is there is room for a certain clarity of thought. I pull my notebook out of my daypack and uncap my pen.

Things considered while flying over the Bay of Bengal:

1. No one stamped my passport when I collected Sumaya and Dom. Why?

2. Speaking of Dominic . . .

3. Point #2 is evidence of the fact that I don't know how to put my thoughts on this man into words.

4. I think he might be growing on me. I refuse to commit to more than that.

5. Something has happened since Sumaya entered the picture. All I can see is his obvious concern for her, and his kindness. It's given me a better look at who he is.

6. Maybe at who I am too?

7. I whispered #6 when I wrote it out, mostly because I remembered what Mrs. Gupta said on the train. Man, that lady could stitch.

8. In any case, once Sumaya is safely with her auntie in Hong Kong, we can flip the switch back into competition mode.

9. After all, this flight is knocking a ton of time off our journey. Suddenly, meeting Teresa Cipher's deadline for the ExLibris position seems—well, not assured, but back within the realm of possibility.

10. Yep. Point #2 notwithstanding, after Hong Kong, all bets are off.

Sometime after we've been in midair for an eternity or two, Klahan waves at us and snaps his fingers. Dom's brows draw together at this, and as he staggers forward, I have a moment to wonder how often Frank Venal summons him in a similar manner. After a moment he's back, and kneels beside me to tell me that Klahan is planning to refuel in Singapore.

"I thought we were flying direct," I say, when the plane gives a giant buck, and Dom's head smacks hard against the metal ceiling of the cabin.

"You okay?" I shout as he drops into his seat and scrabbles around for his belt.

Safely buckled in, Dom smiles. "Luckily I have a hard head," he says ruefully. "But I did bite my tongue."

One wing dips suddenly, and all the saliva dries up in my mouth. Dom reaches over and pats one of my knees.

"Everything okay up there?" he bellows at Klahan.

"No worry—all good," Klahan yells back as the plane shudders again. "We fly over little cyclone. Few air bumps."

Little cyclone? Dom mouths at me.

I swallow hard and glance from him to Sumaya. Her eyes are glued to the window and she's beaming.

No worries there, for sure.

The plane goes through a series of quick lurches, the air beneath us suddenly feeling as if it is made from corduroy, and I clutch both the armrests with a death grip. The act of grabbing the left armrest means I knock Dominic's elbow off, and I can feel his gaze turn to me.

"You okay?" he asks as the plane makes a substantial dip.

It takes a minute for my stomach to catch up to the rest of my body, which so preoccupies me that I don't answer.

The plane's engines rev and we swoop back upwards again. My head bobs, along with all the parts of me that aren't strapped to the seat as the plane shimmies violently. The only other flight I've ever taken—north to Canada for a carnival held in the dead of winter—

had been perfectly smooth, in both directions. Even so, I spent the entire flight with my face buried in my teacher's shoulder.

I find myself wishing I had taken that coaster ride in Coney Island all those years ago, just to have some basis for comparison.

The plane drops again and my stomach gives a tight, painful roll along with it.

"Pretty bad turbulence," says Dom, and awkwardly pats my arm. "Hopefully it'll be over soon."

"Don't say that!" I hiss, and look around desperately. "Find some wood to knock on. Look—touch this, it's paper. That's a wood product."

"What are you talking about?" says Dom, looking baffled as I grab one of his hands and rub it against a small white paper bag peeking out of the seat pocket.

"For luck," I say. "Or—to undo any bad luck from what you said. Touch wood."

"I hope it will be over soon," he repeats, looking puzzled. "What are you—? Oh." His face clears. "Well, of course, I didn't mean . . ."

The plane hits another air pocket, cutting him off.

"See?" I grab the paper out of the pocket and thrust it at him.

"I'm not clear how touching a barf bag is going to bring us better luck," he says, waving it at me.

I recoil in horror. "A barf bag? What do you mean a *barf* bag? I thought it was just an ordinary paper bag."

"Nope." He unfolds the bag and mimes throwing up into it, before refolding and holding it out to me.

I pull both hands away. "I'm not touching that," I mutter.

This makes him laugh out loud. "No one's used it," he begins as the plane lurches again. "At least, not yet."

In the row ahead of us, Sumaya gives a little whoop.

"She's not worried at all," I whisper to Dominic, who smiles almost proudly.

"She's freakin' fantastic," he says. "I'm beginning to think there's nothing she can't do."

The plane gives a little sideways shudder, and the left wing dips enough that I'm flung toward Dominic, jamming my shoulder into his.

"Almost past cyclone," Klahan yells from the front. "Ten minute—maybe fifteen."

"Fifteen minutes?" I mutter. My mouth has gone so dry I'm having trouble swallowing. "It already feels like a lifetime."

And then I grab the barf bag myself, appalled at my own choice of words.

Dom unplugs his other earphone, and reaches out a hand. "Want to hold on?" he says.

I don't hesitate a moment.

"Whoa—that's quite the grip you've got there," he mutters.

"Sorry," I say, but I can't really bring myself to loosen my hold.

He pats the back of my hand. "Okay, time to go to your happy place," he says, and I shoot him a glare. My eyes feel dry and hot, mostly because I think I might be too scared to blink.

"That's not what I meant, goofball," he says gently. "Tell me about your favorite place. Where do you go in your head to feel, you know, truly happy?"

The plane shudders, and I reach over and grab his other hand. It's possible that I'm too scared to actually speak.

As if he senses this—and how could he not, with me crushing his hands?—he leans forward, his warm thumbs running over the backs of my cold fingers.

"I'll start," he says. "My happy place is—well, I was going to say the Crooked Gent, at the end of a long day, with a cold beer in my hand. But I'm not sure that's true."

"What—where's the Crooked Gent?" I manage, the words feeling whispery and weird as they cross my dry tongue.

"Soho," he replies, and the worried creases around his eyes relax a little. "It's the front-of-house bar for the place I've been working lately. After a long day pounding pizza dough in a roasting kitchen—man, that cold beer goes down really easy."

He gives me an encouraging smile. "Your turn."

I shake my head. "No. You said you weren't sure that was it. What's better than the cold beer?"

"Nothing," he says. "At least, nothing in that moment. But you're right, I did say that. I guess the place I think about before I go to sleep is my mom's kitchen, actually."

"Your mom's kitchen? Why is it special?"

His eyes take on a faraway look. "I'm not really sure. I think—maybe 'cause that's where she taught me to bake? Sunday mornings, setting the bread to rise before church. None of the other kids there. I had her all to myself."

He focuses back on me. "Okay, now it really is your turn. Where's your . . ."

"The bookshop," I say before he can even finish. "I mean, I do have to go to the library once in a while, when things get really bad, but the place I'm happiest is in the bookshop, no question."

"The bookshop—okay. But when? At night, when everybody's gone home?"

I shake my head. "I do like the quiet at night, for sure. There's nothing like the smell of old books, right? My favorite time is when it's filled with people, though. Tommy's knitting club on Tuesday nights. All these old guys—and two women—each working on their own little projects. They talk about what they read that week, and maybe who's come out lately, and what's the hottest ticket at the Tribeca Film Fest or whatever. Just—it's so safe, and comfortable."

Dom traces his thumb along the back of my hand. "So Uncle Tommy is a knitter, huh? Can you knit?"

I shake my head. "I get caught up in the conversation and forget to count my stitches. The best I've ever managed was a super-long scarf so I could walk around my high school looking like the fourth Doctor Who."

"That doesn't sound like anything to sneeze at."

"Heh. Didn't meet Tommy's standard, though."

Dom leans back in his seat, and I realize that while the plane has completely steadied out, he's still idly holding one of my hands. And suddenly, I'm in no hurry to have it back.

"Sounds to me like Tommy can be a little hard on you."

"Yeah," I say, thinking of all the times something I've done has come up short in his eyes. "But—the knitting is a good example. He taught me when I was like, fifteen, and that takes patience. And okay, so I've never managed to knit a whole sweater, or even a decent pair of socks, but he always invites me to the circle. Every week."

"Do you go?"

"Hardly ever. But, maybe I will more, now. Now that I've realized it's my happy place."

I make the mistake of grinning at him, and right about then, the engine starts to make a weird surging sound.

Dom and I both instinctively look up at the cockpit, where Klahan is flipping a lot of switches. As if he feels our eyes on him, he glances back over his shoulder. The crazed look from earlier is gone, replaced with a calm, steely-eyed gaze.

"Small change of plans," he yells back at us. "Strap in."

At this point everything happens so fast—so very fast—it's really hard to keep track. Klahan quits responding entirely, so that I'm not even sure he hears me yell that we haven't ever *not* been strapped in, and is there any way to strap in further?

Dominic pats the back of my hand after I say this and I clam up, determined not to worry Sumaya. We're heading down so fast that I'm pretty sure my hair is being blown straight back off my face, but this might only be my imagination.

When the plane breaks through the clouds at last, the first streaks of pink dawn light the sky, and the ground beneath us appears startlingly close. Even Dominic is looking a little tense around the eyes by this time, and when Klahan executes a turn as tight as one of Tommy's hairpins, I swear that Dom lets out a little squeak.

Which he tries to cover with a cough.

Below us, a lush verdant landscape rushes closer. To the south, the enormous city-state of Singapore spreads across an entire island, but we appear to be heading away from it. Out front, a stretch of bright lights appear. A sudden recollection makes me clutch Dom's arm.

"There's no water," I yell at him. "We need water to land!"

Klahan must have heard me, because he shoots a glance over one shoulder.

"Dere's wheels under the pontoons," he yells back at me. "Here we go!"

With a final stomach-departing dip, the plane careens briefly over what looks like far too short a stretch of tarmac. Three endless, lurching bounces later, the wheels finally contact the earth and stay down. Sumaya—who has taken to flying as if she does it every week—cheers lustily at the landing.

Klahan veers the plane off to one side of the runway and lurches to a stop. I peer out the window, but we are nowhere near any buildings. Before I can even formulate a question, he's bounded out of his seat and flung open the door.

"Sit tight," he yells, and then scampers down the stairs.

Sumaya's head pops up over the seat in front of us. "That was brilliant," she says, her smile lighting up her face. "I think maybe I've changed my mind about what I want to do when I'm older. Do you think pilots ever do stand-up?"

Before either of us can begin to formulate an answer to this, Klahan is back. He brandishes a flat sheet of metal, maybe three feet long. It looks like it was originally painted white, but now has rusted around the edges.

"Wing flap," he says succinctly, then points at our seatbelts. "Stay buckle. We need to taxi."

With that, he hops into his seat, revs the engines once, and careens back onto the runway, yelling at someone the whole time over his radio.

Five minutes later, the plane is safely berthed beside a large metal hut bearing a sign that reads "Seletar Airport: Cargo." I can't get out of my seat fast enough, but Dominic still beats me outside.

Then he reaches up a hand to help me down from the plane.

As my feet hit the ground, he picks me up and twirls me around. "Holy shit, I'm glad that's over," he whispers as he sets me down again.

I'm about to reply, when his lips are on mine, and whatever I was going to say is suddenly gone. Instead, I tighten my arms around his neck and kiss him right back.

After a moment that lasts long enough for me to ask myself why I don't do this kissing thing more often, there's a loud throat-clearing noise behind us. We spring apart to find Sumaya rolling her eyes and holding out my suitcase.

"Am I the only one doing all the work around here?"

"No—no," says Dom, and snatches both bags from her arms. "Just—ah—happy to be here," he mutters.

She grins at him and grabs her own small bag back. "Yours is still *inside*," she says, nodding at the open door of the plane. Not looking at either of us, he hurries away.

"Whoo!" I say, my voice coming out louder than I intended. "That was quite the landing, eh? So glad to be safely on the ground!"

Sumaya chuckles. "I can see that," she says, and spreads her arms wide. "What? No kiss for me?"

I stare at her awkwardly for a moment before lurching forward, but when I get close, she folds her arms and steps away. Laughing loudly at her own wit, she marches toward the low hut.

Dominic reappears, this time carrying his own pack. I follow him inside, desperately hoping my face isn't as red as the back of his neck.

He is the first to break the awkward silence while we wait for Sumaya, who has been pulled into the customs office first. When I tried to follow, the door was firmly closed in my face.

"I wonder if—uh—maybe we should try to get a train or something the rest of the way to Hong Kong?" he mutters. "No offense to your pilot, or anything, but it's possible he's insane."

"I think you might be right," I whisper back. "And even if he's not, he never had us clear customs in Kolkata. Is that even legal?"

On the other side of the glass door, I can see the female customs officer nodding gravely as Sumaya speaks. She reaches out and collects the document we picked up in India, and I feel my stomach

clench a little. The man in Kolkata had said there were no guaran-
tees as to the laws of other countries. What if she's denied entry? I
have no idea what the status of refugees is in Singapore.

"What if . . ." I say to Dominic, but stop myself, as he's typing
away into his phone.

"I got into the Wi-Fi," he says, not looking up. "Checking for
train tickets from here to Hong Kong. *What if* what?"

"Nothing," I mutter. The woman talking with Sumaya looks up
and gestures at me imperiously through the glass door. "Gotta go."

As I walk through the door, Sumaya turns and holds up her
hands. Both her index fingertips are blue. "You are guardian?" says
the woman, her tone severe.

I tidy my hair behind my ears as best I can, and nod. "Good," she
says, and slides a document across the desk toward me. "Sign here,
please."

I scan the document hurriedly. It's an immigration document in
English, Chinese, and another language I don't recognize—possibly
Tamil? The whole thing is in black ink, apart from the line:

WARNING
DEATH FOR DRUG TRAFFIKERS
UNDER SINGAPORE LAW

. . . which is printed in bright red.

The woman taps the paper impatiently. "Is approval to finger-
print your charge. We check against the list."

"Okay . . ." I say as I start to sign. "But haven't you already finger-
printed her? And what list?"

Before I've finished, the woman whips the form out from under
my pen, and marches from the room.

Sumaya's eyes are round. "So—no one shares the same pattern?" she asks, holding up one finger. "Let me see yours."

As she scrutinizes my finger, I marvel at a world where this Somali girl can aspire to be a stand-up comic like the ones she's seen on YouTube, and yet has never heard of fingerprints.

Moments later, the customs officer is back.

"Not allowed," she says, pointing at Sumaya. Then she turns to me with her hand out. "Passport?"

"Just a minute," I say. I've been clutching my passport the whole time, but at her words, I hold it behind my back. "What do you mean, not allowed?"

"Papers no good," the woman says. "Passport?"

"We're not staying," I say, trying to keep the fear out of my voice. "We're only passing through, to get to Hong Kong."

I hear the door open behind me. "Everything okay in here?" says Dom, sticking his head through the door.

"You! Close door," the woman snaps.

"He's with us," I babble as quickly as I can. "We're all together. But he doesn't want to stay either—we're going to take a train to Hong Kong."

The woman shakes her head. "No train. If you together, you leave together. Entry denied."

She points past Dominic outside, and the three of us troop back out the door we just came in.

chapter forty-two

IMAGE: Singapore Vending Machines
IG: Romy_K [Singapore, April 16]
#VendingMagic #DeniedEntry
699 ♥

Behind me, the woman closes the door so swiftly that it smacks me on the ass, and I shoot out onto the steamy runway. Beside us, outside the door, a collection of vending machines is lined up like soldiers against the wall, under a broad awning. I don't have any local currency, but I'm desperately thirsty in this heat, so I turn to see if any of them will accept credit card payment.

Turns out? They all do. They are also the most diverse collection of vending devices I've ever seen. Of the five machines, one offers hot pizza, a second will toast a sandwich in a panini grill before serving, and the third offers boxed salads. The fourth, looking more like every vending machine I've ever seen, holds cold drinks—but the fifth? For five Singaporean dollars, you can buy a fillet from the world's first Norwegian Salmon ATM.

Snap frozen in the fjords.

As we're busily buying up a collection from every machine—apart from the salmon, which I'm pretty sure won't keep—Klahan comes trotting up. His beaming smile and air of manic energy have returned in full force.

"Good news!" he crows. "While they fix wing, I trade for Seletar

Flying Club machine. Special double tank for six-hour journey. Already gassed up. We leave in five."

He gestures across the runway. A small man, his shock of white hair shooting straight up from his scalp, waves cheerfully. He's standing beside what looks like a small air force cargo plane.

Klahan waves back before turning to us. "You ready?" he says. "You get food? Go pee? No toilet on board."

After the whole broken wing-flap situation that got us here, I feel unwilling to risk another questionable airborne experience, but it appears we have no other choice.

Sumaya, a slice of pizza in one hand, bounces over to the plane and, unclasping the door handle, swings the built-in step down as expertly as if she's been doing it all her life. Stepping onto the lowest riser, she sticks her head through the door.

"It is very full inside," she reports doubtfully.

And indeed it is.

The plane turns out to be principally intended for use as a skydiving training vehicle. The back is loaded with a number of parachutes, all neatly packed up, along with the rest of Klahan's cargo for transport to Hong Kong. By the time I look inside, Sumaya has climbed in and pulled down one of the jump seats that line the walls.

"Loads of room," she announces cheerfully. "I didn't see how the seats folded flat. It's brilliant!"

Dominic leaps in, bumping into me. When I turn to protest, I see that he's been pushed by Klahan, who clambers in behind Dom and into the pilot seat.

"This fine machine," he chortles as he settles himself in his seat and flips a few switches. "Turbo charge."

"Look, Klahan—before we take off, I need to know. Why no

customs in Kolkata? Are you smuggling this stuff? Including—
including us?"

Without a word, Klahan reaches under the copilot's seat and pulls
out a clipboard.

"Customs paperwork here—all complete before I even meet you,"
he says evenly. "You show me your papers from customs office. No
smuggling. Smuggling for losers."

"It's just when you said there was a change of plan . . ."

He looks so hurt, I take a step forward, but he holds up a hand.
"Change of plan from private runway to Seletar," he says, smacking
his own chest. "I am a marine!"

My face must have reflected my inner turmoil at these words,
because Klahan lifts one arm and points to the seat beside him. "You
sit? Keep tabs, I not a criminal?"

But before I've even shaken my head, a figure zips past me.

"I will!" yells Sumaya, and plops herself down beside Klahan. She
brushes pizza crumbs off her fingers and beams at him.

I try to apologize for insulting his character, but Klahan gives my
stuttering attempts a dismissive wave and hands a pair of headphones
to Sumaya.

I trail into the back as the engine revs, shooting a glance over my
shoulder up at Sumaya. I can only see the top of her head, which now
sports a pair of earphones over her neat blue hijab.

Dom takes a seat across from me, and because of the configuration, our knees are almost touching. He reaches across to pat my
hands, now clenched tightly in my lap.

"I've totally insulted him," I mutter. "We're doomed. He's going
to throw me out with one of these parachutes."

"It'll be okay," Dom says over the noise of the revving engine.
"He's a professional. He knows what he's doing."

And entirely remarkably, he's right.

The plane is noisy and the seats uncomfortable, but once we're up and away, there's little of the rattle and shake that characterized our first flight. Dom almost immediately closes his eyes, his head resting against the pile of parachutes strapped in beside his seat. Up front, I can hear Klahan laughing even over the noise of the engines, a sure sign that Sumaya is testing out some of her new material again. I hope our pilot's good mood extends to all his passengers, even the ones with a perhaps too-obsessive need for the paperwork to be in place.

I pull my hoodie out of my daypack, bundle it behind my head, and lean back. The noise of the plane's engine laboring upward quite perfectly reflects my roiling thoughts at the moment. Across from me, Dom's face has relaxed into sleep, his long lashes wafting across cheekbones that have, I notice for the first time, a scattering of freckles. The cabin is pressurized, but chilly, and even in his sleep I can see goose bumps on his arms. I idly wonder about leaning across and tracing the line of his biceps, where it disappears into the sleeve of his shirt.

Another roar of laughter from Klahan jerks me out of my reverie. It jerks the plane, too, a little, which is unsettling, but nothing less than I deserve. What am I even thinking? Sitting here, mooning at Dominic's arm muscles. And the soft, soft skin of his lips. It's been a long time since I have felt lips so soft. Maybe—never?

Shit. I give myself another shake for good measure. Dominic is the enemy, for goodness' sake. Okay. Maybe not the enemy, but at the very least, he's the competition. When this plane lands, we'll work together to get Sumaya safely into the hands of her auntie, and then? It'll be on again. The race—my race—to save the bookshop. I need to be first across the threshold of ExLibris when this whole thing is over. There can be no other option.

Dragging my eyes away from the slightly damp curls at the nape of Dom's neck, I lean forward to peek into the cockpit. I can just glimpse one side of Sumaya's animated face. She's strapped with two shoulder belts into the copilot's seat, but even so, I can see her gesturing with her hands, eyes bright and a giant grin across her face. My heart swells at the joy that pours off her in waves, and I'm suddenly awash in shame. Any difficulties I've faced making my own way in the world seem embarrassingly dwarfed by everything that Sumaya's been through.

The plane has leveled out, so I risk unsnapping my seatbelt, and shuffle forward, dropping to my knees in the spot between the two pilot's seats.

Sumaya turns her smile on me. "You want a try?" she says, reaching for her seatbelt buckle.

I shake my head hurriedly. "Just checking you're okay."

Her expression shifts to incredulous. "Are you kidding? I'm brilliant!" She waves a hand to take in the endless, deeply green forest, with fluffy clouds like too-thinly stretched cotton, tangled in the treetops far below.

The sight of the view outside the window gives me vertigo, so instead I focus on Sumaya. "I think you might be the bravest kid I've ever met," I blurt.

This makes her laugh delightedly, but when she sees I'm serious, she fires off one of her patented teenage eye-rolls.

"You need to meet more people, Romy," she says, which makes Klahan laugh far more than the joke deserved.

Duly chastised by both of them, I head back to my seat as the plane rumbles through the sky above the dense forests of Southeast Asia.

I distinctly remember snapping myself back into my seat across from a gently snoring travel companion. But the next thing I know, my head is bobbing and my ears crackling. Through the cockpit window, the sun reflects on the deep blue of the ocean below us. We swoop in over a collection of islands—a dozen, or maybe a dozen dozen, poking up through the sea, like the green backs of oddly shaped turtles. The plane circles once, then twice, while Klahan shouts into his headset. And then, gentle as the wafting of a butterfly's wing, we settle down onto one of the smooth, endless runways of the international airport in Hong Kong.

chapter forty-three

IMAGE: Hong Kong Runway
IG: Romy_K [Hong Kong, April 16]
#SouthChinaSea #NotaNewYorkMansplain
580 ❤

From the air, Hong Kong International Airport looks enormous. Perhaps because we are not a commercial flight, our plane is directed over to a small cluster of buildings—hangars and trailers and definitely not the jetways of the mammoth airport I can see across the tarmac. As we roll to a stop, Sumaya yawns and stretches in her seat, and I feel relieved that she got some sleep too.

When Klahan opens the door and swings the steps down, the cabin fills with hot damp air. A diesel-scented sauna. I'm instantly coated in a sheen of sweat.

"You stay," says Klahan, pointing at Sumaya, who blinks sleepily. "And you? Wait with," he adds, gesturing at me. "We mans go. Sort things out."

To give him credit, Dom looks a little startled at this. "I don't know . . ." he begins, but we're on the ground now, and I'm all over this shit.

"Forget it," I say, pushing myself in front of Dominic so I can get right up in Klahan's face. "Sumaya and I don't need a man to speak for us. I'm perfectly capable . . ."

"Who speak in Singapore?" Klahan interrupts.

"I did," I say, but Dom waves me off.

"We both did. Romy's right. She can handle things herself. She can be pretty articulate, when she has to be."

His eyes crinkle and I can see he's doing that thing he does to make light of a situation. To de-escalate, maybe. Mansplaining, still, but at least it's in my defense.

Klahan turns back to me. "*You* speak in Singapore," he says. "And they deny."

He holds his hands up as I try to explain myself. "No bullshit me. I hear on radio. Any case, it's not you, it's her," he adds, jamming a thumb at Sumaya. "Old society, China. Mans still make decisions."

"This isn't China," I retort. "It's Hong Kong. And our company ExLibris, they—she—has applied for our visas. They should be waiting for us."

Klahan crosses his arms over his chest, and inhales deeply through his nose before he speaks.

"I say again. Visas for you, yes. But Hong Kong still China. More than ever. More this year than last year. Next year more still. I think you get in, I do. You two—you leave right away. Need transfer visa. But girl? Girl get in as helper. Big helper culture here. Need mans to sort out. You not in America now. Not everything same as New York."

And this, of course, shuts me up.

Klahan turns and swings himself down the steps onto the tarmac.

"You okay with this?" Dom mutters. "It's only—I've never been here. I think we might need to trust him."

I glare out the door at Klahan's retreating back for a minute, before I throw up my hands.

"Okay—go, go. But I'm *not* happy about this."

I slam down the jump seat next to Sumaya's and plop myself into it. She's shaken off her sleepiness and is bright-eyed once more.

"Just so you know, in law, women are treated equally to men," I say to her huffily.

Her lips curl upwards. "I know this is true," she says. "But sometimes it is good to accept help, yes?"

I slump back in my seat, but before I can muster all my arguments, she speaks again. "I planned for a long time to escape the camp," she says quietly. "I had it all worked out. But some things I did not plan for. The boat taking on water. You and Dom letting me hide on the train."

To my surprise and horror, her eyes fill with tears. This kid has not cried once—not when her tiny boat was sinking, not at the jail in Kolkata.

"Even if I hide on the train, the guards stop me at the end. Send me back to camp. Without you and Dom, I would be back there already."

"No—no," I stutter. So much for being articulate. "I mean, you would have found a way, Sumaya. I've never met anyone with the guts you have."

This makes her laugh a little, and she wipes away the tears as they spill over. "All I am saying is sometimes things don't go as you plan. When someone offers help, maybe if you accept, it makes it easier when it's your turn to help someone else, yes . . . ?"

Her voice trails away, and we sit there quietly, side by side, for a few minutes. This kid is so much wiser than I am, it's depressing. I hope she's right this time too.

Through the open doorway, all the sounds and smells of a major international airport float in on the steamy air. The smell of airplane gasoline is overlaid with something else. Sweet, and floral and lovely.

Still.

"It feels hotter here than in Singapore," I mutter, and try fanning myself with a skydiving flyer, printed in English and Cantonese. This only seems to move the hot air around the cabin even faster, so I stop after a minute or two.

Beside me, Sumaya looks unbothered by the heat. Where my shirt is already bearing two large damp patches under the arms, her hijab rests, unmarked by moisture, against her smooth brown face. She's wiped away all traces of tears, but her eyes are still bright.

"Here they come," she says, leaning forward, clasping her hands.

Sure enough, Klahan is marching back across the tarmac, trailed by a small, dark-haired man and then Dom, towering over them both, bringing up the rear with his long, loping stride.

I reach over and pat her tightly squeezed hands. "Well, let's see where sending the men in has gotten us, shall we?"

The trio stop at the foot of the steps leading to the plane, and Klahan turns to speak to the Chinese man in what I guess is Cantonese. They both bow several times, and then the man hands a manila envelope to Klahan, who bows again as he accepts it. This process is repeated, without the Chinese conversation, as Dom shakes the man's hand, and bows awkwardly.

The man then takes the first step onto the plane stairs, and pokes his head in the door.

"Welcome," he says, and gives each of us a cheerful wave before he steps back out.

After a final round of handshakes and bows, he strides away, back toward the low hut.

Without a word, Klahan marches round to the cargo hatch at the rear of the plane.

Dom bounds on board. "We're in," he says joyfully. "Transit visa only for us, twenty-four-hour limit. We need to get this girl to her auntie's and be on our way."

He holds up three small cards. "Train tickets into the city," he says. "Let's go."

So that's what we do.

Our goodbye to Klahan is short, and gruff, at least on his part. When I try to thank him, he brushes it off.

"I coming here already, bring cargo. Had room to give you a ride. No thanks needed."

But he can't hold on to the gruff exterior when Sumaya throws her arms around his neck.

"My copilot," he says, clapping her on the back. "You fly back see me next time, you have your own plane, yes?"

Her smile says it all.

chapter forty-four

IMAGE DETAIL: Hong Kong Train
IG: Romy_K [Hong Kong Island, April 16]
#AmericansAbroad #NameInLights
3700 ♥

We have arrived at the hottest part of the day, and the pavement around us steams as we step out of the terminal. To one side, the tarmac sweeps all the way down to a spot where it is lapped by the water of the South China Sea. Inside the train station, everything is ultramodern. Unlike most of the MTA stations in New York, these trains have glass and steel doors between the platform and the track. You have to be inventive to throw yourself in front of a train in Hong Kong, is all I'm saying.

We have reserved seats, which involves a trek through the train cars until we find the correct one, but I don't mind a bit. The train is air-conditioned, and I for one am not complaining.

As we glide smoothly along the tracks into the city, Sumaya's nose is glued to the window, and I'm right behind her. The airport itself perches on an island in the South China Sea that, from what I can see, appears to be made up entirely of concrete runways. But as soon as we pull away from the airport, an astonishing range of scenery unfolds outside the windows of the train. We follow a chain of islands linked by bridges all the way into the city. Sumaya, who has borrowed my phone on the promise that once she is with her auntie I will forward all my pictures to her, is snapping away through the glass.

I feel a hand on my arm and turn to see Dominic is holding up his phone. I take it from him and see that he's been searching ships crossing the Pacific. There are two scheduled to depart Hong Kong harbor in the next twenty-four hours. One to Vancouver via Yokohama, and the other straight through to San Francisco.

Bingo.

I hand the phone back, and then, because I can't help it, I reach over and squeeze Sumaya's hand. The thought of carrying on this journey without her, even once she's been safely delivered into the arms of her family, is something I can hardly bear to think about.

Sumaya slides over so I can see out the window beside her. We travel along the azure coastline, the color of the water deepening as the clouds above us begin to break up. The water lies flat, corrugated with tiny ridges, and overslung with bridges linking the many islands. Then, proving the world is far, far smaller than it appears to someone desperately trying to race around it, the train stops at a station, and all the remaining seats are filled by travelers wearing— mouse ears. It's the connection to the Hong Kong Disneyland Resort, and for a short time, anyway, the carriage is filled with accents that remind me of home.

One family approaches the open seats across from ours, and the child, a small girl with a pink polka-dot bow between her Minnie ears, bounces into the seat by the window. The child's mother, no ears but decked out head to toe in Yves Saint Laurent, including handbag, snatches her daughter's hand up and physically hauls her out of the seat.

She ignores Dom and gives me a tight, red-lipped smile. "We're supposed to sit with *our own people*, Maddie-Jo, honey," she says to the girl.

"But I want a *win*dow," whines Maddie-Jo.

Sumaya turns away from the view and smiles up at the mother. "These seats are free," she says politely.

The smile freezes on the mother's face, and she jerks the child out into the aisle. "Daddy's got better seats for us in the next car," she hisses, dragging the now-sniveling Maddie-Jo behind her. "With the rest of the tour group."

They vanish up the aisle.

Sumaya gives me a little shrug and a smile, and turns back to the view. On the other side of me, Dom, who has not said a word during this whole exchange, releases a long breath.

I start to climb over him, but he reaches up and puts a hand on my arm. "Let it go," he says in a quiet voice.

By this time, I have one leg in the aisle, and the other awkwardly jammed between his. As I try to step my second leg into the aisle, he closes his knees, trapping my leg between his.

"Look. They were American. I need to say something."

"Let it *go*," he repeats, this time shooting a glance at Sumaya. She hasn't noticed our little battle of wills, and is still focused on taking pictures. The train takes a hard right, and outside the window the view of the sea is replaced by a busy freeway. Above us, the hillsides are neatly terraced, filled with trees decked in the fresh green of springtime.

His leg strength might be superior to mine, but I'm feeling more furious by the second. "I *need* to say something," I repeat, struggling to free my leg. He's actually crossed his ankles by now, a tactic that does, in fact, defeat me.

Then he gives a mirthless little laugh, and releases me. "You can," he says. "But it's not going to change anything."

"Yes it will," I snap back, glancing up the aisle. Through the glass door at the end of the car, I can see a woman holding one of those little flags used for corralling tourists. She's standing in the aisle, blocking my view, instructing her tour group.

I stand, uncertain for a second, then slump back into my seat.

"She saw two brown people, one of them wearing a hijab, sitting with a white woman," Dom says quietly. "And that frightened her. If you chase her down and shout at her, it will cement her views that we are a threat."

"But we are *not* a freaking threat," I say, still furious. "That's just racist and ignorant."

Dom gives another dry chuckle. "Well, *you're* not a threat. At least, if she met you alone on the street at home, you wouldn't be. But sitting with us? You clearly don't understand what kind of a threat we represent. So you're the ignorant one, in her mind."

"How do you even know her mind?" I hiss at him. "She's an American. Our nation is made up of people of every color and religion. It was *founded* on freedom of religion, for Christ's sake."

Sumaya turns her shocked face away from the window. "Don't swear, Romy. It is very bad to swear. It is blasphemy."

I take a deep breath and then squeeze her hand. "I'm not a practicing Christian, sweetie," I say. "It's not blasphemy if you're not practicing."

She shrugs. The train has entered the city limits, and the trees around us are suddenly sprouting high-rises. "I am not Christian either, but I wouldn't say it. It is disrespectful." She pulls her hand away from mine, and cranes her neck to get a shot of a high-rise towering above the tracks.

When I glance back at Dom, the expression of wariness is gone from his face, but he looks tired.

"Look," he says. "If this is a fight you want, good. But you need to know it's not only here on the train. I think it's more obvious to you right now, maybe because you're not at home. Or because you're with us. But this is nothing new, okay? It's an everyday thing. You learn to choose your battles."

"I get that. But, I feel there's got to be something I can do. Not saying anything to that woman feels like acceptance. Like the way she thinks is okay."

He shrugs and gestures out the window. "Let's focus on what we're here to do. We can talk about this later, if you want, but now? We're here in Hong Kong. Let's find Sumaya's auntie. That's our priority."

My chance to make a point with the tourists is rendered moot, when at that moment, the train stops and the entire tour group vanishes out the door. Seconds later, we are moving again, and I take a deep breath and try to push the American woman's behavior out of my mind. The train hurtles into the heart of the city now, buildings and colors flashing past. We fly by what looks like a giant casino, with English and Cantonese characters running ticker tape style along the roofline. I catch sight of letters spelling both "Rom" and "Dom" mixed in with the Cantonese characters, which makes me laugh out loud, relieving a little of the earlier tension. I've never seen my name in lights before. I mean, what are the chances? But by the time I grab Dominic's arm to point it out to him, we are long past, and sweeping into the final station.

The announcement overhead reminds us to collect up all our belongings, and we start doing just that. Inside the tunnel, the train slows and briefly plunges into darkness, and it's a moment before the lights flicker on. Sumaya drops her head to rummage in the small bag Dominic picked up for her in Kolkata. As the brakes give a final squeal, she pulls out the heavily creased letter she's carried all this way and waves it at me joyfully.

"We're almost there!" she says. "And when we find her, Auntie Nkruna can fix your hair!"

"Tall order," mutters Dom, as he reaches up to pull our bags down from the rack.

Tucking my offending tresses behind my ears, I poke him in the ribs, scoop up my suitcase, and follow an excited Sumaya onto the train platform.

chapter forty-five

IMAGE: Hong Kong City
IG: Romy_K [Hong Kong, April 16]
#VerticalCity #LookUp
6005 ♥

Having been most of the way around the world, I'm starting to feel like there must be few surprises left, but Hong Kong is astonishing. This city is entirely—vertical. I mean, obviously I'm completely comfortable in a big city. It makes me feel like home. So you'd think I could close my eyes a little to the heat—or imagine that it's the middle of July—and this would feel like New York, right?

Wrong.

I've never seen any place like this. To begin with, the city itself is tucked into the most scenic location ever, squeezed between soaring mountains and the sea. The buildings go up forever, many with enclosed balconies jutting out at odd angles, like worn, wooden blocks, carelessly stacked. Every surface is strung with wires and jerry-rigged fans and today's laundry. The noise and the lights and sirens are the same as any big city I've seen so far. But—Hong Kong is different. The energy of the place, even in this kind of heat, is something else. Most of the men engaged in street labor of any description are shirtless. And the scaffolding—even up the highest of skyscrapers—is made of bamboo.

There was bamboo scaffolding in Mumbai too, but far fewer skyscrapers. Hong Kong carries a completely different vibe than Singapore too. What I saw of that city, admittedly mostly from the air, seemed tremendously modern, whereas Hong Kong, for all its tall buildings, radiates history.

According to Sumaya's letter, her auntie's salon is in the Central District of Hong Kong. Half of the city sits on an island, separated by Victoria Harbour from Kowloon, which makes up the mainland side. Central District is on the island half, and we are able to take our train all the way through. We climb the stairs from the station into the heat and chaos of downtown at rush hour. Sumaya turns on her heel, spinning in a slow circle with her head tilted back.

She doesn't say a word, but slowly places her hands over her ears.

Meanwhile, Dominic has collected a free tourist map from a stand near the station exit. It's meant to show the local bus lines, but it also has most of the main streets labeled in English.

"It doesn't look far," he says, tracing an admittedly convoluted route between the station and the address on Nkruna's letter. "Like maybe half a mile?"

"In which—direction?" asks Sumaya, doubtfully. She points across the street. "If it is that way, we have to go straight up the hill."

She looks back at me, round-eyed. "What do they keep in all these tall buildings?"

"Businesses, I guess," I say. Watching her reaction, I realize that this is likely the largest city she has ever seen. Most of her views of India came from inside a train, and seeing a city from the air, as we did Singapore, has much less impact than the full-frontal assault of mid-city Hong Kong. "And people live here too."

I reach across to give her a hug. "This is new to me too," I whisper. "I live in a big city, but this one is very different."

Dom consults his phone. "The mountain ranges of Hong Kong

are famous for hiking," he reads aloud. "And while many see the city as a shopper's paradise, Hong Kong is also a tropical island, dotted in steep climbs."

He looks up at us. "I think we go this way," he says, shouldering his pack and pointing up the hill. "Get ready for one of those famous steep climbs."

"I seriously had no idea," I mutter, scooping up my suitcase. We clamber up the stairs to an overpass, which crosses a freeway beneath us. The overpass is open to the air, but roofed, so it's cooler than the street, with a breeze blowing across from the water. Strangely enough, the length of the entire walkway is lined in sheets of cardboard. Old boxes, broken down and tidily placed inside the line of shade. And on the boxes? Women.

Hundreds of them, just in this walkway alone.

"Are they selling something, maybe?" I ask Dom, as we hurry past.

Most of the women sit in small groups, all tidily dressed, and many with their shoes off and neatly placed to one side. I see a few packed lunches here and there, but no products to sell. Mostly animated chatting, to tell you the truth.

"They look more like they are having a picnic," mutters Dom.

"This many?" I ask. "And why here? Why not in a park?"

"No idea," he says. "People sat on the streets all over Mumbai. How is this different?"

"I don't know," I mutter. "It just is."

Sumaya, whose bag is admittedly lighter than either of ours, trots on ahead. The hot afternoon sun slants between the buildings, and sweat is pouring off me. After a few more blocks straight uphill, I raise my hand.

"Can we . . ." is all I can manage, but Dominic, whose shirt is completely soaked and sticking to his back, stops at once.

He whistles without apparent effort, piercing through all ambient noise. Half a block ahead of us, Sumaya stops and looks around. When he waves at her, she trots back good-naturedly.

"You need to stay with us," he says quietly. "I know you're excited, but this is too big a city. You—we all—could get lost so easily."

Sumaya shrugs. "Mumbai was bigger," she says. "Also dirtier."

"Yeah, well, we weren't running through the streets of Mumbai," he counters. "At least, not after we found the train station."

Sumaya's smile falls away, and suddenly her warm hand is clasping my own.

She's taken Dominic's hand too. "I will pay you back," she says fervently, looking between us. "Both of you. I would never be here without you."

Dominic swings his free arm around her in a slightly awkward squeeze. "That's not true, and we all know it," he says. "You, my girl, are what my mom calls *pono aina*. It means—uh—basically, a force of nature."

As he falls into step beside Sumaya again, I notice a red directional arrow on the wall over his head. Beside the arrow, a sign reads "Central Mid-levels Escalator, under repair. Detour to Stanley Street."

"What's that?" I say as we carry on upwards, trudging past the sign.

Dom pauses to stick his head behind the hoarding the sign is pinned to. "You've got to be kidding me," he says, stepping back out. "They actually have an escalator running up the side of this hill."

Sumaya points to a tattered schematic stapled to the hoarding. "He's right," she says, pointing at a dotted line perpendicular to the streets. "On here it looks like it climbs almost to the top."

I groan and use the sodden sleeve of my t-shirt to wipe the sweat out of my eyes. "Our luck it's broken."

A young man, staring at his phone as he strides past, glances back over his shoulder. "Only this segment is under renovation," he says, not breaking stride. "Up there, past Stanley Street, it's working again."

And sure enough, he is correct. Less than a block uphill, the hoarding ends, and after crossing a narrow laneway, we hop on.

This section is more akin to one of those moving sidewalks in large supermarkets that allow you to ride down to the parking garage with your grocery cart. Personally, I've never had a car to park in one of those garages, but I admit to riding the thing a few times, just for the experience. As we glide upwards, the standard protocol soon makes itself clear. Those who choose to be carried upward—and I count myself among this number—do so by standing to the right. Those who are crazy enough to want to accelerate their climb, do so to the left.

I have the luxury of standing to the right for all of ten seconds before Sumaya casts her imploring gaze on me.

"All right," I grumble and fall into line behind them, marching past the sensible people who know when to take advantage of technology.

It's still vastly superior to running strictly on Romy power, so I don't complain too much.

Soon, I don't have the wind to complain, because the gently sloping moving sidewalk is replaced by increasingly steeper escalators as the incline of the hill increases. Later, I will discover that the entire system has twenty separate escalators and three elevated walkways. But in the moment, I aim my gaze down at Sumaya's feet and follow her upwards.

Over our heads, each segment is protected with a rain cover, and the steeper they get, the more stunning the view behind us grows.

Hong Kong slowly spreads out below our feet, but also still towering above us. It's astonishing.

The walls we pass are alive with neon signs and billboards and even trees—fully leafed trees—whose root systems form a gnarled mass intertwined within the brick walls. I've lost count of the number of escalators we've scaled when Sumaya stops suddenly. I plow right into her, and the force of my momentum causes her to stumble forward. Dom, his reflexes in better shape than my own, scoops a hand under one of her arms, and we all step to the side at the top of this section.

"You okay?" he says. I start to make a smart-ass retort, and then I see her face. Her lips have gone strangely pale, and her eyes are wide as saucers. I turn to see that she's pointing at what looks like a standard storefront. The place is covered in chicken feet logos, and suddenly the air is full of the warm, familiar smell of roasting poultry.

My stomach rumbles.

"Do you need something to eat?" I ask, when Dom nudges me in the ribs. "Not that one, Romy. Next door."

And next door, of course, is a salon, called African Beauty Nails 'n Hair.

Suddenly Sumaya's small, perfect hand is in my sweaty one. "I can't believe it," she whispers. "I can't believe we found it."

Dom beams at her, squeezes her other hand, and as a team we head inside.

chapter forty-six

Nkruna isn't there.

At first glance, at least, I don't see anyone who fits the description of Sumaya's auntie. As we crowd into the doorway, all the heads in the place turn. It's a small salon, with three chairs set up, each in front of a mirror. Two of the chairs are filled with customers, each with a stylist, and a young girl stands at the back with a broom, sweeping hair into a pile on the floor. The scent of hairspray lingers in the air.

Sumaya looks like she's forgotten how to speak, so I jump in.

"We're looking for Nkruna," I say to the stylist working closest to the door. A diminutive Chinese woman with pale purple hair and a lower lip piercing, she's giving her client an elaborate blowout. "Nkruna Warsame?"

"Ismail," whispers Sumaya. "Nkruna Ismail."

"She not here," the woman says, flicking off her hairdryer to answer me. Her eyes turn to Dom, and she gives him a slow perusal from head to toe and then back again. Her eyes linger on where his sweat-soaked shirt clings to his torso.

"You need a haircut?" she says, her voice suddenly breathy. "I give you the *best* haircut you ever have."

I quell a sudden urge to step between them.

Dom clears his throat. "No—no haircut. We're here to meet up with Nkruna."

"What?" says the second stylist. She looks like a slightly younger, less purple-haired version of the first. She's wearing a vivid orange smock over her clothes. "Nkruna's coming back?"

"Wonderful!" says Purple Hair. "How long she stay?"

"Wait till she sees how good my . . ."

"Just a minute!" I bellow, cutting off Orange Smock in mid flow. "Coming back from *where*? Where *is* she?"

Purple Hair begins an elaborate backcombing operation on her client. "Oh, she leave."

Sumaya staggers back, her face blank and shocked, like she's been dealt a physical blow. Dom wraps an arm around her shoulders to steady her.

"Leave?" he says. "What do you mean *leave*? Isn't this her salon?"

"Mine now," says Purple Hair proudly. "She been gone, what— nearly two years, Fan?" she adds, turning to Orange Smock, who nods obligingly.

"Two years?" Sumaya whispers. "That is not possible."

"Uh—well, two years in August. Her sister sponsored her. So, my sister and me, we buy the place, eh?" She points proudly at Fan in her orange smock. "We not African, but we keep name. Good repu-tation."

"Nkruna taught me to braid," adds Fan, who is, in fact, busily braiding as she speaks. "She was the best."

"I thought you said *you* were the best," says her customer, wincing a little.

"I am. 'Cause I was taught by Nkruna."

Between the interaction among the stylists and now the clients,

I'm having trouble following. "Wait a minute," I say. "Her sister sponsored her to do what?"

"To emigrate. That's why she leave."

"To emigrate where?"

The women look at each other and then chorus: "Canada."

"Canada?" My heart sinks. "*Where* in Canada? It's a big country."

Fan shrugs. Her fingers have not stopped moving once over the course of the entire conversation. "Ahh—I forget name. City, but not big like Hong Kong."

"Oh, come *on*," snaps Dom, his patience breaking. "We've come a very long way to find her. *Someone* must know."

"She cannot have gone to Canada," Sumaya says, finally finding her voice. "She would have *written* to me. She would have told me."

Purple Hair pauses in her backcombing and peers at Sumaya's face in the mirror. "Who you?" she asks, and then suddenly drops the comb into the lap of her startled patron. "Not Sumaya! Not little niece Sumaya?"

She throws her arms around Sumaya, who looks like she's about to cry. "Look how tall you get! I'm Le, and this my sister Fan. Your auntie show me pictures of you, but when you were a baby. Like three years old. And look at you now!"

She releases Sumaya from the hug, but holds her at arm's length by her shoulders, and then turns her, as if displaying a prize, to the other stylist. "She look like a young Nkruna, eh? Just like her!"

Fan beams.

"There's got to be a mistake," whispers Sumaya. "I sent her e-mails from the camp. She had to know I was coming. I have her last letter."

I gently disentangle Sumaya from Le's grip and help her over to a low stool by the door. "Show me the letter," I say softly, and Sumaya hands me the envelope.

It's stained with age and has creases so deep the ink has completely faded in places. I slip the letter out from inside and find it wrapped around a tattered snapshot of two tall, strikingly elegant Somali women, standing outside this very shop. Tucking it safely back into the envelope, I carefully unfold the letter. It's brief and has exactly zero words I can read.

"Is this in—Arabic?" I ask her, and she nods miserably. "How long have you had this letter, Sumaya?"

"A long time," she admits. "Five years, maybe. But Nkruna texted Aabe—my papa—in the camps."

Dom flashes me a warning look—unnecessarily, since I pick up the reference immediately. In all the time I've known her, Sumaya has referred to her father exactly once, and that was to tell me that her parents were dead. Still, we need information in order to decide what to do next, so I risk another question.

"So when was the last time you heard from her—from Nkruna?"

Sumaya takes a deep breath. I notice, with relief, the color seems to have returned to her lips. "I don't know. She was sending texts to Aabe, but he got moved to a different part of the camp, so I didn't get to see him. And then . . ."

She pauses for a long moment, and I can feel the daggers shooting at me out of Dom's eyes.

"It's okay," he says in a low voice. "We don't need to go over it now."

But Sumaya smooths down her hijab and stands up. "At least a year," she says, her voice stronger. "It might be more. Since they—the camp leaders—they took my phone away."

Dominic pats her shoulder and then turns back to the sisters, neither of whom has paused in her work.

"Look," he says, and I can hear the edge in his voice. "This is important. Sumaya has come a long way to find her auntie, and now you say she's not here. Was it Toronto? Ottawa? Saskatchewan?"

"That's a province, not a city," I snap, and then almost immediately regret it, since I can't think of another one. "Montreal?" I say, at last.

"Vancouver?" Dom says at the same moment.

Fan's face lights up. "Might be Vancouver," she says. "I think yes."

"Good! That's great," I say. "So do you think you might have an old e-mail or something with her address on it?"

But both Fan and Le are shaking their heads firmly.

Le pulls out an enormous can of hairspray, and tilts her hand over her client's eyes before liberally applying it. "She hasn't contact us," she says, and then coughs a little after inhaling the spray. "I'm really sorry, but no."

Fan reaches over to her sister and pokes her with a long red fingernail. "There's always Nena," she says.

"Who's Nena?" I ask, as she resumes her braiding.

"She used to work here," interjects Le, unsnapping her client's protective cape. "She's good friend to Nkruna—best friend. Maybe they talk since she left? But you never get Nena. She's a nanny now, work way down in Stanley. South Island." She ushers her client past Dom and me, and we shuffle sideways to make room for her to stand at the tiny cash desk.

But Fan's not finished. "It Sunday," she says. "We have picnic. I meet Nena, with Gu and sometimes Joan. She bring her dumpling." She snaps an elastic around the end of the braid, and feeds a bead into place. "Nena make the *best* dumpling."

"What?" says Le to her sister. "Since when you go meet Nena?"

Fan shrugs. "Every few week. She text me." She holds up her phone and waggles it at us.

"Okay, this could be good," Dom says. "If Nkruna's kept in touch with Nena, she might have an address we can use. When are you meeting her?"

"Tonight," says Fan. "After work. I could take you."

"But—you said the South Island," I say to Le. "Is it far?"

Le shrugs. "Stanley one hour, maybe longer, by train."

I exchange a glance with Dom. "Far, then," I say. "If we have to wait until Fan finishes work, the chances of us meeting up with this Nena and still making it back in time to catch the ship home before it sails . . ."

"We can do it," Dom says firmly. "We have to. Can you give us her address in Stanley?"

But Fan is shaking her head at her sister. "No—no. You wrong, Le. I meet Nena *here*, not Stanley. She and Gu, they set up on flyover by Canal Road. Cool breeze there, off water in evening. We have picnic. They bring dumpling."

"Did you say Canal Road?" says Sumaya quietly.

"That the place," agrees Fan, grinning at Sumaya. "Big walkway. Shady with breeze off water."

I hold up a hand. "Sorry—what do you mean by *sets up*?"

Le collects money and shoos her freshly backcombed customer out the door. A young man slips into the chair in her place. Fan is still patiently braiding. The woman in her chair has a bridal magazine open in her lap.

"Oh you know, they get Sundays and some Wednesday afternoons off, so the helpers everywhere," Fan continues. "You must have seen them, climbing up here?"

"Do you mean all the ladies with the sheets of cardboard?" asks Sumaya.

Le clucks disapprovingly, but Fan chuckles. "Heh. Yes. Hong Kong very big helper culture. All family have helper, who live in. Most are foreign, yes?"

"All *wealthy* family," Le interjects.

I lock eyes with Dominic. "Okay, so that's what Klahan meant by the helper culture," I mutter.

The young girl, who has paused in her diligent sweeping of hair to listen in, pipes up for the first time. "Not *all* wealthy," she says in a sweet, high-pitched voice. "I had nanny when I was small, and my family not wealthy."

She smiles shyly at Sumaya, who looks about the same age. "She was more like a granny to me," she says confidentially. "I cry for weeks when she die last year."

"You did, is true," agrees Fan, pausing to hold a mirror up to the back of her client's head.

"It's true," Le adds grudgingly.

I can feel Dom shifting restively beside me.

Le pulls out a pair of lethal-looking shears and starts in at the nape of her client's neck. "All these women," she says. "Mostly women, some men too . . ."

"All gardeners are men," interjects the young sweeper.

"These helpers, they live in. No homes of their own. So on Sundays, they flock to the city. Find a cool place, shady place to sit. They fill streets too much. Get in way."

"You too cranky, Le," says Fan. "Helpers need time with friends. Only fun for them all week."

She winks at me. "I take you. You see."

Dom clears his throat. "What time do you get off work?"

Fan shrugs. "When I'm finish," she says, indicating the woman in her chair. Considering half the woman's hair is still in banana clips, it doesn't seem like anytime soon.

Dom pulls the map out of his back pocket and leans toward me. "We came past Canal Road on the way here," he says to me in a low voice. "I'm sure I can find it on the map. Let's go."

I grab his arm. "They said she's in *Canada*," I hiss. "Our ship is heading to San Francisco. And you know how easy it's going to be bringing a refugee back through the US . . ."

"Not easy. I know." Dom takes a deep breath. "Look. This is *my* problem. It was me who helped her in the first place, and I need to see it through. I'll go locate this Nena, and get Nkruna's address. I'll escort Sumaya to her auntie in Vancouver, and then take a train to San Francisco. You can take the boat straight through."

I roll my eyes. "Oh, right, Mr. Self-Sacrifice. What about your mom?"

"My mom doesn't enter into this. What's important here . . ."

"What's important here is *Sumaya*," I say, jamming my thumb over my shoulder toward the doorway. "After all we've been through— let's get her to her auntie. Together. After that? All bets are off."

He grins at me. "You got a deal." He waves the map at Fan. "We'll find your friend Nena at Canal Street, right?"

"Canal Road," corrects Fan. "We meet at the flyover Hennessy Road. If anyone know Nkruna address, she know."

"Okay," I say. "Thank you very much—both of you." I turn to Dom. "We're going to have to run back down all those stairs."

"Easier than running up," he says, and then his grip on my hand, which he hasn't released, tightens convulsively.

"Ow! What?"

I turn to face the empty doorway.

Sumaya is gone.

chapter forty-seven

IMAGE: Villain-beater
IG: DomBakes [Hong Kong, April 16]
#CurseYourEnemy #StandUpSuccess
19017 ♥

Everything goes to hell for the next few minutes, but after a bit of yelling and cursing in both American English and Cantonese, we determine a few solid facts. Sumaya is indeed missing. But so is the hair-sweeping girl, whose name, it turns out, is Melody.

"Oh—that girl always trouble," says Le, shaking her fist at the darkening doorway.

"This is my fault. I shouldn't have brought up the whole ExLibris thing," I say. "She's gone to find Nena without us."

"Well, if so, she hasn't had a very long head start. We can catch her if we leave now," Dom says. His voice has taken on a panicky tone I've never heard before.

I don't like it, especially when my own stomach is suddenly in knots. One of us needs to keep it together. But he's right. We need to *run*.

After the swiftest of farewells to Le and Fan, we start down the steps that parallel the outdoor escalators. This is no easy jaunt. In the first place, there's a flow of pedestrian traffic in both directions, with an absurd percentage actually hiking up the steps toward us. How they can do this through the steamy, scented heat of a Hong Kong evening seems nothing short of insanity. The steps are worn and broken in places, and at least half of the flights don't have a handrail. Twice I instinctively grab at Dominic's shoulder as he runs ahead of me. The second time he stops so abruptly that I career into his back.

"This isn't safe," he says quietly. "We're not going to do her any good if one of us breaks an ankle on these stairs."

He settles his pack on both shoulders, takes my suitcase in one hand, and laces his fingers between mine with the other. I'm so worried about losing Sumaya that it's a full minute—two flights of steps, with a traffic-laden road in between—before I begin to feel self-conscious about holding his hand. Worse, listening to Dom's quick breathing as we shoot down the stairs makes my own level of desperation rise.

Finally, we're forced to stop at a street where the traffic is flowing far too quickly to dash through. He releases me and bends over, hands on his knees, panting as we wait for the light.

"What is she thinking?" I splutter.

Turning to face me, he uses the back of one hand to wipe the sweat out of his eyes. His shirt is soaked, glued to his skin. This close, he gives off the scent of athletic male, with an inexplicable hint of cinnamon. By contrast, I'm sure I just smell sweaty. I take a self-conscious step away.

"Whatever it is, she means well," he says. "She's operating on a teenage brain."

"She's got to know we're going to come after her," I say as the walk light begins to chirp.

Dom grabs my hand again and we shoot across the road and down the next flight of steps. After another few minutes, we reach the place where we joined the moving sidewalk on our route up. Dominic makes a sharp right onto the main road, and without letting go of my hand, continues our run along the sidewalk.

EIGHTY DAYS TO ELSEWHERE · 321

"Wait a sec," I gasp, and he slows to a trot, and then stops at the corner. It's the worst possible kind of traffic—too many vehicles to allow for jaywalking, and few enough so they can move at a decent clip. Complicating things are the motorcycles and motorized scooters that come shooting out of teeny alleyways, honking—always honking.

"Still not as bad as Mumbai," Dom pants as we wait for the light. "At least we can cross at lights here."

I take a deep breath of the steamy air. "Can I see the map?" I say. "I have an idea."

Dom whips the map out of his pocket and steps over to where we can look at it in the red neon light of a noodle bar sign.

"Look," I say, pointing to the map. "If this is Canal Road, it's only a block away from a metro station. Why don't we hop on the train?"

Dom gives a weary smile. "Best idea I've heard all day," he says. "We might even beat her there!"

By the time we thunder down the steps at the Central Station, the wall clocks are reading 6:00 p.m. We've lost an entire day looking for Nkruna, but having lost Sumaya, too, has made things so much worse. Most of the rush hour appears to have passed, but the crowds waiting for the train are still of a daunting size. Thankfully, the lineups remain pretty orderly, and we're able to crush onto the third train that appears. I spend the ride pushed into a corner near the door, unfortunately nowhere near one of the dangling handholds. Dom squeezes in beside me and then angles himself so his back is to me. He stands a full head and shoulders over most of the crowd, and can easily reach one of the high railings.

"Grab on to me," he whispers over one shoulder as the train lurches forward. As I clutch at the strap of his pack, he winces and turns to face me. "The curse of big feet on a crowded subway car," he mutters. Luckily, the ride is over in a matter of minutes, and the train belches us out at Causeway Bay, the station nearest Canal Road.

A light rain has begun to fall, but there's too much warmth still in the air to feel refreshed. Water trickles down my spine. I have no idea if it's sweat or rain, but at this point it doesn't really matter.

After getting turned around on Hennessy Road, we finally set off in the direction our creased, and now dripping, map tells us is the right one. The pedestrian traffic is heavier here, and the best we can manage is a fast walk, so it's another couple of minutes before we spot the flyover near Canal Road. Around us, the city is lighting up, from neon to lanterns and everything in between. The whole thing reminds me of Times Square on a steamy summer night, apart from the lack of American voices in the air. It's with real relief that I hurry beneath the Canal Road flyover. The atmosphere of only barely controlled chaos along Hennessy is not really any better here, but at least we are under cover from the rain.

As I stop to get my breath, a strange new world emerges before my eyes. The freeway above us is broad, and every square inch of the shelter it offers underneath is packed with things I've never seen before. The smoky air is thick with the unmistakable perfume of incense, and music is spilling out from a dozen different sources, giving the place a festive, almost circus-like atmosphere. Small stalls, mostly in the form of tiny cupboards on wheels, are lined up in haphazard rows. With the doors flung open, the shelves are loaded with fruit and dancing candles and small stone statues. A few have iron bowls on the ground in front, with low fires burning inside.

"I think those might be—altars," I whisper to Dom, who is actually beginning to look a little overwhelmed.

"That one lady is telling fortunes," he says. "But the one behind you? I have *no* idea."

I spin around to see a woman, bent with age, hunched on a stool. In one hand she's holding a worn leather shoe. The old lady is vigorously beating something on the tabletop in front of her, while a small circle of onlookers observe. I shuffle a little closer and see with some puzzlement that she's smacking a tattered piece of pale blue paper.

Beside the lady is another custom-built shrine, this one featuring several golden figurines, along with the more standard piles of oranges, bananas, and dragon fruit. Several of the shelves of her shrine are adorned with paper tigers, and in fact, as I watch, the old lady pauses in her beating to place one of these tigers atop the small brazier at her feet. The flames shoot up and there's a muted murmur from the encircling crowd.

As the flames settle back down, the woman resumes beating the paper effigy, which is now unrecognizable. I can't tell if it was once one of the paper tigers, or something else.

"What the hell?" mutters Dom.

"You want turn?" A small man steps in front of us. "Grandma Chi do *da siu yan* for you. Fifty dollar. Very good deal."

"We're looking for a lost girl," Dom interrupts. "Maybe you've seen her? Blue headscarf, bright . . ."

"No. Grandma Chi no find missing people. She villain-beater. She solve all your problem. Send bad spirit away. Fifty dollar."

"No thanks," Dom says shortly and turns away. By this time, the crowd has grown around us, and it's impossible to move. In front of us, the villain-beater finishes her job with a flourish that sounds a bit like a drum solo, and then tosses a couple of wooden blocks from the table onto the ground.

The crowd cheers heartily, and the old woman gets slowly to her feet and hands the shreds of paper to one of the onlookers. After everyone bows politely, another member of the crowd steps forward, holding out a handful of cash to the woman.

324 · kc dyer

"She's not here," I say to Dominic, scanning the crowd. "Let's keep looking."

"You do that side," he says, pointing at the row of booths behind the lady with her shoe. "I'll go this way, and I'll meet you at the end of the block."

I clutch at his sleeve. "What if you find her?"

"I'll whistle," he promises.

The protected area under the freeway is not so much a market-place as it is a gathering place for street hawkers. It reminds me of the pavement outside Churchgate Station in Mumbai. No real booths, but lots of tarps on the ground, stacked with merchandise. Crowds gather around various street performers, including other villain-beaters.

But no sign of a teenager in a vivid blue hijab.

I scour my side of the street twice, scanning every face. Fifteen minutes later, at the far end of the street, I spot Dominic's head over the crowd. When he turns, I recognize the anxiety in his eyes, but ask the question anyway.

"Anything?"

He shakes his head. "Let's check up on the flyover."

But when we run up the nearest set of stairs, not only is Sumaya nowhere in sight, but the flyover is essentially empty. Not a picnicker anywhere. It's been at least an hour since we left the beauty salon, and a lump of panic has settled solidly right under my heart.

We're thundering back down the stairs when I spot a pair of po-lice officers standing outside the crowd watching the old woman, who is wielding her shoe for yet another customer.

I hurry over. "Excuse me. We're looking for the place where the . . ." I pause, hunting for the word, when Dom pipes up be-hind me.

"The helpers. Where the helpers have their picnics."

The policeman laughs and points outside. "It's raining," he says. "They all go off home."

Dominic's hand squeezes mine convulsively.

"We've lost our little—ah—niece," I say. "She's Somali. About fourteen, but pretty tall? She's wearing a bright floral top and a . . ."

"Blue headscarf?" says the policeman, and then points toward a large crowd. "Behind the villain-beater?"

Both Dom and I whirl around. Sure enough, another large circle has formed right up against the final support pillar beside Hennessy Road. At that moment, the entire crowd bursts into laughter. We lock eyes and race over.

And with her back against the pillar, there she is.

"Thank you very much!" she calls, and there's a spattering of spontaneous applause before the people begin to mill away. I see Melody working the crowd, passing a hat.

"What the heck, Sumaya?" I say as the crowd disperses around us. "Why did you run off?"

She looks puzzled as Melody walks up, jingling a little cloth cap. "I wasn't running away," she says. "I texted you."

I pull out my phone, and sure enough, there's a message. As I open it, Dom sweeps Sumaya up in a hug. "We've been worried sick," he says, setting her back on her feet. "It's been dark for an hour."

Sumaya rolls her eyes at him. "Why didn't you check your phone? I said I'd meet you here at seven."

"She did," I say, holding up my screen to show him.

"How would I know to look at my phone?" he says, the exasperation in his voice tempered by his obvious relief. "*You* don't have a phone to text us with."

Sumaya shrugs. "Melody does. I used hers."

She turns to Melody, who is squatting on the street, already counting the coins. "Half for you," Sumaya says to her new friend. "For helping me find Nena."

"You found Nena?" Dom says.

At the same time I blurt: "Where?"

"We text her too," says Melody, holding up her phone. "No picnic because of rain, but she e-mail me Nkruna's e-mail address."

"I already sent her a message," says Sumaya proudly.

She turns to Dominic. "I'm going to Vancouver to meet her. I need to pay my way."

Melody's phone buzzes, and as she glances down, her eyes widen.

"Got to go," she says. "The aunties are raging."

Sumaya sighs. "Yeah. I remember that."

Melody dumps all the change into Sumaya's hands.

"No—no," Sumaya says. "You need to take your half."

Melody shakes her head. "You're going to need a lot more than that to make it to Vancouver," she says sensibly.

"But—it might make things better with Le," Sumaya adds.

"Okay. I take five bucks. And don't forget to DM me, hey?"

The two girls hug, and Melody disappears in the direction of the subway station.

Dom helps Sumaya gather up all the change into her bag.

"You did pretty well for yourself," he says admiringly. "There's got to be forty or fifty Hong Kong dollars here."

Sumaya looks pleased. "I use my regular English material," she says. "But on the way over, Melody teach me to say "silly tourist" in Cantonese, and that got the biggest laugh of the night."

I check my phone, then look up at Dominic.

"It's only just after seven. If you go now, you can still make the San Francisco connection."

Sumaya steps into the space between us.

"You both have done more than enough for me," she insists bravely. "I should make my own way from here." She thrusts her bag at me. "This is for you. For all the money you have spent on me."

Above her head, I see Dominic's eyes fill with tears. But I'm so wrung out from all the excess emotion of the day, all I can do is laugh.

"Listen, you," I say, stuffing the bag back in her hands. "I know that every kid wants to run away and join the circus, but I'm too invested in your success as a future stand-up comedian-slash-pilot to stop now. We'll say goodbye when you're safely under the care of your auntie, okay?"

"Okay," she says agreeably. She swings her bag over one shoulder and links an arm through each of ours.

Dominic swipes at one eye with the heel of his hand. "When does the other ship leave, again?"

"Midnight, if we can still get tickets."

"Good," he says. "That means we have time to eat, first. I'm starving."

Now the panic over losing Sumaya has faded, I'm suddenly starving too.

She looks up at Dom. "Melody told me about this thing called dim sum that sounds really good."

"Sounds good to me too," he says. "And since you're the one with all the cash, dinner's on you."

chapter forty-eight

IMAGE: Victoria Harbour at Night
IG: Romy_K [Hong Kong, April 17]
#HongKongNeon #ObjectsMayBeSmaller . . .
6903 ♥

The problem, I have learned, with the internet, is that Things Are Not Always As They Appear Online. Case in point: the ship awaiting us at dock in Victoria Harbour.

We pass through customs and immigration without a hitch, and before us, the harbor is awash in neon as we hurry down the pier. The nightly light show that illuminates the waterfront is long over, but both sides of the harbor are lined with tall buildings flashing lights that bounce off the water, giving the entire area a futuristic glow.

As the three of us stride out the doors for what surely must be the final sea journey of the trip, the vessel is not exactly what I expected. When Dom had shown me the listing for a ship willing to take passengers across the Pacific and leaving today, I don't think either one of us had even looked at the size.

The *Arctic Björn* is a Greenpeace expedition ship, scheduled to depart tonight for the Port of Vancouver, after standing down from a whaling protest in Russian waters. The accommodation available is not private, but the ship is crewed by both men and women, and they agree to take us.

Sumaya pauses at the spot where the pier meets the gangway leading to the ship.

"Is this our boat?" she asks, glancing over her shoulder at me. "It is much smaller than the *Wahash Mahat*."

It is.

"It's not a transport vessel," I say, but I can't keep the note of uncertainty out of my voice. "It's only carrying a small crew across to Vancouver."

"It looked bigger online," Dom hisses in my ear.

It did.

Since I did most of the research in the metro on our way over here, there wasn't a lot of time to look into the details. Nevertheless, from what I could read on their site, I learned that normally, signing on as crew to a Greenpeace vessel is kind of a big deal. They ask for marine qualifications, diving licenses—the lot. However, in this case, the ship is returning to port in Vancouver, where a retrofit is scheduled to upgrade the engine. Since a number of their crew have flown off to other assignments, and as no further eco-actions are planned, they have space for us.

We stand dockside, eyeing the *Arctic Björn* as it bobs in the water. Unlike the *Guernsey Isle*, which sat solid, as if rooted to the ocean floor, when at anchor, or even the *Wahash Mahat*, with her shallow draft but enormous length, this Greenpeace ship looks positively wee.

She's a little more than fifty meters long, and is apparently classed as an icebreaker. As I try not to think about Kate Winslet unable to find room for Leo on her floating door after their iceberg, a tall, smiling man strides down the gangplank toward us.

He introduces himself as Captain Jack Kapena, and holds out a hand for our passports. He raises an eyebrow when Sumaya passes over her refugee document. "Lucky we're heading for Canada," he mutters, before handing it back.

However, when he flips open Dom's passport, his eyes widen in surprise.

"Makana?" he says. "Whaaa—Dominic *Makana* Madison? You Hawaiian, brah?"

"My mom's from Waimea," Dom says cautiously.

The captain slaps a hand on his broad chest. "Hilo born and bred," he says, clapping Dom on the shoulder. "One look at you and I knew you were an island boy. We talk later, eh?"

He turns back to the ship and yells, "Margot? Hey—*MARGOT!*"

A woman carrying two storage bins staggers out onto the deck. She drops the bins, and then straightens with an audible sigh. "Uh—hands full?" she says irritably, pointing at the bins.

Captain Kapena grins up at her. "I need you to handle this cargo first, okay?" he says, and then turns back to us. "This is my first officer, Margot Gulama."

Her expression unclouds a little at the sight of us. "Long as I don't have to carry 'em anywhere, we're good," she says, and deserting the bins, clomps down to meet us.

"Cookie needs that stuff ASAP," she says to Kapena in a gentle French accent. Surprisingly, he gives us a wave and then heads up to collect the bins himself.

"You order the captain?" breathes Sumaya admiringly, but Margot shrugs.

"We all have to pitch in, eh? Anyway, it's good for him." She gives us a brilliant widemouthed smile. "He's got a strong back—let him use it."

She eyes Sumaya from head to toe. "You Somali girl?"

Sumaya's eyes light up with pleasure. "Yes! How did you know?"

Margot chuckles. "Oh, I'm one very smart lady," she says. "You will soon see."

Tucking one of her strong brown arms through Sumaya's, she heads back up the ramp. Dom and I follow behind.

"What an adventure you are having!" Margot says to Sumaya as she leads us along the iron deck and then down a narrow staircase. "You must tell me all about it."

She points Dom to a dormitory room, and then directs Sumaya and me to a pair of bunks inside a much smaller room a little further down the passageway.

"Women's quarters," she says. "Make yourselves comfortable. Once you are settled, there's snacks in the galley at the end of the corridor, eh?"

Sumaya, always delighted to find a willing audience, barely drops her small roll bag of possessions on the top bunk before heading off to test out some of her new Hong Kong material on the crew.

"I can try out my English jokes on them," she says to me eagerly. "That way, you don't have to be stuck with me again."

I grin, still filled with relief that we managed to find her. "I don't mind listening to the same jokes again."

She raises an eyebrow. "They're not the *same*, Romy. I picked up a ton of new material in Hong Kong. Besides—some of it might be a bit too risqué for you. You turn red so easily."

And I, of course, can feel my face heating up as I insist this is entirely untrue.

Laughing, she steps over the door sill. "I'll be in the galley," she says and disappears.

After worrying for a while over what a fourteen-year-old might think is too risqué, I decide to leave well enough alone, and turn my attention to posting my latest photo to Instagram.

It's not until I get the picture loaded that I notice my number of followers has taken a massive leap. I've been picking up followers at a steady rate throughout the trip, but to shoot from the hundreds up to well over three thousand seems like a little miracle. It certainly puts me in contention with Dominic, for the first time. But my surge of elation falls away when I flip open Dominic's account only to see his numbers have soared too. Nearly four thousand followers looks a lot less impressive up against almost twenty thousand.

I shut down the app, and open a file for my Hong Kong report. It's only numbers. Determined to find my own way to shine, I begin to type.

chapter forty-nine

IMAGE: External Bridge, Arctic Björn
IG: Romy_K [East China Sea, April 17]
#YetAnotherSea #JapanBound #PirateVibe
6744 ♥

Twelve hours and one delicious sleep later, I'm once again back at my keyboard. As I feel the ship's engines thrum beneath my feet, I look up to see Dominic's head poke through the doorway. "Working on your report for ExLibris?" he asks.

I nod. "I didn't get very far last night. Fell asleep listening to Sumaya practice her jokes."

He grins. "I just heard some of it," he says, pushing the door open and stepping over the threshold. "Her new material is fantastic. That kid is a genius for her insight into the human condition."

"Where is she now?" I ask, sliding my computer off my lap.

He lifts a hand. "Don't worry. She's in the galley with Margot. When I left, they were bonding over tea and memories of Africa. I said I'd go back to collect her in an hour."

"Africa? But Margot's French, isn't she?"

He shrugs, and then leans his lithe form against the door frame. "French Canadian. But, from the sound of it, her family emigrated from West Africa when she was young. Sierra Leone, maybe?"

"Ah. Well, that explains why she connected with Sumaya so easily."

He shrugs. "I guess. We're all from somewhere, right?" He points at my laptop. "How's it going?" he asks.

As I stretch out my neck, he walks over to my bunk. I see he's carrying his tablet.

"This is the women's quarters," I say, pointing to the sign on the door.

He smirks. "Did you read the small print? It says six p.m. to six a.m."

I squint at the sign. "So it does."

He kicks off his shoes and plops down beside me on my bunk. Without another word, he prods the screen to open a document. We type together in companionable silence.

"What are you going to say about not heading for San Francisco?" he says after a few minutes.

I lift my fingers from the keyboard and sigh. "I'm not sure yet. I'm concentrating on giving a really glowing review to Hong Kong, at the moment."

"Good plan," he says.

He's folded his lanky form so that his back is resting against the wall, and with his sock feet on the bed, his knees act as a desk for his tablet. One of his shins is resting, quite naturally, against my knee, and I'm suddenly finding it extremely hard to concentrate on my report.

Dominic is apparently not affected the same way, and resumes two-finger typing at a furious rate.

The pillow is soft behind my own back, and in spite of being worried about what I'm going to report to Teresa Cipher, I'm suddenly aware of the strangest feeling. The ship's engine shifts and I can feel the gentle swell of the ocean beneath us. Three weeks ago, this would have set my heart hammering with anxiety, but right now? It feels comforting. Dom's leg is warm against mine, Sumaya is safely off with Margot, and . . .

I'm not worried about a thing.

A wave of happiness surges over me at this thought, and when my brain kicks in, reminding me there's little more than a week left in the month of April, I take a deep breath and push the thought away.

Mrs. Gupta's words come back to me. *Pick one thing,* she'd said that day on the train. *One thing you can see. One point of beauty, and focus on that.*

The first thing I see when I look up—is Dom's face.

What the hell, I think, and focus on him.

His eyes are locked on his screen, giving me a profile view. His hair, and the little curls forming in his beard along the jawline, are damp, leading me to think he maybe stopped on his way back from the kitchen to have a shower. I risk taking another deep breath in, and yep—there it is. The smell of soap, and clean skin, with that persistent, gentle undercurrent of cinnamon.

Still not shaven, though. I wonder idly if I can even remember what his face looks like without all that hair. Thinking back, I'm pretty sure he was clean-shaven that first morning in the bookstore. Long before he was the Evil Nephew, and when I was still Old Romy who had never been off the block. I glance at the calendar on my laptop screen and realize with a sudden shock that this distant memory took place little more than a month ago.

In a different lifetime.

Dom's fingers stop flying across his tablet keyboard, and when I glance up again, I realize he's closed his eyes. It's remarkable how a person's face changes when the eyes are closed. Dom's irises are light brown, almost hazel, and they light up his face, even when he's tired. But now, his long lashes are brushing his cheekbones. As his breathing evens out, I watch the tiny creases around his eyes relax. The ridge of his cheekbone stands out more sharply in his face than I remember. I'm pretty sure we're both thinner than when we started this crazy quest.

He's still wearing the clothes he had on this morning, mismatched woolen socks and all. We're set to be on this ship for a week, so I have no doubt both of us will make a trip to find the crew laundry, and the Hong Kong stains on his jeans will soon be a memory. In any case, they don't take anything away from his overall look. Since he's had a shower, his usual dusting of flour is missing. Still, even when he's relaxed like this, with his eyes closed, he gives off a kind of pirate vibe.

My laptop suddenly shifts to my screensaver—the photo I took of Sumaya that first day on the *Wahash Mahat*—and it snaps me out of my reverie. Pirate vibe? What the hell am I thinking? As soon as we drop Sumaya with her auntie in Vancouver, *I'm* the one who needs to be a pirate. I need to forget these chiseled cheekbones, and steal this race out from under Dom, so I can collect the bonus from Teresa Cipher.

The future of Two Old Queens depends upon it.

My sense of gentle happiness evaporates immediately on this realization, and to get my mind off the sick feeling that has somehow returned to my stomach, I go back to typing my report with new vigor. When Dom's head slides down the wall onto my shoulder I slip away quietly, close the lid of my laptop, and go looking for Sumaya.

Okay. It's possible that before I leave, I pull my blanket around his shoulders. And maybe I brush a stray lock of hair out of his face, but anyone would do that for another human being. Of course they would. Only common courtesy, after all.

ExLibris Destination Report, submitted by Ramona Keene

CITY/REGIONAL SUMMARY: Hong Kong, Former British Colony, Current Special Administrative Region of the People's Republic of China

TOP PICKS TO SEE AND DO: Don't miss the light show every evening, visible from both sides of Victoria Harbour. Best viewing spot is high above Hong Kong on the Mid-levels Escalator. All the iconic Hong Kong sights are wonderful—Victoria Peak, sunset cruises, and the Tian Tan Buddha—but for something extra special, check out the street art while wandering the back alleys of Wan Chai, and don't miss the villain-beaters under the fly-over at . . .

Luckily, Dom wakes up and joins us in the galley long before eighteen hundred rolls around, so the whole sleeping-in-the-women's-quarters thing doesn't become a problem. His little catnap has done him good, and before long he's wheedled his way through into the kitchen. Every time the door swings open, I can see him in there, apron-clad and showing off for Cookie.

Dinner that night is scrumptious, some kind of roasted white fish, accompanied—why am I not surprised?—by Samoan coconut bread rolls. Captain Jack practically weeps with joy, and scarfs at least a half dozen.

As usual, Dominic has become the most popular person on board. Between his baking and Sumaya's new material, I settle once again into my accustomed role of third wheel. That night we all crash hard, but before I fall asleep, I vow to make my own mark the way I know best—organization. Forget social media followers. There's more to life than popularity.

My Hong Kong report, now safely delivered via satellite Wi-Fi, is a thing of beauty, but I refuse to rest on my laurels. The next day, we make good time traversing the choppy waves of the East China Sea. Thinking ahead to my next report, I head up to the bridge to see if the captain can spare me a few minutes for an interview.

One thing being on board all these ships has taught me is that while every ship's captain I've met loves to talk, they take their responsibilities seriously. This is a busy shipping lane, but at the moment, there isn't any traffic in sight beyond a collection of five or six birds flying beside us, which I assume are seagulls. I assume wrong. They are, in fact, called black-naped terns, and they wheel and dive, riding on the wind behind the *Arctic Björn*. Every once in a while, one of them surges ahead of us, carrying a small fish in its beak.

Captain Kapena is indeed available, as evidenced by the fact that I find Dom on the bridge, leaning casually against a large chart table and chatting with him. I mentally kick myself for, once again, losing the edge to my competitor.

Because, warm hazel eyes or not, that's who he is. This is the way it has to be.

I pull out my phone, hit the "record" button, and listen in while Captain Jack tells stories from the glory days of Greenpeace.

chapter fifty

IMAGE: Yokohama Harbor
IG: Romy_K [Yokohama, Japan, April 18]
#ConcreteSail #JapaneseSushi
6981 ♥

I waken the next morning to an unexpected quiet. The ship's engine is off, and from the feel, we are definitely docked. Which means that sometime while I slept, the *Arctic Björn* has made it to Japan. Sumaya is not in her bunk, so I throw on my hoodie against the morning chill and follow the unexpected smell of bacon to the mess.

The smell is particularly luscious, and for some reason, seems almost decadently foreign. I'm not sure why, until I see Sumaya spooning out the last of a large bowl of oatmeal, while Dominic's plate shows the greasy remains of a full bacon-and-egg breakfast.

Of course. We've been traveling through Islamic countries, but I didn't miss pork at all until I smelled it this morning.

Cookie—land name Susan—slides a full plate toward me through the hatch into the galley. I collect it and walk over to where Dom and Sumaya are sitting with Margot, but I hesitate before sitting down.

"Are you okay with me eating this?" I ask, but Sumaya waves her spoon magnanimously at an open chair.

"No worries," she says as I pull out the chair, and then points her spoon at Dom. "He didn't even ask."

Dom looks puzzled, so I indicate the bacon on my plate.

His expression suddenly changes.

"Oh, shit—I mean—ah, shoot," he amends, looking apologetically over at Sumaya. "It didn't even cross my mind. We haven't had any bacon for so long, all I could think of was cramming it into my face."

She grins over at me. "Cultural insensitivity much?"

I lift my plate. "I can go sit somewhere else . . ."

"I'm kidding," she says, rolling her eyes. "I wouldn't mind trying it myself—it smells quite good."

"No way!" I exclaim, jumping back to my feet. "At least, not on my watch. You can do all the teen rebellion things when you are safely with your family. Until then—you keep . . ."

My voice trails off as I realize I nearly used the word *kosher*.

"Islamic," I say at last.

"Halal," Dom and Sumaya chorus together, then bump fists.

"Right. Halal."

"I'm pescatarian," says Margot as I dig into my food. "So I think you're all terrible people."

Sumaya laughs and gets up to take her bowl into the kitchen.

Margot smiles across the table at me. "Heading into the city today? It's gonna take us three hours to load all the fuel and supplies for the trip, so you have time."

I think about improving my ExLibris report. "I'm not sure," I say slowly. "I haven't exactly ever been to Tokyo before, but . . ."

Margot shrugs. "Well, first place, we're in Yokohama, not Tokyo. A little further south. Still, all the cities run together in this part of Japan, for sure."

"Are you going?" I ask Dom, but he shakes his head.

"I'm thinking customs," he pauses, and glances over at Sumaya, "might be a problem."

I remember the clerk in Kolkata's words: *We cannot, of course, guarantee the reception of the refugee in the receiving country.*

"Good point," I mutter.

"Look," Dom says. "If you go in for an hour, take a few pictures, and get a bit of info on the city for ExLibris, I'll stay here and keep Sumaya busy. She said she'd help me fix my hair."

Sumaya flexes her fingers and beams.

"I'm going in to the market for Cookie," says Margot. "She's going to make sushi tonight, and we need rice and fish for that. I'm happy to show you around, if you want to tag along."

"Deal," I say, grinning at both of them.

chapter fifty-one

Things I learn in Japan that may or may not make it into my report:

1. Yokohama is located south of Tokyo, on the island of Honshu, and is Japan's second-largest city. Also? You can shop till you drop here. So. Many. Shopping centers.

2. Yokohama looks brand-new. The city was devastated by the Great Kanto earthquake of 1923, and then again by American airstrikes in the Second World War. This depressing thought brought to you by the elegance of the Landmark Tower, built in 1993, and by the design innovation of the InterContinental Yokohama Grand, a hotel shaped like a gigantic concrete sail.

3. Japan and North Korea really, really do not get along. Case in point: the Japan Coast Guard Museum has the wreck of a North Korean spy ship inside, with the hull all shot up. Turns out the spy ship blew itself up and sank, so badly did they not want to be captured by the Japanese.

4. Case in second point: an unknown number of Japanese citizens have been kidnapped and taken to Pyongyang over the

years, to aid in spy training. North Korea actually admitted to this, though there is some dispute as to numbers.

5. A few blocks away from the somber museum where I learned all about points three and four, is the CupNoodles Museum, devoted to my favorite Japanese food. A greater contrast in museum subjects I have never seen.

That night, over an excellent sushi repast, as the *Arctic Björn* pulls out into the Pacific Ocean, Sumaya is uncharacteristically silent.

"What—no afterdinner set?" teases Dom, sliding a large wooden spoon across the table. "I thought that's what you were working on today. I've even brought your microphone."

Sumaya arches an eyebrow up under her hijab. "I was in the ship's library," she says, and lifts a book onto the table. "Learning about whales."

She adds that she'd been interested in the history of the ship, so when Dom fell asleep, she pulled a few books off the captain's bookshelf.

"Dom fell asleep?" I ask, shooting him a glance. "What happened to the hair styling?"

"Postponed until tonight," he says with a shrug. "Who am I to get in the way of higher learning?"

Sumaya pulls a heavy set of binoculars onto the table. "When I returned his books, Captain Jack leant me these," she says proudly. "I'm going to keep a close eye out. It's nearly time for the migration of the right whales—they spend their summers in the Bering Sea, and we'll be floating right by there."

"I think whales swim pretty deep," I say. "Don't be disappointed if you don't see much of anything. This is a big ocean, you know."

Sumaya rolls her eyes at Dominic. "Uh, Romy? You do know whales are mammals, yes? Which means they have to surface to breathe."

"Yeah, *Romy*," says Dom, imitating both her exasperated tone and deadpan expression. "What did you think? They scoot along the bottom like submarines?"

The two of them giggle like idiots.

"No," I say stiffly, even though it might be possible the thought had crossed my mind. "I *know* they're mammals."

"Right whales have been around for millions of years," Sumaya adds, flipping open the book. "It says here they've been around since the Mio—the Miocene Epoch," she says, enunciating carefully. "That's longer than Iceland has been an island."

"I did not," I say, shaking my head. Even though I know that she received English tutoring in the camp she was in, I'm constantly stunned by Sumaya's interest in the world around her. Not to mention her mad skills at reading English, which by my count, is her third— or possibly fourth—language.

"And you know what? Now there are only a few hundred left, when there were once thousands—hundreds of thousands—swimming in all the oceans in the world."

"What? Really?"

She slides the book over to me, open to a page with a picture of an enormous baleen whale, leaping high above the waves.

"It's bad enough when people hurt each other," she says softly. "But it seems worse to kill something off that's so giant, and so beautiful."

I nod slowly as she reaches for her binoculars and stands up. "I'm going to spend as much time as I can looking out for them. I wish there was something more we could do."

Tucking in her chair, she grabs the binoculars and heads for the door.

Margot's contribution to the dinner is a bottle of sake, and she slides it across the table to us, as she heads off to bed.

"I don't really drink," I say primly, to which Dom rolls his eyes.

"Since Port Said?" he asks, deadpan.

Margot shakes her head. "Nobody drinks in Port Said," she says. "Muslim country."

I refuse to meet Dominic's eye.

"Anyway," she continues. "There's only a drop left. You two should finish it."

When she leaves, Dom drains the bottle into two glasses.

"That's more than a drop," I say. He tings his glass against mine.

"To our final ocean," he says, and of course, I have to drink to that.

"What's been your favorite city so far?" he asks, leaning back in his chair.

I shake my head, overwhelmed by the question.

He sips his sake and winces. "I really liked Paris," he says, his voice a little hoarse.

I remember my smashed camera, and the dash through the ancient tunnels underground.

"It was—interesting," I admit, hedging.

"I got to tour this tiny apartment in the top of the Eiffel Tower," he says. "Did you see it?"

I shake my head and take another slug of the sake, which is growing on me. "I didn't get a chance to see it. But I may have heard something about it."

He pulls out his phone and shows me a few shots from his Instagram.

The first is a breathtaking panorama of the city, followed by a shot of an elegant dinner set on a tiny table. The plates are rimmed in gold, the cutlery gleams, and a cluster of brilliant gerberas act as a centerpiece.

"That looks really—vivid," I admit. "Were you there on a sunny day?"

He shrugs. "It was pouring, as I recall."

Suddenly I recall it too. "But—how do you get everything to look so bright?"

"I dunno," he says, draining his glass. "Maybe just practice?"

He slides a long finger across the screen, and my own feed pops up.

"No!" I mutter, and reach for his phone.

"Why not? I want to look at *your* work."

"I'm—ah—going for a different aesthetic than you," I say hurriedly.

He starts flipping through my shots.

"Hmm. I see what you mean. Mostly black-and-white. More moody and bleak, right?"

"They're not moody. Or bleak, actually," I say defensively. "More . . ."

The sake prevents me from coming up with the word I'm looking for.

"Gloomy?" he says, grinning.

"Now you're just giving me a hard time."

"No." He shakes his head firmly. "I really am interested."

I shrug. "I've—never thought about it, to tell you the truth," I admit.

"What do you mean? You have to think about these things. It's a choice, isn't it?"

"Yeah, I guess. I dunno, I've always considered black-and-white to be—uh—*better*. More artistically appealing."

"It's more dark, if that's what you're going for."

"Dark?" I lean forward, disturbed by how much his use of the word bothers me. "My pictures are not *dark*. They're stark—they're biting. It's intended as social commentary."

"Social commentary? Okay, now we're getting somewhere."

"Well, what do you think—I'm doing this for fun? I mean, I'm trying to say something, okay?"

"Okay. Which is . . . ?"

"Which is—you don't seriously expect me to sum it up? Each shot means something different, Dom. They're all little pieces of me—of where I'm from. Of who I am."

He leans forward and takes back his phone. "No, you're right, you're right. You shouldn't have to sum up your whole body of work in a few words. Let's pick an example. How 'bout this one?"

He holds out his phone, with one of my earliest Insta shots cued up. It's a picture of the water tank on the roof of the building across from the bookshop.

I look up at him. "That's one of my earliest posts, and I like to think my work has grown quite a bit since then. I mean, my number of followers is way bigger now."

He gives me a crooked grin. "Yeah, mine too. Took a giant surge this week, for some reason. But I don't care about the numbers—I'm talking about the actual pictures you take. So, humor me. Why this shot? It's taken in the rain, right?"

"Obviously. I like roof shots in New York. The roofs are a—a different world. There's all these mundane things like water tanks and air-con units, but up there—there's a freedom you don't feel down on the streets."

His expression changes to something I can't read. "Okay—that's fair. And it explains a lot."

"What does that mean? What are we talking about here? Are you trying to understand me by looking at my pictures?"

"What if I am?"

I'm so surprised by this response, I don't know what to say. Instead, I finish my sake, and catch myself wishing for more.

He's quiet a minute. "Can you pick one to show me? Like, maybe one of your favorites?"

I snatch back his phone and start scrolling through my site. "This is a bad idea. You get to know someone by talking to them, and hanging out, you know? Not by looking at their work."

"So, are you saying your work doesn't reflect who you are?"

I stop scrolling long enough to glare at him. "Well, of course it does. It's just not *all* of who I am." I pause on a more recent picture. "Okay, what about this one?"

We've both been careful to not use Sumaya's face in any of our shots, but the picture I show him is a long shot, showing the refugees on the *Wahash Mahat* right after they were rescued.

"I've seen this one before," he says quietly. "You've taken off the hashtag."

"I pulled it down. I do try to learn from my mistakes, you know."

"Well, you're right. And I really do like this one."

Point to Romy.

"Thank you," I say as graciously as I can manage, considering the sake.

It's not until later that night, in my own bunk, that I notice Dom himself is actually in the picture. He's off to one side, slightly out of focus, a gentle, preoccupied smile on his face. And when I look closely, I realize he's not staring down at the new passengers. He's smiling straight over at me.

chapter fifty-two

IMAGE: Stormy Seas
IG: Romy_K [Arctic Björn, Pacific Ocean, April 23]
#Windswept #Whalers
5921 ♥

ExLibris Transit Report, submitted by Ramona Keene

TRAVEL SUMMARY: The *Arctic Björn*, an icebreaker-class ship, is less speedy than she is mighty. Currently returning to home port in Vancouver from an action against Russian whalers. Destined for a refit.

TOP PICKS TO SEE AND DO: While this is an excellent vessel for whale watching or for adventuresome souls who want to crew on an eco-active ship, I would highly recommend instead, the *Nonsuch Maria*, which sails direct from Victoria Harbour in Hong Kong to San Francisco. Amenities include . . .

In spite of the calendar, the onset of spring seems far, far away on these grey North Pacific seas. The *Arctic Björn* is no container ship—it's not even the size of the stinking refrigeration vessel I took across the Mediterranean Sea. And maybe when we were floating within sight of the coastline of Japan, I noticed the rolling less, but now that we are out—way out—in the Bering Sea, it's really something. The captain muttered something this morning about a low pressure area in the Pacific, which I'm hoping will help speed our journey. At the moment, I feel impossibly far away from New York City, and impossibly close to the end of April. And there's nothing I can do to get there sooner.

"I need a breath of air," I tell Margot one morning as she stands outside the door, effectively blocking the way.

"Of course you do," she says soothingly. "Stomach's probably a mess after that bumpy night, right?"

I haven't actually been seasick since way back on the *Guernsey Isle*, but it's easier to agree.

"Yes—right. Just need a glimpse of the horizon to steady me out."

"Heh." We both clutch the bar on each side of the door as the ship bucks over another wave. "Good luck with that."

She points back behind my shoulder. "Gear up, and you can come out."

Protocol on the *Arctic Björn* requires the crew—which includes us—to be appropriately dressed whenever on deck. This means a heavy-duty grey jumpsuit known as a "float coat" and a bright yellow helmet, tightly strapped under the chin. At the emergency run-through, I looked like a roll of industrial carpet made human.

I turn around with a sigh to find Sumaya, helmet strapped on over her hijab, grinning up at me. "I like these suits," she says, giving a little pirouette in spite of the rolling deck beneath us. "Warm *and* waterproof. Also, fashionable."

I snort and push past her. She's belted the shapeless float coat with her floral headscarf, which means she now looks like a runway model.

"Be quick," she yells in through the door. "I'm looking for whales!"

Ten minutes later, I join her on the deck. We've been relegated to the aft part of the ship, to avoid the small difficulty of being swept off the prow by crashing waves. This part of the ship is marginally less windy, and it's exhilarating to be out on the open sea.

As long as I don't think too hard about how far we are from land.

Clutching the captain's binoculars, and with her legs braced against the railing, Sumaya scans the rolling surface of the seas.

"Any luck?" I yell at her, over the wind.

"Nothing yet," she says, shaking her head. "But I'm hopeful. Margot put the mic in the water overnight, and she played me the recording right after breakfast this morning. Minke whales!"

She dangles the binoculars by the strap around her neck and looks up at me, eyes shining. "They sing to each other, Romy!"

"That's astonishing," I say. "Do you think she'll play the recording for me too? I've never heard a whale sing."

"Remember that bit I read you about the right whales? Margot says there may be a family group near here. She thought she could hear them on the tape."

We grip the railing with both hands as the ship rolls across the top of another white-flecked wave. I keep my knees a little flexed and marvel at how quickly my body has adjusted to being back on the water. These waves aren't much less than the ones that were pitching the *Guernsey Isle* around, and my stomach is handling things much differently.

Half a world differently, I think. *More than half a world.*

The door behind us slams open in the wind and Dominic steps out wearing a self-conscious smile and carrying his helmet.

"Look at you!" I say as he zips his suit up to his chin.

"Like it? It's Sumaya's work."

His low ponytail is gone, replaced with neat dreadlocks.

"Very nice," I mutter, and focus on Sumaya, so my eyes don't give away just how great I think he looks.

Sumaya drops her binoculars again and looks at him critically. "Easier to handle this morning?" she asks, as he straps his helmet on.

"So much easier. I don't know why I didn't do this a long time ago."

"Where did you learn how to make dreadlocks?" I ask her as she prepares to resume her search of the water.

They both burst out laughing at this, and I try hard not to feel hurt, since I entirely do not get the joke.

"Are you serious?" she says at last.

"Yes. And it's not nice to laugh at people."

She immediately looks stricken. "I thought you were joking," she says, patting my arm like you might a stray dog. "My aunties taught me. They are very particular when it comes to doing hair. I have really curly hair, so when I was little it was in locs for as long as I can remember."

"Mine too," says Dom. "Until I was ten, for sure." He points at Sumaya's binoculars and she carefully pulls the strap over her helmet and hands them over.

"Well, you haven't had your hair in dreads since I've met you," I say to her lamely. The truth is, I've only seen her hair once or twice, mostly in her first days on the *Wahash Mahat*, or when she's adjusting her hijab. Every time it's been neatly tidied into a pair of French braids, tight against her scalp.

She shrugs. "When I was eleven, I started trying new things with my hair," she says. "My aunties were gone by then, so I practiced on any of the other kids around the camp who would keep still long enough."

I glance back up at Dom, who is still peering intently through her binoculars. With his hair swept up so neatly under the helmet, the clean broad lines of his cheekbones stand out even further.

"I guess . . ." I begin, but Dom cuts me off with a shout.

"Spout!" he yells, pointing off the starboard side of the ship.

"Where? Where?" cries Sumaya.

Dominic jams the binoculars into her hand again and points her in the right direction.

"I see them!" she yells, bouncing like a pogo stick.

I see them too—three plumes of water shooting above the waves.

"Are you sure it's not only the whitecaps?" I say, but Sumaya shakes her head firmly, glasses still glued to her eyes.

"No! I saw a tail, I think, and maybe a back fin?"

"Dorsal!" yells Dom, and they share a joyful high five.

As they pass the binoculars back and forth, I lean off to one side, feeling the sea spray on my face. I can taste the salt on the back of my tongue, crisp and drying in a way that makes me instantly thirsty. This is good, as it gives me something else to think about other than Dominic.

He's the competition, I remind myself. *After Vancouver, it'll be him against me again. We have to go back to Game On.*

Suddenly losing my taste for being on deck, I'm just heading inside when I spot three ships bearing down on us from the starboard side. The ships are equipped like fishing vessels, and are coming up fast. On the horizon behind them is a much larger ship. Not a tanker. Not really like anything I've ever seen before.

I lean back and put my hand on Dominic's arm.

He automatically reaches out to give me a turn with the binoculars, when he catches sight of the rapidly approaching ships.

"Holy shit," he says, and all the joy drops out of his face. "This can't be good."

"Should we—should we go up to the bridge to let them know?" I ask.

Underneath our feet, the ship's engines shudder, and with a sudden roar, the *Arctic Björn* surges forward.

"I think they might have already clued in," Dom says.

Without another word, we scramble inside.

Upstairs, the bridge is filled to capacity, and everybody's busy.

"You need to go below," says Margot as she hustles past the doorway. "We have a situation. Those ships are whalers, after the minkes."

"But I saw spouts," cries Sumaya. "What if the right whales get in the way?"

"We are between them and the whales, for the moment," says Margot. The ship heaves and she clutches a railing to stop from falling. All the equipment on the bridge, screwed down or not, is shuddering with the effort it's taking the *Arctic Björn* to maintain this speed.

"We're only a few hours out from American waters," Margot adds, pointing at a map on her screen. "If we can keep between them and this pod until then, they'll have to back off."

"I don't have the kind of fuel we're burning to keep up this speed until then," the captain mutters, then jerks his head to the side.

"Get these three down below," he snaps at Margot. "The last thing we need if they fire on us is a kid up here."

"If they—what?" I gasp, but by then Margot's swung open the door.

"Nothing to worry about," she says, pointing down the narrow stairs. "It's all bluff and feint, really. We have a long history with these guys, believe me."

"Where are they from? Russia? Japan?"

She shrugs. "Not sure. The boats are unmarked. We'll do our best, I promise. Now get going!"

Dom and I follow Sumaya as she clatters down the metal stairs, holding the rails on each side as the ship lurches. The engine is even louder down here, and it's making a strange clunking noise I've not heard before.

As we head for the storage lockers, the cook pops a head out of the galley. Her face is dusted in flour.

"I don't know what the hell they're doing up there," she says. "But I've discovered my yeast is dead, and all my help seems to have evaporated. Any chance you could give me a hand?"

Dom's wrapping an apron around his waist before she has a chance to draw another breath. I help Sumaya step out of her float coat and then collect it up, along with Dom's, and the two helmets.

"I'll take these back," I say, and he lifts a hand, already white with flour, in thanks. I close the door behind me as the cook shepherds Sumaya over toward a large bin of dried fruit, and hurry off down the hall.

Jamming the float coats into one of the storage lockers, I race to my bunk and retrieve my phone. If something's going down with these whalers, I want a picture.

chapter fifty-three

IMAGE: Icicles on the Overhangs
IG: Romy_K [Arctic Björn, Pacific Ocean, April 23]
#InternationalIncident #Whoops
6639 ♥

Things I learn during an international incident on the high seas:

1. Time passes very slowly when your vessel is engaged in preventing whale slaughter.

2. Mysterious whaling vessels are small and super speedy. Whoever they are, according to Margot, they're hunting minke whales, not right whales, which—appallingly—is legal.

3. Jurisdiction is a nebulous thing in international waters.

4. Spring storms can be really terrible in the Bering Sea in April.

5. Even one picture of a whale—or a whaler—will be worth it.

By the time I finish my notes and creep back up the stairs, it's all hands on deck. Or, in this case, on the bridge, since no one would last on the deck for long. Huge waves are crashing across the prow, and I can't make out a thing through the window, even with the wipers going full speed.

Outside, icicles have formed on the overhangs, and all the flags and banners on the lines are flapping snaps of brilliant color against the grey seas. I don't know how they measure waves in the middle of an icy ocean, but these ones look as tall and colorless as the roof of any three-story walk-up in Chelsea. There's no pattern to the waves, and they shift and heave in all directions. White foam is flying everywhere.

Inside, the captain is yelling into a phone, Margot's on the radio, and a guy in a striped sweater is calling out readings as he runs back and forth between the various instruments.

No one has time to notice me, so I wedge myself in a back corner, out of the captain's eye line, and start shooting pictures. A strong smell of diesel wafts up from below as I try to get at least one clean shot.

Outside the streaming windows, I watch as one of the smaller rainbow banners rips away from the flagpole and vanishes into the grey waves. The howling wind buffets the ship and rattles the windows in their frames.

Right at that moment, Margot catches sight of me. Grasping the railings, she skips around the perimeter of the bridge to the back corner where I've wedged myself. A set of binoculars that look even larger than Sumaya's swing from her neck as she looms above me.

"The captain sent you below," she yells into my face, and then jams a thumb toward the stairs. "Get going!"

I raise a hand in defeat. "Okay, okay! But are the whales safe?"

She shrugs. "No sign of them since this weather blew up, but that might be the choppiness."

I make my way unsteadily toward the stairs, keeping my knees flexed in order to stay upright. Margot follows, obviously not trusting me to leave on my own.

Behind me, the captain yells something at Margot, and I feel the engine thrust beneath my feet. When she doesn't answer him, he swings around and spots me heading for the door.

"YOU!" he barks. "Get below!"

Stumbling through the door, I glance out the window just as the black shadow of one of the whaling ships veers into view. It surges into a space between the huge waves, only a dozen or so feet from the bow of the *Arctic Björn*.

"Reverse, reverse—all engines," yells the captain, as the prow of the other ship rears up again, this time to the left—the port side—of us. Water streams off the ship's prow, and both ships lurch sideways.

"What the fuck are they doing?" screams Striped Sweater, and slams all the gears back.

The *Arctic Björn* lurches again, and I fly backwards down the stairs.

chapter fifty-four

IMAGE: Emergency
IG: DomBakes [Anchorage, Alaska, April 23]
#RescueChopper #Hospital
25327 ♥

surface long enough to discover that Striped Sweater, whose name I never catch, is also the ship's medic. He's bandaged the cut over my left eye, and offers to give me something for the pain. I have a vague sense of a whirling wind, and a sort of spinning situation during which I'm pretty sure I drift away again.

waken to an intense feeling of pressure in my head. Opening my eyes, Sumaya is holding one of my hands and Dominic the other, but when I struggle to sit up, I find I can't move.

"Hey, you," yells Dom over the wind noise. "You're back just in time."

"In time for what?" I mutter blearily. "Why can't I move?"

"You're strapped onto a stretcher," yells a woman I don't recognize. "How are you feeling?"

"Like I don't want to be strapped onto a stretcher," I say, trying and failing to tug my arms loose.

The woman makes a shooing motion to Sumaya and Dom. "Seatbelts," she says, then turns back to me.

"We're about to land, so I need to leave you where you are for the moment. Hang tight."

I can't turn my head either, for some reason. "Where are we?"

The strange woman's face returns. "About to land at the air force base outside of Anchorage. You've had a head injury, but we'll have you to the hospital in no time."

Then she vanishes again.

And because there's no more frightening word in all the world, I close my eyes and start to cry.

Together people—organized adults, who have control—people like that don't cry in public. They don't melt down right in front of a teenager—a displaced child—who has lost her own parents in the most horrific fashion. They don't cry so hard, they hiccup for an hour afterwards.

I used to think I was a together person.

I was wrong.

It's hard enough to learn this truth, but to learn it about myself in such a public way, with both Dominic and Sumaya making sympathetic eyes at me—it's humiliating.

The tears don't stop until after I've been bundled off the chopper and into an ambulance. Until after the ambulance has taken me to the Providence Medical Center. Until after a determination is made that my neck is uninjured, and in fact, all I need is to have my left eyebrow stitched back together.

The woman, who turns out to be a paramedic named Sara Amaklak, pats my arm with one blue-gloved hand. "I have to head back. Are you feeling better yet?"

"I'm really sorry," I manage, between hiccups.

"No worries. People are scared to fly with us all the time. At least you didn't barf on me."

"It wasn't the flight . . ." I begin, but she's gone before I can find the words.

After she leaves, Dominic slips into the seat beside me.

"I'm sorry," I say to him too. "I've messed everything up."

The taste of the Ativan the nurse gave me before the x-ray is still bitter under my tongue.

He shrugs my apology away, but his face is still puzzled. "Was it the helicopter? You didn't have this reaction in Africa," he whispers.

His head is right beside mine, and the feeling of his breath on my cheek is almost more comforting than the Ativan.

I take a deep, shuddering breath, but at that moment, a nurse enters.

"Just going to get these stitches done," she says to Dominic. "We'll have her back to you in no time."

"I'll be in the waiting room," he says. "Maybe we can talk then?"

I nod, and the nurse wheels me away.

The nurse is right. I've never had stitches before, but she's so fast, I don't even see the needle. In less than ten minutes, I'm sitting on a bench outside the hospital, squinting into the thin spring sunshine while Dominic calls us a cab. Someone has given me a khaki jacket to wear, and I huddle inside it gratefully.

Dominic slides onto the bench beside me. "He'll be here in five."

"Where's Sumaya?" I ask, feeling the bandage over my eyebrow gingerly.

"Don't touch that," he mutters, pulling my hand into his lap. "She's back at the base. Now we know you're okay, there's an armed

362 · kc dyer

forces plane taking us down to Vancouver as soon as we get back there."

"Armed forces? Who's going to pay for that? Is it because Sumaya is considered a threat?"

He laughs. "Not the U.S. Air Force. The Canadians. It's a water bomber on loan for a forest fire up here, so they're heading down to Vancouver anyway. We're hitching a ride."

"That's nice of them," I say, still feeling a bit foggy.

"I think the search and rescue guys pulled some strings, after the whole helicopter thing in Kodiak."

A yellow cab pulls up, and Dom stands to help me into the back seat.

"Wait a minute," I say, slowly, as he slides in beside me. "Kodiak? I thought we were in Anchorage."

He squeezes my hand. "We are. It's April twenty-fourth today, and you've missed a few things."

The rest of the cab ride is taken up with what turns out to be a pretty long story.

chapter fifty-five

IMAGE: Bering Strait in April
IG: DomBakes, April 24
#Alaska #Detour #AFinalGoodbye
27003 ♥

Things I learn in a cab ride in Alaska:

1. Falling down the stairs on a moving ship is not a great idea.

2. My skull is apparently partially granite.

3. After the close call, the whalers did indeed vanish, but the Arctic Björn's engine seized. Captain Kapena's distress call was answered by the search and rescue out of Kodiak, Alaska.

4. KISAR sent a Sea King helicopter to drop a mechanic and fuel supplies to the Arctic Björn. They collected me, my head injury, and my companions and returned us all to Kodiak, where the Sea King refueled and then flew us to Anchorage.

5. I slept through just about all of this.

O kay, that explains a lot," I say as the cab rolls to a halt.

Dominic leans forward. "Wait a sec," he says, handing his credit card to the cab driver. "I'll help you out."

I swing open my door and climb out before he can make it around to my side.

"You should let me help you," he says reproachfully as the cab pulls away. "Head injury, remember?"

"I'm okay, really," I say. "No concussion, even."

"You're still going to have a headache, when the freezing wears off."

In front of us is the gate to the American Air Force base. A cold wind whistles around our feet as we walk up, and a soldier steps out of the booth.

Dominic pulls out a folded paper from the inside of his jacket and hands it over.

"The SAR Buffalo, huh?" the soldier says, scanning the page. "Lemme see your passports. I need to call this in."

He disappears into his booth.

"So, Sumaya is waiting for us here?" I ask.

Dominic nods. "They—ah—wouldn't let her off the base to come to the hospital, because of the no-passport thing." His eyes shift to where the soldier is still talking on the phone. "Technically, they're going with not admitting she's on American soil," he whispers. "If anyone asks, the transfer was straight from the Sea King to the Canadian plane. Less paperwork that way."

I wince. My painkillers are wearing off a little.

He grins at me. "When I left, she was trying out some new material on the search and rescue pilots."

The soldier reemerges. "Sit tight," he says. "Jeep's coming to take you to the plane. Might take a few minutes."

He returns our passports and then lifts the gate. We walk over to a wooden bench tucked against the fence and out of the wind. Behind us, the grey waters of Cook Inlet lay flat and cold. We both fall silent, listening to the wind swirling off the water, around the treeless streets, and between the buildings. The ground is bare—not quite frozen, but dry as a bone, with a few patches of stiff yellow grass.

"So . . ." Dom says, at last. "Why Anchorage?"

"Why what?" I growl, feeling immediately defensive.

"Why were you so upset when you found out where we are? What's so scary about this place?"

I'm about to snap that I don't know what he's talking about, or why it's any of his business anyway, but something about his expression makes the words stick in my throat.

Instead, I take a deep breath.

"I was thirteen years old when my parents went on their second honeymoon. They'd saved up, and made a deal with my uncles for me to sleep over for a week. I was excited, because it was the bookshop. I loved staying at the bookshop."

"Okay," he says, his face still puzzled.

"My dad was a photographer, and he promised to bring a ton of pictures of polar bears and wolves home. He worked for a newspaper then, and he was excited to do some real wildlife photography. Made a change from all the usual urban stuff, I guess."

"So—they came—here?" Dom asks softly.

All I can manage is a nod.

"Car accident," I say at last, but with the words, the tears come again. "On their way to the airport. It's—the reason I've been afraid to go anywhere, for my whole life. If you leave home? You die."

I wipe away the tears, and laugh a little. "Intellectually, I know this isn't true, obviously. And now I've proved it—just about, anyway. I mean, I've been most of the way around the world, and I'm still here. But that's why I never left New York, after the accident. And I probably never would have, without this trip."

"Do you mean to say that you were convinced—in your heart of hearts—that you were going to die if you left New York?"

I sigh, and look away from him. "It sounds so stupid when you say it out loud."

"Romy." He turns sideways on the bench, and puts a hand on each of my shoulders so that I'm forced to look at him. "It's not stupid. It's fucking brave, is what it is. You agreed to race around the world to save your uncle's bookstore, even though you were convinced you were going to die?"

I shrug. "I'm not brave. Sumaya is brave. I'm only an idiot who let a thing—I mean, yes, it was a terrible thing—but I let it ruin my life."

I can feel the tape holding the dressing over my left eye give way, and I push it gingerly back into place. "The whole time, at each stop, I thought—okay, I've made it this far. Maybe I can do it. The West Coast part was supposed to be through San Francisco, right? And then, even in Hong Kong when we learned we needed to take Sumaya to her auntie, we were going through Vancouver. It's Canada, but at least nowhere near Alaska."

I have to stop to catch my breath a minute. Fishing around in the pocket of the stranger's jacket I'm wearing, I find a shred of tissue and use it to wipe my nose.

"On their way to the airport?" Dom says, his voice choking a little on the last word. "On their way home?"

"Their car went into the water. Through the ice. I don't know the details . . ."

He drops his hands, releasing my shoulders, and I slump back against the bench.

"Wait here a second," he says quietly, and then hurries across to speak with the soldier in the booth.

Seconds later, he's back.

"Come on," he says. "I checked. We've got ten minutes. Let's go for a walk."

As I get to my feet, he pauses to do the zipper of my jacket all the way up to my chin. It's a man's coat, and probably looks about as good on me as the float suit on the *Arctic Björn*, but it cuts the wind.

"Where are we going? There's nothing around here," I say as we walk past the guard again. "It's pretty barren."

He reaches to take my hand, and tucks it with his, into his pocket.

"The water's right here," he says, pointing with his other hand toward the rocky shoreline. "Let's go say goodbye."

chapter fifty-six

IMAGE: Vancouver Rain
IG: Romy_K [Above Vancouver, April 24]
#AJoyousReunion
5545 ♥

'm awakened by a shift in the engine as the plane makes its final descent. We're flying in a bright yellow Canadian Armed Forces Search and Rescue plane, returning to Vancouver after dropping firefighting supplies in Alaska.

There are only two windows in this section of the plane and I can't see out of either of them, so there's nothing much to do but sit and think.

The walk to the shore had been brief. I have no idea where my parents died, but I could see commercial planes taking off and landing in the distance, so it had to be somewhere nearby. Dom didn't say anything—just took me in his arms and held me as I stood there on the rocky shore and cried.

By the time we got back to the gate, the jeep was waiting. I'm sure my face was still red when we got to the plane, but Sumaya threw herself into my arms anyway. She was overflowing with the exciting news that she had reached her Auntie Nkruna, who will meet us in Vancouver. Before we left the hangar, Dominic managed to connect with ExLibris via FaceTime, and give Teresa Cipher's assistant a brief update. I kept my stitched-up face well in the background, and let him do the talking. Powell agreed to pass on the information about what Dom referred to several times as our *extenuating circum-stances*, and told us to reconnect with her once we made it to Vancouver.

What neither of us remembered was that crossing the international dateline, somewhere off the coast of Alaska, has bought us another day. All the same, there are now only five days left to the end of April. Five days to cover the whole of North America.

The plane lands with a thump and a slight hop. Sumaya, who has managed to score one of the window seats nearer the front, gives a little squeal of delight.

"It's so green," she exclaims.

"What? The airport?" Dom asks.

Sumaya shakes her head. "No—the city. I've been watching as we landed. So many trees. The whole coast is mountains and trees and . . ."

As the plane taxies to a stop and the engines gear down, another sound emerges, like drumming on the rooftop.

"Rain!" Sumaya finishes. Her smile is a ray of sunshine against the grey light outside.

Dom leans back in his seat and stretches before undoing his seatbelt. "Rain means life in Somalia," he remarks quietly to me.

As I watch him unfold himself from his seat and then turn to help Sumaya gather her things before he collects his own, I know, without a shred of doubt, my feelings for him have completely changed. How can I continue to compete against this person who has shown me—and Sumaya—such kindness?

In the time it takes for the crew to winch open the back door of the plane, we've gathered all our belongings, and are waiting by the exit. Sometime on the flight, I handed Sumaya all the decals I've been collecting, and when I pick up my suitcase, I see it is emblazoned with memories of every country we've been through.

No maple leaf yet, though. I'll have to remedy that.

From behind us, the pilot swings open the door to the cockpit and walks down to join us.

"Welcome to Canada," he says. "Lucky for you, this part of it is less of a frozen wasteland than the rest, at the moment."

Outside, the rain buckets down. Dom and I pause to pull up our hoods, but Sumaya bolts past us and down the ramp. On the tarmac she stops, arms spread wide, and spins in a circle. By the time we reach her, she's soaked to the skin.

"It smells SO good," she says, eyes wide. Her headscarf is plastered to her skull. I think of all she has been through to get here, her new home, and I can't help myself. I hold out my arms and she launches into them—and so does Dom. Suddenly, the three of us are in a laughing, crying, nerd-bouncing hug as the relief of the moment seeps into all of us. We are in Canada. Sumaya is safe at last.

Of course, inside the airport building, there is paperwork. But because Sumaya is designated a refugee, and because she has a relative waiting on the other side of the customs barrier to sponsor her, things progress with a smooth, Canadian politeness that warms my organization-loving heart.

Dominic is approved to move to passport control first, so he heads off, promising to locate Sumaya's Auntie Nkruna. Sumaya and I are ushered into a white-walled room. The border official stamps my passport immediately, but agrees to let me stay with my companion, now designated as an "accompanied refugee minor." Moments later, the door opens and another guard enters. This one is female, and is wearing a hijab.

"Galab wanaagsan," she says to Sumaya. *"Magacayguuwa Sulekha Hussen."*

Sumaya bobs her head. *"Wanaagsan Sulekha,"* she says, grinning. "But I have English, yeah?"

And things move at what feels like an extraordinary rate after that. The session with the Somali-Canadian border official is long enough for her to explain that Nkruna has completed all the preliminary paperwork required to allow Sumaya a temporary admittance to the country.

"Your auntie is very organized," Officer Hussen says. "She has practically the whole Somalian community in the Lower Mainland ready to meet you."

When we finally make it out of the customs area, the doors open on Dominic standing beside a willowy, dusky-skinned woman, with a high forehead crowned in sleek black curls. She is wearing a colorful print blouse over a pair of skinny jeans and Crocs. The resemblance to her niece is striking, though they look more like sisters than a full generation apart. My vision blurs with tears again as she envelops a suddenly very-shy Sumaya in her arms. When I turn away to give them a moment, I spot Dom also wiping his eyes, which makes me feel a little better about crying twice in one day.

After hugging her niece tightly, Auntie Nkruna hands me a business card for her hair salon. Dom holds his up, too, grinning.

"Ten percent off for you both, anytime," she says, and smiles at Dom. "Those locs need some work, bro."

He laughs. "Hey, these were done by a pro."

Sumaya smiles shyly up at her auntie as we follow her past a totem pole standing guard over all our fellow travelers, and out to a small white car.

The sun is setting as Nkruna drives us to her home in nearby

Surrey, for a Somali feast. As we pull to a stop, I can see the house is entirely decked out with colorful streamers and banners, sagging a little but no less cheerful in the deluge of rain. As Sumaya alights from the car, she is swarmed by a seemingly endless group of well-wishers pouring out of Nkruna's front door.

The dinner waiting for us is a feast, with contributions from everyone present. Casserole dishes crowd the table, filled with lamb stew, rice peppered with nuts and raisins, and chicken served over noodles. The competing aromas are warm and spicy and sweet. There are teetering piles of flatbread, tomato and cucumber salad, boiled eggs, and a whole table of sweet fried breads, including an enormous box of Tim Hortons donuts. Excited voices fill the air with conversation in Somali and English and a couple of other languages I cannot begin to decode.

Sumaya is seated with great ceremony at the head of a long table, with Dom and me on either side of her; however, this arrangement doesn't last long. People move their chairs to get closer to Sumaya, to hear news of her village and her journey. Dom is slapped on the back so much, I'm convinced he'll come away cheerfully bruised. My own hand is shaken until it's numb, and I tell the saga of getting my stitches more times than I can count.

Later, over a plate of sorghum salad and flatbread, Nkruna tells me her own story.

"I was in the camps in Eritrea from when I was little girl," she says, her voice low. "My father and both my brothers die in the violence there. My mother and I save all our money so smugglers take us on boat to Malaysia. It was a terrible trip, bad food, bad water. My mother die on the ship." Her voice falters.

"How old were you then?" asks Dominic softly.

"Thirteen," she replies. "Just like Sumaya."

"I'm *fourteen*, Auntie," says Sumaya, walking past with a piece of flatbread in one hand and a donut hole in the other.

At the sound of her niece's voice, Nkruna straightens. "So you are," she says brightly. When Sumaya has been pulled away by a couple of teen girls with an iPhone, Nkruna turns back to me. Her eyes are bright, but I see tears in the corners.

"I work my way to Hong Kong, and build my life there. Then, when I was twenty-nine years old, I came to this country. I want to spare Sumaya all I had to go through as a refugee in Asia, and then a new immigrant here."

Her eyes drop for a minute, and I can see her swallow hard before she is able to continue.

She reaches out and takes one of my hands, and one of Dominic's. "I cannot thank you enough for all you have done for my sister's child. She will be safe here. Soon, all she has gone through to get here will be old memory."

Dominic leans forward, his elbows on his knees, his half-eaten plate of food forgotten.

"My mother emigrated from Samoa to Hawaii when she was in her teens," he says. "She never speaks of the time before she met my dad, except to talk about cooking, of course." His smile is wistful. "Whatever I can do to ease Sumaya's transition into life here, I want to help. My mom does too."

I start to offer my own words of support, but suddenly, Nkruna releases my hand to enclose Dominic's hand in both of hers. As she locks her eyes on him, I remember the lady on the Indian train, and close my mouth.

It's my turn to listen.

"My sisters and I, we have done well in past twenty years," Nkruna says. "We are lucky—we have a trade, and strong backs to work hard."

She smiles proudly. "Today, I have salon here, and my sister has hers in Etobicoke, which is outside Toronto.

"We are forever in your debt for you bringing our family together," she adds, beaming at me again. "Both of you."

I lean forward to return her hug. "I'm pretty sure she would have made it with or without us," I say, and Dom nods. "That girl is a *force*."

Behind me, I hear Sumaya's voice, and I recognize the tone immediately. We turn to find she has everyone under twenty seated against the wall of the small living room. She is standing with her back to us, facing the group of teens, holding one of Nkruna's hairbrushes in her hand.

"You think *you* know rain?" she says, speaking into the handle of the hairbrush. "Let me tell you about the rain *I've* seen . . ."

Nkruna laughs. "I see what you mean," she says. "You know, when she was a little girl, and I used to do her hair, I would tell her there was nothing she couldn't do. At the time, I was thinking, you know—safe place to live, happy family, good career. But this?"

She shakes her head, and then the three of us clink our cups of sweet Somali tea, and drink a silent toast to one remarkable kid.

chapter fifty-seven

IMAGE: Coast Mountains at Sunset
IG: Romy_K [Vancouver, Canada, April 24]
#BeautifulBritishColumbia #CompetitionReignited
8307 ♥

The party spills out of the house into the backyard, which is packed with what feels like every member of the Canadian Somali diaspora, here to wish Sumaya well in her new home. My stomach is full to bursting with all the luscious food, making up for my total lack of appetite in Alaska. As the afternoon darkens, the rain eases up until only a faint mist floats through the evening sky. Everyone is eager to chat with Dom and me, but I am feeling antsy. The clock is ticking.

Apart from the youngsters, it seems many of Nkruna's friends came to Canada in the nineties and early part of the century, when Mogadishu was a war zone.

"It is much better there today, and some of the younger ones, they go back," explains Fawzia, whom I'm fairly certain is another of Sumaya's aunts—Nkruna's sister. "They want to bring investment and safe places back to Somalia."

I think of all that Sumaya went through to come here, and my stomach clenches a little. "And you? Do you plan to return one day?"

Fawzia shakes her head firmly. "This is my home now," she says. "My sisters and I, we work hard to get what we have. But I support the rights of my people to be free to make their own choices. Not everyone has had the same success as we have, coming here."

She points her spoon at a group of young girls circling Sumaya, each vying for a chance to tell jokes into her hairbrush. "Umoja, there in the pink? Both her brothers were lost to gangs. One died in a shooting and one is in jail."

"That's awful," I mutter.

"But some good came from the bad. Umoja's big sister, she works with gang members now. Helping them get back in school, or find jobs. She's very good at it."

"I guess with her brothers to use as examples, she can probably be persuasive," I say, and Fawzia grins.

"She's also much pretty girl," she says, waggling her eyebrows at me. "Especially when I do her hair!"

Later, I follow Nkruna into a little lean-to behind the kitchen. This tiny space only has room to hold a huge chest freezer and two muddy pairs of rubber boots.

"You having a good time?" she asks me, while expertly filling a large ice cream tub with ice from the freezer. "This party to welcome Sumaya, for sure, but also for you and that handsome man of yours. We want you both to know how thankful we are."

"Oh, he's not my—that is—we're not . . ." I stutter, and her eyes widen.

"Are you telling me you haven't indulged in that juicy bit of man flesh you been traveling with?" she asks incredulously.

"It's—it's not like that," I mutter, feeling my face flaming. "We're—uh—colleagues, sort of. With a—a—common goal."

She rolls her eyes in a way that makes it clear where Sumaya picked up her skills. "Girl, can you not see the way that man look at you?"

"Really, Nkruna—it's not like that at all." Changing the subject, I pat my stomach. "Thank you so much for that delicious feast. I don't think I've ever eaten better food in my life. But, I was wondering . . ."

She clunks the overhead door to the freezer closed and drops the newly filled pail on top. "Anything," she says before I can finish my sentence. "Anything you want, missy. Name it. It's yours."

"Just your Wi-Fi code, if you don't mind. I need to get online to find the fastest way back to New York, like right now."

She scoops up the bucket in one hand and sticks her other arm through mine. "Follow me. I've got the router jimmied up in a little closet in my back room, and the signal don't travel out here so good."

After dropping the bucket of ice on the kitchen table, she leads me away from the throng toward a quiet hallway in the back of the small house.

"Thank you so much," I say again. "For everything. It's such a relief to know Sumaya is safely with you. She seems so happy here already."

She squeezes my arm as we pause outside a door. "That girl had some adventures, for sure. She told me about your race," she says, and clicks her tongue disapprovingly. "Seems odd you can't hop a plane to get yourself home."

I can't suppress a sigh, which to my embarrassment comes out sounding more like a yawn.

Nkruna's face immediately looks concerned. "You need rest, Ramona. Let me make bed up for you in my back room." She reaches for the door handle.

I'm so tired, I can hardly think, but I can't even consider sleeping until I've sorted out the rest of the journey. Before I can say a word, the door swings open and Dominic steps out.

"Report filed, transportation sorted," he says, nodding. "Thank you for the quiet space to get it all done, Nkruna." He steps back, swinging the door wide. "You coming in, Romy?"

I slip past, averting my eyes from both of them, but he doesn't seem to notice.

"Good. Got a text from Powell for us to Skype in as soon as possible. Not sure why."

I glance up to see Nkruna, her hand on the doorknob and a funny little smile on her face. "I'll close this to give you two some privacy," she says. She manages one final eyebrow waggle in my direction before closing the door.

All of this is lost on Dominic, who is logging his tablet into Skype.

"I need to get my report in," I mutter, as the familiar Skype tone *bee-boops* through the room. "And I have to figure out where to catch a train . . ."

Dom turns to reply, but is interrupted by a sudden burst of noise from his screen. What looks like a stiff blond helmet emerges, which eventually coalesces into the back of Teresa Cipher's head.

She appears to be at some kind of party.

When she turns to face us at last, it's clear she's on her phone. The sound quality is terrible, and the picture is bouncing all over the place.

"Darlings!" she says effusively. "Are you together? How simply marvelous! Much more efficient this way, absolutely. Powell filled me in about the disastrous crossing. Where have you ended up?"

Dom leans out of the view of the camera and mimes taking a drink. I'm not perfectly clear if he means Teresa's question makes *him* need a drink, or whether he's commenting on her own state of clearly heightened cheeriness.

Maybe both.

I lean in closer to the screen.

"We're outside Vancouver, Canada, Teresa. I've got a report ready to file on the crossing."

"What is that on your eyebrow?" Teresa asks loudly. "Are you all right?"

"I'm fine," I say quickly, and step to one side so Dom can be front and center. "Just a little bump to the head."

"A little bump?" she cries, and her face wobbles in and out of focus as she waves the phone around. Behind her I can see a large round table with a group of men seated around it.

"Honey," says a gruff, strangely familiar voice from somewhere behind her. "Are ya in or . . ."

The voice garbles and then dies as the screen goes momentarily blank.

"You need to hold the phone steady, Ms. Cipher," says Dominic patiently.

The picture returns.

"There. I've propped you against my handbag," says Teresa, and her face reappears, now at a more conventional distance from the screen. "Apologies for the unusual setting for this call, but I'm afraid something rather important has come up that I simply can't afford to miss."

Anything that takes her mind off the fact that we are not in San Francisco is fine by me.

"Our ship was blown off course, and we've ended up in Vancouver," Dom says.

"That's right," I chime in. "But I'm quite sure it's still possible for me to make my way down to San Francisco, and then on to New York before May first."

On the screen, Teresa glances down at her watch before looking up again. She's quiet for a long moment, and I can see the men behind her are playing poker. One of them, wearing a cowboy hat, throws his cards down in disgust.

"I'm out," he splutters, and then Teresa's face fills the screen again.

"Well, in the first place, I'll accept your change in itinerary as inevitable, as storms are considered acts of God, according to the ExLibris principles. I've been to San Francisco dozens of times, and am fully prepared to present that element of the journey to our client myself."

"So—you want us to head straight to New York from here, then?" I ask.

Her expression becomes more serious.

"It seems apparent the two of you have joined forces," she says. "Of course, the May first deadline remains firm. I must remind you that the original parameters of the agreements entered into—with *both of you*—remain intact. Whomever walks through the doors of the ExLibris offices first, having met all the conditions, of course, will be considered the winner."

We both nod obediently, and with a final, haughty raise of her eyebrow, she ends the call.

I flop back in my chair, exhaustion weighing me down. Having Teresa Cipher approve the change in itinerary should feel like a huge triumph, but there's still so much to do. So many miles to go before I sleep.

Dom, on the other hand, looks exultant. "Bullet dodged," he says, dusting his hands off theatrically. "Sumaya's safely with Nkruna and the rest of her aunties, and Teresa isn't holding Vancouver against us."

"That *is* good," I admit. "And listen—I'm grateful you didn't mention the whole thing with my injury. All the time in the hospital cost us at least a day."

Dominic leans back in his own chair, and for the first time, I can see lines of tiredness creasing the corners of his eyes. "You didn't ask to be thrown down those stairs. It could have been any of us," he says. "But right now, all I want is another Timbit. Join me?"

I shoot him a tired smile. He might be my competition, but we definitely share a taste in donuts. "I can't. I need to send this report in, and then find a train that'll take me to New York. *Before* I fall asleep over the keyboard."

I flip open the lid of my laptop and reach for the slip of paper with Nkruna's password.

Dom heaves himself out of his chair. "Okay," he says. "Send your report. But before you walked in here, I looked up the trains, and they run sporadically—at best—this time of year. So I reserved two seats on a ski bus heading into the Rockies. Once we get into Alberta, we can pick up a Greyhound the rest of the way."

"Two seats?" I say. "Like—one for me too?"

He gives a little shrug. "Teamwork got us this far," he says. "I don't see why . . ."

Behind him, the door springs open, and the air is suddenly filled with shrieks of laughter.

"I told you, I told you," giggles Sumaya. "No make-out. You owe me five bucks, Nkruna!"

And ten minutes later, in spite of the fact—or perhaps *because* of the fact—she'd made a game of my embarrassment, Sumaya gives me a giant hug by the front door of her new home. "I'll never forget you," she says, squeezing me tightly. "Now, you need to go ahead and win, okay?"

"Okay," I say as she runs over to hug Dom.

He walks up, grinning. "She told me she wants me to win," he says. "Just so you know whose side she's really on."

Out front, a competition has arisen over who will help us get on our way. Several people offer their cars, including one man who tells me he lobbied to get Uber to Vancouver for three years. "Free enterprise wins out!" he declares, waving his flat cap jauntily.

In the end, one of Nkruna's friends, dressed in his Surrey RCMP uniform, gives us a lift in his squad car to the bus stop in Downtown Vancouver.

"Neighborhood outreach," he says when we offer to pay him for driving so far out of his way. "Thank you for bringing that little girl back to her family."

After waving goodbye, we are the only two people not wearing goggles to climb into the ski bus. And in spite of the noise and the party atmosphere, I curl up in my corner seat near the back and fall solidly asleep.

I don't wake up again until many hours later, when, with the world still enveloped in a pure, velvet darkness, the alarming sound of a shattering axle beneath us brings the bus to a skidding halt.

chapter fifty-eight

IMAGE: Canadian Rail Line
IG: Romy_K [Craigellachie, Canada, April 25]
#BrokenAxel #LastSpike
8651 ♥

like to think the fact I was completely unconscious before the axle broke, and only semiconscious for a few seconds after, plays in my favor. Also a positive? The coach does not spin out or flip over on its side. From my spot near the back, all I feel after the snapping sound, is a jerking side-to-side motion, like being the kid on skates at the end of the crack the whip line.

When the bus finally settles, angled uncomfortably up a snow-bank on one side of the highway, I'm completely unhurt. Not even a wrenched neck.

I do, however, find myself virtually encased within the long limbs of one Dominic Madison. As soon as the bus stops moving, he unfolds himself from around me.

"Ah . . ." he says as I look up at him, speechless. "When I felt the bus go sideways, I assumed the crash position around you, since you were asleep on my lap."

"Right," I say, fumbling for my suitcase. "Right. Thank you for that."

"Pure instinct," he says, and grabs his pack before standing up. "I think we'd better get out of here."

My own good luck—if that's what it was—hasn't extended to the other passengers. By the time we all pile out and clamber over the dirty snowbank on the side of the highway, it's obvious that several of the heartier partiers on board fared less well than I. One guy, who was last seen standing near the front, singing a karaoke version of Shania Twain's "Man! I Feel Like a Woman" had been flipped head first into one of the metal handrails, and was likely concussed. Two other passengers smashed their heads against the window as the bus slewed side to side and have sustained cuts. And the driver has caught his leg between the wall and the gearshift, snapping it neatly—leg, not gearshift—above the ankle.

By the time everyone has banded together to help the driver into a more comfortable position and staunch the two head wounds, the Royal Canadian Mounted Police arrive. The police are not on horseback but in a pretty standard-looking cruiser—lights flashing and with a little convoy of three ambulances following.

"They got here quick," says the driver, through pain-clenched teeth. "Only had to come from Sicamous."

I pretend this means something to me. Some of the passengers have moved him over to what I'm pretty sure is a luggage rack, now rigged up with pillows to make a more comfortable resting place. I'm sitting in the seat beside him, having been given the job of holding his hand.

He closes his eyes and rests his head against the side of the bus, which makes me instantly nervous. My own exhaustion has vanished with the adrenaline rush of the crash. The combination of a few hours' sleep and the reality of being completely unhurt myself has left me feeling almost peppy, and strangely alert. Even my stitches are no longer sore.

"Hey—stay with me," I say to the driver, and his eyes flutter open again. "What's your name, anyway?"

"Stu," he says.

"I'm Ramona," I say, happy he's talking again. "Is that short for Stuart?"

"Just Stu," he repeats. Still, he squeezes my hand, so I take that as encouragement.

"Where are you from, Stu?"

He looks around a little, dipping his head to peer out the window. The faintest line of light is lining the jagged edge of the mountains to the east. "Here, actually," he says. "Craigellachie, that is."

"Whoa—that's a mouthful of a name for such a tiny place," I reply.

He gives me a tight smile. "It's pretty famous round these parts," he says. "Last spike of the railroad was driven in here in 1885. Named for the home town of the Scot who was the first president of the Canadian Pacific Railroad. Spike they drove into the ground was pure gold."

"Is that so?" I say, seeing two ambulance attendants scrambling over the snow with a handheld stretcher.

"Yep," says Stu. "Dug it up right after they took the picture, mind. They *were* Scottish, after all."

Once the injured are all trundled off to the nearest hospital, the rest of the stranded skiers open up the storage locker of the bus, dig out a keg of beer they've been ferrying to the resort, and build a bonfire in a pile of rocks that have recently come down the mountainside. One of which, it turns out, is the cause of our broken axle to begin with.

Most of the skiers are still intoxicated enough that it takes quite a while to get a fire really going. By the time enough of a flame appears to be somewhat worrisome, a fresh set of headlights rolls up behind

386 · kc dyer

our broken vehicle. It is a Sicamous District school bus, driven by a local lady who swings open the front door with a flourish, and identifies herself as Delores.

"I'm here to take you to the visitor's center in town," she says. "They can figure out what to do with you there."

"In town—meaning Craigellachie?" asks Dominic, who I'm pretty sure asks the question because he likes saying the name out loud.

Delores barks a laugh. "Ain't no visitor's center in the Craig. Ain't nothing there but broken promises, far as I can tell."

Unclear on what this means, but equally unwilling to ask, we all troop obediently onto Delores's bus. The skiers line up their gear across several of the back seats, and carefully load the keg in last. As Stu was both tour guide and bus driver, none of the skiers appear to be at all clear how they're going to get to their resort, but I don't hear a single word of complaint. Three of the guys throw snow onto the small bonfire to smother it, and our bus lurches away, leaving the sadly broken vehicle tilted up against a dirty snowbank on the side of the highway.

Turns out that shock absorbers are not really a priority to the Sicamous School District. It's a fifteen-minute bounce-fest to the visitor's center, and I'm relieved when we pull into the parking lot at last. Dawn is breaking, and, according to the sign, the visitor's center doesn't usually open until nine. But Delores has worked some magic, and as we all pile out of the school bus, a car squeals into the parking lot, and a pair of giggling girls who look about fifteen jump out. One of them is still wearing plaid pajama pants.

They might look young and giggly, but between the two of them, they open up the small cafe in the visitor's center, and within twenty minutes everyone inside has a warm drink and a granola bar in front of them. The least inebriated of the skiers has been on the phone, and in short order organizes the group a lift up to a local ski hill called Silver Star. There's a loud cheer at this news, but when Dom pulls out his own phone it turns out to be not so great for us.

Silver Star is in the wrong direction. Also? Neither of us can ski.

The sweet smell of baking dough fills the visitor's center as the last of the skiers pile onto their bus. The silence inside is suddenly so profound, it feels awkward. I chance a sideways glance at Dominic, but he's staring toward the kitchen, drawn, I imagine, by the irresistible aroma. I've learned that if something smells good, he's usually in the thick of it.

We haven't really exchanged more than a word or two since the chaos of uniting Sumaya with her family. I must have slept for at least five or six hours before the ignominious end to our bus trip, but the adrenaline rush of the crash has drained away, leaving me feeling a little sick and a lot worried.

All along—or at least, all along since the train ride in India—my plan has been to see Sumaya safely to her auntie, and then make a beeline straight for New York. Of course, it made perfect sense to work with Dominic to ensure Sumaya's safety, but . . .

The job with ExLibris is still on the line.

I blink my eyes to find Dom is staring right at me. I'm not sure how long I was zoned out for, and suddenly it's awkward again.

"No bus," he says. "No train. As far as I can tell, that leaves only one option."

I glance out through the glass doorway. The parking lot outside, while still surrounded with substantial dust-covered snowbanks, is clear of cars. Not even a taxi to be seen.

Dom stands up and shoulders his pack. "Time for the thumb," he says.

I collect my suitcase and follow him outside, not sure what else to do. In spite of my mercenary feelings of the moment before, the last thing I want is to hitch a ride on this lonely mountain highway by myself.

"I've—uh—never actually hitchhiked before," I mutter as I scurry across the parking lot after him. I still can't hope to match his long-legged stride.

He smiles over one shoulder. "This trip has held a lot of firsts for both of us."

There's a long merge lane leading both to and from the visitor's center, but the vehicles shooting past on the highway are going full speed. Most of them appear to be long-haul trucks—sixteen wheels or more—and none of them appear to be stopping. The wind whipping in the wake of each truck is icy, and the shock to my system feels profound. Ten days ago I was melting in India, and somehow this Canadian April cold feels deeper than anything I've ever experienced in New York.

"You're shaking," Dom says in my ear. "Stand behind me—I'll be the wind break."

"Pretty skinny for a wind break," I say, but I do tuck myself in behind him.

He turns his back to the road and grins down at me. "Generally, I prefer the term *slender*," he says, "or better yet, *buff*. But seeing as I'm pretty sure I've lost at least fifteen pounds on this trip, I'll try not to feel too hurt."

This makes me laugh. "Trust me when I say I would never feel hurt to be called skinny. I think maybe it's a girl thing."

He shrugs into his second strap. "No one would ever call you skinny," he says, hunching his shoulders against the wind backwash from a passing tanker. "You're more . . ."

"Thanks a lot," I mutter as he pauses. "More what?"

His expression changes into something I can't really read. "I was going to say lush," he says, his voice barely carrying over the highway noise. "But maybe . . ." His eyes narrow. "Too descriptive?"

I have to work hard to keep my own face neutral. No one has ever used the word *lush* to describe me before, and I'm completely at a loss. Is it a code word for curvy? I mean, I've always felt that curvy was a code word for fat, invented by women with more self-regard than I can usually muster. "I—I can live with lush," I finally stammer.

He looks relieved, and I stand in the meager shelter of his skinny windbreak and bask in the possible compliment for maybe a full minute.

In that time, six trucks pass us, and with each gust, we get pushed a little further down the road. As the seventh hurtles by, Dom drops his thumb.

"I might be too brown for this neighborhood," he mutters. "Lotta white faces behind those steering wheels."

I roll my eyes. "Delores was brown," I remind him.

"And she stopped for us too," he says. "Anyway, she's native. Lighter brown than I am."

I stare at him critically. There's no doubt he's picked up quite a tan on his face and arms from our time in the Middle East and India.

"That's not going to make a difference," I scoff. "Anyway, I'm tanned too."

He laughs out loud at this, but doesn't answer.

"What? So, yeah, my sunburn's faded, but I'm still a lot darker than I usually am at this time of year."

"Romy," he says quietly. "After going all this way together, you still think anyone mistakes my skin color for a *tan*?" He glances down at his watch. "Sixteen semis have passed us in the last five minutes. Thirteen of them slowed down, and then sped up again. You do the math."

I sigh. "No, I guess not. I just thought Canadians were less racist."

He smirks at this. "Where'd you hear that?"

I open my mouth, when a long line of pickup trucks appears on the highway, and we have to scamper back to the side of the road as they pull into the parking lot.

"Not sure," I mutter. "Maybe we'll have better luck with pickups?"

Scooping up my suitcase, I start walking back toward the visitor's center.

chapter fifty-nine

 IMAGE: Rocky Mountain Morning
IG: Romy_K [Sicamous, Canada, April 25]
#Convoy #ManyNations
9101 ♥

The trucks—in a dozen colors, shapes, and states of repair—turn out to be a sort of convoy, and have come almost the same route that we have. Several of the trucks bear "Protect the Inlet" and "No Pipelines" signs. We return to the cafe in the visitor's center, and sit down at a table next to a garrulous gentleman seated with a woman and a tiny child. When I ask the family group about the signs, we learn the drivers and passengers number about thirty, in total, and are heading to Calgary, which, when it comes to oil and gas, is apparently like the Houston of Canada. Most of the members of this group come from coastal native communities, and are on the road to protest the latest pipeline approval.

"The suits down in Calgary, eh? They make the decisions on land they've never walked on. Most of 'em have never seen the places they run the pipes across. And they don't want to give us a say in the process."

"Do you think you can make a difference?" I ask, but he shrugs.

"Don't matter. I mean—whether we get through to them or not, we still gotta try, right?"

When Dominic sticks out a hand and introduces himself, we learn Ernie George is from one of the coastal Salish nations.

Dominic looks fascinated. "You all from the same Indian tribe?" he asks, gesturing around the room. Ernie winces.

"There's a few families here from my band, but there are six different First Nations represented already," he says proudly. "When we set out, we were hopin' to pick up more, but—life's complicated, y'know?"

Ernie squints his eyes at Dominic through the steam rising from his coffee. "You American, brother?"

Dominic smiles and spreads his hands wide. "I guess it shows, huh?"

Ernie shakes his head. "Plenty of black and mixed-race Canadians," he says, digging into a plate of eggs and bacon. "My cousin Shanna's married to a Haitian fella, down in Toronto. Nah, it's not your looks, it's what I hear. You use words like *tribes* and *Indians*, but up north here we're more inclined to *nations* and *bands*, eh? Yeah, we call ourselves Indian, but that's our choice. You got words like that yourself, I understand? Words that don't sound so great when someone outside the family tosses 'em around?"

"Point taken," Dominic says. "Apologies."

"Those words been hurled at us for generations, too, man. My father is a proud member of the Squamish Nation. And his father before him. My mum's family hail from Nuu-chah-nulth over on the island. Our federation don't see a border—we got brothers down the coast to Seattle too. You gotta understand, we been here a long time. A *long* time. The coast has been our home for eons before the settlers came. Many nations—many voices. And you know what? We ain't no legend. We're still here. We still matter."

The woman beside him, with braided hair reaching below her waist, is called Estelle.

"We lift our voices whenever we can," she adds. "The government is paying lip service to consultation with our nations. Which is why we're heading to Calgary."

When Ernie pushes his plate away, Dom leans forward again.

"We're looking for a ride to the city," he says quietly. "I confess we're ignorant of your fight, but we're willing to listen, and help, if we can."

Ernie grunts, and I realize he's laughing. "Can you pitch in for the gas?" he says. "Kicks my ass to be payin' money to the dudes we're heading down to protest, but if we don't get there tomorrow, we'll miss our chance."

"He's a fantastic cook too," I tell Ernie. "You can put him to work."

And so it is, after Dom and I each fuel up one of the convoy vehicles with our ExLibris cards, we secure seats in the pipeline protest convoy. I climb into the rear seat of Ernie's truck, and Dom slides in beside me, after tossing our luggage into the back.

Ernie drives, and beside him sits Estelle, and Frankie; Estelle being Frankie's mother. She's a thirtysomething native—*First Nations*—woman, with a shy smile and, I discover later, a degree in environmental studies from the University of Victoria. Frankie's not quite five, and she spends most of the drive playing on an ancient Game Boy.

The truck is noisy and has terrible suspension, so conversation is difficult. I pass the time staring out at the passing mountains, which leave the ones we saw outside Vancouver in the dust. These are the Rockies, and they soar above us, their snowy tops stretching to impossible heights against the bluest of skies. The further we travel, the steeper the cliffs that tower both above us and—as the truck begins to labor—below. After a while, I have to avert my eyes from the narrow verge of the road, where only a little snowy gravel and the flimsiest of wire fences separates us from a plunge into the abyss.

The mountains that soar above us are mammoth and snow covered, and yet strangely nothing at all like the Alps. I stare upward,
trying to put my finger on the difference. The Alps were so tall and
pointy, but while a trifle less jagged, the Rockies seem even taller.
They are certainly snowier.

We are still laboring upward when Ernie suddenly slams on the
brakes. The truck slews sideways a bit before stopping, and—while
it's not a full-out scream—I can't stop the little squeak of fear that
escapes me. A spray of gravel shoots off the cliff into thin air.

Peering over Frankie's dark head, I see a row of wooly, bug-eyed
faces placidly gazing back at us through the windscreen.

"Are those—goats?" I ask. The largest of the animals has the
weirdest horns I have ever seen—two full sets, protruding out of his
head so they point front and back at the same time.

The other two look far more sedate, with horns curling around
their heads, like they've tucked them neatly behind their ears.

Ernie chuckles. "Sheep," he says succinctly. "Bighorns. Think
they own the road, the bastards."

Frankie is delighted by the creatures, and insists on climbing out
of her car seat and *baa-ing* at the sheep while Ernie pauses for a
smoke break. I scurry over to the thin verge on the inside of the road,
against the mountainside, only to discover my phone is dead.

Worse, I remember last plugging it in on the ski bus.

When I confess this to Dominic, he shrugs, passes me his charge
cord, and even sweet-talks Frankie into letting me plug in for a while.
There's no Wi-Fi to access in this mountain wilderness, but my
phone is recharged enough to take pictures, and for now, that's all
that matters.

In spite of the many "Elk crossing" signs we pass, the sheep prove
to be the last of our wildlife close encounters for the day. At one

point, Ernie swears he sees a bear in a dense section of forest, but by then it's begun to grow dark, and I really think he's trying to entertain Frankie, who has lost interest in her game and grown somewhat fractious.

Night falls quickly in the mountains, and it's only from the noise of the truck engine that I can tell we're no longer climbing through the Rockies. Bundling up my hoodie into a pillow, I jam it between my neck and the tattered padding on the inside of the truck door and close my eyes. There's no way I'll be able to sleep in this loosely sprung truck, but at least I can give my tired eyes a rest.

I wake up as the truck slows to a halt in a spray of gravel. My head is no longer jammed against the door, but curled into the crook of Dominic's shoulder, and I lie there sleepily a moment, enjoying the peace. Instead of the chugging engine of the Ford F-150, I can hear, in my left ear, at least, the quiet thrum of Dominic's heart.

Slowly, I pull my head away and sit up, determined not to wake him. But his eyes glitter in the dark, and I see the gleam of his smile.

"Good sleep?" he asks quietly. He holds his finger to his lips and points at the front seat, and I realize I must not have been the only one napping. I can hear Frankie's deep breathing now, and I nod my understanding back at Dom. There's no sign of either Ernie or Estelle. My eyes are adjusting to the dark, but I can see firelight reflected on the windshield. Dom reaches across me to quietly open the door, and I unlatch my seatbelt. The truck rocks as I step out, and again as Dominic follows me, but little Frankie stays dead to the world, cozied up in her car seat.

I stretch luxuriously, and then shiver. Beside me, Dom holds up the hoodie I'd been using as a pillow, and I jam my arms into the warmth of it gratefully.

"You were snoring," he whispers.

"I was not," I insist, but his grin only broadens.

"Where are we, anyway?" I whisper to change the subject, but a voice replies from behind me.

"Near Morley," says Estelle, appearing out of the gloom. She's holding a drinking box and possibly a blanket. It's hard to see in the dark.

"This is part of the Stoney Nation, and we're welcome here." She gestures over at what I can now see is an enormous bonfire, surrounded by a milling group of figures, little more than silhouettes in the darkness. "We'll rest here and drive into the city in the morning. It's not much farther."

She turns away from us to unbuckle her daughter, and wraps her, still sleeping, into the folds of the blanket.

Dominic has pulled on his own jacket, with the hood up, and together we leave Estelle to deal with Frankie, and walk toward the flames. Six or seven people, both men and women, pull out skin drums. I stand in the dancing firelight, mesmerized by the pulsing rhythm of the drums, the rising and falling of voices in a language older than any I've ever known.

Sure of nothing—not of making it back to New York in time, not of winning the job at ExLibris, not even of the slow, subtle changes in my feelings toward Dominic, I'm overwhelmed by a sudden wave of gratitude my life has brought me to this place. If I lose everything, I will have seen this.

I will have seen this.

I don't know how long I stand rooted to the spot, but the smell of something delicious makes me turn my head. I look across to see a group of women, busily preparing and filling a long table with food. As the table—a sheet of plywood laid across a handful of sawhorses—is covered with steaming bowls and platters, Dom is busy in the middle of the group, sleeves rolled up, folding and punching dough. His hood is off again, and he's tied his locs back.

He laughs at something one of the women says—they all seem to be laughing, in truth—and looks up at me, eyes dancing, and suddenly?

I'm gone.

Done.

I try to smile back, but instead, I burst into tears.

chapter sixty

IMAGE: Frankie's Sheep
IG: Romy_K [Near Morley, Alberta, April 26]
#FirstNationsProtest #HardTruths
9807 ♥

It's dark away from the fire and the makeshift kitchen, but that's what I need at the moment. I step behind a teepee someone has erected from long poles and a fine, smoothly tanned skin, shivering in the sudden chill of being away from the fire.

I wipe my eyes hard on my cuff, and promise myself—*promise*—to keep my secret. Our lives are complicated enough already. His mother's employer is my family's sworn enemy.

No one can know that I have fallen in love with this man. It takes me a good ten minutes to get enough of a grip on myself to risk heading back to where people can see me.

Ernie pats a spot on a blanket beside where he and Estelle are seated. He's holding the sleeping Frankie across his lap while Estelle eats from a paper plate. A full plate sits in front of him on the ground.

"Go get some food," he says as I approach. "I'll save the place for you."

I fill my plate with brown beans and some kind of dried, chewy fish that tastes almost like cranberries.

"Try this," says Dom, plopping down cross-legged beside me, with his own plate. "It's called bannock. I just learned how to bake it."

It is, of course, delicious—soft and chewy and buttery.

"Another recipe to add to your repertoire," I say, and he reaches across to swipe his piece through the last of the sauce on my plate.

"Already taken a shot for my site," he says, and then pops it into his mouth.

Later, when we sit around the fire, I mostly listen. My world lies on the other side of this continent, and it's my job to try to help out the family that has cared for me all my life. But here, feeling the heat of the fire on my face, and the cold of the wind on my back in such contrast, I listen and learn. The men and women around me debate treaty rights in Canada, and what that means with regard to who owns—or acts as a steward for—the nation's oil and gas.

Estelle tells me there are nearly two hundred First Nations in British Columbia alone, but now we are in Alberta, opinions on pipelines and mineral rights can vastly differ. It's no real surprise how this collection of nations, like any group, holds differing opinions on many topics: mineral rights and global warming and the massive risks faced by First Nations women. The discussion rising and falling throughout the evening is sometimes loud, but is ultimately respectful.

Later, when I want more than anything to find Dominic, and kiss the spot on the inside of his elbow just above the tiny scar from where he burnt himself on the *Wahash Mahat*, I do no such thing. Instead, I take the blanket offered me by one of the three teenage girls, and curl up with them in the back of someone's old GMC Jimmy.

The next morning, I wake early and extricate myself carefully from the group of girls who are curled up like puppies in the back of the truck. As I walk over to the wooden outhouse near the rodeo stand, I see a movement under the tailgate.

Rubbing sleep out of his eyes, Dominic rolls out of his spot on the ground and stretches. His jacket pulls high over his lean stomach, and the sensation that shoots through me is so intense, I have to look away.

"Did you sleep on the ground?" I ask, as he does a few neck circles and then jumps up and down on the spot.

"Yep. And quit grinning at me like I'm a fool. This is good for the circulation, y'know."

The camp is waking up around us, and in no time small meals are eaten or packaged for later, and the convoy gets ready to move again. We've been joined in the night by some local members of one of the Stoney Nations, and they bring with them a small number of magnificent dappled horses.

To Dominic's absolute delight, he is invited to ride with the group, and since the invitation mercifully does not include me, we agree to meet up at the protest itself, at noon.

I end up in the back of a jeep, with two women introduced to me by Estelle. June and Alexis are mother and daughter, and to my delight, June even remembers reading Jules Verne when she was in school. I spend the rest of the morning learning about the horror of residential schools, and the slow and painful reconciliation process taking place in Canada.

The pipeline protest is set to begin on Calgary's pedestrian-friendly Eighth Avenue mall, and following the drumbeat, the parade makes its way to city hall. There, near the end of the protest, a group of mounted riders joins us at last.

Dom winces at me, and it turns out he needs help dismounting, since his legs are so cramped up, he can't actually bend his knees. As he hands the reins off to one of Ernie's friends, the sound of chanting rises up behind us. I turn to see a group—a large group—of counter-protesters has gathered. Turns out, oil and gas production form a significant part of the local economy, and as for pipelines?

Pretty darned popular to many Calgarians.

Things get ugly very quickly.

When a scuffle breaks out nearby, I find myself being hauled out of the fray by one stiff-legged American man.

"We've got to find a train," Dom hisses at me as we hustle away from the milling crowd. "The Greyhound no longer runs in this country."

Above the rising voices, I hear hoofbeats, and suddenly a number of other mounted individuals arrive. This group, however, are all dressed in blue uniforms.

"I thought Mounties only wore red," I mutter at Dom, but he's getting directions to the station from Estelle. She's carrying Frankie on one hip, and is keeping a judicious distance from the counter-protesters.

"It's that way, under the tower," she says. "You can't miss it."

Then, turning to me, she thrusts a book into my hand.

"In case you want to learn something about being an ally."

I add the book, by a First Nations writer called Thomas King, to my growing suitcase library. Both she and Frankie give us big hugs before returning to the protest.

And less than an hour later, Dominic and I nab seats on a mostly freight-laden train heading to Toronto. When the engine pulls away from Calgary, it's towing ninety cars filled with prairie wheat, a single car for passengers, and no actual sleeping berths.

chapter sixty-one

The train picks up speed as it heads east, and outside the windows, it's like the majestic peaks of the Rockies were part of some kind of a fever dream. Within a few minutes, the land rocketing past us moves from a gentle, rolling landscape to a dead flat, yellow-brown pancake, with lumps of dirty snow still occasionally visible.

I turn away from the window to find Dom staring at me. But instead of glancing away when he sees me notice, he holds my gaze. We are both sitting beside the window, facing each other, and he leans forward and puts a hand on my knee.

"First time we've been alone in a while," he says. "You okay with that?"

I'm *so* okay with that.

But instead of saying so, I stand up, and switch across into the empty seat beside him. Outside, the sun is rapidly dropping toward the horizon of the biggest sky I have ever seen. I want to imprint this moment on my memory, but I need to say what's on my mind before I chicken out. I pull my tattered bullet journal out of my daypack, and flip it open to the most recent page.

"You gonna read me something?" he says, with an amused smile.

"No. It's just—my brain dries up when I'm nervous, okay? I have some things to say." I gaze down at the list on the page, not sure where to start.

I take a deep breath. "Okay, number one . . ."

But before I can finish, he pushes the book aside and kisses me.

Things I need to tell Dominic:

1. Without a doubt, the best parts of this trip for me have been the ones with you and Sumaya. The only reason I took on this journey was to help my Uncle Merv, which feels like a pretty good cause, you know? But helping Sumaya get to her only family? That was important. And I wouldn't have been a part of that without you.

2. When you walked me along that Alaskan beach, you gave me my happy memories of my parents back. I will never forget this.

3. I know you need to help your mom. But you are smart and strong and so good at everything you do. I have to hope things will be all right for you both, in the end. But I'm the book-shop's only hope. Without me, Two Old Queens will fail.

4. I need to win this contest. If you hate me for it, it is a price I have to pay.

I never do get around to reading him the list. Which is probably a good thing.

Because instead, as darkness falls and the sky above us fills with

404 · kc dyer

a thousand, thousand stars, we talk about who we were before. And who we might be after.

We make a decision to return to ExLibris together. We can't both have the job, but splitting the bonus money *can* help both our families a little.

At some point, the conductor passes through the cabin, handing out Hudson's Bay blankets to those who want one.

"I could get used to this," Dom says. He's got his seat tilted back, and his half of the blanket pulled up to his chin.

"This, as in . . . ?"

"As in seeing the world out the window of a train. I mean, my heart has always been in the kitchen. But there's something about baking currant scones in the galley of a submarine that adds a little spice to the proceedings."

I sit up and stare at him. "A—submarine?"

He grins sheepishly. "I don't want to oversell it. It was only for three days. But it's how I beat you to the UK—or would have, if that damn storm hadn't blown you forward."

"Wait a minute—where the hell did you manage to hitch a ride on a submarine?"

"Out of Rhode Island, actually. She was a retired Virginia-class vessel, and these days they use her in the film industry. Some director with more money than sense had been shooting a movie off the East Coast, and they needed to move across to get some footage off the Channel Islands. A guy I used to work with does film catering now, and he talked them into taking me."

I flop back into my seat. "You wouldn't catch me . . ." I begin, but my words die in my throat.

"Wouldn't catch you?" he prompts.

I can't help laughing. "I was going to say you wouldn't catch me on a submarine if my life depended on it. But that's Old Romy talking. New Romy squeezed backwards through a hole in the ground to run through an ancient tunnel under Paris. I've ridden a gondola above the Alps. I managed to find my own way through the streets of Mumbai. So much I used to be scared of doesn't frighten me anymore."

He reaches for my hand under the covers. "I've always wanted to travel the world," he says. "I'm glad I got to do it with you."

"Yeah, I bet the part where you had to hold my hair while I vomited up Egyptian street meat was a highlight."

He laughs. "The highlight was kissing you in Singapore," he says. "Know why?"

"Oh, I know why. You didn't think we were going to live through that flight."

He shakes his head. "Nope. It was because it reminded me of this movie I saw a long time ago. It was about this woman, really tall, gorgeous, who travels around the world. And when she gets to Singapore, she falls for . . ."

I sit up so suddenly, the blanket drops to the floor. "Not *Eat Pray Love* . . ." I groan.

"That's it!" he says delightedly. "It was so romantic . . ."

"That wasn't even Singapore," I yell, and then feeling the eyes of the other passengers, I drop back into my seat. "It was *Bali*," I hiss. "Not Singapore."

He shrugs, and pulls the blanket up over both of us. "I don't care," he says. "It was worth it."

The next day, while hunting for Estelle's book in my suitcase on the luggage rack near the rear of the car, I notice a connecting door is ajar. When I stick my head inside, I find a railcar, stacked with bales of hay. To one side, there's a narrow space, open and private, tucked behind a section of tightly wedged boxes. When I disappear a second time, taking Dominic's precious Hudson's Bay blanket, he follows me.

"There you are," he says. "I thought you must be looking at the scenery. It is still entirely flat out there."

I step aside so he can see the cozy hideaway I have constructed.

"Nope," I say. "I've been busy in here. Amazing what you can do with a borrowed blanket or two, isn't it?"

He doesn't answer, instead holding out his arms to me. I step into them, and find the fit to be nothing less than perfect. The sunlight streaming through the door is dappled, the yellow-gold of hayfields outside lighting up the green flecks in his eyes. Suddenly, his eyes darken as he drops his head to kiss me. This close, his usual scents of cinnamon and vanilla shatter into components too complex to parse—cloves and maybe sandalwood and who knows what else. It is entirely intoxicating, and I find I've lost the ability to think coherently—or at all.

After what seems like forever, we break apart. His smile broadens as he points at the door. "Does that thing lock?"

It does.

And that's the last either one of us sees of the Canadian prairies.

Right around dawn on April 30th, something wakes me. I'm alone, cozy under the blanket in our own little corner of the grain car. The fact we've managed to find such a private spot feels like a small miracle, but it's possible all the Canadians on board are just too polite to say anything. No one is awake as I sneak back into the passenger car, feeling weak-kneed, and with straw in places I'd rather not think about too closely.

After brushing my teeth and pulling a strand of hay out of my hair, I return to my seat. Outside the window, the sun glints off a distant body of water, and I feel, for the first time in as long as I can remember, perfectly happy.

With so few passengers on this train, there is, of course, no restaurant car. After a few minutes, I stick my head out and peer down the aisle to see if Dominic is picking up morning tea from the snack trolley. There's no sign of him, so I flop back into my seat by the window. It's not until I'm about to lean into the aisle to look again, when I see the note.

'm not sure how long I sit, staring at the tiny piece of folded card with my name written on the back. Long enough for every worst-case scenario to trumpet through my brain. Long enough for every ounce of good feeling to drain out of me and puddle on the floor. Long enough for the city of Toronto to start whizzing past the windows.

I don't get the nerve up to read the note until the conductor has announced the stop, and reminded us to gather all our personal belongings. Everyone in my car is on their feet, and the train is beginning to slow before I can force my shaking fingers to unfold the card.

Something has come up at home, Dominic writes, *and I have to go. After all we've been through, one of us has to make it. It should be you.*

I turn the note over to find it's written on the back of the card handed to him by Ganesh, first mate on the *Wahash Mahat,* way back when we left the ship in Mumbai.

Looking up, I realize I'm the last passenger on the train. I collect my daypack and suitcase blindly, and head for the door.

Behind me there's a whoosh as the conductor rushes to my side.

"Yours, I believe?" he says, stretching out an arm. My pink bra dangles from one of his fingers.

"Oh, I'm sure that's not mine," I stammer, as a handful of straw flutters to the floor of the train.

I brush past him and take three steps down the platform before I stop, set my suitcase down, and return to snatch it from his hand.

"This thing's carried me around the world," I say. "And it's going to live to carry me another day."

"Lady," the conductor says drily, "I literally give no shits about anything before I have my coffee."

I'm halfway down the platform before he yells, "But you could at least have shaken the straw out of the blanket!"

I don't have time to reply. I don't have time to think about anything. I race upstairs, stop at the first Starbucks, and while they're making my tea, I log on and send a text to Dominic.

What happened? Where are you?

I send the same message by e-mail, and look up at the clock. 8:00 a.m.

For this entire journey, I never really believed I had a chance. And then, for the past week, I've been fighting the certainty that of the two of us, Dominic is the more deserving. I woke up this morning on the train, resigned to losing—or at best, tying—the contest.

But now everything's changed. Sometime since that last, perfect— even with the hay—not-quite-naked moment we shared last night, Dominic has vanished. I don't know why or how. I can't believe he's morphed back into the Evil Nephew I so despised when I started this journey. All I do know is that, against all odds, there's still a chance for me to do what I set out to do.

It's 8:00 a.m. on April 30th, and I have sixteen hours to save Two Old Queens.

chapter sixty-two

IMAGE: CN Tower
IG: Romy_K [Toronto, Canada, April 30]
#Ghosted #LastDay
8846 ♥

Union Station is the cavernous main train station for the city of Toronto, and can easily go mano a mano with any of New York's stations when it comes to marble pillars and soaring ceilings. But my too-new-to-even-use-the-word boyfriend has vanished, and time is running out, so admiring majestic architecture is definitely not on the menu. When, after collecting my tea, I still haven't heard back from Dominic, I plug my phone in and start to research the fastest way home.

I'm one measly international border away from my home state. My two limitations: time and commercial aircraft. Since I'm in a train station, I check—and eliminate—that option first. The fastest trip by VIA Rail doesn't arrive in New York until tomorrow. There *is* a train leaving from Niagara Falls that can get me home on time, but I have to get there first.

I waste almost a full hour investigating my next choice, which is to throw cost to the wind and hire someone to drive me to New York. While I can't find any actual rules prohibiting crossing the border, I also can't find any ride-share drivers willing to take me.

In the end, I decide on the Niagara Falls option, mostly because

I can catch a bus right here, outside the station. I prepay for my Amtrak ticket online, which, if it doesn't hit a cow on the tracks, is scheduled to pull into Penn Station by eleven tonight.

As soon as I press "confirm" on the train ticket, I check both my text and e-mail again. Considering I have them set to push notifications through, it shouldn't be a surprise to see there's nothing from Dominic.

Have I been ghosted?

The thought makes me sick, but I can't think of a single reason that would justify his total disappearance. I mean—even in an emergency, a quick text is so easy.

Clutching the handle of my suitcase firmly, I swallow down the hurt that wants to eat my head right now, and hurry outside to find my bus. Above Union Station, the CN Tower points its needle nose at the sky, and I pause long enough to take my requisite tower shot.

Spotting a line of coaches across the street, I leap aboard the first one I see with "Niagara Falls" on the sign roller, and slap the last of my Canadian currency into the driver's collection bin.

"Pedal to the metal, James," I mutter, dropping my suitcase onto the luggage rack behind his seat.

Unfortunately, the driver turns out to have excellent hearing, and informs me that his name is Abdul. All the same, I feel like the credit for the speed with which we surge out of the parking bay belongs to me.

The bus trip is scheduled to take two and a half hours to circle around the perimeter of Lake Ontario, but Abdul and his pedal to the metal makes it in just under two. This final last day of April brings a few scattered showers, and there's still a trace of ice along the highway. Unlike the fresh and verdant environment we left in Vancouver, the climate here is closer to the snowy reality of the prairie landscape. I'm hoping by this time tomorrow, I'll be enjoying tulips bursting out of all the window boxes in New York City.

In any case, two hours is far too long to dwell on climate. In spite of all my efforts not to, I check my phone at least a dozen times in the first hour. What if Dominic really has ditched me? What if everything I thought we had was a ruse?

I finally stagger up to the front of the bus to tuck my phone into my suitcase so I won't look at it again. And for the first time since Paris, I pull out my poor broken Canon to take back to my seat. There are no pictures to remind me of Dominic here—the Parisian purloiners saw to that by smashing the lens. But holding the camera in my hand again brings the strangest sense of loss sweeping over me. This trip, this journey of a lifetime, is almost over.

Back at my seat, I can see the lens is truly beyond help, with little pieces of glass and plastic still tinkling around inside when I hold it up.

But the body of the camera—even the delicate shutter mechanism—seems to be functional. Maybe if I have a job at the end of this crazy journey, I can look for a new lens.

"Canon, eh?" says a voice from across the aisle. "I prefer this old Pentax, m'self. Course, they don't make 'em like this anymore."

An old man in a pristine Tilley hat and pressed chinos holds out his camera for me to admire. "Max Hammer," he says, patting his chest as I take his camera.

It's an old one, for sure, covered in dents and scratches. "You shoot on film?" I ask incredulously. "Isn't that massively expensive?"

He shrugs. "Old habits die hard," he says, caressing his camera fondly, as I place it carefully back into his hands. "Spendin' my retirement shootin' this country from coast to coast to coast."

I can't help grinning at him. "One too many coasts in there, Max."

He waggles his eyebrows at me under his hat. "We got three oceans, Missy. Don't forget the Arctic!"

"That you have," I agree, remembering the size of the grey waves splashing across the bow of the *Arctic Björn*. "So, are you adding a little taste of America today, then?"

He gives me a mischievous look. "No chance of that. I've taken a stand against the current administration. When they clean up their act, I'll go back."

He busies himself polishing the lens of his camera, and I get the sense our conversation is over, but I'm puzzled. "You *do* know this bus is bound for Niagara Falls?" I ask. "Niagara Falls is in New York State."

This time his smile takes on a pitying tone. "Indeed it is, young lady. But this bus is headed for the Canadian side of the falls."

My look of shock prompts him to reach over and pat my hand, which is gripping the rail on the back of the seat in front of me, at the moment. "Not to worry, though. If you're headed for the other side, you can zip across the bridge in under ten minutes, I'm sure."

I hop out of my seat, and trot up the aisle to stand beside Driver Abdul.

"No standing while the vehicle is in motion," he intones, so I swing myself into one of the empty seats behind him. Which doesn't exactly facilitate conversation. Nevertheless, I persevere.

"Are you driving through to New York State, Abdul?" I holler.

"No distracting the driver while the vehicle is in motion," he hollers back.

"I only need to know where we're going, dude!"

I'm pretty sure the desperation in my voice wins him over. Or maybe he likes being called *dude*.

He taps the paper schedule taped to the dashboard beside the door-opening crank. I stand up to read it, and he jabs his thumb toward the back of the bus. "No standing while the vehicle is in motion," he repeats, and I beat a hasty retreat.

But not before I have seen the words "Niagara Falls, Ontario" on his schedule.

I yank my phone back out of my suitcase, and take ten minutes trying to log on to the sketchy Wi-Fi. This bus might be destination Ontario, but Max Hammer is right. A bridge stretches between the two Niagaras, open twenty-four hours a day.

As I'm about to close my phone, it pings with an e-mail from Tommy. I haven't heard anything from him for ages, so I open it nervously. He's not castigating me this time, but not welcoming me home either. Instead, he wants me to know that Rhianna has been missing more than a week, and that Merv is devastated. The e-mail is short on detail, but he adds they are planning a going-out-of-business sale to coincide with my return.

Please don't give up yet, I back desperately, but there's no reply. With the state of the Wi-Fi on the bus, I'm not even sure it's gone through.

I try calling, but Merv's phone goes straight to voice mail.

In desperation, I call Dominic's number too. Nothing.

What's wrong with these people? Who doesn't answer their phone?

Across the aisle, Max is out like a light. His hat tilts rakishly over one eye and he is snoring so hard, one side of his moustache is flapping gently. I envy his serenity and am furious at his ability to relax, all in the same moment.

Leaning back in my seat, I try to practice yoga breathing. So close now. I'm so close. In a few hours, I'll be home. This crazy journey will be over. And the bookshop will be fine.

It's got to be.

have my suitcase in hand before Abdul has even stopped the bus, and I leap out into a town that reminds me of nothing so much as Coney Island. Casinos, wax museums, and souvenir shops mingle with "like real" Falls experiences. Who wouldn't want to watch a 4-D—maybe they throw water on you?—movie of the Falls in a theater, when the real thing is thundering right outside the door?

There's no time to look at any of it, of course. I wave goodbye to Max Hammer and his Pentax and sprint off the bus in the direction of the Rainbow Bridge—a fairly generic green, considering its name—spanning the Niagara River. The air is misty and the thunder of the falls overlays everything.

The wind coming off the water still bears winter's edge, and as I get closer to the Rainbow Bridge, I can see the water in the gorge is filled with shattered ice. Water falling on the American side carves fantastic shapes through the still-huge blocks of ice at the base.

There's no Wi-Fi, but I do one last desperate scan of my text messages, and then run toward the American border, jamming my phone into my pocket. The entrance to the Rainbow Bridge is through a glass door, behind which are coin machines that accept both Canadian loonies—dollar coins—and American bills. To cross, one must feed four quarters into the turnstile, hence the change machines.

This means I have to leave and run back across the street to get money from an ATM. I feel pathetically grateful when it gives me a choice of currency, and in seconds, I have American money in my hand for the first time in over a month. I feed a dollar bill into the machine, and holding my suitcase over my head, push through the turnstile.

In seconds, I'm through and onto the pedestrian walkway to the bridge. I dodge the dozen or so tourists posing for selfies and family shots with the frosty falls in the background, and trot toward the American side. The center of the bridge features a plaque and two flagpoles ceremoniously marking each side of the world's longest undefended border. I know I should be taking pictures for ExLibris, but I'm too close now. At the far end of the bridge, by some miracle, there's no lineup at customs. I force myself to walk up to the glass door, and the officer waves me inside, ready to welcome me home with open arms.

The second I place my passport into his hands, immediately behind me, there's a piercing scream.

chapter sixty-three

IMAGE: Frozen Waterfall
IG: Romy_K [Niagara Falls, US/Canada Border, April 30]
#NiagaraIce #AFallOvertheFalls #ABrokenRainbow
9919 ❤

How to tell things are bad: When a sweet-faced, thick-necked American boy in uniform swears at you. With a *gosh* or even a *goldarn*, you know there's a problem. More than that? The writing is on the wall.

Or in this case, over it.

Customs Guy stamps my passport, and flips it over onto his laser reader, but as he glances over my shoulder, his smile freezes.

"Jesus Christ," he says. "A car seat just went over." And in one of the smoothest moves I've ever seen on ice or off—and I'm speaking as an Islanders fan here—he smacks a big red button, and vaults over the gate separating the guards from the great unwashed.

As in me.

He spins me around as he shoulders past, and I find myself facing back through the glass door I've just entered. Outside, I see a small family staring, openmouthed, over the railing of the bridge.

Even in the raw horror of this moment, I do not lose sight of my goal.

Snatching my passport back, I run for the last glass door separating me from the country of my birth—but I'm too late.

Customs Guy's red button has put the place into lockdown.

I knock on the door, trying to gain the attention of the woman on the other side. She is wearing an identical uniform to Customs Guy's, and she has her back to me.

"He's passed me through," I yell at the glass, and wave my passport for good measure. "Look! He's given me my passport back."

She shoots me a side-eye, so I know she's heard me, but turns her back on me all the same. Crossing her arms, she spreads her feet wide, and holds her position.

I decide Customs Guy is now my only hope.

Turning around, I race back outside to find a phalanx of guards—these ones wearing Niagara Parks Police insignia—have cleared everyone off the bridge, with the exception of the car-seat-less family, and me. The pedestrian bridge is separated by cement blocks from the vehicle bridge, but there are no longer any cars either.

An icy wind whistles up from the churning water below.

The family is car-seat-less, but clearly not baby-less. The father is holding the baby, whose nose, I have to add, is running in a ghastly fashion, while the mother speaks to Customs Guy. She has a shock of blond hair piled up in the patented "I haven't brushed this stuff on my head for a week now, but I'm still unwilling to part with it" style, topped with rain-speckled sunglasses. Her husband's plaid jacket flaps in the wind over a t-shirt reading "Saskatchewan Flour Power."

"It was my fault," the woman says patiently. "I wouldn't let him use the selfie stick. I'd only propped the car seat on the railing to get it out of the way of the picture."

Customs Guy has pulled a radio off his belt. "I saw it go over," he says, gesturing with the antenna. "There was something inside."

The father shakes his head, and holds up the evidence. "No—no. Jenna's right here. It was only the seat." He turns back to his wife and points an accusatory finger. "*You* are going to have to be the one to tell your parents. That thing cost 'em three hundred bucks, and you know they're going to hold this against me."

"Honey—it was my fault. Don't worry," she soothes.

"Object overboard reported to be an empty car seat," Customs Guy says into his radio, and then touches his earphone. "I—uh—no, I can't confirm that."

He glances back at the couple and says, "Roger that," before replacing the radio in his belt.

"You two are going to have to come with me," he says, and makes a sweeping gesture with his arms toward the Canadian side of the bridge.

The baby sneezes, thoroughly spraying both the father and Customs Guy in the process. I stare at the child in disgust.

Look. I cannot be happier the baby is safe, okay? Can*not* be more delighted. That doesn't stop me from wanting to murder her parents with my bare hands.

After being ushered back to the Canadian side, all the guards will say is that the bridge will be closed briefly.

"Pardon me for interrupting," I say. "Before you go, can you open the door to let me through?"

Customs Guy looks at me as though he's never seen me before.

"I'm sorry, ma'am," he says. "But there's been an object overage incident on the bridge. Until it's resolved, all traffic has to be halted."

"But you've already returned my passport," I say, and wave it at him. "Stamped it and everything."

"We have to follow policy, ma'am," he says.

"No one was hurt," I say to the officer, whose gloved hand is gesturing firmly in a direction I do not want to go. "You can see the dad has the baby. It was only a car seat."

He gives me the tight smile I'm sure he reserves for idiot tourists to whom he is forced to be polite.

"The bridge will be closed until the incident is declared resolved," he says, reaching out a hand to guide me on my way.

I dodge his hand on instinct. Before I know it, I've bolted back inside the American customs area, and am pounding on the window at the woman who is still patiently settled on the other side.

Which is how I find myself with an armed escort, each holding one of my elbows, for the remainder of my march back across the bridge into Canada. Luckily, these guards are members of the Niagara Parks Police and not the RCMP. During the course of this march, I explain to them several times how I have a train to catch, how my uncle is being forced to sell his bookshop, and how I need to be back in New York City today. The guards, in turn, point out all the grounds on which they can arrest me.

By the time we step back onto solid ground, we have reached an agreement which involves me not being arrested on the condition I not set foot on the Rainbow Bridge again today.

I have enough sense left in me to obey.

A light drizzle begins to fall as I hurry away from the police lights flashing at the end of the bridge. It feels much colder than it should for this time of year, thanks to the icy wind swirling up from the water. Also, thanks to the fact that I was sweating my ass off in Singapore what feels like mere minutes ago.

The remaining tourists have done the sensible thing and gone to watch the 4-D version of the falls, inside where it's warm.

Alone on the bank, I stare out glumly across the railing at the thundering waterway standing between me and the state of New York, and burst into tears.

Public displays of emotion are generally not my thing. Every time I've hit bottom on this trip—and thinking back over the last month, there have been plenty—I've had to duck into a shadowy corner somewhere to get a grip on myself.

This time, as the rain patters down and mingles with my tears, no one can tell. I'm the only idiot still standing out of doors beside the falls. Equal parts soaked and discouraged, I cross the street and step under a familiar green Starbucks awning, only to have the corner of it give way, cascading yet more water into my eyes. As I scramble to find a tissue in my pocket, I dislodge my wallet, which—naturally—falls in a puddle. After wiping my eyes, I use my last remaining tissue to dry off the outside of the wallet, and then check inside to ensure my passport is still dry. The handful of American bills are fine, and only the edge of a white card appears to have been soaked. It's the card Dominic's note is written on. The water has washed away his message.

The symbolism of this is not lost on me, but as I'm about to lose it completely, I turn the card over and Ganesh's name leaps out at me. Dominic's message may have been in water-soluble ink, but Ganesh's info is printed with tougher stuff.

As I hold the soggy remains of the card, I remember his words to Dominic as he stepped off the *Wahash Mahat*.

"If you ever need any help, call. My whole family is on the sea. You never know—maybe we can assist."

I brush away a stray raindrop and study Ganesh's name, and his cell phone number.

The display on my own phone indicates I have two hours until the train departs from a station on the other side of a thin ribbon of water. A station I can almost see from here.

Two hours.

I lean against the damp Starbucks window, and start to text.

E ven though it must be the middle of the night for him, when I send the text, I get a response almost immediately. To my surprise, he calls me.

"This has to be costing a fortune," I gasp, instead of the usual *hello*.

I can hear the smile in his sleepy voice.

"We're in port, and it's FaceTime. Your message sounded a bit too urgent for text, eh?"

He's right, so I give him the quickest rundown I can.

"I've run out of people to call, Ganesh. When I found your card, I remembered how . . ."

"There's always a way," he says, cutting me off. "If it was summer, I have an uncle who pilots the Maid of the Mist, but at this time of year . . ."

His voice trails off, and I think for a moment the line has gone dead.

"Hello?" I say, and then he's back again.

"Leave it with me," he says. "Give me five minutes. No planes, correct?"

"Right. No commercial aircraft."

"Okay. Give me a few minutes, I'll call you back."

"Thank you," I yell into the phone, but he's already rung off.

I use the time to dash into the unisex washroom inside Starbucks. I'm reaching for the toilet paper when my phone rings again.

"Where are you?" Ganesh barks at me.

There's such a thing as too much information. "In the Starbucks," I hiss. Someone outside the cubicles is washing their hands. "Near the—I don't know what it's called. The promenade, I guess. Overlooking the falls."

"American or Canadian?"

"Well, obviously I'm on the Canadian side . . ." I begin, but he cuts me off.

"Which falls?"

"American," I say quickly. I flush the toilet with my foot and hope it sounds like Niagara.

"Cross the street and look down," he says. "Straight down. Tell me what you see."

I yank up my yoga pants and dash out the door. On the street outside, I jaywalk right across the center of the block.

What have I become?

Gasping for breath after the mad dash, I drop my suitcase and lean over the railing. "I see a couple of little railcars for going up and down . . ."

"Funiculars," Ganesh interrupts. "And below them?"

"There are a bunch of guys in yellow, running around two grey rafts—is that what you mean?"

"Ah—brilliant!" he says cheerfully. "Now, Romy, you have to move fast, understand? You should be quite near the entrance to the boat tours, yes?"

"Yep."

"Is anyone near?"

"Nope."

"Good. Jump the gate, then take the stairs beside the funicular. You need to catch that Zodiac."

"The raft? What do . . ."

"Just go! My uncle says they were supposed to leave already. If you make it, you have a chance."

By the time he finishes this sentence, I'm over the railing and halfway down the stairs.

"Which one is your uncle?" I pant, trying not to slip as I clamber down. The iron stairs are corrugated, but covered in a thin layer of frost.

"My uncle is not there. But his friend Winston is SAR, and they have to go collect a baby seat that—uh—went over the falls, I think?"

"Right," I say as I hit the rocky beach and aim myself at the group on the shore. One of the Zodiacs has already set out, but the other hasn't left yet. A figure in yellow lifts a hand to me.

"He sees me, Ganesh. Thank you so much! Next time you're in New York, I'll take you for dinner."

"Ha!" he replies. "Next time I'm in New York, your man can bake me some of that rum cake, eh?"

He rings off before I can explain.

So it seems that Ganesh's uncle, the tourist boat captain, is friends with the head of nautical search and rescue. His name is Winston Tubbs, which I learn as he unceremoniously hauls me into the boat.

"Usually we're fishin' out bodies," he says, tossing me a giant yellow raincoat. "The only reason I agreed to taking you is today's target is apparently a baby seat, hopefully empty. Piece of cake job."

He zips up his own coat to the neck and chuckles. "Also? I owe Shiv a favor. So this is your lucky day, baby girl. Now put that life jacket on and sit yourself down there."

He points to a spot on the floor of the Zodiac near the back, and I do as I'm told.

Revving the engine, he follows the other boat out onto the Niagara River.

This close to the water, I can see the ice floating in jagged pieces, under the surface. It looks like we are flying across a mosaic of broken glass.

Within seconds, my hood has flown back and my face is frozen solid. I squeeze my eyes closed against the unrelenting cold.

In under a minute, the engine gears down and I risk opening my eyes again. The first Zodiac is bobbing nearby, and a yellow-clad figure near the prow of the boat is reaching into the water with a long hooked pole. He needs both hands to wrestle his catch into the boat, and in fact, the driver has to come forward to help. Seconds later, the missing car seat splashes onto the deck of the other Zodiac. As the driver makes his way back to the motor, the man in front holds up something to wave at us.

It's a sodden and fully naked baby doll.

The other boat peels away, back to the landing stage, when Winston holds out a hand.

"Shiv tells me they stamped your passport?" he says. "Let's see it."

I dig it out of my bag and hand it over.

"Cause I ain't riskin' the law for smuggling no immigrant," he says, peering closely at the stamp on the page.

Satisfied, he holds a thumb to the radio attached to his shoulder, says something into it, and points the prow of the Zodiac away from the falls.

"You taking the Amtrak?" he asks.

When I nod, he bends over the huge motor.

"Right then. We'll go for a little ride upstream. Less notice that way, an' closer to the station," he says as the engine roars into life.

We speed past the bridge and around a little section of land near

EIGHTY DAYS TO ELSEWHERE · 425

the far side in no time. Outside the immediate influence of the falls, a low fog rolls in over the water to greet us.

As the engine gears down, Winston waves me to my feet. "I'm gonna drop you at the old dock," he says. "There's steps up the side, but they're steep and rickety, so take care, will ya? From the top, it's less 'n a mile to the station, across the Scenic Parkway."

He waves off my thanks as I clamber onto the dock with my suitcase. As I toss back his life jacket, it lands on the deck of the Zodiac beside him, but somehow my phone goes with it. Even though I drop to my knees and plunge both arms into the water, it slips away beneath the ice-crusted surface, and vanishes deep into the Niagara River.

Winston roars off into the fog without seeing what happened. In any case, there's nothing to be done. I wring out my sleeves, and turn to face the precipitous wooden staircase, in the last light of this April day. Thanks to Ganesh, a Tamil sailor on a ship half a world away, I've made it back into the nation of my birth. After eleven countries— counting the stop in Singapore—only a single train ride stands between me and the end of this race. Clinging to the icy wooden railing, I scale the steps, which are as rickety as advertised, and race through the darkening streets of Niagara Falls, New York.

chapter sixty-four

No phone. No camera. No Insta post.
April 30
Niagara Falls, New York

Against all odds, the final train trip of the journey unfolds without a single mishap. This is possibly due to the worst having already happened. Now, I've not only lost Dominic, I've lost my phone too.

Nevertheless, I fall asleep in my seat almost instantly, waking long enough to stumble blearily to the washroom. Forgetting all my hard-won travel lore, I splash my face with water from the tap. It's not as cold as the Niagara River, and it only revives me long enough to get back to my seat. The minute I pillow my hoodie under my head, I'm gone again.

I wake as the train slows, chugging a little, into the lights of the city.

My city.

Slinging my daypack over my shoulder, and clutching the handle of my suitcase, I step off the train onto the platform of Penn Station, a full minute before 11:00 p.m. on the 30th day of April.

I'm home.

The sleep has revived me somewhat, and I literally hit the ground running at the station. A deep longing for a large cup of highly caffeinated tea grips me, but there's no time for that now. My suitcase is so light, I tuck it under one arm to make the running easier, and feel all my pockets for my phone—twice—before I remember it's at the bottom of the Niagara River.

Glancing up instead at the mammoth old clock on the wall, I watch the minute hand move to four minutes after the hour as I flash my ticket at the sleepy employee by the gate. The fact that I finish this quest alone, exactly the way I began it, slams me with a pang of disappointment so strong, it makes my mouth taste sour. Taking a deep breath, I head up through the main concourse of the station. Merv and Tommy need this. It will be worth everything I've gone through.

It has to be.

I take the stairs two at a time up to the street. It feels so weird to be home, I have to stop at the top and breathe in the unmistakable New York smell, and get my bearings. If I go through to the subway at Herald Square, I can pick up the M line, which will take me right down to the ExLibris offices.

Above me, the lights of Macy's gleam down, and there are tulips in the little garden boxes at each entrance.

The streets are still busy, and I even have to dodge a little traffic before the steps to the Thirty-Fourth Street Station appear. I thunder down, and then have to stop at the bottom to dig my transit pass out from the deepest pocket in my wallet.

As I run down the escalator, there's a low rumble from the approaching train. I hit the platform as the train roars up, and the doors swish open. At this hour, there's no crowd off-loading, so I step inside and drop my suitcase at my feet. Glancing up at the map above the door, I confirm I need to go two stops. Only two stops and I'll be at ExLibris. I take a step forward to look up at the digital clock on the platform. It's only 11:30.

I'm going to be early.

Outside, the whistle goes, and I step back as the doors slam shut in front of my nose. As I do, a figure comes shooting down the escalator, but the train has started to move. I catch a glimpse of long legs and flying dreads.

"Wait—Dom?" I yell, and run down the aisle inside the nearly empty car, but the train is moving too fast already. I smash my face against the window, but it's too late.

"What the actual hell?" I mutter.

A drunk guy, flopped across a whole row of seats, peers up at me blearily.

"You givin' up that suitcase, lady? 'Cause I could use a nice suitcase."

I snatch it up, and go stand at the far end of the car.

By the time the train hits the stop at Twenty-Eighth, I have a plan. Leaping off, I race down to the far end of the platform, and position myself in the best strategic spot for watching the next train. If it *was* Dominic, he will have hopped on, and I will see him as it pulls in. If it wasn't, I hop on and take it the final stop to ExLibris.

I'm so hyped up on adrenaline, I can't stand still, so I pace in small circles near my spot. There's no one on the platform, since all the waiting passengers have climbed aboard the train I just hopped off, which means there's no one to side-eye my pacing, or more importantly, to make a play for my suitcase.

After five minutes, I start to freak out. Where's the next train? I risk leaving the case where it is, and trot down closer to the electronic sign board, but where it usually lists the next arrival, only the current time is on display.

11:43, it says in red LED lights.

11:44.

At 11:47, I can't stand it anymore. I know the trains become less frequent at night, but this is ridiculous. Where is it? They never stop before midnight. But it's five full city blocks to ExLibris from here. Can I run five blocks in thirteen minutes?

What choice do I have? Walk in late, complaining of poor service on the MTA?

Not *this* New Yorker.

Clutching my suitcase, I fly up the stairs, and hit the exit turnstile at full velocity. By the time the tall tower housing the offices of Ex-Libris comes into view, I'm panting like a Mumbai street dog, but the iron clock on Fifth Avenue reads four minutes to midnight. The comparatively deserted streets of New York have helped, but my land speed has definitely improved on this journey.

The front doors are open, just as they were that early morning, another lifetime ago, when I entered to persuade Teresa Cipher to give me the job. I run straight through and into an open elevator. Inside, I hit the number for the fortieth floor, and then button-mash it at least a dozen times before the doors finally close. For an elevator in an empty building, it takes an eternity to climb to the top. But when the doors open on the fortieth floor, the office inside is not only dark, but totally deserted.

I leap out anyway. "I'm back, and I'm in time," I yell, but my voice is swallowed by the empty office space.

Down the hall, the clock in Teresa Cipher's office begins to chime. After everything I've been through, this? Is a total anticlimax. No one is even here to witness my arrival.

On Powell's desk in front of me, a large-screen monitor flickers into life. There's no sound, but on it I see a room filled with people.

Everyone is holding up what look like glasses of champagne. Teresa stands in front of the throng with her assistant, who hands her a fluted glass. A large form blocks the frame for a moment, but as he steps away from the camera, there's no doubt who it is.

Dominic.

So. He made it first, after all.

On the screen, everyone, including Dom, raises their glasses toward the camera.

I slump back against the elevator doors, feeling completely defeated. Behind me, the doors slide open, and I lurch backwards in the elevator and trip over my own suitcase.

This is the final indignity. The doors close, and I don't have the strength to do anything but lie there on the floor.

To tell you the truth, it's a relief to put my feet up.

After a minute, the elevator lurches into movement, and I pull myself to my feet. It's not until I'm standing that I realize it's going up instead of down.

"Oh, that's not spooky at all," I mutter, shivering a little. This endless day is finally catching up to me. At the sight of my tangled hair in the elevator mirror, I yank up my hood and turn back to face the doors. As they slide open, I smack the lobby button, and the doors begin to close again.

Suddenly a large, perfectly manicured hand reaches inside. The doors bounce back and Teresa is standing outside, looking a little shocked.

"I think perhaps I shouldn't have used that arm," she says, rubbing it. Using her body to block open the elevator doors instead, she ushers me out into a cheering crowd.

This penthouse office is essentially a glass room, and the view is, as once promised by Teresa's assistant, breathtaking. Somehow, the view serves to drive home my loss even more strongly, and I have to take a deep breath to stop myself from sobbing. I've never taken acting lessons, but there's no way I'm willing to show my disappointment in front of all these people.

Who the hell *are* all these people?

Feeling completely gobsmacked, I turn to look back at Teresa, who is not looking at me at all, but at someone behind me.

It's Dom, of course. Before I can say a word, his mouth is on mine, and his arms are around me, his fingers caught up in my hair.

Literally caught up. My hair hasn't been brushed since sometime in Saskatchewan.

"You made it!" he says when he finally releases me long enough to breathe. He scoops a pair of champagne glasses off a passing server's tray and holds one out to me.

I drain it in one gulp.

"What the actual hell, Dom?" I explode. It's taken me a minute to recover my mental faculties after that kiss and remember why I'm mad at him. "Why didn't you answer my messages?"

He stares at me. "I did. I said I'd meet you here, and—here I am."

He holds out his arms, including the one attached to me, as evidence.

"You didn't! I haven't heard a thing since you disappeared from the train. I thought you'd dumped me."

"Dumped you? Are you crazy? I left you a note. And I answered all your texts and e-mails as soon as I could get my phone charged up again."

Suddenly, the memory that I've been using his phone cord since I left mine on the ski bus returns to me.

"That's *no* excuse," I mutter. "You can get another phone cord anywhere."

"I did," he says patiently. "But my mom's in the hospital. As soon as I found out how she was doing, one of the nurses charged it up for me."

I swallow hard. That *was* an excuse, and a good one too. "Your mom's in the hospital? Is she okay?"

He nods and sips his champagne. "Yeah, thank God. But it was meningitis, and when Teresa texted me, things were looking really bad."

He narrows his eyes at me. "I sent you all the details this afternoon, as soon as I could. Check your phone, you'll see."

I shake my head. "My phone didn't make it across the Niagara River," I say, adding, "Long story," at his puzzled look.

Instead of telling it, I paste on a smile, and clink his glass with my empty one. "Congratulations. I'm so happy for you."

"Me too. It's a huge relief to find out she's okay," he replies, and kisses me again.

I do not kiss back, and his face is puzzled as he pulls away.

"You *do* know I took a commercial flight, right?"

"You—what? When?"

"To get here. This morning, at the crack of dawn. I took a commercial flight, and Teresa knew all about it. I tried to meet you at the train station, but . . ."

A voice comes from behind me. "I knew all about what?"

It's Teresa, who is wearing a long bandage dress in carnelian red, and four-inch matching stilettos.

"My flight," Dom says.

Teresa waves a hand dismissively. "Oh, that—of course. I'm just glad your mother is going to be fine. Look—Powell's got the tape cued up, finally. She's going to play it again."

She steps back, and points upward. On the wall above the elevators is another CCTV screen, identical to the one on Powell's desk. I watch myself, in crystal-clear black-and-white, racing into the ExLibris offices. Someone freezes the image when I have one foot in the air, and zooms in on the wall clock, visible in the background. The minute hand is frozen at two minutes to midnight.

A cheer rises up around us again.

"You made it," Dominic repeats, like he's talking to a small, slow child. "This is all for you."

"Who are all these people?" I hiss, and this time he laughs.

"Your new coworkers," he says. "Turns out ExLibris is a pretty large company."

He leans down to kiss me again, and I'm feeling so slack-jawed by the situation that I barely remember to kiss him back.

But somehow? I manage it.

When we break apart at last, Teresa is beaming at me, and beside her for some inexplicable reason, stands Frank Venal. He looks exactly the same as he did the day I first met him, right down to the orange spray tan and the open topcoat. Minus the cigar, I realize.

"Congratulations," says Teresa. "And welcome to ExLibris." She hands me a check made out in my name for $10,000. "Your bonus."

I manage to stammer something resembling a thank-you, and then immediately turn and hand the check to Frank Venal. My loathing for the man is, for the moment at least, replaced by a wild sense of relief. My uncles are out of danger. The bookshop is safe.

I grab another champagne flute and drain it to cut the pain of holding so much money for so short a time.

Venal's blank expression shifts into a furtive grin as he folds the check in half. He reaches for his inside pocket, but before he can tuck it away, Teresa Cipher plucks it out of his fingers.

"Oh, Frankie," she says disapprovingly. "You know that's not in the cards."

"Frankie?" I mutter, looking up at Dom, who laughs out loud as Venal stomps off.

"Good one," he says, and Teresa gives a tiny bow before returning the check to me and floating away.

Staring from her retreating back to Dom, I open my mouth with the first of approximately a million questions, when the crowd of revelers parts, and Sumaya appears. She finishes stuffing an appetizer into her mouth, wipes her hands on a napkin, and then throws herself into my arms.

"What the . . . ? How?" I give up trying to speak coherently, and concentrate on hugging her back fiercely.

"Nkruna's here too," she says as her aunt steps through the throng. "And if you're done with all the kissing, Terri said she'll give me the mic for a five-minute set."

Auntie Nkruna, dressed in a robe and matching head wrap patterned in vivid blues and greens, rolls her eyes.

"I keep trying to interest her in hair, or even esthetics," she says with a shrug. "But it's always with the jokes, this one." Turning to Sumaya, she says: "Five minutes only, young lady. It's long past your bedtime."

Later when a second tall, beautiful black woman comes up, it takes me a minute to realize it's Jersey.

"What are you doing here?" I hiss in her ear, as she kisses me.

She shrugs. "Handed in my dissertation, and I needed to see this in person. A friendship can't exist on Instagram posts alone." She flashes me her wide, beautiful smile, and I'm so happy to see her, I do a total Sumaya and throw myself into her arms.

"That man of yours is *fine*," she whispers, when I finally release my grip. "Where have you been hiding him?" She narrows her eyes. "Oh, I get it—he's the Javier Bardem in your little *Eat Pray Love* scenario, right?"

I can't even muster a rebuttal.

Instead, I pull a fresh champagne glass off the tray, and watch Dom laughing with Nkruna and Sumaya. "He *is* fine," I mutter. "But . . ."

"No, you're right," says Jersey, contemplatively talking right over me. "He's definitely more of a young Khal Drogo than a Javier. Nothing wrong with that."

Nothing wrong with that, at all.

Sometime later, after Sumaya—wearing her Bowie t-shirt—has brought down the house, I manage to corner Teresa on her own for a moment. She tells me that after Frank Venal's run-in with Merv, he'd stomped into ExLibris to demand an explanation. Instead, Teresa Cipher, who knew Venal through her poker club, goaded him into a little wager over the outcome. At stake?

Ownership of a bookshop.

chapter sixty-five

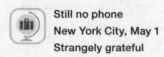
Still no phone
New York City, May 1
Strangely grateful

I wake up in my own bed for the first time at five, to the outline of a very naked man silhouetted against the blinds.

"Are you bolting?" I croak. "Because . . ."

I never get to finish this thought, because his lips are on mine, and—it's distracting.

"Not a chance," he whispers. "You're stuck with me now. It's just—my interior clock is all screwed up. I was thinking about checking in with my mom. She's due to leave the hospital this morning."

I sit up in bed before I remember I, too, am naked. I make a quick grab for the covers, but Dom is faster than I am. He pulls them back down and then slides over to sit on them.

"Don't worry about the bedclothes," he says, his fingertips tracing a line along my ribs. "It's pitch dark in here. I can't see a thing."

His fingers continue their journey, pausing to rest lightly at the base of my throat.

"You're so warm," he murmurs, and I can feel my heartbeat speed up under his touch.

"Didn't you say you were going over to the hosp . . ." I begin, before his lips find mine again. Pretty unerring aim for someone who claims he can't see a thing, is all I'm saying.

"I was. I am. Just not quite yet," he mutters, and then makes an entirely convincing case for a departure delay.

I wake up the *next* time to find Rhianna curled up on my stomach. When I stretch, she kneads the covers with her claws, eyes tightly closed.

"Tommy thought you were lost, girlie," I whisper, and she rubs her chops along my finger. "But you were waiting for me here, right?"

"Uh . . ." says a voice from across the room. "You're only half right, actually."

I look up to see a freshly showered man standing in my doorway, smelling of the fragrant, but unlikely, combination of mint shampoo and bacon.

He is disappointingly fully clothed.

"I made breakfast," he says. "Even though it's now officially afternoon."

Rolling over, I check the clock sitting on the stack of books that has been my temporary nightstand for the past two years. It reads 12:01.

"Why only half right?"

Dominic winces a little. "You might want breakfast before you look inside your sock drawer."

What I want, before anything, is the bathroom. As soon as I sit up, Rhianna bolts off the bed. I climb over my suitcase and slip inside the bathroom door. Once the essentials are out of the way, I peer into the mirror while I brush my teeth. New Romy is grinning like a fool back at me, looking happier than I can ever remember, at least during a morning toothbrushing. My hair is piled in a rusty, chaotic mass on my head, and I'm wearing a Grateful Dead t-shirt I've never before laid eyes on, at least three sizes too large.

It smells of cinnamon and vanilla—that is to say, of Dominic. I may never take it off.

Tossing my toothbrush, I pull on a pair of yoga pants, in case breakfast turns out to be a formal affair. When I open the bathroom door, Dominic is standing beside my tiny stove with a cup of tea in his hand.

"First things first," he says, and holds it out to me.

I think I may have to marry this man. But I have a few questions first.

Things I learn before looking in my sock drawer:

1. Dominic has never heard of ghosting, and claims to be insulted that I even considered the possibility he had dumped me. Counterpoint: He made breakfast, which I read as a conciliatory gesture.

2. I have never eaten French toast this good before.

3. Dominic and Teresa had a chat at the party, and she offered him a job overseeing the ExLibris adventure-travel cookbook division. He accepted on the spot.

4. She also connected him with another member of her poker club, a lawyer with a specialty in immigration law.

5. When Teresa registered her wager against Frank Venal with her Hong Kong bookie, he opened the betting up to the public. Which means that I actually did see my name in lights in Hong Kong. And which also means I owe my giant bump in social media followers more to illicit gambling than to my skill as a

photographer. I'm pretty sure they'll all dump me, now that the race is over. No regrets.

6. Most of what I learned at the party last night has vanished from my head. I remember meeting a few ExLibris employees who all seemed nice, and something about Teresa having quit smoking.

7. I'm going to need to spend some of my bonus money on new socks.

When Dom leaves to go see his mother, I gently pull out my sock drawer and carefully carry it down the stairs.

Merv is beyond delighted to have Rhianna back, but Tommy takes one look into the drawer, screams "Kittens!" and bursts into tears.

My return didn't elicit half this emotion, is all I'm saying.

I head upstairs to dump and sort the gross laundry out of my suitcase—and, to be clear, it's *all* gross laundry—to upload the contents of my photo file onto my backup drive, and to deliberately not strip my bed. Like the t-shirt, the pillow case still smells of him, and I'm not ready to give that up.

I *do* make my bed, though. I mean, change doesn't always have to be radical, right? One step at a time.

Just as I finish my bed, the bell on the front door tings. Tommy and Merv are still celebrating the arrival of Rhianna's new family, so I thunder down the stairs and into the shop.

Inside, Teresa is standing with Dominic, who's carrying a bag that smells suspiciously like cookies. He looks bright-eyed and not at all like a man who was engaged in an energy-intensive workout at five this morning. I can feel heat rising up my neck at the memory, and find I can no longer meet his eye. Instead, I focus on Teresa. She has changed her red sheath of the night before for a one-piece ski suit, which looks, I have to admit, slightly incongruous on the first of May. She's got red sunglasses propped on her head, and she's holding an empty cigarette holder in one hand.

Some habits die harder than others, I think. One step at a time, even for Teresa.

She beams at me, and as I introduce Tommy and Merv, the bell tinkles behind us, and the front door opens.

"Darling!" cries Teresa, and before I know it, she's greeting Frank Venal with a kiss on each cheek. Frank, also, seems too-warmly dressed for the balmy day, in a bright blue puffy jacket over pin-striped suit trousers. He gives Teresa a sheepish smile, then firmly—and proprietorially—links his arm through hers.

There are no customers in the store, so once the introductions are done, our little group stands for a moment in awkward silence.

Teresa, who has been glancing around the store with an apprecia-tive smile on her face, clears her throat. "We felt—Frank and I—that it was important to make this exchange formally, which is why we've asked you all to gather here this afternoon," she says.

Beside her, Frank rolls up on his toes, all evidence of his previous mobster-like demeanor completely absent.

Teresa glances down at him fondly. "Frankie, dear?" she says, after a pause.

"Oh—right, right," splutters Venal, and jams a hand into his in-side pocket. "I believe this belongs to you, my dear," he says, and passes Teresa an envelope.

She removes the title deed from the envelope.

I manage to catch Dom's eye. *WTF?* I mouth at him, but he shrugs and raises his eyebrows at me.

Teresa turns to Merv.

"We have a firm policy at ExLibris of supporting our staff," she says, handing Merv the deed. "A happy staff is a loyal staff, yes?" she adds, raising an eyebrow at Frank, who nods vigorously.

"A good staff is like family," he says, sounding not at all like Don Corleone.

Merv accepts the envelope and immediately chokes up as he tries to thank her.

"Nonsense," she says, patting his arm gently. "This arrangement can only benefit ExLibris, after all. It makes perfect sense that we affiliate with an independent bookstore. I have big plans to feature some of your collection on our site. It's a marvelous chance to offer up more variety to our clientele."

"Of course," says Merv eagerly, having found his voice at last. "Whatever we can do."

He and Tommy beam at each other, and I have to look up at the ceiling to keep a grip on myself.

Teresa strides over beside me. "We have the ideal liaison in Ramona, of course. I assume you are fairly conversant with the stock of the establishment?"

I take a deep breath and try to focus. "Of course," I say. "Intimately."

This makes Dom wiggle his eyebrows at me again, dammit.

Teresa appears not to notice. "Excellent. An absolute added-value to our clients."

"I've always thought it was a nice space," says Frank, glancing around appreciatively. "If we clear away some of these books, maybe we can do poker here on Friday nights?"

Oblivious to the collective expressions of horror around her, Teresa pats his hand. "We'll see, honey," she says. "I may have other ways of keeping you busy on Friday nights."

Okay, so I'm ashamed to admit that it's not until this moment the penny drops for me. In my own defense, I have been somewhat distracted since my arrival home. Not much sleep. I blame Dominic.

I stare at the moony expression on Frank's face, and everything comes clear.

"You two—are a couple?" I gasp, and to my utter shock, Teresa gives a girlish giggle.

"We've been playing in the same poker group for months," she admits. "But somehow, even after fleecing him three weeks running, *including* winning the bookshop . . ."

"I stole her heart," Frank says, beaming.

"He's a bit of a hard case," Teresa admits with the teeniest shrug, "but I've always been a gambler, after all."

Merv, still emotional from becoming a recent cat grandfather, wipes his eyes with the back of one hand and holds up the title deed to the bookstore. "Are you sure about this?" he asks Teresa.

"I don't have time to look after the day to day in a bookshop," she scoffs. "In fact, now that I have two such capable new employees to handle things at ExLibris, I think I've earned some time off."

She flips down her sunglasses. "I am—that is—*we are*," she corrects, squeezing Frank's arm, "heading for Reykjavík."

"Iceland?" I blurt, astonished.

"Indeed. Your eighty days to elsewhere have inspired me. After we send our client out on the re-creation of Fogg's journey the two of you so ably put together, I need to scout a few locations for other Verne books." Her smile widens. "There's a lava cave in Iceland I need to check out," she says, waving her phone. "Frank and I plan to Snapchat our way to the center of the earth."

Venal leans over to me. "I've never been outta the Big Apple before," he says in a stage whisper. "But now that I've found the right escort, I'm ready to see the world."

EIGHTY DAYS TO ELSEWHERE · 443

"Escort's maybe not the best word in this case," mutters Dom, but Venal ignores him.

Truthfully, I'm finding it impossible not to grin back at Venal. His smile lights up his face, the creases around his eyes erasing a lifetime of frown lines in an instant.

"He has a few things to learn about treating people decently," says Teresa, patting Venal's hand. "But I can't think of a better way than travel to open his eyes."

As Venal reaches up to kiss Teresa on the cheek, she snaps a selfie of the two of them with her phone. Then she turns, gesturing imperiously at Dom and me.

"Enough dillydallying. Back to ExLibris, you two," she says. "Powell is waiting for you. There's work to be done."

And smiling, she and Frank sweep out through the door and into the sunny May morning.

Dom turns to follow the new couple out the door, but I hold up a hand. "Wait a sec—I've got something for my uncle."

I reach behind the desk and grab my almost-empty daypack. From the back section, I pull out the copy of Verne's book that he handed me a whole lifetime ago. "Here's your book, safe and sound," I say, unwrapping it from Ganesh's waterproof cloth.

The cover is a little more battered than it was when he gave it to me, but all things considered, it's still in pretty good shape.

"I've tucked pictures of all the stops we made inside," I say, flipping open the back cover to show him the collection. "And now that it's actually been around the world, maybe it's worth even more?"

"The extra wear on the cover doesn't help," sniffs Tommy, but Merv snatches the book up.

"Are you crazy?" he says. "This is going on display in the front window. Your trip saved our shop, Romy! The book needs to go in a place of honor."

To my utter shock, Tommy actually cracks a smile. "Well. I did notice our Instagram account just hit three hundred followers. So, I guess you were right all along, Ms. Social Media Queen."

I lock eyes with Dominic, who grins and doesn't say a word.

Once I promise Merv that I'll always be there when he needs me, I kiss his cheek and follow Dom out the door. He pauses outside the front window, watching Tommy clear space for Verne's book in his featured display.

"Did you get things sorted with your mom?" I ask, and he nods.

"She's—ah—maybe not as forgiving as Teresa. He's going to have to find another housekeeper. Once she's feeling better, she's going to set up the daycare full time." He holds up the paper bag. "These are from her. She wanted to deliver them in person, but I told her we had to go to work."

Inside the bookshop window, Tommy blows up an inflatable globe.

I unfurl the bag, and breathe in the scent of chocolate chip cookies. But before I can take one, Dom reaches out and wraps his arms around me.

"You did it," he says softly. "You made it all the way around the world, and in way less than eighty days too. Can you believe it?"

"*We* did it," I correct him. "Don't pretend this wasn't a team effort. I would never have made it out of Suez if you hadn't booked us on that helicopter."

He snorts. "Spending all our money in the process. We were lucky Teresa was on our side."

I cuddle deeper into his arms. "I was lucky the whole way round. I mean, I was supposed to be racing you to the finish, but I kept getting distracted. African refugees, the First Nations protests in Canada, even the fight for the whales . . . Not exactly great at staying on task."

He squeezes me gently. "You seemed pretty focused to me. And that stuff was important. What we learned—who we met. I mean— can you imagine *not* knowing Sumaya?"

I grin up at him. "Nope. But that's what I mean. I feel so lucky to have met her. To be a part of her life."

A laugh rumbles in his chest. "I feel lucky we survived that plane ride."

"Me too. And all the helicopters, and ships, and trains . . ."

"Don't forget that rik in Kolkata."

"What about the cable car over the Alps?"

"Now, see, I missed that one." He gives my shoulders another little squeeze. "I took a balloon instead."

The memory of a rainbow-colored balloon, bobbing once above the gondola in Italy, makes me laugh out loud.

He grins back at me. "Look, you've even won over Tommy. Which means there's *nothing* you can't do."

"Oh, don't fool yourself. There's lots I can't do. But at least I learned I can tolerate a little chaos, now and again."

Inside the window, Tommy leans Verne's book against the inflated globe.

Dom is quiet a moment, and the warmth of his breath is in my hair.

"Okay. But here's a question for you. Was it worth it? You've come home empty-handed, and exhausted, and . . ."

"With three new stitches I didn't have before."

I can feel his laugh through my back. "Okay, besides the stitches. Do you regret any of it?"

I turn and bury my face in his chest, breathing in the warm, delicious scent of him. "Not for a single second," I say, and the kiss he gives me then proves me to be completely correct.

Behind us, there's a sharp, disapproving knock on the window.

Dom jumps so guiltily, I laugh out loud. "See? There are some things even a Social Media Queen can't get away with."

Reaching into the bag to collect a cookie, I give Tommy a jaunty wave, and then take Dom's hand again.

It's time to get back to work.

ACKNOWLEDGMENTS

Eighty Days to Elsewhere is my eighth published novel—the twelfth that I have written—but never, NEVER, have I had more of an adventure in putting pen to paper. Or fingertips to keys, for that matter. I love to travel, but the truth is, I am most often to be found at home in the woods, surrounded by dogs and rain and copious quantities of strong tea. But for seven weeks last year, I set out on a research quest that took me, quite literally, around the world.

I blame you, dear reader, for all that followed. To make sure I got the details right, I crawled backwards through a muddy hole in the floor of a railroad tunnel, ancient passages deep under the ground in Paris. I rode a cable car up the world's highest vertical ascent, soaring through the thin air and indigo skies above the Alps. I dodged traffic like I've never seen on the streets of Mumbai during an Indian heatwave. I toured a North Korean spy ship in Yokohama and the earth trembled beneath me as I sat in an airport in Tokyo. I scaled outdoor escalators in Hong Kong, idly reading street posters that decried the "repatriation" of activists; a situation that would explode into fiery protests the day I left the city. I visited Fogg's Reform Club in London and libraries and independent bookshops in every city from New York to Singapore. I managed to acquire poison oak in Hong Kong, had my pocket picked in Paris, was pummeled by mammoth hailstones in Milan, and tasted monsoon rains in both Singapore and India. I walked the Rainbow Bridge across the Niagara gorge, hung out with Patience and Virtue at the public library in New York, and watched *Hamilton* on Broadway. I flew around the entire globe, and every place I went, I was met with kindness.

My goal was to take you with me—to bring the dusty whiff of drought and the tang of sea salt and the gasp of not quite enough oxygen in the cold, still air—to anyone who might open the pages of this book. But as it did with Romy, this research brought transformation to me too. Travel changes a person. No matter how closed the mind is upon departure, it is forced open when faced with the shocking contrasts and terrible beauties of this earth. Every traveller discovers both how vast and how tiny our planet is, and the reminder that good people are the same, world over, is an excellent lesson to learn.

And so, I must thank the people who helped me, and thus Romy, make our frantic—and fantastic—way around the world. I am lucky enough to have the friendship and support of some absolutely wonderful writers, and I owe them all a tremendous debt of gratitude. There is not enough chocolate in the world to thank the lovely Hallie Ephron for the inspiration that ultimately led to this book. Thanks, too, to my dear friend and writing partner, Kathy Chung, who makes me laugh, and will cry with me or hold my hand whenever I need it. Thanks to both Pamela Patchet and Tyner Gillies for their undying love and support; proof that friendship doesn't see distance. Much love and appreciation goes to the brilliant Diana Gabaldon for her warm heart, generosity of spirit, and good advice. Thanks also to that quintessential Jekyll & Hyde of writers Michael Slade, whose ostensibly evil exterior masks the big-hearted Jay Clarke, regularly cheering me on and offering advice in equally enthusiastic measure. Special *bisous* to Laura Bradbury for her unending enthusiasm, support, and translation help. Thanks also to Mahtab Narsimhan, for fantastic feedback (and food!), and sharing her friendships with me on the other side of the world.

Thanks to Lee, James, Rob, Sarah, Rick, and all the Scoobies, big and little, for friendship and for always bringing the crazy. As ever, to my whole SiWC family—your support means more than I can say. And while I was gone, Magdalena Koryzna kept my canine boys fed and the home fires burning—*dziękuję bardzo*, my friend.

A cross the globe, my gratitude goes out to Khursheed Kanga for not only touring me through the streets of Mumbai, but ensuring I was optimally fed and housed. Thanks also to Karen Vaz for feeding me perhaps the best meal of my journey, in a little spot near her office in Mumbai. I am grateful to Helen Wang for her guidance in Hong Kong, and without whom I would never have stumbled upon the incredible villain-beaters, and to Su-In Kuah for tips on navigating the many faces of Singapore. *Merci beaucoup* to the king of the Parisian underworld, Gilles Thomas, for touring me deep under the ground in Paris, and successfully dissuading the *cataflics,* when they came to arrest us. (If you want to learn more of the depths beneath that city, Gilles's book *Atlas du Paris souterrain* is the definitive work.)

Thanks also to my amazing literary support crew—my superagent Laura Bradford (and her team at Bradford Literary) with whom all things are possible, and to Taryn Fagerness for her support of Romy's story overseas. Thanks also to the incredible Cindy Hwang and her team at Berkley, including Angela Kim, Scott Jones, and Stacy Edwards. Peter and Alicia, and Mim and Jürgen, thank you for your patience (and worry!). You will always have my heart.

Finally, I'd like to send out my deepest appreciation to you, dear reader, for buying this book, or borrowing it from the library. Thank you for sharing this journey with Romy and Dominic and Sumaya and their friends.

This story is fiction, but because it is set on a planet we all share, I want to remind you that any mistakes herein are entirely my own. Of course, if you point them out to me, I may have to go on another research trip.

Don't say I didn't warn you.

Eighty Days to Elsewhere

to

Elsewhere

kc dyer

QUESTIONS FOR DISCUSSION

1. *Eighty Days to Elsewhere* is a story about a journey—around the world, yes, but also a journey of the heart. In this adventure, Romy sees the world for the first time outside the pages of the books she has read, so everything feels brand new to her. Have you traveled to another country? What was the biggest cultural difference you experienced?

2. Romy's first impressions of Dominic harden her heart against him, even when his behavior shows him to be a better person than she believes. Have you ever had a terrible first impression of someone, only to end up close to them?

3. With all her years of education, and her obvious abilities, why do you think Romy is still working at the Two Old Queens bookshop? Just like in this story, sometimes taking the easy, comfortable choice is no longer an option in the real world. Have you ever been forced to step up and make a difficult life choice?

4. Romy has a strong support group at home, with her uncles, her friend Jersey, and even the librarians at the New York Public Library are available to offer support when she needs it. But when she takes on the ExLibris challenge, all that changes, and she is on her own for the first time in her life. Have you ever faced a challenge alone, without the support of family or friends around you? What advice would you give Romy when she steps on board the ship that will take her away from New York for the first time?

5. What possible circumstances could compel you out of your comfort zone at home? Do you think you would be able to go on a journey like Romy's, with limited finances and options for transportation?

6. Does Dominic's motivation change over the course of the challenge? Do his priorities change, or is he just able to find a compromise that works?

7. Both Romy and Dom encounter unexpected adventures and a huge learning curve about their own planet in their race around the world. Meeting Sumaya shows Romy that the world is both much larger and much smaller than she ever expected. How does the interaction with this Somali teenager change Romy? And how does it change the tenor of the competition between Romy and Dom?

8. Romy has a definite worldview before she sets out on her journey. Did you find yourself judging her because of her choices? As the story progresses, Romy begins to question herself on some of her first-world values. Has travel ever changed your worldview?

9. Compare Romy and Dom's reactions to the encounter with fellow American travelers on a train in Hong Kong. How are Romy's own perceptions changed by traveling with Dom and Sumaya?

10. When Romy first departs, she takes her old suitcase along as sort of a talisman. As the journey progresses, what she puts into the suitcase, and the value of the case itself begin to take on a heightened importance. Why is this particular object so significant to Romy? How does her inadvertent arrival in Alaska bring Romy's past and future both into sharper focus?

11. If you had a chance to press pause in the frantic pace of this journey, would you have liked Romy to linger longer in Paris—or perhaps Eritrea, or Japan? Is there some other part of the world you would like to see more thoroughly through Romy's eyes—or your own?

12. If ExLibris was setting up a literary expedition for you, which book would you choose? What adventure would you most love to reenact for yourself?

Keep reading for an excerpt from kc dyer's next novel . . .

An Accidental Odyssey

Coming soon from Jove!

chapter one

FRIDAY
NEW YORK FRIES

A recipe in prose by Gia Kostas, staff writer

I like my fries like i like my guys—a little greasy, a lot salty, and soft on the inside. This is a recipe that tastes hot off the street cart . . . and if you're a purist, I've got a quick and dirty ketchup recipe waiting for you in the side-bar.

To feed four, all you need to begin are six large potatoes—Yukon Gold, if you can get 'em, six cups of sesame cooking oil and a whole lot of finely ground sea salt.

To begin . . .

Reaching across my keyboard, I click the "return" button and my piece shoots off with a tiny, audible zing into cyberspace. In reality, this means it travels all the way to the far end of the floor, behind a closed door and into the in-box of my editor. I can't suppress a sigh as I lean back into my chair. My final assignment submitted. I should be celebrating.

As if on cue, a head pops up, appearing above the cubicle wall. The wall is one of those soft, grey fabric jobs, designed to absorb sound in an open-plan office. The grey color is soul-crushing on the best of days, and I'm not sure the things do much for absorbing the sound either. Mine is mostly covered with mouth-watering food shots destined for Instagram, recipes, and a map of Manhattan with push-pins in all the places I've written pieces about.

The head belongs to my cubicle neighbor, Janelle. She beams at me, her face poised above the shot of a beautifully plated selection of sushi that adorned an article I submitted last week.

"Drinks at five?" Janelle says, and waggles her keychain at me. The keychain bears a little martini glass, complete with tiny olive. "Billy Rae's has two-for-one Fridays for the whole month of May."

In spite of my interior gloom, I can't help grinning back at her. Janelle's smile is infectious, her wide mouth bracketed with a pair of dimples on the left, and a single on the right. The effect is just off-kilter enough to charm the hardest heart. She jingles the keychain again, clearly not convinced by my expression, and steps around the wall and into my cubicle.

"I heard your story go through," she says, tapping my monitor with her pen. The pen, I can't help noticing, exactly matches the shade of lipstick she's wearing. Which, in turn, perfectly comple-ments the blouse beneath her neatly tailored suit. "That means you're done, right?"

Janelle's ability to look uncreased at the end of the workday is a skill I've not managed to master in my time here. I sigh again, and reflexively run my palms across my own crumpled skirt.

"Yeah, that was the last piece. Apart from edits, I guess I *am* done."

Janelle's grin widens. "And I've just finished the last of my three-parter on this year's local Michelin stars. So it's a celebration, then. Excellent." She perches on the corner of my desk, scrolling through her phone screen. "They do a classic Gibson too. Perfect for a rainy Friday."

My back crackles as I push back my chair and stand up. "I'd love to, but I can't," I mutter, not quite able to meet her eye. "I promised Edward I'd meet him at Hudson Bakery. Cake tasting."

"Hudson Bakery? Christ, Gia—that's the most expensive place in the city." Janelle, shocked out of her menu scrolling, drops her phone on the desk. "Forget drinks. I'll come with you for the tasting. I'd give my right arm to taste their chocolate raspberry truffle cake again."

I think about Edward's reaction to me showing up with a work colleague. Considering he'd already vetoed me bringing Ruby—my maid of honor—I didn't think it would go over very well.

"This is special, Gia," he'd said that morning. "We're never going to have a day like this again. Who cares what everyone else thinks? Let's choose something we both love."

And so it was decided.

"I'd love that," I say, entirely honestly. "But he's planned a special date night for us, with the tasting as the centerpiece. Sorry."

Janelle leans forward and puts a hand on my arm. "God, Gia—you are *so* lucky. When I got married it was all I could do to get Gord to show up for the ceremony. 'It's your day,' he'd say, every time I asked for help making a decision. 'You just need to tell me where to stand, and I'll leave the rest up to you.'" She sighs. "I'd have done anything to have such a supportive partner."

There's a fine line between supportive and bossy, but I don't want to admit that to Janelle. Instead, I haul out an old box I've been hoarding from under my desk, and start loading it with pictures off

462 · kc dyer

the wall of my cubicle. In spite of the fact that the clock has just ticked past five, my boss's office door remains firmly closed. Charlotte Castle, my no-nonsense, incredibly organized supervisor, offered me a polite farewell when we passed in the hallway just after lunch, and wished me well. But she hadn't offered me a job.

"Last day and no job to go to on Monday," I say, gloomily. "I kinda wish I'd made a better impression on the powers that be."

Janelle folds her arms across her chest, and a careful look comes into her eyes. "Look," she says. "It's not just you. It's a rough time for journalists everywhere. NOSH is a small company—one of the last independents. Charlotte has nothing but good things to say about you—you'll get a fantastic reference, for sure."

I step around her and begin pulling recipe clips off the wall. "I know. It's just . . ."

"Besides," she says, catching hold of my left hand as I reach for the last clip. "You've got cake to look forward to, right?"

She turns my hand so that the diamond catches one of the last rays of the setting sun gleaming in through the window.

I slip my hand out of hers and shoot her a wry grin. "The wedding's not until the summer. And I'd rather be thinking about my next story here, to tell you the truth. This whole big wedding thing has me a bit freaked out."

"Girl? Edward Hearst is one of the city's most eligible dudes. I wouldn't give working another thought, if I was in your shoes. I'd be sitting back, drinking a bellini, and leafing through *Billionaire Bridal*."

Rolling my eyes, I jam the last of my tear sheets into the box. "Janelle Olsen, you're the last person I thought would tell me to quit work because I'm getting married. What is this, the 1950s?"

As I say this, I drop the framed photo of Edward and me from the day we got engaged on top of the box. With all personal traces removed, the cubicle looks like what it is. Empty space for a temporary intern.

Janelle grins and hands me my coat from the hook by the entrance to my cubicle. "Don't look so gloomy! All I'm saying is that you don't have to worry financially. You can take some time, plan the wedding, and keep an eye on the job market for when your schedule lightens up."

I'm just about to nail her again for this suddenly archaic attitude when my phone rings. It's slipped down inside the box, and I need to pull out my stapler and the framed photo to get to it. The photo is a little out of focus, since it was taken from the Jumbotron at a Yankees game. It shows me standing on the infield, looking stunned—and with one eye half-closed—as Edward beams straight into the camera from his position, down on one knee.

I shove the photo aside and grab the phone, which is displaying a number I don't recognize. "Gia Kostas," I say, and hold a finger up to Janelle to let her know she's not off the hook with me just yet.

But whatever I was planning to lambaste her with vanishes in the next moment.

"It's Beth Israel ER, Ms. Kostas," a voice says through the line. "Your father has just been admitted with symptoms of stroke."

The NOSH offices are just off Union Square, so it's actually faster to run to the hospital than taking the L line. Janelle scoops up my box for me, offering to drop my belongings at my place on her way home. I give her a quick squeeze before tossing my heels into the box and slamming my feet into Nikes. Charlotte's office door is still firmly closed, so I make an executive decision to call in my goodbyes, and then bolt for the stairs. This building was renovated sometime before the turn of the last century, and a person can age out before the elevator arrives.

As a native New Yorker, I am nothing if not an expert at texting on the fly, so by the time I hit 14th Street, I've already left a message for Edward and a voice mail for my best friend. Edward keeps himself on a strict communications schedule, so even though he doesn't reply, I know he'll be checking his texts on the hour. Ruby's residency is in the Ophthalmology department in the hospital, and while I don't expect her to pick up either, it's a relief to know she'll be nearby. It's not until I jog up to the front of the building that it occurs to me to call my mother, but the sight of an ambulance unloading pushes the thought out of my mind. I can call her when I have actual news. For now?

I just want to see my dad.

So. My dad.

Professionally, Dr. Aristotle Kostas is a well-regarded academic. He's got a string of initials behind his name, and more degrees—earned and honorary—than I've ever actually counted. He's retired now, but still holds a post as professor emeritus at NYU in the Classics department. Which mostly means he hangs out there on weekdays, puttering around and giving the graduate students grief.

On the personal side, though, I can't really say things are as successful. My own relationship with him was totally rocky, at least while I was growing up. I almost never saw him, and my mom didn't have much to say that was positive. But lately—mostly since he's retired—things between us have been on the mend. My dad considers himself a life-long romantic, and has told me many times— usually after too much *ouzo*—how helpless he is in the face of love.

I know for a fact that others, out of his hearing, are less charitable. Having a reputation as a bit of a dog wasn't such a problem in the twentieth century, but it doesn't carry very far in the era of #MeToo. My dad's been married three times; his last wife being my mom, who is twenty-five years his junior—because they met when she was one of his students. By then, he was already a father to two boys. Both of my half-brothers are much older than I am, married with families of their own. Alek lives in Los Angeles and Tomas in Boston. With the uncomfortable situation between our respective mothers, we have never even exchanged Christmas cards.

But since I started college and moved out on my own, things have warmed between my dad and me. Not having my mom in the room when we talk these days doesn't hurt, though I have to admit their relationship has improved, too, now that she's remarried—and moved to Connecticut.

Since he's retired, he makes more of an effort to spend time with me. He's a life-long season-ticket-holder for the Yankees, and I'll tag along and take in a game with him now and then. During my whole internship at NOSH, he's taken me out for lunch at least once a month. And now? The thought I might lose him just as I'm finally getting to know him is terrifying.

The hospital is a maze, and by the time I find the right floor and skid into his room, I'm sweating and breathless. A nurse, standing just inside the door, raises her hand to stop me from going further. Curtains encircle three beds, with a fourth partially drawn. I can see my dad inside, propped up in the bed, an IV tube taped to his arm. He's in conversation with a woman who appears to be holding his hand.

"Dad!" I gasp, and they both turn to look at me.

". . . entirely out of the question," the woman says, unclipping something from one of his fingers. She hands a tablet computer to the nurse, who steps around me to receive it, and I hurry over to the bed.

"My daughter Gia," my dad says, warmly, as I bend to kiss his cheek. "Gia, this is Dr. Patil."

I nod at the doctor and reach for my dad's hand. "Are you okay, Pops? They said you had a . . ."

"I'm fine," my father says, airily waving the arm attached to the IV. "A small anomaly, nothing more."

My dad is a Greek male, who would lose a leg before admitting to a bit of a scratch, so I turn instead to Dr. Patil. "They said it was a stroke. Is there such a thing as a small stroke?"

The doctor nods, tucking her hands into the pockets of her lab coat. "Small, yes, but worrisome, nevertheless. We'll need to monitor your dad for the next forty-eight hours at least, just to rule out any further complications."

She turns back to him, and gestures at a stack of books piled on the side table, partially covered by my dad's overcoat. "That means bed rest, young man. Time to stay put and catch up on your reading." Raising an admonishing finger, she adds: "No exertion of any sort, you hear me?"

My phone buzzes in my pocket, and I pull it out long enough to flick the sound off.

It's a text from Edward. I decide to take it later, and as I drop the phone back in my pocket, the doctor shoots my dad a final grin and follows the nurse out past the curtain.

"Exertion?" I ask, yanking the lone chair closer to his bed. "What was that about?"

He rolls his eyes at me. "Overreaction. There's nothing much on my scan—I spoke with the radiologist, and that guy really knew his stuff. It's no big deal, trust me. Who's on the phone?"

"Just Edward. I can talk to him later—this is more important. Start at the beginning. What happened?"

"Nothing, really. I was late this morning and missed my breakfast, so I had a little dizzy spell on the subway. When I got into the office, it returned, and . . ."

"They said it was a stroke, Dad. That's different from a little dizzy spell."

"Not a stroke—a TIA. You heard the doctor. Completely different kettle of fish, *matakia mou.*"

I glance around pointedly at all the equipment. "So, is TIA medical short-hand for a stroke?"

"It stands for *transient ischemic attack,*" he says, falling into his teacher voice. "It mimics the symptoms of a stroke, but usually leaves no lasting damage."

"Usually?"

"Almost always," he says, cutting me off with another dismissive wave. "I'm fine. The dizziness is gone. They're giving me blood-thinners, and bad food." He sips ginger ale through a paper straw and grimaces. "All I need at the moment is some decent souvlaki. Was that Edward on the phone? Do you two have plans for the evening?"

I admit we were supposed to be tasting cakes. "But I can bring you some souvlaki, Pops." He pats my hand and shakes his head.

"Martin is already on his way over. He's—ah—bringing me some papers from the office, and he said he'd stop at Spiro's on the way. Don't worry about a thing, little girl. Papa will be fine. Go out and enjoy your Friday night. Eat cake. Have fun."

"Uh—don't you think I should stay and keep you company awhile?"

"I'm fine, darling, I promise you," he says, gesturing at the pile of books. "Reading to catch up on, remember?"

The adrenaline that carried me up here has drained away, replaced with a combination of annoyance and dismay at being so summarily dismissed. Then I feel guilty for feeling this way, when he's stuck in bed with a tube in his arm.

"But what about . . ." I begin, when his cell phone starts buzzing over on the table beside the books. I leap up and hurry around the bed to grab it, but he scoops it and answers before I can take more than a couple of steps.

"Martin!" he says cheerfully into the phone. "I'm fine—never better. Just hold a second, will you . . . ?"

He pulls the receiver away from his ear. "This is going to take a few minutes, Giannita. Off you go. I'll speak to you in the morning, yes?"

"Are you sure, Pops?" I ask, the guilt surging again. "I can stay until Martin . . ."

"Go—go," he says. "That man of yours keeps a tight schedule. It's good for him to eat a bit of cake too, no?"

I step out of the room once it becomes clear that he's not getting off his phone anytime soon. In the hall, I pause to lean against the wall and check my text from Edward. I click on the message with a little trepidation—my dad isn't wrong about Edward and his schedules. But against all expectations, the text is nothing but sympathetic.

Don't worry about a thing, babe. Stay with your dad as long as you need. Managed to reschedule the tasting for tomorrow, noon. Call if you need anything—turned the ringer on. Love you! Xx

As I begin dialing, a nurse gives me the evil eye, so I sidle toward the elevators before I push "send." The doors slide open on Martin, my dad's most recent graduate student and resident dogsbody. His arms are piled with books and papers, and he's so intent on getting in to see my dad that he hurries by me without a second glance.

I sigh, and step onto the elevator. I can check in again in the morning, before the rescheduled cake tasting. It's only as the doors begin to close that I realize my dad never answered my question. Just what *had* the doctor been warning him against, anyway?

Photo by Martin Chung

kc dyer loves to travel. When she's not on the road, she resides in the wilds of British Columbia, where she likes to walk in the woods and write books. Her most recent novel—a bestselling romantic comedy—is *Finding Fraser*, published by Berkley, and which *Us Weekly* called a "humorous but relatable self-discovery tale," and Bustle named "a Must-Read for Outlander fans."

For teens, kc's most recent work is *Facing Fire*, a sequel to the acclaimed novel *A Walk Through a Window*, published by Doubleday / Random House. kc is represented by Laura Bradford of Bradford Literary Agency.

She sweetly tweets at @kcdyer and you can find her website at kcdyer.com.

AS
FAR
AS
THE
EYE
CAN
SEE

AS
FAR
AS
THE
EYE
CAN
SEE

Reflections of an
Appalachian Trail Hiker

David
Brill

RUTLEDGE HILL PRESS
Nashville, Tennessee

Published in Nashville, Tennessee, by Rutledge Hill Press, 211 Seventh Avenue North, Nashville, Tennessee 37219. Distributed in Canada by H. B. Fenn & Company, Ltd., 1090 Lorimar Drive, Mississauga, Ontario L5S 1R7.

Typography by D&T/Bailey Typesetting, Inc., Nashville, Tennessee

Library of Congress Cataloging-in-Publication Data

Brill, David, 1955-
    As far as the eye can see : reflections of an Appalachian Trail hiker / David Brill.
      p.   cm.
    ISBN 1-55853-401-6
    1. Backpacking—Appalachian Trail.   2. Hiking—Appalachian Trail.
3. Appalachian Trail—Description and travel.   4. Brill, David,
1955- I. Title.
GV199.42.A68B75   1990   90-45387
796.5'1'0974—dc20   CIP

Printed in the United States of America
  3 4 5 6 7 8 — 99 98 97 96

I went to the woods because I wished to live deliberately, to front only the essential facts of life, and see if I could not learn what it had to teach, and not, when I came to die, discover that I had not lived.

Henry David Thoreau, *Walden*

Contents

Preface

On September 27, 1979, I ascended the mile-high summit of Mount Katahdin, a broad-shouldered peak rising from the Lake Country of central Maine. The fall frost had tinged the sugar maples bright red, the birches shone like burnished gold, and their color stretched away endlessly from the base of the mountain to the horizon.

Mount Katahdin ranks as one of the most majestic peaks east of the Mississippi, but for me it held special significance. It marked the northern terminus of the 2,100-mile Appalachian Trail, and it signaled the completion of a five-month wilderness journey that traced some five million steps through the eastern wilderness over hundreds of other peaks, through fourteen states, and dozens of small mountain towns.

When I began planning for my trek, friends and relatives seemed puzzled by my interest in forsaking the conveniences of modern society for a months-long sojourn in the wilderness. "Why are you doing this?" they asked, finding my commitment to the trail a bit extreme. All I could tell them was that hiking the Appalachian Trail was something I wanted and needed to do.

Today, I realize that my decision to hike the Appalachian Trail wasn't as capricious as it might have seemed at the time. My pilgrimage toward the trail began years earlier, in fact, with my first exposure to the natural world as a child and at the hand of my grandmother.

Our family made weekly trips to her house, which sat on a quiet side street two blocks from a large, forested hill.

Each Sunday, after we had finished our early afternoon dinner, Grandma asked my brother and me if we wanted "to go up on the hill." Then, clad in her floral print dress and walking shoes, she ushered our small hiking party out the front door and toward the woods.

Through the eyes of a child, the hill loomed as large as the Appalachian peaks I would ascend years later. Though it was nothing more than a glorified nob, one of many punctuating the hilly geography of southwestern Ohio, for me it was a magical place that exposed me to countless discoveries.

Each week, as we walked along the well-worn trail, wending higher and higher up the hill, Grandma shared her knowledge of the woods. Though she hadn't completed high school, she knew so much. She could identify scads of wildflowers—Dutchman's breeches, jack-in-the-pulpit, violets—and she knew the names of almost all the birds.

She showed us how to nip off the ends of honeysuckle blossoms, slowly draw out the pistils, and taste the sweet drop of nectar that clung to the tip. She held grasshoppers by their wings, saying, "Spit tobacco," and on command they would deposit a small drop of brown juice from their mouths onto her index finger. She could join small twigs into crosses or squares by peeling back some of the flexible green bark and using it as twine. She knotted clover blossoms into necklaces and draped them around our necks or tied them around our wrists.

When we passed the small brook that cascaded down the hill, she pointed to tadpoles wriggling across dark pools. She overturned rocks, revealing crayfish or slithering, spotted salamanders. Then she provided us with nature's play dough. After scooping soft gray clay from under the falls, we molded it into figures of people or animals and set them out to harden in the sun.

But Grandmother taught me much more. A serene, shy woman, who seemed to prefer the company of trees over that of people, Grandma often retreated to the woods, alone, to struggle with problems or just to think. She lived in communion with nature and seemed thoroughly at ease

ambling along a wooded trail. By watching the ease that accompanied her into the woods, I learned to trust the wilderness while embracing its gifts.

We sometimes sat on rocks or downed logs for long minutes and looked down on the orderly rows of houses and streets in the distance. Or we just sat, listening to the cacophony of woodland sounds until sunlight waned and it was time to return to the house. My brother and I often made our descent by rolling down a long, gently sloping hillside covered with grass, and we arrived at the bottom giggling and dizzy, giddy from sheer joy.

I balk when I try to explain how it felt to be in the woods with my grandmother. The feeling was so sublime, so serene, so personal. In the woods I found hope, peace, healing; no matter how sour my mood, the woods seemed always to soothe me, to resurrect sagging spirits. In the woods there was a sense of being at home, of being where I ought to have been all along.

Like my grandmother, I've often walked to the woods to think, to reflect, to sort things out. Even as an adolescent, when I encountered difficult times, I sought the peace I knew I would find there. In high school, when my grandmother died, I instinctively followed my grief to the hill where I sat for an hour or more, looking, listening for an answer. And I believe I found it at the brook that, to this day, traces the clay banks down the hill, just as it did on my first visit years ago.

Years would pass before I learned about the Appalachian Trail in 1977, during summer break before my senior year in college. At the time, I was working on a landscaping crew, and one day during our lunch break I sat in the cab of the truck with Jim Koegel, a quiet, intense man, four years my senior. A radio news program came on, and the announcer made some reference to the Appalachian Trail. Between bites of his sandwich, Jim mentioned that he had hiked it the year before.

I had no idea what the trail was or where it went, so I probed him for information. He explained that the trail extended 2,100 miles from Maine to Georgia and that he had hiked it from end to end the summer before, starting in Georgia. At first I was incredulous: could a person really walk that far in one summer? Then I pressed Jim for details, asking the same questions I would face dozens of times while on my hike: Was the way marked? What did he eat? Where did he sleep? Did he hike alone? Did he encounter wild animals? What did he do when it rained?

As the summer passed, I drew more and more information from Jim, not so much the information that pertained to logistics or miles but more about the experiential value of his summer in the wilderness, how the trail had changed him, and what lessons it had taught. And I became ever more captivated by his varied experiences.

At the time, I was primed for a challenge. The years of my adolescence had been difficult ones, not just for me but for most of the men and women of my generation. To some extent, we had been shaped by the Vietnam War and all the events it had precipitated. During those years the country was rife with conflict and chaos.

Evenings, we watched the nightly news with our parents and saw mangled corpses being dumped into body bags. We watched reports of the 1968 Democratic National Convention in Chicago, where Mayor Daley's police thrashed panic-stricken protestors. We heard our hard-line elders denigrate the unpatriotic hippies and peaceniks who protested the war. Meanwhile, race riots ripped the inner-cities and in ways reached our snug, middle-class suburbs. I was surprised to learn from a friend that his father slept with a loaded shotgun under his bed.

Amid all the chaos there was excitement, and it reached into every living room, every institution, every life. Everyone was full of passion, regardless of beliefs or convictions. So much was at stake. Men of draft age who had exhausted the deferment process faced war, prison, or escape to Canada. Blacks and other minorities faced

continued oppression. And the establishment—middle-class Americans—feared an end to traditional values.

For those of us yet to come of age, there was a sense of an impending showdown. How would we respond when we received our draft notices? Would we go to war and earn the respect of our elders? Would we flee to Canada and face being disowned by our families? Would we be secure enough in our opposition to the war to accept a prison term by refusing to do either? Like most young men my age, I deferred the decision until I was forced to choose.

When I graduated from high school in 1974, I was eighteen and ready for the passage into adulthood, but by that time the matter had been rendered moot. The war was, in effect, over, and the government had begun pulling troops out of combat. The protests had ended. The commotion died. The era drew to a close. And everyone seemed badly in need of rest.

As the fury died, I was left feeling like a man who had spent years preparing—mentally, emotionally—for a test, only to arrive a day late to a darkened classroom and to realize that I would never know how well I might have done.

In the years following World War I, there emerged a generation of young Americans termed by Gertrude Stein, "the lost generation." It was a generation of restless young men and women, including Hemingway, Fitzgerald, Ezra Pound, T. S. Eliot, and others, who had fled America out of disgust or boredom for the excitement of Paris. Once there, the expatriates pursued a life of abandon—living, drinking, loving to excess—while trying to make sense of their world and times.

Then, after World War II, novelist Jack Kerouac chronicled the attitudes of a similar generation, the "beat generation," in his book *On the Road.*

It seems that there follows in the wake of war a pestering complacency that sends youthful seekers out in search of excitement and meaning. Those of us affected by Vietnam were no exception.

I won't go so far as to say that I envied my peers who had been born five years earlier, but at least they had been forced to examine their beliefs, to make decisions, and, once made, to put them to the test. I envied them the personal growth they had derived from being in the core of the revolution or in the heart of the battle.

But for me there was no war, no showdown. Instead, there was only college and a continuation of my comfortable life. Once in school, and without having made the slightest sacrifice, I savored all the privileges won by the young people who had preceded me and had waged the social revolution.

During my first year in college, the resident radicals who had orchestrated the college protests during the war years still appealed to the students to support one cause or another, but by that time they had begun to resemble caricatures of themselves. By the time I graduated in 1978, benign indifference had supplanted the zeal of the late sixties. Oxford-cloth shirts and khaki pants had replaced jeans and T-shirts, and the emphasis had shifted from pursuing spiritual, sensual, and political goals to securing high-paying jobs. The whole scene left me flat.

I graduated, fulfilling an obligation to my parents who had helped pay my way through college and expected me to finish. The rest of my life was my own, but I had no idea what I wanted to do with it. I only knew that I craved experience outside of the cozy environs that had sheltered me for the first twenty-three years of my life. I wanted to be challenged. I wanted to confront something new and different. I wanted to find out what I was made of.

Thanks to Jim Koegel, I knew just where to find such challenge. After hearing his tales of adventure in the eastern wilderness, I made the Appalachian Trail my quest. I had heard so many people lament lost dreams, things they had longed to do but never found the time for. I was determined to see that that didn't happen to me. The trail would pose a wonderful setting where I could live, as Thoreau expressed in *Walden*, simply and deliberately, with room to grow, to breathe, to change, to discover what really mattered to me.

In the end, the Appalachian Trail provided all those things and more. Like every one of the other several thousand or so end-to-enders who have hiked the trail since its completion in 1937, I emerged from the Maine woods transformed.

This book is a collection of experiences and encounters, stories of fear and courage, of risk, of friendship and intimacy, of the power and beauty of nature. It contains one hiker's reflections and is one of several volumes that chronicle the Appalachian Trail experience, each different in its focus and impressions, yet each predicated on the same essential truths that have always beckoned man away from civilization and back into the wilderness.

For more than fifty years, the Appalachian Trail has offered footloose seekers a wooded path to spiritual and physical growth, to communion with the natural world, and to discovery of self. May it continue to do so.

The Author

Acknowledgments

I would like to thank the following people for their support while I hiked the Appalachian Trail and, later, while I wrote about it.

Dan, Paul, and Nick, and all the other backcountry travelers whose companionship has enriched my life.

The Appalachian Trail Conference and all the trail volunteers for their devotion to the trail, its maintenance, and its preservation.

Jean Cashin, for her boundless enthusiasm for the trail and its people.

Earl Conn, Larry Horney, and Jon Hughes, who nurtured the writer in me.

Benton MacKaye, who in 1921 conceived the outlandish notion of an Appalachian Trail.

My wife, Susan, most of all, who loves me despite the chaos that often attends a writer's life.

AS
FAR
AS
THE
EYE
CAN
SEE

To Dad,
who believed in my quest—and in me—long be-
fore he understood either
and who taught me that compassion is at the
heart of all worthwhile journeys

CHAPTER • ONE

Fear

*I'm lying under a wind-and-rain-buf-
feted tarp in a mountain gap in Georgia. I can hear wind
gusts begin miles away, then gather intensity and plow
through the gap, and with each gust the tarp sounds as if it's
about to rip from its tethers. The trees creak, and I can hear
limbs crack. I am terrified and awed by the power and violence of nature, and I realize that there's nowhere I can go to
escape it. I never appreciated how vulnerable I'd feel away
from the shelter of a roof and four sound walls.*
                 —April 24, 1979, Tesnatee Gap, Georgia

Just before a spring thunderstorm ham-
mers the mountains, the animals disappear. The songbirds
stop singing. The chipmunks stop scurrying. The spring
peepers stop peeping. The crickets stop grinding. And an
eerie quiet settles over the woods.

When twisters accompany those storms and rip their own
random trails across the landscape, you nestle down in the
deepest part of your sleeping bag and hope that your luck
holds.

You also swear that you will never, ever, camp in a mountain gap again. Tornados, like the pioneers of centuries past,
often follow the gaps across mountain ranges. I know that

21

now, but on April 24, 1979, as I lay under a nylon tarp in Tesnatee Gap, Georgia, I didn't.

There was, however, one thing that I knew for certain that night. I was frightened.

I had watched the storm approach from the west in the late hours of the afternoon. Columns of cumulo-nimbus clouds lumbered into view above the faraway hills, erasing the sun. The air smelled and felt pregnant with moisture, and, as the first winds began to buffet my camp, the atmosphere took on a sick, green cast.

By 6:00 P.M., it was dark, and I lay ensconced under my rain fly, waiting, as the first peals of thunder rumbled a few miles away. I had learned that by counting the seconds that lagged between each lightning flash and peal of thunder, I could estimate my distance from the heart of the storm. A five-second lag meant the storm was roughly one mile away. At 6:30 P.M., the storm was four miles away and approaching fast.

By 7:00 P.M., the counting game ended when the storm enveloped my camp. The ground rumbled beneath me, and the wind and rain raged above. I had experienced storms in the lowlands, secure inside four walls, but never in the mountains. At three thousand feet, I was wrapped in the low-slung clouds and, thus, inside the storm, and the thunder seemed to surround me before rolling away to the valleys.

Lightning bolts cast stark silhouettes of tree branches against the nylon of the tarp. First the flash, then immediately after, the resounding crack of thunder, like the slow splintering of huge bones. Then there was the rain, which fell so heavily at times that the tarp sagged under its assault and brushed against my face, and I could hear torrents of water channeling downhill, carving away earth and stone.

The wind howled and churned like an errant locomotive, and its force all but deadened the sound of the thunder and falling rain. I could hear walls of wind originate miles away in the valleys, then thrash toward me gathering intensity as they approached. They plowed through the gap, bowing the trees, scattering leaves, and snapping limbs. As each passed, the rain fly popped and bucked and surged, and I feared that

it would tear from its tethers and disappear into the darkness, leaving me exposed and even more vulnerable.

I cowered under the fly, feeling utterly helpless, like a prairie dog trapped under the hooves of stampeding cattle, and I prayed for the storm to deliver me unharmed. Through the night I felt like a victim, as if all the storm's violent energy had been directed at me and as if raw vengeance bolstered the wind and powered the rain. Though I wouldn't realize it until the next morning, a twister had already cut a swath through another gap a few miles to the north. I had been spared.

When day broke, I surveyed the damage wrought through the night. Tree trunks had been splintered, severed branches lay scattered about, and uprooted trees criss-crossed the trail with gray clay and stone still clinging to their dying roots.

At that point, I was four days and thirty-seven miles into the Appalachian Trail. I had begun my hike at Springer Mountain, the trail's southern terminus some sixty miles northeast of Atlanta, and I was determined to trek all the way to Mount Katahdin, the trail's northernmost point, in central Maine.

A month earlier I had resigned my job as manager of a Washington, D.C., tennis shop and had committed myself and my meager $1,500 in savings to completing the trail. I wanted to become one of several hundred "thru-hikers" who had navigated the route from end to end in one summer, but other reasons, too, had drawn me toward the trail. Among them was the desire to confront and overcome my fears, but in the wake of the storm, I realized that I had only begun to identify them. Moreover, I acknowledged that I couldn't hope to banish my fears until I had pushed deeper into the eastern wilderness and probed much further into myself.

Though fear is a solitary condition, at least I had not had to endure the storm alone. I had shared my camp with Dan Howe, a twenty-three-year-old former

architectural planner for a large oil corporation who had swapped his business suit and fast-track career for a pair of lug-soled boots, a backpack, and 2,100 miles of adventure. When we had set out on the trail, we had known each other just over a month and had met face to face only a half-dozen times.

Dan and I had first met during a program on the Appalachian Trail at a Washington-area backpacking shop. The program featured Ed Garvey, a well-known thru-hiker and author who had hiked the trail in the early 1970s. I had arrived for Garvey's talk fully reconciled to the notion that I would begin and finish the trail by myself, despite the fact that my previous backpacking experience had been limited to four or five overnighters; the longest duration had been three days. Over the previous months, I had telephoned every friend I had, and even a few casual acquaintances, in hopes of cajoling one or more of them into taking up the trail with me.

Most of them, like me, were in their first year out of college but, unlike me, had devoted their energies to charting career paths rather than ambling along wilderness trails. While they regarded the Appalachian Trail as a romantic pursuit, they also recognized its potential for stalling a career climb, and one by one they declined my invitation. So I had attended Garvey's presentation with the dim hope of finding a partner there.

As Garvey concluded his presentation, he asked if anyone among the thirty people in the audience intended to attempt the trail that summer. Tentatively, I raised my hand and then quickly scanned the room. One other hand waved in the air, and it belonged to a sandy-haired, bearded man who appeared to be about my age. After the meeting disbanded, I approached him and introduced myself, trying not to seem too eager or needy and realizing that to ask him abruptly if he would commit to spending the next five months with me was tantamount to proposing marriage on a first date.

Within a half-hour, Dan and I sat at a nearby tavern drinking beer and discussing our hopes, dreams, and expectations

for our months on the trail. As we talked, I discovered that
we had planned to begin the trail at about the same time—
late April—and that we shared many common attitudes.
Both of us had lived through the turbulent years of the late
1960s and early 1970s, and we both had emerged with a
sense that if society failed to provide the peace and stability
we sought, we might find it in nature.

While I had begun the trail seeking nature's healing
powers, over the first four days I had found only disappointment, discovering that nature was capable of more violence
than I had ever experienced in civilization. I found disappointment, too, in discovering the fear that dwelt within
me.

In the throes of the storm, I had lain awake, my heart
thumping like that of a snared rabbit, while Dan slumbered
peacefully beside me. Through the long night, my head
churned a maelstrom of doubt and anxiety, and I began to
suspect that I possessed neither the courage nor the
stamina to reach Mount Katahdin more than two thousand
miles to the north. I also suspected that I had invested my
hopes in a folly that would break me the way the wind had
cracked away the branches of the surrounding trees and that
I would limp back home wounded by failure. Those feelings
may have been amplified by the storm, but they had just as
surely accompanied my first tentative steps on the trail four
days earlier.

Early on the morning of April 21, my
parents had driven Dan and me up a ten-mile stretch of
gravel road to Nimblewill Gap, which reaches within three
miles of Springer Mountain and represents the nearest road
access to the southern terminus of the Appalachian Trail.

An alternate route to the top follows an approach trail,
which begins at Amicalola Falls State Park and ascends
nine miles to Springer. We had heard stories about the stiff
vertical ascent from the park to the trailhead, reputed to be
among the trail's most difficult sections. This was especially the case for neophyte hikers who lacked the fitness

and stamina that hundreds of miles on the trail would later provide. Among the dozens of hopeful thru-hikers who abandon the trail each year, in fact, many stumble back down the mountain—defeated—before ever reaching the summit of Springer. We didn't want to be among them, and by starting our hike at Nimblewill, we reasoned, we would at least make it as far as the official starting point.

We arrived at the gap in my parents' new sedan, and Dan and I climbed from the car smelling of soap and shampoo, fresh from our last hot shower for many days. Once out of the car, Dan, a seasoned woodsman who had logged countless miles on backcountry trails, hefted his pack from the trunk and slid effortlessly into its straps. The process wasn't quite as easy for me.

First, there was the actual heft of my pack. I realize now that there is no more reliable method for gauging a hiker's confidence than studying the contents of his pack. The least experienced hikers labor under a yoke of fear and worry, cluttering their packs with devices they hope will duplicate the security of more familiar environments. Veteran hikers, whose packs are characteristically Spartan, have discovered that a well chosen poem or quotation, which weighs nothing once committed to memory, can provide more solace in the face of fear than a welter of gadgets and trinkets.

Since I was a novice, my backpack burgeoned with expendable items that catered either to my fears or to my vanity but which served no purpose other than to occupy space with their bulk and stress my knees with their weight. While Dan's pack weighed a respectable thirty-five to forty pounds, mine surpassed fifty-five. I had read and reread backpacking how-to books, which sang the praises of lightweight packs bearing only the essentials. In the months before the outset of my hike, I had loaded the pack dozens of times, and each time I tried to assess honestly the merit of each item I slipped into the pockets. Gradually, I had pared the pack down to forty pounds. As the day of departure approached, however, my doubts and fears reversed the trend,

and I found myself sneaking small items back into the pack until the scales again topped fifty-five.

On the eve of the hike, I had down-loaded the pack one last time, and I resolved to leave it just as it was. To assuage my fears, though, I had stashed the discarded items in the trunk of the car. As I wrestled the pack onto the ground in Nimblewill Gap and glimpsed them for the last time, each suddenly seemed essential, and I realized that once the trunk was closed, I would be forced to live without them.

Wouldn't the two-pound pair of binoculars in their leather case bring me closer to wildlife and help me identify the denizens of my new environment? Wouldn't the plastic egg-carrier and fifty feet of braided marine rope prove indispensable? What about the extra cook pot, aluminum plate, and oven mitt? Would one pair of long trousers be enough, and did I need a third pair of wool socks? Would the sheath knife, with its six-inch blade, protect me from wild beasts, or would my Swiss Army knife be sufficient? Would the package of firecrackers and can of dog repellent chase marauding bears from our camps? Would the metal pocket mirror, which doubled as a signal mirror, become an invaluable grooming aid or even save my life if I became lost? Wouldn't the one-pound hammock help make my leisure hours more comfortable? Would my health fail without the three-month supply of vitamins and the bulky first-aid manual?

As I deliberated, Dan shifted impatiently, and I resolved finally that the egg-carrier, binoculars, oven mitt, sheath knife, and marine rope would stay behind. The mirror, the first-aid guide, the firecrackers, the hammock, the extra pair of socks and trousers, the supplemental pot and plate, the vitamins, and dog repellent, I reasoned, would justify their weight.

At the time, my pack, as heavy as it was, seemed far less burdensome than the emotional and physical challenge that awaited me, and as I glimpsed the trailhead, I first registered the full impact of what I was about to do. I had been raised by conservative and protective parents, who tended

not to venture far from the cloister of their snug middle-class environment. From the time I was young, my life had been predicated on safe decisions. Now I was about to embark on a five-month journey through the unknown where I would face risks more real than any I had known before.

Fueling my fears was the knowledge that once I entered the backcountry I would leave behind the familiar trappings of the civilized world—electric lights to chase away the darkness, television sets and radios to help fill the idle hours, modern appliances to ease the chores of daily life—and the comfort they provided. I had fully enjoyed the morning's hot shower and the meal at the hotel restaurant. I felt no shame in ascending into the mountains inside the climate-controlled environment of the car, and I wasn't at all sure I could endure life without those and other amenities.

In some ways, the act of climbing from the car was tantamount to exiting the womb: I faced a strange and forbidding new world. At least in the first instance I had been blessed with conscientious parents who shepherded me clear of major pitfalls. Once I entered the woods, I knew that there would be nothing to shield me from hardship and danger except my own resources, which I had never really tested.

When the time to leave came, I embraced my parents and hoped they would offer some advice or guidance, yet I realized that I was about to enter a realm they knew little about.

"Be careful," said my mother, with tears welling in her eyes.

"Yes, and have fun," Dad advised, as I took the first of the five million steps that would lead me to Mount Katahdin. After a few hundred feet, I turned one last time to see the white sedan disappear in a cloud of dust as it descended the gravel road. For the first time in my life, I was truly on my own.

Within an hour and a half, we reached Springer, a rounded mountain cloaked in hardwood trees, their branches tipped with opening buds, and we discovered a sign-in book wedged into a mailbox planted on the summit. We took the

register to a grassy clearing and basked for a few minutes in the eighty-two-degree sunshine as we read the entries logged by other hikers who had begun the hike in previous days and weeks. Dan and I noted that eight hikers, all bound for Maine, had signed in over the weekend, and we were two of the nearly five hundred who would set out on the northward pilgrimage that summer. At that point, none of us knew who would be among the one hundred or so who would reach our goal.

I penned a brief message about my dream of reaching Katahdin and then signed my name. Under it I drafted the thru-hiker symbol: a capital T nestled under and joined with the crossbar of a capital A. Beside it I printed the letters GA, the designation for Georgia, with an arrow pointing to the letters ME, the abbreviation for Maine, and added the year: 1979. In so doing I became an official Appalachian Trail thru-hiker.

Before continuing north, Dan and I posed for pictures beside a forest service sign. It listed Springer Mountain and its elevation of 3,782 feet along with the distance to a few major mileposts ahead. The last entry was Mount Katahdin, mileage two thousand miles (since the sign had been erected, trail relocations had added about one hundred miles). From the perspective of the wooded hills of Georgia at the base of the Appalachian spine, the northern terminus wouldn't have seemed more remote if it had been located on the surface of the moon.

For the next several days we traversed the three thousand-foot peaks of the Chattahoochee National Forest. I count those days among the most difficult I have endured. I spent most of them absorbed in the rigors of survival in an environment that seemed foreign and hostile. In short, I was consumed by apprehension and fear.

I was afraid of my own ineptitude. I fumbled with my new stove, lost track of items stored in my pack, and listened at night as mice gnawed through my foodbag before I learned to hang it out of their reach. I had no idea how to bushwhack down a mountainside to locate a water source, what to do to protect myself on an exposed ridge in a thun-

derstorm, how to patch myself back together after I had sliced myself with my pocketknife, how long to boil lentils and rice, how much stove fuel to carry for the days and nights between supply stops, and how much and what type of food I would need to keep from starving.

I was afraid of my own weakness. My lungs burned, my thighs were seared, and my feet throbbed as my boots rubbed my tender heels to blisters on the first few steep ascents, and I wondered if I had the fortitude to keep pushing on through the pain. When late April storms drenched the woods, I dreaded leaving the dry warmth of my shelter to set out for fifteen miles through the downpour. I was afraid, too, of facing my friends back home if I failed to meet those challenges and had to pack it in.

I was afraid of being alone. Dan's woods-sense far exceeded my own, and I stuck by him like moss on a log, worried that if I let him out of my sight, I would never catch up to him and would be left to earn my proficiency through hardship and failure. As it turned out, Dan taught me much, and we remained a team to the very pinnacle of Mount Katahdin. During our five months on the trail, we propped each other up when our spirits flagged, fought like badgers when our egos pulled in different directions, and shared our food, our shelter, and our thoughts. When the trip ended, we had spent more than 150 days and nights together and had forged a friendship that will endure no matter how much time and distance separate us.

I was afraid of the vast mystery of nature. The chilling echo of hoot owls, the distant drumming of male ruffed grouse beating the air with their wings, the constant rustling in the brush around our camps after we'd extinguished our evening campfires were all unfamiliar sounds that fueled my fear.

And I was afraid when, under a tarp in Tesnatee Gap, I first experienced the raw power of nature.

The fear inspired by that first spring storm—and all the fears that accompanied me along my first miles on the trail—soon fused into a pervading sense of dread. As I watched Dan confront the trail's challenges with courage

and confidence, I began to resign myself to the belief that I wasn't quite suited for an extended stay in the woods. One evening, while I sat on a log downcast and preparing to tell him that I had decided to leave the trail, a toy collie strayed into camp. Though I didn't realize it at the time, I was about to learn the first, and perhaps the most enduring, lesson about life on the trail. Put simply, if one is receptive and open to change, the trail—and in a larger sense, nature itself—seems always to answer one's questions and meet one's needs. It sounds mystical, and I wouldn't believe it if I hadn't experienced it so many times along my journey.

Just behind the dog, a woman in her late fifties labored up the trail, the huge pack she carried dwarfing her slight frame. Her legs appeared much too frail to support her own weight, much less the weight of the pack, and her face, framed by silver shoulder-length hair, registered the pain of every step.

She paused for a few minutes, leaning on her walking stick, and told us that her name was Elizabeth and that she was hiking alone. Her destination, like ours, was Mount Katahdin. She told us that her husband had died the previous year and that she had taken up the trail to ease her grief and to chart a new direction for her life. She said she covered twelve to fifteen miles per day, beginning at dawn and continuing until dark.

She declined our invitation to join us in our camp, saying that she hoped to cover a few more miles before it became too dark to navigate the boulder-strewn trail. Soon she called to her dog and resumed her slow, deliberate pace.

Later, as Dan and I sat beside the fire plotting our mileage for the next several days and as I struggled with the decision to continue on or abandon the trail, I couldn't shake the memory of Elizabeth. It had taken me five hours to cover the twelve miles to camp that day; she had been plodding along for nearly twice that long. At the end of each day, my twenty-three-year-old thighs and feet ached. How, then, must hers have felt? I had shuddered as the storm blew through our camp, and I had flinched in the darkness when the trees creaked and wild animals crept unseen through

the underbrush. Yet I had the comfort of a companion. How did she contend with such fears during her solitary days and nights on the trail? How had she become so brave?

Frankly, in spite of her apparent courage, I had dismissed Elizabeth's goal of completing the trail as foolhardy. Yet one evening some five months later, while Dan and I camped in the woods of central Maine, a toy collie entered camp. As soon as we saw it, we looked at one another and smiled. Then we turned and looked up the trail. A slender figure soon emerged from the trees. It was Elizabeth.

Although the previous five months had wrought physical changes in all of us, the rigors of trail life had completely transformed Elizabeth. Her face was wan and haggard, and dark circles had formed under her eyes. Her legs seemed to have lost what little muscle tone they had had, and her silver hair had billowed into a tangled mass. Her gait seemed even more painful and unsteady than when I had first seen her.

Once she joined us in camp, she explained that she had made it as far as New England before realizing that at her pace, she could not hope to reach Katahdin before the end of October, when Baxter State Park officials bar access to the mountain because of unpredictable weather. She had decided to "flop," as do many of the slower-moving hikers, and travel to Katahdin, then hike south to where she had left off. I later learned that she reached her goal.

When I refer back to my journal entry on the night we first met Elizabeth in Georgia, I find a message of hope. There I termed her "Our Lady of the Trail" and wrote that "she seems weak and distant and unaware of the difficulty of the task that awaits her. We have heard about other hikers who have already gotten discouraged and gone home. But after these few days, she is still here, still moving north. How, I don't know. She will always be an inspiration to me."

Thereafter, Elizabeth became my guiding spirit, like a figurehead on an old wooden ship leading frightened sailors through uncharted seas. When my confidence began to fail, I would think of her and her frail body, facing the wilderness alone with no one to ease her fears or share her discoveries.

From then on I resolved that although I could not conquer my fears outright, I could at least confront them squarely. As I did, they seemed to lose their power over me.

As the weeks passed, my blisters began to heal, and my thighs grew hard and strong. My camp routine became well enough ingrained that I could fetch water, fire the stove, cook and eat dinner, and hang my food without a wasted motion. My pack and its contents became more familiar to me than my dresser drawers at home, and I eventually discarded the spare socks, extra cook pot and plate, vitamins, firecrackers, dog repellent, and several other pounds of extraneous gear. I gave the extra trousers to a fellow hiker who had ripped the seat out of his own, and soon my pack dipped to a manageable thirty-five pounds.

From then on I carried only the essentials. As the load in my pack decreased, my initial fear of the wilderness mellowed, and I began walking my fifteen to twenty miles each day alone, fascinated with the process of spring awakening around me. I even began to regard thunderstorms, which weeks earlier had pitched me into panic, as among nature's most formidable and entertaining displays, more potent and grand than anything I had witnessed in civilization. Many evenings, as storms approached, I scrambled to an open perch on a ridge-line from which to watch them, as their charcoal-gray sentries floated across dusky skies stretching to the horizon. I sat captivated as their silver talons raked nearby mountain peaks and their thunder shook the earth. As I watched, I began to realize that my transformation from visitor to resident of the wilderness had begun and that there was much yet to learn about my new home.

Chapter • Two

Learning to Walk, Learning to See

This lifestyle certainly allows plenty of time for introspection. Most days I spend six or seven hours alone, walking, out of sight and sound of any other human being. Some days my thoughts turn inward, and I pass the miles exploring memories of people and events that have shaped my past. Other days my mind nestles into a meditative daze, and I sense myself connected to the birds, the plants, the flowers, the trees, like a man floating on the breeze through a boundless garden.
—May 29, 1979, Iron Mountain Shelter, Tennessee

We often define ourselves by our primary occupations. A person who busies himself painting houses, for instance, is a painter. A person who devotes his energies to growing crops is a farmer. In that sense, during my months on the Appalachian Trail, I was a hiker, and the simple act of hiking—lifting each boot, planting it squarely, and biting off another three-foot section of trail—came to define who I was.

Though simple in terms of mechanics, hiking proved to

be a complex process that evolved over time into an almost meditative act that touched me daily in physical and spiritual ways. But before I could savor the more sublime virtues of hiking, I had to submit to an often demanding apprenticeship, one that I undertook at the heels of my companion, Dan.

There was a grace inherent in Dan's gait, and I detected it the first time we hiked together. On our first shakedown hike, a two-day trip to the Shenandoah National Park, we covered fifteen miles under a constant downpour. During the first day I watched in awe as Dan approached a rain-swollen stream, leapt from the ground onto a downed tree spanning the creek, and crossed without breaking stride. The tree was maybe six inches in diameter and had been stripped of its bark, making it as slick as a greased iron post. The murky stream had spilled over its banks and roared beneath. Adding to the challenge were the hard-rubber soles of our hiking boots, which provided precarious footing at best on a wet surface. Nonetheless, Dan ambled across the log as surely as if he were traversing a flat dirt path wearing baseball spikes, and once on the other side he stopped to watch me make my pass.

I eased onto the log, feeling my muscles tighten, and after taking two unsteady steps, with my arms and legs tracing hula hoops in the air, I plunged waist-deep into the stream. Dragging myself up the far bank, I unleashed a string of expletives as Dan, laughing, disappeared up the trail. That night, while I slumbered restlessly in the tent, I had a dream that fashioned my frustration into a metaphor.

In the dream I awoke in the darkness and found myself clinging to a life raft that was being dragged through rough seas at high speed. As the foam spattered my face, I spied through the darkness a long rope tethered to the raft and leading a few hundred yards forward to the stern of a huge cruise ship. The ship was kicking up a fearful wake, and I could see Dan standing aboard ship and peering at me from the deck.

I didn't require an analyst to interpret the dream. I obviously was worried that I would never match Dan's speed

or agility, and I saw myself forever in the wash, slogging along the trail in wet boots and sodden clothes, careening into every stream and tumbling over every obstacle. What I failed to realize at the time was that the problems I encountered did not lie in any inborn lack of balance or coordination. Rather they lay in my inexperience, which made me regard the pack as an accessory, rather than an extension of my physical self.

Once on the trail in April, I underwent a period of adjustment during which I gradually learned to accommodate the load on my back through subtle shifts in muscles and balance. Actually the change took place unconsciously, much the way a mail carrier might gradually lean in one direction to offset the weight of the mailbag. It would be weeks, however, before I had accomplished the necessary changes and could stride surely across such obstacles as fallen logs. Eventually the pack became a part of me, and I soon felt only partially clothed without it.

Once I had adapted to the pack, I began to experience the opposite problem and discovered that my balance wavered when I took it off at the end of a long day. I wasn't alone in that regard. I recall watching many of my fellow hikers arrive in camp and, once relieved of their loads, stumble like drunken men.

Balance was one component of hiking; strength and endurance were others. During our first days on the trail, the twelve- and thirteen-mile days seemed interminable, and as each day passed, I grimaced as I glanced up the trail and beheld yet another ascent lurking ahead. The trail seemed to be a never-ending continuum of ascents that taxed my thighs and descents that stressed my knees, with hardly a flat quarter-mile stretch to ease the twitching in my fatigued muscles.

At the same time, I suffered a pestering preoccupation with distance, how much mileage I had covered through each day and how much remained ahead until I would reach camp. I even wore a pedometer attached to my belt to measure my progress by the length of my stride. It worked, in a sense, but by wearing it I became like the motorist who

fixes on the odometer while excluding the scenery rolling past. Like such a motorist, I never seemed to draw much closer to my destination.

Beyond my daily mileage, there was the larger perspective—the distance to the northern terminus of the trail—and I found myself constantly subtracting the miles I had covered from the total to Mount Katahdin. Even at the time that struck me as ludicrous, like counting every chisel stroke invested in carving the presidents' heads into Mount Rushmore, and it imparted little sense of motion. Such a means of gauging my progress—focusing on the remaining miles to the trail's end rather than taking each day in turn—reminded me of a line from T. S. Eliot's poem, "The Love Song of J. Alfred Prufrock," about a man who ponders his misspent life and concludes, sadly, that he's measured out his life "with coffee spoons." Prufrock had his coffee spoon; I had my pedometer.

Thru-hiking was not, after all, a race, though some hikers seemed inclined to view it as one. Over the summer, each of the dozens of thru-hikers I met seemed to fall into one of two categories. First were those intent on savoring the trail experience, while still viewing Katahdin as the ultimate goal. They tended to measure the miles in terms of quality—of events and experience—rather than quantity. These were the hikers who, I believe, learned and grew the most while on the trail. Most of my colleagues fell into this camp. Shortly after discarding my pedometer, I joined their ranks.

There were others—the peak-baggers—who viewed completing the Appalachian Trail as a Spartan feat that would enhance their sense of machismo without reconfiguring their attitudes or values. To many of them, the trail became an ultraendurance footrace that, once completed, would provide another certificate to hang on their walls and another patch to sew onto their backpacks. Covering the 2,100 miles with their hearts and minds fixed on the final peak, they missed the important peaks that led to it.

Among us were men and women who embodied the extremes of each philosophy. There were, for instance, hikers

who dallied too long in trail towns or who sacrificed too many days by refusing to walk in the rain. In the end, completion of the trail eluded them. I recall a pair of hikers from New Jersey who hiked when they felt like it and lounged around in camp or hitchhiked into town when they didn't. Most of the time they didn't, and, as far as I know, they never reached Katahdin.

There were others who dallied not at all and dashed up the trail as if pursued by demons. Late one evening in a shelter near Erwin, Tennessee, for instance, a hiker arrived in the dark, at 9:30 P.M. After a hasty greeting, he munched a few handfuls of dry trail mix, unrolled his bag, slept until 5:30 A.M., munched a few more handfuls of Good Old Raisins and Peanuts (GORP), and hit the trail by 5:45. As he ate, I propped myself on one elbow, disinclined to leave the warmth of my sleeping bag, and asked him a few questions.

I discovered that he had less than three months to finish the trail before he had to return to school, and he covered twenty-five to thirty miles each day. What's more, he had not taken a day off since he had left Springer and was fully reconciled to the fact that his entire summer might pass without a single idle day to laze around town or wallow in a mountain lake. As I listened, he outlined his schedule for the next several weeks: Harpers Ferry by this date, the White Mountains by another, and Katahdin by another, leaving him less than a week to digest the trail experience, return home, gather his books, and return to school. The schedule could not have been more oppressive if it had belonged to an overworked corporate executive.

Another such hiker, George, a Massachusetts native known as Pigpen because of his stolid refusal to bathe, had secured a four-month leave of absence from his accounting firm in Boston. The leave left him just enough time to finish the trail, baring any unexpected problems. I hiked with George for several days in Georgia and North Carolina before he blasted ahead under the strain of his deadline.

I learned later that once George reached New England, the trail had worked its magic and his priorities had shifted. The threat of losing his job and his single-minded deter-

mination to reach Mount Katahdin, which had propelled him ahead at his furious pace, suddenly seemed to contradict the essence of the trail experience, that it's the journey itself, not the journey's end, that offers the greatest reward. George finally called his boss, asked for and received an extension, finished the trail, and eventually returned to the office. The last I heard, he was considering chucking both his navy-blue suits and his job to take up long-distance cycling.

By late May, the trail had begun to affect me too, and I began to view my daily mileage as a wholesome addiction. I had reached a level of physical stamina that I had not known before and have never achieved since, and each day's end found me feeling energized, cleansed, and relaxed, with endorphins (the body's natural opiates released by exercise) coursing through my system. I soon settled into a constant three-mile-an-hour pace, no faster or slower than that of my fellow hikers, Dan included. The pace seldom varied, whether I was climbing or descending, unless of course I decided to throttle back to take in a view or study the flowers lining the trail.

I had come to relish hiking and the feeling of physical prowess that accompanied it, but it wasn't until the day in late May when we ascended Roan Mountain, a hulking six-thousand-footer in northeastern Tennessee, that I first experienced the sheer bliss of foot travel. The ascent to the top led up two thousand vertical feet, which would have destroyed me a month earlier. A freak snowstorm had blown in the previous day, layering the entire wilderness in a crystal glaze, and I remember the climb as a continuum of fairytale scenes and vistas: the surrounding snow-clad peaks, pink rhododendron and delicate mountain laurel blossoms frozen in full flower, and ice-laden spruce boughs shimmering in the sun. Along the steep ascent, utter fascination supplanted any concern I might have had over distance or altitude. As I reached the open, sun-drenched alpine meadows at the top, I realized that I would gladly have scaled four thousand more feet just for the opportunity to see it.

After the ascent, I realized how effortless climbing could be if one simply let the muscles and lungs work while savoring the beauty of each mile in its turn. Hiking soon evolved into a meditative act. There was euphony in the measured, purposeful sound of motion: the rhythmic rise and fall of breath, the thump of the heart, the cadence of boots crunching soil and rock, the steady tap of the walking stick, the bending of knees and the flexing and relaxing of thigh muscles, calf muscles, hip muscles.

There were days when I focused on the scenery, and I ambled along the trail feeling connected to the birds, plants, flowers, and trees, like a man floating on the breeze through a boundless garden. There were other days when the trees melded into two green labyrinthine walls that contained and guided me, and my mind traced other trails, scattered with people and events drawn from my past.

Memories I had lost or forgotten seemed to surface of their own accord, bringing with them vivid images, sensations, emotions, and voices, and I spent hours in their company. I relived my first date—with a shy brunette—in eighth grade; I embraced my high-school lover in the back seat of my old blue Impala; I circled the bases as a Little Leaguer after hitting my first and only grand slam home run; I sparred with a high school rival at a Friday-night dance over the affections of a young woman; I relived the long summer afternoons as a child with my grandmother, exploring the woods and identifying wild flowers; and I relived the night my father entered my bedroom and, crying, told me she was dead.

And so—lost in thought—I passed the miles, and often by day's end I was jarred from my reverie by the sound of companions ahead in camp. I would then realize that I had traveled six or ten or twelve miles without recalling a single step.

I began to notice, too, how changes in the weather conjured up different moods. When gentle rains came, the woods swirled with mist, the leaves drooped, the ground became sodden brown, and the air hung rich with the smells of damp humus and musky ferns. On rain days, I

cinched my parka hood around my face and drew within, enshrouded in the same clouds that swallowed the treetops and muted vibrant colors to hues of brown and gray.

Rain days were quiet days, with the *hisss* of a million drops plinking the palms of leaves and drowning the sounds of birds and wind and even the cadence of my boots. Often during such days, I delved into the repertoire of poems I had memorized since grade school—poems by Frost, Coleridge, Yeats, Kipling—and recited them aloud as I hiked, confident that no one could hear.

Or I bellowed lyrics of favorite songs into the indifferent face of the rain and fog. One of them, "Taxi," a Harry Chapin song, always seemed to fit the mood of the rain: "It was raining hard in Frisco; I needed one more fare to make my night. . . ." The song, about a taxi driver who encounters his former lover on a dismal night, seemed doubly tragic in the rain, and I always enjoyed the pang of sadness it aroused.

On the other hand, sunny days were expansive days, especially when the trail snaked across bald-topped mountains or over exposed rock ledges where one's perspective was as broad as the horizon. Spence Field, in the southern section of the Great Smoky Mountains National Park, offered such a view, and we lazed for an hour or more in the grassy meadows there, tracing the mountains to where they yielded to the foothills and beyond to where the hills gave way to the plains and further still to where long-fingered TVA lakes probed into hidden coves.

If my experiences during my first weeks on the trail taught me a new way to walk, they also provided me with a new way to see. Much as a novice audiophile might fail to appreciate the subtle qualities—tempo, pitch, melody, harmony—hidden in a musical composition, I, too, failed to notice many of the woods' subtle offerings before I had developed a sensitivity to the sounds, rhythms, and sights of the wilderness. There were bald-faced hornets' nests hanging in branches; songbirds and

flitting among the leaves; lizards and snakes slithering across sunbaked rocks; groundhogs burrowing among fallen leaves; hawks and buzzards circling on thermals; bears nestling in treetops. And there was spring in the Appalachians. Each day, as the frail-green phalanx of opening buds crept up the mountains, the trail revealed new secrets.

Seasons

The colors of the leaves are incredible! In just the past few days they have broken into full fall color. Reds and oranges predominate in the lowlands, and dark evergreens contrast with yellow birches on the mountain tops. The foliage should be at its peak when we climb Katahdin within a week, and we're all grateful for the perfect timing. The arrival of fall marks the fourth season we've walked through, completing the cycle. When we began in April, winter clung to the upper elevations as spring began its slow ascent. Then, summer overtook spring. Fall, like winter, takes the opposite route, beginning at the mountain tops and working its way down the slopes, sparking summer green to fire as it advances.

There is no describing the hiker's-eye-view of the changing seasons and living the continuous transition day by day, hour by hour.

—September 22, 1979, Cooper Brook Falls Lean-to, Maine

Even today—more than fifteen years after I completed the trail—I suffer pangs of nostalgia with spring's onset. When those first spring days arrive and the whole world seems charged with passion and energy, I sit at a traffic light, bound for work in some climate-controlled

office, and roll down my windows to savor the spring air, fragrant with the aroma of a million blossoms. I eye the landscaper, the carpenter, the maintenance worker seated in the truck beside me. I see him clad in work clothes, with the first ruddy traces of sun coloring his cheeks, and I envy him for his days spent outside and his intimacy with the seasons.

I realize that I, with my desk job, will witness the spring in scattered glimpses, while paused at traffic lights, at lunch hours spent on park benches, on weekends spent tilling my garden. And I realize, sadly, that one day the spring will have passed and it will be summer, and I will remind myself, as I always do, to pay closer attention next year. But I seem never to succeed at it; too many things distract me. At such times, I fondly remember my journey through the Appalachians where, in my memory, it is always spring.

The trail forever changed my perspective on the seasons. On the trail I *lived* the seasons. I *experienced* them moment to moment, sensing one season's gradual surrender to the next. There was no urgency, just the perennial cycle of death and life played out in slow, fluid motion, every morning providing new evidence of change.

First there was winter, gripping the higher elevations where barren limbs rattled in icy winds and where everything was dormant brown except the green conifers, the clusters of shiny galax, and the scatterings of aromatic wintergreen. Meanwhile, at the lower elevations spring's most resilient sprigs probed through layers of decaying foliage and buds burst open on deciduous trees. A phalanx of frail green marked the place where the two seasons met.

I remember the first time I saw it. I had ascended Albert Mountain, a boulder-strewn nob topped with a fire tower in North Carolina one hundred miles north of Springer Mountain. It was April 29, and as I looked out across the surrounding ridges and valleys, first I saw the deep green swatches of fir trees. Then I noted the barren mountain crests. Far below were lowlands tinged in green. Between, an asymmetric line of the faintest green traced the boundary between death and life, between winter and spring. If

someone were to have asked me at that moment where and when spring arrived, I could have provided an answer. Pointing to that line I would have said, "There, this very minute, along that faint green line, spring is overtaking winter." And if we had paused long enough and were patient enough, we could have watched it move. Naturalists claim that the line ascends at a rate of six feet per day, three inches every hour.

As we traced the line of the ridges and dipped into saddles and sags on our way north, we crossed that boundary countless times. As the days passed, the last vestiges of winter retreated higher and higher up the mountains until finally, by June, spring had surmounted even the six-thousand-foot peaks. Meanwhile, deep in the valleys summer awakened and began its own slow ascent.

There was so much to see in the spring; every parcel of trail presented a colorful floral display. Dan carried a wildflower identification book in his pack, and evenings in camp, he reported his latest findings. Together we learned to call each flower by its rightful name.

There were delicate bluets, their four lavender lobes emerging from a golden, star-burst center and their needle-thin stems rising out of trailside grass. Wild irises, their rigid spiked leaves deep green and their blossoms curled like lips into a rich purple kiss. Jack-in-the-pulpits, with their green mottled leaves curled around and over a phallic spadix, a legion of upright preachers ministering to the emerging vegetation of the season's fertile rite. Lady's slippers, with their soft pink labia transmitting a similar, though more delicate, message. Trilliums—pink ones, yellow ones, purple ones, striped ones—with their tri-lobed heads and leaves nourished beside rotting logs.

Bloodroot, with its variegated leaves, shaped as if by elfin scissors, sheltering a shy white flower. Buttercups, with tiny, waxen gold pedals. Yellow and purple violets. Mayapples, with tight-wrapped leaves slowly swirling open like green picnic umbrellas, shading a round, white flower. Flame azalea trees, burning like fire with bright orange blossoms visible from hundreds of yards away. Fiddlehead

ferns, uncoiling like cobras along the trail. Dutchman's breeches, with white blossoms dangling from a pale bowed spike, like tiny trousers hung on a line to dry. Showy orchids, a two-tone blending of violet and pure white. And the dogwoods decked in white and pink.

As the forest floor began to teem with flowers, the birds also awakened. Scarlet tanagers lit in dogwood trees, lending their red plumage to the bouquet of white blossoms. The brown wood thrush, with its auburn head, brown wings, and brown-spotted belly, trilled its lyrical flute-like song, of which Thoreau wrote, "Whenever a man hears it he is young, and nature is in its spring." Pileated woodpeckers, with their oversized, tufted red heads and narrow necks, screeched through the woods like winged banshees. Indigo buntings glowed iridescent purple in the sunlight. Chickadees, tufted titmice, and rufous-sided towhees seemed to inhabit every tree and bush. Hoot owls' eerie four-syllable calls echoed through the trees around our camps, and we joked that they were really saying, "Whooo cooks for yooooo?"

And then there were the whip-poor-wills that irked us through many nights with their frenetic calls, beginning their arias about the time we climbed into our bags and often continuing until dawn. We frequently lobbed rocks in their direction but never scored a direct hit. More often than not, our mortars seemed only to intensify their maddening songs.

By late June, the spring buds had given way to the first of summer's flowering plants. Softball-sized rhododendron blossoms, ranging from rose-red to pink-white, exploded in such profusion that they washed entire mountainsides with their color. Mountain laurel, with its white, star-shaped blossoms punctuated with ten rosy dots, offered itself to us from bushes that draped over the trail. Pink musk thistle, white daisies, and golden black-eyed Susans bowed to summer breezes in open fields and along country roads. Turk's-cap lilies, their knifelike petals curled into spotted orange turbans, grew as tall as seven feet and peered down on us as we traversed ridge-line trails through Virginia. Firepink and

Indian paintbrush advertised their presence along the trail-side with neon-red, dime-sized blossoms.

The bounty of edible plants and berries enhanced the beauty of the forest in bloom. Ramps, wild leeks with drooping green rabbit-ear leaves, thrived along the trail in Georgia, North Carolina, and Tennessee. The Indians used the plant's essence to treat insect bites; hikers use the bulbs and leaves to add garlic tang to soups and stews.

We had been searching for ramps for days after encountering a mountain woman, clad in a gingham dress and carrying a woven basket, who scoured the trail for ramps, wild mushrooms, and edible snails brought out by spring rains. She had shown us a ramp and slit open the bulb with her thumbnail, inviting us to sniff. The aroma brought tears, and we reasoned that anything with such a potent smell would pose an easy quarry. We were mistaken, and after plucking from the loam dozens of trout lilies, which also boast drooping green leaves but no tang, we were ready to abandon hope. Then, as we passed through Beech Gap three miles north of the summit of Standing Indian Mountain, I spotted a trio of green leaves and determined to make one last try. I tugged on the leaves, which snapped off in my hands, and realized I had found our illusive ramp as the odor of garlic filled my nostrils.

That night, camped at the Carter Gap Shelter, we had a rampfest, slicing, dicing, and chopping the leaves and bulbs and dropping handfuls into our evening stews. One of our more daring colleagues, who experimented by eating an entire bulb raw, soon sat weeping over his cook pot, a beatific grin spreading across his tear-stained face.

Unfortunately, while the mountain woman had cited the culinary virtues of ramps, she had said nothing about their disastrous side effects. The morning after our ramp orgy, the shelter reeked in spite of its open face. Well into the next day, acrid ramp burps curled my tongue, and I would have parted with my sleeping bag and pack for a single roll of antacid tablets. As my stomach churned, I swore off ramps, vowing to starve before I ever sampled another bulb. Unfortunately, my hiking buddies were not so inclined, and they

continued to spice their evening meals with ramps until the leaves toughened later in the season, and the plant sprouted a cluster of white flowers.

I soon learned that although eating ramps is pure bliss for the strong of stomach, for the abstainer, living alongside anyone who has eaten them is pure hell. The pungent aroma not only stays on the breath but is exuded through the skin, taints the sweat, and lingers on clothing for days afterward.

Fortunately, most of nature's bounty was more sweet than acid. The same woman who had helped us identify ramps also showed us lemon balm, a member of the mint family with a square stalk, reddish-green variegated leaves, and a tart lemony smell. We steeped the leaves in boiling water, added honey, and drank lemon-balm tea.

Near Hot Springs, North Carolina, thirty-five miles north of the Smokies, a toothless wanderer who shared our camp disappeared at dusk and returned with an armload of poke, a green edible weed with poison roots and dark red-blue berries later in the season. He boiled the leaves, dumped the water, and boiled them again. Once done, he smothered the leaves in butter from a squeeze tube and offered them around. The poke "salit" was rich and slightly bitter but good, and it provided us with the fresh greens that our standard menus of noodles, rice, and lentils lacked.

Into southern Virginia the blossoms yielded to fruit on flowering trees. As we descended through a grassy meadow into Newport, I felt something crawling along my calf, and when I glanced down I spotted a legion of wood ticks creeping up my socks. After brushing them off, I spied hundreds of red berries nestled beneath green variegated leaves. Wild strawberries! Soon Jeff, a blond hiker from Kansas, and Mark, a long-haired eighteen-year-old thru-hiker from Maryland, joined me, and together we filled a gallon-sized Ziploc bag before continuing into town. We made our first stop the general store, and soon each of us sat under the store's awning savoring dollops of vanilla ice cream smothered in fresh berries.

Through Virginia the trail frequently followed abandoned

wagon and carriage roads past remains of eighteenth- and nineteenth-century settlements. We often walked along rusted barbed-wire fences past decaying homesteads. One day we encountered a fresh-water spring near where the hand-hewn timbers of a cabin had rotted away from an erect, field-stone chimney. As we sat in the shade envying the former inhabitants their idyllic setting and simple life, I looked up and noticed that we were surrounded by cherry trees, their branches hanging heavy with ripe red fruit. We soon emptied our quart water bottles and filled them with sweet cherries. We sat for an hour munching fruit and spewing pits into the brush. But the cherries, too, posed uncomfortable side effects, and for the next several days toilet paper was at a premium.

Further north, we plucked blackberries and raspberries from tangled thickets of briars. But even fresh native fruits and berries could not mitigate the less desirable effects of summer—oppressive heat, humidity, and biting insects. The summer months, which ushered us through the trail's central states—Maryland, Pennsylvania, New Jersey, and New York—posed the most difficult miles of the trail for most of us. Not because of the difficulty of the terrain. On the contrary, passage through the central states brought with it a pestering boredom. The elevation of the mountains dipped below three thousand feet; there were few stunning vistas; and miles of trail coursed along roads and through congested urban areas. So frequent were the road crossings and encounters with developed areas that we had little sense of being in the woods at all. In the 161 miles through New Jersey and New York, the trail is crossed by 64 roads, an average of one in every two-and-a-half miles. The most auspicious road crossing is the Interstate-80 overpass, where the trail crosses the busy four-lane freeway via a fenced-in cement walkway. A green highway sign posted on the walkway alerts motorists that they're passing under the Appalachian Trail. In my travels between Washington, D.C., (where I lived the year prior to my hike), and my parents' home in Cincinnati, I passed under the bridge a half-dozen times, and with each pass I wondered how a hiker

would feel to exit the woods onto a platform above four lanes of thundering semis and speeding automobiles.

During the summer, we constantly sought relief from the heat and boredom by wallowing in mountain streams and lakes. Evenings we wrestled with the decision to bake in our sleeping bags and thus avoid the swarms of mosquitoes and gnats, or to sleep—cooler—on top and awake to find our arms, legs, and faces swollen and itching from insect bites. I carried a bottle of jungle juice, a potent insect repellent developed for use by U.S. troops in Vietnam, which kept the bugs away but at a cost. It burned, and we joked, only half in jest, that it removed the top layer of skin. A few of us carried black-fly hoods—head-coverings sewn from mosquito netting—and evenings we resembled a corps of mournful beekeepers. Jimmy, a young man who hiked with us for several days and who had a knack for spinning macabre trail tales, used the hood as a theme for a fireside story about the Black-Fly Hood Murderer, who allegedly prowled the New Jersey woods, stalking unwary hikers and arriving in their camps after dark to hack them to bits with his hatchet.

Through the summer our clothes stayed drenched in sweat, and our fluid intake escalated as the water levels of backcountry streams and springs dwindled. Gone were the cold, free-flowing springs of the South whose water we quaffed without a thought as to its purity; we were forced to take water from stagnant bogs and slow-moving creeks. We expended precious stove fuel boiling the water, or we doctored it with iodine tablets that left behind a rancid chemical taste. This routine also tended to turn our dinners an unappetizing shade of blue when the iodine reacted with the starch in our pasta. Increasingly, we left the trail to ask for tap water at nearby houses.

On the day we crossed Bear Mountain Bridge, which spans the Hudson River in New York, the temperature soared into the hundreds. As we climbed into shallow caves along the route, we spent blissful rest breaks in their constant fifty-degree temperatures.

Through the midsummer months, we longed for the ar-

rival of fall and a return to the larger mountains we knew we would find in New England. It turned out that we encountered both on the same day. We had just exited New York and were covering the forty miles of trail through Connecticut. On August 6, as we began our hike, the heat, as usual, bore down on us, but as the day progressed, a stiff wind blew in from the west and slowly began to sap the humidity from the air. When we ascended to the summit of Bear Mountain, a 2,316-foot peak near the Massachusetts border topped with a crumbling stone edifice built in 1885, the summer, with all its attendant misery, was gone. Crisp blue skies replaced the haze; billowy tufts of cumulus clouds floated by on the wind; and the air temperature plunged into the seventies, holding the promise of fall.

In Connecticut we reentered the wilderness and began to scale larger mountains, mountains with views. The springs and streams, which had dwindled to murky, mosquito-infested puddles, again gave forth clean, cold water. When we descended Bear Mountain, crossed into Massachusetts, and descended into Sages Ravine, with its series of falls and deep pools, the air was too cool for swimming.

Once we arrived in New England, the trail still held a vestige of the wild fruit we had enjoyed in the South. On the day I crossed the open rock ledges leading to Bear Mountain, I suddenly noticed I had lost my companion, Paul, a long-legged strider, who normally blazed by me. Dillon, a New Englander, had recognized the scrub berry bushes, while I, absorbed in the views, had passed them by. He had slowed his pace, raking the bushes for fruit. Hours later, when he finally arrived in camp, his purple grin and red-stained fingers brought laughter from the rest of us who had wondered what was taking him so long. For days afterward, the berries became a morning staple, finding their way into our pancakes, granola, and hot oatmeal.

By the time we crossed into New Hampshire on August 22, we had had our cold-weather woolens sent back to us. Crisp mornings found us layered in sweaters and windbreakers, and our evening fires provided warmth and smoke screens to drive away biting insects.

Then, in Maine, a state rich with birches, sugar maples, and oaks, the fall colors arrived on the heels of Hurricane David, which blasted the northern woods with wind and cold rain in early September. By the time we had reached Monson, the last major town for the trail's final 116 miles, the frost had tinged the maples blaze-red, the birches mottled entire hillsides in gold, and the oaks dappled the mountains in bursts of orange and yellow.

Our ascent of Mount Katahdin brought with it a taste of winter. Ice layered Thoreau Spring, situated a mile below the summit, and the wind pierced our layers of nylon and wool. But if it was a day of ice, it was also a day of fire. Sprawling away from the base of the mountain, fall flames fringed the cool blue ponds of the Lake Country.

Over the course of five months, we had traced the cycle of the seasons, from the wintry peaks of the southern Appalachians in April, through the months of spring and summer, to the fall and the brink of another winter in central Maine. Though I have lost the intimacy with the seasons since my hike, I retain the sense of perfect order, of graceful succession and surrender, and of the bold brilliance of fall leaves as they yield to death.

CHAPTER • FOUR

Our Gang

I proceed for all who are or have been young men,
To tell the secret of my nights and days,
To celebrate the need of comrades.
> Walt Whitman, "In Paths Untrodden"

By the time Dan and I entered Virginia June 1, we had become a trio. Nick Gelesko, known on the trail as the Michigan granddad, a fifty-seven-year-old retired engineer from Dawagiac, Michigan, had joined us. By the time we reached New Jersey, we were a foursome, having adopted Paul Dillon, a twenty-year-old, long-legged former competitive skier from Peterboro, New Hampshire. From then on, we were virtually inseparable.

Of all the trail's gifts, none was more precious to me than that of friendship. We were a corps of men and women united by our common love of nature, by our shared needs and experiences, and our affection for one another was as real and enduring as the love of brothers and sisters. We lived side by side, and we shared of ourselves—our thoughts, our fears, our hopes, our experiences past and present—as freely as we shared our food and shelter.

I remember a series of nights in the company of trail friends, some spent around campfires, others in open, star-lit fields, some under rain-pummeled tin roofs, many beside churning brooks, and I remember talking, sometimes for hours, about love, death, God, spirit, nature. Or about more earthy concerns: blisters, bent tent poles, wet boots. Perhaps more significant than the ease with which we discussed our feelings were the remarkably unself-conscious stretches of silence when we were content just to have close friends nearby.

Evenings, each of us followed his own interests. At dusk Dan often retired with his penny whistle to a stream, where his notes mingled with the melodic tumble of water. Paul, our trailside Lord Byron, frequently scribbled odes about love or nature in his journal, which he shared with us around evening fires. Each night after dinner, Nick, squatting on his haunches, meticulously measured, mixed, and stirred his beloved chocolate pudding, as his baritone voice hummed some forgotten ballad from the 1950s. The rest of us always knew that when he finished, we would find a dollop of dessert left in his cook pot for each of us. While my colleagues pursued their evening diversions, I pursued my own, reclining against a tree and recording the whole wonderful scene in my journal.

These are the things I remember about my trail family.

Dan

Dan, a former architectural planner for a major oil corporation, had left a promising fast-track career to walk in the woods. He may have left the job, but he retained his gift for organizing, leading, orchestrating, planning. Dan was our field marshal who, perhaps more than the rest of us, kept his eye on our daily progress, constantly measuring the months against the miles and making sure we reached Katahdin before winter snows closed the mountain down in October. In spite of his drive to cover the miles, he was just as attuned to natural wonders as the rest

of us—perhaps even more so—and he frequently called our attention to plants, animals, or birds that had escaped our notice.

Unlike Dan, I had become oblivious to accumulated mileage and more inclined to amble and roost when I found a snug nest along the way. Had it not been for Dan and his intense desire to drive north, I suspect I might have whiled away the summer lazing in mountain lakes or stooped over fresh-scented flowers and might have missed my date with Katahdin altogether. On most occasions, we yielded to Dan's scheduling and advanced at his pace, but not always happily.

In mid-Pennsylvania, after Nick had slowed his pace to hike with his wife, Gwen, who had joined us for a couple of weeks, and before Paul had joined our group, Dan and I were again a twosome. We decided to do an easy day out of Duncannon to a campsite sixteen miles away. Once we were out of town and over the broad bridge spanning the Susquehanna River, Dan blasted ahead, while I throttled back, taking extended rest stops and rummaging through my food bag for the candy and other sweet treats that always attended my departure from town. At 5:30 P.M., I arrived at our scheduled stop, ready to relax. Instead of finding Dan scribing in his journal, I discovered a hand-written note. He had arrived in camp early, become restless, and decided to push on an additional eleven miles, making for a twenty-seven-mile day.

Hiking, like most other endurance activities, is a mental as well as physical pursuit. That is particularly true when you face high-mileage days. Even hikers in prime condition suffer aches, pains, and fatigue after long miles. Most often, when we confronted twenty-plus-mile days, they were planned, allowing us time to psych ourselves up for the long stretches. In the days prior to a long-mile hump, we ate more, rested more. Consider that a hiker who maintains a three-mile-an-hour pace, which is about as fast as one can travel mountainous terrain on foot with a loaded pack, will walk continuously for a full nine hours to cover twenty-seven miles. That includes no time for eating, drinking,

resting, or smelling the flowers. Discovering at 5:30 P.M. that I faced an additional eleven miles did not make me a happy camper.

I would have stayed the night where I was, but there were a few complicating factors: Dan carried the guidebook, half of the tent, and half the stove. Without a guidebook, I had no means for gauging my progress over the remaining eleven miles other than by multiplying my average speed (three miles per hour) by the elapsed time and stopping when my watch indicated that I had covered the distance. I also was left without means for protecting myself from the elements, and I was not about to hack down perfectly healthy trees to make a den. At the time, I saw one option: to bust ass and catch Dan.

If I hustled, allowing no food or water breaks, I surmised I would reach the shelter by about 9:10 P.M., a half-hour past dusk. That is, provided I could find the blue-blazed side trail to the shelter in the darkness. Never mind the hundreds of fist-sized rocks—Pennsylvania is famous for them—that tottered with each step and gouged the soles, and never mind the thriving population of rattlesnakes inhabiting the area—Pennsylvania's second most notable distinction. I wolfed down two high-energy breakfast bars, gulped down a liter of water, and set out.

At about 7:00 P.M., still seven-and-a-half-miles from my destination, I passed a group of day-hikers on the trail. Had they seen Dan, the low-life son of a bitch who had abandoned me a few miles back? Yes, a high-school-aged girl answered.

"He figured you might be a little upset," she said.

"And be careful up ahead," she called after me. "There was a big rattlesnake coiled in the middle of the trail!"

I never saw the rattlesnake, but then I didn't look for it. Anger, it seemed, has a wonderful way of dampening one's fear.

By 9:15 and now moving through dusk, I slowed, looking for the blue-blazed trail to the shelter. Blue blazes are difficult enough to spot in the daylight, let alone after dark. Besides, during July, such side trails are frequently overgrown

and barely discernible. By 9:20, now following the beam of my mini-flashlight and with my thighs twitching and the soles of my feet feeling as if I had trodden across hot glass shards, I still hadn't spotted the blaze. As I was about to roll out my bag in the weeds and eat a cold dinner, I finally spied it. Soon I was wheeling along toward the shelter. When I reached it, Dan greeted me tentatively. Until my temper calmed, I said nothing at all.

What followed had all the makings of a backwoods lovers' spat. I explained that I could appreciate his yen to cover more miles but didn't appreciate being left with no stove, shelter, or guidebook. Dan sympathized but went on to explain that this was his trip and that he was going to do it his way. That hurt. It reawakened the feelings I had confronted in Georgia, the fear that I couldn't keep pace with him, that I was bogging him down.

I suggested that perhaps it would be best if we split up, dividing the gear, he taking the stove and I taking the shelter and both of us making arrangements to acquire the additional equipment we needed. I'm thankful that it didn't come to that. We both seemed to realize that after investing so much time and energy in the relationship, it would have been a shame to dissolve it. I know I would have missed his company, and I suspect he would have missed mine. Besides, what would our backcountry neighbors have said when they learned that Dan and Dave, one of the more stable trail marriages, had separated? The next morning we continued north, our union intact after surviving our first quarrel.

The next time Dan's drive for miles provoked a rift, we were four—Nick and Paul had joined us—and this time our voting bloc prevailed. It happened in Vermont on August 12, the day we hiked through the spruce-clad northern Berkshires to the 3,491-foot summit of Mount Greylock, the highest peak in Massachusetts. That day we confronted some of the worst weather the Appalachians can muster: the temperature hovered just above freezing. Wind and cold rain stung our faces and hands, and we frequently stepped ankle-deep into mucky spruce bogs as we picked our way to

the top. By early afternoon we arrived at Bascom Lodge, an ample rough-hewn summit house built in 1937. Once over the threshold, I was convinced we had perished on the trail and had passed into hiker heaven. A fire blazed in each of two three-foot-square fireplaces, one in each of the two thirty-by-twenty-five-foot great rooms. There were hot coffee, hamburgers, junk food. Old furniture—great comfortable couches and easy chairs—sat in the warmth of the fires.

After peeling off our wet clothes, we sat by the fire sipping hot coffee. When Dan suggested that we take it easy for an hour or so then push back out into the rain for a few more miles, we were incredulous. We held fast and finally reached a compromise: We would stay the night at the lodge and make up the lost mileage over the next few days. The four of us helped wax the scarred wooden floors in exchange for the night's lodging. I spent most of the evening perched at a wooden table, facing a bank of large picture windows. Through the glass I glimpsed the wind-buffeted spruce trees and the swirling fog and rain—the very misery we had escaped—and I slept that night thoroughly content with our decision to stay. I suspect Dan did too.

Maybe Dan was driven, but he was also endowed with other attributes that allow people to thrive in the wilderness. Though slight in stature, at five-feet-ten-inches tall and 145 pounds, and with straight, sandy-blond hair and brown eyes, Dan was rock steady, courageous, and tough. Over the five months we spent together, I never saw his courage falter. He was crazy, too. Crazy to expand his margins and experience new things. More than once, in the midst of a cold spring rain, I watched him strip off his clothes and step under a frigid waterfall or plunge into an icy pool just to savor the rush it would bring.

He demonstrated those hard-edged qualities again and again over our months together, but never more convincingly than on the trail that led us out of Hanover, New Hampshire, in late August.

We had just left the road and had begun our ascent back into the mountains. I led and soon pulled away from my three companions. About a half-mile up the trail, I encountered a hand-written note attached to some evergreen boughs that had been arranged across the trail. The note warned of a bees' nest ahead and advised us to skirt around it. I looked ahead and saw a hole two feet in diameter seething with yellow jackets, and I called back to the others a couple hundred yards behind to be careful. Nick, ahead of Dan and Paul, nodded, though in retrospect it is clear he hadn't understood my warning. I veered into the brush, passed around the nest, and continued up the trail.

In seconds I heard Nick shout, and I turned just in time to see him break into a run. He had overlooked the sign and had continued right over the nest. Though he had escaped being stung, he had pitched the bees into a protective frenzy. Then I watched and listened—helplessly—as Dan began flailing and emitting a horrible series of screams, each marking a sting. I wanted to run and help him, but I realized that there was nothing any of us could do; we would just have become targets ourselves. The attack—and the screaming—lasted for nearly a minute before Dan reached a safe distance from the nest and the swarm retreated. Once it was over, I reeled from spent adrenaline. All of us did.

Anyone who has ever been the victim of a yellow jacket knows the instant, throbbing acid burn of a single sting. In all, Dan had suffered twenty-six stings. The bees had pierced his bare face, arms, and legs and had swarmed inside his shorts and shirt. He was a mass of red, acid-oozing welts, and I realized that if he were allergic to the venom, as many people are, he would die quickly. His breathing tube would swell shut, and he would asphyxiate.

Within minutes Dan had completely regained his calm. He sat quietly on a rock, focusing, pulling himself back together, as Nick, Paul, and I buzzed frantically around him offering to help, though I'm not sure how we could have eased his discomfort. He declined our offers and continued

to sit. Within five minutes of the attack, he rose and, unbelievably, started walking back toward the hive.

"I dropped my walking stick," he said.

Dan had found the stick, a twisted, gnarly branch, on Springer Mountain, and he had grown attached to it. I would learn later that he aimed to deposit it, in a private ceremony, on Mount Katahdin, making it a 2,100-mile stick. He crept cautiously to within three feet of the hive, picked up his staff, returned to where we stood, climbed into his pack, and continued up the trail. Meanwhile, the rest of us—stunned—fumbled into our pack straps and followed.

Some days later, I too became a yellow-jacket casualty. Though stung only four times, I cursed and shrieked, wheeled and spun, flailing at unseen adversaries. Afterward, as I stood panting and shaking, I wanted to sit in self-pity and lick my wounds, but, remembering Dan's example, I glanced ahead to the next white blaze and kept on walking.

Nick

We met Nick Gelesko over a vegetarian dinner at the Inn in Hot Springs, North Carolina. The Inn, a restored nineteenth-century resort hotel, had once served an upscale clientele that sought the healing powers of the hot mineral springs located a few blocks away. Though the springs had passed from vogue years earlier, by 1979 the Inn—which featured bountiful vegetarian meals, new age music, and hundreds of books—reigned as a mecca for hungry hikers.

Seated at the round wooden table, Nick wore a khaki shirt bearing an Appalachian Trail patch and a matching pair of khaki pants. He was Sean Connery handsome, with a tanned face, sharp features, bright brown eyes, and, like Connery, a bald pate. Dressed as he was in his khaki uniform and surrounded by an air of confidence and authority, I initially mistook him for a park ranger. Through the meal

Nick assumed the role of table host, drawing out some of the more reluctant hikers and sharing bits of his own stories. I soon detected in him irrepressible charm and charisma.

Over the ensuing summer, those attributes made Nick an endearing sidekick. They also became a secret weapon, one we employed countless times in asking for—and receiving—favored treatment from townsfolk along the way.

Because of his age, at first Nick posed a fatherly threat to some of us younger men who were out on the trail to exert our independence, to find our own way and shed the tethers of adult authority. He had fought in the South Pacific during World War II—our fathers' war—he had raised his children to adulthood, and his attitudes were decidedly conservative. At many of our fireside chats early on, he represented the establishment point of view while we argued in behalf of the new order.

But the trail, along with the social healing brought on by the 1970s, had softened many of Nick's attitudes about the younger generation, just as it had altered our attitudes regarding his. One night near the end of the trail Nick discussed his relationship with his son who had fled to Canada during the Vietnam War rather than face the draft. As a veteran, Nick had initially responded by severing ties with his son and his family, but eventually his love for his son and his increasing sympathy for the young men who had become entangled in the complexities of the conflict changed his thinking, and he and his wife, Gwen, had made a trip to Canada.

As our relationship developed and we became more closely bound by our shared experiences, Nick and the rest of us found common ground on many issues. Soon our age differences were as insignificant as the regions of the country we hailed from.

Nick ultimately became one of my closest friends and companions, a man whom I still admire as much as anyone I've ever known. Whatever courage it took for me—a twenty-three-year-old man—to face the wild, his was greater. Though the body of a fifty-seven-year-old man can't

cover the miles at the same clip as men less than half his age, he kept pace with us, never complaining about his ailing knees and feet while many of the rest of us vented our physical woes almost nightly.

As for our secret weapon: Nick was charming, so charming, in fact, that I'm convinced that, given time, he might have persuaded Donald Trump to turn over his casinos, all of his rental properties, all his worldly possessions, all of his lands, and that once the deal was struck, somehow Nick would have left him feeling that he—not Nick—had profited in the transaction. What's more, Nick was confident enough to ask for anything from anybody, and his older, more mature countenance stood him in good stead with local folks, many of whom were distrustful of us younger guys. The combined effect of his charm, chutzpah, and maturity became our ticket to a bounty of special privileges.

The first time I saw Nick work his magic, I ascribed it to luck. Dan and I had arrived at the road crossing where a little-traveled Virginia highway cut the trail, and we had arranged to meet Nick, who was some distance behind, in town. While Dan and I baked in the sun, our thumbs eagerly thrust in the air, car after car inhabited by sour-faced people zoomed by. Some of the drivers were so leery of us that they swerved into the oncoming traffic lane to be sure we didn't leap through the open window and commandeer their vehicles. After we had spent nearly an hour of smiling, waving, and looking as harmless as possible, a huge Buick slowed, swung onto the berm, and stopped. I immediately recognized Nick's tan porkpie hat and grinning face through the windshield of the passenger seat.

"You fellas need a lift?" he asked.

After we loaded our packs into the trunk, Nick introduced us to the driver, a middle-aged man whom he addressed with the familiarity of an old friend. Thoroughly charmed, the man had agreed to drive us into town, to wait while we bought our groceries and washed our clothes at the local laundromat, and then to shuttle us back to the trailhead to resume our hike.

The next time it happened, I began to suspect that there

was more to Nick's good fortune than simple dumb luck. On a similarly isolated stretch of highway a few days farther north, we repeated the same scenario, with Dan and me— thumbs in the air—ruefully watching an armada of cars and trucks roll past. Then a battered flatbed swung off the road and stopped, and a familiar, grinning face topped with a porkpie hat poked from the passenger's window.

"Come on over," Nick called through the window. "I'd like for you guys to meet my friend, Martin, who's been kind enough to give us a lift into town."

From then on, in a slightly skewed version of the old hitchhiker's ruse in which the alluring blonde flags down a lift while her male friend hides in the bushes, Nick acted as our front man. He stood prominently on the highway while Dan and I lingered just out of sight until Nick called us over to meet our chauffeur. Once we got to town, we loaded our packs at the local store, and Dan and I sat on the store stoop while our envoy roved through the store lot, scanning the parked cars for those that offered ample room for three hikers and their packs. Then he waited. When the owners arrived, he launched into his routine, which went something like this:

"Good afternoon (morning, evening), ma'am (sir, young man, young lady), my name is Nick, and I'm out hiking the Appalachian Trail. I just want you to know that my buddies and I sure are enjoying the scenery around (town name here). In fact, it's some of the most beautiful country we've seen so far, and the people sure are friendly. Hey, by the way, we're trying to find a way back up (highway name and number here) to the trail junction so we can continue our hike. Would you know of anyone around here who might be willing, say, to earn a few extra bucks by giving us a lift?"

More often than not, the first contact would assent, but if not the first, always the second. Soon Nick would motion us over to meet his new friend. Often, en route, the drivers handed us a couple of cold beers, a bag of chicken legs, or a ham sandwich, and in spite of Nick's offer to pay for the lift, few of them accepted our money. They were just happy to help us out.

After weeks of practice Nick became thoroughly proficient at procuring food, drink, and transportation from strangers, yet we exhausted our vocabularies in searching for a word to describe what he did. It really wasn't "scamming." Sure, Nick sometimes exaggerated the direness of our circumstances by insisting that we were "bone weary" or by claiming that our hunger or misery was so abject that we might perish if we didn't get to town soon. But he never knowingly deceived anyone, and he never attempted to force anyone to help us. In some ways I think the donors benefited from their contact with us, particularly the drivers, who often seemed hungry for company and welcomed our companionship. And everyone enjoyed our trail stories. But still, what to call Nick's magical process? Finally, after weeks of searching we fixed on a term for Nick's natural aptitude: *Geleskoing*, derived from his last name.

Gelesko-ing: the use of tact and persuasion by Appalachian Trail hikers to influence local townsfolk to provide goods and services free of charge.

We applied the word in the following ways:

"Where did you get that sandwich?"

"I *Geleskoed* it from some picnickers a few miles back on the trail."

"How did you get into town?"

"I *Geleskoed* a ride from a nice couple returning from church."

"Where did you stay last night?"

"I *Geleskoed* a family into letting me stay in their guest bedroom."

Among Nick's most notable coups, I count the following: We were staying the night in a ski lodge on Sugarloaf Mountain in central Maine. The lodge, a circular structure with a massive central fireplace and walls of windows looking out on the surrounding peaks, was abandoned but had been left open as a refuge to hikers. We laid our bags out on the wooden benches surrounding the fireplace and stoked the flames from the ample pile of firewood provided by the caretaker.

Midafternoon, I heard a clang, then the clattering of

gears, and ran to one of the windows. I turned to the lift cables, which had sat idle since we had arrived in the early afternoon, just in time to see Nick's hat through the rear window of a gondola descending toward the mountain's base. Where was he going? He had left without giving us a clue. It turned out that the caretaker, who just happened to be in the lodge, had been Geleskoed into operating the lift in spite of dangerous winds. Before we could probe him for information regarding Nick's mission, he had left the lodge and begun hiking down the mountain.

Several hours passed, and the winds increased. At one point, the wind howled so fiercely that when I stepped outside to dump a pot of dishwater, the wind ripped the pot from my hand and threw the water back in my face with such force that it stung.

More time passed. Still no sign of Nick. Just before dusk, I heard the gears grind into motion, and far down the mountain I could see a red gondola ascending the cable. The car bucked and swayed like a carnival ride run amok, and when it neared each of the towers that supported the lines, it stopped. Inside, I could see Nick, swinging back and forth, captive in the round red pendulum. He would swing left, toward the tower, then as he swung right, away from the obstacle, the motor would again engage, and the car would advance, each time barely missing the tower on its backswing. The process was repeated at each of the half-dozen towers, and the lift operator at the base of the mountain would gauge the rhythm of the swinging car as he rocked it past the tower. At last the car entered the gondola shed, the engine stopped, and Nick emerged carrying two grocery bags.

One of the bags contained three half-gallons of ice cream. The other contained several bags of cookies and a bottle of wine. It turned out that Nick had made his tempest-tossed voyage in search of sweets, and as we all attacked the bounty of confections, he explained his adventure.

Struck by an irrepressible craving for sugar, Nick had consulted his map. Noting that the road at the base of the mountain led into Stratton, he had approached the care-

taker (who also served as the lift operator) for a ride to the bottom. When the caretaker refused, explaining that the wind conditions made it unsafe to operate the lift, Nick persisted. Finally, the caretaker agreed to send Nick down the mountain. Once at the base, Nick had persuaded— Geleskoed, rather—some kindly local folks into giving him a lift to the grocery store. After cleaning out the ice-cream freezer at the store, he had persuaded another kindly local to give him a lift back to the gondola. Then, after waiting futilely for a full hour for the winds to calm, he had cajoled the lift operator, who by now had returned to the base, into giving him a ride back to the top. As a result of his expedition, Nick may well rank as the only Appalachian Trail hiker ever to risk death for a few half-gallons of Breyer's vanilla ice cream.

Then there was the night in Rangeley, Maine.

We arrived in Rangeley on September 6, driven from the woods by the tail end of Hurricane David, which whipped the surface of Lake Rangeley into a froth of rolling white caps. Rangeley is a quiet New England resort town set on the shores of the lake and cluttered with quaint shops and restaurants competing for the tourist trade.

In several towns along the trail, local churches had opened their doors to hikers, providing them a place to sleep for the night. According to the scuttlebutt on the trail, a Protestant church in Rangeley was one such place. We had made our requisite stop at the local grocery store and, after scampering along rain-drenched streets, found our way to the church just after dark.

Once inside, we made ourselves at home in the recreation room, which featured a full kitchen and a number of banquet tables. We soon commenced the ritualistic food binge that accompanied our arrivals in town by preparing heaping root beer floats. Nick had wandered into the sanctuary and had found a Bible, and as we sat slurping our floats, he began flipping through it, looking for familiar passages. Soon we were engaged in a discussion of Christian ethics and the role of Christ as teacher and provider, which inspired us to give thanks for having such a snug refuge from the storm.

Though we frequently discussed religious philosophy, we didn't often discuss the specific tenets of Christianity. But this night the topic was Christ: His resurrection, the redemption He offered the world's sinners. Christian love, we determined, whether the doctrine behind it was or was not the only way to salvation, was a beautiful force at work in the world. After all, we agreed, though the congregation of this church did not know us, they had opened their doors to us.

At 8:00 P.M., our discussion of Christian love was brought to an abrupt halt when the church caretaker arrived and, explaining that hikers were no longer welcome to stay in the church, threw us out into the bleak, cold night.

We made our way from the sanctuary into the gutter, arriving some minutes later at Doc Grant's, a local watering hole perhaps best known for its alleged location precisely halfway between the equator and the North Pole. The placemats at the bar depict a map bisected by a line. In the upper half is a sketch of an Eskimo clad in mukluks and a fur coat. In the lower half is a rendering of a hula girl in grass skirt.

We sidled up to the bar, ordered a round of cold beers, and watched reruns of the "Andy Griffith Show." Meanwhile, we had no notion of where we might be sleeping that night. The hotels in town were decidedly upscale and priced beyond our budgets, and the hurricane had made conditions outdoors insufferable. Our tents would have been ripped to tatters by the wind and rain. We had asked—begged really—a place to stay from every patron at the bar but received no firm offers. On our march from the church to the bar, we had noticed a theater marquee sheltered by a large overhang and decided that, if worse came to worst, we could always sleep there. For the first time on our trek, we were plum out of tricks. Or so we thought. That's when Nick went to work.

While the rest of us sat at the bar, Nick got a few dollars' worth of quarters and a phone book and walked over to the pay phone. First he called the local hotels. It was prime tourist season, and there were no available rooms. Then he

called all the local churches. Still no luck. After learning the names of the town's elected officials from the barkeep, he called the mayor. Even he balked. Then Nick called the chief of police and finally struck pay dirt. Smiling, he rejoined us at the bar.

"Our ride will be here in five minutes," he said, returning to his beer. And so it was. In a few minutes the chief of police, clad in a rain slicker, entered the bar, asked for Nick, introduced himself, and ushered us out of the bar into a waiting cruiser. We soon arrived at the police station, our home for the night. It was the first and only night I've spent in jail, and I couldn't have been happier.

Only once did I see Gelesko's charm fail. We had arrived at Farmers Mills Shelter, set two hundred feet off a back road near Stormville, New York. The shelter, our scheduled destination for the night, turned out to be a fetid, cinder-block hovel surrounded by heaps of trash and a mosquito-infested swamp. Gelesko took one look at it and decreed that he wasn't about to sleep there. Soon he moved on up the country road to make other arrangements. With the rest of us in tow, he approached a nearby house that boasted a large garage and knocked at the door. When a middle-aged woman cracked open the door, he began his pitch.

"Good afternoon, ma'am. My name is Nick Gelesko, and a few buddies and I are hiking the Appalachian Trail."

"Yes?" she asked suspiciously.

"Well, it's been so darned hot the past few days, and that shelter up the road is really a mess, you know, with trash and mosquitoes, and I was wondering if you know of anyone around here who might have, well, say, a *garage* where we might roll out our bags and sleep the night."

At that point, Nick, having emphasized the word *garage*, turned and casually glanced at its counterpart around the corner of the house.

"Sure don't," the woman answered without hesitating.

Undaunted, Nick continued. "You know, a *garage* or some place we could lay out our bags? We sure would be grateful."

"No, I'm sorry."

"You know, if someone were to have a *garage*, we'd be more than happy to do a little cleaning up to help pay for the kindness . . ."

The three of us stood within ear shot, and, frankly, we couldn't believe what we were hearing. Was it actually possible for someone—anyone—to resist being Geleskoed by Gelesko himself? Gradually the woman began to soften.

"Well, I can't let you stay in my garage because my husband's out of town, and he wouldn't approve. But there's a young guy up the road who lives in a barn, and he might take you in."

On her advice, we pushed up the road until we arrived at a red barn that had been converted to a suitable, though drafty, residence. Nick knocked at the door, and a young man answered. In less than a minute, Nick waved us all toward the door. His magic was back. He introduced us to our host for the night, and soon we were upstairs, sipping cold beers and flipping through the man's record supply, blissed out on rock 'n' roll music.

Paul

When we encountered twenty-year-old New Hampshire native Paul Dillon in Pennsylvania, he was making his third attempt on the Appalachian Trail. Paul had begun the trail at Springer Mountain in 1976, reaching as far north as the Cumberland Gap in Pennsylvania. He set out on the trail again in 1978 and reached as far as the Blue Ridge Parkway in Virginia. He returned to the trail in 1979, starting his hike where he had left off in Pennsylvania, and Dan and I met him just north of Port Clinton. As it turned out, the encounter would benefit all of us.

Dan and I had suffered our first major battle of wills a few days earlier over the planned sixteen-mile day that evolved into a twenty-seven-mile marathon, and though we were speaking to one another, our relationship lacked any semblance of brotherly affection. Paul's inclusion in the group

immediately eased the tension between us. At the same time we offered Paul the two things he seemed to need most. First was companionship. He had mistimed his first and second ventures on the trail and had missed the mass of northbound thru-hikers. After spending days and nights alone, he had decided to leave the trail. The second thing we offered Paul was Dan's knack for organization and goal setting, which would impose a schedule on Paul and the rest of us and would guarantee to lead us to the summit of Katahdin by summer's end.

Despite his thwarted attempts on the trail, Paul possessed an aptitude for wilderness travel. While Dan and Nick tended at times to muscle their way along, confronting obstacles with will and determination, Paul seemed inclined to abide by whatever nature threw his way and to try to make the best of it. As far as Paul was concerned, whatever we encountered along the trail was okay, as long as he was able to glean some significance from it. For Paul, miles did not measure linear distance so much as they traced units of experience. Paul sought the sadness, the happiness, the beauty, the wisdom lurking in the wilderness, and he translated those things into the verses and songs he composed along the way. While the rest of us orally recounted the highlights of our days as we sat around campfires, Paul was often inclined to apply his thoughts to paper and, once finished, to share them in the group.

Paul had carried his penchant for poetry so far as to have had a friend embroider a verse onto the front flap of his green nylon framepack. The verse, taken from *On the Loose*, Jerry and Renny Russell's book on adventure and the environment, reads:

> So why do we do it?
> What good is it?
> Does it teach you anything?
> Like determination?
> Invention?
> Improvisation?
> Foresight?
> Hindsight?

Love?
Art?
Music?
Religion?
Strength or patience or accuracy or quickness or tolerance
or which wood will burn and how long is a day and how far is
a mile and how delicious is water and smoky green pea
soup?
And how to rely on yourself?

The verse embraced the essence of the trail quest, but
more than that, it captured the grace and rhythm that
seemed to govern everything Paul did, whether writing a
poem or traversing a ridge.

I will forever picture Paul ambling along the trail, smiling
and shirtless, his lanky, six-foot-one-inch frame clad only in
blue corduroy Ocean Pacific shorts, knee-high gaiters,
socks, and boots, and with his shoulder-length brown hair
bound by a red bandana tied pirate-style.

A former competitive downhill skier and college tennis
player, Paul had been an accomplished athlete long before
taking up the trail. Though he was lean, his strength and
endurance powered him past most other thru-hikers on
long ascents, and his physical poise and skier's balance allowed him to dance effortlessly down steep, rock-strewn descents where most hikers crept cautiously along.

I didn't fully appreciate just how graceful Paul was on his
feet until we reached the White Mountains in New
Hampshire, where the open, treeless ridges allowed us to
glimpse other hikers from miles away. On the afternoon
that Dan and I arrived at Lakes of the Clouds Hut, nestled
below the summit of Mount Washington, we dumped our
packs and climbed to the top of Mount Monroe, a secondary
peak a few hundred yards from the hut.

From our perch a couple of hundred feet above the trail,
we watched hikers wend their way along the rocky path
heading north. As practitioners of the art of walking, we
had developed a habit of evaluating the style of other foot
travelers. Among those we scrutinized that day, some
cullumphed along like human jackhammers, assaulting the

trail with their heavy footfalls. Others surged ahead like jack rabbits, stopping to rest at two hundred-yard intervals before surging ahead again. A few labored painfully along like arthritic octogenarians, pausing after each step to peer ahead, hoping to glimpse the hut and the termination of their misery. After watching them pass, Dan and I fixed on a lone hiker who, unlike the others, eased effortlessly across the open ridge.

"Look at that guy move," Dan said, pointing.

"God, he's graceful," I said. And he was. Every step, every aspect of his stride, from the bend of his knees to the pivot of his torso to the plant of his walking stick, was as fluid as a brook coursing its way between and over the boulders of a streambed.

It wasn't until he neared the base of the mountain that we recognized the familiar green backpack and red bandana as belonging to our own poet laureate, Paul.

Linear Community

Whatever concerns I had about this trail lacking human companionship were resolved this evening. There are nineteen hikers and two dogs wedged into the shelter. Further cramping our space are hikers' packs and foodbags, which hang like ripe fruit from the rafters—to keep them from the mice, rats, and skunks who also call this place home. There are hikers here from Indiana, Illinois, Ohio, Tennessee, North Carolina, Massachusetts, Virginia, and Georgia, and though we all have different backgrounds and come from different parts of the country, we are unified by our shared love for the wilderness. Here are nineteen strangers existing so peaceably, sharing food, thoughts, equipment, and trail tips under conditions that would pitch most city dwellers into panic. What is it about our society that inhibits such wonderful—and spontaneous—acceptance and sense of community?
—May 6, 1979, Russell Field Shelter, Great Smoky Mountains National Park

Many people envision the Appalachian Trail as a remote, isolated wilderness path where hikers pass days—even weeks—in utter solitude and with no access to roads or towns for supplies and companionship.

75

Even some novice trail hikers maintain such a skewed vision of the trail. A pair of would-be thru-hikers I met near Springer Mountain in 1987, for instance, believed that once a person had set out on the trail, there was no means of egress and that the hiker was committed to traveling at least as far as Harpers Ferry, nearly one thousand miles north, before he could bail out or acquire fresh supplies. As a result, the two wretched souls carried nearly one hundred pounds of gear each, including extra boots and a two-month supply of food.

I'll acknowledge that the image of a hiker confronting the eastern wilds alone is romantic. Perhaps the trail's pioneers, including Earl Shafer, who logged the first end-to-end hike in 1948, did experience such isolation. By 1979 the trail attracted dozens of hopeful thru-hikers and thousands of "weekenders" or "short-timers" who visited the trail for one- or two-day hikes. According to Appalachian Trail Conference statistics, as many as four million people visit the trail each year.

No, the Appalachian Trail was not a lonely place. On the contrary, Dan and I passed few days without encountering at least one other person on the trail. In the more popular sections—through national parks—we often met and talked with dozens of people. For those who sought isolation, the trail's human population may have been a disappointment, but for others—most hikers, really—the thriving backcountry society only enhanced the experience. Any hiker who has spent weeks along the route knows that the real story of the Appalachian Trail is found among the people who walk it.

The social quality of the trail inspired Nancy Sills, wife of Normal Sills, a Connecticut native who thru-hiked the trail in 1985, to dub the trail a linear community, and of all the descriptions applied to the trail, I find hers most fitting. My experience is that if the trail was a community, it was a community predicated on trust, fellowship, and sharing— values that too often seem lacking in the more "civilized" society we had left behind.

During our days of hiking through the Smokies—the

most heavily used national park in the country—we met dozens of other hikers. Many, like us, were thru-hikers bound for Maine, but there were also many day-hikers and weekend backpackers. On the night we slept in Russell Field Shelter, tucked in a hardwood grove seventeen miles south of Clingman's Dome, the highest point on the trail, as daylight waned, hikers continued to arrive at the shelter until nineteen people and two dogs occupied a space designed to accommodate twelve. Among them was a woman who lived in a tepee in Massachusetts; another woman and her bearded boyfriend, both from North Carolina, who had packed in a glass bottle of tequila; two college students from Dayton, Ohio; and others who hailed from Indiana, Georgia, Virginia, and Illinois.

Because of the cramped conditions, late-comers, and the two dogs, slept on the floor. Once all of us and our gear were ensconced inside, the nineteen packs and accompanying foodbags—of orange, blue, red, maroon, turquoise, and brown nylon—hung like ripe fruit from the shelter's rafters.

That night chatter filled the shelter as hikers swapped backpacking tips, compared equipment, and talked of faraway home towns. For me it marked the first time I had experienced the communion shared among hikers in the backcountry. It did not matter who you were, where you were from, or how much you were worth. If you were a backpacker, you were okay.

The rigors of life on the trail tended to screen out most undesirables, while those same rigors tended to unify those of us who were tough and committed enough to forge on. We climbed the same mountains; we plodded through the same rainstorms; we suffered the same aches and pains as our bodies adapted to the physical challenge of fifteen- to twenty-mile days. We drank from the same springs; we stopped at the same towns to resupply; we experienced the same insatiable hunger—which I termed "hiker's disease"—as our bodies metabolized as many as six thousand calories a day. We carried the same equipment; we swatted the same mosquitoes; and we slept in the same three-sided, rough-hewn shelters. We shared the same quest.

We learned to depend on one another. If a hiker failed to arrive in camp by nightfall, we mounted a search party and set out with our flashlights. The night we camped at Ice Water Springs, four miles north of Newfound Gap, the midway point of the Smokies, a hiker in the shelter expressed concern that his companion had not yet arrived in camp a half-hour after dark. Though beautiful by day, the Smokies posed certain hazards by night, among them bears and the roving herd of three-hundred-pound wild boars that use their formidable tusks to scavenge for food after dark. We organized a search party, left the security of the fence-enclosed shelter, and followed our flashlight beams into the darkness. As I pushed up the trail past the darkened groves of hardwoods, a line from Robert Frost's poem "Stopping by Woods" kept tumbling through my mind: "The woods are lovely, dark and deep . . . ." And they were. Every sound and shadow teased my imagination. Rocks wore faces, tree trunks sheltered gnomes, branches shivered and squeaked.

Within a half mile, I detected a beam of light sweeping the trail ahead and realized that we had found our lost hiker. He had taken a wrong turn at a trail junction a few tenths of a mile back and had followed it a couple of miles before realizing his mistake. He was relieved to see us, and his gratitude was our reward. I knew, without really knowing much about him except that he was a backpacker, that he would have done the same for me.

In a similar way, if someone ran short of food, we delved into our food bags and shared what surplus we had. Within minutes the famished hiker would find himself stationed before a mountain of Ziploc bags of rice and noodles. And if someone turned an ankle and twisted a knee, we carried some of the weight from his pack until his injury healed. Victor, an upbeat man in his early twenties from Northampton, Massachusetts, who had linked up with Dan and me in Georgia, pulled a calf muscle the day we entered the Smokies. As we moved north and Victor's limp became more and more conspicuous, we volunteered to carry some of his weight. When he refused, we insisted. Unfortunately,

it was not enough, and Victor then wrestled with the decision to abandon the trail.

When Victor seemed to have reached his limit, we encouraged him to plod on, and, in spite of his injury, he continued on to Hot Springs, North Carolina, thirty-five miles north of the Smokies. Realizing that if he continued, he would just slow us down, he bought a bus ticket home. When he departed the trail, we embraced him and wished him well, and for days afterward we felt that an important part of our family was absent. The separation proved to be only temporary, however. Months later when we entered New England, Victor rejoined us for weekends and joined us for the final 120 miles of the trail.

Though most hikers shared the same experiences, we were all different in terms of ages, backgrounds, and regions of the country. On one night at Muskrat Creek Shelter three miles beyond the North Carolina–Georgia line, I shared the shelter with a sixty-five-year-old mathematics professor from Ottawa, who had navigated a mountain bike loaded with bulging panniers to the shelter; a seventy-two-year-old retired army sergeant and veteran of World War II and Korea; two tattooed heavy-metal mavens in their early twenties from northern Kentucky; and a clean-cut twenty-six-year-old butcher from Washington, D.C. It occurred to me that if we had met under any other circumstances, we probably would not have had much to talk about. We had all arrived at the A-frame shelter after walking through a driving thunderstorm, and, although we were virtual strangers, we spent the evening packed under a ten-by-twelve-foot roof, discussing religion, philosophy, and our personal reasons for being on the trail, while swapping samples from our cook pots. At bedtime we slithered into our sleeping bags in the dank shelter illuminated by a single candle, and as the rain peppered the roof, someone told a joke, then another, and another. For more than an hour we lay awake listening and laughing together. The barriers of age, education, and social status couldn't have mattered less.

A couple of hundred miles farther north, at Cherry Gap

Shelter, a day's hike south of Roan Mountain in the northeastern corner of Tennessee, we had a similar experience. It was May 24. We had been on the trail for just over a month, and the continuing warming of spring had inspired Dan and me to ship our woolens, gloves, and heavy sweaters home from Erwin, believing that we had suffered winter's last blast. We were mistaken.

Dan and I began shivering soon after we arrived in camp that afternoon. The temperatures during the day had lingered in the sixties and seventies—too warm to induce shivering—and so we ascribed our chills to the flu-like effects of bad water. By dusk, however, we realized that the air temperature had dropped more than thirty degrees. The next morning we awoke to two inches of snow. It blanketed the ground and bowed the trees, now in full summer foliage. As we prepared to leave the shelter, a combination of snow and sleet began to fall, and we abandoned our travel plans for the day. We spent the morning hours drinking herbal tea and reading, and by noon the first of our benumbed colleagues began to arrive. Some of them had slept under ponchos through the night's storm. By midafternoon eleven hikers were wedged into a shelter designed to sleep six, and only by alternating head to foot could we squeeze everyone in.

Nestled in our sleeping bags, we read our books, wrote in our journals, munched surplus food, or stared out into the icy woods. Someone passed around a plastic bottle filled with Jack Daniel's, and by dusk we were one very happy family. Through the evening hours we sang verses of a blues song, creating new verses as we progressed, and joking about the wicked weather, the flatulence that resulted from our heavy dietary regimen of legumes, our ailing feet, or the wild stench that rose from eleven filthy, pressure-packed bodies. What had the makings for a bad scene still endures among my most cherished memories of the trail. It was a prime example of making do with what nature throws your way and finding contentment in companionship and simple pleasures.

If there was any sense of isolation from being on the trail

for months at a time, it was isolation from world and national news. We spent from three to ten days at a stretch between resupply trips to town. We didn't carry radios, and during our stopovers we rarely picked up newspapers. Frankly, there wasn't much going on in the world that interested us. The big news during the summer of 1979, for instance, was the gas shortage and the fuel rationing programs in effect in major cities. We heard stories about escalating gas prices, long lines at the pump, and the occasional shooting that resulted when someone edged his way into line. To us, the gas crunch meant only one thing: by the end of the summer it cost us eight, rather than six, cents to fill our fuel bottles.

Much more important to us was the latest trail news. We gleaned most of this news from the spiral notebooks left in many of the trail shelters. On these pages hikers signed in, mentioned the highlights or low points of their days, described the weather, listed the other hikers in their parties, drew caricatures of themselves, and sometimes waxed philosophical about the vicissitudes of life on the trail.

Through the summer, we followed the exploits of other thru-hikers: Otel (who, according to rumor, sometimes hiked in the buff) and his dog A.T.; Al and Moonie, a couple of good-natured cutups from New Jersey; the Phillips brothers, Paul and Robin, two siblings from Florida, who packed heavy photographic equipment; Woodstock and Nancy and Phil and Cindy, two of the trail's few man–woman teams; Byron and Jimmy—Byron, who had a ready joke for every occasion and who eventually lost his pack to a trailside thief, and Jimmy, who, we heard, recorded humorous and bawdy trail tales in the registers. On later trips to the trail I followed Sunshine and Daydream, a newlywed couple from Connecticut; Captain Kangaroo, an Australian hiker who became a friend; Pigpen, an accountant from Boston who refused to bathe; the Bluegrass Boys, a trio of hikers from northern Kentucky.

Through register entries, we came to know each of the hikers who plodded along anywhere from a few hours to days and weeks ahead of us before we even met them. We

learned of their likes and dislikes, the types of food that filled their bellies, their struggles, their triumphs, the professions they had left to hike the trail, and even what they looked like, the styles of packs they carried, and what they wore. When we caught up with them, we could call them by name before they had a chance to introduce themselves, just as the hikers behind us would often come into camp and without hesitation announce, "You must be Dan and Dave. I've been on your heels for two weeks."

We often used the registers to communicate messages to those behind us, urging them to hustle to catch us for a beer bash or a megafeed at a town stop or telling them, sadly, when someone in our party had reached his limit and had gone home. At times the efficiency of our primitive communications network amazed us. Near the end of June, for instance, Dan and I approached Harpers Ferry, West Virginia, headquarters for the Appalachian Trail Conference and the unofficial halfway point. As we progressed north, we left a series of entries inviting other thru-hikers to hitchhike the fifty miles from Harpers Ferry into Washington, D.C., for the Fourth of July celebration on the Mall. We planned to meet at noon at the Jefferson Memorial.

By noon on the fourth, nearly a dozen hikers—many of whom we had never met—straggled to the memorial. We spent the afternoon swapping trail stories and enjoying the bounty of junk food available from sidewalk vendors.

Southbounders on the trail—those who had begun their hike in Maine rather than Georgia—became another source of trail news. When we encountered them, we often slipped from our packs and shared a bag of trail mix while we exchanged data. Our news was as vital to them as theirs was to us; each could provide the other with information about what lay ahead: the friendliest towns, the cheapest hotels and restaurants, the most taxing ascents and descents, the locations of reliable water sources.

Through the summer we leapfrogged with dozens of other northbounders who had left Springer about the same time we had. Among them were the Phillips brothers, Jeff Hammons from Kansas, North Carolina native Gary Owen,

and Mark Gornick from Maryland. We would link up with them for several days, or even weeks, losing them after we or they had stopped for an extended stay in one place. Two or three months later, we would catch them at a shelter farther north and spend hours around the campfire detailing the important events of our lives and discussing how we had changed.

In terms of our appearance, the changes were obvious. One night in Maine I rejoined Al, a solitary hiker from New York, whom we had last seen in Hot Springs, North Carolina. Al had adopted a mongrel dog he had found near Wayah Bald in North Carolina and had named the animal Wayah. Wayah had contracted a bad case of mange, and as Dan and I left Hot Springs, Wayah—completely bereft of fur—lay wheezing in the grass. Both Dan and I wrote her off as a lost cause.

Yet some four months later, Al and Wayah, the latter sporting a luxurious new coat of fur, entered camp. We laughed at Wayah's changed appearance, and Al laughed at ours. Al, who had started the hike with a billowy beard, really hadn't changed much, but we had. I had started the trail with a haircut, a clean-shaven face, ten pounds of unwanted fat, and a crisp new hiking outfit. I had long ago surrendered my threadbare khakis and now wore a pair of tattered fatigue trousers with holes in the knees and seat. My beard had grown to three inches, and I had hardened, having lost ten pounds.

Although the trail provided an ample measure of male companionship, during my five months in the wilderness, I suffered a pestering hunger for the physical affection of a woman. Along the trail, when virtually all of one's sensibilities became attuned to sensual cues and when one spent his days surrounded by beauty, peace, and harmony, it seemed natural to hunger for touch and to surrender, like all of nature's creatures, to the attraction of members of the opposite sex. The problem was that the pickings were slim.

Though the ratio of men to women is becoming more balanced each year, in 1979 we met fewer than ten women who aspired to complete the trail. If we did want to meet women, it seemed, we would have to create them in our own imaginations, which we often did. One night over a few ounces of bourbon by a campfire, Dan and I created mythological Venuses we dubbed the "Scandinavian hiking queens." In our minds they were beautiful, lithesome women who would love us, share our experiences, and provide feminine companionship. They became the object of our hormone-inspired quest, although neither one of us ever imagined we actually would encounter them in the flesh. Against the odds, in the White Mountains of New Hampshire I met a woman who more than matched my fantasy.

The White Mountains, for all their stark, alpine beauty, also tend to attract throngs of hiking enthusiasts, which for us created nightly contests for shelter space. On August 29 we had left Garfield Ridge Campsite and in a cold New England rain pushed on toward Ethan Pond, a campsite that included a six-man shelter and several tent platforms. Though none of us wanted to acknowledge concern over finding shelter space for the night—to have done so would have smacked of the competitiveness we had shunned in greater society—the rain inspired a quickening of our pace, and each of us discreetly counted heads and jockeyed for position over the last few miles to the pond lest we be left out in the rain.

By that stage of the trip, my rain fly, which had served as a groundsheet as often as a shelter, bore visible holes and admitted almost as much rain as it repelled. I didn't want to suffer a cold, clammy night beneath it.

When we arrived at Ethan Pond Campsite, we encountered six sullen faces peering out of the shelter into the rain. Dan managed to secure a space in the shelter after persuading a reluctant weekender to shift his body, along with his staggering assemblage of gear, over a few inches. If the shelter had been full of thru-hikers, I have no doubt they would have accommodated me too, but weekenders were notori-

ously protective of their personal space, and there clearly was no room for me.

I walked out to the tent platform, a ten-by-ten-foot elevated square of rain-soaked wooden slats, and began erecting my pitiful shelter. The task proved counterproductive in the rain, so I decided to wait and see if the rain would quit and walked back to dump my pack under the shelter's eaves. A while later, feeling crowded, I left the shelter and returned to the tent platform, somewhat reconciled to the notion that it would be my home for the night. Nearby, I noticed a large olive-drab tent mounted on another platform.

Just outside the tent, I met its occupant, a friendly, long-legged woman with brown hair topped by a blue wool watch cap. I eyed her ample shelter, and without presuming to ask if there was room inside for an extra boarder, I began complaining about my leaky digs for the night. Sensing my misery, she asked me to join her for a cup of hot tea inside the tent.

A large gas stove had heated the tent to a comfortable seventy degrees, and a steaming kettle sat on the burner. From it she poured two cups of herbal tea, and, as we sipped our drinks, we talked about her frequent trips to the White Mountains and about my experiences along the trail. She was a bright, cheerful woman whose knowledge of the wilderness amazed me. At dusk I rose to leave, but she seemed to sense my reluctance and asked if I'd like to stay the night in her tent. Without hesitating, I accepted her offer.

After we had finished our dinners, we sat close to a candle, and she showed me clippings from many of the edible plants that grew in the area: wood sorrel, a tart, tri-leaved plant that resembles clover and provides vitamin C; reindeer moss, a fungus of light green skeletal tines that boasts a musky mushroom flavor; and Labrador tea leaves, taken from a low-growing evergreen heath, which she steeped in boiling water and served to me with honey.

As we sat close over the candle, I wanted to move closer, to smell her hair, to kiss her. I wanted to hold her, not necessarily make love to her, but just hold her. For all of its gifts,

the trail deprived us of that one thing—touch—which I believe we all craved. As we prepared to climb into our bags, I gently touched her back, and she drew away from me. I apologized and backed away, explaining how lonely for affection I had grown over the past few months and how much I enjoyed her company.

Moments later, with the candle out, I heard her slip from her clothes and enter her bag. I, too, lay naked in mine. Then I felt her hand reach for mine, and for an hour we lay silent, just stroking one another's hands. I reached over and kissed her, and she took me in her arms, kissing me back. Soon, we had rearranged our bags, laying one on the tent floor and covering ourselves with the other. We kissed and embraced through the night, sleeping and awakening in each other's arms, never making love but succumbing to blissful, innocent intimacy.

Near dawn she suggested that we walk outside to experience the cold rain against our skin, then return to the warmth of our sleeping bags. We did, and we ran naked and barefoot through the rain along the trail. Back in the tent, we climbed under our sleeping bags, still warm from when we had left them, and fell asleep. Soon, in spite of my desire to prolong the night forever, it was morning.

Over breakfast, she asked me if I would like some company for the morning hike. Yes, I told her, and in a dramatic overture that might have been lifted from a grade-B romance movie, I suggested that she accompany me to Katahdin. She hugged me, laughing at the suggestion. Once I realized how ridiculous it must have sounded, I laughed, too. I realized I was falling in love; *all* relationships, it seems, develop rapidly in the rarefied environment of the trail.

Together, we left Ethan Pond and descended into Crawford Notch. As we began the long, three-mile ascent to the Presidential Range, the sun emerged and the temperature rose. Midway up the climb, she stopped me and asked if I would be offended if she hiked topless, explaining that she didn't want to sweat in her last clean T-shirt. I hiked shirtless, so it seemed natural for her to do the same.

Besides, how could I pass up a chance to view her beautiful body in the daylight? She pulled her shirt off and slipped back into her pack, and we continued up the trail.

From time to time, as we ascended, I glanced back at her and admired her perfect, full breasts moving sensuously with her stride. I was struck by how her natural beauty complemented that of the wilderness.

As we neared the ridge, I spotted one of my fellow hikers, a quiet, contemplative Connecticut native whose face displayed little emotion, that is, until the day he caught a glimpse of a beautiful, topless woman bounding up the trail. The hiker, who sat on a rock munching trail mix, looked up, spotted me, nodded a silent hello, and returned his glance to the bag of trail mix on his lap. When his glance rose again, my hiking partner had come into view, and his eyes beamed like duel harvest moons. As we passed, the hiker, always a man of few words, was stunned totally speechless.

My friend left me at the Mizpah Hut, six miles short of Lakes of the Clouds Hut, our destination for the day. For the rest of the trip, I replayed our night together often in my mind as I walked alone through the woods, and I savor the memory even now. As it was, it was a perfect union of two free-spirited souls—a man and a woman—both searching for some meaning in the eastern wilderness and finding unexpected intimacy. If it had lasted longer, it might have lost some of its intensity. If it had not lasted as long, I would have regretted every second that was lost.

When I think of her, I think of a line from Whitman's "I Sing the Body Electric":

I have perceived that to be with those I like is enough,
To stop in company with the rest at evening is enough,
To be surrounded by beautiful, curious, breathing, laughing
    flesh is enough. . . .

CHAPTER · SIX

Bad Company

We had our first encounter with lowlifes last night at Roan Highlands Shelter. A couple of gun-toting hoodlums in leather jackets and a drunken woman had hiked the half-mile from the road, and they commandeered the shelter for their private party. Only the Phillips brothers were bold enough to demand space inside. The rest of us were content to sleep in our tents.

A couple of weeks ago we heard a hiker tell a story about being abducted at a road crossing by some locals in a pickup truck. Apparently, they demanded that he help them rob other people or that he would himself become their victim. He was able to escape when the truck stopped at a backwoods road junction, as a car just happened to pass. He leaped from the truck, grabbed his pack, and ran into the woods. They searched for him for a few minutes, and he escaped unharmed. We've also heard stories from other hikers about moonshiners at backwoods road crossings who offer to sell them hooch. Seems that such encounters take place where roads intrude into the wilderness. Not much good results when their world and ours collide. Even in the face of such risk, I feel much safer out here on the trail than I would in any major city.

—May 26, 1979, Roan Highlands Shelter, Tennessee

It was a Sunday evening in the early spring 1987, and I shared Addis Gap Shelter in Georgia with a married couple, Kit and Candy, and their pit bull, A.T.

As we arrived at camp, the sun dipped behind the ridge. We quickly unrolled our bags and dressed in our camp clothes, ready to settle in for the night and enjoy the tranquil setting that had once been the site of the Addis family homestead. A grove of Carolina silver-bell trees sprinkled the ground with delicate white blossoms shaken free by the breeze. The slanting rays of the sun traced long shadows across the clearing, and a small brook sluiced away from the shelter down a hillside. Amid all the beauty, however, there was one unsettling feature: a gravel forest service road that wound up the mountain came within a few hundred feet of the shelter.

Most hikers have learned to apply the following postulate to their wilderness wanderings: the quality of people increases in proportion to the distance from the nearest road and the difficulty of the terrain. In other words, the bad guys don't have the gumption or stamina to hump heavy packs into the heart of the backcountry.

Service roads linked the backcountry with the outer world and invited intrusion, and occasionally they attracted an often belligerent corps of locals who drove their fat-tired 4X4s up into the mountains to fire their guns, drink beer, and sometimes harass foot travelers. Often such backwoods crossings were choked with discarded trash, littered with spent shotgun shells and empty whiskey and beer bottles, and gutted by all-terrain vehicles. We needed only to view the scattered refuse to know that our nemeses had been there, and we could only hope that our arrival would not coincide with theirs. I can't speak for other hikers, but I know that I always tensed when I approached such crossings, realizing that if I did emerge from the woods and face trouble, there wasn't much I could do to defend myself.

In all my days in the woods, I met only one hiker who had stowed a weapon in his pack. The rest of us felt that to walk armed would violate the true spirit of the trail. It also would have violated the law against carrying concealed weapons in national parks and forests. Besides, in view of our preoccupation with cutting weight, it would have been uncon-

scionable to supplant one pound of food with one pound of steel.

During our night at Addis Gap, the road brought unwelcome visitors. As the three of us sparked our stoves and set about cooking our dinners, we heard a vehicle approach.

"That had better be a government truck," Kit said.

I hoped so, too, but realized that it probably wasn't. It was Sunday, late in the day. By that time most government employees were off the clock. Then we heard a volley of gunfire echo through the woods, which resolved any doubt.

A brown pickup truck soon rounded a bend and came into view. From the distance of several hundred yards, I noticed that the cab carried four people. As the vehicle drew nearer, I saw that it contained two men and two women. The truck continued until it reached the end of the road, thirty yards behind the shelter. Now out of our sight, the driver killed the engine. We heard the doors swing open.

"Oh, shit," I said under my breath. "We've got company."

I heard the two women giggling like adolescents. One of the men cursed them, telling them to shut up.

The four then stepped around to the front of the shelter. The two women—plump and in their midthirties, dressed in double-knit shorts and halter tops—stayed in the background giggling, while the men took seats at the picnic table perched in front of the shelter. I expected the protective pit bull to charge over my shoulder and confront the men, but I peered behind me—amazed—to find her snoozing peacefully at the back of the shelter.

The two men held beers in their hands and reeked of alcohol. The tall, gaunt man with dark eyes, a black beard, and stringy shoulder-length hair, glared into the shelter for a time before he spoke.

"You know these shelters are for everyone," he said, sternly. Then he smiled at his friend, a portly man with red hair and bloodshot eyes. The man smiled back. "They're not just for you backpackers."

We told him we knew that.

"Most hikers think they own these places," he continued. "But it ain't that way."

"Y'all want something to drink?" asked the friend, still wearing a queer smile. "We got some liquor and some beer. Done smoked up the pot, though."

There was a fresh ripple of giggling from the women.

"No, that's okay, but thanks," I answered.

"Naw, y'all gonna drink a beer," commanded the dark-haired man.

His friend returned to the truck. I suspected he might return with the beer *and* a weapon. While he was gone, his dark friend glared into the shelter at us without talking. I'm sure our apprehension was palpable. The redheaded man soon returned, proffering two beers.

As the women continued to giggle, the dark man snapped to his friend, "Hell, we ought to take them two out and shoot them!"

The redheaded man laughed, and I tried to muster a smile but couldn't. I knew that it was unlikely that the man would make good on his threat, but there was always a chance. These mountains were thoroughly isolated from the law.

The men stayed for nearly an hour, without talking much, but just glaring into the shelter. The pit bull continued to sleep. As night fell, they discussed staying at the shelter but finally decided to move on, saying they might be back later with some friends.

Relieved, we watched the truck wind away down the road and disappear around the bend.

"Think they were trying to scare us?" I asked.

"Well, they succeeded," Kit answered.

We discussed whether to move on up the trail or stay in the shelter and risk facing the men and a group of their hiker-hating allies later in the night.

Then we heard the truck stop and the doors open. Two shots rang through the trees, rousing the pit bull, who sat bolt upright growling.

There was no need for further discussion. Quickly, we were all on our feet, frantically stowing our gear. Within ten

minutes we were racing north on the trail through the darkness. We spent a restless night on a mountain shoulder half a mile beyond the shelter, and I awoke several times through the night to hear the pit bull, tensed and alert, growling at shadows in the woods. From where we lay I spotted a string of lights marking faraway backwoods houses extending down through the valley, and in my sleepy daze I imagined a pack of militant rednecks stalking us through the woods with flashlights.

A few hundred miles farther north, I had confronted another weapon-toting yokel, not on the trail but in Erwin, a small trail town in northern Tennessee. Because of intolerance for hikers among some of the town's residents, in the late 1970s Erwin ranked as one of the trail's least hospitable stopovers. Erwin's most enduring legacy, it seems, involves the lynching of an elephant some years ago. As the story goes, during a circus in a nearby town, an elephant squashed a young spectator, and after a brief trial the town hired a crane operator in Erwin, who summarily executed the hapless creature by hanging.

Over the last decade the town has made great strides to clean up its reputation. The Nolichucky Retreat Campground and Nolichucky Expeditions, a rafting outfitter located on the banks of the Nolichucky River, now offer hikers comfortable and friendly accommodations. But in 1979, in some ways Erwin seemed almost as inhospitable to hikers as it had been to clumsy pachyderms.

After we arrived in town, we found our way to the YMCA, a dingy edifice, and we welcomed the chance to take a hot shower and sleep under a roof, such as it was.

The shelters we had passed on our approach to town had posted warnings to hikers advising them not to interact with locals and not to divulge their travel plans. The signs made it clear that there had been trouble with some of the people from the area.

Though the town offered us little in the way of amenities, it was the first "wet" town we had passed through in many days, and after dropping our packs at the Y, Dan and I walked to one of the town's few taverns, several streets

away. The tavern was nothing more than a long, dimly lit room with a chipped linoleum floor, a row of rickety stools, and a large cooler filled with iced quarts of Iron City Beer. Seventy-five cents bought a quart of beer and a styrofoam cup.

As soon as we crossed the threshold, I realized that we had made a mistake. Fifteen bleary-eyed patrons swung their faces toward the door, and as they did, conversation ceased. Most of the men wore work shirts and billed caps advertising chewing tobacco, fishing gear, or four-wheel-drive trucks. Some of the men had wads of tobacco bulging in their cheeks and sluiced the juice right onto the floor.

Clad in our hiking clothes and boots and with our long hair and beards—both emblems of the counterculture in 1979—we made ready targets. The men recognized us immediately as hikers or, worse, as hippie hikers who had chucked the work ethic to wander through the woods. Their values and ours, at least as they perceived them, were at odds, and I confess that I was guilty of making snap judgments about the men and their attitudes toward us myself. It turned out that my snap judgments weren't too far off.

Dan and I sidled up to the bar, ordered the house specialty, and soon sat in front of two frothy styrofoam cups.

"Hey, what the hell you fellows doin' walking when you can drive!" said one of the men. Laughter. "Wall, look at 'em boots! 'Em's some fancy boots!" More laughter. "You all walk in 'em cute little shorts?" Again, more laughter. I noticed that Dan's beer had vanished in one quaff, and he fixed me with a look that said, "Let's get the hell out of here. Now."

I took a long pull at my beer, hoping that the onslaught would end and that the men would focus their attention on something else. They didn't. The man on my left, who tottered unsteadily on his perch, turned a red, haggard face toward me and started raving about something. I'm sure he had a definite message in mind, but under the influence of a few dozen beers, all that came out was a string of garbled syllables. From the few words I could understand, I learned that the man was angry with a fellow named Rufus or Verl or some such, who had taken liberties with his daughter.

About that time, he rested his elbow on my shoulder and reached his free hand into his work pants and pulled out a small silver handgun.

I had had a terrifying experience in college when at a barn dance a drunken lunatic who had infiltrated the college crowd pulled a western-style revolver, poked it into my chest, pushed me back, and leveled the gun at my heart before someone wrestled the weapon from his hand. The experience left me with a dread of handguns.

Now, in this dingy Tennessee tavern as the sodden man waved the loaded gun in my face, I felt a twinge of panic. I looked at Dan, and for the first time since I'd known him, I saw he was frightened.

The man continued to bellow about this Rufus and how he was going to "kill that son of a bitch," when the man seated on his left intervened.

"Jack, you can't kill Rufus," he said. "He hanged hisself in prison last week!"

With his primary target gone, I imagined that the man might turn his sights on me. At that, Dan rose, sensibly figuring that this was an appropriate time to leave.

Just then our savior—a disabled young man with a vacant smile, a bum leg, and an atrophied right arm—entered the bar. He was, in the lexicon of this rural hamlet, the reigning village idiot, and the tavern denizens aimed their abuse at him. They jeered him and mocked him, but his smile indicated that he enjoyed the attention, derisive though it was.

The man's presence seemed to boost Jack's mood, and he called the crippled man over to the bar. As the young man approached, Jack pulled the clip from his gun and withdrew a single 22-caliber round. He then told the man that he had a game he could play, and he demonstrated how to pound the butt-end of the cartridge against the sharp metal edge of the bar with the slug pointed at his head. He handed the bullet to the man and backed away. As he did, Dan and I made our way toward the door.

My last memory of the tavern was of the pathetic man, the silly grin still playing across his face, pounding the bul-

let against the edge of the bar while the men stood clear of danger, laughing and waiting for the round to discharge.

Within a week, on May 26 at the Roan Highlands Shelter in Low Gap four miles north of the summit of Roan Mountain, we had another bizarre encounter. Six of us—the Phillips brothers; Mark, an eighteen-year-old thru-hiker from Maryland; Jeff, a Kansas native; and Dan and I—arrived at the shelter as it began to drizzle. Inside were two rough-looking men clad in black leather jackets who had hiked in the half mile from the nearest road. With them was an attractive woman with long dark hair and brown eyes. She and the men swilled whiskey from a Jack Daniel's bottle that sat on the floor beside a healthy store of tin cans.

The men seemed irked at our arrival and they made it clear that they planned on making good use of the shelter that night and did not welcome our company. The woman, though drunk, seemed happy enough with her two companions.

Most of us decided to avoid a confrontation and set up our tents and rain flies outside the shelter. The Phillips brothers, nonetheless, determined to wedge their way into the shelter, and after a few minutes of tense negotiation, the men grudgingly yielded. To insure their privacy, the men hung two rain ponchos from the shelter eaves, one dividing the shelter in half, and the other closing off the front.

Through the evening, as we huddled around a smoky fire, the three continued to party. At one point we dived for cover when we heard one of the men shout at the woman to put down the gun. Having discovered that the men were armed, we spent a restless night inside our nylon tents. The next morning we were packed and on the trail before the hung-over revelers awoke, and as we walked, the Phillips brothers shared what they had overheard from beyond the nylon partition.

"One of the men had sex with the woman a couple of times, and then he called his friend over," he said. "He told the girl that he wanted her to have sex with his friend." The woman, who was all but comatose at that point, initially resisted but then willingly accommodated the man's re-

quest. The men apparently took turns with her through the night.

As we distanced ourselves from the shelter, we wrestled with our judgment, wondering if we should have intervened on the woman's behalf. After some discussion, we decided we had done the right thing. The woman seemed to be a willing participant, and if we had intervened, what would the outcome have been if we had confronted the two burly, armed men in defense of a woman whose honor seemed as dubious as theirs?

The gun-wielding southern rogues were intimidating, but even they did not rattle us nearly as much as the illusive nocturnal demon that sent us fleeing from the shore of Tiorati Lake forty miles outside of New York City.

It was July 30, and I was traveling with Paul. Dan had pushed a day ahead, and Nick lagged a few days behind. We had veered off the trail ten miles south of Bear Mountain Bridge, where the trail crosses the Hudson River, and at dusk we found ourselves following the paved roads through Tiorati Circle.

At that point, we had become thoroughly at ease in the wilderness, yet the prospect of mixing with the denizens of the nation's largest city, which lay a scant forty miles away, left us spooked.

Initially, Paul and I had decided to camp on Tiorati Circle, a paved loop a few yards off the trail that ran along the shores of Tiorati Lake resort. When we got there, we encountered riotous commotion that left us feeling like back-country immigrants newly arrived in a society devoted to noise, hedonism, and excess. One camper, a plump man in his early thirties, sat in a lawn chair basking in the glow of a Coleman lantern beside a small card table cluttered with a three-foot water pipe for smoking pot, a quart bottle of whiskey, and a massive sound system that blared disco dance music. In the site beside his, a family outfitted with

an equally outsized boom-box blasted their hard-rock strains into the night. Several young men in souped-up cars had converted the circle into a racetrack, and they sped around the oval squealing their tires, shouting to other drivers and blaring their own music through open windows.

At the outset of my hike, I would have welcomed the security of having other campers—even such boisterous ones—gathered around me, but the three months on the trail had changed my perspective. These disrespectful urban campers seemed to violate the peaceful sanctity of the wilderness while they violated my own peace of mind, and Paul and I wanted nothing to do with them.

Before making camp, we decided to push up the road to find a less frenetic setting, even though it was now dark. Within a half-mile, we passed a group camp area where a dozen inner-city children—most of them from Harlem—sat clustered around a campfire grilling hot dogs and hamburgers. The delicious aroma of cooking meat tempered our wariness, and we ambled over to the fire. Soon we sat swapping tales with the children while sharing their dinner. Just before we left, a raccoon strayed into the camp, and the children scattered, screaming, from the fire. One young boy shrieked, "Bear! It's a bear!" as he ran.

Paul and I couldn't help but laugh at the irony. These kids had grown up on some of the meanest streets in America where they had no doubt witnessed muggings, shootings, stabbings, and other violent crimes. Yet, to them the wilderness and its harmless creatures were unfamiliar and strange, evoking fear and panic. A dozen armed gang members could have wandered into camp and not raised an eyebrow, but a ten-pound raccoon sent the children fleeing for their lives.

Paul and I thanked the children and their counselors for the kindness and pushed on. Faced with the prospect of bumbling through the brush in the dark looking for a suitable place to sleep, we opted instead to take our chances amid the noise and confusion back at Tiorati Circle.

We rolled out our bags along the fringes of the lake and decided not to hang our food, convinced that the noise from

our neighbors would at least protect us from scavenging animals.

Minutes after we had climbed into our bags, we heard the horrible call. It wouldn't have been more unsettling if it had risen from the throat of a Godzilla. Instead, it was the call of the dread *homo sapiens intoxicatus,* and it came from the campsite nearest ours.

"Ahhhhhhh!" it began. "Ahhhhhhhhhh! Somebody stole my friggin' radio!"

Seconds later, a dark form was crashing through the bushes, and soon a bearded man in a white T-shirt and ball cap tottered above us as we cowered in our sleeping bags.

"I'm gonna kill the son of a bitch who stole my radio!" he shouted in our direction. "Yoos guys seen my radio?"

No, we explained, we hadn't. But we'd be sure to keep an eye out for it.

After scanning our Spartan camp, he seemed convinced of our innocence and staggered on through the weeds toward the next site. "Ahhhhhhhhhhh! Somebody stole my friggin' radio! I'm gonna kill the bastard who stole my radio . . ."

Serenaded by the squealing tires, blaring music, and the mournful call of the radio-less man, we eventually fell asleep. But the urban reign of terror wasn't over for us quite yet.

About 3:00 A.M., after even the most devoted partyers had drifted off, I heard it. I shook Paul in his bag.

"Listen," I said.

It was the sound of something large, plunging with its paws and splashing through the water of the lake. It was moving toward our camp.

"What is it?" Paul asked.

"God, I don't know," I continued, "but I think we ought to hang our food."

Still half asleep, we slipped from our bags, and I fumbled through my pack for the fifty feet of parachute cord I carried for hanging our food. As I did, I could hear the strange creature plunging through the water toward us. I found the rope and, as Paul fixed his flashlight beam on a branch above us, tied a rock to one end of the rope before hurling it toward

the branch. It missed. As I felt along the ground for the rope, Paul swung his flashlight toward the advancing creature.

"I can't see anything, but it's still moving toward us," he said.

"Yeah, and we'd better get this food up before it gets here," I said.

Before I could take another shot at the branch, the creature had cleared the shoreline and began moving through the brush.

I'm not sure if it was my imagination, but I swear I could see the whites of Paul's eyes bulging, and before I could stop him, he tore off through the trees in the opposite direction. Not one to face peril alone, I followed on his heels, and together we charged willy-nilly through the woods, peering over our shoulders to glimpse the mystery predator. Although we couldn't see what or who pursued us, we could hear it rustling through the brush a constant fifteen yards behind us, matching us stride for stride.

At one point I grabbed Paul's arm, and we stopped to listen. As soon as we stopped, the creature stopped. After a few seconds, we spooked again and sped off howling through the trees. The creature again was on our heels, fifteen yards behind us. I spotted the light of the bathhouse and raced toward it, thinking that we'd finally get a good look at our pursuer.

When we arrived under the light, we peered behind us. Still nothing. Then I cast a glance down at my boot and started laughing.

"What's so funny?" Paul asked.

"We are," I answered. "Look at my boot."

Looking down, he saw the parachute cord tangled around my ankle and started laughing too. I had been dragging the parachute cord through the weeds, and we had been fleeing from the dread rock monster I had secured to the other end while I was trying to hang our food bags. We may have identified one of our assailants, but the other, the bizarre aquatic demon that had plunged through the water toward our camp, remains a mystery.

Wasted Along the Way

No matter how poorly prepared I feel for this trip, there is always someone less prepared, less well equipped, less conditioned. Some of the people out here are like harlequins in hiking boots. Some have never read a single word about this trail or hiked a single mile before setting out, and their misadventures tend to encourage me. Compared to some of them, I am a virtual expert on backwoods living. I've discovered, too, that there are a few hucksters out here, who seem to be preying on them.
—May 5, 1979, Fontana Dam, North Carolina

A white gauze bandage crusted with a yellow stain clung to Mark's forehead, a reminder of his rather inauspicious introduction to the Appalachian Trail. His eyes, glazed and distant, peered lifelessly from their sockets.

He curled in his cotton flannel sleeping bag in the recesses of the Springer Mountain Shelter, staring blankly out into the greening, rain-drenched forest while his partner, Don, a tiny man who stood five feet tall and weighed 105

pounds, set about building a fire. Don may have been small, but he was mightily armed. A massive hunting knife—a machete, really—hung from his belt and extended below his knee. In his right hand he held a full-sized axe, which he wielded fiercely against the unyielding trunk of a very large and healthy maple.

After assaulting the trunk for several minutes with no results, he lowered the axe. Wheezing like an asthmatic, he scanned the woods for a more accommodating target, locating a smaller, though no less healthy, green maple. Straining to bend the small tree nearly double and struggling to secure the top to the ground with his foot, he grunted as he drove the axe into the midsection. The axe head rebounded like a Superball and struck Don square in the forehead, knocking him to his knees.

"Oh, shit," muttered Mark. "Now this."

The two of them were not having a good day. In fact, it had been a pretty miserable week. Only a few days earlier Don and he had had such high hopes for their journey on the Appalachian Trail. They had been planning for weeks, organizing their equipment, purchasing food, sharpening their axes and knives. But things hadn't worked out the way they had hoped, and their dreams, along with Mark's head—and now Don's—had been dashed.

Mark's head injury had occurred before they even reached the trail. After becoming entangled in his pack straps, Mark had stumbled off the bus that had carried them to Atlanta and had landed solidly on his forehead. The ambulance ride to the emergency room was an unexpected side trip, but Mark was relieved when the doctor glanced at the X-rays and reported that he had not fractured his skull. He had, however, suffered a wicked concussion, which had left him dazed and confused, and the medication they had given him to quiet his nerves had only compounded the problem. Against the doctor's orders, he had checked out of the hospital two days later. After purchasing two twelve-packs of Budweiser, Mark and Don had set out for Amicalola Falls.

The eight-and-a-half-mile hike up from the falls to the official start of the Appalachian Trail hadn't exactly met

their expectations, either. Neither had trained for the hike, and the stiff uphill grade soon exhausted them. It also made them thirsty. They hadn't bothered to fill their canteens with water before leaving the park. Why bother? Each carried 144 ounces of beer, and as they struggled up the mountain, they left a trail of empty twelve-ounce aluminum cans behind them.

Near the halfway point, Mark began to suffer another spell. His vision blurred, and he spun and collapsed into a heap beside the trail. After Don assessed the situation, he became convinced that his partner was dehydrated and decided to go for water. Had they carried a map or guidebook, they would have realized that a perfectly good spring spouted water within a few hundred yards of their emergency bivouac, but the twelve cans of beer had already made their packs unmanageably heavy, and they had left the trail guide behind.

As his partner lapsed deeper into a daze, Don humped the four miles to the top of Springer Mountain, located the spring at the shelter, filled his canteen, then spun back down the mountain to his friend. By the time Don returned, Mark was sitting up, cradling his throbbing head. By now it was dark, and the two rolled out their sleeping bags—heavy cotton flannel models—in the brush and tried to ignore the rain that pummeled their faces and drenched their bags. It seems they had also neglected to bring a tent.

That was the end of day one.

The next morning, the two arose. Don arose, rather, while Mark, pale and wan, lay in his bag, his lifeless eyes cast toward the heavens. Don revived him with a tepid Budweiser, and after a breakfast of Fig Newtons, the two once again embarked for Springer more determined than ever.

Late that afternoon, long after they had exhausted their cache of beer, they arrived at the shelter, Mark tottering unsteadily and Don dragging his sodden sleeping bag behind him like a thick serpentine tail. While Mark lay in the shelter, his partner set out to build a fire to warm them and dry their wet clothes. Since no dead trees lay within two hun-

dred yards of the shelter, in the interest of convenience, he opted to fell a few live ones, which was not proceeding well.

After Don thumped himself on the noggin with the butt end of his axe head, he soon staggered to his feet and turned his attention to yet another living maple, this one a mere sapling. On *this* diminutive twig his axe found purchase. Soon he had harvested a bundle of twigs and placed them in a tangled heap in the middle of the fire pit. But how to light them? Igniting green wood is tough enough; igniting *wet* green wood is nearly impossible. But the very enterprising Don doused the branches in a pint of white gas, struck a match, and at the cost of his eyebrows and forearm hair successfully kindled a fire that emitted a cloud of wet green smoke. Returning the axe to its sheath on his belt and swaggering like a gunfighter who had just dropped his arch nemesis, Don returned to the shelter.

Soon the dense smoke was billowing into the shelter, driving all of its occupants out into the rain, except Mark, who was too dazed to move. Squinting through tears, Don joined his partner at the back of the shelter where the two set about preparing dinner by peeling the plastic wrappers from a half-dozen SlimJims.

"What do you think?" Don asked, biting off a finger-length portion of his evening entree.

"About what?"

"About the trail."

"I dunno. What do *you* think?" asked Mark, still staring into the void.

"Do you think we can make it?"

"Where?" Mark asked, suddenly alert. "To Maine? Are you crazy! After all this!"

"No," Don answered. "Back down to Amicalola Falls."

"Well, if we rest up another day, I think I might be up to it."

And so, two days later, after the supply of SlimJims was spent and some of the color had returned to Mark's cheeks, the two again took up the blue blazes and retreated to Amicalola Falls, promising to return next year—better equipped, better prepared, better conditioned, in better health—to hike the entire Appalachian Trail.

Sadly, this tale of woe is true. I met Don and Mark on Springer Mountain while I was on the trail in 1987. They will forever epitomize the misadventures that often befall poorly prepared hikers who—eager but clueless—take up the trail.

As it turns out, the odds are against the hundreds of hikers who each summer leave Springer aspiring to reach Maine. During most summers, only about 20 percent will achieve their goal. Owing to a welter of possible complications, the others become wasted along the way, many before they even clear the seventy-eight miles to the North Carolina border. For one thing, there is injury. The Appalachian Trail is, in effect, a nearly continuous, five-month endurance event and, like any athletic pursuit, it poses limitless potential for injury. Rick, a hiker we had met in Georgia, who seemed to have the mental toughness and stamina to make it all the way, made it only as far as Virginia before he took a spill on a stretch of wet, rocky trail and opened a tendon-deep gash in his knee.

Victor wrenched a calf muscle in the Smokies and, after hobbling along and grimacing for a week, made the painful decision to depart the trail in Hot Springs, North Carolina.

There were less predictable obstacles, too, that led hikers to abandon their hopes. Byron, whom we had befriended in Tennessee, made it as far as New Jersey, we heard, before someone stole his pack while he was off in the brush relieving himself. Without a pack or the funds to buy a new one, Byron was forced to end his hike. One day in Shenandoah National Park in Virginia we discovered a note pinned to a wooden park service sign at a road crossing. The note, addressed to a hiker behind us whom we didn't know, read:

Dear ———,
Your father has died of a heart attack. Call your sister for details. Please return home immediately.

There were the psychological factors—boredom, loneliness—which also reduced our ranks. But more than anything else, it was poor planning and conditioning and

overloaded packs that led to failure. Springer Mountain served as a magnet for legions of uninitiated hikers who bumbled into the woods and who, often just as quickly, bumbled back out. Incredibly, there were people who had quit their jobs and drained their bank accounts to hike the trail without ever having read about it or explored any of its miles. They based their expectations on their own romantic visions or secondhand information gleaned from friends and acquaintances.

Though I never consciously derived pleasure from the misfortunes of others, I confess that I did find solace in their often ridiculous, sometimes humorous, misadventures. During my most difficult days, in fact, no matter how unfit I felt for life on the trail, I found that reflecting on some of the unforgivable gaffes of my colleagues could leave me feeling like Kit Carson.

We met many of them face to face on the trail, and we read the accounts of others in shelter registers. More often, we learned about their desperate straits by the gear they had left behind. All through Georgia, for instance, shelters were cluttered with heaps of discarded items: axes, shovels, survival knives, shoes, boots, socks, shirts, pants, underwear, bras, rain ponchos, canned goods, cook pots, gallon cans of white gas, plant books, first-aid books, Bibles (full-sized leather-bound editions), books of poetry, novels, bird books, insect books, cookbooks.

Often the items were accompanied by notes that, with some variation, expressed this sentiment:

> I am miserable. My pack is too heavy. My feet hurt. I've decided to cut weight by leaving behind this garden spade, cast-iron skillet, twelve-inch survival knife, and two-pound tin of Dinty Moore beef stew. I have not had the opportunity to use them but hope they'll be of service to someone. Heading north. Hoping things improve.

A hardliner would call such disposal of goods littering. Most of the items became permanent fixtures in the shelters. After all, what reasonable hiker seeks to *increase* his load once he's entered the woods? But then who condemned

the pioneers who lightened their loads by heaving their heirlooms and other expendable items overboard in hopes of successfully crossing the prairies?

We learned that there were other means of lightening one's load. One hiker Dan and I encountered less than one mile below Springer had kindled a trailside fire, which he stoked with heavy volumes on first aid, edible wild plants, birds, and bugs. We stood by watching him feed the flames. Like a backcountry merchant, he had set out his store of canned goods in orderly stacks, inviting passersby to take whatever they wanted. As if he hadn't suffered enough already under the weight of his pack, he tore the seat out of his trousers when he squatted to extract more extraneous items from his pack.

Then there were the two women I met as I neared the summit of Springer on a later trip. It was raining, and as I glanced ahead, I spotted the two of them shuffling along as if their legs were bound. In a sense they were. It seems that one of the women, a seamstress, had crafted "front" packs to supplement the storage capacity of their fully loaded backpacks. The packs, which fastened around the waist, had never been fieldtested, and after a few miles on the trail they had slipped down, settling around the women's upper thighs and reducing their strides to a series of baby steps.

But the women had other problems, too. Once in camp, I watched as each woman withdrew from her pack an entire spice rack, crafted from twelve-inch strips of Styrofoam and equipped with twelve or fifteen plastic bottles. Then came the stoves: propane torches and foot-tall iron tripods borrowed from a chemistry lab where one of the women worked. These were not modest propane burners, but heavy foot-long tanks with brass nozzles. The stoves were designed not to heat metal pots but to *melt* them. The cooking outfits also included a metal support for the torches, which directed the blue blade of flame through the ring of the beaker stand and onto the base of the cook pot. After twenty miles of abject misery, the women veered off the trail at the first crossroads, which led into Suches, Georgia.

Once in town, they dumped the front packs and torches before buying more suitable gear and continuing on.

Then there were the two fellows from Atlanta who had set out under the mistaken assumption that once on the trail there was no means for egress or acquiring supplies. Their determination—and knees—gave out after twenty miles, and they too bailed out in Suches.

There was the sweet, naive woman from New York. Plump and in her early twenties, she had set out on the trail by her parents' choosing, not by her own. Her parents had hoped to help their daughter boost her self-confidence and drop a few pounds in the process, and they decided that a 2,100-mile hike along the Appalachian Trail might do the trick. So they bought her a pack, a pair of boots, and a bus ticket to Georgia.

Her first days on the trail were torturous, and it was remarkable that she made it as far as she did. Had it not been for Byron, who found her blubbering in the weeds on the trail in the Smokies, she might still be stranded there. Byron hefted her pack, along with his own, and led her, sobbing, to the next shelter. Once there, Byron assumed the role of big brother and urged her to bail out. She heeded his advice, sort of.

Over the next several weeks, she evolved from an Appalachian Trail hiker to an Appalachian Trail groupie. Frequently, we arrived in trail towns—through most of Georgia, North Carolina, Tennessee, and even into Virginia—only to find the woman waiting for us there. She had given up hiking, but not hitchhiking, and as we would pick up the trail out of town, she would hang her thumb for a lift into the next stop. Bryon repeatedly urged her to go home, fearing that some deranged motorist might take advantage of her, and he went so far as to buy her a bus ticket home, but she persisted. Eventually, she became the basis for a series of bets among hikers: would she or wouldn't she be waiting for us in the next town?

After Byron had purchased the bus ticket and extracted a promise from her that she would use it, he was so confident that he bet a group of us a milk shake each that when we

arrived in Damascus, Virginia, she would be gone. When we entered town, we spotted her waving from a hotel and hoofed it directly to the local Dairy Queen to collect on our bet.

Where there are sheep, there are also wolves, and on the trail, where there are such poorly adapted hikers as the young woman from New York, there are hucksters out to take unfair advantage of them. The trail's reigning flimflam artist was a man known variously as Mack, Mountain Man Mack, and Ranger Mack. A portly, indigent man in his early twenties who hailed from some backwoods settlement, Mack had developed an ingenious scam.

Clad in a forest-service green uniform and wearing a pack, Mack would arrive on the trail in late April as the fresh corps of thru-hikers set out from Springer. He presented himself as an agent of the national forest service, and he carried a bogus badge and a small side arm. He explained that his mission was to serve as guide to hikers on the Appalachian Trail. Mack boasted that he had hiked the trail end to end, that he knew virtually every edible plant, and that he could steer a hiker safely through even the most formidable disasters. Having won the hikers' confidence, he would then amble along with them, gauging their gullibility as he inventoried their stores of cash and food.

To hikers ill-suited for the rigors of life on the trail and needing guidance, Mack was a godsend, or so he seemed. In exchange for a few dollars a day and a share of their food, he would shepherd them through the woods. Slowly. He stolidly refused to walk in the rain, and even on sunny days he seldom covered more than five or six miles.

Dan and I met Mack at Rocky Knob Shelter in Georgia the day after a tornado had ripped through the woods a few miles from our camp in Tesnatee Gap. Peering inside the shelter, we spotted Mack with four other hikers. Among them were the woman from New York and a bizarre, bearded man from Maine who seemed to be daft. Both

posed perfect targets for Mack. They, along with the other two, had signed on with the shyster, who now sat fat and happy in the shelter eating their food. Why they never became suspicious of him or his alleged background I can't imagine. If he were an official of the forest service, why did he require food? If he refused to walk in the rain, how had he completed the trail? And if he had completed the trail and continued to spend his days hiking, why was he so fat?

We learned later that one morning near the edge of the Smokies, the hikers had awakened to find themselves alone in the shelter. Having bilked them out of money and food, Mack had vanished. It seems he had an aversion to the Smokies, and later in Hot Springs we would learn why.

A few days after we arrived in Hot Springs, Elmer, the owner of the Inn, explained that Mack, who lived off the kindness—or ignorance—of hapless hikers, was as much a part of spring in the southern Appalachians as the budding flowers. Years earlier he had been arrested for impersonating a government law enforcement official and for carrying a concealed weapon without a permit. Even now, Elmer explained, there was a warrant out for his arrest. It seems that while Mack felt comfortable working his scheme along the little-traveled trails of the national forests, he feared the trails of the national parks, which were populated with armed, *bona fide* rangers.

Elmer was right. Later, while on an early spring hike with a friend near Hot Springs in 1986, I arrived at Deer Park Mountain Shelter four miles south of town. We sat eating lunch when a shirtless hiker approached from the south, his gut flopping over the hip belt to his pack. He wore stereo headphones connected to a Walkman.

"Been damned hungry the past few days," he said, scratching his protruding belly after shedding his pack. "I hain't had a decent meal for the last four days, and I'm damned near starvin'." He flashed us a toothless grin as he eyed the bag of trail mix that lay on my lap. I offered him a handful, and when I did he snatched up the entire bag. Then his glance moved to the plastic bottle of whiskey beside me.

"That wouldn't be sippin' whiskey, would it?" he asked.

Though irked by his shameless mooching, I handed him the bottle. Then he spotted the tin of snuff in my shirt pocket. "And might I trouble you for a dip?" he continued. "Hain't had a dip for nigh on a week." Again, I obliged.

"God, I'm hungry," he continued.

"You know there's food in town," I suggested. "The Inn has some of the best meals on the whole trail."

"I hain't sure I can make it that far, I'm so darned weak, and my stomach's so empty it hurts," he continued, patting his healthy roll of flab. "And I hain't got no money. A couple guys robbed me back at the last shelter."

It had been years since I had last seen Mack, and though I didn't immediately recognize the face, his *modus operandi* was unmistakable. I decided to confront him.

"Your name wouldn't be Mack by any chance?" I asked.

An alarmed look spread over his face.

"Well, ah, some people call me that."

"Mountain Man Mack?"

"Well, yeah."

"Ranger Mack?"

"Uh-huh."

I started laughing. In seven years the trail hadn't changed one bit. The spring was just as beautiful—and Mack just as corrupt—as ever. The reason he was so reluctant to push on into Hot Springs, I surmised, was that he was known there by too many people, people who were wise to his game and might have turned him in to the authorities. He realized he would fare better, and eat better, if he stuck to the trail and plied hikers for food.

"Well, I think it's time to be moseying. Mack, I hope you get some grub," I said as I piled my gearack into my pack, stood, and climbed into the straps. My friend, who threw me a baffled glance, did the same. As we left the shelter, Mack tried one last ploy to separate me from my cash: "Hey, I'll sell you this Walkman for ten dollars." I ignored the offer and, still laughing, kept on walking. Over the few miles to our camp, I explained to my friend that he had met one of the trail's most notorious con men.

Initially, I viewed Mack—and others like him—as a

scourge of the trail, but in time I've come to regard him in a kinder light. In many ways he was the same as the mice, chipmunks, raccoons, skunks, feral dogs, and other opportunistic critters who lingered around the shelters and grew fat on our mistakes. But he was different from his four-legged counterparts in one regard: once I was on to his tricks, he seemed a lot less clever.

CHAPTER · EIGHT

Gear

I never imagined that existence could be so simple, so uncluttered, so Spartan, so free of baggage, so sublimely gratifying. I have reduced the weight of my pack to thirty-five pounds, and yet I can't think of a single thing I really need that I can't find either within myself or within my pack. The pack contains all essentials, as well as a few luxury items: a book, a Frisbee, a quarter-pint of whiskey, and a poem I photocopied at a library a few miles back. Today as I walked, I memorized the poem, "She Walks in Beauty" by Lord Byron, and tonight I will use the paper to kindle a fire and thereby reduce my weight by another ounce.

—September 9, 1979, Poplar Ridge Lean-to, Maine

I live with my wife and two daughters in a century-old, two-story farmhouse in Tennessee. Our collective possessions occupy seven indoor rooms, a porch, and an outdoor shed. Together, they sprawl, they clutter, they choke. I open closets and confront boxes whose contents remain a complete mystery. I open drawers, searching for pencils or scissors, and sift through a chaos of knickknacks. In the work shed I forage for tools through a tangle of gadgets whose functions I have long ago forgotten.

Returning from the shed, I spot my former dwelling hanging on a nail in the enclosed porch. A green nylon frame backpack with a capacity of 2,500 cubic inches. It features one large main compartment, a front pouch, and four side pouches. The largest pouch—in the front—measures nine inches across, seven inches from top to bottom, and two inches deep. Below the pack bag is a vacant section of frame for my sleeping bag.

Eleven years ago, that pack was more than ample to contain the sum total of my worldly possessions—thirty-five to forty-five pounds worth. It included everything—absolutely everything—I really needed:

Two cotton T-shirts, two cotton bandanas, one pair of nylon running shorts, a pair of cotton army fatigue trousers, one wool shirt, a pair of wool gloves, a coated-nylon rain jacket, two pairs of wool socks, two pairs of thin liner socks, one pair of lug-soled boots for the trail and a pair of running shoes for camp, a stove and one-liter fuel bottle, a two-quart cook pot, a nylon foodbag, one plastic film canister filled with salt and another filled with pepper, a steel drinking cup, one metal spoon with bent handle, two one-liter plastic water bottles, a six-ounce plastic bottle for distilled spirits, one bottle of water-purification tablets, a toothbrush and small tube of toothpaste, a three-ounce bottle of biodegradable soap, a fifty-foot length of parachute cord for hanging food, a synthetic-fill sleeping bag rated to thirty-five degrees, a closed-cell foam sleeping mat, a first-aid kit, a trail guidebook, a paperback book, a spiral-bound notebook in which I recorded my journal, a billed cap, insect repellent, a Swiss Army knife, a butane lighter, and a partial roll of toilet paper.

How would I begin, I wonder, to prioritize what I own today and select thirty-five pounds from all this tonnage, thirty-five pounds that would answer my needs and leave me feeling as secure and well outfitted as I felt in 1979? I suspect I couldn't. Even if I were to fill my pack with the same items, I realize I could not resurrect the sense of self-sufficiency. Or the freedom that came from knowing that

wherever I found myself at noonday or nightfall, my house and its goods rested beside me.

No. The years away from the trail have softened me, made me reliant on creature comforts. Certainly, I can and do release my hold on them when I return to the trail for a few days or even a week, but for five months? I would feel naked, vulnerable. I would, in spite of myself, imagine a host of dire what-if contingencies requiring the addition of first one item, then another and another, until my pack strained at its seams and refused to accommodate any more.

At one time my pack was an extension of myself. It accompanied me everywhere I went. When I carried it, it rode on my back as naturally as a flesh-and-bone appendage. And even after I took it off, my hands probed its pockets and hidden folds as precisely as I might have reached to scratch an unseen itch. I could locate any item, no matter how small or deeply buried, as quickly and surely as I might have raised a finger to touch my nose or flick an insect from my ear. I was like a snail or turtle whose den is a fixed companion along all the miles of its life.

Someone on the trail once shared with me a simple principle for reducing my pack to the bare essentials. "If you don't use an item at least once a day," he said, "get rid of it."

It was sound advice. With the exception of the items in my first-aid kit, some of which, thankfully, I never used, I abided by that principle. In the interest of economy, like most hikers I devised methods for extending the utility of the items I did carry.

My sleeping bag, for instance, fulfilled its primary task of insulating my body from the elements. It served almost as efficiently as a refrigerator. A quart of ice cream nestled at the core of a sleeping bag in its stuff sack would survive summertime heat and provide a refreshing dessert hours and miles out of town. My closed-cell foam pad served equally well as a beer or soda cooler or as a comfortable sleeping mat. I could roll three chilled cans tightly in the eight-foot-long pad, stopper the ends with wool socks, and enjoy a cold beer with dinner six or eight hours later. And

when laid against a tree trunk, the pad served as a chaise longue for afternoon naps.

The plumber's candles I carried were effective fire starters, and when set on an overturned drinking cup, they provided ample light for reading or writing after dark. The flexible round screen—made from heavy-gauge aluminum foil—that circled my stove and shielded it from the wind, doubled as a lantern reflector. If I folded it in half, bent it into an arc, and then placed it behind a candle, it would illuminate an entire shelter. The windscreen also served as a spout if laid amid the rocks in a slow-moving spring that trickled down a hillside.

The fifty feet of nylon parachute cord I carried served several functions. Evenings, I tied a stone to one end, hurled it over a sturdy branch, secured the end to our nylon food bags, and hoisted it out of reach of raccoons and bears. The line served equally well as a clothesline, and I found that if I doubled the cord and twisted it before securing it to two trees, I could hang my socks, bandana, shirt, and shorts by threading the fabric between the twisted filaments. Even the stiffest breeze could not pluck them free. And once, when my pack bag tore from one of its grommets, I used the cord to secure the bag to the frame.

The needle and packet of dental floss I carried in my first-aid kit provided sturdy, waxed-nylon thread for repairing packs, clothes, and boots. My metal drinking cup held my evening tea, but it also served as a bowl for my morning oatmeal and a scoop for drawing water from pools too shallow to accept a water bottle or cook pot. My Frisbee provided postdinner diversion and served as a fine plate.

Once filled, my two-and-a-half-gallon waterbag, a plastic pouch housed in a purple nylon sack and outfitted with a rubber nozzle, contained ample water for evening meals and drinks. Once emptied of water and inflated with air, it made a comfortable pillow.

My two one-liter water bottles doubled as rehydrating containers, and a handful of dried beans or lentils dropped into a bottle of water in the morning would be swollen and ready to cook by the time I arrived in camp in the afternoon.

The rain fly I carried provided emergency shelter and doubled as a groundsheet, protecting my sleeping bag from damp earth. The coated nylon anorak, a light jacket I carried, repelled rain, and in cool weather I layered it over my wool shirt to retain body heat.

The three-and-one-half-ounce tuna tins I carried as my primary source of protein served, when empty, to thwart the critters who attempted to pillage our food bags at night. I baked the empty tin in the fire to remove the odor and then poked a hole in the can's bottom with my knife. Then I tied a knot halfway down the line from my foodbag and threaded the cord through the hole before I hung the bag. The upside-down can, situated midway on the hanging line, presented an impasse for the craftiest of mice.

Even my wool gloves served a dual purpose. They warmed my hands on chill, wet days, and they acted as hot pads for plucking boiling pots from the coals. Hikers caught by cold temperatures without gloves, found that wool socks doubled as warm mittens.

If the contents of our packs couldn't answer our needs, we turned to the forest for aid. Our ingenuity, combined with the raw resources of the wilderness, resolved most problems.

Stiff rhododendron leaves or short sticks split in half and cleaned of their center core provided spouts when inserted into slow-trickling springs. When downed deadwood was drenched by rains, we could always find dry kindling by shaking the trunks of standing dead trees. The trunks telegraphed and amplified the swaying motion to the tops of the trees, which whipped furiously and cracked, releasing a hail of dead branches. Because of their vertical orientation, those top branches escaped the brunt of drenching rains and dried quickly in the air circulating through the treetops.

When our cook pots became crusted with baked-on food, we used nature's scouring pad, a handful of sand and pebbles from a streambed. A cook pot laid in a stream and anchored with a stone on its lid would cool instant pudding, and forked sticks driven into the ground near the fire and spanned with a wooden crossbar would provide a perfect drying rack for wet socks and clothing. We used the same

spits for dangling pots over the flames. Flat rocks served as cutting boards for chopping vegetables and as dining tables.

If we weren't turning to the wilderness for solutions, we turned to it for amusement. Through the five months I spent on the trail, I do not recall ever once being bored for want of something to occupy my time in camp. There was always something to do or see.

Just before we reached the Lake Country in Maine, for instance, I had my parents send me my telescoping fishing rod, and I spent evenings angling for supplemental protein and for fun. The rod provided dinner for a half-dozen hikers when we reached Antlers Camp, an abandoned fishing camp on the shores of a pristine backwoods lake fifty miles south of Mount Katahdin. Situated on a rocky peninsula, the camp contained a series of old log cabins, the main cabin featuring a wood-burning stove and an iron skillet; it was perfect for a fish-fry. After arriving in the early afternoon, I pulled on my wool shirt, grabbed my fishing rod, and followed the curve of the shoreline three-quarters of a mile from camp. Perched on a rock and surrounded by flaming sugar maples and golden birches, I reeled in a dozen lake trout. Two hours later, when I arrived back in camp, I discovered that Dan, Paul, and two other two hikers who shared our camp had spent the afternoon harvesting freshwater clams from the rocky shore.

That evening Dan played chef, frying our fillets and mussels in butter, and we took our evening meal on the shoreline in front of a fire. As we ate, we watched the red sash of sunset ripple on the wind-buffeted surface of the lake.

Then there was stargazing, a diversion I could never get enough of. There were always mysterious specks—satellites, probably—floating in the seas of the heavens, which invariably led to discussion regarding life on other planets or extraterrestrials. And meteors. We would lie on our backs in open fields under the canopy of a real-life planetarium and fix on the star-flecked heavens. Although we

had witnessed dozens of meteor showers, we could never contain the *ooohs* and *ahhs* that escaped as the bright orbs arced across black skies spilling trails of golden glitter.

Bird watching became another favorite pastime. I once sat at the base of a hardwood tree in Maine watching a pileated woodpecker probe the bark for grubs directly above me while his manic excavation showered me with wood chips.

And night hikes. As fearful as I had been in my first days in Georgia of the dark woods and mysterious night sounds, I later found in the dark woods a sanctuary where I could sit alone and think in the company of the animals. I often strayed away from camp, following the beam of my flashlight until I found a comfortable roost on a rock or fallen log. Then I switched off the flashlight and instantly was enveloped in the womb of darkness. Without my sense of sight, my hearing and touch became heightened, and I could follow the progress of large and small creatures as they moved around and past me. Chipmunks, skunks, mice, and squirrels scurried, while deer cracked and thudded. As deer approached, I could hear the branches snap and feel the ground vibrating under the heavy impact of their hooves.

But the night woods weren't always serene. One night in Connecticut I left camp and found a seat in a grove of hemlock along the Housitanic River. It was perfectly still when a hoot owl perched in the tree behind me suddenly unleashed its eerie call. From a distance of twenty feet, it boomed as if through an amplified speaker. Spooked, I started and jumped to my feet. Equally startled, the owl took flight, and I heard its wing tips slap the hemlock branches as it retreated.

Streams were favorite spots for evening reveries. They titillated the ears and the eyes. If we listened, we could hear the lapping water trace the entire musical scale in a random melody of ethereal notes and chords, and if we probed the water with our flashlight beams, we could watch scads of bizarre performers—nymphs, water spiders, crayfish, minnows—as they ducked and darted, scampered and scuttled in and out of the spotlight.

There were times, too, when we used the streams as aquatic sports arenas. In mid-May, for instance, Dan and I camped near a stream in Devils Creek Watershed in Tennessee, where we staged the Devils Creek Regatta. We used our pocket knife to carve small boats from dead wood. Rocks wedged into the boats' undersides provided ballast, and we even went so far as to gouge holes for masts. We established a starting line at the head of a thirty-yard stretch of flat water; a chute where the water narrowed to a falls marked the finish line. For two hours, until darkness made it impossible to follow the course of the boats, we ran the river, and before it was over, each of us skippered a fleet of six or eight boats, some built for speed, some built for stability, and others built for the sheer beauty of their intricate hulls.

There were other games, too. In Maine, after we had resupplied in Caratunk, we left town and covered thirteen miles before deciding to hole up in an abandoned barn near a road crossing. After we sat idle for half an hour, Nick discovered a length of wire, which he soon wound into four rings. We drove sharpened stakes into the ground, twenty yards apart, and engaged in game after game of Appalachian Trail horseshoes.

My favorite pastime, though, was reading. Along the trail, I read a dozen books, mainly on nature or the environment. Among them were Thoreau's *Walden*, Annie Dillard's *Pilgrim at Tinker Creek*, Whitman's *Leaves of Grass*.

I had read Whitman and Thoreau in high school, but in the classroom of the Appalachian wilderness, their writing came to life. I could peer up from any page and find living examples of the words.

I recall reading a passage from *Walden* while I was camped in the Lake Country of Maine less than one hundred miles from Katahdin. We were literally following in Thoreau's footsteps, he having visited the area in 1846. Though we explored those mountains 133 years later, the words were written about me, about us, about our carefree existence, and about anyone who seeks communion with the wilderness:

Remember thy creator in the days of thy youth. Rise free from care before the dawn, and seek adventures. Let the noon find thee by other lakes, and the night overtake thee everywhere at home. There are no larger fields than these, no worthier games than here may be played. Grow wild according to thy nature, like these sedges and brakes. . . . Let the thunder rumble; what if it threaten ruin to farmers' crops? That is not its errand to thee. Take shelter under the cloud, while they flee to carts and sheds. Let not to get a living be thy trade, but thy sport. Enjoy the land, but own it not. Through want of enterprise and faith men are where they are, buying and selling, and spending their lives like serfs.

Stopping Along the Way

Last night in Port Clinton, Pennsylvania, Dan and I learned once again that the magic of comradeship does not end at the trailhead but often extends into the small towns along the route. We spent the evening at the Port Clinton Hotel bar in the small blue-collar town with Chuck the snake handler, the boom-pa lady, and a handful of other colorful personalities, and we departed town this morning with a new page of names in our address books.

Those hikers who blast in and out of town, stopping only long enough to fill their stomachs and their foodbags, are missing a vital part of the trail experience. But even though I've been on the trail for months and have on many occasions been greeted with warmth and acceptance by total strangers, I still occasionally struggle with feelings of mistrust. I'm left wondering why someone would open himself to me when all he stands to gain in return is my own trust and acceptance. Such feelings, I suspect, result from lessons we're taught from the time we're very young. I wonder if they'll survive beyond completion of my hike.

—July 21, 1979, Allentown Hiking Club Shelter, Pennsylvania

April 24 introduced me to new extremes of experience. The previous night we had weathered a fierce thunderstorm that left the woods strewn with splintered branches and uprooted trees. The following day wasn't much better. After leaving camp, we trudged through cold rain and ankle-deep muck, and over the long afternoon my thoughts turned again and again to the comforts of town.

By early evening, when we finally slipped down an embankment and landed on paved Georgia Highway 75, we faced a decision: we could continue up the trail through more muck and cold rain, or we could follow the road to more inviting surroundings. Though we had not planned a town stop for another few days, we consulted our maps, hung our thumbs, and set out for Helen, Georgia, a tourist resort of alpine chalets and quaint restaurants nine miles to the south.

After scoring a ride from a sympathetic local in a big car, Dan and I, along with four other sodden hikers, were soon ensconced in a cut-rate motel room—twenty-six dollars a night for the bunch of us—and drawing lots for the shower. En route to the motel, we had cajoled our driver into stopping at a local package store and a pizza joint before he deposited us at the motel office.

Six showers and an hour later, the room lay in shambles. Fetid shirts, shorts, boots, and socks lay in dank, aromatic piles in corners and on counter tops. Pack covers and rain parkas dripped from curtain rods. Pizza boxes and empty beer bottles cluttered bedside tables. In the bathroom, dirt-smudged towels steeped in standing water, and a dark water stain crept along the all-weather carpet from the bathroom into the bedroom. The soil we had rinsed from our bodies formed a miniature delta at the drain in the bathtub.

But none of us seemed to notice the clutter, or if we did we didn't much care. We were too busy indulging our wanton appetites. It wasn't until we switched on the television that it occurred to us that our few days on the trail had already wrought some changes.

We watched a special program about the life of American novelist Thomas Wolfe. The story of Wolfe, a true icon-

oclast, appealed to our own sense of freewheeling independence. Then a commercial came on the screen. It was an
unremarkable advertisement—for corn chips or glass
cleaner or hair spray—but it had an unusual effect. We
laughed. We roared. We howled. We cried. Not so much at
the product itself but at the realization that the world of
fresh-smelling houses, clean-shaven faces, sporty sedans,
dutiful housewives, and industrious husbands no longer
connected with ours. The commercial clearly had been directed at someone else.

The next morning we made a quick stop at a local grocery
store, hitchhiked back to the trailhead, and again picked up
the white blazes. Even though we faced another day of rain
and muck, those things seemed much less dismal. Our
twelve hours in town had restored us, but the town stop had
done more than that. It had provided evidence that by following the trail we had strayed into a strange new realm
where the attractions of civilization, though still appealing,
had assumed a new role, and I realized that with months
remaining ahead of us, this shift in attitude was only the
beginning.

Helen, Georgia, was our first town stop,
and over the next several months we visited dozens of vil-
lages, cities, back-road hamlets, and crossroads. As it
turned out, those outposts of civilization were in some
ways as vital to the trail experience as the mountains themselves.

The towns allowed us to phone friends and relatives to
catch up on important news from home. News from home
that did not reach us via the phone lines usually awaited
our arrival at the local post offices, where postal clerks pro-
cessed and held scores of boxes—boxes of supplies, care
packages, and letters—addressed to us in care of general delivery.

Towns afforded us breaks from the routine of big-mile
days, and we celebrated the long, steep descents that led us
into those settlements just as working men and women

might have welcomed the five-o'clock whistle that marked the onset of a holiday.

Towns also exposed us to the distinctive people and cultures of the various regions of the eastern United States. Along the way, we encountered open, slow-talking Southerners; circumspect residents of the populous mid-Atlantic states; and wry, taciturn New Englanders. Each region and town provided its own brand of succor.

Most important, towns provided needed supplies. Without them we would have been forced either to carry five months' worth of food on our backs or to subsist on roots and berries. The first option, I suspect, would have left us crippled; the second might have left us dead, owing to our familiarity with only a few edible plants.

Food. Though we cursed it for all the weight a five- or seven-day supply added to the pack on the stiff ascents out of town, we also celebrated it when, during the first days along a new section, the foodbag promised both plenty and variety.

Then, toward the end of that same stretch, when our reserves ran low and we subsisted on the dregs of the food sack, we became obsessed by food, talked about it incessantly, craved it, longed for it. Mountains of ice cream, bags of cookies, slabs of red meat, bowls of crisp greens, and boxes of pastries, cakes, and pies—these were the stuff of hikers' dreams during the last few days and nights before a resupply stop.

Consider that most long-distance hikers eat and metabolize as many as six thousand calories a day. After the first couple of weeks on the trail, when exertion tends to suppress a hiker's appetite, most end-to-enders succumb to an incurable case of "hiker's disease," an affliction characterized by an appetite that simply cannot be satisfied.

I could not count the number of times I confronted stunned expressions on onlookers' faces as they observed my colleagues and me wandering along the aisles of a food market dazed and bewitched by the abundance while trying to decide what to consume first, second, third. . . . We were, in effect, prisoners of want suddenly freed in a climate-

controlled environment of excess, and in weaker moments my companions and I were likely to consume half-gallons of ice cream, pound bags of cookies, and quarts of fruit juice before returning to the store for the second course.

Our binge eating wasn't limited to grocery stores. In Elk Park, North Carolina, for instance, three other hikers and I arrived at a restaurant soon after it opened on a Sunday afternoon, paid our three dollars each, and consumed the entire contents of a salad bar before the owner politely but firmly invited us to move on.

In a northern Virginia town, I spent five hours at an all-you-can-eat restaurant with another hiker, downing dozens of plates of steamed shrimp. We finally left the establishment more to ease the finger cramps that resulted from peeling so much shellfish than because we had eaten our fill.

The challenge we faced as caloric consumers, as I liked to describe it, was to "toe the fine line between bliss and nausea." Regrettably, I crossed that line on occasion and suffered the consequences. On one such night in Gorham, New Hampshire, after first visiting the local McDonald's, I ate five heaping bowls of a vegetable stew we had prepared in the kitchen of the Congregational church where we were permitted to stay. When I had choked down the last spoonful, I staggered out onto the church lawn, unbuttoned my pants to relieve some of the pressure on my bloated abdomen, and lay in the grass, moaning like a pregnant mare in the throes of labor. As I did, I prayed for the nausea to pass and vowed never to eat that much again. I kept my resolution only until we arrived in the next town.

Once we had purchased our supplies at a market, it was customary for us to sit on the store's stoop, alternately loading supplies into our packs and wedging morsels into our mouths. The process of taking products from the shelves and preparing them for the backcountry became known as "throwing away Madison Avenue." Essentially, the process involved stripping off the boxes, wrap-

pers, bags, and canisters, which catered more to the whims of marketing executives than to the needs of backcountry travelers. Once we had removed the items from their packages, we deposited them in plastic bags. The bags were durable as well as flexible, and they allowed us to take full advantage of every available square inch of pack space. Eliminating Madison Avenue also spared us several pounds of useless heft.

Though at times it seemed that we hikers took more than we gave in each of those towns, filling our stomachs and food bags before moving on, I like to think that an equitable exchange took place when hikers visited civilization. Because many of the trail towns lay far off the main roads, townsfolk often embraced us as ambassadors of good will and seemed never to tire of our tales of adventure from the surrounding woods.

Local merchants welcomed our business, and they stocked their shelves with dietary staples—macaroni-and-cheese, pasta noodles, rice, peanut butter, English muffins, lentils, summer sausage, instant oatmeal, sardines, granola bars, honey—that were perfectly suited to our transient needs. Innkeepers often allowed us to pile as many as ten hikers into a room designed to accommodate two, and they often adjusted their rates to ease the jolt to our meager budgets.

Most townsfolk were accustomed to having legions of straggly foot travelers loose in their streets, and they afforded us all the courtesy of temporary residents. We brought curious stares from tourists unfamiliar with the trail, and they often seemed puzzled and fascinated by our peculiar avocation. Their questions seldom varied: Where do you sleep? What do you do when it rains? What do you eat? Seen any snakes? Seen any bears? Don't your feet hurt? Where did you start? Where are you headin'? Why are you doing this? Our responses soon became as pat and predictable as the questions themselves, but I, for one, enjoyed sharing my experiences with anyone interested enough to listen.

Along our journey, we logged a series of fond memories of

our stopovers, some because of novelty, others because of kindness shown us. A few were because of the rich relationships we enjoyed with our hosts.

At Wesser, North Carolina, a settlement set on the banks of the Nantahala River 137 miles north of Springer, we sat for hours in the rustic health-food restaurant eating fresh-baked herb bread and peering through picture windows at kayakers navigating the rapids below. In Damascus, Virginia, known as the friendliest town on the trail, we lodged in a two-story hostel dubbed The Place, which was owned and operated by the Methodist church. We spent the evening swapping tales with our brothers and sisters on two wheels—transcontinental cyclists—who had embarked on the Centennial Route that passed through town and continued on to the West Coast.

In Charlottesville, Virginia, Dan and I crashed in a dilapidated fraternity house with walls and doors pocked with fist- and head-sized holes, and we spent the evening in a local pub listening to live country music.

In Duncannon, Pennsylvania, on the Susquehanna River, we shared the basement of the city firehouse with a foursome of teachers who worked with mentally disabled children.

Dan and I arrived in Port Clinton, Pennsylvania, on a Saturday afternoon and found our way to a covered pavilion that the city had designated as an overnight area for hikers. By dusk, after cranking a hand pump and washing the grit from my face, arms, and legs, I wandered through the streets of the working-class town. The place looked drab and depressed, and had it not been for the experiences that awaited me, I would have forever viewed Port Clinton as a decaying, lifeless burg on the verge of economic ruin.

On the way back to the pavilion, I strayed into the lounge at the Port Clinton Hotel and took a seat at the bar. Once inside, I suspected I had strayed into another establishment of the Erwin, Tennessee, ilk. The working-class locals perched on bar stools studied me closely, but none acknowledged me directly. I ordered a beer, which cost me twenty-five cents, and as I sipped it, I noticed that the bartender had

deposited a handful of small plastic tokens in front of me. I finished the beer and ordered another, but when I tried to pay for it, the bartender motioned toward the tokens. "Son, the rest of your beers have already been paid for."

These stone-faced locals, it seems, were not as sour as they looked. Once I realized that I sat surrounded by bene-factors, I hefted my mug and toasted them. Whatever doubts I had had about the character of those folks vanished with my next draught, and in minutes I sat surrounded by local men and women, all hungry for news from the trail.

After a half-hour of chatter about the trail, a woman in her mid-thirties entered the room carrying a curious con-traption that resembled a pogo stick adorned with cymbals, bells, a tambourine, a snare drum, and a squeeze horn. She greeted me, walked over to the juke box, and dropped a nickel into the slot. Soon Bobby Vinton's voice crooned the "Beer Barrel Polka" through the speakers. She then began lurching around the dance floor, bouncing the contraption, which unleashed a cacophonous din of clangs and crashes in time with the music. After a brief demonstration, she handed the device to me.

"This is called a 'boom-pa,'" she said. "And it's custom-ary for the guest of honor to play it on the first song."

I was both honored and mortified. By now the bar had attracted a standing-room-only crowd, and all eyes were turned on me. Again, she selected the Bobby Vinton tune on the juke box, and I tentatively stepped to the center of the dance floor and, laughing, began pounding and clanging with as much enthusiasm as I could muster. The bar's pa-trons soon encircled me, raising their beer mugs and cheer-ing me on. When the tune ended, I returned to my seat to a round of applause. I had been duly initiated.

The boom-pa's clamorous din and the crowd noise had apparently carried several city blocks to the pavilion and reached Dan's ears. Drawn by his curiosity, he followed the sound to the bar, and when he passed through the door, I announced to my newfound friends that it would only be fitting to afford Dan the same honor they had extended to me. Soon the polka tune roared through the speakers, and I

sat back and laughed as Dan plied the boom-pa and received the same frenzied response.

Normally cool and composed, Dan sat with his mouth agape for some minutes after his boom-pa debut, and I felt obliged to explain our good fortune. As I explained the bargain beers, at twenty-five cents a draught, and the juke box, where a quarter bought five plays, he, too, began to amass the small tokens. Before long, both of us were gloriously drunk, sitting at the bar and hobnobbing with the other patrons as intimately as if we had shared the same parentage. Among them was a toothless fellow named Chuck, a self-described snake charmer who claimed to keep rattlers in his car as insurance against thieves. Though Dan and I were accustomed to providing tales of wild adventure, we yielded to a more masterful storyteller and passed the evening hours listening to Chuck relate fascinating—though unlikely—Indian legends, mountain ghost tales, and sorcery yarns.

When Dan and I departed Port Clinton the next morning, the town appeared much more vibrant and alive than it had when we arrived.

Several weeks later, we again encountered good fortune near Unionville, New York, at the lakeside home of Gary, a new age minister, and his wife and two sons. Dan and I— along with Paul, who had since joined our group—had met Gary at a road crossing a week south of Unionville when he stopped to give us a lift to the local grocery store. Back at the trailhead, he gave us his phone number and invited us to call him when we reached Unionville.

A few days later, we phoned him from the trailhead, piled into the back of his car, and soon arrived at his house. That evening, after we had enjoyed a lavish gourmet feast on the lakeside deck, Gary, an accomplished musician, uncorked a bottle of wine, lighted a candelabra, and serenaded us with beautiful classical music on his baby grand piano. It was the first music we had heard for weeks, and Paul and Dan, both musicians themselves, sat rapt through Gary's performance.

The next day we accompanied Gary and his wife to a for-

mal lawn party. The host and his family occupied a massive country estate with manicured grounds and a private tennis court. A live rock band performed in a covered gazebo. Most of the few dozen guests sported designer-label togs. Dressed in our cutoff fatigue pants, rag wool socks, and tattered shirts, we looked like a trio of vagabonds who had strayed away from the local mission, but we soon discovered that our shabby dress, and our status as Appalachian Trail thru-hikers, only enhanced our romantic mystique among the hippie-turned-yuppie partygoers.

Paul and I borrowed a couple of rackets and spent the afternoon on the tennis courts. Between sets we raided the twenty-foot banquet table heaped with enough food to pitch a famished hiker into delirium. There were steamed clams and crabs, roast beef, ham, deviled eggs, salads, fresh fruit, fresh-baked bread, and kegs of iced beer.

After a two-day stay with Gary, we returned to the trail. Over the next several weeks we frequently found packages filled with books, food, and tidings waiting for us at post offices, courtesy of our zany friend.

Farther north we splashed in a lake with children from Pawling, New York. While in Pawling, on a dare I had my ear pierced. In Hanover, New Hampshire, we dined on five-star dormitory fare in Thayer Hall at Dartmouth—one of the more expensive colleges in the United States—and stayed at a former fraternity house that then housed both men and women and where the term *coed* applied even to the showers and the bathrooms.

Our passage through New Hampshire's White Mountains—the most punishing section of the trail—was fortified in part by a visit by Paul's mother, who lived in nearby Peterboro. When our gang—Nick, Dan, Paul, and Victor, the friend who had left the trail in North Carolina—reached Franconia Notch in North Woodstock, New Hampshire, we thumbed the few miles to a park at Profile Lake and met Mrs. Dillon, a jovial woman in her mid-forties. She had arrived in a station wagon brimming with things that trail life had deprived us of: a guitar, cold beer, and food. As we shuttled the food from the car, Mrs. Dillon confessed that she

had been cooking for the better part of a week, and it showed. There were pans of fried chicken, plates of deviled eggs, a half-dozen cakes, cookies, and salads: potato salad, tossed salad, macaroni salad, Jell-O salad, cole slaw, fruit salad.

Throughout the long, sun-drenched afternoon, we sidled up to the picnic table, ate our fill, and rolled into the grass, only to begin the cycle again an hour later. Despite our efforts to find the bottoms of all the bowls, plates, and pans, there seemed to be no end to the food, and when we said good-bye to Mrs. Dillon, we loaded all the surplus we could carry into our packs and happily strained up the trail as if we had shouldered a load of gold bricks.

In Rangeley, Maine, the town of dowdy, vacationing retirees, a snooty teller in a posh tourist's bank glanced at my shabby clothes, refused to cash a one-hundred-dollar postal money order, and told me that no one should visit Rangeley without sufficient cash. A few blocks up the street, the teller at an austere, prefab workingman's bank cashed my check without a blink and for a half-hour engaged me in conversation about the trail.

Monson, Maine, is the last outpost of civilization for one hundred miles for hikers headed north, and a church converted to a boarding house provides lodging for most hikers passing through town. For some days prior to reaching Monson, we had heard stories about curious goings on in the town, which is situated on the fringe of the northern wilderness. There were stories about a haggard alcoholic—a resident at the church—who was prone to pestering hikers and pleading with them for spare change to feed his habit.

Though many stories grow with each telling as they're passed from hiker to hiker, the word on Monson was, if anything, muted compared with what we discovered when we arrived there.

Once in town, Paul opted to spend the extra money and stay at Shaw's Boarding House, a quaint bed and breakfast run by Mr. and Mrs. Shaw, while Dan and I, both watching our budgets, chose to stay at the church.

When I arrived at the church, a square-jawed man in his

sixties sat on the stoop. He wore thick glasses, seemed alert and well mannered, and asked me about the trail. After he helped me find a bunk in the church loft, he ushered me through the converted church while I kept an eye open for the belligerent drunk I had heard so much about.

I didn't realize it at the time, but I had already met him. After about an hour, the man approached me and asked me for seventy-five cents. Still disinclined to believe this was the man who had inspired the rumors, I handed him a dollar. He took it and walked directly to the local package store, where he bought a pint of Old Duke wine. By 2:00 P.M., he had finished his first bottle. Through the afternoon he systematically begged enough change from other hikers to buy his second, third, and fourth rounds.

By early evening, his eyes were bleary and glazed, his speech was slurred, and he had become the gruff, abrasive character we had been warned about.

"Break my arm, son," he muttered to me, thrusting his stout forearm in my direction. "Ain't no man can break my arm."

I learned later that he was challenging me to arm-wrestle. When I declined, he moved along and challenged other hikers. Soon one of the other hikers called his bluff and squared off with him over the kitchen table. In spite of the muscular physique he had developed while working as a logger, the drunken man offered little resistance, and the hiker slammed his arm to the table. Tears welled in the old man's eyes, and he stumbled back to his room to the companionship of the Old Duke.

He emerged some time later as Dan and I fixed dinner in the church kitchen. Though he was still drunk, his disposition had softened somewhat, and he sat muttering unintelligibly at the table. As we ate our dinner, he disappeared and returned a few minutes later with a stack of ancient black-and-white photos. "This is my mother," he mumbled, pointing to an attractive woman in turn-of-the-century dress. "This is me," he continued, indicating a much younger, smiling version of himself surrounded by classmates in a grade-school photograph. A later photo

showed him—young and strong—in a military uniform, his shoulders straining the seams of his shirt and his stout neck encircled by a tie.

"Then I could break any man's arm," he said, tapping the picture. He curled his arm and pointed to his biceps.

As he continued through the photos, he began to cry. The cry became a moan, and soon he sat alone in a corner of the kitchen, weeping, his eyes closed.

As I sat watching him slump, blubbering, into unconsciousness, I wanted to cry with him. The schoolboy he had pointed out to me in the photo had, no doubt, viewed his future with as much hope and promise as his classmates had. Where had he gotten off track? What had destroyed him?

That evening I climbed the loft to my bed at 10:30 P.M. and slept soundly for several hours. Then I heard a sound I'll never forget. It started at 2:00 A.M. from below the rafters and jarred me awake. It was, simply, the most pitiful sound I've ever heard. It began with the sound of retching, as if the old man were coughing up his heart and lungs. For a half hour, he gagged and vomited, and when the wave of nausea had passed, the retching was replaced by moaning and wailing. Then more retching. And more moaning. So it went through the night.

By dawn, he apparently had purged his guts and his emotional reserves, and I found him sitting in the kitchen early the next morning, his eyes clear. He was alert, and the belligerence was gone; he was the same polite, quiet man I had met upon arriving the previous day. He was ready to start a new day, to meet new hikers, to ply them for more change, to follow the same worn path to the package store, to run through his dog-eared photographs, and, finally, to pass the night gagging on bile and despair.

Out of town and back on the trail, I found a cluster of young ferns, picked a few sprigs, and rolled them between my palms. I held them to my nose, breathed in the sweet musk, and rejoiced in knowing that one hundred miles lay between me and the next town. As I walked, for the first time in my life I wondered what it would be like to grow old.

CHAPTER • TEN

Hot Springs Rhapsody

We're back on the trail again, after spending ten days in Hot Springs, North Carolina. I've never been one to abide traditional religious values or to put much stock in spiritual transformation or rebirth, but I know that my stay in Hot Springs showed me more, taught me more, and changed me more than any other experience of my life. During our stay, after working in the fields and talking with Randall and Elmer, I felt as though I had awakened from a long sleep and for the first time began to experience the reality of the world around me. I left town today, not only renewed physically but utterly transformed spiritually. After this, I wonder what other experiences await me farther north.
—May 19, 1979, Spring Mountain Shelter, Tennessee

"'Tis a gift to be simple, 'tis a gift to be free, 'tis a gift to end up where you ought to be," Randall sang, giving life to an old Shaker hymn as he scratched the bow across the strings of his fiddle. I joined in the chorus. Dan did, too. The words seemed to capture the essence of what we had experienced since arriving in Hot Springs, North Carolina, a few days earlier.

As I stood at the edge of a furrowed field bristling with newly planted sorghum shoots, I was surrounded by friends: Dan, Randall, the proprietor of the farm, and Elmer, Randall's business partner, who operated a restored Victorian hotel three miles down the serpentine two-lane in town. The hotel, dubbed the Inn, had become a new age mecca for hikers where dinner time brought lavish five-course vegetarian meals and conversation that invariably explored philosophy, religion, and politics. Both Randall and Elmer, as ordained ministers and children of the sixties, were well versed in all three topics. Elmer had studied at Duke University, Randall at Yale.

Above and around the expanse of cleared farmland, the densely forested peaks of the Pisgah National Forest probed a cloudless blue evening sky. Randall, a tall, thin man in his mid-forties with a bushy beard that reached to his chest and shoulder-length hair coiled into a bun at the top of his head, continued his serenade, which he explained was more for the benefit of his crops than for his human audience. Randall's grandpappy, who had lived and died a farmer in these mountains, had told his grandson that fiddling to a newly planted field would ensure a healthy crop.

"'Tis a gift to be simple . . ." Randall continued.

The lyrics of the hymn might have been written about Randall himself and his bohemian lifestyle, and they characterized the wonderful dichotomy he represented. On one hand, he was a man who had traveled the world and had been educated at one of the nation's most prestigious universities. On the other, he was a man born and bred in the nearby mountains who had returned from his travels with a yen to regain his roots, to embrace the solitude provided by a back-country farm, to "wind up where he ought to be." In spite of his theological education, or perhaps because of it, he believed in the magic of such simple mountain folkways as fiddling to a field of fledgling crops just as fervently as he believed in the inherent goodness of the earth. Standing there beneath the mountains and in the company of friends, I began to believe in it too. Dan and I had spent the preceding five days in Hot Springs, at the Inn and on the farm, and in that time I had

discovered that this small North Carolina hamlet was more than just another resupply stop. It was Eden, a place where hikers could find nourishment, love, acceptance, awakening. For me it provided all those things and more.

Randall and Elmer were two spiritual teachers who had risen out of the ashes of the sixties, preserving all the finest precepts of that era—brotherhood, sharing, love, peace, respect for nature—and carrying the banner into a new age. Because of them, my stay in Hot Springs showed me more, taught me more, and changed me more than any other experience on the trail. When Dan and I resumed our hike after a ten-day rest, I left the town renewed physically and awakened spiritually.

We had arrived in Hot Springs on May 11, tired and haggard from our first three weeks on the trail. Though our blisters had healed, we had encountered the second, and in some ways more debilitating, stage of physical afflictions that plague long-distance hikers. Under the pounding of fifteen- to twenty-mile days, our joints—knees and ankles—constantly ached; we had covered the sixty-eight difficult miles of trail through the Smokies in only four days. Making matters worse, the cuff of my boot had irritated the Achilles tendon of my left leg, and as I hobbled along, each step brought searing pain. I had been forced to walk in my running shoes, which provided little support, and I had tethered my boots—along with their five-pound heft—to my pack.

Then there was the fatigue. Our systems seemed to be wearing down, and each day left us more tired than the previous day. In short, we were ready for a break. We had learned from a southbound hiker that Hot Springs was a five-star stop, and in spite of our fatigue and my pestering leg pain, we pushed the last twenty-three miles into town in one day.

Once out of the woods, we arrived at the hiker hostel operated by the Jesuits, dumped our packs, and continued into town.

The town of Hot Springs consists of a main street, an eighth-mile stretch of hardware shops, grocery stores, a laundromat, and a couple of cafes. Populated by farmers and

mechanics in work clothes, it looks like any other small southern crossroads town. That is, until you spot the Inn.

As I neared the main intersection in town, I peered off to the right and through the trees spotted a magnificent two-story Victorian edifice painted white and appointed with a sharp-peaked roof, ornate columns, and a verandah that circled the entire second floor. The building—surrounded by gas stations, modest frame houses, and streets lined with rusting pickup trucks—would not have looked more out of place if it had been set on Fifth Avenue in New York City.

I stepped onto a covered porch, cluttered with bicycles and hanging plants, and opened the door into the kitchen. Inside, Elmer, clad in faded overalls and a flannel shirt and with a bushy salt-and-pepper beard, stood poised over an antique black cast-iron stove that spanned the wall opposite me. Randall stood by the sink, washing greens—onions, lettuce, and spinach—grown on his farm. Once in the room, I was enveloped in a cloud of savory aromas. Dill, curry, sage, and garlic wafted away from a quartet of pots simmering on the stove, mingling with the scent of bread baking in the oven. As I stood breathing the aroma, Elmer approached, gripped me in a hug, and welcomed me to the Inn. Here, I learned, everyone was greeted with a hug. Then Randall introduced himself, and he, too, welcomed me with a hug.

After the greeting, Elmer invited me to explore the Inn, while the two returned to the task of preparing dinner for the twenty-plus hikers and other guests who would soon arrive for dinner.

I set out from the kitchen and made my way across a wood-paneled hallway and into a sitting room. The room had lost none of the Victorian charm it must have possessed when, near the turn of the century, the Inn catered to the wealthy clientele who journeyed to Hot Springs to bask in the town's natural mineral baths just two blocks away. A woven rug covered the hardwood floor; a wood-burning stove probed into the center of the room; and horsehair couches and easy chairs nestled in corners next to antique tables and lamps. Original art work from the 1920s hung between and above bookshelves that lined the walls. Many

of the volumes were old leather-bound classics, and there were dozens of more modern coffee-table books of photography and art. But most of the books were devoted to nature, religion, philosophy, travel, and adventure. As I scanned the shelves, the ethereal strains of one of Bach's Brandenburg Concertos filled the room, reminding me of how much I had missed music while on the trail.

As I continued to explore, I found my way to the main dining room, outfitted with a half-dozen antique wooden tables and chairs. Two of the Inn's bedrooms opened off the main floor; the rest were upstairs. Most featured antique four-poster beds draped with patchwork quilts and doors leading out onto the verandah. At every turn I encountered more books, and arrangements of fresh-cut spring flowers sat on tables in each room.

At the time, a room for the night cost eight dollars, and four dollars bought a four- or five-course vegetarian feast of gourmet soups, salads, breads, stews, and desserts—all made from scratch and served family-style. After our self-guided tour, Dan and I quickly retrieved our packs from the Jesuit hostel and took up lodging at the Inn.

Our first dinner there began, as all of them do, with a welcome from Elmer. After a brief prayer he invited guests to introduce themselves to the group, and each hiker shared a bit of personal history and a general reaction to life on the trail. Then the steaming platters of food arrived: spinach salad with vinaigrette dressing, black-bean soup, rice stew, whole-wheat bread, and fresh apple and berry pies, all hot from the oven. We washed it down with iced herbal tea.

After dinner Elmer hosted a wine-tasting party, which drew a crowd of the artists and artisans—photographers, painters, poets, woodworkers—who had begun to settle in Hot Springs, turning it into a sort of backwoods Renaissance community with the Inn as its cultural epicenter. While Elmer entertained the more highbrow guests, Randall, whose cultural tastes were a shade folksier, hosted a collection of twelve hikers who lingered in the kitchen. The artists sipped wine and listened to classical music, while the rest of us pursued more down-home forms of amuse-

ment, sipping Tennessee whiskey and clogging to strains of mountain music from Randall's fiddle and the guitars of two of his friends. Soon the cramped kitchen erupted into a regular hoedown, with hikers swinging arm in arm and stomping the floor with lug-soled boots.

Later that evening, when only Dan and I remained, Elmer suggested we take a drive; he wanted to show us something. We climbed into a rickety, decades-old Rambler and set off up the mountain. A few minutes later we stopped at a pull-off on the quiet, two-lane highway and got out. Below us spread a scene of such stark beauty that I'll never forget it.

Several hundred yards below, miles away from the nearest incandescent light bulb, lay Randall's farm, its rolling fields shining silver in the moonlight. Above it rose the dark sil-houettes of the mountains. In the center of the plot of cleared fields, a rustic two-room cabin perched on a hillside above a mountain brook. Moonbeams sliced through the skeleton of a rickety barn that stood beside it.

"We try to keep this place secret," said Elmer. "But it's so special that we like to share it with some of the people who come through town who we think might appreciate it."

Randall went on to explain, in his thick Carolina drawl, that he had purchased the farm several years earlier, and since then it had become his haven, his retreat, a place where he could pursue a simple, honest life of self-suffi-ciency that would keep him grounded in the earth. The cabin had no electricity or running water, and he worked the farm without chemical pesticides or motorized tools, tilling the fields with a horse-drawn plow and spreading cow manure as organic fertilizer. Oil lamps provided eve-ning light, and he warmed his dwelling and cooked over a wood-burning stove.

As we stood mesmerized by the scene, Elmer broke in. "We've really enjoyed the two of you, and we'd like for you to consider a proposition. If you need a few days' rest, we'd love to have you stay with us. You can help around the Inn or work on the farm for room and board, and you're wel-come to stay as long as you like."

As far as I was concerned, there wasn't much deciding to

be done. I needed rest, and the Inn and farm promised to expose me to a new way of life, one that my city upbringing had deprived me of. I voted to stay. Dan thought for a few seconds, then assented.

"This trail is about experiences," he said. "And I think there's a lot we could learn from this place."

So we took up residence in Hot Springs, like dozens of other hikers before and since who have wandered into town for a one-day stopover and wound up staying for days, weeks, or even years, living and learning from those two remarkable teachers.

And we did learn. For the next ten days, we shuttled between the Inn and the farm, working the fields through the morning and afternoon hours and in the evenings serving meals at the Inn. Each day brought new discoveries, new insights. For me, most of them occurred at Randall's farm, where I spent my nights, while Dan stayed at the Inn.

On the farm mornings began at dawn with plates of hot beans and cornbread Randall had cooked on his stove. After breakfast Dan and I, armed with hoes, acted as organic weedkillers, severing the necks of weeds that encroached on the tender, new sorghum sprigs. One day as we hoed, Dan and I sang choruses of old Negro spirituals, the sun warming our shirtless backs. When the hoeing was done, we rode a horse-drawn cart, spreading manure along uncultivated fields that Randall would soon till behind Bill, his chestnut-brown workhorse.

Afternoons always ended with a hike up the mountainside to a spring-fed stream dammed into a series of cool, thigh-deep pools where, naked, we splashed the sweat and dirt from our bodies before walking to the Inn to serve the evening meal.

Mornings, I hovered close to Randall as he entered the barn and soothed his cow, Molly, now nine months with calf. On Mother's Day morning Randall summoned me to the barn, where Molly lay licking her limpid, gangly offspring, which Randall named Daisy. She had been born only minutes earlier, and for the next several days Molly's milk was rich yellow with colostrum, which tasted heavy and sweet.

Other days, I worked little, instead spending the day with a fishing pole, rock-hopping along the mountain brook spanned by the rickety swinging bridge that separated Randall's spread from the quarter-mile dirt road that led to the highway.

Evenings were always special times. After we had finished our chores at the Inn, Elmer, Dan, and I walked or drove the three miles from the Inn to the rutted, quarter-mile dirt road that led back to the swinging bridge and Randall's farm. On one beautiful spring night the four of us sat on the front porch of the cabin on a dilapidated car seat salvaged from an old Volkswagen. We filled metal cups with whiskey mixed with fresh mint leaves and cold spring water dipped from an old barrel that sat on the side of the porch. A rubber hose led from a spring high up the mountain down across a field and onto the porch, where it constantly infused the barrel with ice-cold water. The barrel, which was outfitted with a hinged door and a series of shelves, served as Randall's refrigerator. There he kept Molly's milk stored in a gallon glass jar.

That night at dusk, the sun burned like fire when it touched the ridge line, and it spread into a beautiful horizontal blaze of red, pink, and magenta. We had front-row seats for the pyrotechnics, and after the sunlight began to fade, Randall took up his fiddle and, like a new-aged pied piper, led us out to the edge of the plowed field where he began stretching out the old Shaker hymn to encourage his crops to grow. Even today, when I hear the hymn, I fondly recall my days in Hot Springs.

That night, after Elmer and Dan had returned to the Inn, Randall lit the stove to heat water for tea, and we sat down over the small kitchen table draped with an oilcloth. A single oil lamp illuminated the scarred, rough-hewn walls hung with mementos from Randall's life. There were Japanese watercolors from his travels to the East to study Eastern religion during his years at Yale. There were photographs of his two sons, Randall, Jr., and Laird. There were mobiles crafted from bird bones or chips of quartz. There were shelves lined with hundreds of the knickknacks Ran-

dall had collected since moving to the farm: colorful stones, deer antlers, snakeskins, and turtle shells. They were, like the dwelling itself, beautifully austere, things most people would have swept aside to make room for more elegant furnishings. But they were Randall's most prized possessions, and not one of them had cost him a cent.

We had grown very close over the previous few days, and I had begun to feel like a student in the presence of a wise teacher who instructed through precept and example without ever seeming to teach at all. Randall had a way of asking questions—thoughtful questions—that inspired introspection.

We had talked easily for a half-hour or so, sipping tea, when Randall staggered me with an ostensibly simple question that begged for a deeper response. "Will you share with me who you are?" I laughed, but I realized that it was a question I had been asking myself daily since I started the trail.

As I began to answer, I sensed that I was on the verge of a cathartic outpouring. For the next seven hours we talked, and it was the most honest, revealing, illuminating encounter I've ever had. I traced my history, not only exploring important events, but finding myself realizing for the first time the impact of those events, their meaning, how they had shaped me, led me in one direction or another, and how, ultimately, they had led me to the trail and here to Randall's farm.

As the night passed and Randall refilled our tea mugs, I shared things about myself that I had never broached before. I confessed. I voiced regrets. I expressed hopes. I talked about the kind of person I wanted to become: a person who loved and trusted more, a person who gave more, a person who fully appreciated life's simple blessings. As I spoke, I began to believe that such changes were possible.

I talked about the trail and how in three short weeks it had dazzled me and introduced me to a new world, one I had never imagined existed. A world full of goodness and beauty.

After I finished, I asked Randall the same question, and he shared his story with me. About the incompatible lifestyles that had divided him from his wife, she being drawn to the city, he to his primitive farm. About his sons, whom

he loved desperately and saw too infrequently. He talked about his spiritual search that had led him to Yale and later to the Far East. About his entry into the ministry and the rejection that resulted when his new-aged Christianity clashed with the Fundamentalist values of his conservative neighbors. Finally he talked about his decision to drop out, to abandon the mechanized world and sow his hopes for a better life here on the farm.

Near dawn Randall rose from the table and put his arm around me, thanking me for the soul-deep dialogue we had shared. After bidding him goodnight and with an oil lamp in hand, I climbed the ladder to the open-air loft where I slept. Before settling to sleep, I extinguished the lamp and walked to the edge of the loft, which looked out over the silent fields and shadowed mountains. The evening chill felt clean and good against my face, and I watched the steam of my breath billow and fade. Beyond, I could see the dew twinkling in the moonlight, and I detected the faint smell of manure, the sweet bite of hay, the perfume of clover. The rich tang of wood smoke hung in the air, and I heard Molly and her new calf lowing softly in the barn. I heard the water lapping over the stones in the stream. Suddenly, the boundaries separating me from the tranquil night world disappeared. The mountains engulfed me, and I began to feel as if I had just been born into a world filled with peace.

I experienced such an intense swell of emotion that I could hardly contain it, and for the first time in my life I knew that God and all His goodness lurked in every rock, in every tree, in every blade of grass, and in me. I walked to the mattress, climbed under the quilt, and lay—awake—until dawn, fearful that if I slept, I would awaken to find the feelings gone.

But several days later, when Dan and I said good-bye to Elmer and Randall and departed Hot Springs on May 19, those feelings were still as surely connected to me as my pack and walking stick. From then on the trail seemed different—more inviting, more filled with wonder, more charged with excitement. And as we picked up the white blazes, heading north, I realized that what I had discovered in Hot Springs was just the beginning. Hundreds of miles lay ahead, miles full of promise.

CHAPTER • ELEVEN

Critters

I'm learning that nature can be as harsh as it is beautiful. I watched tonight as Randall's cat crept up into the open loft of the cabin, crouched, and uncoiled, seizing a bat that had been fluttering around the rafters in the lantern light. The cat then walked past me down the ladder with the bat still wriggling in her jaws. The act was so quick, so efficient, and yet so horrifying to me, perhaps because I haven't watched many living things die. Afterward, it occurred to me that predators like the cat are playing out their roles in this theater without malice or spite or cruelty, which we humans tend to ascribe to them and their killing acts.
—May 16, 1979, Randall's Farm,
Hot Springs, North Carolina

In many ways, the Appalachian Trail was a thriving biology lab or, more precisely, a biology theater where myriad critters—many I had no idea existed—bustled, stirred, buzzed, tittered, slithered, and scrambled about, entertaining and educating us with their antics. Through them we received a firsthand survival lesson.

But the animals offered us more than that. Over time, they became our colleagues, appealing to our sense of sight or sound through all of our days and nights on the trail and

147

reminding us always that man, the animal, is never alone, never wanting for companions. There was the screech of the pileated woodpecker winging unseen through densely foliated tree tops. Graceful hawks and buzzards spiraled effortlessly on thermals. Barred owls or wild turkeys glided agilely on four-foot wings through dense hardwood forests. Woodchucks, chipmunks, squirrels, rummaged through the underbrush for seeds or insect larva. Skunks sauntered slowly across the trail with their young in tow.

There was the collective drone of millions of insects— the rhythmic tweep of crickets, the rasp of cicadas, the oscillating buzz of bumblebees weaving through the underbrush. The flutelike trill of the brown thrush and the incessant banter of the whip-poor-will violated the sanctity of night; and we could hear the tapping and pawing of white-tailed deer as they foraged through open meadows after dark.

In our daily and nightly encounters with the animals, it became difficult not to view them as paradigms, as living symbols of simplicity, contentment, and clarity of purpose in the often charitable, sometimes hostile, world of the wilderness. For the animals, to live was enough. Whitman captured that sentiment so well in *Leaves of Grass:*

> I think I could turn and live with animals,
>   they are so placid and self-contained,
> I stand and look at them long and long.
> They do not sweat and whine about their condition,
> They do not lie awake in the dark and weep for their sins,
> They do not make me sick discussing their duty to God,
> Not one is dissatisfied, not one is demented with the
>   mania of owning things,
> Not one kneels to another, nor to his kind that lived
>   thousands of years ago,
> Not one is respectable or unhappy over the whole earth.

I saw my first black bear in the Smokies as I hiked alone from Ice Water Springs to Cosby Knob in the northern section of the national park. He was a great three-year-old male, and he sat in the middle of the trail with his feet

splayed outward, back erect like a Buddha in brown fur. Placid and self-contained, he seemed to embody the spirit of Whitman's tribute.

When I first spotted him, I wanted to shout, to share my excitement with my companions behind me on the trail, but I realized that to do so would have sent the animal fleeing through the trees. Instead, I stood trembling, like an adolescent who has just discovered sex, studying the bear as he swept the branches of a small bush into his gaping mouth.

The bear wasn't beautiful, and he wasn't majestic. In fact, he was somewhat waggish, with his abundant fat and baggy skin draped around him like an outsized black overcoat and with a vacant, blissful expression spread across his face. But he was also astonishing, astonishing because he was there at all: a massive wild beast pursuing his simple livelihood not forty yards in front of me.

After two minutes I ventured closer and snapped his photograph. Because I was positioned downwind, his powerful sense of smell—many times more acute than my own—didn't register my scent, and he was left to evaluate me through his rather feeble eyesight. After scrutinizing me for several seconds, he showed no alarm and remained where he sat until he had eaten his fill and decided to move on. I followed his clamorous passage down the mountain by tracing the heavy thud of his footfalls and the rustle of snapping branches.

When he was gone, I felt blessed to have been permitted such an intimate glimpse of one of North America's largest creatures, and I realized that our encounter was vastly more honest, more revealing, than ever might have occurred in a zoo. He and I had met on equal terms. No fences separated us; no manmade walls sealed him in or kept him out. He was free to roam as he pleased, freer in many ways than I, who adhered to established trails while he, guided by whim or instinct, created his own.

Taken alone, the encounter with the bear was enough to thrill me for weeks, but it was only one of three major wildlife sightings I had logged over the previous few days.

Two days earlier I had stood within ten yards of a six-point buck. I had left my backpack on the ridge at Spencer Field, at five thousand feet, and had wandered down a sunlit trail to fill my water bottle at a spring. As the chilly water tumbled over my hands, I heard a twig snap and looked up to see him peering at me.

My heart pounded as I watched him, certain that at any moment he would spook and vanish through the trees. But he never did. After several minutes, he strayed away at an easy pace, rooting for acorns as he went.

Then there were the wild boars. As I ascended from Spence Field toward the summit of Thunderhead late in the afternoon, I peered ahead to see an ample brown rump disappear into the brush. An eighth of a mile farther up the trail, I glanced thirty yards below me and saw an entire herd of twelve to fourteen wild boars—from three hundred-pound sows to cat-sized piglets—scampering through a thicket. I later learned that the boars were descendants of the Russian wild boars introduced to the area in 1910 by a lodge keeper who had imported them to serve as game for his clientele. The boars proved an elusive quarry, and the hunting lodge soon closed its doors, but the animals went on to thrive in the park.

Later that evening when I reached Derrick Knob Shelter, six miles north, I met a ranger on horseback. Slung over his shoulder was a shotgun mounted with a spotlight. He was boar hunting, part of a park-wide effort to eradicate the animals, which already had destroyed acres of foliage by rooting for acorns with their tusks. Above three thousand feet, the ranger would drag his kill off the trail and leave it as food for the carrion eaters.

Through the spring and summer, the ruffed grouse also became an important woodland symbol and a perfect emblem of the passing of the seasons. The game birds were always willing to share the secrets of their life cycle and their tactics of self-preservation with any passerby willing to look and listen.

I heard the birds long before I first glimpsed them. On our second night on the trail, for instance, I heard an eerie drumming sound that resembled the noise of a basketball being dribbled with increasing tempo on a carpeted floor. I heard that sound again and again over the next few days, yet neither Dan nor I had the slightest notion of what it was. We learned later that the dribbling sound arose from a male ruffed grouse beating the air with its wings to attract a mate.

Several days later as I ambled along a tranquil stretch of trail lost in thought, a sudden explosion of thundering wings jarred me to attention. Out of the corner of my eye, I spotted two birds the size of large game hens beating their wings and flying erratically through the trees. Their black, brown, and tan feathers provided perfect camouflage, and when they lit in trees several hundred feet away, they virtually disappeared into the background colors of the wilderness.

As the weeks passed, I found myself repeatedly startled by the grouse. Even though I encountered them every few days, I never learned to anticipate their frenetic, graceless retreat. Yet with each encounter I learned more about them. I soon learned, for instance, that when spooked, the male fled to a faraway tree, while the hen stayed near the nest. Though separated by some distance, the two birds maintained a constant communication of staccato squawks, perhaps a verbal assessment of their two-legged intruder. I also found that if I ignored their decoy and instead located the now-abandoned nest, I could glimpse tiny, perfectly camouflaged chicks darting for cover in the underbrush.

One day as I walked along the trail through the Blue Ridge of Virginia, I encountered a nest and, as usual, the male grouse scattered while the female clung to the ground. When she noticed that I had spied the nest, she employed her first diversionary tactic, which no doubt was intended to decoy predators. She hopped onto the trail in front of me, staggering drunkenly and feigning a broken wing. When she looked back and realized that I had called her bluff, she shifted to her second tactic, one that I still regard as the most perfect act of

selfless devotion I've ever seen. Now twenty feet ahead on the trail, she turned to face me and billowed out her feathers until she had doubled in size. Squawking maniacally, she charged.

I held my position as the protective mother approached, but when she began nipping at my legs with her beak and thrashing me with her wings, I suddenly found myself fleeing down the trail—more amazed than afraid—with the enraged hen in hot pursuit.

As the spring yielded to summer, the chicks continued to grow with each sighting. By summer's end the chaos of dozens of thrashing wings greeted me whenever I encountered a nest, with father, mother, and offspring together taking wing in retreat.

Other birds had adapted more graciously to our presence and approached rather than withdrew from us. While I hiked through the Green Mountains of Vermont, for instance, one day I stopped in a spruce grove to have a snack. Pulling a granola bar from my pack, I sat on a rock, but no sooner had I peeled off the wrapper than a gray Canada jay landed squarely on my shoulder. At first I suspected that I had been visited by a winged demon, but soon the jay roosted on my finger and nibbled from my hand.

Through the north woods, the plump, round-headed birds, also known as scavenger jays or camp jays, became invited dinner guests and even entertainers. On the last night of our hike, in the twin shelters at Katahdin Stream Campground, one hiker in our group plugged both of his nostrils with bread, lay on his back, and soon catered a buffet for two jays. While the birds roosted on his chin and picked the bread from his nose, the rest of us howled, more shocked by the behavior of our own species than by that of the animals.

The jays were perhaps the most loveable among the camp raiders that abounded on the trail. The others engaged us in a never-ending battle of wits, but while we often disdained their efforts to pillage our supplies, we also marveled at their pluck and adaptability. They had learned to regard humans as hosts, not intruders.

Mice. When Dante described the inferno, rife with fire and darkness, he omitted one detail: mice. Millions of them, with rasping teeth and clattering claws.

I had my first encounter with mice on my third night on the trail. I had slept beside my foodbag in the shelter, certain that no creature would venture close to a sleeping human. I awoke to find a quarter-sized hole leading through the green nylon and into each of the half-dozen plastic bags inside. As it turned out, the stealthy mice had sampled from the bags, mingling their tiny brown droppings with the contents of each. The next night, I hung my foodbag from a nail driven into a shelter eave, thinking I had surely outsmarted them. I awoke the next morning to discover new ports of entry and freshly laid turds.

Determined to observe the rapscallions at work, the next night I lay in my bag, gripping my flashlight. As soon as I blew out the candle, the frantic chorus of scraping and gnawing began. The more brazen shelter denizens crisscrossed the shelter eaves, and when I clicked on my flashlight, their tiny eyes glowed red in the beam. Finally, one reached the nail that supported my foodbag and scampered down the line. Now in the spotlight, he gnawed insouciantly at the nylon until I drove him away with a well aimed stone.

I was baffled and prepared to offer nightly sacrifices— small heaps of food—in hopes that the mice would leave the larger portion alone. The next day a more experienced hiker taught me how to pierce a tuna can in the center, invert it, and suspend it midway along the line to discourage even the most enterprising rodents.

The barrier prevented them from reaching my food, but I soon discovered that the mice did more than assail foodbags. Once they realized our edible supplies were beyond their reach, they turned their sights on our wool socks and shirts and even raided our rolls of toilet tissue. The shredded tissue and frayed wool provided soft, warm batting for their dens, and close inspection between the shelter logs almost always revealed cushy nests heaped in colored wool and white tissue.

We soon learned to leave the pockets of our packs un-zipped, to allow the critters free access. Otherwise, their teeth would have made quick work of the pack cloth if a pocket contained so much as a crumb of bread or a single rolled-oat flake. I awoke one morning in a shelter to find a trio of rigid mouse tails projecting from flaps and pocket openings, and when I picked up my pack no fewer than a dozen mice leaped for safety. Thankfully, because I had left the pockets open, they had left my pack intact, though lib-erally sprinkled with feces.

Though personal assaults were rare, they were not un-heard of. The night we slept at Sassafrass Gap Shelter, seven miles north of Wesser, North Carolina, one of the other shelter occupants woke us all with a shout in the wee hours of the morning. A mouse had blazed a path across his fore-head, stopped near his nose, and emptied its tiny bladder into his eye. And it wasn't unusual for an errant mouse to take a wrong turn and wind up inside a bag occupied by a slumbering hiker, an accident that usually resulted in a chorus of squeaks and shrieks as man and beast scrambled to escape their odd bedfellow.

While most of us faced the mouse menace with resigna-tion and even good-natured fascination, others devised grim methods for reprisal. One hiker, for instance, carried a sup-ply of traps that he rigged each night before he turned in. Within minutes of lights out, we would hear the clatter of spring-loaded jaws; the hiker then slipped from his bag, tossed the casualties out into the brush, and started the pro-cess over again.

Everyone soon began to consider his pesticidal mission an exercise in futility. The mice were so populous that while a few strayed into the traps, dozens of others pillaged the shelter with impunity. Before abandoning his calling al-together, however, the hiker resorted to more drastic mea-sures. He rigged a tiny hangman's noose and suspended a dead mouse from the rafters in a Virginia shelter, a warning to others that they might suffer the same fate. His mouse lynching, like his efforts with the traps, backfired, and he soon found himself besieged not only by mice but also by

fellow hikers who considered his tactics cruel and inhumane.

In the war against the mice, it seems the best we could hope for was a truce: if we stashed our socks and shirts and hung our foodbags properly, the mice contented themselves with the scraps spilled from our dinner pots.

Some shelters harbored larger, more daunting scavengers. Ice Water Springs Shelter in the Smokies, for instance, served as home to a resident skunk. While I slept in the shelter on the bottom tier of wire-mesh bunks two feet above the ground, I awoke at 3:00 A.M. to see the skunk's tail passing inches from my nose as he scoured the floor for food.

One evening in the Shenandoah National Park, Dan and I camped in an open field, and shortly after dark we heard a frantic rustling at the base of the tree that bore our foodbags. We soon trained our flashlights on an enterprising raccoon who spent the better part of the night devising tactics to reach our food, which dangled from a stout bough fifteen feet above the ground. First, the animal tried to untie the knot that secured the cord to the tree trunk. When that failed, he scampered up the tree and worked at the line where it draped over the branch. Finally, he suspended himself from the limb, grabbed at the line, and set the bags swinging back and forth. Though the animal never reached the foodbags, I had to resist a temptation to reward him for his perseverance and cunning.

Raccoons weren't the only animals that employed ingenious techniques. In the Smokies, a park ranger related a story about a notorious camp raider known as the Suicide Bear. The bear was known for hoisting himself into trees and, like a portly trapeze artist, flinging himself in the direction of the dangling foodbags. More often than not, the ranger explained, the bear would crash to the ground empty-handed. Undaunted, he would scale the tree and leap again and again until finally, bruised and battered, he limped off into the woods.

Occasionally his plan worked. He would leap, snatch the food bag in his paws, cling to it until the line snapped, and

then scamper off into the brush with his pilfered dinner. According to the ranger, the bear's fur was a mass of scabs and bald patches, but he also sported an ample layer of fat, proof that his leaps into the void were sometimes productive.

Vermont was porcupine country, and the scavengers' teethmarks scarred everything that bore a trace of salt from hikers' sweat. The sharp edges of shelter planking, forest service signs, and even outhouse seats had been gnawed smooth. Pack straps, boots, and walking sticks posed equally tempting morsels, and we hung them along with our foodbags. Though I never saw a porcupine, the gnarled wood and piles of stones—antiporcupine artillery—left in shelters attested to bitter night battles between hikers and the bristling marauders.

The animals' behavior patterns weren't always as endearing as those of the grouse or as comical as those of the camp raiders, particularly when they embraced the harsh and sometimes gruesome world of predators and prey.

Near the streambed of Sages Ravine in Connecticut, for instance, I watched, horrified, as yellow jackets descended on a butterfly in such numbers that they completely obscured the body, covered the wings, and swarmed over the ground in a wriggling mass two feet in diameter. Initially, the butterfly struggled, but within seconds the battle was over. As the predators continued to work, the dead insect's wings waved pathetically as the wasps' mandibles gnawed through the tissue that attached the wings to the body. Perhaps the butterfly had strayed too close to the nest, or maybe the yellow jackets had sought him as food to be chewed to pulp and fed to their larvae.

In Virginia I watched a giant cicada killer, a two-inch-long wasp with a bulbous, gold-spotted abdomen, swoop onto a cicada that clung to a tree trunk. The wasp arched its abdomen and drove in its stinger. When the cicada had stopped twitching, the insect dropped with its prey to the

ground. It then lumbered into the air, still clutching its victim and flying like an overloaded transport plane to its den where, I learned, it would lay its eggs on the body of the paralyzed host. When the eggs hatched, the larva would enter the body of the cicada and eat the insect alive from the inside.

During my stay at Randall's farm in Hot Springs, North Carolina, I witnessed another staggering display of predatory skill. Nights at the cabin, I slept in an open-air loft with no walls separating me from the night air. One evening, as I poked my head through the trap door leading to the loft, I spotted a bat swooping through the open space under the eaves. An oil lamp dangled from my hand, and from its position below the trap door, it infused the loft with a faint, eerie glow.

As I watched the bat zig and zag along the rafters of the open room, Randall's tailless cat, Ichtar, slipped up the ladder, brushed past my chest, and crept onto the floor beside my head. Her body remained still while her head swiveled, tracking the bat's erratic course.

Though I had no idea what was about to happen, I was transfixed by the scene: a domesticated cat, but a predator, crouching, silhouetted against the dark walls of the loft, while the bat, seemingly drawn to the new life presence in the room, swooped closer with each pass. Finally, the bat flew within striking distance, and Ichtar's body uncoiled with such force and quickness that I missed the motion completely.

Still perched on the ladder, I lifted the lamp onto the loft floor and saw that the cat held the wriggling bat in her jaws. She moved back down the ladder, brushing past my chest, as serenely and purposefully as when she had arrived, while I, with racing heart and trembling hands, felt unnerved, as if I had just witnessed a murder.

Miles farther south, in Georgia, I had experienced a similar pang of disgust and frustration after I witnessed a suicide. Four of us sat by a fire and noticed a pale green luna moth—as large as a small bird—swooping close to the flames. Having watched countless insects scorch them-

selves in our candle flames, we knew what was likely to
follow. While we had had little concern for the self-destruc-
tive bent of smaller, less spectacular insects, the imminent
self-immolation of the luna provoked a response in all of us.
We rose, flailing our arms attempting to block the insect's
path back to the fire. But our protective efforts posed little
deterrent for the moth, and it easily maneuvered past us.

Inexorably programmed on its suicidal mission, the insect sputtered through the flames and careened to the
ground on the far side of the fire. Mortally wounded, it lay
on its back, wriggling its seared legs and fluttering its
singed wings until it had righted itself. No longer able to fly,
it limped along the ground, scaled one of the rocks ringing
the fire, and heaved itself into the pyre. There, without apparent fear or despair, it vanished in a brilliant flash of green
flame.

CHAPTER · TWELVE

Where I Live

I believe I have finally found my niche, and it's here in the woods. I thrive here. I relax here. I feel so right here. And I've begun to realize that I have become a resident of the wilderness: I no longer leave society to visit the woods. Rather, I leave the woods to visit society. When I'm in town, I feel uprooted and often suffer pangs of separation. When I'm in town, I constantly wonder what natural displays I'm missing, and it's also sometimes difficult to sleep because the air seems stale and all the familiar night sounds are muted by walls and windows.
—August 17, 1979, Little Rock Pond Lean-to, Vermont

None of us who ventured out on the Appalachian Trail for weeks at a time could resist being transformed by the experience.

Some of the changes were obvious. "There's something different about thru-hikers," Richard Bramley, the owner of a package store on the trail in Cornwall Bridge, Connecticut, once told me. Bramley, who offers free drinks to thru-hikers, has spent hours on his front porch listening to the stories of end-to-enders. "Once you've spent over two or three weeks on the trail, you're into a different head. You've begun to change. You've left the rest of the world behind,

and it shows." People like Bramley who frequently encounter thru-hikers claim there is an unmistakable aura about them, a lean, hard look and a beatific demeanor.

Our clothes were perpetually soiled and often tattered, and the backs of our T-shirts bore permanent gray streaks where the aluminum crossbars of our packs had oxidized. Our boots were scuffed and scarred by rocks and roots, and our hair and beards grew unencumbered. By the time I reached Maine, for instance, I could no longer negotiate a comb through the tangle that billowed from my face.

Our leg muscles became sharply defined, and whatever fat we had carried along the early miles through the South soon disappeared. We covered miles—whether climbing or descending—at the same brisk, three-mile-per-hour pace. On long ascents we frequently blazed by weekend hikers who swore and grunted their way to the top. Our packs truly looked like mobile homes, with socks, bandanas, and surplus shorts and T-shirts tethered to the outside to dry in the sun.

Other changes were more subtle. After weeks on the trail, primitive instincts began to awaken. Away from the bombardment of loud music and the din of rush-hour traffic, our hearing became sensitized to the gentle cues of the wilderness. Never silent, the woods were constantly astir with the titter of birds, the rustle of wind through the leaves, the scurry of chipmunks scattering through the underbrush, the drone of buzzing insects, the rumble of distant thunder clouds, the crackling of approaching footsteps.

We developed a knack for predicting changes in the weather. By reading shifting winds, cloud formations, subtle changes in pressure, or the smell of dampness in the air, we could often forecast impending storms hours before they struck.

At the same time, the sounds, smells, and sensations of civilization became foreign and at times even threatening to us. The clamor of trucks and cars streaking along highways contrasted so starkly to the sounds of the woods, for instance, that I became edgy whenever the trail crossed a main road.

Other sounds pitched me into panic. I recall the night we

camped beside Pierce Pond in the wilderness of central Maine, miles from the nearest road. I had finished my dinner and had climbed out onto a large rock that jutted into the water, and as I lay on my back, gazing contentedly at the night sky, I dozed into a tranquil sleep only to be jarred awake as a fighter jet from Pease Air Force Base a few hundred miles away roared across the lake at treetop level, shooting flames from its afterburners. The incident left me shaken and disoriented, unable to sleep.

Other, less invasive, aspects of civilization disturbed us too. The stench of car exhaust burned our nostrils as we descended into towns from the fresh, clean air of the mountains, and the odors of perfume, deodorant, and soap on the well scrubbed people we encountered in towns almost sickened us at times. In one instance I was positioned in a line of a dozen tourists in a grocery check-out aisle in Rangeley, Maine, when the collective assault of a dozen bottled fragrances left me wondering if I could clear the register and exit with my supplies before I gagged. I suspect that my own rank aroma left my fellow shoppers wondering the same thing.

We could smell the acrid odor of tobacco smoke ahead of us on the trail from as far as a quarter-mile away. We also began to notice that day hikers carried on their clothes the distinct odor of their houses and the foods they had cooked for dinner. Often, as they passed me on the trail, I instinctively raised my nose to the air, reading their scents on the wind.

There were other changes, too. Over my five months on the trail, the very rhythm of my life settled down. I had no deadlines, no commitments, no job awaiting my return, no schedule to keep beyond reaching Maine before my cash reserves ran dry. I ate when I was hungry, slept when I was tired, hiked alone when I felt crowded or with friends when I felt lonely. I rose at dawn and covered my daily mileage with ample time to tarry at mountaintop vistas or soak my feet in streams and still make camp with enough daylight to roll out my bag, boil my noodles, write in my journal, and brew my evening cup of tea before sunset. My wrist

watch became just another trinket to weigh me down and clutter my life, and I sent it home. Today, if I could revive any element of the trail experience, it would be that wonderful feeling of escape from mechanized timekeeping and the sense that the daylight hours provided more than ample time for fulfilling my obligations.

But the most notable change in me was the evolution from visitor to resident of the wilderness. It was such a gradual change that I can't say exactly when or where it happened, and I tried to explain it to Victor, the Massachusetts hiker who had departed the trail in North Carolina and joined us for weekends as we passed through New England. On an afternoon hike through the Green Mountains of Vermont he asked me what it was like to spend so many days away from civilization. As we walked through a fir grove, across exposed rock outcroppings, up boulder-strewn climbs, and finally to camp beside a tumbling brook, I explained that I felt as if I were ushering him through my home the way someone might walk a visitor through his house, pointing to the kitchen where he ate his meals, to the den where he sat with his evening tea, to the bedroom where he slept.

I explained to him that my layovers in town had become progressively shorter, and that I quickly became "homesick" for the woods. I told him that for every minute I dallied in town I realized that I chanced missing the natural wonders occurring in the mountains: hawks circling on thermals, bears lumbering away in retreat, scavenger Canada jays eating from my hand, deer pawing through camp at dusk, stellar sunsets rippling the horizon in waves of purple, red, and blue, and golden meteors blazing across black night skies that always left me with goose bumps no matter how many times I had seen them.

I explained to him that many of the trappings of my life in the city—electric can openers, microwave ovens, television sets, blow driers, daily hot showers—seemed excessive, wasteful. I explained that I had lost my lust for material things and could not think of anything I really wanted that wasn't already in my pack.

If the wilderness was my home, then many of the trail's 230 shelters served as my domiciles, linking passage through fourteen states and the 160 days of my trek. I could never resist the thrill of counting down the day's last mile, of feeling my pace quicken in anticipation, and finally glancing ahead and spotting the blue-blazed side trail or the shelter roof through the trees and knowing that the day's labor was complete, that it was time to rest.

The shelters were Spartan, fifteen-by-ten-foot open-faced lean-tos with sloping roofs and fieldstone walls or walls hewn from native timbers. Some of the shelters were spectacular relics of the 1930's, of the trail's earliest days and of the craftsmanship of the Civilian Conservation Corps. Some, like the squat Cable Gap Shelter seven miles south of the entrance to the Great Smoky Mountains National Park, were constructed of stout, two-foot-broad logs. A few of the shelters boasted four, not three, walls and included doorways, lofts, and shuttered windows. The Roan High Knob Shelter on the shoulder of Roan Mountain and the Blood Mountain Shelter, thirty miles north of Springer, were two such places.

Many shelters perched on the ridge line and afforded spectacular views of the surrounding mountains. Vandeventer Shelter, for instance, rests on a rocky ridge some one thousand feet above Watauga Dam, thirty-three miles south of the Virginia border. During our night on the ridge, we watched as the daylight waned and tiny lights shimmered like earth-bound stars, each marking a house or a barn or a church. The next morning we awoke to find the lake and her civilization gone. Instead we saw a stratus of dense silver clouds probed by the round green nobs of surrounding mountains.

Other shelters—Ice Water Springs, Russell Field, Spence Field, Derrick Knob, all in the Smokies—were crafted of fieldstone and equipped with indoor hearths and fireplaces.

Some, particularly those through the Lake Country of central Maine, nestled alongside pristine ponds whose tree-lined shores were scattered with rocks and driftwood

bleached white in the sun. There the wild, maniacal laughter of loons echoed across the still water after dark.

Though simple, those accommodations afforded us more pleasure than a welter of more extravagant, more civilized, offerings ever could. A roof to keep off the rain. Three walls to block the wind. A timber platform on which to sleep or sit and watch the gradual arrival of nightfall. A sixteen-penny nail driven into the shelter eaves, a place to hang damp shorts, a waterbag, or a parcel of food. A spiral-bound register filled with pages and pages of hikers' tales, experiences, reflections, insights. A nearby spring spouting delicious fifty-degree water. A stout tree to cradle one's back.

Once at the shelter, I would slip from my sweat-soaked clothes and wander to the spring to fill my waterbag and splash the day's grime from my skin. Then I would pull on a pair of dry socks, a clean cotton T-shirt and wool shirt, a pair of long trousers, and a pair of ragged sneakers that seemed to weigh nothing at all after a day in hiking boots. If it was early in the evening, I might have four or five hours of daylight to do exactly as I pleased: to write, to read, to feed the fire, to talk with friends, to explore the environs of my temporary home. Or to do nothing at all and feel that the time was just as well spent.

Special Attractions

Talk of mysteries! Think of our life in nature—daily to be shown matter, to come in contact with it—rocks, trees, wind on our cheeks! the solid earth!
—Henry David Thoreau, The Maine Woods

Before assaulting Springer Mountain, I had heard or read accounts of the trail's "special attractions," those sections that possessed the grandest vistas, posed the most grueling ascents or descents, harbored the largest and most varied populations of wildlife, boasted the most exhilarating traverses, or offered other qualities that made them especially memorable to hikers.

For the northbounder, the trail seems to arrange those sections in perfect sequence. As hikers move north and develop physical and mental stamina, they encounter progressively more demanding terrain and more challenging experiences.

It begins with Springer Mountain, an unremarkable peak, really, at just over three thousand feet and shrouded in hardwood trees. For thru-hikers the mountain ranks as a major milestone, marking either the outset or completion of their months-long trek.

Some 165 miles farther north, hikers enter the Great Smoky Mountains National Park, which teems with wild-life—bears, boars, skunks, deer. As the most frequently vis-ited national park in the country, it teems with human life, too. Through the park we ascended through rhododendron groves, along cascading brooks tangled in dense, rich under-brush, and across bald-topped mountains, and we scaled the tallest peak on the entire trail, Clingmans Dome, at 6,643 feet.

The 106 miles through Virginia's Shenandoah National Park led us through open meadows and over rocky promon-tories. In other places through Virginia we traced the trail over centuries-old carriage ruts past abandoned homesteads and settlements whose flower gardens still blossom and whose cherry and apple trees still yield fruit.

Much farther north, six and one-half miles beyond the Maine–New Hampshire border, the Mahoosuc Notch offers a mile-long scramble under, around, and between bus-sized boulders. The Notch is regarded as the trail's toughest mile, but for me it ranked as a gray, lichen-covered amusement park where we followed a series of white arrows that marked the *only* route through the jumble of granite blocks. The tight passages through the rocks frequently required us to shed our packs, tie them with parachute cord, and trail them behind us as we wedged through the cracks and fissures. Midway through the notch, we stopped to rest and dipped our drinking cups into a spring that courses under the rocks. As I withdrew my cup, the sides immediately fogged with condensation, even though the air temperature hovered in the fifties, and when I touched the cup to my mouth, the water was so frigid that it stung my lips.

Those were all special places, yet the trail offered three sections that, for me, represented emotional or aesthetic highlights of my trek: the White Mountains of New Hampshire, with their barren, windswept ridges that reach above timberline with the stark grandeur of the Swiss Alps; the Kennebec River, in southwestern Maine, an optional ford across 150 feet of roiling, waist-deep rapids; and Mount Katahdin, the lone granite sentry that rises out of the Lake

Country of central Maine and which I regard as the trail's most perfect mountain.

The White Mountains

We have been blessed with beautiful weather for our passage along the Franconia and Presidential ridges where the trail reaches above tree line. Having heard descriptions of the rawer aspects of the weather in these mountains—and of the deaths that have resulted—we're both relieved and grateful. Crossing the Whites in fog, sleet, summer snows, dangerous winds, or any combination of those things would have made for tough going, but the worst part would have been exploring these mountains without being able to see them. We had heard that the terrain is challenging here, and I suppose that it has been, but I've been too absorbed in the grandeur and beauty that greets us at every turn even to notice.

—August 30, 1979, Lakes of the Clouds Hut,
White Mountains, New Hampshire

On April 12, 1934, the weather station on the barren summit of Mount Washington clocked winds in excess of 230 miles per hour, the stiffest winds ever recorded on the earth's surface. To put that figure into perspective, hurricane-force winds begin at seventy-five miles per hour. As the story goes, after the incredulous meteorologist confirmed the reading, the gauge broke, and winds continued to gain in intensity.

The winds and harsh winter weather have sculpted the ancient granite of the Whites into vast bowls, cirques, and windswept ridges stripped bare of all plant life but scrub vegetation, alpine flowers, and tundra grass. Along the Franconia Ridge and through the Presidential Range, the trail lopes above timberline and often stays there for miles, crossing the summits of Mount Lincoln (5,089 feet), Mount Lafayette (5,249), Mount Jackson (4,052 feet), Mount Pierce (4,310), Mount Eisenhower (4,761), Mount Franklin (5,004), Mount Washington (6,288), and Mount Madison (5,363).

For most of us who had passed the previous 1,700 miles cloaked in hardwood forests and shrouded in lush vegetation, our first forays above timberline seemed accompanied by magic. For every wonderful vista we had enjoyed through the twelve states leading from Georgia to Vermont, we had scrambled over hundreds of less spectacular peaks that, day after day, offered no vistas, no break from the often monotonous routine of ascents and descents. The Whites were different, in fact, majestic, a term I would be reluctant to apply to any of the other ranges we passed through en route. They were majestic because their stately summits towered as many as three thousand feet above tree line and provided unbroken, panoramic vistas in every direction.

The terrain above timberline boasts exaggerated proportions, where mountains swell like barren, well-muscled biceps; where clouds don't float, but shoot across the sky like ice splinters; and where the wind assaults you in sudden gusts that tug at your watch cap, billow your parka and pants, and leave you tottering and lurching for balance. Above timberline, the absence of trees scrambles your sense of distance and size. Open vistas make a dozen miles appear like a few hundred yards until you spot another hiker, a tiny black form advancing along a gargantuan crest, and your perspective returns and you begin to feel as small as the distant hiker appears.

Above timberline, the trails themselves meld into the Hobbitlike landscape. You can glimpse ahead a mile, five miles, ten miles, and follow the serpentine cut of the trail as it meanders across ridges, slumps into saddles, skirts around peaks, disappears, then emerges again as it strays back into your line of sight. The trails snake to the horizon, becoming ever more faint, narrowing with the distance, and you walk them with your eyes before you and explore them with your feet. Ahead, you can see where you will stand in one hour, two hours, a day.

At the same time, the scale turns the landscape into a living relief map, and hiking becomes a lesson in living geography. You begin to understand how one peak links to the

next, how streams follow the folds in the ridges and converge into rivers.

Our days along the Franconia Ridge and through the Presidential Range to the summit of Mount Washington were marked by blue skies and moderate temperatures. We visited several of the eight high-elevation huts operated by the Appalachian Mountain Club (AMC), which provide lodging and gourmet meals for short-term hikers who may spend several days to a week in the Whites, but none of us had the cash to pay the twenty dollars per night. Often we arrived at the huts just after breakfast and gobbled up left-over whole-wheat pancakes and muffins at five cents apiece.

On August 30 we reached Lakes of the Clouds Hut, a rustic T-shaped lodge sided with weathered cedar shakes. This, the largest of the AMC's eight huts, accommodates as many as ninety guests. Though we couldn't afford to pay for dinner and a bunk, the hut crew members allowed us to sleep on table tops in the dining room for two dollars. The next morning, the sun glinted through the windows, and we knew we were in for a beautiful summit day. Along the 1.4 miles to the top, we battled forty-mile-per-hour winds, which formed horizontal spikes of rime ice on the windward sides of trail signs and rocks, but the day remained clear. As we soon discovered, not everyone who explored the mountain had been so fortunate.

The same features that render the alpine ridges of the Whites majestic also make them deadly. Days earlier, as we neared the top of the three-thousand-foot ascent leading from Franconia Notch to the ridge, we confronted the first of several yellow warning signs posted at timberline. They read: "Attention: Try this trail only if you are in top physical condition, well clothed, and carrying extra clothing and food. Many have died above timberline from exposure. Turn back at the first sign of bad weather." The conditions are particularly harsh on Mount Washington. Later I would learn that the average June temperature on the mountain is forty-five degrees; in July it's forty-nine; and in August,

forty-seven. The mountain routinely receives snowfall all months of the year.

The message did not strike home until we approached the summit of Mount Washington and encountered a series of weathered, wooden crosses wedged into the rocks. The crosses, we learned, marked the spots where hikers had died of exposure. One of the crosses, less than a quarter-mile from the summit house, served as a stark memorial to two hikers who had perished in a blizzard on July 18, 1958.

In the summit house a list hangs from one wall with the names of the mountain's victims. Since 1849 more than one hundred people have died of exposure on Mount Washington, nearly a quarter of them during the summer. Often their bodies were recovered only a few hundred yards from shelter. The scenario is often the same: fog materializes from nowhere or a sudden snowy whiteout descends, and visibility vanishes in minutes. Hikers clad in shorts and T-shirts, who might have been basking in warm sunlight only minutes earlier, suddenly find themselves drenched, shrouded in fog or snow, and buffeted by fifty- or sixty-mile-per-hour winds—the perfect recipe for hypothermia. The limited visibility leads to disorientation; the indistinct trails—snaking across boulder fields—disappear; and hikers stumble in circles. Soon their body temperatures plunge below critical levels, their mental faculties dim, and they lie down in the snow and yield to death.

Where there is death, there are tales of ghosts, and the Whites are no exception. Since 1979 I've returned to the Whites three times, and while on a magazine assignment there in 1987, I had what remains my only paranormal experience. I was working on a story about the high-elevation huts of the area and was on the trail with Charlie, a college-aged hut keeper who had spent the preceding summer working in Lakes of the Clouds hut. For the better part of a week, Charlie and I traced the Appalachian Trail through the region, stopping each evening at a different hut.

One evening we arrived at Mizpah Spring Hut, six miles south of Mount Washington, just before dusk. After the evening meal as darkness descended, Charlie and I sat with the few dozen guests in the hut reading and talking in the golden glow of propane lamps. At 8:30 P.M., the hut keepers extinguished the lamps, and we navigated our way to our bunk rooms with flashlights. Though ours was ample to sleep a dozen hikers, Charlie and I were the room's only occupants.

Soon after we climbed into our bunks, the mountain sounds became amplified in the darkness. As the wind surged against the sides of the hut, every sash whined and every rafter creaked and moaned. At the same time, I heard the distinct sound of someone—or some thing—pacing across the floor above us. I didn't know it at the time, but the storeroom was directly above us. With its steeply pitched roof and large stores of flour sacks and other dry goods, it was unlikely that anyone could have navigated across the floor, much less stood upright while doing so.

The footsteps continued. A rhythmic, light step moving from one edge of the ceiling to the other, turning and pacing back. I asked Charlie, who had spent several summers working in the Whites, if he had any notion of what it was.

"Mice?" he ventured, as perplexed as I.

"Uh-uh," I said. "If that's mice, they're damned big mice, and they're wearing shoes."

"What else could it be?" he asked after pausing to listen for a few seconds.

We drifted off to sleep to the sound of the incessant pacing.

At about 3:00 A.M., I had a dream. I call it a dream because I don't know what other term I could apply to it, but it was different from most dreams in that I experienced it in the semiconscious stage between sleep and wakefulness. It was too vivid to have been a dream.

It was night, and I was alone in an old abandoned house ascending a long stairway. At the top I arrived at a door that was ajar, and I pushed it open. Inside, the windowless room was dusky, not completely dark. There was no furniture on

the scarred wooden floor, and on the right I spotted a brick fireplace smudged with soot. A rusted flour tin rested on the hearth, and as I spied it, it began to move, scraping in slow circles as if moved by an invisible hand.

As it moved, something across the room caught my attention. I peered to the left, across the floor toward an alcove at the far end of the room, and there I saw a shaft of gray light, like a translucent form, stretching from floor to ceiling. As I watched, it glided back and forth, tracing the width of the alcove. Though it had no shape—no discernible form, no features—I felt a strong presence in the room. Somehow, I knew—I just knew—it was a woman, a young woman. A tingle surged up my spine, and I felt my hair stand on end as if I had just passed into a strong electrical current.

That's when I awoke and called to my friend, who slumbered in the bunk across the room.

"Hey, Charlie, I just saw a ghost!"

"Huh? You saw what?"

"I'm telling you, man, I just saw the ghost of a woman!"

"Are you sure it was a woman?"

"Absolutely!"

"Wow," Charlie said. "Listen, in the morning tell the hut crew about this."

"Why?" I asked.

"I'd rather not say, but just do it."

The next morning, I recounted my experience to Mark, a hut keeper at Mizpah in his early twenties. After I had finished, he calmly explained that over the summer dozens of other hikers had reported the same experience: first the footsteps, then the ghost. "Her name is Betsy," he said.

Betsy, he explained, was a young hiker who had drowned in a rain-swollen stream several summers earlier. The hut keepers had found her body near the hut. Because they were unable to transport the corpse down the mountain in the dark, they wrapped her in a sheet and placed it in the hut basement overnight.

"A short time later," Mark said, "people began to complain about the ghost."

The Kennebec River

Paul, Dan, and I forded the Kennebec River today, and I have never experienced a more sustained or intense rush in my life. When I reached the northern side, I lay in the grass quaking for the better part of a half-hour, feeling exhausted and exhilarated at the same time. The exhaustion soon passed, but the sense of accomplishment has remained with me through the day and I suspect I'll carry it with me for months to come.

We had timed our crossing badly, as the dam upstream had already released its load, and when we reached the bank, the rapids churned and roiled. As we prepared to plunge in, my resolve began to waver, particularly when I watched some of the other hikers in our group climb into a ferryman's boat for a risk-free ride to the other side. As I watched the boat leave the shore, I realized that I was committed, and the reality of what I was about to do scared me shitless.

I'd been contemplating this day for hundreds of miles, wondering if I'd have the guts to follow through. The crossing was as difficult—more difficult, in fact—than I had imagined, but in a similar way, my strength and concentration exceeded my expectations, too.

—September 16, 1979, abandoned barn near
Moxie Pond, Maine

The Kennebec River, which sluices south through the center of Maine toward the Atlantic Coast, cost me more adrenalin, and, once I had crossed it, left me with a greater sense of accomplishment than any other stretch along the trail. Since then, it has served as the yardstick by which I measure the extremes of fear and exhilaration.

After feasting on an all-you-can-eat pancake breakfast at the Carrying Place, a backwoods pancake house, we eased north to the banks of the Kennebec at 8:00 A.M. on September 16.

The Kennebec represented an important emotional passage for me, and it allowed me to measure the courage I had

gained over my months on the trail. Back in Georgia, I had been frightened by chipmunks rattling the underbrush. At that time, the notion of fording the Kennebec seemed foolhardy and dangerous, and I probably would have walked an additional 2,100 miles just to avoid it. But by the time I reached Maine, my self-confidence had soared, and the Kennebec loomed more as a challenge than as an invitation for disaster. I realized, too, that facing the Kennebec would put my triumph over fear into a tangible perspective.

Positioned below a dam that releases thousands of tons of water each morning, the river crossing is known for its unpredictable conditions. At times it is nothing more than a shallow ford that laps at the shins. At other times it rages, exposing hikers to a belt-deep channel of torrid rapids.

When we reached the river, we realized that our timing was unfortunate. The dam had released its load, and the 150-foot-wide column of water was alive with riffles and eddies.

Paul, Dan, and I eyed the surface and located a ragged line of riffles breaking on the surface, which marked the shallowest crossing. The shallowest stretch, we realized, also marked the fastest water. We clustered on the bank in the weeds for fifteen minutes or more reviewing our strategy and donned our fording gear. Because the riverbed was strewn with rocks and boulders, we decided to leave our boots on. To attempt the ford in bare feet would leave our flesh tattered by the jagged rocks. There was another consideration, too. The current was so swift that without the added support provided by the boots, if a foot had wedged between submerged boulders, ankle or shin bones would have snapped like green twigs, leaving us crippled *and* submerged.

There also was the question of traction. Along the trail we had all careened into the weeds when our Vibram soles had glanced off damp rocks, and we knew that wet Vibram on wet, silt-covered stones would have provided us no purchase at all, never mind the tug of the current. So we opted to pull on a pair of rag wool socks over our boots. The wool,

similar to the felt worn by fishermen on the soles of their waders, would provide at least some grab.

Next, each of us foraged through the brush for an additional walking stick to supplement the one we already carried. The notion was to form a tripod, with the anchored foot as one base, and the stick in either hand as the second and third. That way there would always be three points in contact with the bottom, and if we happened to totter, we would have a chance to arrest our fall using one or both sticks.

Then each of us unhooked his pack waistbelt. Over the years, the Kennebec has felled more than a few hikers. Those who were fortunate surrendered their packs to the current and reached shore drenched and shaken, but alive.

If our waistbelts had remained secured and we had taken a spill, the outcome would most certainly have been grim. The combined effect of the current, the unwieldy burden of a loaded pack, and the panic of being awash in a raging river would have left little hope of escape. With the belt unfixed, we stood a much better chance of jettisoning our packs if we submerged.

I chose not to dwell on those possibilities. In fact, I tried very hard not to think at all. If I had, I certainly would have pursued the sensible, risk-free means of crossing the river available to us at the time: as the three of us stood on the brink, a local boatman loaded several of our colleagues into his dinghy. For a few dollars, he would carry them safely across. Since 1985 when a woman drowned while fording the Kennebec, the Appalachian Trail Conference has admonished hikers to ferry across rather than ford, and the organization, in concert with the Maine Appalachian Trail Club, now subsidizes a ferry service through the summer months.

"Woooow, shit, Brill," shouted Dillon. "Do we really want to do this?"

"Just think about how great it will feel to get to the other side," I answered, as much to bolster my own failing confidence as to convince Paul of my commitment.

"Who's going first?" Paul asked. But even as we stood quaking on the shoreline, his question had already been answered.

Dan was twenty yards away from the bank and sinking up to his pack straps in rapids. As we watched, I noticed that for the first time since I had known him his motion had lost its grace. I could see that he was straining against the current, fighting it with everything he had. On his upstream side, the water curled like a hydraulic battering ram where it struck his body.

As Dan reached the halfway point, Paul stepped into the water, and I watched the water lap farther and farther up his thighs and finally reach near his waist. Then I knew that my moment of reckoning had come.

Paul and Dan were both endowed with long legs, while I am of a rather squat construction. My legs are strong, but they are also short. While the water reached just below Dan's and Paul's waists, it would reach to the middle of my own when I stepped into the deepest point.

As soon as I stepped in, I confronted an added hazard, one I hadn't anticipated. As I glanced at the rocks on the bottom through the rushing water, they seemed to waver, and within a few feet I began to suffer the effects of vertigo.

Within a few feet, I realized, too, that I had vastly underestimated the force of the current. It felt as if the combined force of all those millions of tons of water was pinioned against my thighs, threatening to pull me down, pull me under.

I soon lost perception of time and space. Was I moving? The distant shore didn't look any closer, but the water had gotten progressively deeper. Yes, I must be moving, yet progress was so slow, measured in inches. Lift the upstream—the left-hand—walking stick. Force it into the current. Plant it. Lift the left foot. Keep the thigh and knee stiff against the current. Advance it several inches. Ease the muscles enough to allow the boot sole to bounce along the bottom until it wedged against a rock. Plant it. Lift the right stick. Plant. Lift the right leg. Plant.

Soon a remarkable thing happened, something that I have

experienced neither before nor since: I became so thoroughly focused on my task that motion seemed to cease, and I became lost in such complete concentration that the surrounding woods disappeared and the roar of the rapids faded. There were only the water, the rocks, the current, and I, fighting against all of them. There was the feeling that if one muscle twitched, if the wind buffeted one strand of my hair, I would lose it. And there was the feeling, too, that there would be a release in surrendering, in letting go the fight and yielding to the current.

As I reached the halfway point, I heard voices and whistling coming from the northern bank, and I glanced up. Paul and Dan stood on the bank waving frantically toward my right—downstream. It seems that I focused too intently on the riverbed and had strayed upstream into deeper water. Now I faced the added burden of adjusting my course while continuing the ford.

Above the thunder of the water, I could hear my heart pounding in my ears. At the same time, I could feel surge after surge of adrenaline sparking my muscles.

Finally, the water began to inch down my stomach, then down my waist, my thighs, my knees. And I was safely across.

As I collapsed on the bank, the three of us recounted each step of the crossing like comrades who had survived the same battle. In many ways it was a battle—a battle against current, rocks, vertigo, and fear. I had just experienced a rush so intense, so sustained, that for a few minutes afterward my muscles refused to respond at all; they only twitched.

As I lay on the bank, I began to understand the addictive power of risk. I could fathom why skydivers, high-elevation mountaineers, race-car drivers—people whose relative risk was much greater than what I had faced—willingly laid their lives on the line. Yes, the experience had been frightening. But somehow the mental clarity I had experienced during the crossing overrode the fear, and a sense of peace and security settled over me when I finally reached the northern bank of the Kennebec.

Katahdin

Climbing Katahdin didn't produce the emotional catharsis I had expected it would. Instead, the climb was like the last frantic dash to touch home plate. With each step, my anticipation of triumph grew, but when I finally reached the summit, I felt a surge of sadness at realizing what I was about to leave behind. All of it: the rain, the cold, the mornings and evenings, the ascents and descents, the peaks, the friends, the seasons, the plants and animals, and the intimacy I've come to know with this world. I thought, too, about those things that I had already left behind. The continuum of my life has been broken. There are the events that occurred before the trail; then there is the trail. Those events seem thoroughly disjointed, as if from different lifetimes. The me of five months ago is a stranger. I am changed—forever.
—September 27, 1979, Mount Katahdin, Maine

I caught my first full broadside glimpse of Katahdin from the shore of Rainbow Lake Pond, twenty-seven miles and two days south of the trail's northern terminus. The sun shimmered off fall foliage, and I could see where the ruff of red sugar maples and yellow birches yielded to scree and rock at the timberline. Katahdin was, and is, the most beautiful mountain I've ever seen, so perfect in shape and so solitary amid the sweep of flatlands.

As I viewed the mountain, I wanted to stop, to settle in and spend days or even weeks thinking about what those final few days meant. At the same time, there was an irresistible urge to confront the mountain, to trace its boulder-strewn shoulders, to reach its rounded, mile-high crown and complete the final leg of my journey. Katahdin had been the image in my sights for five months, especially in the early days when the peak seemed so distant and remote that we had little hope of reaching it, but when I actually beheld the mountain, I knew I would finish and realized that my days on the trail were coming to an end.

On September 26 we reached the twin shelters at Ka-

tahdin Stream Campground. By that point our ranks had swelled to nearly fifteen. Over the previous weeks we had left entries in trail registers urging our fellow thru-hikers to adjust their mileage so that we could make our summit bid *en masse*. Among those who joined our foursome were the Phillips brothers from Florida, Kansas native Jeff Hammons, newlyweds Phil and Cindy (who had honeymooned on the trail), North Carolina native Gary Owen, Jim Shaffrick from Connecticut, and Victor Hoyt, the Massachusetts hiker who had departed the trail in North Carolina.

We awoke on the morning of September 27 to clear blue skies. As we departed the shelters, the temperature hovered just above freezing.

The ascent to the summit of Katahdin is one of the stiffest along the entire trail: four thousand feet in just over five miles. In places the ascent requires hand-over-hand scrambling along boulder-strewn pitches, and in other places iron bars protrude from the rock and provide the only secure hand-holds.

But I think I speak for most northbounders when I say that the difficulty of the ascent is negated by the sheer excitement of reaching the end of the trail. But there were other factors as well that eased the strain of the ascent. For one thing, we were all in top physical form, having logged 2,100 miles of stiff ascents over the previous months. For another, before reaching the base of Katahdin, we had ambled through the rolling Lake Country without facing a major ascent for more than seventy miles, and our disdain for constant ascending and descending had passed. Our loads were much lighter than what we had become accustomed to, and we had supplanted our expedition packs with day packs since we would be following the same route to the summit and back down to Katahdin Stream Campground. Then there was the beauty of a perfect fall day. At every turn, autumn colors blazed, and as we emerged above timberline at three thousand feet, every foot of elevation gained brought new vistas of the surrounding sphagnum bogs and shimmering lakes that captured parcels of the azure sky on their surfaces.

Despite the beautiful surroundings, I soon found myself so thoroughly absorbed in a tangle of conflicting emotions that I felt as though I were climbing alone when in fact I was surrounded by companions. To reach the summit, I realized, would mean that I had achieved the goal, but then it occurred to me that I had already achieved other, more important, goals over all the miles that had led me there. Katahdin was a formality, a definitive end point.

Once we reached the rock cairn that marked the top, Dan and I embraced. We surveyed the vast flat Lake Country that sprawled for miles away from the mountain's base, and we studied the blue pockets of water fringed by acres of red and gold. Then we sat peering silently toward the south, back across five months and 2,100 miles to Springer Mountain. There were so many things to say, yet none of them could be articulated.

If the white blazes had led farther north, I'm certain that all of us would have followed them. But they didn't. We had reached the end of the trail. It was time to leave the wilderness and return home.

CHAPTER • FOURTEEN

Coming Home

We've reached the end of the trail, and we're heading back home to people and things that once were so familiar. Yet I'm a bit apprehensive about how I'll respond to them and how they will respond to me. Will this experience make sense to anyone? Will things at home seem changed? Will I readjust? Will I remember all that I've seen, felt, learned, and shared over the past five months? Will I, in time, lose my intimacy with nature and begin to feel like a stranger when I visit the wilderness?

Tonight there are fourteen of us gathered in adjoining hotel rooms in Millinocket celebrating the completion of our trek. Tomorrow, I say good-bye to friends whom I've come to know and love so well. Then I will pile into a car for the trip home. The adventure continues. . .

—September 27, 1979, hotel room, Millinocket, Maine

Mount Katahdin represented the only peak along the Appalachian Trail that proved more difficult to descend than ascend, yet that difficulty had nothing to do with terrain. For me, the 2,100 miles from Springer Mountain north had represented an unbroken continuum, a journey along a ridgeline corridor that was neatly contained between woodland walls and the southern and northern

endposts. As long as I remained within those boundaries, my foremost designation was that of Appalachian Trail hiker, and my primary goal remained to reach the trail's northern terminus.

Once I had reached Baxter Peak, I realized that my next footfall would stray outside those boundaries and would lead inexorably away from the trail and away from the white blazes that for 150 days had provided all the direction I needed. The next step would lead away from a world of simple routine, away from a world governed by weather and shifting winds where sun and seasons were the only time-keepers and where the measure of a day was in miles passed and insight gained. For the first time in more than five months, my path into the future was unclear.

As I reached the base of Katahdin, I confronted a tangle of conflicting emotions. I was proud of what I had accomplished, but I wondered what place my trail experiences would occupy in my life in the years that followed. I wondered if the lessons I had learned would be of use to me back home, and I wondered what I would do if I discovered that my new values clashed with those of civilized society. Would I have the courage to set off in my own direction? It would take me years to find the answers to those questions.

As daunting as the transition had been back in April when as a neophyte woodsman I had struggled for security in a foreign environment, I suspected the transition back would be more difficult still. And more abrupt.

Twenty-four hours after reaching the summit of Katahdin, I had said a painful good-bye to my trail friends, and was sitting in the passenger seat of a car cruising south along Interstate 95. As the car accelerated, I gripped the dashboard with white knuckles. Was it necessary to travel so fast, I asked the driver, a friend of Dan's who had agreed to shuttle us from Maine back home to Washington, D.C. He laughed and pointed to the speedometer. We were moving at fifty-eight miles per hour, yet compared to the three-mile-an-hour pace I had maintained along the trail, it seemed as though we had broken the sound barrier.

Once we were out of Maine and away from the mountains

and the accommodating residents of the trail towns, the people we encountered during our rest stops seemed to regard Dan and me, with our long beards and shabby clothes, as drifters or vagrants. Shopkeepers were abrupt, sometimes even rude. Diners at nearby tables glanced in our direction and muttered among themselves. As I confronted more and more suspicious faces, the pride that had evolved over the previous months began to ebb, replaced by self-consciousness and a feeling of being out of place. These people were clean and well dressed. I was filthy. After several consecutive showers, I began to notice my pack and clothes reeked of sweat and campfire smoke. While these people abided by rules of etiquette, I attacked my food like a famished savage. As we exited a fast-food restaurant in Pennsylvania, I recall joking to Dan, "Well, Toto, I don't think we're in Kansas anymore." It occurred to me then that if, after leaving the trail, I had strayed into a fairytale world peopled by dwarfs and witches, it wouldn't have seemed more skewed than this vision of mainstream America.

After a week back in Washington, the transition continued as I trimmed my beard, shed my trail clothes, and slipped into a navy-blue suit to be best man in a friend's wedding. Because I was penniless, the week after that I sought work through a temporary employment service. On my first assignment I spent four interminable days working as a file clerk and general lackey at a small corporate office. When a middle-aged woman chided me for misfiling a document, I wanted to explain to her that after five months in the wilderness, the disposition of a file didn't seem all that vital to me, but I didn't. Instead, I resigned myself to the fact that to the woman, my trail experiences were somewhat trivial while my ability to alphabetize files was of paramount importance.

Two weeks after that I returned home to Cincinnati and moved in with my parents. Though they had been supportive of my trail quest, they soon began to query me about my plans for the future. As it turned out, they weren't asking me anything that I hadn't been asking myself.

What followed was a slow, sometimes painful process of

reentry, marked by incidents that, taken together, made me wonder if my trek had been a tangential journey into the darkness rather than a pilgrimage toward self-discovery.

In October I attended a party with some friends. By then I had upgraded my wardrobe, and although, in the sartorial sense, I fitted in with the rest of the partygoers, my attitudes and theirs seemed at odds.

"What have you been up to?" asked a friend whom I had not seen for several years.

"Well, I've spent the past five months in the woods, hiking the Appalachian Trail," I said, somewhat tentatively.

"Oh, is that right?" he responded. "My wife and I spent ten days in Europe this past summer."

He detailed his trip, then described his job as a sales representative for a large corporation. He told me how well he was doing and asked if I had noticed his new car parked out in front. I hadn't. He insisted on leading me outside to show it to me.

Afterward, he returned to the party while I settled into a rocking chair on the front porch. It was a cool October night, and I found relief in the breeze rustling the fallen leaves, the crisp smell of fall, and the stars—the same stars that had adorned night skies while I passed through fourteen states. But beyond the glow of city lights, they seemed to have lost much of their luster, and I found myself wondering if my trail buddies had encountered the same difficulties. I wanted desperately to be with them. I knew Dan had abandoned his corporate career and had returned to Hot Springs. There, at the Inn, in the shadow of the mountains and surrounded by men and women who shared his trail values, he became an apprentice to a harpsichord builder. I regretted not having followed him there.

A couple of weeks later I shaved my beard and, clad in dress clothes, set out to find a job. A career counselor who helped me prepare a resume advised me not to include any mention of the Appalachian Trail among my accomplishments. He even suggested that I try to cover the gap it had created in my employment history.

"No one will see much value in your hiking experi-

ences," he said. "They will only see that you were unemployed for those months."

I bristled at his suggestion that I should hide my adventure between lines on a resume or, worse, twist it into a nonevent, something that I should deny ever happened.

Despite his advice, I *did* include the trail on my resume, and it has appeared on every resume I've drafted since. I eventually landed a job in a backpacking shop, and though the position didn't pay much, it kept me in touch with people who, like me, lived for weekend forays into the woods.

During my tenure at the backpacking shop, in my years as a writer, and in all the relationships and roles that have occupied my life since 1979, I have drawn on my experiences from the trail. Though it took awhile to realize it, the trail had shaped me, had given me a philosophy and had toughened me in some ways, softened me in others, and taught me lessons I will never forget: lessons on survival, kindness, strength, friendship, courage, perseverance, and the ways of nature. Those lessons have affected everything I've done since.

From weeks of living out of a thirty-five-pound pack, I learned to find contentment in simple things and to rely on myself and my resources to surmount obstacles. From long days spent tromping through rain and cold, I learned that whenever I felt beaten, spent, exhausted, and ready to quit, there was always something left and that if I delved deep enough, I could always find the strength to keep moving forward. From watching the seasons yield one to the next, daylight surrender to night, and darkness give way to morning, I discovered that in the midst of chaos order and purpose are present for us. From the unqualified kindness shared among travelers in the back country, I learned that for all the cruelty loose in the world, people care deeply for their fellow creatures. And I learned that whenever I lose sight of those lessons, I can regain them by returning to the trail.

In the spring of 1987 I left my job as an editor with a large southeastern publishing company—a job that never really felt right for me—to pursue a full-time career as a free-lance

writer. The transition was not as graceful as I had hoped, and I passed months of despondency when the assignments I sought didn't come. I decided to quit, but before I did, I loaded my pack and set out for Springer Mountain. The trail had answered my needs once before, and I had faith that it would do so again. Over the following weeks I mingled with the new class of thru-hikers and formed new, lasting friendships as I ambled along flower-speckled trails and savored the verdant arrival of spring. I also discovered that, though the circumstances of my life had changed, the trail had remained the same—just as charged with life and hope as I remembered it. A month after I began and 335 miles farther north, I was healed and returned to my chosen occupation more determined than ever. In time, I succeeded.

Since 1937 more than two thousand seekers have coursed along the trail's miles, each pursuing a personal mission, each in search of something enduring and real. Among those hikers I came to know, there was Elizabeth, who took up the trail seeking relief from the grief of losing her husband. There was Nick, who forged a new direction for his life after retirement. As for Paul, Dan, and the rest of us, fresh from college, we set out to learn the lessons of the wilderness before we learned the lessons of the professional world, and somewhere along the way, we all found what we were looking for. The answers may not have been exactly what we sought, but I believe they were precisely what we needed.

I suspect that the trail will continue to work its magic on the hundreds of future end-to-enders who in years hence will arrive at Springer, sign the log book, and point their boots and hopes north. I suspect, too, that years and years from now, after we have followed our new technologies and grand urban schemes into a new century, the trail will remain a sure route into our past, a route along which technology will always surrender to strength and spirit and the laws of nature.

Over the past eleven years, my memories of the months on the trail have survived as a time of sublime happiness, a time when I felt my neurons being switched on for the very first time. The mention of the trail still evokes images of lush, green mountains; of great gray clouds of mist wafting through virgin stands of hemlock and oak; of bald-topped mountains with views that roll out across miles and miles of blue-hazed hills; of hawks swirling above sun-drenched granite ledges; of springs that ran so cold they made my teeth ache.

My other memories also grow more vivid and precious with time. No matter how many times I have hefted my backpack, picked up the white blazes, and trod my favorite sections of trail, the excitement—the sense of discovery—has never failed me. I doubt that any other event of my life will choke me with as much emotion, fill me with as much pride, or define more clearly who I am than my summer on the Appalachian Trail.

Appendix

For information about the Appalachian Trail

If you would like to learn more about the Appalachian Trail, write the Appalachian Trail Conference, Post Office Box 807, Harpers Ferry, West Virginia 25425-0807: or call (304) 535-6331.

Suggested Reading for Hikers

Appalachian Odyssey, Steve Sherman and Julia Older. South Greene Press.

Appalachian Trail Hiker, Ed Garvey. Appalachian Outfitters.

The Complete Walker, Colin Fletcher. Alfred A. Knopf, Inc.

Leaves of Grass, Walt Whitman. Modern Library.

The Man Who Walked through Time, Colin Fletcher. Random House.

The Monkey Wrench Gang, Edward Abbey. Avon Books.

The Nick Adams Stories, Ernest Hemingway. Charles Scribner's Sons.

On the Road, Jack Kerouac. Penguin Publishing.

Pilgrim at Tinker Creek, Annie Dillard. Harper and Row Publishers.

Sand Country Almanac, Aldo Leopold. Ballantine Books.

The Snow Leopard, Peter Matthiessen. Penguin Publishing.

Walden, Henry David Thoreau. Doubleday & Company, Inc.

Walk across America, Peter Jenkins. Fawcett Juniper.

Walk West, Peter and Barbara Jenkins. William Morrow and Company.

Walking with Spring, Earl Shaffer. Appalachian Trail Conference.

A Woman's Journey on the Appalachian Trail, Cindy Ross. The Globe Pequot Press.

Zen and the Art of Motorcycle Maintenance, Robert M. Pirsig. Bantam Books.